THE BETRAYAL

BOOK 2 OF THE HOLLYWOOD PRINCESS SERIES

DANA AYNN LEVIN

Park-Hill Press

The Betrayal: Book 2 of the Hollywood Princess Series

The Betrayal: Book 2 of the Hollywood Princess Series is a work of fiction. Names, characters, places and incidents either are the product of the author's imagination or are used fictitiously. Any resemblance to any person, living or dead, or any events or occurrences, is purely coincidental.

Cover design by Caiti Reid Levin

Cover image used under license from Shutterstock.com

ISBN: 0990737039
ISBN-13: 978-0-9907370-3-2

DEDICATION

"Heaven has no rage like love to hatred turned,
Nor hell a fury like a woman scorned."
- The Mourning Bride (1697), William Congreve

CONTENTS

ACKNOWLEDGEMENTS

Writing a novel, nevertheless a series, was never my aspiration, but then Elizabeth and Daniel's story came to me, and it wouldn't stop. So thank you Elizabeth and Daniel for being such compelling characters that I had to continue. You make my job easy.

Thank you also to my husband and children for allowing me to sometimes pay more attention to Elizabeth and Daniel than to you, but I never missed the important stuff.

Finally, thank you to the readers who started the journey with Hollywood Princess, and now continue with The Betrayal.

PROLOGUE

Moonlight, filtered through sheers covering floor to ceiling windows, cast an ethereal glow on the man and woman sharing the king-sized bed. It was a testament to the hurry they had been in that neither had stopped to consider pulling the heavy outer drapes closed. But that was okay.

On the twenty-second floor of the Four Seasons Hotel in Vancouver, privacy was a given. Yet it was far from quiet. Despite its lofty position, the spacious suite with its city views was not immune from the noise of evening traffic, or the glow from distant streetlights and neon, for it was not that late.

The couple didn't care. Naked, in the throes of passion, each into the other and the moment, ambient noise and light made no difference. Nothing would interrupt them.

Luxury bedcovers and sheets askew, throw pillows tossed about; the couple ignored these.

Loud moans and heated panting built to a crescendo. Their climax was nearing. The man, tall with rippling muscles, moved effortlessly in synch with the woman beneath him. Long, slender legs wrapped around his waist, while similarly long, slender fingers gripped his back.

Straight dark hair splayed out across the white pillowcase. One final grunt and the man collapsed into the satisfied woman. Then silence enveloped them.

"Let's give them something to talk about," Bonnie Rait's voice cut through the stillness. Bonnie Raitt?

"My phone," the man mumbled. He reached across the slender woman to the nightstand. His shaggy dark blonde hair, in need of a trim, fell across his brow.

"Now?" The woman was unhappy with the inopportune timing of the interruption.

Bonnie Raitt began a second chorus.

"It's my girlfriend," the man explained as he picked up the iPhone. The woman grimaced.

Now alert, "Hey, baby," he said, all sugary sweet.

"Tired?" A girl's voice coming through the phone asked.

Sapphire eyes glanced at the brunette, now lying against his side, her bony fingers resting across his chest.

"Another hectic day. Call was at seven," he replied. "I don't have your cushy ten to six job," he teased.

"Oh. I'm sorry. You are tired. I'll call earlier tomorrow. I love you, honey."

"I love you, too, baby. Sweet dreams." The man placed the phone beside his hand on the mattress.

"Now, where were we," the woman trilled.

She reached her hand to the man's face and pressed her lips to his.

Again, the phone rang, a standard ring-tone. This time the woman groaned in disbelief as the man picked up the phone.

"Oh, no!" Then he answered the phone. "Hey, Dad. What's up?"

By now the woman, covering herself with the sheet, had sat up.

"You should go," she said without rancour in her voice. "First your girlfriend, now your Dad. I'm getting a case of bad karma here."

CHAPTER ONE – ELIZABETH

Malibu, California

What a great day! I sensed it already, and I'd barely woken. Having showered, shampooed, and completed all those other mundane morning bathroom routines, I threw open the sliders and stepped out onto the bedroom balcony. Breathing deeply, I took in the fresh, salty air. Ah! This was heaven!

There was no better way to start the day. Well one thing would make it better; if Danny were here with me. But it was Friday. By evening that would be solved. Already packed, I was ready for my four o'clock flight to Vancouver for our weekly reunion.

I hated admitting this, but sometimes it was great being Elizabeth Jacobs. Though I had fled the Hollywood A-list trappings I'd grown up with to attend Donnelly College in New York last fall, this summer I enjoyed taking full advantage. The daughter of superstar Miranda Jordan could leave work whenever she wanted, and fly up to visit her boyfriend on location. No questions asked.

Today I was turning nineteen. What a year it had been! When I turned eighteen, I had been full of trepedations. Freshman year of college was fast approaching. For the first time, I was attending a school where I didn't know anyone. Typical student insecurites haunted me; social, academic, overall fear of failure. Underlying it all was my desire to blend in, and not be identified as Miranda Jordan and Michael Jacobs' daughter.

That plan lasted for about one week. Within days of arriving at Donnelly, I had reunited with my childhood friend and fellow freshman, Daniel Newman. In contrast to me, Danny was not trying to hide from his identity as Academy Award winning director Steven Newman's son. As my father had attended college with Danny's parents, our families were closely associated. With Danny on campus, my identity could not remain hidden.

Within a few months, Danny and I had become a couple. It always wasn't easy. Danny was a difficult man to love. He had not wanted a girlfriend. He feared commitment. Dating your parents' goddaughter was as commited as it could get. We'd experienced ups and downs, but as summer began, Danny had worked through his issues.

I'd never had a boyfriend to celebrate my birthday with. Knowing Danny, this would be the best birthday ever! He would have something special planned. Danny would not disappoint, but first I had to get through the workday. Anticipation was killing me.

I was the third "J" at J⁴ Productions, and I took my responsibilities seriously. When the summer began, I had been insecure in my position as the most junior of junior development executives. While composing coverage, I worried that I would recommend passing on a future blockbuster.

Dad, my boss, explained that it wasn't about my personal tastes but was rather an objective assessment of the characters and plot. Equally important, did the script have that intangible quality that made it worthy of being produced by Michael Jacobs. Soon, I gained confidence, and learned that most scripts were not worthy of pursuit.

Dad often invited me to sit in at meetings. He would proudly introduce me, and I would quietly observe, absorbing as much as I could. Then Dad would solicit my opinion, as though I were a trusted colleague. Privately, I expressed my surprise.

"Elizabeth, you may be my daughter, but you're a bright, capable young woman. I'd be a fool not to court your opinion."

The phone startled me out of my reverie, and I hurried inside to retrieve it from the nightstand.

"Hi, Daddy," I said cheerfully, and I plopped down on the bed.

"Good morning, birthday girl!" Dad laughed. "Can you be ready to leave the house by eight?"

I glanced at the clock. Seven-fifteen! I was still in my bathrobe; wet hair dripping down my back. If I didn't dry my hair, I could. My thick auburn waves took forever to dry. I sighed. A braid would suffice.

"I guess so. Why? Early meeting?"

"I'm sending a car for you. You plane leaves Santa Monica at nine. Happy birthday, Sweetheart!"

"Daddy! Are you sure?" I was touched by his unexpected generosity.

"Honey, I know where your head is today. You'll be useless."

"Thank you, Daddy. You're the best!"

"I already told Steve to send his driver to meet you, and I swore him to secrecy. I know you'll want to surprise Danny."

"Oh, I will! I get tired of Danny always surprising me. I never seem to surprise him. Not that I don't love his surprises."

"You surprise Danny much more than you think, but this one he'll love."

"Let me go. I have to get dressed if I'm to make that plane! I love you, Daddy."

Now I was in a rush. I had forty minutes to do hair, makeup, get dressed and finish packing. Ugh!

The phone was ringing. I didn't have time for well-meaning birthday greetings.

"Hello," I answered, without even checking the caller ID.

"How's my birthday girlfriend?" Danny exclaimed.

"I'm fine now," I giggled. "Aren't you at work?"

"Early call today. I only have a minute. Can't let anyone think I'm taking advantage just because my wife is the boss' favorite. More important, you're my favorite. I can't wait for tonight."

"Me neither," I laughed. "This will be the most awesome birthday ever!"

Sailing English Bay was magical. After taking several lessons over the past few weeks, it was our first time out on a boat by ourselves. Initially insecure, Danny's bravado put me at ease. I was in awe that he could seemingly do everything.

By mid-morning as we successfully navigated the sparkling clear waters, I achieved a state of zen. British Columbia's shoreline took my breath away. With its many coves and inlets, and small islands dotting the surface, it was picture postcard perfect. The splendor of the majestic trees, the clean sand beaches, and the glamour of downtown Vancouver's skyscrapers, combined to fill me with joy.

The late-June sun beat down full-force. I unbuttoned the cuffed-up chambray shirt I had worn, tails tied at my waist, and removed it, leaving me in a strapless bikini top. As I folded the shirt and placed it in my tote bag, a loud whistle caught my attention . I laughed at Danny's boyish grin, and he shrugged.

"Why don't I drop anchor and we'll have our picnic," Danny suggested.

"I'll lay out the blanket."

I lifted the lid on the teak bench and removed the vinyl-backed blanket. After smoothing it out on the deck, I carefully placed the wicker picnic hamper on a corner to prevent the blanket from flapping in the breeze. Meanwhile, Danny wrapped the line from the lowered main sail in careful figure eights around the cleat.

"Ready," I cheerfully announced.

"Me, too," Danny answered, and he wrapped his arms around my back.

Danny held me as close as he could, and crushed his lips to mine. Reflexively, my lips parted, weldoming his exploring tongue, and my hands clasped around his neck. I held Danny's face to mine, drinking in his love, and his hands caressed my back.

Danny opened the button and zipper of my denim cut-offs. I gasped from his masculinity as he pressed against me. Danny pushed my shorts off my hips, and when they fell to my ankles, I stepped out of them, leaving me in an audaciously revealing orange bikini bottom.

One of Danny's large hands lingered on my rear as his other held me close around my back. His touch was intoxicating. Our lips remained joined. My heart beat rapidly. Danny's did the same. I gripped him tighter. He was hard against me through his swim trunks. One of Danny's hands crept up my back and unhooked my bikini top. It fell to the boat bottom.

I gasped, but Danny's tongue exploring my mouth silenced me. My pulse raced and my nails dug into his back. Danny's hand entered my bikini bottom. Long fingers slipped into me and I moaned.

I stared at Danny, disbelieving. We were on a boat! His pace increased. I held tighter, unable to stop my rhythm against his palm. His throaty groan pushed me to the edge and my quiver became explosive.

"Hey, birthday girl," Danny whispered. He grinned, more than satisfied by his obvious success. "I love you."

Danny brought his face back to mine. Our noses touched. His eyes sparkled, full of love, and our lips joined again.

Then Danny took my left hand and admired the platinum bracelet he had given me last night. The sun hit the diamonds, and danced off in all directions. The facets burst forth in multiple sunburst ions.

"Nice bracelet," Danny smiled, proud of his gift.

"I love it almost as much as the man who gave it to me," I whispered.

Danny lifted me up, and I wrapped my legs around his waist. His hardness pulsated against my bikini, silently urging its removal.

"You know what I want?" he whispered.

"Me?" I giggled, still so aroused. My birthday celebration continued.

CHAPTER TWO – DANNY

"Welcome back, Mr. Newman. Miss Jacobs," the uniformed doorman with ramrod straight military posture, greeted us on our return to the Four Seasons.

I responded with a nod and guided Eli into the hotel. Securely holding her hand, we crossed the lobby toward the Concierge.

"Enjoy your picnic, Mr. Newman?" he asked as I placed the basket on his desk.

More than he could ever imagine. "It was great. Thank you again for arranging the sailboat," I answered.

"You're most welcome. I'll take your basket," he offered.

"Thank you,"

Eli hid a yawn behind her hand.

"Can we please have a five pm wake-up call?" I asked. "Too much sun. We need a nap or we'll never make it to dinner."

"Certainly. Consider it done, Mr. Newman."

"Thanks," I said as I slipped him a twenty while shaking his hand.

I led Eli to the elevator bank and took her hands. We exchanged smiles, content. Then I gathered Eli in my arms and kissed her.

"This is a public lobby, Danny," Vanessa admonished.

I hadn't heard the elevator doors open, but they must have. Eli and I broke apart except for our hands. She blushed deep red. I grinned.

Vanessa was dressed in gym shorts, a fitted tank top hugging all her curves, and running shoes. Her hair was pulled back in a severe ponytail. Vanessa had one iPhone earbud inserted, while the other hung down her chest. Ultra-dark sunglasses perched on her head were ready to be lowered over her eyes the moment she reached the exit.

"You're right Vanessa," I answered smugly, "But I really don't care."

I was proud to be seen kissing my girlfriend. CNN could even air it if they wanted.

"If you didn't already have a room here, I'd tell you to get one," she said sharply.

"And that's exactly where we're going," I snapped.

Confused, Elizabeth stared at Vanessa and then at me. Vanessa shook her head with disdain.

"Where are you going, Vanessa?" the always polite Elizabeth Jacobs asked pleasantly.

"I'm off on my morning run."

"Morning run? But it's the afternoon?" Eli cocked her head to one side, puzzled.

"I slept in. I'm transitioning my internal clock in preparation for Monday's night shoots. You should do the same, Danny."

"I'll be alright. I've pulled all-nighters."

"Well, I suppose." Vanessa gave a haughty laugh. "Nobody cares what a PA looks like."

"I care," Eli chirped. "And I'm glad you havea night shoot on Monday. I get to stay an extra day,"

"I'll take you to the airport Monday afternoon and then I'll report to the set."

"I'd like that," Eli sighed. "One more night together."

Vanessa rolled her eyes. "I'm so out of here," she declared.

"Later, Vanessa," I said.

The elevator finally landed, and the doors opened discharging its passengers. Eli and I quickly jumped in, barely making it before the doors closed again.

Upstairs Eli and I stripped off our damp clothes and crawled under the covers. As we snuggled together I broke the bad news.

"Baby, night shoots go through Saturday."

"Saturday?" Eli frowned. "Then I get to spend next weekend watching you sleep?"

"No. This is where you gracefully agree to spend next weekend at home because it's pointless watching me sleep."

Eli quietly pouted. "You're frowning, babe."

"I'm not happy," she complained.

"I'll miss you too. Let me make it up to you in advance, right now."

CHAPTER THREE - ELIZABETH

Danny ushered me into a trendy restaurant in the Yaletown section of Vancouver for my birthday dinner. A crowd of well-dressed men and women filled the entrance, blocking me from seeing through to the bar. Still, I caught a glimpse. Could it be?

"Mom? Dad?"

What were they doing in Vancouver? And Ellen too! I had expected Jim and Tom to join us, but Mom, Dad and Ellen? When did they fly up?

"Happy Birthday, honey!" Dad exclaimed. He crushed me in a bear hug.

Then Mom pecked my cheek. "Happy birthday, Elizabeth."

"I can't believe you're here!" I squealed.

"Where else would we be? It's your birthday," Mom laughed. "Nineteen years ago today…"

"Yeah, yeah. I know. Under cover of darkness Dad snuck you in through the back door at Cedars while the paparazzi staked out the front, waiting in the icy June air."

Danny laughed. "Is that true?"

"Yes," we answered in unison.

"Well, maybe not the icy part," I added.

But Danny continued grinning like the Cheshire Cat.

"You knew they were coming? You're usually terrible at keeping secrets."

Danny laughed. "That's why I'm glad you distracted me today," he choked out. "You made me forget I had a secret."

Dad smirked. Mom rolled her eyes. And Ellen smiled.

"We went sailing," I explained. "What a perfect day!"

"Yeah, Eli was perfect," said Danny.

"No, you were. Danny knew exactly what to do," I said proudly.

"I certainly did," he laughed.

Ugh! Danny knew damned well that I was referring to his prowess as a skipper, not a lover.

"Really?" Dad asked, raising an eyebrow.

"Danny is an excellent captain," I said.

Then Danny took my hand and kissed it. "Hey, show the folks your birthday present."

"Of course." How could I forget?

I held up my wrist. Mom carefully examined the platinum link bracelet.

A sizable round diamond with three smaller diamonds on each side was mounted on a narrow platinum bar. The piece was at once elegant while remaining everyday casual.

"It's beautiful," Dad declared.

"Michael, it's better than beautiful," Mom pronounced. "Honey, that's a stunning bracelet. Daniel, you have excellent taste."

"Thanks, Randi." Danny beamed with pride.

"Come see what Danny gave Elizabeth," Mom said to Ellen who was standing a few steps away with Steve.

In an instant, jewelry expert Ellen was at our side examining the bracelet. "Danny, you outdid yourself. It's gorgeous."

"A local artist designed it," Danny explained. "Whenever Elizabeth wears it, she'll be reminded of this summer."

I glowed. I would always cherish the memory of this summer.

Later, we gathered in the elegant YEW Bar at the Four Seasons for a nightcap. Danny and I shared a table with Mom and Dad while Steve and Ellen lingered at the bar.

"How long are you here?" I asked Dad.

"I'm up for the week," Dad answered. "It's about time I visited the set and saw how my investment was doing."

"I'll tell you Mike, Dad certainly is relieved that you're here. He's been trying

"Danny, I don't want Steve stressing you," I said.

Danny drained his drink and hailed a passing waitress. "I'll have another, please," he requested, and he handed her his empty glass. "Babe, don't worry." Danny twirled a lock of my hair. "I'm only doing my job. Dad expects me to run interference."

"Eli worries way too much," Danny explained to my folks.

"Honey, I'll keep my eyes on Danny all week for you, so don't worry."

"She cares too much," Danny said.

"She's supposed to, Danny," said Mom. "Elizabeth loves you."

The waitress stopped and handed Danny a fresh gin and tonic. "Thank you," he said. Danny immediately took a large gulp.

"Danny, please," I cautioned.

"E, I'm fine. It's not like I have to drive anywhere. We live upstairs."

I frowned, disappointed. Each time I visited Vancouver, Danny's drinking increased. Something was eating at him, but what? Except for the drinking, all seemed well. I looked forward to debriefing Dad when he returned home.

"Randi, how long are you here?" Danny purposely changed the subject.

"I'll be on Elizabeth's plane, Monday."

"No," I groaned.

"What's wrong with me sharing your flight?"

"It's the car. I planned on alone time with Danny."

Danny laughed and hugged me around my shoulders.

"Then I'll take my own car," Mom said, annoyed.

"I wish Ellen was coming home with us. With Steve working nights this week, won't she be bored?"

Mom and Dad glanced across the room. Danny and I followed their eyes to the bar. I giggled. Mom smiled. Dad snickered. And Danny glared. Steve's arm was wrapped around Ellen's shoulder, and they were kissing like newlyweds, completely oblivious to their surroundings.

"That's disgusting!" Danny spat out.

Mom and I laughed. Dad smirked. "Now you understand why Ellen's staying," he said.

"That's gross, Michael," Danny sneered.

"It's no different than you and Elizabeth," Mom laughed.

"But we're kids," Danny protested, even as he began to laugh.

Vanessa entered the bar on the arm of a distinguished-looking man in his forties.

"Who's that with Vanessa?" I asked.

Three heads turned as one in Vanessa's direction. Danny's hug tightened. Steve abruptly stopped kissing Ellen, but kept his arm protectively around her. We turned away, not wanting our collective curiosity to be noticed.

"Never seen him before," Danny said.

"Looks like a local," Dad added.

"Who cares? It has nothing to do with us," Mom declared. "Vanessa's single. She's allowed to date."

"Baby, I'm tired. Let's go," Danny said, and he rose.

Danny didn't seem tired. Maybe he was getting ideas from his parents.

"Hello, Steven, Ellen," came Vanessa's frosty greeting.

"Good evening, Vanessa. Ellen and I were just leaving," Steve responded equally cool.

I stood up. "We'll see you tomorrow."

My parents rose to bid us good-night. Mom and I embraced.

"Happy birthday again, Elizabeth."

Just as Dad and I were about to embrace, Vanessa appeared with her date.

"Why, hello," she said pleasantly.

Danny grabbed me back into his arms as though it were for my protection. But it was only Vanessa and her businessman. What was there to protect me from?

"Elizabeth and I were leaving," Danny said curtly.

"Good evening, Vanessa," Dad said pleasantly. "Have you met

Miranda?"

"Miranda Jordan," Vanessa mused. "I've never had the pleasure. How nice."

"Good to meet you," Mom said graciously, for she outranked Vanessa.

"And this is Robert Smythe. Robert, Michael Jacobs' family plus, uh, Steven Newman's son."

"Eli, let's go," Danny urged, his impatience increasing.

"The Newmans certainly are sleepy this evening," Vanessa remarked. Her gaze turned in the direction of Steve and Ellen, now exiting the bar.

"I'm coming," I told Danny. "Good night, Dad," I said, and I turned to him for an embrace.

"Happy birthday, honey," Dad said as I returned to Danny's arms.

"That's right. It's your birthday," Vanessa remarked with syrupy sweetness. "Did you have a happy one?"

"Oh, yes," I answered. "The best. Look at what Danny gave me." I held out my wrist for inspection.

"Elizabeth, I'm sure Vanessa doesn't care. Let's go," Danny insisted.

I gaped at him, taken aback by his rudeness. Was the alcohol doing this?

"It's lovely, Elizabeth. Danny, you have excellent taste," Vanessa sneered.

"Eli, c'mon," he urged.

"Thank you, Vanessa. Good night." I barely got the words out as Danny dragged me me out of the bar.

"What was that about?" I asked Danny through gritted teeth as we made our way across the lobby to the elevators. "You were so rude to Vanessa."

"She's getting on my nerves. Everywhere we turn, there's Vanessa."

"We only ran into her at the elevator this afternoon," I pointed out.

Danny pressed the call button for the elevator. "I still don't like it," he grumbled.

I sighed. I didn't understand Danny's problem with Vanessa. He could be so difficult at times. But it was my birthday, and if I wanted the evening to end on an up-note, I would have to get Danny out of his funk.

As we waited for the elevator, I slipped under Danny's arm and wrapped mine around him. Then I reached for his face and smiled into unusually flat sapphires. Danny took my hand and kissed my palm. He smiled.

"Oh Lizzie," he sighed. "I'm never down for long if I'm with you."

I kissed Danny's cheek. "Ready to end my birthday in style?" I winked, and Danny laughed as the elevator door opened on our floor.

"Definitely," Danny answered, and he squeezed my butt.

CHAPTER FOUR - DANNY

Bonnie Raitt? Eli! At once, I disengaged from the tangle of sheets. Somehow I reached my jeans, dug the phone out of its pocket, and answered by the end of the second chorus. Elizabeth could not discover my whereabouts.

"Hey, baby," I said.

The girl whose bed I had just vacated looked expectantly at me.

"Hey yourself, honey," Eli responded cheerfully. "I wanted to chat before I went to bed."

"E, I'm saying good-night to the guys." I cradled the phone between my ear and shoulder while I struggled to pull on my jeans. "I'll be home in half an hour. Hold on a second."

The somewhat attractive, but otherwise unremarkable, dirty blonde haired girl had served a purpose, and that was all. I glanced back toward the bed, found my polo shirt, and pulled it over my head. The girl glared, and pulled the sheet up, covering her naked body. A moment earlier she had not been modest.

Stupid bitch! What did you expect when you picked a guy up at a bar?

"Sorry. I couldn't find my valet ticket," I said to Elizabeth. "Let me call you when I get home and we'll Skype."

"Okay. I love you, Danny. Drive safely," Elizabeth said in ignorant innocence.

"Always do. I love you too, babe."

I jammed the phone into my pocket, and shoved my feet into my Topsiders lying at the side of the bed.

"You have a girlfriend." The girl stated the obvious with scorn.

"She lives in New York," I lied. What did she expect? Of course I had a girlfriend.

Buoyed by adrenaline-fueled anger, the girl rose onto her knees, the sheet slipping, and with all her strength, smacked me with a pillow.

"Ouch!" I exclaimed, and I quickened my pace.

"Get out of here!" she shrieked. "You bastard!"

Grabbing my sweatshirt, I glared at her with disdain, and fled before the girl found an instrument more lethal than a pillow.

Fortunately, she lived on a busy street. I easily found a cab and arrived at the Four Seasons within minutes.

"Great," I groaned while I paid the driver. Dad! He was getting out of his car. Dad was the next to last person I wanted to run into. The last sat waiting by her laptop, curled up in the bed we shared in Malibu.

"Danny!" Dad called. Ugh! There was no way to avoid the coming inquisition.

"Hey," I said in a subdued tone.

Dad and I entered the lobby together. He grimaced as he examined his disheveled son.

"What have you been up to Danny? You're a mess."

"I was out with the guys," I answered, giving no specifics. After a week of night shooting, we had welcomed a free evening.

"You look like you just got out of bed," he said as we waited for the elevator.

I ignored this truthful observation, smoothed my hair. As the elevator doors closed behind us, I yawned.

"It's late, Dad. I want to shower and call Eli. She's expecting to Skype."

"Good idea. Shower. You can't let Elizabeth see you looking like this."

"Dad…" I hated when he acted like a parent.

Dad sidled closer, scrutinizing my appearance. I swear he even sniffed me.

"I only drank a couple of beers," I snapped. "I'm legal in Canada."

Was he judging my level of intoxication or discerning whether or not I was stoned?

"You smell like sex," Dad said in a voice filled with disapproval, and he followed me off the elevator.

"Dad," I said as I opened the door to my room, "Eli."

"She won't mind if you're. You can blame me." Dad entered behind me and closed the door.

I ignored Dad by opening a drawer containing sleep clothes and clean underwear, but to no avail.

"Danny, what the hell are you doing?" Dad asked slowly and deliberately. "You have a girlfriend! An exquisite young woman who adores you, and whom you profess to love. So what the hell were you doing? Do you want Elizabeth to break up with you?"

"Of course not. I love Eli." There was no good explanation for my behavior.

Dad glared.

Guilty as hell, I sighed. "I made a mistake, okay. I'm human. Like father, like son."

"This is not about me. I learned the hard way. Thankfully Ellen forgave me."

"I haven't seen Elizabeth in two weeks. I miss her."

"Do you miss Elizabeth, or do you miss the sex?"

"I miss Elizabeth," I answered without wavering. "Dad, I'm a man. I have needs."

"A real man controls himself so he doesn't hurt the woman he loves. You can't go two weeks without a girl?"

"Dad! It's not like that," I began defensively. "I went out with the guys, and these girls approached our table. One of them hit on me."

"And you couldn't say no?"

"I did say no. The girl went to the restroom, and the guys were all over me. They wouldn't let up until I gave in."

"You caved to peer pressure? Is approval so important that you'd jeopardize everything?"

"Dad!" He was right. I wanted the crew to forget I was the director's son and include me. "It shouldn't have gone that far. I walked the girl home so the guys would see me leave with her. That sounds so pathetic," I admitted.

"It does," Dad agreed.

"I was being a gentleman, but we reached her apartment, and she was all over me. I had no choice, Dad."

"You had a choice, Daniel. There's always a choice. You made the wrong one. Think about Elizabeth when she visits the set? You've set her up to be gossip fodder."

Crap! I hadn't considered that. And there was no way to keep Elizabeth from the set.

"I'm sorry," I said contritely.

"I'm concerned about your commitment to Elizabeth. Your girlfriend is living with you in a house owned by me. That puts me in the middle."

"Mom said we could. You didn't want Eli moving into my old bedroom, did you? That would have been so weird."

"No. No, I mean. Danny, I overheard your conversation with Elizabeth. Not that she needs your money, but you handed her your paychecks."

"I love Eli. I want to support her."

"That's my point, Danny. When you live with a woman and you support her, she has certain expectations."

"Like faithfulness," I answered sadly. I felt like such a failure.

"And that's only the beginning, Danny."

"I'm not ready for diamond rings, Dad."

"So why are you behaving like you're Elizabeth's husband?"

Dad had me there. I knew why I did, and it hurt to admit it.

"Because I love her. I'm miserable when we're apart. Dad, I'm afraid of losing Elizabeth. If she doesn't live with me, she might find someone else, and where would that leave me?"

"The same place you'll be if you don't stop cheating. Alone," he stated firmly.

Dad was right. I knew it all along, but hearing it verbalized added impact.

"Dad, I was wrong," I said contritely. "Can you keep this quiet? I swear, I won't ever do it again."

Dad smiled, and he embraced me. Then he clapped me on the shoulder.

"You're a good boy, Danny. I know you want to do the right thing. Now, go take that shower and call your girl. Elizabeth will be up Thursday, right?"

"Two more days."

"You're counting, huh?" Dad smiled. "I'll give you my RV for a private lunch when she arrives. You and Elizabeth need immediate alone time, Danny."

I smiled sheepishly. I doubted Eli would want to be so obvious. Dad had a killer RV though. His mobile estate rivaled the Four Seasons for luxury accommodations.

"Thanks, Dad," I answered.

Dad finally left. My Skype session would be late. Eli wouldn't mind when she learned I'd run into Dad.

"We break in ten minutes," I explained to gaffer Darren, shortly before one on Thursday afternoon.

I glanced at the shooting schedule on my iPad. "After lunch, Steven will be ready for the next set-up."

"I'm on it, Danny. Tell Steven everything will be ready."

Light tapping on my shoulder, and Darren's smile as he departed, gave away my guest's identity. A broad smile lit my face as warmth from my heart spread. I reached for the soft fingers and spun around.

An electric smile and sparkling emerald eyes greeted me. Eli was here!

"Oh, babe. It's you," I said, brimming with pleasure.

I pulled Elizabeth into my arms, my equilibrium restored.

"Hi!" Elizabeth's perky voice muffled against my shirt, greeted me.

"Hi, back," I answered.

Elizabeth responded with a girlish giggle. I held her face upturned in my hands. That winning smile never failed to dazzle me. I brought my lips to hers. How I'd missed them!

As I drank in her sweetness, Elizabeth wrapped her dainty hands around my neck. She didn't want to part either. My arms holding her tightly ensured that we didn't.

"I missed you so much," she whispered.

Like attracting magnets, our lips drew back together. I had no choice. I couldn't resist. We both wanted more, but had to content ourselves with kissing for now.

Lost in each other's love, we barely heard Dad's interruption.

"Hello, Elizabeth," he laughed.

We abruptly broke apart.

"Steve!" Eli laughed, embarrassed.

"I know you miss him, but this is a workplace, not a hotel," Dad laughed.

Elizabeth blushed. "Sorry, Dad." I apologized for both of us.

"Danny, after lunch why don't you show Elizabeth to my R.V. Honey, if you want to rest from your flight, you can use the stateroom. I never do."

"Thanks, Steve. It has been a long morning."

"Danny, take your time," Dad added as he walked away.

I love you, Daddy. I must be the only man in America to have their boss give them permission, not to mention a cozy location, to have a quickie with their girlfriend during the workday.

"Why don't we skip lunch? We can always snack on craft service," Eli suggested. A mischievous glint lit her eyes. She had correctly interpreted Dad's message.

The bedroom wasn't the only section of the two-story mobile estate that Dad hadn't used, at least not on this shoot.

When Mom and I first laid eyes on the 1200 square foot behemoth on wheels upon our arrival in Botswana two years ago, our jaws had dropped. Mom had worked with the design team in Los Angeles, but it was quite different studying fabric swatches and wood samples to seeing the completed animal. We were awestruck.

In the remote section of Botswana, at the edge of the Kalahari Desert, where Dad had been filming, the vehicle had made sense. With two bedrooms, it provided five-star accommodations for our family in a region thus lacking. It's conference table and desks provided Dad with office space. The touch-of-a-button screening room was utilized daily.

Parked on the set in Vancouver where modern office space and screening rooms were plentiful, and where Dad and I were housed at the Four Seasons, the mobile estate seemed excessive. Frankly, it embarrassed me. Until today, I'd even kept Eli from it.

"Oh my god!" Eli exclaimed as we neared the vehicle.

She rushed toward the door, pulling me along.

"Grant Barnes has one," she gushed, "But I've never been inside!" Elizabeth was as excited as a five year-old on Christmas morning.

Punching in the keypad code, I unlocked the door and led her inside. Elizabeth's eyes scanned the spacious kitchen/dining/living room, taking in the full-sized appliances, seating and dining space for ten, and the 42-inch television.

"This is great! Why doesn't my Mom have one?" Eli exclaimed, oozing RV envy as she entered the kitchen.

Elizabeth opened a cabinet and examined its contents. She opened and closed the oven door.

"Mom has got to get one of these."

Then Elizabeth opened the Sub-Zero refrigerator and giggled when she found it nearly empty.

"Anything to drink in there?" I asked.

Eli removed two bottles of water.

"Just this," she answered, and handed me one.

Eli's fingers purposely lingered on mine, and she smiled. I pulled back, unscrewed the bottle top, and took a long pull of water. At once I felt uncomfortable and shy. I didn't know why.

"Let me give you the tour," I suggested.

"That can wait. I want to see that stateroom Steve offered me."

Eli pressed against me and her lips were on me in a nanosecond. I held up my hand to stop her.

"Baby, later, okay?"

I realized the root of my discomfort. It would be awkward to have sex with Elizabeth, step out of the R.V., and run into the guys I'd gone out with the other night.

"Danny, Steve told me to use his stateroom. We both know what he meant."

"I know, but Eli, Dad isn't the one who has to face everyone afterwards."

"Since when are you shy, Danny?"

Elizabeth led me toward the back of the first floor. The bed was visible through the open door. Once inside the custom appointed stateroom, Elizabeth pulled her top over her head revealing a lacy pink bra.

"E, the moment we return to the set everyone will guess what we've been up to."

"I don't care," she pouted. "I missed you."

Then Eli unzipped her skirt, and it fell to the floor. Her thong matched the bra.

"It's the middle of a work day," I protested.

Eli wrapped her arms around my neck and pressed against me. When I didn't respond, she pulled back, hurt evident in her darkening emerald eyes.

"Daniel, what's going on? We haven't seen each other in two weeks. I thought you'd be as eager as I am."

Shit! Elizabeth eyed me suspiciously. After this week's elicit adventures, I was not in the mood. Dad's lecture had gotten to me. From the moment Elizabeth had arrived extraordinary guilt had quashed my desire.

Now here Eli was, the only woman I should be having sex with, standing before me wearing lacey silk undies and completely valid expectations.

Time was running out. Uncomfortable questions were forming in her brain. But simply put, I wasn't in the mood. I would have to fake it or Eli's heart would be broken. My acting chops were about to be put to the test.

I enveloped Elizabeth in my arms.

"Of course I am, baby." I inhaled and welcomed her unique Elizabeth scent, a mixture of light floral and citrus. "I'm worn. It's been a stressful morning."

Elizabeth flinched. "Danny, I'm so sorry. Of course. You've had a long day already. I wasn't thinking. Can you forgive me for being so selfish?"

Pangs of regret stabbed my heart. I was the cad here and Eli was apologizing.

"Babe, you are the farthest thing from selfish."

"We can wait until later when you're rested."

I pressed Eli against me. Then I delicately ran my fingertips across her back and thighs. Elizabeth gasped, then shuddered. I smiled as my resolve softened. Then I unhooked her bra and pushed it off her narrow shoulders.

Elizabeth looked at me, confused. "I thought you were too tired."

"I am, but I can never resist you. I may need some coaxing though."

Eli threw her arms around my neck, completely happy once more.

I crushed my lips to hers, my fire igniting. She had no idea how unworthy of her love I was. With any luck, she would never know.

CHAPTER FIVE - ELIZABETH

The ringing phone roused me from my nap. Stretching across the bed I fumbled to reach it, and I picked up on the third ring.

"Hello," I mumbled, sleepy.

It was my six o'clock wake-up call. Once Dad told me yesterday he would let me take off work not only tomorrow as planned, but also today, I was determined not to disappoint him.

Grateful that he understood how much I missed Danny, I had stayed up until four o'clock reading two screenplays and typing coverage. Once I pressed the send button to email my reports to Dad, I grabbed two hours of sleep before rising to make my flight out of LAX.

After my reunion with Danny had sapped what little energy I had, a car drove me to the hotel. I dragged myself through the lobby of the Four Seasons to the elevator. Once upstairs, I changed into Danny's shirt, and collapsed into bed. I didn't expect him back from the set until seven o'clock.

Hot, steamy water falling over my tired limbs felt so good. I luxuriated beneath the pulsating jets. Forever would not be too long to stay in this shower.

Knock, knock, knock! My heart jumped. It was too early for Danny. Who was in my room? Then I remembered the door was locked. The noise must be from the next room. I picked up the lavendar-scented bar of French-milled soap and began making a lather.

"Can I join you?" a man's voice asked.

My heart took another abrupt leap. I gasped, ready to shriek.

"Babe, it's me." Danny announced his entrance.

Of course it was. I could breathe again. Who else but Danny would be in my bathroom? How foolish of me to have been scared.

I poked my head out from behind the curtain. Danny's electric smile met mine. He was already stripping off his clothes.

"You didn't wait for my answer," I giggled.

"Eli?" Danny raised his eyebrow.

"What's taking you so long?" I gave him a saucy grin.

Danny finished knotting the belt of the oversized white hotel bathrobe at my waist. Designed to fit a man, it fell to my ankles. I held out my arms like a small child and he cuffed the sleeves for my wrists to show and my fingers to function.

Then Danny pulled me against his wet chest and kissed me. He hadn't even toweled off yet. He rubbed against my robe, and we laughed.

"I am not your towel, Daniel."

"Too bad," he laughed again.

I reached for the thick white bath-sheet. Then I dried Danny's chest, his arms, and his legs. Finally I tied the towel around his waist. The bath sheet covered Danny's legs to mid-calf.

I reached my hand against his stubbled cheek and kissed him. Danny took my hand and kissed my palm.

"I'll be out in a minute, Eli. I want to shave."

Rapid knocking on the door interrupted our moment.

"I'll get that," I said. It sounded urgent.

I slipped out of Danny's embrace and left the bathroom with a small towel in my hand. Rivulets ran down my back from my freshly shampooed hair. I vigorously rubbed my wet mane with the towel as I opened the door.

"Vanessa?" Huh?

"Elizabeth? What are you doing here?" Vanessa stuttered.

I'd never seen Vanessa lose her composure before. She was flummoxed by my appearance, which made no sense.

"This is my room," I answered curtly. Why should she be wondering why I was here? I belonged here.

"Are you looking for Danny?" I asked, though I couldn't imagine why.

"Where's Steven?" she stammered. "I thought Danny might know."

"Baby, who's at the door?" Danny called out from the bathroom.

Before I answered, Danny's towel-clad body strutted into the room.

"Vanessa?"

She and I both stared at the handsome boyish face atop the perfect toned body. What woman wouldn't? Hollywood's finest wasn't an actor. Water drizzled down from Danny's wet shaggy hair to his cheeks. A spot of shaving cream remained smudged on an earlobe.

Danny reached for the hem of his towel to wipe his face, then thought better of it. The shaving cream could wait. Instead he wiped his eyes on my robe-covered shoulder.

"Thanks, babe."

"Anytime," I chuckled.

"Vanessa?" Danny turned back to her. "We're sort of busy here."

"Do you know where Steven is?' she asked with urgency.

"Last time I saw Dad he was at the set. You have his phone number. Call him," Danny answered curtly.

"I'll do that," she answered, and Vanessa backed out the door that Danny re-locked at once.

"What was that about?" I crinkled my nose in distaste. "And Vanessa seemed so surprised to find me here."

"That's Vanessa. She thinks everyone is on call for her. Don't sweat it, babe." Danny pulled me into his arms. "Our private lunch kept your arrival a secret, miss."

I smiled into Danny's twinkling eyes, grinning at the memory we'd made in the RV stateroom. Then I whipped off his damp bath sheet, and I rubbed my hair with it.

CHAPTER SIX - ELIZABETH

Malibu, a few weeks later

"It's perfect!" The muralist had completed his installation, and not a moment too soon. Production had wrapped, and with Danny due home at the end of the week, I wanted everything perfect.

"Thank you so much," I told the artist as I walked him to the door and closed it behind him. Then I returned to the mural, mounted above the sofa and admired it.

"Ellen, isn't it wonderful? Do you think Danny will like it?"

Ellen and I had spent an enjoyable mother/daughter day in Malibu, beginning with shopping in the morning before returning home for lunch on the patio. Ellen should be the first to see the completed mural. She owned the house after all.

Ellen stepped back and appraised the piece. The seascape reflected the view from the patio of the beach and the Pacific Ocean beyond on a cloudless day. Standing in the breaking foam, a young couple held hands. The woman had long, auburn waves cascading down the back of her flowing white dress. The much taller man had shaggy, dirty blonde hair. He wore khaki shorts and a white shirt, sleeves rolled up, tails hanging out.

The couple stood to the right of center. On the left, in the near-ground, two young children, a boy and a girl, child versions of the adults, sat playing in the sand, filing pails and building a sandcastle.

"That's you and Danny when you were little."

"Yes," I nodded. "Do you think Danny will like it?" I asked again, anxious.

"Oh, yes. It's lovely, Elizabeth. But it's not actually a mural. It's on canvas."

"I wanted flexibility. What if we move? We can take a canvas with us. Same if we renovate. Danny is always talking about renovating. I want to keep this mural forever."

"You've really thought this through. Danny will love it."

Tuesday I went shopping. Again. It took most of the day, but in the end I found the perfect welcome home outfit; a short slip dress in blush rayon chiffon worn over a lace-hemmed slip. The lace peeked out from the bottom of the dress. Over the dress was a bolero length openwork cream-colored vest. Cowboy boots completed the look.

The pale colors of the dress set off my contrasting deep tan. I would wear my hair loose and natural. Danny couldn't resist.

Wednesday was spa day. I giggled to myself when I checked in. Mrs. Daniel Newman needed to be perfect when Mr. Newman returned home. And perfect I would be, from the top of my head down to my toes.

My day began with a facial followed by a hot stone massage. After a light lunch, I enjoyed a full-body scrub and a seaweed wrap. As I lay on the table covered in plant matter, I smiled imagining how much Mr. Newman would enjoy touching my soft skin after this treatment.

Last came a luxurious spa manicure and pedicure with magenta Shellac polish. I wouldn't have to worry about any chipping while I busied myself in the kitchen tomorrow and Friday.

Thursday I shopped for food. I was planning an impressive welcome home dinner. Danny would see I could cook. And bake, too. Flora had taught me her amazing apple crumble recipe, and Danny loved any dessert made with apples.

Tonight I would bake the crumble. Then tomorrow while we dined, I would warm it in a low-heat oven and serve it with vanilla ice cream. Or whipped cream. Whichever Danny preferred, his choice. I'd buy both!

But first I visited Williams-Sonoma. I was short on those kitchen implements Flora used because Mom had accumulated them over the years. I needed a pie pan, a peeler, and an apple corer. But while I was there…. It was impossible to leave with only the three items on my list.

The perfect apple crumble, piping hot, with the penetrating aroma of cinnamon and nutmeg was out of the oven, resting on the ceramic trivet painted with apple motif, that I had purchased this morning.

I glanced around the kitchen. What a mess! It was ten o'clock, and the counter was covered in flour and brown sugar, plus it was sticky from juicy apple slices. The sink was full of mixing bowls and baking tools. Exhausted, I whipped out a sponge. The kitchen had to be made spotless.

An hour later, Martha Stewart would have been proud. Except for the masterpiece sitting on the counter, there was not one trace of my labors.

I stumbled up the stairs for a night of good, deep sleep. After changing to Danny's shirt and brushing my teeth, I slipped between the sheets and turned off the lights. Wired in anticipation of Danny's arrival, I couldn't fall asleep!

While listening to the breaking waves, I fantasized about tomorrow night and grinned. Danny would be lying beside me. Danny would hold me, he would love me. Danny would… amazing! It was so real, I could almost feel him.

But if I didn't get to sleep, I would look like hell tomorrow when I wanted to give Danny perfection.

CHAPTER SEVEN - DANIEL

The cabin of a Gulfstream is a cramped space when you're forced to share it with someone whom you feel such extreme animosity toward that the sight of them triggers an allergic reaction.

Such was the state of my affairs on the flight home from Vancouver with Dad. I wouldn't talk to him. I couldn't even look at him without cringing. A quick glance in his direction confirmed Dad was avoiding me as well. He stared out the window, a stony expression on his face.

So I ceded half the plane to Dad, the better half, and I suffered. I desperately needed sleep, but the sofas for stretching out were in Dad's quadrant. I didn't dare claim the stateroom, either. Instead, I was relegated to a club chair.

Chronic exhaustion plagued me. Three grueling months of hard work, erratic schedules, and insufficient sleep, had taken their toll. My body and my brains no longer needing to perform, they had now collapsed. I existed like a zombie, empty and dead.

I had to get some sleep! I just had to. Dark circles rimmed my eyes. Eli would freak when she saw them. I needed energy too. Eli's expectations required vigor. I couldn't disappoint her.

We hadn't been together in two weeks. Eli wanted me so badly, and she assumed the feelings were mutual. I thought they were. Exhaustion had put me in such a state, I was no longer certain about anything.

Eli was a trooper. She would understand if all I wanted to do when I got home was to crawl into bed and sleep. Sleep. Sleep.

Somehow I dozed, though not long enough. I rubbed the sleep out of my eyes, yawned, and looked out the window. We were beginning our decent. Soon I would see Elizabeth waiting on the tarmac. I yawned again. It would take more than an hour's nap to right me.

"Mr. Newman," Deliah, the flight attendant, interrupted my reverie. "Seatbelt, please. We're preparing to land."

I complied with her request and returned to starring out the window. I imagined Elizabeth standing beside her car, scanning the skies over Santa Monica for the Gulfstream. She would wear something new to please me. Her hair would be worn loose. Eli knew how sexy I found those thick auburn waves.

The plane touched down, a soft kiss to the tarmac. Sure enough, there was Elizabeth, standing beside Mike's white BMW X5. The Range Rover was garaged in New York this summer.

Gathering my belongings with all deliberate slowness allowed Dad to deplane first. From the doorway, I watched Dad and Eli embrace. She seemed happy to see him. And why not? She didn't know the truth, and I intended to protect her from it.

Dad kissed Elizabeth's cheek as I strode down the stairs. He uttered some words to Eli. What, I wished I knew.

Then as my feet reached the tarmac, Dad left Elizabeth for his car. My eyes locked on hers. I grinned. Elizabeth smiled, thrilled to see me. She was literally a sight for my sore eyes.

"Eli!" I called out.

"Danny!" She shrieked.

At full-speed, Elizabeth ran into my waiting arms, threw her hands around my neck, and jumped up, wrapping her legs around my waist. All the while we laughed, me at her exuberance, Eli joyous, thrilled to see me.

"I missed you so much," she squealed.

"I missed you too, babe."

I grabbed Elizabeth's head through her wild mane and crushed our lips together. Incredible! I needed this. Elizabeth's kiss tasted sweeter than sweet. She felt soft and feminine. Perfection.

The silk of her dress matched the smoothness of her skin. I held her firmly, my hand supporting her shapely bottom, now peeking out from beneath her short skirt that had risen high on her thighs.

"E, your dress," I scolded. I did not want Dad or the crew getting a free show.

"Whoops," Elizabeth giggled as I gently placed her back on her feet. I pulled her in for another kiss.

"It's so good to be back," I told her.

Wrapping my arm around Eli's slender shoulders, we walked to the car and waited for my luggage to be brought over. I wouldn't let her go.

"I can't wait to get home," I whispered.

"Oh, yes," Eli giggled. Then she examined my face. "Danny, you look like hell."

"Thanks, babe," I answered drily.

Elizabeth stroked my three-day beard with her delicate fingertips. They paused on my cheek and she kissed me.

"But you're the handsomest hell I've ever seen."

"You're awfully quiet," Elizabeth remarked as she turned north on Pacific Coast Highway. She was right. I had no energy, and probably hadn't said more than a handful of words.

"Don't mind me," I said. "I'm tired. Let me be quiet."

And she did. Stopped at the Topanga Canyon traffic light, I reached for

Eli's hand and kissed it. She shouldn't interpret my quiet as me ignoring her.

My pulse quickened as we neared downtown Malibu. Familiar landscapes excited me. The waves on Eli's side of the car cracked against the shore. This was home!

"I'll bring the luggage in later," I announced as Eli parked the car in the garage beside my Porsche. My Porsche! How I'd missed my beloved car.

After I climbed out of the X5, I ran my fingertips over the hood of the black Carrerea, and sighed with pleasure. When Elizabeth came around from her side of her car. I reached for her hand and pulled her into my arms, pressing against the Porsche. Eli shouldn't suspect I was numb and going through the motions.

"It's good to be home," I said.

Eli reached around my neck, a smile lighting her face, those emerald eyes showing her love. Again, I reached through her tangled waves, and brought her lips to mine. The strength of our love bound us together.

Eli stood on out-stretched toes. I lifted her gently off the ground. Instinctively she wrapped her slender legs, strong and flexible from years of dance, around my waist.

This time, I didn't mind Elizabeth's skirt riding up. I eagerly reached beneath the silk fabric to support her firm but satiny smooth bottom. With Elizabeth pressed into me, well maybe I wasn't as tired as I thought.

"Let's go upstairs, Mrs. Newman," I whispered.

Eli giggled. She loved when I called her 'Mrs. Newman.'

"I was wondering when you would ask," she teased.

"Oh were you," I laughed. "Let's go."

I set Elizabeth back on her feet, took her hand, and opened the door to the house. I led her towards the stairs with urgency.

Upstairs in the bedroom, I was in awe. Elizabeth hadn't redecorated, but the room was so welcoming. They say 'absence makes the heart grow fonder,' but for furniture? Too many nights in an impersonal hotel, I guess?

There on the table was a vase filled with fresh white roses, and nestled in the center, the silk rose that would never die, just like our love.

I turned to Elizabeth and wrapped her in my arms. "It's so good to be home," I whispered. "Now where were we?"

Elizabeth grinned. "Right here," she giggled, and then she pulled her dress and its slip over her head. In her blush-colored bra and matching thong, Elizabeth was breathtaking and my pulse raced.

I gently fluffed her hair, admiring the contrast of dark auburn against pale silk. Eli smiled, pleased with the happiness only she could provide. I lifted her into my arms, amazed by her lightness. Devouring her lips with my kiss, I carried her to the bed and delicately placed her down before joining her.

I kissed her shoulder and her neck. Eli shivered. Then she arched her back, begging for more.

"I can't resist you. My wife, you are the most beautiful, sexiest woman ever."

I pulled off my shirt while Eli yanked opened my shorts and pushed them off. She reached for me and smiled provocatively. I deftly removed her bra and thong.

"I've missed you so much," I whispered.

Our lips crushed together again, our bodies joined, and I entered her with force. Searing pleasure spread throughout us. Sharing our powerful love, we soon exploded.

Afterwards, Elizabeth cuddled against me. Her head on my shoulder, there was wild auburn hair everywhere. I brushed strands off my face before I found them in my mouth. Eli giggled at my struggle.

"I love you babe, but now I've got to get some sleep."

Eli kissed my cheek and ran her fingertips over my stubbled cheek.

"I'm sorry," Elizabeth giggled. "I wore you out."

"No, you're not sorry. Be honest."

"You're right. I'm not." Eli kissed me again. "But I'll let you sleep."

Elizabeth began to rise. I reached for her arm.

"Stay with me, Eli. You know I don't like sleeping alone."

She considered my request, and lay back down. "How did you get through the summer?"

"Maybe that's why I'm so tired. Wake me when it's time for dinner. Where do you want to go?"

"Nowhere. I'm cooking tonight."

"Yeah, right. Elizabeth, all you can do is make a tossed salad."

"Mmmmm," I murmured, having been woken by the sweetest kiss.

As my eyes slowly opened, I reached for Eli's fingers and pulsed them.

"Hey," she said cheerfully. "Feeling better?"

I tried focusing on her face, but needed my eyeglasses.

"Here," Eli said. As though reading my mind, she carefully placed them on my face.

"Thanks, babe. Now I can see your beautiful face."

Eli blushed, as I knew she woud. I yawned. "I think I'm awake," I told her.

"Good, 'cause it's time for you to shower. Dinner is just about ready."

"I can't believe you're cooking. Do you have a back-up pizza in the freezer?"

"Daniel!" she scowled, and swatted my hair.

I laughed. "Just kidding, Elizabeth."

Running down the stairs, I inhaled the warm aroma of a well-cooked meal. Could the beef I detected possibly taste as delicious as it smelled? I shook my head. Doubtful. No matter what she said, Eli couldn't cook. But the smell… mmmmm.

The lovely chef stood outside, laying silverware on the table beside china I didn't recognize. Eli had also changed clothes; to a long, gauzy apricot-colored skirt with a belted white tank top that emphasized her tiny waist and narrow hips.

I headed toward the sliders to join Elizabeth on the patio. On my way through the living room, a painting taking up the entire wall behind the couch begged my attention.

The seascape reminded me of the view from our bedroom window. A young couple and two children playing in the sand were its subjects. What a nice family. One day that might be us. Perhaps that inspired Elizabeth's purchase of the piece.

I caught up with Elizabeth as she completed setting the table. She flashed me a winning smile, and I took her hands.

"Hey, babe," I mumbled as I kissed her cheek. "Everything looks great."

"Still tired?" Elizabeth was surprised.

"Yeah," I said while massaging my temple. "I'm fuzzy-headed."

"But you slept for six hours." I shrugged. "Hmm. Well, just take a seat. I'm getting the salads out."

I obediently did as told while Elizabeth strode to the outdoor kitchen and removed two plates from the refrigerator. While I waited for her to serve, I picked up my salad fork and mindlessly twirled it between my fingers.

Meanwhile, I examined the china. The large round charger plate was unfamiliar. White with a wide black band, it was modern and very attractive, but…

"Where did this come from" I asked Elizabeth as she set down the coordinating salad plates.

"Geary's," she answered. "They're Kate Spade."

"Nice," I responded without enthusiasm.

What else was new? It was as though I'd landed in a honeymoon cottage without any notice. Kate Spade? Geary's? Had Elizabeth signed up for the bridal registry? The whole notion left me uncomfortable. Although I had instructed Eli to make the house our home, and buying dishes made sense, the reality my words had spawned weirded me out.

"Baby, everything was amazing," I told Elizabeth as I carried the dinner plates to the kitchen sink. The Shrimp Louis salad dressing had just the right tang. The beef tenderloin with its peppery crust was a perfect medium-rare pink.

"When did you learn to cook like this?" I asked, duly impressed.

Eli beamed with pride, and rightly so. When I'd left for Vancouver, the girl could slice and dice veggies and cook a few simple dishes, but not an entire gourmet meal like the one she had produced this evening.

"Flora gave me a few lessons, and I watched Food Network."

"You learned all this from television?" I laughed.

Elizabeth laughed too, understanding the absurdity. "It gave me confidence, and I picked up some tips. Now Danny, go back outside and sit down. I have desert to serve."

"Yes, ma'am," I saluted.

Moments later, Elizabeth appeared at the table carrying desert plates. I didn't need to look. The enticing aroma, a blend of cinnamon and sweetness, announced my favorite desert, Apple Crumble!

I grinned from ear-to-ear as Elizabeth placed the warm plates on the table. A small scoop of vanilla ice cream with a squirt of whipped cream on top of the crumble was already melting. I hadn't felt this good in weeks!

"I hope you like it," Eli said eagerly as she sat down beside me.

"Well, yeah. It's my favorite. Thanks, babe."

Eli's eyes were glued on me. She stared as I lifted my fork and took the first bite. My eyes opened wide in delight. The sweet cinnamon syrup, the tangy apple, and the crumb topping combined for a full-fledged orgasm on a plate.

"Amazing. It's really fantastic."

"You're not just saying that?" Eli asked, but she was giddy.

"Yeah. This is the best apple crumble ever. Where'd you get it?"

Elizabeth was glowing. "Our kitchen, silly," she answered. "I baked it."

"Get out of here! This is great! Is there any more?"

"There's a whole pan." she trilled.

Eli had tried so hard to please me, and she more than exceeded expectations.

"Good. 'Cause I want another slice." Eli grinned, so proud. "Who would ever have imagined, my spoiled Hollywood princess could cook!"

Eli giggled. "Well we can't eat every meal at The Café once we move out of the dorm, and all you can do is grill."

Move out of the dorm? Elizabeth's assumption left me flat. It wasn't unexpected. An apartment made perfect sense. We lived in our own home here. Why wouldn't we do the same in New York?

This was the logical next step, I didn't want. Not yet.

CHAPTER EIGHT - ELIZABETH

Tomorrow Danny and I were flying back to Donnelly. Summer vacation finally over, and not a moment too soon.

I never imagined I would be relieved to leave Malibu. The week I had waited all summer for had come and gone. Rather than a time for creating cherished memories, it had become a nightmare.

Almost from the start, Danny had not been himself. It wasn't what he said; he used all the right words. And it wasn't that Danny didn't show me his love; he certainly demonstrated his passion. But something wasn't right.

Danny seemed off in that subtle way only someone who knows you as intimately as your spouse could discern. Even after his initial exhaustion passed, Danny's spark did not return. He was lethargic.

Most telling was two evenings ago at Dodger Stadium, the last game we attended before leaving Los Angeles. The easy Dodger victory over the Pirates should have elevated Danny to euphoria, but didn't.

For the first time in a lifetime spent with Danny, I found myself working at it. Our usual easy repartee felt clumsy. Whereas normally the smiles and laughter came naturally, I now made an effort.

I didn't know what to do. Should I confront Danny or wait for it to pass? The uncertainty of a confrontation frightened me, so I avoided one. Now I hoped returning to Donnelly would restore Danny. Perhaps my love wasn't sufficient. Perhaps he needed his friends and the hard partying I dreaded.

I hoped a return to the familiar routines of classwork, studying, and Donnelly social life, would bring Danny back. If not...

For probably the first time in the history of Danny and I being Danny and I, we were dining with my mother tonight, and I was glad. If I could spirit Mom away from Dad and Ellen... I desparately needed her advice.

By evening's end a tete a tete with Mom had not materialized. With Steve back in Vancouver for the week, Mom didn't leave Ellen's side, and this conversation needed to be private.

Oh, well! While dining at my parents' house, the old Danny re-emerged. From the moment we arrived, Danny's warm, easy-going smile returned. He lavished me with the attention I craved, whether it was holding my hand, whispering in my ear, or subtlely touching me.

After dinner when we repaired to the patio to enjoy dessert, Danny pulled me onto his lap and held me close, his strong arms affectionately wrapped around my waist. Our parents smiled, acknowledging their pleasure in seeing us so happy.

I returned home with renewed hope the crisis had passed.

Danny's mood change held the next morning. Unfortunately our plane was leaving at ten so we couldn't linger when the alarm clock signaled. But Danny slapped it off and pounced on me anyway.

Sapphire eyes twinkling with full strength had their desired effect. I melted. My heart galloped. Danny grinned, and he pulled the sheet out of the way. Right as our lips crushed together, he entered me.

Conscious of the time, we couldn't enjoy each other for long. Soon, Danny gave me one more kiss and removed the arm holding me pressed against him.

"Time to rise, sleepyhead."

I groaned, unhappy. Then I playfully climbed on top of him, straddled his hips, and looked Danny straight in the eyes.

"I don't want to leave," I complained.

Danny kissed me as he brought himself up to sitting with me still on top. He swept my hair out of my face and placed his hands on my shoulders.

"What difference does it make?" Danny asked. Ferocity filled his eyes.

Huh? Was he nuts? "Danny, we just woke up in our own home. Tonight we're sleeping in a dorm room," I cried.

I didn't want to, I knew it was childish, but we'd had this discussion so many times. What did Danny still not get about my disappointment with our housing situation? And why wasn't he equally as unhappy? I broke down sobbing, distraught.

Danny wrapped conforting arms around me.

"Shhh, shhh, Eli. Don't cry," he said softly, trying to soothe me. "As long as we're together, wherever we are is home."

"It doesn't bother you?"

"It does, but we'll make do," he answered tersely.

Now with two hours left before the Gulfstream touched down, Danny was napping, his head resting in my lap. I mindlessly stroked his soft, thick hair while I sat on the sofa brooding, starring out the window at the endless blue sky.

Maybe Danny was right. Maybe as long as we were together the accommodations wouldn't matter.

Who was I fooling? Of course it mattered. Last year I might have been excited that being a sophomore meant having a single. As a freshman, the prospect of any room without roommates pleased me. Now, no longer. I was used to so much better.

Upon opening the door and entering my room, I broke down again. Sobs wracked my body. Danny ushered me over to the bed and sat me down on the bare twin mattress, holding me in his arms. I didn't want to live here.

"It's awful," I cried. "Danny, how are we supposed to live like this?" I wanted a house! Or at least an apartment, and I wanted it now!

The dorm room measured perhaps seven feet wide, and possibly fifteen feet long. There wasn't even a real closet; just a freestanding wardrobe. How would our clothes fit? In another century, these rooms had not been designed for the wealthy girls who attended Donnelly, but rather, for their servants. Servants didn't require space for designer wardrobes! Upstairs, Danny had nearly an identical one.

"We'll figure it out," Danny responded, but I didn't see how that was possible.

With Danny owning the larger bed, we were sleeping upstairs. If I had to trek down here every morning to get dressed, ugh! This was no better than last year. My head slouched into my knees. I was depressed.

Danny massaged my shoulders. Usually his strong hands kneading my muscles cured me. Not this time.

"You're tired, babe. Let's eat. You'll feel better. Then we'll unpack."

Save for freshmen, the dining hall was empty. We enjoyed a quiet dinner at our usual table, staking our claim for the year. After, my hunger sated, I admitted Danny was right. I felt better physically. But my mood was just as pissy.

Sleep did not come easily. Danny's full-sized bed felt foreign and small. Dorm sounds; doors opening and closing, and rowdy voices oblivious to us trying to sleep, distracted me. But Danny slept peacefully, undisturbed. How could he?

I missed the sound of waves breaking, and the scent of salty ocean air. Only the strong arms wrapped around me seemed familiar, but I wasn't sure if they held me in affection or for safety, to keep me from falling off the bed and onto the floor.

Unbelievable, the morning was worse. Upon stepping out of the shower, we encountered two guys in shorts and tees shaving at the sinks. They starred, gawking actually. Had they never seen a girl in a bathrobe before? Or were they envious of Danny, his sculpted chest and flat abs prominent above the towel wrapped at his waist. Perhaps they were jealous because Danny had a girl and they didn't.

So awkward! And we couldn't escape. Our toiletries waited on the shelf above the two middle sinks, trapping us between the ones being used by the guys who continued staring. I didn't want to brush my teeth in front of strangers.

Danny lived on this corridor last year. How did they not know us? Freshmen! Crap! More than six hundred new students to discover we were

Miranda Jordan's daughter and Steven Newman's son. How many already knew we attended Donnelly but didn't recognize us?

Over six hundred new students whose trustworthyness we would have to decipher. Ugh! I hated this. Count me out! I had my friends. I didn't want additional ones. It was too much work.

Danny had the same realization. He smiled at the guys and warmly asked, "You're freshmen, right?"

"Yes. I'm Sam," said the slender one with dark, curly hair.

"And I'm his roommate, Ian," added the other whose short sandy hair stuck up in a frizzy bedhead.

"Danny Newman and Elizabeth Jacobs, sophomores."

"Hi," I said uncomfortably, "I'm his roommate, too."

"Yes, she is," Danny smiled.

I relaxed. I didn't want Sam and Ian thinking Danny had picked me up for the night.

"Sophomores," Ian pondered. "Know where we can find a good party?"

I'd let Danny handle this one. "We checked in late last night. Don't let your RA hear you asking me," Danny chuckled.

Perhaps we should introduce Ian to Duncan. As a freshman last year, Duncan Lebeau had established a reputation as the most notorious partier on campus. Much to my chagrin, Danny spent too many evenings with him at a housing enclave at Donnelly called the Village. My contempt for Duncan's friends intensified after Danny had a fling with one of their girls and we nearly broke up.

"Eli, it's like you're paralyzed, babe."

Danny was right. After returning to our downstairs room after breakfast, I sat on the bed starring at the two suitcases left untouched last night, and a stack of cartons that had spent the summer in storage.

"I don't know what to do. There isn't enough room upstairs for everything."

"So don't decide today, Elizabeth. Let's get your stuff unpacked. We'll deal with that later."

"Danny, it would be different if your room was on this hall. I can't function with my bed upstairs and my clothes down here. What if you hang your winter stuff in this room? Then we'll have room upstairs for what I'm wearing now. When it gets cold, we'll switch."

"Eli, you're obssessing. Start unpacking. If you want to keep stuff upstairs, do it gradually. Like last night. Where are your clothes from yesterday?"

"Upstairs. I hung my skirt in the closet and the rest is in the laundry bag."

"And when it comes back from the laundry, it'll go upstairs. See? Now please, let's unpack."

Soon all the clothing was put away, but my mood did not abate. Surrounded by cartons, I didn't know what to do next. I didn't want to do anything. I was numb.

"Let's make up the bed," Danny suggested.

"Why? We're not sleeping down here."

"This room is depressing, Elizabeth. If we make the bed, the linens will make it cheerful. Maybe then you'll get out of your funk."

"It's still depressing," I moaned once the pink and white Kate Spade linens neatly dressed the bed.

"Now let's tackle these cartons," Danny urged while ignoring my previous remarks.

"Danny, don't unpack them. We'll be moving soon. Why do it twice?"

Danny took me by my shoulders and leaned in to make eye contact.

"Eli, it might be awhile. Classes are starting. We don't have time to search for a place?"

"It's not like buying a house. Securing a rental won't be difficult."

"Baby, maybe we should wait until second smester."

"Are you kidding?" Tears formed. I blinked hard to prevent my crying.

"Our parents have paid for this semester. Moving now would waste their money."

I couldn't believe those words came from Danny's mouth. Anyone else's perhaps, but not Danny's.

"Since when do you care about the cost of anything?" I blurted.

My world was caving in. I ran to the bed, burrowed my face in the pillows and sobbed. What the hell? Last week Danny seemed off, but before we left Malibu he appeared to have returned to his usual self. Now he had no interest in finding an apartment?

Danny strode to my side, and brushed the hair off my wet cheeks. "E, don't cry."

I lifted my tear-stained face and came eye-to-eye with him.

"Danny, is something wrong here? We've been discussing this move for months."

"No, babe. It's just… I… oh, Eli. As soon as we landed, I realized I missed my friends. It won't be Donnelly without Cam and Shane living down the hall. Baby, we're sophomores. I'm not ready to live off-campus yet. I want the full college experience."

"But what about us?" I cried, my voice rising. "Are you saying you only want to live with me when we're in L.A.? Cause we're barely there, Danny!"

"That's not it at all," Danny snapped. "I love you, Eli. I'm just thinking Donnelly is a difficult school to live off-campus at because everyone else lives on it. We'll have no social life."

"So where does this leave us?" I fretted.

Danny smiled impishly. "Inconvenienced," he answered. "We'll live upstairs but you'll have to leave most of your stuff down here."

"That's not living together. That's sleeping together," I complained.

Danny smiled. "It's living together, collegiate style."

"I don't like this," I mumbled.

"I know you don't, but you love me, so we'll do it."

"I want to go home!" I wailed.

Danny pulled me into his arms and hugged me tight.

"Babe, I know this is difficult," he said soothingly. "You'll see. Give it a couple of weeks and we'll be used to it."

Danny lifted my chin and kissed me. At first I forced myself not to respond, but my body wouldn't listen. I relaxed, gave in, and enjoyed the kiss.

"Feel better?"

"You think all you have to do is kiss me and I'll get over anything, but this time I'm not."

"Liz, you're killing my self-esteem here," Danny said with mock dejection.

Then he tickled me and we both laughed, though I tried not to.

By mid-afternoon, we completed unpacking the cartons and setting up my room. The predicament was still depressing, but the room no longer was.

While I waited for Danny, who had gone upstairs for a few things, I uploaded photos I took in Malibu last week. The perfect view from our bedroom balcony of the sun setting over the breaking waves cheered me. A few quick keystrokes and…

"What are you doing, babe?" Danny had let himself back in.

"Designing a poster," I answered. "Want one?"

"Move over. Let me see."

I relinquished my chair to Danny and sat cross-legged on the bed while he scrolled through the photos on my laptop.

"This is the one I want, but only a 5x7. It's going on my desk."

I glanced at the screen. The photo was of me! Taken on the patio, I was relaxed, seated on a lounge, wearing Danny's grey cashmere pullover and a bathing suit. My knees were pulled up, and I was laughing, green eyes mischievously flashing, because Danny had been making funny faces. Even I had to admit, it was a great shot.

"That way even when you're not home I can see your beautiful smile." As an afterthought Danny added, "And a wallet sized one too. You'll always be with me."

We may be living in a dorm for now, but knowing Danny wanted me with him every minute of the day, even when classes and activities kept us apart was more than adequate compensation. I smiled. Could it be the real Danny was finally back?

CHAPTER NINE - DANIEL

"Leaving?" Shane asked as we ran into him in the parking lot.

"Man, it's great to see you."

I greeted Shane with a heart-felt embrace, like brothers who hadn't seen each other in years. Had it only been three and a half months? It seemed like forever.

Shane hefted two large suitcases onto a luggage trolley, leaving his Jeep Wrangler packed with cartons and clothes on hangers. Cam was also returning today. I looked forward to hanging with the guys this evening.

"Elizabeth!" Shane exclaimed when we broke apart.

"Shane!" Eli squealed. "I missed you!" She jumped into his arms for a hug.

"You're still with this guy?" he teased. "I thought you'd come to your senses by now."

"I know, right? I'm a masochist," Elizabeth laughed.

"Cam will be disappointed," Shane smirked. Eli smiled at this reference to Cam's short-lived crush on her early last year. I grimaced.

"Where are you going?" Shane finally asked.

"Running errands," Elizabeth answered.

"Eli's having a difficult time adjusting to dorm life so we're picking up posters we made from photos we took at the beach."

"Shane, it's awful here," Elizabeth protested. "These freshmen in the bathroom gawked at us this morning."

"And there was no spa tub! Poor, you!" Shane laughed. He enjoyed needling Elizabeth

Eli rolled her eyes, not amused.

"Of course they were gawking. They're freshmen," I laughed. "The prettiest girl they've ever seen is standing before them dripping wet in a bathrobe. That doesn't happen in high school."

Shane nearly doubled over laughing. I couldn't stop laughing either. What was funnier, Eli's naivety or Shane's hysteria?

Elizabeth glared. She didn't get it. Eli didn't understand the power of her beauty, and I was glad.

"Enjoy your summer, Shane?" I choked out as my laughter subsided.

"I waited tables. A lot of hard work," Shane stammered as he tried stopping his laughter. "My parents still like their beach house so they won't give it to me like yours did. It may have been the Hamptons, but it was living with Mom and Dad."

"That sucks for you," I said.

"Tell me about it," Shane continued. "I'm surrounded all day by hot babes in bikinis and I have nowhere to bring them at night."

"Poor thing," I laughed.

"It's not funny, Newman. What I wouldn't give for your set-up."

Later we returned to my room to continue unpacking.

After a break for a surprisingly solid nap, I woke with the realization that this was not what I needed. With Elizabeth, still deep in sleep, lying next to me with a lovely smile playing on her lips, the realization struck; I did not want to be here.

I felt trapped, afraid to move for fear of waking her. Elizabeth would want, no she would expect, that we would make love and I didn't want to. I had no desire.

What was wrong with me? The stunning woman whom I loved, a girl who turned heads wherever she went, lay next to me, naked, and I had no interest.

Visions from Vancouver consumed me. My stomach sank. The nightmare haunted me though I was awake. Flashbacks were particularly powerful. The pain was unbearable. My breathing became shallow. Get out of my brain!

I closed my eyes and tightly squeezed them together, an attempt at blocking out the disturbing memories. That only made it worse. Without Eli in my line of sight, the darkness was more vivid.

Immediately I opened my eyes and concentrated on Eli, trying to replace the evil vision with one of beauty and goodness.

It didn't work. I had to get out of here! One more night and I feared I would have an actual breakdown. How I longed to hang out with Shane and Cam. And Duncan should also be back by now. Ian wasn't the only one wanting to party

When Eli woke I would lay down the law. If she didn't like it, I didn't care. After a summer spent under Dad's watchful eyes, what I wanted more than anything was a night with the guys. I desperately needed to get wasted.

There! Decision made! I felt infinitely better, my attitude adjusted. Time to wake Eli. My desire had returned.

CHAPTER TEN - ELIZABETH

This morning I desperately wanted to give Danny the cold shoulder, but I didn't.

Last night after Danny left to join the guys I could have hung out with Rachel and Chloe, but I just couldn't. The girls would read through my shallow smiles and know that all was not perfect in the Jacobs-Newman household.

When Danny finally stumbled home at three in the morning, he reeked. Last year I often slept through these arrivals, but Danny clambered through the door, not seeming to notice or care that I was sleeping. Why so inconsiderate?

Pretending to sleep, I ignored him. But when Danny climbed into bed, it became impossible. The stench of marijuana and beer overwhelmed my senses.

Then just as I dozed off again, Danny bolted for the door, jarring me out of my drowsy state. When he returned, I was relieved that my senses had not been assaulted by additional noxious odors. I assumed he made it to the toilet in time.

When Danny bolted a second time, I sat up, wide-awake. I was furious, but I loved Danny too much not to be concerned.

Like a good wife, I found the bottle of Extra-Strength Tylenol, shook out two caplets, and placed them on the desk beside a fresh bottle of water whose cap I first loosened.

Danny took longer this time, but when he returned, I understood why. Dripping wet and wearing a towel around his waist, he carried his soiled clothing in a bundle and deposited them in the laundry bag.

Eying the Tylenol, Danny grabbed the caplets and swallowed them with half the bottle of water.

"Thanks, baby. I'm sorry," he said, contrite. I turned my back to him.

Moments later, Danny crawled into bed. He wrapped his arm around me and leaned over to kiss me. I didn't want his kiss, but I couldn't help responding to his minty-fresh breath.

"Don't be angry, Eli."

Sapphire puppy-dog eyes pleaded for my forgiveness. When he gave me that look, I was defenseless and Danny knew it. I caved.

I brushed a lock of damp hair off his brow, my hand lingering on his cheek. "I'm not angry," I assured Danny. "It's late. Let's get some sleep."

Danny tenderly kissed me. "I love you, baby," he whispered.

"I know you do," I answered. "I love you too. You'll feel better in the morning."

And Danny did. We both did.

"Great bracelet!" Chloe said when Danny and I joined our friends for lunch.

"Thanks," I answered, and I beamed with pride.

I had kept my gift in its box since arriving at Donnelly. I didn't want it getting damaged while I unpacked.

"A little trinket for m'lady's birthday," Danny added. He grinned, pleased by the attention his gift received.

"Well, it's stunning," Chloe said. "Danny, you can shop for me anytime."

Danny laughed. "Sorry, Chloe. My Amex card has already been spoken for."

Chloe grinned. I kissed Danny's cheek.

"Hey, guys!" Rachel had arrived.

"Rach!" I cried, and I jumped up to embrace her. Rachel was the Donnelly friend whom I missed the most this summer and I hadn't seen her since our return.

"I'm surprised to see you guys," Rachel said as she took her seat after embracing Danny.

"Where else would we be?" I asked. "It's noon."

"I didn't mean lunch," Rachel explained. "After a summer in Malibu I thought you'd transfer to UCLA and live at the beach."

"Rach, don't go there," Danny warned.

"We discussed it," I said flatly.

"I like Donnelly," Danny said with deliberateness. "And you do too."

"I thought you'd at least live off-campus," said Chloe.

"We will. Soon. Danny only got home from Vancouver last week so we didn't have time to look for a place," I explained.

Then I turned to Danny and tugged his arm, excited. "Oh, oh, oh! I forgot to tell you. I passed by the housing board. There's a posting for the perfect house. It's three bedrooms and two baths."

"Why do you need three bedrooms?" Shane asked. "Isn't that large?"

Was he kidding? Three bedrooms isn't large.

"One bedroom to sleep in, one to study in, and one for guests. We can't have guests sleep on the couch," I said indignantly.

"You wouldn't dare to offend Martha Stewart," Rachel answered, her voice tinged with sarcasm.

What didn't Rachel get about having a guest room? Everybody at home had at least one if not more.

"Danny, Steff wants to visit from DC this year. And I bet Zach will come down from Boston. And maybe Hannah can visit!"

"Eli, you don't like your cousin," Danny pointed out.

"Hey! Hannah's family," I retorted. "Danny, I'm calling right after lunch. It's freshly painted, has new carpets, and the kitchen and bathrooms are recently renovated." I paused to think if I left anything out. "Oh, and it has a two-car garage, and the posting said it's walking distance to Donnelly. It's perfect!"

"Elizabeth, that sounds great," Chloe agreed.

"We have to call right away," I explained. "The landlord will love us when he learns we're ready to make a three-year commitment."

"A three-year commitment?" Danny exclaimed.

"Well, yeah, through graduation. I don't want to move every year. We can pay the rent over the summer even though we're not here. Won't that be great, not having to pack and unpack?"

"Eli, shouldn't we settle into our classes first?"

"Danny! It's only $3,500 a month. I don't want someone else to snatch it first. Who knows if we can find another place this nice, and so close to Donnelly."

All summer we had discussed moving out of the dorm. Why was it now that I'd found a place, Danny seemed so tentative? Who knows? Perhaps this wouldn't be the right house. All I wanted was to call and book a showing.

If Danny was concerned with the time-consuming nature of house hunting, I could do it alone. I made up my mind. I would screen any potential rentals and only show him the promising ones. Once Danny saw the actual house, he was certain to share my enthusiasm.

"Loved that photo of you on the boart, Elizabeth," Cam said a little later. "You were scalding! We're you even wearing anything?"

"Of course I was wearing something! I had on a bikini." I glared at Cam. How dare he embarrass me like this!

Damn that photographer! That had been a private birthday outing. Now, thanks to the internet, everyone was leering at me. Thank goodness he hadn't been shooting from a glider. I would have been mortified if what had happened next had found its way to the web.

"We're never going to live that down are we?" I complained to Danny.

"Probably not," he answered. Then Danny sat up a little straighter. "What a great day. Everything was perfect," he said wistfully.

I grinned at Danny. My heart fluttered, excited by the memory. He caressed my back, but it lacked emotion. Oddly too, Danny's smile was tinged with sadness.

"Oh, yes," I added, forcing cheer. "It was my birthday. Even the weather was perfect. Excellent sailing conditions."

Again I smiled at the memory. "We did a lot of sailing in Vancouver. We're going to buy a boat next summer," I announced.

"Or maybe when we graduate," said Danny, sounding more sedate. "That day was supposed to be private. A man can't even take his lady sailing…"

"How did they get that picture?" Chloe asked.

"Long-range telephoto. They're pros."

"Yeah, I guess so," I groaned. "Ever since those pictures from the premiere hit 'People,' what is this, like the third or fourth time somebody has photographed us going about our lives? Last time we were coming out of Ralph's supermarket. Just because our parents are famous doesn't mean we want to be. Hell, we're just students! Danny and I have done nothing to warrant attention."

"Face it Eli, we're marked for life unless we move to the remotest part of Manitoba or something like that. They're probably waiting for the scoop when we split."

"Happy thought, Daniel," I said crossly. "Still why the interest? All we do for a living is study. How boring is that?"

I hadn't noticed Danny absent-mindedly twirling a lock of my hair until he abruptly stopped doing it.

"I need another iced tea. Want anything?"

Again Danny's voice sounded dull and lifeless. It was difficult for me to remain upbeat for both of us. I hoped if I sounded sunny long enough, Danny would get out of his funk. So far he hadn't.

"Thanks," I answered cheerfully, "But no, I don't need anything."

Danny rose and left the table. Lackluster.

"What's with him?" Rachel asked.

"I don't know," I fretted. "Danny's been like this since he returned from Vancouver. He hasn't said that anything's bothering him. I'm thinking it's post-production exhaustion. It happens to Mom when she wraps a movie. I'll let Danny sleep this weekend and…"

I stopped in mid-sentence as Danny returned with his tea.

"What were you saying about me that you stopped?" he asked.

"Nothing really. Just that I'm concerned by how worn out you are. But you don't have class Monday until the afternoon. I'll put out the 'do not disturb' sign and see that you get your sleep this weekend."

"Uh, yeah, right. Thanks, Eli," Danny responded with no enthusiasm.

CHAPTER ELEVEN - ELIZABETH

After political science class, Danny was unusually quiet. We walked back to Berkeley Hall after stopping to get me an ice cream cone at The Cafe. Danny didn't want one, and he didn't want to linger either. On a beautiful day like this we always snagged a table on the patio. We enjoyed the time together, socializing with any friends who passed by. We spent entire afternoons this way.

Something bothered Danny, but I was clueless. Since his return from Vancouver, Danny had behaved inconsistently. At times he was the loving, attentive man I expected. Other times he was distant and brooding, like today.

I would give Danny until after dinner. If he didn't open up by then, tonight I would sit him down and get to the bottom of it.

We had just entered Berkeley Hall when Danny stopped in his tracks. "Elizabeth, let's talk," he commanded in a soft voice.

Perhaps I could cancel tonight's discussion. I accompanied Danny down the hall to my room without speaking. Danny didn't hold my hand. What the…? My heart beat rapidly. I had to remember to breathe.

Danny unlocked the door, and I padded into the room after him. He sat down on the bed and reached out his hand for me to join him. As I sat, Danny took both my hands in his large, warm ones. His well-tanned hands were soft and radiated strength.

Danny's eyes met mine. The sapphires did not twinkle. They were flat and worn. Sadness filled those eyes.

"What's up?" I asked, trying hard to sound upbeat.

Danny stared at our joined hands. He rubbed my fingers, a blank expression on his face.

"Elizabeth, no matter what, please believe that I love you. Always."

"Of course," I stammered. "I'll always love you too."

If Danny hadn't been holding my hands, I would have been twisting the fabric of the comforter trying to calm my fraying nerves. Instead my mouth went dry.

"Eli," Danny glanced at me. His voice was low and lacked energy. "I'm going through a tough time, baby."

"I'm here for you, Danny. You know that."

Danny nodded, but the worry etched in his handsome face made me anxious.

"This is very difficult," he began. "So difficult. I look at you and I see the most wonderful woman I've ever met."

Danny took a deep breath, rubbed my fingers and sighed audibly.

"Eli, I'm bad news."

Huh? Confused, I locked onto Danny's eyes. Vacant, lifeless blue orbs blinked. Danny was depressed. His body slouched as though a large weight held him down. I wanted to cry. It hurt just looking at him.

"Baby, I'm drowning."

"What does that mean?"

"I'm not in my right mind. Three weeks ago my world came crashing down. You've noticed I'm different. E, you try to hide it, but I can read you. Elizabeth, you vacillate between pretending all is normal and overcompensating with forced cheerfulness. Baby, I appreciate what you're doing, but please stop."

"Danny, I love you," I said tearfully. "I'm here for you. Always. I'm signed on for life."

"Same. That's what makes this so difficult."

"I will do whatever it takes to help you or see that you get the help you need," I said with urgency. "Danny, we're a team. But you have to tell me, how did your world come crashing down?"

Three weeks ago? That was the week before Danny came home from Vancouver. He had not hinted that anything was wrong during our frequent phone calls and text sessions. What had changed?

Danny shook his head sadly. The life had been sucked out of him.

"E, you're the best part of my life. I love you so much. Always know that because I doubt you'll love me anymore, baby. I messed up this summer. Big time." Tears choked his voice.

"Danny, you're scaring me. Why won't I love you anymore?" There was only one reason, and it petrified me to acknowledge it. "Danny," I said slowly, "Did you cheat?"

How could he! Before leaving for Vancouver Danny had indicated that when he returned he would finally give me the commitment I wanted. At home in Malibu, I spent the summer anticipating his return for just this reason.

"I had an affair," he said slowly. "We both understood it was a casual relationship that would end when filming wrapped, but we spent most of the summer together."

No! Why would Danny say this? What kind of sick joke was he pulling? One look at Danny's sorrowful face confirmed it was the truth. My heart beat so rapidly I swore it stopped. My stomach dropped, consumed with nausea.

"You couldn't be faithful for half the week?" I cried.

"I wanted to be."

"You bastard."

The tears I had been holding back flowed freely, the floodgates opened. I buried my head in my arms resting on my knees.

My platinum and diamond birthday bracelet pressed against my cheek, an uncomfortable reminder of our love, now evaporated.

"Was this to buy my ignorance?" I spat out.

"Of course not. Eli, I wanted to give you the best birthday ever," Danny said. "I love you, baby."

How could Danny say that? He didn't know what love was. My tear-streaked face tilted up at him, stunned.

"Are you in love with her?" I whispered.

"God, no Eli. You're the only one I'm in love with. Her I hate."

"Hate? How do you have an affair with someone and hate them?" I asked.

Danny didn't answer. He turned away, ashamed. Then it hit me. He said the affair lasted all summer.

"Do I know her?" The answer terrified me, but I had to know.

"She worked on the set," Danny answered, but he looked down, avoiding my eyes.

"She saw us together!" I exclaimed. What a fool I made of myself! "Everyone must have laughed at me."

"Nobody laughed at you. Nobody knew. We kept it secret."

"I can't believe some PA would keep quiet about sleeping with Steven Newman's son."

"She wasn't a PA."

Then Danny looked up at me. Sorrow tinged his eyes, or was it shame. "I had an affair with Vanessa."

"Vanessa!" I gasped.

I was horrified. Then I remembered, "That day Vanessa stopped by our room. Now it makes sense," I stammered." I never understood her surprise at seeing me in my own room. Now I understand. I ruined her plans! She thought you were alone."

The image of Danny with Vanessa was more than I could bear.

"You… Vanessa… in our bed," I wailed.

"Never. Vanessa was never in our bed. That's sacred."

Sacred? I hugged myself tightly, trying to find comfort.

"But you say you hate her?" That made no sense. None of this did.

"Vanessa was playing a game, Eli. A sick, evil game and I was her victim."

"Victim? I'm her victim, not you," I answered bitterly.

"Baby, I'm so sorry," Danny pleaded. "I've tried so hard to protect you."

"You've failed miserably, Daniel."

"It's complicated, Eli. I can't even discuss it. I'm devastated. I've ruined everything good in my life."

"You're right, Daniel. You have ruined everything. And Steve? I can't believe he'd let you do this to me."

"Dad would have killed me. He didn't find out until we wrapped. By then it was too late."

"The media? Is that why you're confessing? Are pictures on the internet?" Panic crept into my voice.

"God no, Eli."

"You're certain?"

"Absolutely. We used discretion. Vanessa didn't want it to go public either."

"Well, that's a relief," I said sarcastically. "At least it's a private humiliation, not a public one."

"Eli, please don't hate me," Danny begged.

"I can't hate you," I cried. "I love you."

Tears flowed down my cheeks again as I sobbed. Danny pulled me into his arms and held me against his powerful chest.

"I want my life back," I wailed.

"I know you do, baby," Danny said gently, and he even kissed my hair. Then Danny took a slow breathe before continuing.

"Now I have to do the most painful thing I've ever done. This hurts more than anything. Baby, I can't be with you right now. I need to work this through, but I have to do it alone."

"You're breaking up with me?" Unbelievable! I should be the one breaking up, not him.

"No, baby. I'm not breaking up with you. I need a hiatus."

What? I stared at Danny, numb and unable to function.

"A hiatus?" I shuddered deep down inside. Nothing good ever came from being put on hiatus. Television programs put on hiatus by the networks were almost always cancelled, but at a later date. Was Danny cancelling me without having the balls to do it outright?

"I missed you so much this summer," Danny continued, "But I can't give you what you need. I can't give you promises. My head is not in a good place. I need a break from us, Eli."

"What happened to forever? We live together. In our beach house. Forever," I stammered, blinking hard to keep from crying again. "You said when you returned you would give me what I wanted. This is not what I want."

How could this be happening? My life was crashing down, and I still didn't understand what Danny meant when he said that his had.

"I know. I meant all of that, baby. Eli, Malibu is still our home. It will be forever. But not now. I'm not capable of doing this now. Forever can't start yet."

"I don't understand," I whimpered. "We were so close. Between texting and Skype, I only felt apart when I crawled into bed at night. And then I surrounded myself with your things so it would seem like you were there."

"And I did the same," Danny said mournfully. "I love you, baby. One day we'll get married and be together for life, but right now I have to work on me."

"I can't help?" I sniffled. "I'm your best friend."

Danny smiled for a brief moment, but it faded just as fast.

"Nobody can," Danny answered sadly.

"What about Steve and Ellen?"

"I can't tell Mom. It would kill her. And Dad and I aren't talking."

"What!" They had always been so close.

"We haven't spoken a word to each other since the night Dad found out."

"Oh, Danny!" This was worse than I had imagined. I felt as though my heart had been ripped in two by a serrated bread knife, never to be intact again.

"When Dad found out, only the knowledge that it would break Mom's heart kept him from disowning me. I can't ever go home."

My heart went out to Danny even as mine was breaking. I couldn't imagine my parents cutting me off no matter what I'd done.

"Eli, I'm no good for you, babe. I'm poison."

"Danny, don't say that."

"I'm broken, baby."

I had nothing more to say. I felt empty inside. Sobs consumed me.

Danny pulled me to his chest, a place I used to find comfort in but no longer could.

"I'm hurting, Elizabeth. I love you, and I know I'm making the worst mistake. You are the only girl I ever want to spend my life with. But first I have a lot of growing up to do. And it's not a ride I want you to take."

Danny wiped my tears away with his thumb. "Eli, it might get ugly. You could get hurt, even worse than this."

"Worse? That's not possible."

"It will take time, but I don't know how much time," Danny said with sorrow, his head hanging down, eyes filled with regret. "Eli, we'll get past this."

Body wracking sobs, more powerful than before overtook me. Ashamed of my weakness, I turned away from Danny and held myself. My insides felt hollow. I was shaking. I was cold. It was ninety degrees outside. So many thoughts bubbled through my brain. They collided and resulted in no thoughts. I drew not one valid conclusion.

Danny said he loved me, but he'd had an affair with Vanessa. Danny said he loved me, but he wasn't ready to commit to me. Danny said he wanted to spend the rest of his life with me, only not now. Not now.

Reality was blatantly obvious.

"You don't want me anymore," I whispered. "I gave you my... my everything," I stammered. "Now you don't want me anymore."

My shaking intensified, uncontrollable. I shivered from shock. Danny wrapped his arms around me to warm me.

"I do want you, baby. You're my girl. Eli, you are my everything. Always. You have to believe me," he pleaded.

I tried squirming out of Danny's hold but he was too strong. My sobs intensified as my mind turned to memories of all the pleasures those arms used to bring me. The warmth and the love they had given me. The many nights I had spent sleeping wrapped in them. I couldn't stop shaking.

Danny guided my head to his shoulder and let me cry. He held me tight, stroking my hair and rubbing my back. The feel of his hands, the familiarity of his sculpted chest couldn't contain my tears.

Danny's physical strength had always protected me and kept me safe. Danny's hands on my body had always held magic. Never again would I experience the shiver they generated. Never again would they undress me and stroke my bare skin. Never again would their touch be a prelude to the pleasure only he provided.

The realization that I had given him all I had to give, and it hadn't been enough, was too much for me to take. Danny knew he was the only man I'd ever been with. I thought that was important. Danny had told me it was.

Now he would be gone. I wasn't like Danny. I didn't want other lovers. I wanted him. The thought of being with another man repulsed me. Other girls found new boyfriends easily enough. Not me. My heart belonged to only one.

Paralysis set in once Danny left my room. After my crying tapered off, he held me tight, allowing me to bury my face in his shoulder while I composed myself.

Danny, affectionate as ever, stroked my hair. He tenderly kissed my lips, took my hands and gazed into my puffy, red eyes.

"Please understand, I have to work on me. I'll be a better man for you."

"I don't think I can understand," I responded sadly.

"It's for the best in the long run, you'll see."

Then Danny lifted my chin and kissed me. I felt through this contact that he did love me. My lips responded, parting for his exploring tongue. We were all lips and hands, undressing each other with urgency.

Soon we fell asleep, spent from the emotional turmoil, and sated from sharing our love the way we did best.

When I woke, the sky was turning from dusk's purple orange hues to early evening's darkness. Danny and I were entwined on the narrow mattress like so many times before. His arm draped around me, holding me close as though I were his most precious possession. I smiled, knowing that despite what he said earlier, I was.

In sleep he looked so beautiful. Danny's hair was a sexy mess and his closed full lips upturned, appearing content. He was calm, his breathing slow and steady, a picture of serenity.

Soon Danny would stir. I was on borrowed time to figure out my next move. Anger and hurt consumed me in equal measure, but dissolving our relationship should be my decision, not his. I was the aggrieved.

After all the progress we had made, it was incredible that Danny would cheat again. Vanessa meant nothing to him. Danny would never do it again. She had been convenient. I would rescind our break up, and out of gratitude Danny would consent to the couple's counseling we so badly needed.

Time to work my magic. Danny didn't want to break up. It was a purely emotional response to his guilt. Danny would see that only I could fulfill his needs.

Danny would soon be stirring. Slowly, I didn't want to wake him until I was ready, I moved my hand down and began delicately stroking him. Danny's eyelids fluttered, regaining their awareness.

"E?" his bewildered voice, groggy with sleep, answered.

I had scant moments left to captivate him. I slid down on the bed and began sucking on his hardening length.

"Mmmm, Eli," he quietly moaned, not completely comprehending.

I continued sucking, swirling my tongue around his tip, teasing Danny's hardness.

"E," he moaned, "What are you doing?"

Ignoring hin, I picked up my rhythm, and Danny responded, flexing his hips. I hated this, and Danny knew it, but desperate times called for desperate measures.

"E, I'm going to come in your mouth," Danny warned, yet his hands holding my head in place were a complete contradiction.

"E, stop!" Danny said firmly, though his sapphire eyes twinkled in delight. "Please, stop," he softened. "I want to come inside you."

Victory! I smiled and stopped. Then I gripped his well-developed biceps for support, and eased myself on to him. Flashing Danny a mischievous grin, I began our shared rhythm anew. Soon we exploded together.

How could he possibly leave the girl who wakes him like this? Surely our love would negate everything Danny had said earlier, and we could begin our next happy chapter together.

I could not have been more wrong. Instead of saying, "I'll see you at dinner," Danny's parting words were, "I love you Elizabeth, but this doesn't change anything. I need to be single right now."

So here I was, still lying naked beneath the sheets, totally humiliated. Devastated. I despised Danny for letting this happen. I hated myself even more for thinking seduction was the solution.

Finally, I willed myself out of bed and put on my robe. A hot shower would not repair my psyche, but I was desperate to rid myself of Danny's scent. Scrubbing every body part twice and double shampooing wasn't enough, but it would suffice for now.

Afterwards, I put on a pair of old gym shorts and a plain tee-shirt, items Danny had never touched. I threw open my closet and drawers and found the few things I had worn since returning to school that were not already in the laundry bag. An obsessed person on a mission, I sniffed at the rest. Anything even remotely smelling of Danny, I yanked off its hanger.

A sizable pile amassed on the floor. I collapsed in the heap, sobbing into the fine cottons, linens, and silks. Surrounded by the faded scent of Danny's cologne, my new reality overwhelmed me.

The knife plunged deeper into my heart as I imagined the pleasure this would have brought me only yesterday. Paralyzed once more, I held the clothing to my nose and inhaled deeply. I hoped Danny experienced the same agony when confronting my light floral scent in his closet, and in his bed.

Time passed. Lying atop a pile of dirty laundry was not healthy. I forced myself off the floor. I noticed my disheveled bed mocking me, taunting. I should strip it. My linens must be laundered.

I couldn't bring myself to go near it. This act would be too final, too painful. I wasn't ready to eradicate Danny from my consciousness, not yet. Nineteen years washed away in one evening. It was too much to process.

I sat on the bed holding myself, shaking and crying again. Gathering the top sheet around me, I felt so alone. Where was Rachel? Chloe?

I glanced at the clock. Nine-thirty. Why had nobody come looking for me? The answer was obvious. They assumed I was with Danny. I picked up a pillow and punched it with all my strength before forcefully throwing it against the wall.

Mom! I might be nineteen, but I needed my mom. She was the one person who would understand. Mom would be on my side. At home it was six-thirty. Was Mom with Ellen? I couldn't take the chance.

The laundry. I could sort the pile. It was a productive, mindless activity. Perfect for my numb, shell-shocked, brain.

I stuffed the machine washables into a pink mesh laundry bag. The dry clean only items I returned to the closet, placing their hangers in the front, ready to grab in the morning. Then I settled at my desk, reading to kill time until I tried Mom.

Near midnight, I was proud that I had not cried in over two hours. Reading had required just enough concentration to keep my mind occupied and off Danny.

But I couldn't hold it together any longer. The book slipped from my fingers. The shaking began. I felt cold both inside and out, despite the sticky summer weather. I crawled into bed, pulling the covers up to my chin.

Resting my head against the pillows, Danny's scent overwhelmed me. How dare Danny break up with me! He had confessed to cheating. I was supposed to do the dumping. Those were the rules.

Robbed of my only emotional outlet, tears spilled out in torrents. I worked at keeping them silent, pulling my knees up to my chest in an attempt at self-comfort that failed.

My hand reached for my throat. Unconsciously, like so many other times since last December, I fingered my golden heart. My golden heart. Memories of the night Danny gave it to me, our first night spent together, came flooding back as powerfully as though it were yesterday. That had been the happiest evening of my life. Pure magic. How did everything go so wrong?

I overlaid the events of this afternoon with those of that evening. Both times Danny told me he loved me. Both times we made love. That evening Danny stayed and our journey together had begun. Today he left me cold and alone. We no longer had a future.

I couldn't reconcile it. How could Danny tell me he loved me and at the same time not want me anymore? After Danny's confession, how did I still want him? I trembled. I cried. I stared at my diamond bracelet. No longer a symbol of our love, it was an albatross around my wrist. I couldn't remove it.

I reached for my phone and dialed. Mom's private line forwarded to her cell phone after the fifth ring. She would answer no matter where she was. I got her outgoing message. Mom must be at an event, her phone buried in her purse. What more would go wrong today?

The beep sounded for me to leave my message. "Mommy," I whimpered, "I need you. I don't care how late it is. Call me."

CHAPTER TWELVE - DANIEL

Groggy from getting high, hung-over from the beer consumed for dinner, and suffering indigestion from the pizza ordered at midnight, no words existed strong enough to describe my condition when I woke. I was the most contemptible person on earth for breaking the heart of the most wonderful girl who I loved more than anything.

Bastard! Only a total fucking bastard could have hurt Eli the way I did.

Yesterday had been the worst day of my life. Worse even than learning of a death because the responsibility rested solely with me. The pain inflicted on Eli came from me, only me. I would have to live with the consequences for the rest of my life. So far I wasn't doing very well.

I consoled myself that it was for the best. I couldn't keep hurting Elizabeth in small increments. How much disappointment would Eli have tolerated before casting me out of her life forever? This way it was a clean break. I wouldn't feel guilt for being an immature twenty year old, and she would be free to find a new, more dedicated boyfriend.

Picturing my Elizabeth with another man, sharing her bed with him and not me, was not what I wanted. My stomach churned again. I reached for the half-empty bottle of Tums.

Who would Eli want to be with? Would her new boyfriend be someone I knew? Elizabeth enjoyed being spoiled. Would he live up to her expectations? Part of me, an extremely large part, hoped she wouldn't be interested in anyone, not ever. I wanted her for myself, just not now.

I smacked my head with a pillow. Argh! I must be the most spoiled, self-centered person in the world for having these thoughts.

Something inside of me had snapped this summer. Domestic bliss ceased being on my agenda. I was far from proud of my behavior, but I saw no reason to reform.

After Dad forbide Vanessa and I from socializing, we managed the impossible; carrying on a location affair without so much as one person suspecting. When Eli visited on weekends, even she remained clueless.

Being with a woman as stunning and powerful as Vanessa, I felt invincible thinking I could get away with anything. I even enjoyed a couple of isolated pick-ups too. Hell! I was Danny Newman. I could, and I did.

Vanessa's worldly sophistication stood in sharp contrast to Elizabeth's naïve vulnerability. I would never feel protective of tough as nails Vanessa. I could never love a woman like Vanessa. I knew she didn't love me either, but the knowledge that Vanessa chose me left me cocky.

In the end, Vanessa left me in incredible pain I couldn't come to terms with. I broke every promise I'd made to Elizabeth, and now my self-esteem was shot. To know that Vanessa seduced me as part of a larger scheme was unbearable. Now there was no one I could share my pain with. Vanessa had ruined that for me.

Normally, Eli would have been there to pick up my broken pieces. She would have helped me through my anger and my personal doubts. But this I couldn't share with Eli. She had expected my love, and I betrayed her.

That was the worst part. Eli was innocent, yet she was the one most victimized. No matter that she still seemed to want me, and I couldn't understand why she did, I wasn't worthy of Eli's love anymore. Would I ever be?

I didn't know if I could be redeemed, and I didn't know what to do. I desperately wanted Eli's love, but not in my damaged state. Until I figured things out, I didn't deserve Eli. But I couldn't live without her.

My dark journey to the abyss thus began. How I would crawl back up I didn't know. Would I ever be able to? Doubt petrified me.

A knock came on my door. "Danny, you up?"

Shane! What time it was? Judging by the sun it was daytime. Morning or afternoon? I couldn't read the blurry numbers on the clock.

"Give me twenty minutes," I called back.

Shane must want to eat. Shane always did. Whichever meal it was time for, I didn't know.

With deliberate slowness, I pulled myself out of bed to shower and get dressed. The hell with shaving. Elizabeth's tender face no longer concerned me.

Twenty-five minutes later, Shane and I entered the dorm lobby from the stairwell, and Cam caught up to us.

"You look like hell," he said.

Scruffy in shorts, a tee-shirt, and flip-flops, eyeglasses partially hidding puffy red eyes, I shrugged my agreement.

"I feel even worse," I answered.

"Hey man, I'm sorry about you and Elizabeth," Shane said. "I thought you were solid," he shrugged. "Well, now you can have fun again. You're not married anymore."

"I **was** having fun. Eli's the best," I brooded.

"Did you see?" Cam interrupted. "Limo in the parking lot."

"Danny, is it yours?" Shane chuckled.

"Of course not," I snapped. Still it made me think. Who besides me…? Shit!

"Miranda Jordan!" Cam, awestruck, provided the answer.

"Oh, crap!" I muttered, glad to be surrounded by my posse.

Randi! The last person I wanted to see today. Of course Elizabeth had called home. I imagined the lioness had hopped on her Gulfstream, and here she was protecting her cub from its prey. Nala never had it so good.

I felt lower than low, but I had no choice but to cross paths with Randi if I wanted to exit the building.

Nostrils flaring, brown eyes glaring with a look that about killed me, or perhaps it was guilt, Randi stormed toward me.

"Hi, Randi," The words stuck in my arid mouth.

Not yet eleven o'clock, Randi must have traveled all night to get here. Not a good sign for Team Danny, an exclusive club with a membership of probably less than one. In this matter, even I wasn't on my side.

"Don't you ever go near my daughter again," she said sharply.

"Good to see you too, Randi." Yes, that was flippant, but I felt so awkward I couldn't respond otherwise.

Randi fumed, even angrier, if that was possible. Steam spouted. I had just further screwed myself with my own parents. When Randi failed to show at their weekly Friday luncheon today, my mother would learn what a disrespectful, shit she had for a son.

"Don't you ever speak to me again, Daniel!" So much for godmotherly love.

Enraged, Randi raised her perfectly manicured right hand, smacked my face with all her strength, and stormed off toward Eli's room.

"Damn it! My face!"

I winced from the sharp pain. My hand shot up to cover my cheek. It was the same side I had injured at rugby last fall. Shane and Cam stared in disbelief as did the other half dozen or so students who'd been passing through.

Everyone stopped in their tracks. Nobody was passing through anymore. It wasn't everyday you witnessed a world-famous actress smacking a student's face in a dorm lobby.

Blood trickled down my cheek. My hands flew to my face to stop it, and I adjusted my glasses, now askew. My face throbbed. Randi's sizable diamond ring must have been turned around for maximum effect because the force of the blow really hadn't been that powerful.

"I need an ice pack," I ordered Shane who ran off to get one.

"I can't believe Miranda Jordan just smacked you, Danny," said a star-struck Cam, stunned from my unexpected encounter.

"Miranda Jordan didn't smack me. Randi Jacobs did. I deserved it, and probably much more." Cam's expression twisted, puzzled.

The small group of students that had gathered around made me uncomfortable. This was a family matter, and I did not desire witnesses for my moment of shame.

Shane returned and handed me an ice pack. I pressed it to my cheek. "Thanks," I said.

I turned to retreat to my room, but couldn't. Bonnie Preston-Smith, the Birkenstock wearing wife of our faculty resident, Joseph Preston-Smith, followed close on Shane's footsteps.

"I heard there was an altercation," she said in the voice of a thirty year-old Girl Scout out to solve a Nancy Drew mystery.

"Miranda Jordan slapped him," someone eagerly volunteered.

"Does she live in this dorm?" Bonnie's innocent question raised a chorus of giggles from the other students. I tried hard to stifle my own desire to laugh.

"The actress," someone said.

Bonnie was confused. She and Joe were new to Berkeley Hall and were unaware of the A-list parentage of one of our sophomores. Elizabeth had not made it to the list of troubled and/or trouble-making students for them to be looking out for. Had I?

"Bonnie," I said, "I'm fine. It's a family matter."

I really just wanted her and everyone else gathered around to go back to whatever they would have been doing had drama not erupted in the lobby.

"But she hit you," Bonnie insisted. "Let me see."

Reluctantly I lifted the ice pack from my cheek.

"It's bleeding. You should go to the Health Center and I should make a report."

"You'll do no such thing, Bonnie. This is between Randi and I. She's Elizabeth Jacobs of Room 105A's mother, and I deserved it. Randi's also my godmother."

"I have a responsibility toward your parents, Danny."

"My parents." I hadn't considered them. "When my parents find out, they'll be disappointed that Randi didn't hit me harder. They'll be on her side."

CHAPTER THIRTEEN - ELIZABETH

I woke lethargic and confused, my eyes dry and sticky with sleep. I glanced down. Gym shorts and a baggy tee? No Danny? His presence was strong, but he wasn't in my bed as usual.

Then the nightmare that defined yesterday came flooding back. I buried my head in the pillow. Hollow emptiness and tears followed. When they subsided, I couldn't move from the security of my bed. Where would I go anyway?

There was rapid knocking on my door. Someone was at my door. Danny? Had he come to apologize? Please.

"One moment," I called out.

An unexpected adrenaline rush pulled me out of bed and I made it across the room in three strides. Flushed, I turned the knob and swung open the door.

"Mommy!" I cried, and I collapsed sobbing into her warm, welcoming arms.

Mom took charge, quickly packing my overnight case. Then she ushered me into her waiting limo, and whisked me away to the Mayflower Inn in Washington Depot, a small town in Litchfield County, Connecticut.

Two days of spa treatments and motherly advice was just what I needed. While I remained heartbroken, I felt refreshed, energized and, attractive again. The force of Mom's personality would not allow otherwise. Though depressed, once more I was functional, my behavior and appearance no longer frightening either of us.

Upon returning to Donnelly, I had three hours before dinner to reflect and prepare. Mom and I strategized that I would not hide. Danny and I had too many friends in common. I would not give them up because of him. Let Danny be the uncomfortable one.

Publicly I would behave as though nothing were the matter. Dinner would find me at my usual table. If Danny didn't like it, he could move. This was his fault anyway. I'd even study with him on Sunday evening as we always did. Yes, I would be the mature one, and give friendship a try.

By four-thirty I was antsy. If I had to wait more than another fifteen minutes before getting Rachel, I would wear a hole in the hardwood floor from pacing.

My reflection in the mirror caught my attention. Red, puffy eyes had been replaced by clear, green ones. Subtle eyeliner and mascara gave them some life, but their flatness was still obvious. I might fool a casual observer, but not Danny.

I resigned myself to my appearance being the best I could manage for today. As time passed, the sparkle would surely return. Time would heal me, Mom had said. I had to believe she was right.

A few locks of hair were out of place, and I reached for my hairbrush. How many times had I brushed my hair already? Too many. I had lost track.

A knock on the door saved me from becoming truly obsessive.

"Rach!" I exclaimed, happier than I had known I'd be to see her. I had not seen Rachel since Thursday at lunch.

Rachel gave me a comforting hug and closed the door. "Elizabeth, I'm so sorry about you and Danny."

I bit down on my lower lip determined to keep the tears at bay.

"Yeah," was all I had the energy to say.

"You look great though. You're holding up much better than I'd have thought."

"I'm not holding up, Rach. I'm a mess. I've been stabbed through the heart and I've lost my best friend. I'm a wreck."

For the first time since I'd known her, Rachel was at a loss for words.

"Well you look great," she repeated.

I smiled. "Thanks. You wouldn't have said that on Friday. I'm lucky Mom came and took me to a spa in Litchfield."

"The Mayflower Inn?"

"You know it?" Of course! Rachel lived in Westport.

"I've never been there, but my parents go every year for their anniversary. They say it's amazing."

"It's sweet," I answered.

"Sweet? You are depressed. It's the best hotel in Connecticut."

I sighed loudly. I didn't have the energy to emote about anything.

I sat quietly on the edge of the bed staring at Rachel, waiting for her to continue the conversation. Anything I said would make me cry, and I didn't want to spoil my makeup or cause red puffiness to return to my eyes this close to dinner.

"Should we sit at a different table?" Rachel asked. "Danny told me he'd understand. But I told him, and now I'm telling you, Elizabeth I'm friends with both of you. I will not take sides so don't ask me to. And do not, absolutely do not, put me in the middle. If you have something to say to Danny, you say it to him. I will not be your messenger or his."

Tears threatened again, and I forced myself to glance away from Rachel. Her speech brought the reality I had avoided all weekend, crashing down on me. Nervously I twisted my fingers, afraid to face her while I formulated a response.

I answered tentatively. "I plan on sitting at my usual table, with my friends." Then with renewed resolve I added, "If Danny doesn't like it, he can move. I won't drop my friends because of him." I looked up at Rachel. "Why is it always expected that the girl should fade away?"

Rachel gave me a supportive smile. "I hoped you'd say that."

"Head up, smile on," I thought as I neared the dining table.

Danny was already seated beside Shane. My pulse quickened as my stomach sank. I took a seat beside Rachel, across from Shane, and generated little reaction.

My plastic smile lasted only a minute, replaced by genuine concern when I peeked at Danny.

"What happened to your face?" I exclaimed.

His cheek had a sizeable purple bruise on it.

Danny smiled at me and laughed. His smile, filled with his usual affection, was difficult for me to consume. His eyes twinkled, too. Pain shot through my heart. I chewed on my lip. How could Danny show love with his eyes and not want me anymore?

"You haven't heard?" he asked.

I shook my head "no."

"I had a run-in with Randi," Danny sheepishly confessed.

"My mother did that?" Now I was the one laughing. Mom did not go around beating up people.

"Glad you find it funny Elizabeth. Randi got me with her diamond."

"Poor ring!" I laughed.

"What about poor me?"

I stared directly into Danny's sapphire eyes for impact and said, "now you know, Daniel. Don't mess with Jacobs women."

Shane and Rachel were silent, eyes on Danny. The ball was in his court.

Rising from the table he replied, "I deserved it, and probably worse."

I smiled triumphantly, but it was short-lived when Danny added, "You forgot your iced tea, babe. I'll get it."

Babe? I was dumbfounded. Shane and Rachel stared at Danny and back to me. "Thanks," I mumbled.

Why would Danny call me babe and bring me iced tea? Did he still care or was it an ingrained habit?

When Danny returned, he handed me the glass instead of placing it on the table. Staring directly at me, his gaze penetrating my entire being, Danny brushed my fingertips with his, and smiled at my resultant shiver. What game was he playing?

Despite this, I relaxed, and even enjoyed dinner. Danny was apparently using the same playbook I was; behaving normally. Our friends followed our cues. But it was Sunday. What would happen next?

Once we cleared our dishes and exited the dining hall, Danny approached me.

"Hey, Eli," he began tentatively, "Are we studying tonight?"

I gasped, shocked. Is this what the tabloids meant by an amicable separation? That seemed to be the only way people in Hollywood ever split if you followed the gossip websites.

"You're serious?" I asked.

Rachel cocked her head in our direction, curious what I would decide. I couldn't blame her. I was too.

"We have Dennison's class to prep for."

"I'll try," I answered truthfully.

"I'd like that. I'll meet you in the lobby in fifteen."

This was very odd, but if I wanted Danny to see what he was missing, it played right into my strategy of being "just friends."

"E, you look great," Danny said upon greeting me. Sadness tinged his eyes. Regret perhaps?

"Thank you," I stammered, hoping Danny didn't detect the quiver in my voice.

Danny and I checked into our favorite study room. On the walk over he had wanted to know all about my weekend with Mom. Every detail about the Mayflower Inn was of utmost importance to him. Danny even concluded by saying, "It sounds romantic."

"Yeah," I laughed, "If I had been with you instead of Mom."

Instantly I regretted my words. I did not like the new normal of filtering my words spoken to Danny.

Danny smiled thoughtfully. "We'll go sometime," he said.

My stomach clenched. It took all the strength I could muster not to break down.

Had Thursday's heart-wrenching breakup been nothing more than a short-lived nightmare? If I was no longer his girlfriend, why was Danny suggesting a romantic getaway in the future? Was this what he meant by a hiatus? A weekend off from each other?

The mixed signals continued at the library with Danny sitting close to me. In the past, it had been natural, comforting even. Tonight, it was causing my heart to flip-flop.

During a break, I stood by the vending machines sipping bottled water. Danny stood opposite me, one hand holding a cup of coffee, the other pressing against the wall above me. His head tilted toward mine, ensuring eye contact, his sapphire gaze powerful. As we chatted, I thought how passersby would not dare to interrupt the happy couple.

Back in our study room, as I searched for a specific quote in the material we were reviewing, Danny leaned in close, placing his hand on my shoulder.

I felt his breath on my neck, and shivers went up and down my spine.

When I found the passage, as I pointed it out to Danny, I tilted my face up toward his. He smiled his easygoing smile that always melted me. Then Danny lightly brushed his lips against mine, and I gasped.

What the hell?

Danny escorted me to my door after we returned to Berkeley Hall. Before I unlocked it, I insisted on saying goodnight.

"I'm tired," I said.

"It's been a long weekend."

"Yeah," I agreed smiling into his twinkling sapphire eyes.

We stood staring at each other, unsure of what to do next. If I had any sense, I would enter my room and immediately close the door. This moment would be ended. Danny would leave. That was the best solution, but I felt rooted in place.

Danny didn't budge. His sapphire eyes fixated on me. Finally Danny broke what seemed like an interminable silence, but was likely moments long.

"Elizabeth?"

"Daniel?" I trembled from the electric current between us.

Danny's thumb gently tilted my chin up, his touch full of promise, and he kissed me, slow and sweet. My insides quaked, leaving me short of breath.

"I'll always love you, Elizabeth," he said with quiet emotion.

Speechless, I entered my room and locked the door.

With sweat dripping down my neck, I dragged myself into the dance department locker room. Beginning at eight, I had been through ballet and then jazz; three straight hours of dance.

Slouched on a stool by my open locker, a towel around the back of my neck absorbed the sweat. Kelsey and I sat quietly chugging water from liter bottles. I stared into space thinking about Danny's kiss. Conclusions failed to materialize.

"Elizabeth, you're ringing." Kelsey's voice brought me back to planet Earth.

"Huh?"

"Your phone. It's singing."

"Right." Flustered, I reached for my phone. It was a text message from Danny. "Missed bkfst. Hungry. C u @11:15."

Like an idiot, I grinned at the phone.

Kelsey raised an eyebrow. We were dance friends, not confidantes. She was not privy to my personal life. All Kelsey knew of my relationship with Danny was that I had one.

"Early lunch date," I told Kelsey, and I texted back "c u then".

I pulled gym shorts over my leotard, stuffed my towel in my large dance bag, and let the locker door slam closed.

Normally, I would have showered and changed clothes, but I had a scant ten minutes to cross the campus. Danny would have to understand that this would be a short lunch. I refused to go to my afternoon class in a sweaty leotard.

Danny was waiting when I arrived at the dining hall. He looked perfect, reading for the country club. Danny was clean, freshly shaved, and wearing pressed khaki shorts with a polo shirt. What a mess I was! The contrast was startling. At least he knew I hadn't dressed for him.

Danny's smile and twinkling eyes fixated on my body lit up his face. Only wearing footless tights, a tank leotard and gym shorts, I felt practically naked. With my hair dirty from sweat, and pulled back in a ponytail, I was not attractive.

"Hey, Sweetheart," Danny greeted me with a chaste kiss on my cheek. My heart fluttered. It was impossible not to smile.

"Why so early?" I asked.

Danny took my hand. "I wanted you to sit next to me."

"Maybe not. I'm stinky from dance." I replied.

Danny tucked a damp lock of hair behind my ear. "Your sweat smells sweet." Huh? I looked at him as though he were nuts.

Cam and Rachel soon joined us, but I badly needed to shower so I didn't linger.

After I finished my salad I stood up and said, "I've got to shower. I'll see you guys later."

"I'll walk you," Danny eagerly volunteered.

"You can stay. I think I can find it."

Danny's dejected expression was laughable.

"Hi, Mom," I cheerfully answered the phone. I planned on spending the evening alone in my room, getting ahead in my readings, and avoiding Danny too. A win-win for me.

"Elizabeth, what's going on? You sound… happy?"

I blushed, embarrassed that Mom could read me in two short words. I leaned back against my desk chair uncertain how to respond. I sighed. Why fight it? Anything short of the truth, Mom would see through.

"Not quite," I admitted. "It's Danny," I began.

"That much I assumed."

"I'm confused." Then I explained the goings on of the last twenty-four hours.

"What does Danny want Elizabeth?" Mom was furious. "Have you confronted him?"

"No." I was embarrassed for being such a wuss. "I'm hiding in my room tonight. Danny makes me uncomfortable."

"So you haven't asked why after breaking your heart he's now pursuing you?" Mom sounded like a prosecutor. She intimidated me.

"No. I haven't," I responded sheepishly.

"You're impossible. Elizabeth, you don't want the answer, do you? You're hoping Danny's changed his mind, but you're afraid you could be wrong."

"Is that so terrible?"

"He cheated, Elizabeth," Mom firmly reminded me, "And not for the first time. Danny's not to be trusted."

"I'm aware of that, Mother!" I answered defensively.

"This is the strangest breakup. Until you speak to Danny directly you're going to keep torturing yourself. Elizabeth, you have to find out where you stand, even if it hurts. Get it over with."

Mom was right, but I was afraid to take the risk. Maybe I didn't want to confront reality. I was scared. Part of me, a large part, needed to believe Danny desired me again.

Midway through Professor Dennison's class the next afternoon, I decided that painful as it might be, Danny and I had to have a heart-to-heart.

In my mind I replayed lunch, where again Danny had sat so close. Then, after eating, Danny had helped me into my raincoat and wrapped his arm possessively around my shoulder as we left for class. I was forgetting that Danny wasn't mine anymore. That's how I knew it was time to have the discussion.

Rain was falling when class ended. I enjoyed the envious glares directed my way as Danny again helped me into my raincoat. Overly solicitous, Danny gently lifted my hair out of the collar and straightened the lapels, all the while keeping his dark sapphires locked on me.

Danny's smoldering eyes melted me as he assumed they would. I had to avert my gaze to remain upright. If only the jealous girls glaring at me were aware of what a difficult man he was to live with. They would no longer be envious of this display of courtly good manners.

After belting my Burberry mini-trench that was more fashionable than functional given the sheets of rain falling, I reached into my canvas tote bag and removed the matching mini umbrella I had grabbed at the last minute. When opened, it became full-sized.

"I'll carry your bag if I can put my books in there," Danny offered.

I giggled at my advantage. Danny wore only a cotton hoodie. At least it covered his head, but Danny would get drenched if I didn't quickly offer him some kindness. We fast approached the building door.

I opened my tote for his books and smiled. "I'll do you one better. I'll carry the bag, you hold the umbrella."

"Thanks, Eli. You're my lifesaver." Danny kissed the top of my head.

Buckets of rain assaulted us. No matter how close Danny and I huddled under the umbrella, we still got soaked. Chilly air was being ushered in by the storm. The calendar didn't say it, but summer was ending.

Steaming cups of hot chocolate topped with lots of whipped cream was the perfect antidote. Danny handed me my mug after he paid for our drinks at the Café. Our fingers touched, unleashing an electric current. Danny flinched. He felt it too.

"Your hands are ice cold. Let me."

Danny took my hands and gently massaged them. My insides warmed and tingled. Then he tenderly kissed the top of each one.

"Better?" Danny asked, those potent sapphire eyes meeting my gaze.

"Much," I smiled, and I sipped my drink. Then I nibbled at my cookie. Danny did the same. Our eyes never left each other. I grinned like a fool, enjoying Danny's pursuit.

Difficult as it was to keep my wits about me, I summoned the strength to broach the uncomfortable subject. I had to do this, and it had to be now. Uncertainty never sat well with me. I could not let this continue. Sitting alone at this quiet table in The Café provided the privacy I required.

"Danny, what's going on? With us?" I asked tentatively.

"What do you mean, Elizabeth?"

Ugh! Danny answering my question with a question was so predictable.

"You know what I mean. Thursday you broke up with me. It's only Tuesday and you're kissing my hands."

Danny smiled shyly and leaned forward in his chair.

"You were heartbroken," he said softly.

"Danny, you confessed to an affair, and then you had the audacity to brake up with me," I scowled. "I wanted to do the dumping."

Danny grinned, then he turned serious. "I didn't realize how bad off I left you until I saw Randi. I thought if she had traveled all night... I never wanted to hurt you, Eli. You have no idea how awful I feel."

"Good." I said emphatically.

"I deserve that."

"You do," I agreed.

"While you relaxed at your five-star spa, do you know what I did last weekend?"

"I'm sure it's no concern of mine," I said coldly. I didn't want to hear about the girls he picked up while partying.

"Probably not, but you should know. I spent the weekend alone and wasted. I couldn't face myself, because I had hurt the most important person in my life, and by Sunday I didn't understand why. I'll give your mother credit though. Randi hitting me got my thinking started."

"Mom's good that way."

Danny rubbed his bruised cheek. "It still hurts."

"I'm sorry."

"No you're not. Be honest."

"I'm a little sorry?"

"Nice try. Alright, I'll believe you," Danny laughed. "When I saw you at dinner Sunday, I was confused. You looked so beautiful and you weren't upset. I was hurt because you didn't seem hurt."

"Danny, how could you have been hurt?"

"I assumed you'd be distraught."

"You wanted me to be distraught?"

"Of course not. But when you weren't, I thought I could have been wrong about us. Perhaps I didn't mean as much to you as I thought I had."

I smirked. "You couldn't really think that?" Wow! Danny had insecurities just like everyone else. That didn't seem possible

"Part of me was having doubts, Eli. That's why I insisted on our study date."

"You sat so close. It didn't make sense."

"You behaved so coolly. I was testing your reaction. You quivered, so your coolness was a façade."

"Is that why you kissed me? Another test?"

"No. Once I confirmed you didn't hate me, I regretted what I had done."

"What exactly do you regret?"

"Everything. Especially the part where I broke up with you. That's the dumbest thing I've ever done."

"I'm glad you realize that."

Danny reached for my hands and gazed intently into my eyes.

"Can we reset the clock and pretend it's still last Wednesday? Please?" he asked in a voice resembling a small child wanting forgiveness from his mother.

Wednesday? "I don't remember Wednesday."

"That's my point. Wednesday was before I made a mess of everything."

"Danny, you made a mess of everything way before Wednesday. I don't think we can go back to Wednesday unless you have a potion that can make me forget Thursday."

"I was afraid you'd say something like that." Danny smiled, his eyes crinkling.

"Danny, you may want to reverse breaking up with me, but that leaves issues of trust and commitment. You admitted to some intolerable acts."

I was treading in dangerous waters where I didn't know how Danny would respond. In those old procedural courtroom dramas the star always followed the maxim, "don't ask the witness any question you don't already know the answer to." My acusation had just violated Rule Number One.

"You're right, Elizabeth."

"Think about it, Danny. You know what's important to me."

"Help me with my thinking, Eli."

"How can I do that?" I asked, confused.

Danny took my face in his hands. With tender passion he pressed his lips against mine and kissed me like so many times before.

"Oh," I said, my wide eyes, showing pleased surprise.

CHAPTER FOURTEEN - ELIZABETH

The advantage of being part of a group of friends where no one is dating anyone was that Thursday at dinner we made group plans for the upcoming weekend.

Talk about having your cake and eating it too. How often does that happen? I would enjoy Danny's company without pressure because our friends would be with us. But first I needed to get through tonight.

Danny walked me back to Berkeley Hall after dinner expecting to spend time with me. He was tired of my rebuffs, but I didn't want to be alone with him. In fact, I feared it.

As we stood in front of the door, Danny inched closer. With every step he took forward I moved backwards. Within three moves Danny had me trapped against the door, staring into his magnetic eyes. Danny smiled, his sapphire eyes laughing at my futility.

"C'mon Elizabeth. This is silly. Let's go inside."

"No," I said nervously.

A smile stretched across his face. "If you don't open that door, I will say something embarrassing in a very loud voice so all your neighbors hear," he teased.

"Grrrr," I scowled.

Then Danny laughed.

"You are so infuriating."

Against my better judgement, I unlocked the door and opened it.

Like a gazelle, Danny pounced through the door, and in what seemed like one graceful movement, landed on my bed. I would not go there. Nothing would make me go near that piece of furniture.

Crushed against my pillows, Danny appeared as comfortable as though he were a permanent fixture. You could almost hear the linens saying, "Welcome home. We missed you." Perhaps that was my heart. My head wanted no part of this conversation. I deliberately sat down on the swivel desk chair.

"You've made your point. You can go now," I said firmly.

"And what point is that, Elizabeth?" Danny grinned, enjoying my discomfort.

"That you could worm your way back into my bed. You win. You're in my bed, but I'm not joining you, so you lose."

Danny considered this for a moment. "I don't like to lose," he said.

"That's obvious." I smiled, and I waved, "bye-bye".

Without warning, Danny sat up, leaned forward and pulled the chair so quickly that I lost my balance and fell on top of him. Danny caught me, holding me tight in his strong arms. Then he kissed my startled lips.

"I don't like to lose," he repeated slowly as his fingertip traced my lower lip.

Our eyes met, his smug with victory, mine open wide, surprised at how against my stated desire I now lay in bed on top of Danny.

"Our clothes stay on," I warned.

"Agreed," Danny said. He reached for my face and our lips pressed together.

"You should go," I whispered. It was eleven o'clock. My lips were bruised and swollen from lying in Danny's arms the past three hours kissing.

Good to his word, Danny had never tried taking it further. Yet that made it one of our most erotic evenings ever. The excitement and chemistry between us was stronger than ever. Danny's kisses were a persuasive reminder of the pleasures I was denying us both.

Eventually Danny pulled himself up from the bed taking me with him.

"Can't I stay?" he asked, holding me close with his eyes full of mischief.

"No," I laughed.

Danny gave me sad puppy dog eyes. He knew my answer without me saying it. Then Danny got down on his knees and took my hands.

Sapphire eyes gazing up at me he pleaded, "Please Eli? I'll make it a night you'll always remember."

It already had been a night I would always remember.

"Nope," I smiled. "I have my reputation to consider, and the neighbors are nosy," I smirked, referencing Rachel.

I pulled Danny up from the floor.

"You win," he said, and Danny walked toward the door.

When it appeared that he would walk out the door, Danny grabbed my hand and pulled me into his arms.

"Eli, you need a proper good-night kiss," he declared.

This was ludicrous given how we had spent the evening. Danny and I laughed as he held my face and kissed me yet again. My hands clasped around Danny's neck and twined in his hair, drawing Danny even closer as his hands across my back held me firmly. Breathing was nearly impossible. Bolts of electricity glued us together, making us unable to separate.

"I love you, E. I'm so glad you saved me from blowing it."

One more kiss, and Danny finally left. In a dream-like state I changed to pajamas. Then I collapsed into bed, hugging the pillows close, deeply inhaling Danny's scent absorbed into the percale.

A combination of head in the clouds coupled with anxiety gripped me the next day. The cure; I would hang out at the yearbook office. This early in the year with the workload light, I could catch up with friends I hadn't seen since May.

On my way upstairs I stopped at The Café for a bottle of water and a large chocolate chip cookie, my third cookie this week. They certainly were delicious; baked crispy around the edges, softer in the middle, with a combination of semi-sweet and milk chocolate chips. But if I didn't watch it, my jeans wouldn't fit anymore.

Jackson Shaw greeted me with a warm welcome hug and a smile that wouldn't quit. From the beginning when I joined the staff last year, we had hit it off and become good friends. A senior, Jackson was Editor-in-Chief. My official title, Sophomore Editor, was not much different from last year, though my responsibilities increased. I would play a larger role this year in the book's layout and creative design.

Last year I enjoyed being on the yearbook staff. The perks – front row seats at events attended on official business, and the staff camaraderie, fulfilled my deep-seated desire to become part of the fabric of Donnelly College life.

Even better, the yearbook was a Danny-free zone! I doubted that anyone on staff other than Jackson had ever even met Danny. At yearbook, I was Elizabeth Jacobs; just Elizabeth. And that was fine by me.

"Elizabeth, great to see you." Jackson said after giving me a kiss on the cheek.

"Good to see you too, Jackson. Enjoy your summer?"

"I interned at the Huffington Post," he said, his voice laced with excitement.

"Awesome!"

It was common knowledge that Jackson hoped to land a job at an important news outlet or financial publication when he graduated in the spring.

"How about you?" he asked.

"I worked for my Dad and commuted to Vancouver on the weekends."

Jackson grinned, but he asked anyway, "Still with Danny?"

"For the time being."

No need for anyone outside my inner circle to know about our breakup especially as Danny and I were sure to be reconciled by the end of the weekend.

Jackson raised an eyebrow. "Trouble in paradise?"

"No. I'm just being cynical today. You can never assume anything, no matter how great it seems."

"You don't have to discuss it. I respect your privacy."

Why so negative, Elizabeth? All was good again, and about to get better.

Other staff members soon filed into the office. The hot topic of conversation was the summer. As upbeat as I tried sounding, mine hadn't been as idyllic as I had thought. It was embarrassing confessing to working for Dad. The upperclassmen had worked for companies and people unrelated to themselves.

Dad had given me real responsibilities, but it was still Dad. Though I had worked very hard, it was in the telling that it didn't sound right. I sounded like a spoiled rich kid unable to make it on her own.

I vowed to begin searching now for what I would do next summer. The more challenging the opportunity, the better. Proving to others, perhaps more importantly to myself, that I was capable of succeeding in a world where the names Jacobs, Jordan and Newman were unknown was of paramount importance.

I had no idea what I would do, but I had to get away from Los Angeles next summer. Danny would understand. I'd have him come with me. We could rent a loft in Soho. Finding jobs in New York should be easy.

"Everyone is waiting," Danny said as he entered my room.

A rarity; I was running late. Danny had caught me still fussing with my hair. I was trying to pull back a few strands on my left side with a faux sapphire and diamond-encrusted clip.

"This isn't working." I was frustrated.

"Let me try."

"You can do girl hair?"

"No, but I'll try if you promise to give up when I fail so we can get going."

"Fine," I sighed.

I felt like a small child standing before its mother as Danny carefully lifted a few strands off my face. His fingertips lightly brushing my cheek caused my heart to flutter. His smile told me he knew.

"There," he declared.

Danny had easily affixed the clip just where I wanted it.

"Thanks," I said, surprised. "It's perfect. It matches…"

"Elizabeth, what does this clip match?"

Danny stared at the autumn colored silk shirt I was wearing over a short russet denim skirt.

"Your eyes," I said, looking directly at him. "It matches your eyes."

"My eyes?" Danny was taken aback, "That's different."

"And so am I," I answered, and I kissed his surprised lips.

We were going with our friends to the movie theatre across the street from Donnelly. Danny held my hand as we walked. My fingers felt snug entwined in his, and the warmth of his touch radiated through my entire being. I didn't stop smiling and neither did Danny.

Danny and I ended up sitting in the middle of our group, between Shane and Rachel. I would have preferred either sitting on the end, or ditching them altogether. Our friends' presence had become an unwanted intrusion on our evening.

"Forget they're here. I have," Danny whispered, having read my mind. Then he brushed his lips against mine and I smiled.

The lights went down, and the previews began.

"I'm so sorry about everything," Danny said in a voice so soft only I heard him. "Eli, I can't live without you, baby."

"I can't live without you either." I thought last night had made that apparent.

Danny leaned in and crushed his lips to mine. The hand not holding the popcorn bag held my face. I touched his cheek with affection. Danny's stubble felt so right.

"Popcorn, babe?" Danny asked as our lips parted. I giggled.

Without waiting for my answer, he leisurely placed a few kernels in my mouth. The slowness with which Danny did this, his fingertips lingering on my lips, caused my shudder. It was so erotic.

In return, I fed Danny a few kernels of popcorn. He smiled and took my hand. Danny languidly sucked the butter off my fingertips. I gasped, starring at his sensuous smile, and mischievous blue eyes. This was way too intimate for public consumption.

"It's your mother!" Rachel interrupted.

"What?"

I turned toward her. For the moment I thought Mom was in the theatre, ready to swoop in and prevent me from going home with Danny. Then I realized it was a preview for her new film due out in November.

Danny pressed my hand against his face and kissed my palm.

"I thought Danny broke up with you last week," Rachel whispered.

"He did."

"Then why were you making out with him?"

"Because it's this week," I retorted, and I turned back to Danny.

"I don't want to look at Randi," Danny whispered, "I want you."

My cheeks reddened, flushed with joy. Danny lifted my chin and kissed me. My lips parted, and my heart beat rapidly. How I wish we were alone.

Danny put down the popcorn bag to hold me with both hands. Our kiss became urgent. My lips parted, eagerly letting his tongue explore my mouth while his hand trailed down my side, up my skirt, and squeezed in between my thighs.

Through the fabric of my panties he stroked me. I gasped. My eyes popped open wide in disbelief. Surrounded by our friends, I was moments from an orgasm. I summoned my inner resolve and pulled his hand away.

"We should behave now," I said.

"What about later?"

"We are definitely not behaving later," I giggled.

Throughout the opening sequence Danny tenderly massaged my knuckles. As the credits began against dramatic music, Danny shifted the popcorn bag to his left knee. I glanced at him, quizzical. I still wanted to eat. As I released my left hand from Danny's right to reach across for some popcorn, he laid his right hand on my thigh.

As I munched, Danny's fingers tip-toed up my thigh, beneath my skirt again, and I shivered. Mischievous sapphire eyes met my frustrated emeralds. Oh, no! Why couldn't he wait? Danny grinned in answer to my unasked question. His fingers crept higher. Shit! Not now!

Stifling my gasp by biting my lip, I grabbed the popcorn bag and settled it onto my right knee, shielding his handiwork from Rachel were she to turn my way. Then Danny's fingers reached inside my panties. Unwanted waves of pleasure radiated through me. A moan rose from my throat. My muscles clenched. I was too far-gone, and I was stuck. Danny knew protesting would draw attention.

My brain was angered, but my body was so aroused. Danny inserted two fingers into me and began their rhythmic seduction. Oh, no!

It took all the concentration I could muster to keep my hips still, and my eyes fixed on the screen. I bit my lip, hard, hoping the pain would keep my moans silent, and counteract the wave building inside me. Danny's rhythm sped up. I dug my nails into his denim-covered thigh.

Just as I thought I couldn't hide my impending orgasm any longer, Danny smashed his lips to mine, his deep kiss muffling my uncontrollable moans as I exploded around him. Then grinning, pleased with his success, Danny withdrew his fingers. He patted my skirt into place, and reached for the popcorn. My racing heart tried to settle.

"I so own you," Danny whispered before placing a kernel of popcorn in my mouth, silencing me.

He was right. I didn't like that he was.

It turned out to be a much better than I had expected psychological thriller. And when the film ended, I walked back to campus happy, nestled under Danny's protective arm. Life was back to normal, last week's heartbreak a thing of the past.

Cam, Shane and Chloe parted for the Cellar before we reached Berkeley Hall, leaving us accompanying Rachel. As Danny and I turned for the stairwell to his corridor, Rachel stopped us.

"We've got to talk," she said to Danny with urgency. "Alone. Now."

Danny glanced at me and I shrugged.

"I won't be long," he promised. "Baby, you have your key?"

While Danny had his curious chat with Rachel, I striped off my clothes, and put Danny's way too large navy bathrobe on over my underwear. I wanted to brush my teeth. Danny deserved better than a girlfriend with popcorn breath.

I found my toothbrush in Danny's bathroom cubby, right where I'd left it last time I'd slept here, and I giggled. Not much of a break-up.

Flossing and brushing done, I was ready for Danny's return. As I reached for the mouthwash bottle, the bathroom door opened. It was Ian. Why did I always run into him in the bathroom? It gave me the creeps.

A tall, skinny girl with mousy hair, was wrapped around him. Ian was supporting her weight. She giggled, obviously intoxicated.

"Around the corner, sugar," Ian slurred, while pointing in the direction of the toilet stalls.

While holding the wall, the girl continued giggling as she managed to stumble in the direction of the toilet stalls.

"Its Newman's girlfriend," Ian sneered, "I heard you broke up."

"Well, you heard wrong," I answered curtly.

Then I sipped a capful of Listerine Zero and gargled.

"So I'm not the only guy on this hall getting lucky tonight."

Ian's audacity caught in my throat. I choked on the rinse, coughing and spitting it out of my mouth, into the sink.

"How dare you compare me and Danny to your drunken one-night-stand," I replied with superiority.

I returned the cap to the bottle and stowed it in Danny's cubby. Without waiting for Ian's answer, I strode out of the room, the door slamming shut behind me.

Back in our room, I returned Danny's robe to the hook on the door. I stood before the wardrobe in a pale orange lace thong and matching cropped camisol bra and hung my clothes away.

Soon Danny entered and locked the door. His eyes opened wide with pleasure. Without hesitation, he pulled me into his arms, kissing me with urgency.

"Baby, I've missed you. Now, where were we?" Danny whispered.

The excitement of his hands gripping my bare skin clouded my common sense.

"You were finger fucking me," I laughed, and Danny smiled.

Going up on toe and holding his broad shoulders for support, I chastely kissed Danny's lips. Then I grabbed the bottom of his tee-shirt, pulled it over his head, and tossed it near the corner laundry basket.

Danny grinned. "I like when you take the lead," he said.

I peppered Danny's chest with delicate kisses, unbuttoned his jeans, and pulled open the zipper. Then I went down on my knees. As my final kiss landed at his waistband, I yanked his jeans and underwear down, and Danny stepped out of them.

His hard masculinity sprung free, and I planted a kiss on his firm tip.

"What did Rachel want?" I asked. I took him in my mouth and sucked.

Danny gasped as he answered. "She warned me not to do what I'm about to do."

I paused. "You're not doing anything. I am," I answered, and I stroked him with my fingertips.

"She doesn't want me to hurt you again." I kissed Danny's tip, and his hips flexed.

"I'm afraid too."

"You don't seem afraid," Danny answered, and he pressed himself into my mouth. I stopped to swallow.

"Promise me you won't hurt me again."

"Baby, I can't promise you anything right now," Danny said and kissed my hair.

"Why not?" I asked while stroking him again.

"It wouldn't be honest," Danny whispered, his breath more shallow. "I want you so desperately I would say anything right now to get my way."

I smiled shyly and resumed sucking, my tongue flicking at his impressive length.

"Babe," Danny said breathlessly, "You don't like giving blow jobs."

Danny reached for my head, which he gently disengaged.

"E," he said in a soft voice, "Let me make us both happy."

Danny lifted me up by my shoulders, and I wrapped my legs around his waist as he carried me to the bed.

"I thought you'd like that," I pouted.

Didn't he understand? Danny had to realize all his needs could be met by me, and me alone. He didn't need to go elsewhere for anything.

"I do like it," Danny said, his breath shallow. "But no, not really."

I frowned, confused.

"It feels good, Eli. Just not in here." Danny patted his heart. "I love you, E. I only want to do what we both enjoy."

My legs still wrapped around his waist, Danny delicately laid me down. He leaned over and kissed my lips. Then Danny reached for my cami and pulled it over my head. He slowly pulled off my thong.

Danny's eyes were bright with merriment, and he bent down to kiss me. "Blow jobs give me a release with no strings," he explained. "And it gives the girls I won't have sex with the thrill of blowing Danny Newman."

My eyes shot open, gaping in shock at his arrogance.

To stifle the protest he knew was coming, Danny crushed his lips to mine, sending shudders throughout my core. At the same time, he thrust himself into me, and soon we exploded together. How I'd missed this.

I woke feeling content. With the morning sun filtered through the edges of the window shade, I found the arms of my beloved warmly wrapped around my middle. I snuggled closer, pressing Danny's arms against me. As I desired, sleepy lips pressed against my shoulder. I tilted my head to face Danny, and gave him my happiest, brightest smile.

"That's blinding me, Elizabeth."

I pressed my lips against his and experienced his happiness through our kiss.

"Good morning," I whispered.

"It certainly is," Danny answered as I turned my body to his and his lips melted to mine.

Danny's heart beat rapidly as did mine. Our kisses increased in intensity. Danny's hands knew exactly how to touch me to drive away all reason. We entwined, sharing our passion and love the way we did best.

Forever would not be enough mornings to wake up like this, I decided as we snuggled in each other's arms sharing gentle, satisfied kisses.

"I have rugby practice," Danny whispered. I gave his bruised cheek a gentle kiss.

"Watch your face. I have a vested interest in it. I'm tired of people saying there goes Elizabeth Jacobs and her damaged boyfriend."

"Nobody says that. If they do, who cares? You know what I really look like."

"I sure do," I responded, flirting all the way. I wrapped my arms around Danny's neck and kissed him until he pulled his lips away.

"Don't start, Elizabeth. I need my energy for rugby."

I smiled and kissed Danny's cheek again before climbing on top of him.

Eventually Danny pulled himself out of bed while I remained under the covers. It was later than we thought and he needed to get to practice or risk his teammates' wrath. Fooling around with your girlfriend would not be an acceptable excuse for being late. It was rugby. Broken bones and death were the only acceptable excuses.

"Can we go on a real date tonight?" I asked. "Just you and me? No entourage."

Danny laughed. "You don't want chaperones again?"

"If that's what they were, they did a poor job."

"They sure did," Danny answered and kissed my lips. "Disappointed?"

"Not at all, Daniel."

"What do you want to do?"

I shrugged. "I don't care. How about bowling or fast food? As long as we spend the evening alone."

"You bowl and eat fast food? Right."

"They're just examples. We don't have to do anything special as long as it's only us."

We did much better than fast food. The cool late summer evening was perfect for dining on the patio of an elegant little bistro on the other side of town. A discovery of ours last spring, the bistro had an excellent menu that changed depending on which locally produced ingredients were available. And they made unexpectedly excellent Margaritas given that its cuisine was modern French.

Later, we connected with our friends at The Cellar. What a difference one day made! Tonight they accepted that Danny and I were back together.

CHAPTER FIFTEEN - ELIZABETH

Great! It was raining. Again. It had been marginally overcast earlier, thus all I had for protection when political science ended was a light sweatshirt. I glanced at Danny. He was no better off, but at least he'd brought his backpack so our laptops would be protected.

"Let's make a run for it." Danny said at the front door of the building.

From the looks of it, there appeared to be no end in sight to the downpour. We had no choice.

Danny and I pulled the hoods of our sweatshirts up and tightened the drawstrings. Taking my hand, we made a dash for it, jogging, sloshing through puddles along the way. Thoroughly drenched, but laughing at the absurdity, we arrived at Berkeley Hall.

"I feel like a wet rat!" I laughed as we entered the lobby and were greeted by a blast of air conditioning. Right away I began shaking.

Danny smirked, and he pulled me into his arms. "Babe, you're freezing. Let's get you upstairs." Danny vigorously rubbed my arms to warm me.

Upstairs, Danny removed a navy bath sheet from the upper cupboard. I was trembling non-stop, though the bedroom was substantially warmer than the lobby.

"Let's get you out of those wet things."

I nodded like an obedient little girl as Danny swiftly removed my sweatshirt and then my shirt and bra. He draped the towel around my shoulders, vigorously rubbing to dry my skin and dripping hair. Then Danny leaned down to remove my waterlogged shoes, and he opened my jeans. We laughed as the saturated denim clung to my legs, making removal difficult. Again, Danny rubbed me dry.

"E, get under the covers while I lay these out," he instructed.

Obediently following orders, I crawled into bed, letting the damp towel fall to the floor. Cozy, I pulled up the covers up to my chin.

As best as he could, Danny found places for our wet clothes. My sweatshirt was already on the back of the chair, the jeans and bra he hung on a hook, and my shirt he placed on a hanger dangling from another hook. Finally, Danny removed his own wet clothing, laid them over the open wardrobe doors, and dried himself with a fresh towel. He shuddered from the chill air.

"Come. I'll warm you up," I smiled, and twinkled emerald eyes at him.

"I'm sure you will," he chuckled. Danny dropped the towel and dove under the covers.

"You're like ice!" I exclaimed.

"Not for long I'm not," Danny answered. Playful, he wrapped his arms around me, and covered me with kisses.

An afternoon in bed was the perfect way to pass a rainy day. Both of us warm and sated, we lay in each other's arms, enjoying the strength of our bond.

"You know, you're the only girl I've ever had sex with in the afternoon."

"I am?" Danny had only been with other girls at night? Interesting.

"Yeah. If you have sex with a girl in the afternoon she'll expect you to dine with her, and spend the evening, and possibly even the entire night with her, maybe even the next day, too. One afternoon, and boom! You're married."

"Where do you come up with this stuff?" I giggled.

"Don't you expect to eat dinner with me?"

"We were going to anyway, Daniel."

"That's my point. You're not expecting anything I wasn't already planning. That's why I can make love to you in the afternoon. I already wanted to spend the evening with you."

"What if I don't want to?"

"Of course you want to."

"That's so arrogant, Daniel. Now I'll have to spend the night alone just to prove you wrong."

"No you won't. I won't allow it. Elizabeth, I love you and I really want to spend the night with you."

"Okay, because I love starting my day in your arms. And I love you."

I turned to Danny and kissed him. A contented moan rose from his throat, and he tightened his affectionate embrace.

"You know besides you and Juliette, I've never slept with anyone."

"I find that hard to believe."

"It's the truth, Elizabeth. I don't want to wake up the next day saddled with some girl I'm only having a fling with."

"That's so rude."

Danny grinned. "I risk them taking it too seriously. Except for you. I know I want to spend the day with you. I always do. And you're so beautiful in the morning."

"I am?" I grinned. Keep the compliments coming, Newman.

Playful, Danny ruffled my hair.

"Elizabeth, I love the way your hair is a mess all over the pillows. And you wake with the happiest smile, like there's no place you'd rather be."

"There is no place I'd rather be. Danny, this is why I can never say no to you."

I lay quiet once more. All this romantic talk was raising my expectations.

If I was going to enjoy my time with Danny, I shouldn't think about it. Yet at times like this, I couldn't help it.

I refused to analyze the situation, knowing that only time would change Danny. But would it change me too? Could I trust him until then?

Stop! I was ruining an amazing afternoon.

As though reading my mind, Danny, who was caressing my fingers, said gently, "I can't tell you what you want Eli, not yet."

There was sadness in his sapphire eyes as though he regretted it. Whatever had gone on in Vancouver had damaged him. Danny needed to heal. If only he was strong enough to share it with me. It would be painful, but in the long run he needed to do so for our relationship to succeed. Danny needed to find the strength.

I turned away, afraid of crying.

"No pouting, Elizabeth. This is why I wanted a hiatus. Because it makes me sad and it hurts you."

"Some break-up," I said trying to keep it light.

Danny turned me to face him, and he smiled.

"I didn't consider the strength of our love, or how we can't keep our hands off each other." Danny tickled my neck with my hair.

"Then why can't you...?" I squirmed. "I'm ready to help if you'd open up."

"I know you are," he said sadly. "I can't. Not yet. It's too raw. I'm sorry baby. After what I've been through, I'm not ready to be married. I don't want to make promises I can't guarantee."

"Since we decided not to be on hiatus, it's been great."

"Because I'm more relaxed. E, I thought you finally understood and accepted how things have to be for now. Was I wrong?"

I nodded, no, and I asked, "Danny do you want to break-up again?"

"Of course not. Whom would I have afternoons sex with?" Danny winked, took my face in his warm hands, and pressed his lips to mine.

Instinctively I responded, wrapping my arms around his neck and pulling him closer, our bodies tight against each other, becoming one again. My head said "no" but my body, so excited by his touch, was not listening, and I welcomed our shared explosion.

Sated, Danny held me while I drifted off, content in his warm embrace.

CHAPTER SIXTEEN - ELIZABETH

Wednesday I gave myself the night off from Danny. I'd experienced so much turmoil lately. I welcomed the solitude of a quiet evening alone.

My phone rang shortly after ten.

"Hey," I answered, my voice soft. Cozy, propped against my pillows, I was ready for sleep. "Did you enjoy your evening?"

Danny had gone to The Cellar with Cam and Shane.

"Mellow. Tired. Can I come down?"

"I'm… ," I yawned. "Exhausted."

"Baby, go to sleep. I'll see you tomorrow."

Thursday was a beautiful late summer afternoon and Danny suggested that we play tennis after our last class. We're both competitive on court, and a heated match had the potential to bring out the worst in us.

"I want to make you happy," Danny explained. "You love tennis."

It did make me happy. Tennis was my sport. I was a better technical player than him, though Danny had more power.

Danny did not run at full speed to reach my cross-court backhand giving me a game point early on. He should have stretched his six-foot frame to easily get his racket on it. My shot wasn't even the powerful pinpoint bullet I was capable of. Oddly too, Danny had earlier double-faulted. Tennis had been his idea. Why throw the match?

"Let's get lemonade," Danny suggested after I handily defeated him. With sweat dripping off my forehead and arms, cold lemonade sounded enticing.

At The Café, I opted for the healthier banana-orange smoothie while Danny ordered lemonade and soft pretzels, his slathered with spicy brown mustard. Seated across from him at a table in the shade, I waited for the proverbial other shoe to drop. There had to be a reason my competitive boyfriend let me win.

"What?" I finally blurted.

Danny hesitated, "Nothing. You won't like this."

"What won't I like?" I raised an eyebrow, suspicious.

"Duncan. I ran into him last night. I'm jamming at The Village tonight."

"Great," I said with sarcasm.

"That's why I couldn't tell you," said Danny, exasperated.

"Am I invited?" I countered.

Danny shifted in his chair. He struggled to make eye contact. "Baby, it's been a long time. I want to let loose. I can't do that if you're there."

"Sorry I cramp your style," I muttered.

"Elizabeth …," Danny said with tenderness, and he lifted my chin with his fingertips. "You never cramp my style. This is about me, not you. You're always my girl, but sometimes I want to hang with the guys." Danny's lips brushed against mine.

"All the kisses in the world won't make me happy, Daniel. It's still Duncan."

Actually it was Amelia and the memory of Danny's fling with her last winter that rankled me. But she transferred to Dartmouth this semester to be with her boyfriend. I let it go.

"Elizabeth, I'm not asking you to like Duncan. Please accept that he's my friend, and I enjoy spending time with him."

"I accept that he's your friend, but when you're with Duncan you always get drunk or wasted. Then you become a different person and I don't like that Danny."

Danny chuckled. "It's still me. The same man who adores you." Danny kissed me again.

Why fight it? Danny would hang out with Duncan whether I liked it or not. The best I got was extracting the promise that no matter how late he returned, Danny swore he would spend the night with me.

I could deal with Duncan and the guys that frequented the Village party scene. The heavy alcohol and drug consumption didn't make me uneasy either. The clique of slutty girls, equally wasted, who had no compunctions about sleeping their way around the room regardless of a guy's relationship status, did.

They didn't care that Danny had a girlfriend. It made him that much more exciting to target as a conquest. Last year I had over-heard their ringleader, Phoebe plotting. They wanted to give Danny whatever they assumed he was missing by dating me. I laughed. The only thing Danny was missing was exposure to STDs.

Uneasy, I paced my room until midnight before deciding to try sleep. The last thing I wanted was for Danny to catch me waiting up. I put my Bose Wave on sleep mode, checked once again that the door was unlocked, shut the light, and crawled into bed.

My favorite love song woke me with sweetness at eight o'clock. The sweetness was short-lived. Still sleepy I reached over and found no Danny. I snapped to attention.

Where the hell was he, I fretted.

I grabbed my phone and confirmed I hadn't slept through any calls or texts. Then I jumped out of bed and opened the door. A quick check confirmed the door remained unlocked. No notes had been left.

Panic. My heartbeat accelerated. Had something happened? Did Danny get into an accident? Be logical, Elizabeth. If there had been an accident, Steve and Ellen would have called, even in the middle of the night.

Maybe it had been so late that Danny went to his own room to actually sleep. Danny had no classes today. He could sleep all day if he wanted to. I considered calling him, but instantly dismissed that idea. Calling this early would signal a lack of trust on my part.

Trust. I gasped.

It crystallized in that one word the reason behind my panic. I didn't trust Danny. It filled me with unavoidable heart-stabbing pain. That's what had been gnawing at me all week, and now it had surfaced. I loved a man I didn't trust.

Trust should be a two-way street. Danny could implicitly trust me in every facet of life, and in our relationship. But what about Danny? For certain he loved me, and I trusted him with my life, but regrettably, not with our love.

Was a one-way street the equivalent of a dead-end? I would analyze this later. My dance classes soon started, and I needed yogurt and fruit or I wouldn't have the energy to get through them.

I ran into Shane while eating breakfast.

"Have you seen Danny?" I asked.

I tried sounding casual. How absurd it must seem that this early in the morning I didn't know where my boyfriend was.

"Isn't he with you?" Shane asked.

"Would I be asking you if he were?" I snapped.

"Good point. I haven't seen him since about midnight. I was leaving Duncan's. Danny said he'd be coming in a few. Said you were waiting for him. He was so wasted."

Great. Not what I wanted to hear.

Dance classes, with their complex combinations take a lot of concentration. If I didn't want a repeat of last year's sprained ankle, I needed my mind unoccupied to successfully negotiate the moves. I cleared Danny from my thoughts for now.

After, while in the shower, my mind wandered. Like a bolt of lightening, and equally welcome, I realized the painful truth and shuddered. I knew what I needed to do, and it took all the strength I had not to break down sobbing in the locker room. My long-term sanity and self-esteem were more important than the pain I would have to inflict and endure.

While getting dressed I received a one-word text message from Danny. "Lunch?" it asked. I answered immediately, "10 mins." Better to get this over with.

Whether Danny had crashed at Duncan's or had ended up in bed with a slut, that I couldn't trust him not to have been with another woman was not a place I wanted to be.

If only Danny would commit to me. Until he did, whenever Danny failed to be where he should be, I would have doubts. How ironic; one small sentence pledging his fidelity, and I'd believe anything Danny wanted me to believe.

At lunch I played with my food while Danny was his usual affable self. His concerned glances and hand squeezing made it obvious that he sensed something was amiss. Danny would not ask in front of our friends.

A cheerful Danny held my hand all the way back to the dorm. Deja-vu, the sensation that you've been there before, swept through me as we neared my room.

"Danny, we need to talk," I said, my voice tinged with sadness.

Danny raised an eyebrow as he followed me into my room. We sat down on the bed, like last time. Danny took my shaky hands. I frowned and looked into his puzzled blue eyes.

"Where did you sleep last night?" I began.

He laughed, relieved. "That's what this is about?"

I nodded, although I was certain Danny had interpreted my nod different from how I intended.

"I'm so sorry, babe. You must have been worried sick by my absence this morning. I apologize for not texting. I couldn't drive so I crashed on Duncan's couch." Danny ended with a smile.

When I didn't return his smile, Danny grew concerned.

"You believe me, don't you?"

Gathering my courage, I responded, "Yes, of course I do."

Again Danny looked relieved. I looked down at my fingers twisting the fabric of my sweatshirt.

"Eli?" he asked tentatively.

I took a deep breath before continuing. This was so difficult.

"Danny, I shouldn't have to ask you in private about last night. It should be a question I could ask in front of everyone."

"Then why didn't you?"

"I didn't know the answer," I said, deflated.

"You thought I was with another woman?" he asked flatly.

"It was a possibility. Do you know how awful that is?"

"Babe…" Danny protested.

"This morning, I realized I didn't trust you."

"Elizabeth, you can trust me."

"I want to so badly, but no Danny, I can't. It hurts, so much." I trembled. Tears spilled down my cheeks. "I won't give you an ultimatum.

That's not me," I stammered. "But until you can promise, I can't trust you. I want to trust you, Danny. I love you," I sobbed. "This hurts so much!"

Danny wrapped me in his arms. I pushed away. He took my hand.

"Elizabeth, I love you," Danny pleaded. "Please don't be saying this."

"I have to. I will not keep you on a leash. I need confidence not to be concerned about other women. I don't have that. Danny, I deserve better. I want better." Tears continued streaming down my cheeks.

Danny stared at my fingers he was playing with. He looked at me, shaken. Danny understood.

"You're right Elizabeth. You deserve much better. Trust is important for a relationship to be successful. I don't know how you've gone this long without it."

"I kept hoping you'd change. You had changed. Then came Vanessa. I convinced myself it didn't matter. Today I realized it matters. It matters a lot."

More tears spilled down my face. I didn't bother wiping them away.

"So now what? Where does this leave us, Elizabeth?" Danny asked. His eyes were downcast, full of sorrow, sensing what he knew must be coming.

"This is awful. I love you so much. You know I do," I paused, steeling myself. "I hate this. I really do. Danny, we need a hiatus until you figure yourself out. We can't see each other. If we do, we'll be back together again with nothing resolved."

"Eli, no…" Danny was stunned. "I love you, baby."

"This is the hardest thing I've ever had to do. We're too close. We have too much love. I hate this Danny."

"It's all my fault. What can I do, Eli?"

"It's both of our faults. I should have believed you long ago, but I enjoyed us too much. There's only one thing you can do, but you have to want to. I can't make that happen. Until you do…" My voice tailed off. My insides convulsed.

Ashen-faced, Danny was shell-shocked, not comprehending my words. Any more talk would not make a difference.

I rose, and Danny followed suit. I squeezed his hand and looked into very sad sapphire eyes. Kissing Danny's cheek for the last time was agonizing. I could barely speak.

"Good-bye, Daniel."

"Eli, no!"

"I love you. I always will."

CHAPTER SEVENTEEN- ELIZABETH

"Tell me again why we're having dinner with Juliette?" Rachel asked.

Rachel and I were trekking across the Donnelly campus to The Exchange, the cooperative housing center where Juliette, now a senior, lived.

It was a reasonable question. Juliette was Danny's last girlfriend before he and I became a couple last fall. They had dated for about a month. Juliette ended the relationship when I'd broken my ankle and Danny was taking care of me.

I smirked at the memory, bittersweet now. Juliette wouldn't tolerate me staying in Danny's room. At the time, nothing was going on between us, but Juliette understood what Danny could not admit at the time; he was in love with me. It was a few more weeks until our first date, and several more weeks passed before Danny confessed his love.

"Because she invited me," I answered curtly.

"But she's Danny's ex. Isn't this more than just a little awkward?"

"We're adults, Rachel. If Juliette thought it was too awkward, she wouldn't have called."

"Elizabeth, you have nothing in common with her. What can you even talk about besides Danny?" Rachel shook her head in frustration.

That much was true. I had zero in common with Juliette. That had been Danny's problem with her too. Even without his feelings for me, their days as a couple had been numbered.

Juliette was an ethereal, hippie earth-mother type, seemingly leftover from the 1960s. Her waist-long hair was white-blonde, and her skin was so fair she must never spend time in the sun. She favored gauzy long dresses and flat sandals, too.

And Juliette was a vegan, which I respected. I enjoy meals without meat, lasagna and penne alla Norma are my favorites. But as a romantic relationship for Danny, it had been comical. Nothing makes him happier than a juicy burger. The one or two times I dined with him and Juliette, I deliberately ordered one to annoy him.

"It'll be fun. Juliette's a nice girl," I answered.

"Does Danny know?"

My heart felt sick at the repeated mention of Danny's name. I had to tell Rachel about us, and soon, but how? It hurt so much to say it. Telling her would make it real.

I smoothed my hair and refrained from answering Rachel's question.

Distracted, and despite the flat heeled boots I was wearing, I tripped twice in quick succession.

Rachel had reached her limits and stopped dead in the path.

"What's wrong with you?" she asked. "You're acting so strange."

I couldn't look at her. My eyes blinked back tears. I played with the leather fringe hanging from my small shoulder bag.

"It's Danny, isn't it?"

I looked up and met Rachel's gaze with sad, dull eyes.

"Danny didn't break up with you again, did he?"

I peeked at her through my lashes, nervous. "No. I broke up with him. This afternoon," I confessed, and I bit my lip to staunch the tears.

Stunned, Rachel stared at me with wide eyes. "But you love Danny!"

Then I explained everything.

"You'll get back together," Rachel declared with confidence.

"I don't know. Not anytime soon," I stammered.

"Your last break-up lasted for what, three days?"

"More like five. This is different. I don't want that again."

"I do know this. Danny cannot live without you, and you can't live without him."

"We'll have to try. I told Danny we need a clean break. Absolutely no contact."

"Why can't you be friends while you work things out?"

"There's nothing to work out. We didn't have a fight. We're still in love."

"Don't you want Danny anymore?" Rachel asked, shocked that perhaps I didn't.

"Desperately," I answered sadly, trying my hardest to fight back the tears stinging my eyes. "Rachel, I want Danny on my terms. And he agrees. If I can't trust Danny, what's the point? Eventually he would lose all respect for me."

"Elizabeth, you don't mean that?"

"Yes, I do. Depressed as I am, my self-esteem is the highest it's been in a long time. No matter what happens, I won't let Danny use me anymore."

"Danny loves you. He didn't use you."

"Well, maybe not exactly, but Danny knew he could do whatever he wanted because I was always there. I'm empowered. For the first time in my life, I turned away Danny Newman."

"But why not be friends? You've been friends for almost twenty years."

For the first time I started crying. Rachel embraced me.

"That's the worst part," I wailed. "Danny's my best friend. Now that's over too."

"It doesn't have to be," Rachel said in a comforting voice.

"It does. Our love is too strong. You saw what happened last week. If we socialize, we'll end up back in bed with nothing resolved, and I'll really be the loser. Then Danny will definitely walk all over me."

CHAPTER EIGHTEEN - DANIEL

Thick fog shrouded my every movement. What was I even doing here, at the dining hall? I didn't care which food I chose. Whatever was on my plate, I practically threw down on the table. I wasn't eating it anyway. I had no appetite. Life had been sucked out of me.

I loved Elizabeth, and now she was gone. Gone. Elizabeth, my rock whom I depended on. Elizabeth, my best friend, and lover. I had never been in love before. I doubted I ever would be again. It hurt too much.

My thoughts rambled. I hated myself. It was all my fault. If only I could have confessed to Elizabeth. Then she would be sitting beside me, gazing at me with her adoring emerald eyes, secure in my love. But I couldn't. It was too humiliating.

I looked forward to escaping from the dining hall and getting totally wasted to stop thinking of Elizabeth.

"Where's your wife?" Cam asked, jarring me from my thoughts.

"Huh?" I responded.

My wife? So this is how divorce feels; empty, devastating, completely demoralizing. No wonder my parents had fought tooth and nail to stay together.

I had no idea where Eli was, but I feared admitting it to my friends.

"She went off-campus with Rachel," Chloe piped in from beside me.

That's right. I remembered Eli telling me this the other day, but that seemed an eternity ago now. Thanks, Chlo. I hadn't even realized she was sitting next to me.

"Yeah. Chloe's right," I slurred, a by-product of the beers I had consumed.

"Danny, you look awful," Chloe exclaimed.

"You reek, man," Shane added. "Mrs. Newman will not be happy."

Mrs. Newman. I couldn't respond.

Chloe took my hand. Kindness and concern etched across her pretty face.

"Danny, you're drunk," she said softly. "What's going on? This isn't like you."

I stared blankly past her highlighted blonde hair. Some guys like that. Not me.

"Danny, tell me," Chloe urged. "I'm your friend. I can help."

Chloe was right. She was my friend, but I doubted she could help. Humiliated, I was unable to make eye contact with Chloe.

THE BETRAYAL

"Eli broke up with me," I blurted out.

"No!" Chloe exclaimed, her brown eyes wide with concern.

Cam and Shane stared in disbelief.

"I thought she was crazy about you," said Cam.

"And you her," Chloe added.

"She is. I am," I answered mournfully.

Shane expressed shock. "You and Elizabeth are always doing it."

"Shane!" Chloe scolded.

"Sorry, Danny. Just trying to make sense of this."

"There is no sense," Chloe replied. "Give Elizabeth some time. She'll come make up with you."

"No, she won't. This time it's final," I said woefully.

"That can't be. You're meant for each other."

"Chloe's right. She'll come back. Give her some time," said Cam.

"She's gone. Damn it! I blew it. Eli's gone!"

I pushed back from the table and stalked out. I was out of beer. Time to get wasted.

CHAPTER NINETEEN - ELIZABETH

"Give me your phone. I'll call us out. You can be sick." Rachel demanded as we neared The Exchange.

I shook my head. ""I told Juliette we'd be there. I'd feel guilty." I had enough guilt swirling through me as it was. I didn't have to court any additional.

"This is too weird. Dinner with Danny's two exes," Rachel muttered.

"One ex. Juliette was just a fling."

"For a month?" Rachel rolled her eyes.

"Don't say a word!" I said sharply. That was the last thing I needed, giving Juliette validation.

Part of me doubted the sincerity behind tonight's invitation, but I had been too stubborn to decline. If Juliette's motivation was to laugh at an uncomfortable fish out of water, I determined to prove to her holier-than-thou crowd that this Hollywood princess was anything but.

Elizabeth Jordan Jacobs could do anything she put her mind to, and do it with aplomb. I would eat tofu or anything else they served as a substitute for meat, and smile throughout. I would. No matter how awful the taste.

I would roll up my sleeves and wash dishes too. I'd even wipe down the tables if that's what they expected from guests at The Exchange. I did it at home in Malibu. Danny and I didn't have staff. Only Graci, and she came just once a week to do the laundry and the real cleaning.

Malibu. The thought of my beautiful home, empty, waiting for that day when Danny and I returned, a day that might never happen, brought me to the edge of tears.

Don't cry, Elizabeth. Keep it together.

"I think tonight will be good for me," I said to Rachel, trying to sound upbeat, wanting to convince myself. "I'll be forced to concentrate on Juliette and her friends. There won't be time to think about Danny."

"Aren't you forgetting the obvious?" I cocked my head in Rachel's direction. "You're only aquainted with Juliette because of Danny."

A willowy blonde with a pixie cut and a tan greeted us. A tan? Juliette was usually albino pale.

"Elizabeth! Rachel!" Juliette exclaimed, and she warmly embraced us.

"Hi," Rachel said quietly.

I pulled back and examined Juliette's appearance. For the first time that I recalled, she wore jeans and a polo shirt. She looked healthy. She looked great.

"Juliette! I love your hair," I said. Why the total transformation, I wondered?

Juliette fingered her short locks, a sharp contrast to her formerly waist-long straight hair. "I needed the right cut for job interviews," she answered sounding embarrassed.

"Well you look great," I said.

I dug my fingers into my palm so I wouldn't laugh. Last year Juliette had been critical of girls who dressed in the typical collegiate preppy style. Her wardrobe had consisted of long, hippy dresses.

"I'm glad you came," Juliette said in her lighter than air voice when we sat down to dine. "I wanted you to experience who we really are. Maybe you'll consider living here next year."

Like that would ever happen.

Surprisingly, the residents of The Exchange were a diverse cross-section of Donnelly students. They were warm and friendly, pleased to welcome guests to their close-knit community.

Dinner impressed me. Cooked by the students, everything was delicious. Large bowls of whole-wheat spaghetti with homemade marinara sauce were served family style. Salad greens and bowls of sautéed zucchini and mushrooms also made the rounds. Most unexpected, a platter of sliced chicken breasts was on each table, an add-on for those who were not vegetarian. And there was freshly baked bread!

"How do you cook such large quantities?" I asked. How did they have time?

At home, despite my mother loving to cook, we never had more than eight people to dinner without it being professionally catered, except for Thanksgiving. At The Exchange they served triple that at every meal. With class schedules, I marveled at how they accomplished this.

"We cook in teams," Juliette explained. "Monday through Friday, but Saturday and Sunday, you fend for yourself."

"Cooking in teams is a great way to get to know each other," the girl next to her added. "We do everything in teams. It's the philosophy of The Exchange."

I wished I lived there now. Being part of a team, engaged in tasks, that was exactly what I needed to get my mind off of Danny.

With my thumbs, I broke open a flaky dinner roll. Buttermilk crumbs scattered across the table and onto my lap. I plucked them off with my fingertips. As I reached for the last of the crumbs, my hopes sank as I confronted ten perfect, Shellac French-manicured nails. I knew in my heart,

The Exchange was not the place for a girl who kept a standing appointment every two weeks for a Shellac manicure.

A quick glance at everyone else's nails confirmed this. Forget Shellac, none of the girls even wore self-applied drug store polish. They didn't wear make-up either, though the local mall had a Sephora.

Somewhere, apart from Danny's bed, there had to be a place for a girl like me. The Exchange was not it.

After taking a hot shower, I crawled into bed, exhausted. Then I turned out the desk light, settled beneath the covers, and… the phone rang.

"Oh, bother," I moaned. "Who on earth is calling me this late at night?" It was nearly midnight.

I turned the light back on and grabbed my phone. I smiled. Grandma Margie! What a pleasant surprise.

"Grandma! Why are you up so late?" Then I laughed, remembering the obvious. It was three hours earlier in Sherman Oaks.

"I'm just back from dinner. I was at services. Shabbat Shalom, Elizabeth dear."

"Uh, right," I answered awkwardly.

At home, I rarely attended services, and at Donnelly I never considered it. "Shabbat Shalom to you too, Grandma," I stammered. Grandma had a knack for dishing out Jewish guilt.

Although Grandma had strayed from her Orthodox roots, she regularly attended a popular Conservative synagogue near her home, and she kept kosher. My lack of religious observation was probably an embarrassment to her, but she never hinted at it.

"Mom tells me things are rocky with Danny," Grandma got directly to the point.

"That's one way of putting it," I answered. Then I filled her in on the latest.

"Elizabeth, I'm so sorry. I thought Danny was it for you."

"Thanks, Grandma. So did I."

"Have you thought about what's next?"

Tell me she wasn't going to suggest that I join Hillel? Or worse, JDate.

"There is no 'next' yet. Grandma, the ink's not even dry on the divorce papers."

Then I told her about dinner at The Exchange. "I don't know if this qualifies as a 'next,' but I realized tonight that I need to discover who I am and find my place. I've spent the past year in Danny's world. I don't know what Elizabeth's is."

"Good girl! You're on the right track."

"Grandma, I'm a mess. I'm not on any track."

"Elizabeth, I discussed you with the rabbi."

"Oh, no!" I was right; Hillel. I groaned, loudly.

"Elizabeth, don't give me attitude. At least let me tell you what she suggested."

"Whatever," I answered disrespectfully.

"It's probably too late for you to apply for this school year, but you could go during the summer."

"Go where?" I asked, disinterested.

"Israel. The rabbi told me about programs for college students."

"You've got to be kidding," I said. "You are kidding, aren't you, Grandma?"

"I knew you'd say that. It's your father's fault, you know. I love Michael, but he wasn't raised the same as Miranda. Until your mother met Michael, she went to Shabbat every week."

"She had no choice, Grandma. Mom lived with you."

"They should have moved to Beverly Hills. They have real rabbis in Beverly Hills. The leader of a congregation should not look like George Clooney. And that cantor sounds like he should be on Broadway."

"Grandma!" I protested. "I love our Rabbi Klein. He's a great man. He's smart and compassionate, too. So he looks like George Clooney. He can't help it."

"Whatever, Elizabeth. It's all you've known. The sanctuary is not a soundstage."

Grandma was a progressive, modern woman except regarding religion. Any movement more liberal than Conservative Judaism she considered borderline Christianity. Although she agreed with the modern tenants of the Reconstructionist congregation my family belonged to, she was unfamiliar with this movement.

"I'm emailing you the links the rabbi gave me. I won't force you, but I want you to promise me you'll at least read through the websites and consider them."

"Grandma..." I objected.

"Elizabeth, reading websites is not a commitment."

"Fine! I'll read the websites. This does not mean I'm going to Israel. I might spend the summer in New York. That's just as Jewish."

"You'll see, Elizabeth. Getting in touch with your roots may be just what you need to find your place in this world."

"My roots are on the Brooklyn boardwalk, not the Middle East. Maybe I should spend the summer at Coney Island eating Nathan's hotdogs while playing pinochle with a bunch of pudgy old men wearing wife-beaters."

"Elizabeth!"

CHAPTER TWENTY - DANIEL

"Damn it Lizzie!"

I knocked back a shot of Jack Daniels and slammed the glass down hard against the round wooden table. Sturdy little fucker. It didn't break.

I picked up the glass and examined it. I rolled it in my palm, my thumb caressing its solid surface. Glass, not plastic. Hmmm.

Cam slid into the chair adjacent to Shane seated beside me.

"How many is that?" Cam asked Shane.

"I've lost track," he answered.

I reached for the pitcher of beer and carefully poured into a glass, barely spilling a drop. Then I took a large swallow. I had no idea of the time, or how long I'd been sitting at this table in The Cellar.

My goal was to get completely plastered, and I was well on my way to success. The hell with everyone! The world be damned!

"Fuck you, Dad!" I exclaimed as I gulped down the rest.

"We have our hands full tonight, don't we?" Cam said to Shane.

Did they think I was deaf? "Hey! I don't need you or anybody else," I scowled. Well, maybe I needed Lizzie. My heart ached.

I grabbed the nearly empty pitcher and claimed its remaining contents. Shane clapped a supportive hand on my shoulder.

"We're here for you, man. We know you're hurting."

"I used to think Elizabeth was a great girl, but not anymore," Cam said. "What kind of game is she playing? I can't believe Elizabeth got you to go back to her just so she could dump you."

I took another large swallow of beer for fortification. How dare Cam criticize my Lizzie. I poured the rest of the beer into my glass.

"Never talk about my wife like that," I cautioned though my voice slurred. "Lizzie is a goddess. She is."

"Danny, get real," Cam blurted. "She manipulated you. Then she stabbed you."

"Fuck you, Cam! Lizzie's not like that!" I drained the beer. "We need another pitcher, and a shot of Jack," I called to a passing server. "You don't what you're talking about. So don't."

"But, Danny," Shane began.

"I did much worse to her, and I did it first," I confessed. "Leave Lizzie alone!"

A fresh pitcher of beer along with my shot was served. This time when I poured, I spilled a little. Cam had me agitated. Didn't he understand? My Lizzie is perfect. I'm the fucked-up SOB.

I slouched against the back of my chair and took a swallow of beer. A sort of cute girl with straight brown pixie hair made eye contact with me before stopping at my side.

"Hey, Danny," she greeted me with a cheerful smile.

I recognized her from someplace, but I couldn't recall. Her name was…? Andy? No, that's not right. Girls aren't named Andrew. Randi? It better not be Randi. One Randi in my life was more than I could handle.

"Intermediate Macro sure is tougher than Intro," she chirped.

Or course! That's where I knew her from – Econ! Now what was her name? Andy? Candy? Not Randi. Sandy?

"Mandy!" I exclaimed with relief.

Mandy was taken aback by my enthusiasm. I took another swallow of beer.

"Maybe we could study some time," I suggested. Like me, she was a top student.

Mandy smiled brightly. Shit! What the hell had I just done? Now to reverse it without hurting her feelings, but how?

"Can I have a glass?" Mandy asked of my beer. She was carrying an empty glass.

"Sure," I answered. Cam and Shane starred at me.

Mandy settled in to the chair next to me. I picked up the pitcher and poured. My hand wobbled, and Mandy placed hers over mine to steady me. Her touch was soft and warm.

Glass full, Mandy released her hand from mine, but she directed a smile my way. Shit! Mandy was interested.

"Where's your girlfriend?" she innocently asked.

Mandy was smart. Why flirt with a man if he was taken?

"My wife and I have separated," I said sadly before swallowing more beer. My heart hurt simply saying the words.

"Your wife? Separated? I didn't know you were actually married. I thought she was just your girlfriend."

"They weren't married," Shane corrected, "But they just broke up."

"We did not break up," I slurred with finality.

"I'm so sorry," Mandy said with sympathy. She leaned toward me and placed her hand on my forearm.

"We're separated," I explained.

"Of course," said Mandy. "I understand. It's difficult to acknowledge when a long-term relationship ends."

"It did not end!" I barked. Mandy jerked back in her chair, startled.

"Right. You're not divorced. You're separated," Cam snickered.

"What does that mean?" Mandy asked, calm again, her hand had returned to my arm.

"It means we're on a god-damned hiatus," I snapped.

"I feel your pain, Danny. Let me cheer you up."

"Not tonight," I answered.

I peeled Mandy's fingers off my arm to reach the Jack Daniels. I threw back the shot and winced at the sting of the warm amber flowing through my veins.

I leaned back against my chair and wrapped my arm around Mandy's bony shoulder.

"Mandy, darlin'," I drawled. "I am one fucked-up dude."

"You're southern?" she asked, surprised by my new accent.

"No, he's drunk," Cam explained. "When Danny gets drunk, he speaks Texan."

"Odd, but it's kind of cute."

"Mandy, I am not kind of cute. I'm fucked. But you are kind of cute. You're a nice girl. You're smart. If you're looking for a boyfriend, I am not your man. I'll study econ with you, I'll share a coffee after class with you, but that's it. My heart belongs to my wife. I am bad news for nice girls. Lizzie is the sweetest girl there is, and I hurt her. I messed with her real bad. She says I can't come home until I fix my head."

"Elizabeth found out about Reggie?" Shane asked.

"More or less," I answered sadly.

I turned to Mandy, her kind face confused. "Mandy, I'm such bad news. Unless you want a one-night-stand, but not tonight. I'm too fucked-up even for that."

I poured another beer, this time sloppy. I was beyond buzzed, well on my way toward being blitzed.

"Danny, you're drinking too much," Cam said with concern.

"Probably so," I answered.

"Elizabeth won't want you back like this."

"Yes, she will. Lizziebeth loves me. One day we'll get married and have a bunch of babies, all as beautiful as my Lizziebeth."

CHAPTER TWENTY-ONE - ELIZABETH

"Everything has a season, everything has …"

My phone! I had already changed my ringtone from Danny's singing to the Pippin soundtrack. I couldn't bear Danny's smooth tenor voice singing a love song every time someone called. I'd left it programmed for only when he called. If he called.

"…a time. Show me a reason and I'll…"

What time was it anyway? I reached for the phone and looked at the time. Falling asleep had been difficult enough. The last thing I needed was the phone waking me.

"…soon show you a rhyme. Cats fit…"

Two o'clock! Only bad news comes at two in the morning.

Instantly awake, I sat up. I pushed the on button without even glancing at the caller ID.

"Hello," I answered abruptly, unable to disguise my panic.

"How's my Lizziebeth?" a very inebriated Danny asked.

Great. Danny's plastered and I'm on his speed-dial. No. Wait. Pippin. Danny had borrowed someone's phone. "Danny, I'm sleeping," I growled.

"Yeah? Can I join you? Please?" His voice brightened for a moment.

"No," I answered curtly.

"C'mon Lizziebeth. I miss you baby," he slurred in a little boy voice.

"No," I repeated, less harsh. "You're drunk Danny."

"I am that, Lizziebeth. Totally wasted too."

My heart caught in my throat. It was my fault that Danny was trashed. My eyes welled up. I didn't want to cry with him on the phone.

"Get some sleep, Danny," I stammered. "It will be better tomorrow."

"Please, Lizziebeth," Danny pleaded. "I feel sick, baby. I'm scared to be alone."

Danny sounded like a five year old; my very own, beautiful little boy.

"I know," I said tenderly. How I ached for him.

Some time after the buzz started wearing off Danny became his most vulnerable. He was petrified by the prospect of being alone when he might get sick.

Guilt consumed me. Tears rolled down my cheeks. I hated his pain. I hated that he was alone. Worse, I was frightened that he wouldn't wake up if he fell asleep, and it would be my fault. But I had to stand firm.

"Can you get Shane?" I asked through my tears.

"He's here."

"Put him on."

"It's my beautiful Lizziebeth," Danny slurred as he passed the phone to Shane.

"Elizabeth?"

"It's me."

"Danny needs you. He's a mess."

"No, Shane. I will not deal with this."

"C'mon Elizabeth. Can't you and Danny kiss and make up?"

"Shane, I'm not discussing it with you at two in the morning. Or ever. I am not coming."

"Elizabeth, please."

I ignored Shane's pleas. "Danny needs you, Shane. Promise me that you'll spend the night with him. He's scared. I'm scared too."

"All right. Fine."

"Thank you. Please put Danny back on."

Danny must have been listening. He grabbed the phone immediately.

"Lizziebeth?"

"Danny, Shane will stay with you tonight."

"What about tomorrow?"

"Don't do this tomorrow."

"It dulls the pain."

"I know." His honesty rattled me. It smacked me in the face. "I hurt too."

"You do?" Danny asked softly. "Oh, Lizzie." The drunken soul transformed into my caring lover again.

"Yes," I wept. "I hate this."

"I do too. Are you crying?" Danny's tender voice was filled with concern.

"Yes," I trembled.

"Lizziebeth, please don't cry. I love you."

Now the tears wouldn't stop. "I love you too, but it has to be this way."

"Lizzie…"

I was incapable of speaking. "I gotta go, Danny. Feel better," I stammered.

I turned off the phone and buried my face in the pillow, sobbing. Danny loved me. I loved Danny. What had messed his head so badly?

Eventually I fell into a fitful sleep.

When morning came I felt ravaged. My head hurt from crying and my heart was hollow. Guilt consumed me too. I was to blame for Danny getting into such a state last night.

"No! Don't go there!" I scolded myself. That Danny needed a healthier way to channel his disappointment was not my fault. My subconscious sounded like a shrink.

But Danny wasn't disappointed. He was heartbroken, his anguish palpable last night. I had broken Danny's heart. What had I expected? Men do not call their mothers and cry. I felt lower than low.

I loved Danny. I didn't want him to hurt. Last night his wasted little boy voice had been unbearable. Would he now hate me? That would be even worse.

I hate clichés, but as I stood soaking in the hot steam shower, one kept going around and around inside my head. "Today is the first day of the rest of your life. Today is the first day of the rest of your life."

"Oh shut up!" I silently screamed as lather from the shampoo splashed in my eye. Ouch! The sharp, stinging that momentarily blinded me made me wince. Was this punishment for hurting Danny? God had sent me careless shampooing. Preposterous as it sounded, I was willing to believe anything today.

After last night's phone call, I amended my approach. Forget socializing, I could not risk crossing paths with Danny. It was too painful, yet I understood the necessity.

If I went to lunch later, and used the line on the left instead of the right, it would put me on the opposite side of the dining hall. Of course it would also leave me completely alone, but I had to take the risk.

Mom had taught me well. I donned my oversized Chanel wrap-around sunglasses that hid most of my face. I stuffed my iPad into my totebag and steeled myself for a lonely meal.

My confidence vanished as I entered the dining hall. I clenched my jaw and squared my shoulders. I could do this. I had arrived alone before, but always with the expectation that one of my friends was already seated at our table or would arrive shortly.

Our table, where Danny and I held court as Donnelly College's most intriguing couple, was no longer my home. Freshman year I ate every meal at that table. It was such a given that our group sat there, even if we were late, nobody dared to claim it. I didn't have a place at that table anymore. I didn't have a table.

So I headed to the left. Although identical to the one on the right, the left service line seemed foreign with every food station backward. Was that girl at the salad bar starring? Elizabeth Jacobs belonged on the line to the right.

I held my plate of food, an iced tea and a handful of cutlery that I almost forgot to grab. Now what? Where to sit? A quick glance around the room didn't help. Everyone was settled at their own tables with their own friends. Students are creatures of habit. My group wasn't the only one with set dining patterns.

I opted to sit alone at a small table. I would read my iPad, pretend to study, and take note of anyone I remotely had a relationship with who sat on this side. Then I would figure out how to get them to invite me to join them. People liked me. This shouldn't be too difficult.

Wrong. I'd forgotten my intrinsic shyness. It had been easy to forget. Rachel and Chloe had been my roommates last year. From the first we naturally dined together. Then I met Cam in French class. Danny and Shane were his roommates. We organically formed a tight-knit group. I never gave it a thought.

Sitting alone, hiding behind dark glasses, flipping cyber pages, I felt like such a loser; an unpopular reject. How embarrassing. Miranda Jordan's daughter shouldn't be seen this way.

I hunched over my plate, making myself smaller, hoping to stay hidden from curious eyes. Would the truth I dreaded admitting; that without her popular boyfriend by her side Miranda Jordan's daughter didn't have any friends, be revealed?

I gobbled down my food and left before anyone posted a photo of me on the internet. Thankfully tonight was the yearbook staff pizza party. I wouldn't endure this humiliation again until tomorrow.

Joining the yearbook staff last year now proved to be one of the most intelligent decisions I'd made since arriving at Donnelly. Not only did it require full immersion, but I enjoyed the company of the other staff members.

The low-key pizza party was just what I needed. This casual gathering of a varied group of friends, strong acquaintances actually, but perhaps some could become friends now that I had time to devote, promised to be fun.

It was our kick-off event, an evening of bonding. Only staff members; no dates allowed. Perfect. Danny couldn't have accompanied me anyway so nobody would question his absence

Unfortunately, this party ended early. Despite dragging the evening out by helping with clean-up, it was not yet midnight when I returned to my room. In the past I welcomed the hour of quiet solitude before sleeping. Now, it reinforced my loneliness.

I couldn't escape dwelling on last Friday night when Danny and I returned from the movie and spent the remainder of the night sharing our love. Had it only been last week? Impossible!

Distraught, I felt desolate, empty. My body trembled. Curled up on the bed, I pulled my knees up to my chest, and sobbed into my pillow. This didn't help. The pillows held the faint but unmistakably masculine scent of Danny. I wept some more.

How long would Danny's scent remain? I feared it growing fainter each day. Would his love? I might never wash these linens if I could stay connected to Danny a little longer, a few more days. I missed him so much!

A knock on the door woke me the following morning.

"Coming," I called out sleepily.

As I rose from my bed I looked down at myself. Oh my god! Yesterday's clothes! What I must look like! I was horrified. This was a new low; falling asleep fully clothed.

I let Rachel in.

"What did you do last night?" Was that an accusation or surprise?

No Rachel, I hadn't gotten drunk or wasted.

"It's not what you think." I flushed, embarrassed. "After yearbook I couldn't stop crying. I didn't even know I'd fallen asleep."

"Do you need babysitting too?" Rachel asked.

"No. I promise to spend the day in pajamas if that's what it takes to be appropriately attired tomorrow morning," I answered sarcastically.

"Don't go that far. We're having a hard enough time handling Danny. I'm on duty tonight."

"On duty?" Oh, no!

"You were right. No matter how much Danny loves you, he wasn't giving you what you deserved. But Danny can't handle it. No girl has ever dumped him before."

"I'll be notorious," I lamented.

"No. A guy like Danny needs to be told no. You'll be back in his life if he lives long enough."

"If he lives long enough? What does that mean?"

"Shane told me Danny drunk-dialed you Friday night. Last night he was worse if that's possible."

My head dropped into my hands. Tears of grief unleashed, rained down my cheeks. I couldn't handle it. Poor Danny!

"Don't cry, Elizabeth. Cam spent the night with Danny, and tonight's my turn."

"That's what you mean by on-duty?" I sniffled.

"Yes."

"Rachel, what have I done?" I wailed.

"Elizabeth, you stood up for yourself. You're not putting up with Danny's crap anymore. I'm proud of you. When Danny's sanity returns, he will be too. He doesn't want a dormouse. Danny wants a girlfriend he can respect."

"He sounds so bad off, and I've done this to him."

"It's not your fault. Don't you dare feel guilty!"

I continued sobbing. Rachel laid a comforting arm around my shoulders.

"Danny will be all right. We've given him until the end of the week. If he doesn't improve, I'll call his father."

"Okay," I whimpered. "Steve will kick his butt."

"Now, go shower and put on clean clothes. We'll go to brunch."

Brunch with Rachel almost seemed normal enough, though I insisted we dine on my side of the dining hall. With Rach at my table, I didn't feel like a friendless loser.

Casual talk did not come easily. I had already relegated Danny to never discuss status, but he was all that was on my mind.

"It's too painful, and it accomplishes nothing," I explained to Rachel.

Rachel and I had other issues. She wanted to remain neutral. I respected her decision, but Rachel needed to declare if not allegiance, then a preference. Was she choosing Danny over me? Eating alone was unbearable. Yesterday I went to a local market and stocked up on Ramen noodles and protein bars. A defection by Rachel would not leave Danny alone. He had Cam and Shane.

"Join me for dinner?" I asked trying to sound casual. "I'll buy."

Rachel hesitated, then she smiled. She understood this was a bigger deal than I let on. "I can't. I'm babysitting tonight, remember?" she said with remorse.

"I thought that was later."

"My shift starts with picking Danny up for dinner. He doesn't know the plan."

"Oh." I sounded dejected. I was dejected.

"Tomorrow. Let's do dinner tomorrow."

I nodded my agreement, but I needed a friend tonight.

"How about Chloe? I may not be imploding, but I need babysitting too."

I sounded pathetic, but I was just as depressed as Danny.

My friends knew he'd been my first and only love. Why didn't I get their attention? Was it because I refused to binge drink and take drugs? Or was something more going on? Did they consider me the bad guy because I'd finally had enough?

"I'll speak to Chloe," said Rachel. Then, as if reading my mind, she hastily added, "If it's any consolation, I don't know how you put up with Danny's BS for this long."

So Rachel knew. Danny must have confessed. I knew I hadn't. I was so ashamed.

The first few weeks challenged me. I forced myself to change my schedule and avoid the places where I might see Danny.

The library became my new safe house though I couldn't escape the panic that overwhelmed me whenever I entered or exited the building. Would Danny be there, lurking just on the other side of the heavy, antique paneled doors? Would those sluts from the Village whom I imagined Danny hooking up with, be gossiping about me as I sat hiding in my favorite carrel in the stacks?

Forget nights at The Cellar. I considered going to the under-21, alcohol-free campus club, "The Aerie," with Rachel or Chloe, but I wasn't in a social state of mind. I didn't attend parties anymore either.

Meals I dreaded. With classes in full swing, mid-day social arrangements were fluid and unplanned. I could handle breakfast and lunch alone. There was no stigma attached to going solo. Lunch spent with a book was acceptable at this academically competitive campus.

Dinner I obsessed over daily. I was too shy to take a chance and sit with casual acquaintances though logic told me nobody would turn refuse my company. By mid-October I still had no one to regularly dine with.

Each evening, I entered the dining hall a skittish bundle of nerves. My eyes opened wide like a deer caught in headlights. Immediately I grabbed a fistful of cutlery if for no other reason than to have something to occupy my twitchy fingers with as I waited for the service line to progress.

Don't look to the right! How long before I stopped reflexively veering that way? Had Danny caught my glance, I would have died, mortified. Left. Go to the left. Go to the left.

I couldn't get past the desolate emptiness of dining alone, or the immobility from the awkwardness of not having standing dinner partners. Consequently, I took fruit from lunch back to my room for in-room dinner. And on weekends, I hoped a late lunch at the mall food court would hold me until morning.

I stopped begging Rachel and Chloe to join me. Occasionally, very occasionally, one of them would remember and join me. I assumed by now everyone knew I was no longer with Danny. Why that didn't lead to overtures, I didn't understand.

Resentment toward my so-called friends festered. Where were they? Real friends would be here for me. Steff and Emma, my dearest childhood friends, never would desert me. I missed them so much! Why did they have to be so far away at Duke and George Washington? If I weren't so depressed, I would plan a weekend visit.

Rachel was my biggest disappointment. I thought she was a genuine friend. I trusted her as much as Steff and Emma. I had been so wrong. Her behavior demonstrated that her career came first. She wouldn't dare desert Steven Newman's son. Friendship with Danny could lead to immediate employment after graduation, and entrée to the right people who would read her scripts. Her career would be accelerated by years. But the same coud be said of friendship with me. Dad would give Rachel the world if only she would dine with me.

There was one place where I couldn't avoid Danny; Professor Dennison's twice weekly class. Arriving at the first Constitutional Law class after our break up, I changed my seat. I would no longer sit next to Danny. I grabbed an empty desk on the far left side of the room. I had no option. It was either that or withdraw from the class.

Now that cooler autumn weather had arrived, I wore the most form-fitting jeans I owned, usually tucked into boots. I always wore softly feminine shirts with the necklines open as much as possible, making my gold heart visible, even across the room.

I couldn't remove the heart, and I often fingered it. The necklace brought me solace while I struggled to control my emotions. I didn't remove my diamond bracelet either. They reminded me that for once I had found love. I still loved Danny, and through his gifts, I fantasized that he was still in love with me. When I became strong enough to put my jewelry away, then I knew it was over and I was ready to date again, but not before.

I obsessed over being prepared for political science class. Danny should see that I didn't need our Sunday study sessions to be on top. I read every optional book and article the professor suggested, and I found my own supplemental pieces as well. I even went on-line, subscribed to Lexis-Nexis, and found case law to quote in class. When you have singular determination, you can do this.

Danny had always been an active participant in class. He added intelligent, insightful opinions to the discussion. In the past I would contribute, but not often. Now we became locked in an intellectual battle. No matter what opinion Danny expressed, I'd mastered both sides of the issue and chose the opposing side to defend, whether I agreed with it or not. Let him see what he was missing.

CHAPTER TWENTY-TWO - ELIZABETH

"Elizabeth?" Jackson interrupted me as I was designing a section layout one Friday afternoon in late October.

Seated in front of a Mac desktop in the yearbook office, I glanced up.

"We need rugby pictures before the season ends."

My heart sunk. Please, not rugby. Any fall sport but rugby.

"There's a tournament tomorrow. Please cover it."

"Jackson, please no." Rugby was the last place I wanted to be. "Can't Kyle cover it?"

Jackson smirked. "He's on the team, Elizabeth. I think he'll be busy."

I blushed. I knew Kyle was an athlete. That's why I'd thought of him. Why did he have to play rugby!

"Oh," I answered, disappointed.

"If you're studying, I understand, but it'll only take a couple of hours."

"Jackson…" I protested but to no avail.

"Thanks, Elizabeth. You got the best action shots last year."

Of course I had. They were predominately of Danny.

Saturday morning dawned crisp and sunny, a perfect day for rugby. I parked my car at the gravel covered rugby field lot. Ugh! What was I doing here? It was my fault, too. If I weren't so damned secretive, Jackson would have known the truth about Danny and I. He would have assigned someone else.

But Jackson was a senior, and he no longer lived in Berkeley Hall. Our paths never crossed anymore except at yearbook. Jackson didn't know my status with Danny.

"Elizabeth, are you okay?" Chloe asked as I grabbed my camera from the back seat of the Range Rover.

"I don't know," I answered honestly. "I'll deal with it," but I wasn't sure how.

Recently, Chloe had emerged as my go-to friend. In matters of the heart, she was more compassionate than Rachel. She'd suffered through her own disappointments and understood.

"Chloe, thank you for coming today. If I had to be alone, I'd die."

Chloe warmly embraced me. "That's what friends are for, Elizabeth."

Even I smiled. Her words warmed me. It felt good to know I had her as a friend.

As we strolled to the sidelines, Chloe said with confidence, "When

Danny sees you, he'll regret everything. You look killer."

Wearing skinny jeans tucked into flat black leather knee-high boots, a cropped V-necked sweater, and a studded black leather jacket, every curve was accentuated by the waist-nipping ensemble. My attire was casual but chic, Beverly Hills rugby babe.

Prepping my camera provided a needed distraction. I so desperately did not want to run into…, oh hell, of course I did. Why else had I dressed like this when Donnelly logowear sweats would have sufficed? The match could not start soon enough.

I eyed Danny out on the field warming up. He finished short sprints and began stretching. Butterflies beat up my stomach as I stared. Danny's shaggy hair needed a trim. The sapphire eyes smiled as he exchanged good-natured words with a teammate. Well-defined muscles flexed his sinewy legs. My heart filled with longing to be held in Danny's strong arms, against the sculpted chest, showed off to perfection by his team jersey. The memories were powerful.

"I can't do this, Chloe," I fretted.

I bit my lip, and blinked furiously to hold back tears. My eyes were thankfully hidden by dark Ray-Bans.

Chloe's eyes followed mine to Danny.

"He's too hot," I complained.

"Elizabeth, I'm so sorry," Chloe answered.

"I'm pathetic. After all these weeks, I still want Danny so badly."

I wiped a tear I couldn't contain with my forefinger.

"Of course you do. You love Danny. And he is hot."

I nodded, afraid to speak.

"But don't cry now," Chloe smiled. "We're at rugby. Save it for after the game."

I laughed at her logic. "Right. If we lose, it'll be appropriate."

Returning my attention to my camera, I was pleased to have something to do to keep my mind off of…

"Elizabeth?"

Despite my awareness of Danny's every move on the field, his smooth tenor voice saying my name jarred me. The camera slipped from my hand. I gasped, fearful it would fall. But the strap was firmly affixed to my shoulder, so it simply banged my hip. Ouch!

"Danny," I responded, trying to recover my composure.

Danny smiled warmly; the sapphires twinkled at me as in the past.

"I'm so glad you're here," he said with sincerity.

Chloe stepped back, giving us privacy.

I held up my yearbook badge. "I'm working." I didn't want Danny to think I was there to see him.

But then Danny took my hands. His gaze melted my heart, but

hopefully not my resolve. "Be here for me, Eli. I need you here for me," he said softly.

"I know you do," I answered weakly, barely holding it together.

"You look incredible."

"Thank you," I stammered, breathless.

"Baby," Danny began before those arms I dreamed to be held by pulled me to the sculpted chest I longed to rest upon. "I love you, babe," he whispered.

Several tears spilled onto his jersey. Embarrassed, I wiped them away. Then Danny took my damp hand and kissed my fingertips. His smiling sapphires met my emeralds.

"I shouldn't, but I love you too," I admitted.

Danny smiled. Then he reached for my face and he held it between both hands, while his lips met mine for a kiss.

"This is so wrong," I whispered, my heart beating out of control.

"Yeah, but it sure feels right."

"Didn't they break up?" we heard someone behind us whisper to their neighbor.

Danny and I shared a laugh.

"Didn't we?" I asked him.

"No, it's just a hiatus until I get my act together."

Then Danny kissed me again, and I willingly complied. I enjoyed knowing our physical attraction bought us time. At least a few girls were now re-crossing Danny's name off their lists.

I smiled warmly. "You're impossible," I told Danny.

In the distance a whistle blew.

"Newman!" One of his teammates yelled.

"I gotta go, babe."

"Danny, have a safe game," I said quietly. For no matter what, I would never want Danny to get injured.

"Thanks, baby."

Then Danny quickly kissed me before running off to join his team.

When the whistle blew ending the match, Danny smiled at me and winked from his downfield position. I blushed and smiled back. He had played a good game and had emerged unscathed.

"Chloe, let's get out of here," I said with urgency.

I did not want another encounter with Danny. He knew he owned my heart, and he could find me if he was ready to claim it.

The following Thursday, arms loaded down with books, my hip pushed open the heavy wooden front door of Berkeley Hall. I cast my eyes downward. I did not want to make eye contact with anyone and be forced to engage in pleasantries. I wanted to retreat to my room and enjoy a cup of blueberry yogurt. Enjoy? Wrong word. There was nothing enjoyable about today.

Until September, I had been looking forward to today, the anniversary of the most important day in my life. Incredible that a year had passed since my first date with Danny; the date that almost wasn't. We had spent the two-hour drive to the Lake House Inn as friends. But once seated at our table in its elegant Beach House restaurant, Danny finally admitted we were on a date. He even kissed me to prove it. My lips still felt the bruising from that evening.

In retrospect, he had warned me even then. Danny was uncertain whether he could make the commitment needed for a successful relationship. At the time, I assumed it was one of those man things, a 'cover-your ass' out-clause. If we didn't work out, Danny could say, "You should have heeded my warning." We more than worked out. I should have heeded his warning anyway.

I blinked away the threatening tears. I hoped to make it to the privacy of my room without being stopped. Hard as I tried, it was impossible to keep the next thought from forming, and it would bring a torrent. Danny would have taken me to the Beach House today for the weekend. Friday classes be damned.

I bit my lip and dug my nails into my palm until it hurt. I had to get to my room!

"Elizabeth!" Someone called my name? Shit! I didn't want to stop. Please don't force me to be social.

"Elizabeth!" I heard my name again. Wendy, the student manning the lobby desk called to me. I hadn't realized it at first because she was hidden behind a large vase of flowers. I was glad they finally decided to add some color to the drab lobby.

"What's up, Wendy?" I forced a smile.

"These flowers are for you."

"Me?" Not for dorm lobby beautification?

"New beau?" Wendy asked, hopeful.

"These are for me?" I said, taken by surprise. Why me?

"Elizabeth, I'm glad you have a new boyfriend," Wendy said to be kind. "Danny is a schmuck." Students who worked the desk knew all the dorm gossip.

"Thanks, Wendy," I stammered, "No, he isn't." Danny was a lot of things, a philandering bastard maybe, but not a schmuck.

I lifted the heavy vase filled with a breathtaking display of pink, red and white flowers, mostly roses, and I turned in the direction of my room.

"New boyfriend? You didn't tell me," declared Rachel.

She had appeared seemingly from out of nowhere. Rachel was on her way out of the building. Was she nuts? Me? New boyfriend? Right. Rachel knew better.

"I don't have a new boyfriend," I answered. "Give me a hand?" I asked.

Rachel removed the burden from my shaking hands. I was so surprised to receive the flowers I risked dropping the heavy gift.

I grabbed the larger than standard gift card with its fine cream-colored envelope, and recognized the messy penmanship.

"Danny!" I gasped.

"Danny?" Rachel parroted my surprise.

Once inside my room, Rachel placed the vase on the desk while I carefully opened the navy-lined envelope of Danny's personalized Crane stationary. I removed the cream-colored paper with navy border and DMN monogram.

"Pretentious, isn't he?" Rachel remarked. I snarled at her, and opened the folded sheet, holding it close to maintain privacy.

My insides quivered. I sat down, and silently read to myself.

"*E-No tears, baby,*" the note began. I smiled at how well Danny read me, and I wiped a tear from my eyes. Then I steeled my nerves to read the rest, hopefully tearless.

"You don't think I'll remember what today is, but of course I do. Who could forget the most important day of their life?

I know you're hurting. Me too. If I could, baby I would take you in my arms and make everything good again. But I can't, not today. You need honesty, and I can't give it to you. Not yet.

I'm going through a real bad time, but I've got to work it out by myself. I'm failing miserably baby, but I love you too much to bring you down.

I hope I have your support. I do, don't I? Your love has always been so pure. I have your back too, but you know that.

Under other circumstances, we'd be on our way to the Lake House for the weekend. We'll get there, baby. Not this time, but we will. Elizabeth, that's a promise. You know I always keep my promises.

Please enjoy the flowers. It's the best I can do for now. Baby, I love you, more than anything. I always will. – Danny. P.S. – As always, you were the hottest girl on the rugby sidelines."

I sunk my head into my hands, and sobbed. Rachel lifted the letter from my fingers and read.

The anniversary flowers left me feeling emptier than ever. To understand how strong Danny's love was, yet know he was powerless to change, was unbearable. I felt as dead as the flowers were once two weeks had passed and Danny had not approached me. I desperately wanted his attention, and I resorted to the only tool available.

CHAPTER TWENTY-THREE - DANIEL

Coach gave his approval for us to carpool to Poughkeepsie provided we swore not to be late for the pre-game warm-up at Vassar. I insisted on doing the driving, and I herded my boys into the car extra early.

With the season winding down, I wanted to impress the coach with my sense of responsibility. I tasted a captaincy for next year.

Shane joined Cam, Duncan and I for the road trip, though he didn't play on the rugby team. We drove down because we planned to spend the night partying. Shane's cousin, a senior at Vassar, promised us a good time. A good time; I was ready for a good time. It had been almost two months. I needed a good time.

"What were you thinking!" Rachel howled when I met her at breakfast prior to departing for Poughkeepsie.

Rachel's accusation stung. She didn't understand. Elizabeth did. The dressing-down that followed informed me that Elizabeth had reacted to the flowers exactly as I knew she would.

Emotionally bankrupt and full of regret, I'd pounced on the opportunity the anniversary afforded. It had been important to convey to Elizabeth that she wasn't alone even if we were apart. She needed to understand I loved her. She shouldn't feel abandoned. Elizabeth looked so hot last Saturday.

Ironic that we were playing at Vassar. I'd almost matriculated there. So similar to Donnelly, I had gone back and forth debating which school to attend after I received acceptances from both.

Elizabeth would never learn what finally sealed the deal with Donnelly. I had overheard Randi telling Mom that Eli was applying early decision to Donnelly, and was not even considering Vassar.

Friendship, not romance had been my impetus. With Elizabeth initially wait-listed I'd been crushed. Months later I was over the moon happy when she was finally admitted. After four miserable prep years at Bromley Hall, I was thrilled that my best friend would also be attending Donnelly.

"A toast to us," I joyously proposed to my victorious mates.

We raised our beer glasses high and tapped them together. Then Shane, Cam, Duncan and I chugged and slammed the empty glasses down.

"Hey, hey, hey! Remember, you're in our bar," Shane's cousin Alex laughed.

"Whatever you say, Alex," Shane laughed, then added, "loser!"

The pert waitress delivered a new pitcher of beer to our table in The Mug, Vassar's counterpart to The Cellar. We were in celebration mode. Except for Alex and his friends. They did not share our glee, for Donnelly had readily beaten Vassar this afternoon.

Good friends, good beer. Tonight I refused to get depressed by thinking about Elizabeth.

Acknowledging our anniversary by sending Elizabeth flowers had freed me. I didn't understand it, but putting my emotions on paper had proven therapeutic. Reaffirming our love, I shed the malaise I didn't realize afflicted me.

A group of co-eds, friends of Alex's, stopped at our table. Prospects for an enjoyable evening were looking up.

A cute brunette with long, straight hair caught my eye. Her pink logo t-shirt clung to all the right places. Snug, well-worn jeans revealed a shapely ass. For the first time since my last time with Elizabeth, desire stirred. Time to turn on the Newman charm. I was determined not to sleep alone tonight.

Allison proved to be as lovely as her name, warmly welcoming me into her room and her bed.

"Spend the night?" Allison asked when she opened the door.

"I wondered when you were going to ask," I answered with an irresistible twinkle in my eye that always made women melt.

Allison was not shy, and she harbored no inhibitions either. Upon closing the door to her room, she pulled her t-shirt over her head and let it carelessly drop to the floor. My educated eye recognized pale pink Victoria's Secret, not the exclusive designer bras favored by Elizabeth.

I couldn't let thoughts of Eli spoil a sure thing.

"You smoke?" I asked Allison, and I pulled a joint out of my pocket.

"Sure," Allison answered, and she unbuttoned her jeans.

While I lit the joint, she pulled off the jeans and let them drop to the floor, revealing a matching pale pink thong.

After a quick hit, Allison led me to her bed. She inhaled again, slowly this time, then passed the joint back to me.

Hands free, Allison went to work opening my jeans. Could it get any better than this? An attractive girl down to her underwear was eagerly begging me to join her. Sometimes it's great being me.

A few more hits, and I tapped out the joint. Getting wasted would be counterproductive.

Allison removed her bra and welcomed me into her arms. Before removing my jeans, I reached into the back pocket and retrieved a condom. Welcome back to the living,

Afterward, I rolled over, turning my back to Allison. Unexpected regret filled me. I should have been with Eli. I never turned my back on Eli. With

Eli, it was love making, slow and deliberate. With anyone else, it was just sex, quick and easy.

With Eli, the best part was always after. We held each other, kissed, and engaged in intimate conversation, discussing what we couldn't during full hectic days. We even planned for our future.

Stabbing pain shot through my heart. If I didn't find the courage to come clean, there would be no future for us, planned or otherwise.

It was unsettling to find my arm holding Allison and not Elizabeth when I woke. I'd had no choice. The only other bed available was Alex's couch. So, I did the unthinkable. I spent the night with a girl who wasn't Eli.

"Good morning," I whispered when I saw Allison stirring.

"Let's have sex," she suggested.

Being direct evidently bore no relationship to whether or not Allison was imebriated.

While I complied, I wasn't sure I like this much directness. I preferred waking to Elizabeth's gentle kisses and caresses, her desires implied.

So much for keeping me company on the drive back. Duncan slept in the seat beside me, and Shane and Cam stretched out in the back, doing the same. The solitude of a long drive punctuated by the snores of my passengers would either lead to an epiphany or send me spiraling downward. It was too early to know.

Progressing though bucolic upstate New York, the trees now bare of their autumn glory, blocking out thoughts of Elizabeth was impossible. I pictured my beautiful girl, rising from bed, wearing my shirt; her auburn waves tumbling wildly down her back. She scampered over to the vase of anniversary flowers.

Eli inhaled deeply. I had purposely filled the bouquet with plenty of roses, her favorite. The biggest smile crossed her face. In my daydreams, Eli always smiled. Now she texted me three simple words, "I want you."

In an instant I was in her room. Her arms wrapped around me as though she would never let me go.

"I want you back. I don't care what happened. I can't live without you."

"I can't live without you, either."

"We'll get through this together, Danny. I love you."

Our lips joined. I carried Elizabeth to her bed. In one swift motion, life was back to normal.

The slow traffic at the toll plaza brought me back to reality. I didn't have an EZPass. This metaphor for the current state of my life did not escape me. But if I summoned the courage, perhaps my daydream could become reality. Maybe it was time.

After paying the toll, I floored it. The emptiness in my soul was unbearable. The sooner I reached Donnelly, the sooner I would reach the stash hidden in my desk and treat the pain.

CHAPTER TWENTY-FOUR – ELIZABETH

This morning I dressed with utmost care, and I finger-dried my hair to make it full and flowing. With anticipation, I timed arriving in Professor Dennison's class just after it had begun; my grand entrance.

The professor raised an eyebrow at my tardiness while I flashed him an enchanting smile. I kept the smile and aimed it directly at Danny. He smiled in return, a warm, easy-going smile.

My heart beat rapidly, a welcome distraction, as I took my seat. How would I concentrate? I had this feeling; positive intuition for once. Today was the day. I was certain. Why else would Danny send me flowers? He would beg my forgiveness and ask me to take him back. He had to.

Danny didn't wait for me. He didn't wait outside the building either. Instead he quick-stepped out the door the moment class ended. I hadn't even put my laptop away when I glanced in Danny's direction and found him, gone!

Crestfallen, my eyes filled with tears I wouldn't spill in public. What had been the meaning behind sending those flowers if not to smooth the way to reunite? How could I have been so wrong?

I raced back to my room and spent the afternoon sobbing, heartbroken all over again. Starring at the beautiful flowers, I re-read the note that accompanied them. Danny said he loved me. Then why wasn't he here?

It was the next morning before I left my room.

Grabbing Danny's attention twice a week in the safe environment of our class was all I could do. Academic victory over Danny closed my wounds ever so slightly if only for brief moments. The attention that came with showing him that I was the top student lifted my hopes, if fleetingly, that Danny would miss what he didn't have.

Professor Denison finally lost his patience during a discussion of Brown vs. Board of Education of Topeka, Kansas.

Danny had just completed a brilliant analysis of the landmark civil rights decision when I raised my hand. I didn't dispute the validity of the Brown decision, so instead I launched into a dissertation on the attorney for Brown, Thurgood Marshall. I cited key cases he had played a part in either as an attorney or later as a Supreme Court justice.

"Miss Jacobs," Professor Denison interrupted, "what has any of that got to do with the Brown case?"

I turned scarlet. All eyes, including Danny's turned toward me. Of course nothing I had said had anything to do with the Brown case. That was beside the point.

"It gives us a greater understanding of Thurgood Marshall." I stammered knowing my response was lame.

"When did this college open a law library?" the professor mused. "Miss Jacobs, where did you find these case citations?"

That I answered confidently.

"I logged onto my father's Lexis-Nexis account."

This was the truth. Sort of. Earlier in the semester I had opened an account with the legal research site, and charged it to Dad's credit card. Technically it was his account.

The professor looked at me, brow quirked, questioning.

"My father's an attorney," I said proudly.

"Really?" said the professor who damned well what Dad did for a living.

Across the room, Danny burst into laughter.

"Mr. Newman?" Professor Denison asked with a condescending tone and glare.

Danny, still laughing, answered, "Eli's father isn't an attorney. He's a movie producer."

I turned purple with rage. If Danny wanted to humiliate me, he was doing an excellent job.

"My father," I said slowly, and with emphasis, "is a graduate of the UCLA School of Law, and he's a member in good standing of both the California and New York bars."

"C'mon Eli. When was Mike ever in a courtroom as the attorney?"

I wanted to answer, "When you were thirteen and Steve was arrested for drunk driving at three in the morning. The police found cocaine in his pocket, and his passenger was a woman who wasn't your mother. So he called the only attorney whose name he could remember, and whom he could trust to keep him out of the news, his best friend, my dad."

But I couldn't do that. That would have been cruel, not just to Danny, but to Ellen, too.

Instead I said nothing, and took my public flogging. Tears filled my eyes, and I blinked hard to hold them back. I wanted to run out of the room and cry. How dare Danny publically stab me! But I had to keep Steve's secret.

"Daniel, enough," Professor Denison said in his commanding voice. "I want to see you and Miss Jacobs after class."

Panic, sheer panic. For the first time since he'd kissed me at rugby, I would be standing beside Danny. I didn't now how I would handle it. I feared either breaking down or blurting out the truth about Steve. Whatever the professor wanted, I would acquiesce simply to end the meeting as quickly as possible.

My stomach ached, twisting from nerves. I could not concentrate on the class. I kept my eyes on my laptop avoiding eye contact with anyone who might have glanced my way. Between the professor's berating and Danny's insults, I wanted to disappear.

After collecting my belongings and putting on my jacket, I joined Danny at the front of the room. Whether it was the predicament with the professor, or Danny's close proximity, I didn't know, but I began shaking. I couldn't look at either of them.

"I'll be brief," Professor Denison began, and my eyes looked up. "First, Miss Jacobs, please stick to the syllabus. We are all tired of your digressions, well researched as they are, into areas beyond what this class covers. I have enough material to cover that actually is on the syllabus. Perhaps you should enroll in an independent study."

"Yes, professor," I whispered.

"Second, your personal lives are not my business or anyone else's. Clearly something ugly is going on between you. Keep it out of my classroom."

Danny and I mumbled, "Yes, sir."

I couldn't control my shaking anymore, and I gripped my jacket for warmth.

"That will be all," the professor said, dismissing us.

I bolted from the building, tears streaming down my face. Humiliation, anger, and hurt, consumed me in equal measure. My emotions, hidden just below the surface for so long finally bubbled up. A complete breakdown threatened.

I didn't hear Danny following me until he caught up and spoke my name.

"Elizabeth," he said softly.

Instinctively I stopped and turned, my tear-filled green eyes meeting his clear, dry blue ones.

"Elizabeth, please, can't we talk?" Danny pleaded.

"I don't have anything to say," I stammered, tears choked me.

"Don't cry, baby."

I lost it. I couldn't hold back any longer.

"Don't call me that," I cried.

"Elizabeth, you're always my baby. I love you."

"I love you, too," I found myself answering against all sensibility. "Those flowers are beautiful."

Danny took my face in his hands, his palms warm and strong. Then he pressed his lips against mine. No! No! No! I lifted my hand, aiming to slap his face. Danny anticipated my movement and captured my wrist. This pulled me into his arms.

114

I could no longer resist. I never could. Without wanting to, I found myself responding to his lips and to the touch of his hand around my waist.

Danny smiled when we broke apart. I did not. Our love and our physical attraction were undeniable, but I had gone so long without them. True, I felt like an empty shell of a woman going through the motions of life, but it had to, it had to improve. I had to believe.

Danny ran his fingertip along my jawbone. I took his hand, cradled it against my face and kissed it.

We quietly gazed at each other. Then sadness replaced Danny's smile. I took back my hand. His change in demeanor spoke volumes. Danny wasn't ready to end our impass.

"Can't we be friends again? I miss you, baby."

I shook my head. "It wouldn't work. We'd end up back in bed."

Danny grinned. "Would that be so bad?"

The thought made me shiver. My body remembered his touch. "I miss you too," I admitted. "But we can't be."

Danny frowned. "I'll let you go," he said and he kissed my cheek.

I smiled and walked back to Berkeley Hall, feeling better than I had in weeks. Perhaps Danny was changing.

My good mood was short-lived. Alone in my room, reality returned. The glimmer of hope I'd experienced earlier dissolved into frustration. When Danny had the chance, he'd suggested only friendship. Knowing Danny loved me but seemed powerless to do anything about it, depressed me.

I considered packing up and heading home. Nobody there would think anything of it. It was Los Angeles. I could become an actress. Not that I wanted to be one, but with my name, that would be an acceptable option. Hollywood would welcome me with open arms. Hell, it probably made more sense to many than attending Donnelly.

Yes, I would enroll in acting school and rent an apartment. But where? There had to be a neighborhood where struggling actors lived. I couldn't remember its name. I'd never given it any thought before.

Who was I fooling? I would never be struggling. I was too well connected, and I had a trust fund. What would I talk about when it became known that I didn't need roommates, didn't wait tables or didn't do office temp work? Actual struggling actors would ostracize me. I couldn't live surrounded by people who resented me.

Instead, I would buy a condo in Beverly Hills or, Santa Monica. Maybe I'd buy a small house instead, with a yard, and a fluffy dog for companionship. The Westside was dotted with small houses. No, wait! Los Feliz! That's where young Hollywood lived, and I would have no memories of life with Danny that far east of the 405.

Mom's agent would represent me. Or I could be the rebellious daughter and call Lee Greenberg. The head of T.A.G. would enjoy representing the daughter of the player he could never sign. I would get cast in small parts or television based on nothing more than my name and looks. Perhaps a fragrance or cosmetics company would make me their "face." If it turned out that I actually had talent – bonus!

The clubs of the Strip would be my home each evening. I could rotate among them. I would hang-out with my friend, Grant Barnes, the young sex god actor, and we'd behave badly together. On name alone the paparazzi would eat it up. I'd be dubbed, "EJay."

Danny would read about me in gossip blogs and feel guilty. He would beg me back knowing it was his fault.

But what if he didn't? I could drown my sorrows in every substance known to mankind. No I couldn't. I was still me, the sane, sober girl I'd always been. I'd better just stick with becoming an actor.

Fame? Clubs? Grant Barnes? Would any of this make me happy? That was the critical question. The answer, probably not. Without Danny sharing my successes, they would be hollow. Other young actors jump when their phone rings hoping it's their agent with an important audition, or a booking. I would jump hoping it was Danny begging my forgiveness and wanting me to take him back.

None of this was guaranteed. If I knew for sure that Danny would come after me, I'd go home in a heartbeat. But I didn't know if he would. If I was going to be miserable and lonely, I might as well stay at Donnelly where at least I was happy.

CHAPTER TWENTY-FIVE - DANIEL

Who was I fooling? After my encounter with Eli I was wired. No way could I read the book resting on my lap, my long legs stretched out, I knew the antidote that would relax me. But today I didn't want to lose touch with a pleasant memory.

Elizabeth still loved me.

The last few weeks had been filled with despair. After returning from Vassar, I'd lost my confidence and didn't speak to Eli. I was a coward, and angry with myself for being one. Now the only time I saw Eli was in Constitutional Law class. Considering we lived in the same building, and shared many of the same friends, I didn't understand how we never crossed paths. Was she avoiding me?

So the two times each week when I saw Elizabeth were all the more precious. Except Elizabeth was often so hostile, attacking every opinion I voiced in class. I disliked this bitter Elizabeth immensely. Revenge had not been in my plans today, and I felt bad that I verbally accosted her in class.

It was a guttural reaction to Elizabeth's ongoing behavior. Declaring Mike wasn't an attorney had been a low blow. I lied to make Eli feel small. I knew damned well that Mike had represented Dad on several discrete matters over the years. My parents never told me the particulars, nor was it even discussed at home, but there had been a lot of arguing, so I could only imagine the subject.

Standing beside Elizabeth as she was dressed-down by Owen, she appeared so vulnerable. Elizabeth had trembled. It was difficult not to draw her into my arms and offer comfort.

At such close proximity, Elizabeth's cologne, a fragrance I had selected, proved too intoxicating to resist. So I followed her.

A knock came on my door.

"It's open," I called, knowing it was Rachel.

She entered the room and closed the door.

"You summoned me, your highness." Rachel was certainly in a surly mood today.

"All right, I deserve that, but please no sarcasm today."

Rachel rolled the desk chair to the edge of the bed. Straddling the chair, she leaned against its ladderback.

"What's up Danny? You're smiling."

"I talked to Eli today."

"And that smile means?"

"She still loves me."

"Of course she does."

"It was probably dumb to do it, but I couldn't help it. I told Eli I loved her and then I kissed her."

"Did Elizabeth smack you?" Rachel asked.

I smirked, remembering what happened next.

"Eli wanted to at first, but instead she kissed me back and told me she loved me too."

"So why are you pretending to read instead of making up for lost time?"

"I can't give Eli what she wants."

The nightmare had woken me again last night. Until I could protect her from Vanessa, Elizabeth was safer away from me.

"You are a hopeless, pathetic loser, Daniel!"

"I probably am."

"Would you please do us all a favor and see a therapist already?"

"You're so melodramatic," I laughed.

"I'm serious, Danny. At least go with Elizabeth to a marriage counselor."

"We're not married."

"Doesn't matter. You're close enough," Rachel answered, frustrated. "Danny, I'm your friend, and Elizabeth's, so I get it from both sides."

"And you've been great at keeping neutral."

"Yes, I have. Do you have any idea how mental you sound?"

"No, not really," I laughed uncomfortably. Yes, I did know.

"This is you. I love Eli. She loves me. We could be ecstatically happy but I'd rather make us both miserable because my parents married too young, so my father spent the next two decades cheating on my mother. I don't want to hurt Eli that way, which is admirable, so I won't commit to her. Instead I'll watch her wallow through depression, while I exist in a drunken, drugged state of self-pity waiting for a sign from god. Then I'll race to my fair maiden's side, tell her I've seen the light, and we'll live happily ever after."

Rachel's version of my life was not only accurate, it was embarrassing. "Okay. I get it," I answered awkwardly.

"Good. So what are you going to do?"

"Nothing. Get wasted. That sign from god hasn't come yet."

"Grrrrr… Daniel!"

"I'm sorry, Rach. That's just how it has to be. But there is something I'd like you to do."

"What?" she snapped.

"Elizabeth felt bony. She's lost weight. Can you please see that she eats properly? I'm worried about her."

"If you're so concerned, why don't you take her to a restaurant. I can recommend one on a beautiful lake in the Adirondacks. It'll take you only two hours to get there, plenty of time to kiss and make-up. I think you're familiar with the place."

Why did Rachel have to bring up my first date with Elizabeth? I knew why. My heart became heavy with the memory.

"Rach, I can't do that, and you know it."

"I am so frustrated! Elizabeth has lost weight, and it's because she's been skipping meals. She doesn't have anyone to sit with."

"I have Shane and Cam. Eli's shy. She needs you."

"You're sure? You won't mind?" Rachel hesitated.

"I don't need babysitting, Rachel." She fidgeted uncomfortably. "I know what you guys were doing," I smiled.

"We were that obvious?"

"Yes. It was sweet."

"You scared us."

"I scared me too. I'm lucky. I have great friends. Now, if I promise not to abuse any substances until after dinner, will you leave me alone and take care of Eli. She needs you badly."

"Okay," Rachel promised. She rose from the chair and kissed my cheek. That surprised me. Rachel never kissed me.

"Danny, you may be mental, but I'm glad you love Elizabeth this much."

CHAPTER TWENTY-SIX - ELIZABETH

Rachel found me Skyping with Mom when she stopped to pick me up for dinner. She politely pulled up a chair, and pretended not to be eavesdropping as Mom and I discussed plans for winter break, nothing Rachel could not be privy to.

"Mom, I will not go to Aspen," I was adamant. "I'd rather stay home alone."

"Dad will be disappointed, honey."

"Don't do this," I insisted. "Dad will understand."

"Elizabeth, you love Aspen."

"I can't Mom. It's too depressing. I'll spend the entire break crying." Last year with Danny was magical. What didn't she understand about that?

"It's family time. Teddy will miss you."

Mom was really pushing the guilt-trip buttons.

"Mom! I'll miss Teddy too, but I have to think about me. Why can't Dad and Teddy go to Aspen, and you and I can go somewhere else? Think about it. I have to go. Rachel is here. Sorry my divorce is such an inconvenience."

Mom rolled her eyes. "Elizabeth, I love you."

"Love you too, Mom." I pushed the off button, stared at the screen, and growled at it. Then I turned to Rachel. "No way on earth will I go to Aspen!" I declared.

"If it helps, Danny is spending the break in New Orleans."

"New Orleans? Danny doesn't speak French."

Rachel crinkled her eyes in dismay.

"He doesn't have to. It's in the United States. He's visiting Duncan."

"Right," I responded, distracted. Then refocused, I added, "Guaranteed trouble. I still won't go to Aspen. The house reeks."

I picked my keycard off the desk. "Let's go. I'm starving." It had been several days since I'd last eaten dinner.

With Rachel by my side, I relaxed and felt nearly normal again. I piled my plate high with pasta marinara, an extra portion of broccoli, and two pieces of thick garlic bread. Rachel's plate appeared sparse in comparison. She gave me that, "you've got to be kidding," glare as I placed the plate on the table.

After skipping dinner the last few days I really was that hungry. Well, maybe not. After a few bites, I realized my eyes were bigger than my stomach. Much bigger.

"You're less morose than usual," Rachel remarked half-way through our meal.

I was surprised to hear her say that. It contradicted how I felt.

"Actually, I'm sadder," I answered, and I explained my encounter with Danny.

"It didn't make you happier hearing Danny say, 'I love you'?"

"It did for a moment. 'm so frustrated. Rachel, why can't Danny give me what I need when he loves me?"

"I told him to see a therapist."

"You what!" I exclaimed, and for a beat, I giggled. Then I sobered and sat up straighter. "Wait a minute. You knew about this?"

"Danny told me this afternoon. I wanted your take."

"Oh."

"He won't go."

"I doubted he would," I said sadly.

"You should see a marriage counselor together."

"I don't think so."

"I bet Danny would go if you asked him."

"Did he say that?"

"No, but I know Danny. He would go if you asked him to."

"Absolutely no. I won't do it."

"Why not?"

"For one, we're not married."

"You don't have to be."

"The therapist would be on Danny's side. Think about it. He'd say, 'miss, Danny's twenty years old. What do you expect? So either take him as he is or say good-bye.' And as I've already said goodbye, I don't need a therapist telling me to do it again."

Rachel sighed. "It would get you talking."

"Danny has to want to change, and he's made it perfectly clear he doesn't want to."

"You're both hopeless. That's why you're perfect for each other."

"Can we drop this? I don't want to discuss Danny, not now or ever. It makes me more depressed.

Saturday evening found me in my room studying, my usual weekend entertainment of late. What good is date night when you don't have your date anymore? It was safer to hide than go out.

A knock on the door startled me.

"Come in!" I called out, grumpy.

These days, interruptions ticked me off. Mindless dribble, someone's futile attempt to cheer me, both passed through me, ignored with no impact.

Chloe! She entered with the light breeziness of the first warm day of spring. It was in sharp contrast to the thick, bleak cloud of winter following me around. Her resolute cheerfulness seemed completely out of place in the dark cold of my room.

Chloe stared at me dressed in sweats, and boldly threw open my closet.

"Chloe!" How dare she!

Searching through the hangers, Chloe pulled out an orange and white silk chiffon shirt with attached camisole, and a pair of skinny jeans.

"I'm sick of this, Elizabeth." She shoved the clothing in my face. "You're putting these on and going with me to the party in Reilly. I'll pick you up in an hour. I won't take no for an answer." Chloe was adamant.

I pushed the hand holding the hangers out of my face. "Thanks, Chloe. I know what you're trying to do, but I'm not going."

"C'mon, Elizabeth! You can't stay buried away forever. It's like you're in mourning and as far as I can see, nobody died."

"I died. If you can't understand that."

"I do understand, but you're not a widow."

"I wish I were. Then everyone would leave me alone to grieve."

"You don't mean that. You don't want Danny dead."

"Of course I don't want Danny dead! I just meant nobody would expect me to go to a party this soon afterwards if he were."

"Elizabeth, you'll have a great time. Trust me."

I appreciated Chloe's intentions. She meant well, and she was being a good friend. But Chloe didn't understand the reality of the situation, or the depth of my hurt. I took a deep breath. I didn't want to offend her.

"Chloe, I'm sorry," I said. "I can't go. The time isn't right."

"Elizabeth, it's been two months. It's time to start living again. I won't leave your side. I'll be there supporting you," Chloe said, full of encouragement.

"Thank you. Chloe, you have no idea how much I appreciate this. You're a great friend. But I can't go," I said, nearly hysterical. "Everyone will stare at me."

"No they won't."

"They already do."

"No they don't. They have their own lives."

"I walk into that party, people will look at me with pity. They'll be whispering, 'poor Elizabeth, I wonder why Danny dumped her.'"

"Nobody will do that."

Then Chloe looked at me, surprised.

"Didn't you dump Danny?"

"I did, but that's besides the point. Everyone assumes Danny dumped me because how could anyone dump Mr. Perfect." I rolled my eyes. "Even worse, some are gleeful. They don't want me with Danny. They're happy I'm miserable."

"You sound either self-centered or paranoid delusional. I can't decide which."

"Chloe! It's true. And then there are the vultures who seeing me alone will leave to find Danny so they can pounce on him."

"Have you looked in the mirror lately? You forgot the men who will see *you* alone and want to pounce on you."

"I know what you're doing. I'm not the girl that gets pounced on."

"If I didn't know you so well, I'd say you were losing it."

"It's possible," I answered seriously.

"Then you've got to get your mojo back. It's the best cure."

"Not for me."

"Rachel says you're hanging at The Exchange. What on earth...?"

"Juliette invited m a couple of times," I answered defensively.

"You're committing social suicide. They're certainly not cool."

"Maybe I'm tired of cool. I spent all last year being 'Mrs. Coolest Guy on Campus,' and where did it get me? It's safe at The Exchange. They don't care who I am, or where I've been. They don't want anything from me. They're happy to welcome me."

"Of course they are. You're Hollywood royalty. You lend them panache. They can deny their geekiness by citing you as a member."

"I've only gone a couple of times," I repeated. "That doesn't qualify me as a member. The Exchange is simply a nice group of kids who don't pressure me, and they don't mention Danny any more than he would be likely to turn up there."

"A Danny-free zone. That's why you like it."

"Exactly. I can be me and, not the former Mrs. Danny Newman."

CHAPTER TWENTY-SEVEN - ELIZABETH

As November progressed I gave up all hope. My heart stopped jumping every time the phone beeped, or a knock came on the door. It wasn't Danny, and I knew it. I felt emptier and emptier, emotionally vacant.

It didn't take much; nothing actually, to start the tears the moment I was alone in my room. A hollow pit in my chest permanently replaced my heart. Numbness replaced all previous emotions.

Depression stole every desire, including eating. Despite Rachel's company at dinner, my appetite remained non-existent. I continued losing weight. My formerly tight jeans weren't, and even I was shocked when I stepped on the scale for my dance costume measurements, and it registered under one hundred pounds.

Thanksgiving with Rachel at her family's home in Westport, Connecticut would hopefully do me some good. The change of scenery would keep me from dwelling on last year, and the unforgettable evening in New York when Danny and I realized we were in love.

Once we exited the Merritt Parkway, Rachel and I drove down street after street of large homes, mostly colonials or modern farmhouse style. Many were set back from the road with massive front lawns and stately maple and oak trees, bare now but they must have enjoyed magnificent color in October.

In sharp contrast to Los Angeles, most of the fences were decorative pickets or low stone ones evocative of the colonial era, neither built for security. This was so different than walled-in Los Angeles. And everybody in Westport seemed to have both large houses and large lots. In Los Angeles, only wealthy families could afford both. Rachel's neighborhood looked like a movie set with the story set in affluent east-coast suburbia.

Rachel's mother, Denise, warmly greeted us at the door of their mission-style farmhouse when we arrived just before noon on Wednesday.

"Elizabeth! Welcome!" Denise declared as she guided us to the kitchen for lunch.

Every room on the first floor was designed with warm-toned woods. The kitchen, living room, and library each contained wood-burning fireplaces with stone surrounds. Wood was stacked, ready to be lit. Stickley seemed to have furnished the home.

"Are you ill, Elizabeth?" Denise asked with motherly concern.

She had last seen me in May when she picked Rachel up for summer vacation.

"I'm fine," I stammered looking to Rachel for support. Why would she ask that?

Denise ignored my answer. "I hope you haven't developed an eating disorder. Elizabeth, you're positively skeletal."

Did I really look this bad? Rachel grimly nodded, reading my mind.

I forced myself to eat half a bagel covered in cream cheese and topped with lox. After I finished, I stayed in proximity to Denise. A former high school counselor, she had a wealth of experience ministering to students with eating disorders. Denise would soon see I wasn't an anorexic, or a bulimic forcing myself to throw-up.

When I went to the bathroom, I lingered in front of the mirror. Although I looked in the mirror at least a few times each day while washing and grooming, I must not have been looking carefully enough.

My reflection frightened me. When did my cheekbones get so pronounced? My eyes looked dull and sunken. Even my collarbone stuck out. Auschwitz survivors didn't look much worse.

Later, when we prepared for bed, I weighed myself on the scale in Rachel's bathroom. Ninety-three pounds! And it was evening. I probably weighed only ninety-one in the morning, fourteen pounds below my ideal, one hundred five.

At one hundred five, I looked and felt great. My stomach was flat, I had no flab, and I had curves in all the right places. At one hundred three, I could afford to splurge. When I reached one hundred eight, I cut back for a few days or added more exercise. But ninety-one! I hadn't seen ninety-one since I was twelve years old. I was becoming that scrawny kid Danny remembered from before prep school.

"Elizabeth, are you okay?" Rachel asked from her bed as I re-entered her room.

Ironically, the theme of her décor was "Hollywood." That made perfect sense for film major Rachel, but left me mildly uncomfortable. The framed poster hanging above my bed was from a movie that had won a Best Director Oscar for Steve. Even in Westport I couldn't escape the Newmans.

If it fell off the wall during an earthquake and hit me on the head, I would die knowing Steve had caused my death. Reality check, Elizabeth; Connecticut rarely has earthquakes. It was safe to sleep here.

"Elizabeth, are you okay?" Rachel asked again.

"No. I'm not okay." I cried, and Rachel came over to my bed. She took my hand like a sister.

"Rach, I need help. I'm scared."

For the remainder of the weekend, I forced myself to eat proper portions. By Sunday I was pleased to find a gain of three pounds. If I didn't come home for winter break weighing at least one hundred pounds my parents would freak and I would willingly go for counseling. It would be a clear indication I was no longer capable of handling life.

The following Saturday promised to be the absolute worst day. It was the anniversary of my first night with Danny, my first night spent with any man. I fingered my heart necklace as I frequently found myself doing. After all this time, I couldn't bring myself to remove it or my diamond bracelet.

A year ago, Danny had surprised me by bringing champagne, caviar, and the necklace back from New York. He had devoted the day to spoiling me as the prelude to my seduction. That evening had been magical.

Rachel and Chloe understood. They bought tickets for Saturday's concert at the Times Union Center in Albany. One of my favorite bands, *Streetcar,* was headlining. It's lead guitarist, Gibby Palmer, was my good friend Zac's father. Rachel and Chloe had even reserved a hotel room for the night so I wouldn't have to come back to an empty dorm room.

Without telling them, I contacted Gibby who upgraded us to VIP status. We now had passes to watch the concert from the side of the stage, and of course Gibby couldn't wait to see us. Sometimes it's great being me!

"Backstage passes! No!" Chloe exclaimed when I told her and Rachel.

Chloe had a crush on the hot drummer in the opening act. Now she would meet him. I didn't have the heart to tell her the drummer was an egotistical jerk, but when you're a budding rock star, people put up with you.

Unbelievably, now I couldn't wait for Saturday.

It didn't disappoint.

"Elizabeth!" Gibby exclaimed, upon seeing me enter the Times Union Center.

We had been escorted in for the soundcheck. Rachel, Chloe and I found ourselves at the front of the empty arena enjoying our own private concert.

Gibby blew me a kiss from the stage, and I, in exaggerated motion, caught it. As soon as the song was over, he jumped off the stage to greet me, embracing me warmly.

"I'm still clean," he proudly whispered in my ear.

"Fantastic," I responded as we hugged. And it was.

Gibby had been through rehab several times, and this time, at over a year of being clean, it appeared to be working. Fingers crossed.

The concert was amazing! The excitement in the arena and the energetic performance absorbed me. Rachel and Chloe were in awe; their faces glowed. And I thoroughly enjoyed watching my friends experience for the first time, the perks I was so accustomed to receiving.

Seeing we were friends of Gibby's, the hot drummer held his ego in check when we were introduced in the green room after the concert. Their lead guitarist was cast in a bit part in a movie last year, and he had acting aspirations. His buddy wouldn't blow it by being rude to Michael Jacobs' daughter and her friends.

Rachel and Chloe acted like children locked in a toy store. They were excited beyond belief to be hanging with the bands. And Chloe's dream came true when she engaged in conversation with the drummer. I thoroughly enjoyed watching my friends!

Sunday we slept in and enjoyed the hotel's brunch. It was one of those endless buffets with waffle stations, omelette stations, carving stations, bacon, ham, bagels, muffins, spreads of all kinds, lox, pasta, a carving station, pastries, and even healthy options like fruits and vegetables. You name it. Even I overate!

We returned to Donnelly bloated, but thoroughly satisfied.

When Mom called that evening, she was excited for me.

"I'm so glad you enjoyed the weekend," she exclaimed. "Gibby's such a dear friend."

After I rapidly filled her in on all the details, Mom explained why she called.

"Hawaii!"

Now that was more like it. Mom's new winter vacation plans were perfect. "How many days?"

"Ten days, at a resort, not a house, so there's a spa, and plenty for you to do."

"Just you and me, right?"

"Can Ellen come with us?" Mom cautiously asked,

"What! I love Ellen, but she's a Newman," a member of the enemy clan, I complained.

"But Elizabeth, Steve's joining Dad and Teddy in Aspen, and Danny is, uh, wherever, so Ellen's all alone."

"Mom! That's so unfair. If I say no, I'll feel so guilty it'll ruin our trip. And if I say yes, I'll be thinking of Danny all week which will ruin it for me."

It was unbelievable that I could break-up with Danny and then find his family completely entwined with mine for the holidays. And my parents thought this was okay?

"Ellen and I discussed this already. She swears not to mention him."

"She doesn't have to," I scowled. "Just looking at Ellen is a reminder."

"It won't be that bad."

"You do realize how incredibly odd this is?"

"Yes, but it'll be worse for Danny. He'll see Ellen's pictures of you in a bikini."

"Mom!" and we laughed together for the first time in months.

CHAPTER TWENTY-EIGHT - DANIEL

"Dan, how are you so wasted when it's only ten o'clock?"

Phoebe sidled next to me on the couch. She smiled and kissed my cheek.

"Just lucky," I answered in a hazy stupor.

Party time had started early this evening. Rather it had started immediately upon my arrival at Duncan's with nothing to do but mourn the memory of last year.

Phoebe pressed against my arm. "Let me help you," she offered.

"I'm good," I answered. I lifted the joint from Phoebe's fingers and inhaled.

"It's Mary Poppins, isn't it? You've been up here often lately."

"I'm not discussing it."

I inhaled again, and then I smiled. "My personal life is just that; personal."

I wasn't about to reveal the intimacies of my complicated life with Eli. Again, I inhaled deeply. Then I sighed.

"You are so wasted," a similarly inebriated Phoebe observed.

"Yep." I burst into uncontrollable laughter. How absurd. No way would I ever confide in Phoebe. She would never understand the importance of today.

Tonight was the anniversary of taking Elizabeth's virginity. One year ago, I had driven to New York City and spent the day shopping, with one goal; spoiling my lady. I'd purchased caviar and champagne at Petrossian. Then I'd gone to Tiffany's and bought the gold Peretti heart necklace that incredibly Eli still wore. Everything had to be perfect.

I smirked at Phoebe. What a slut. Had she ever even been a virgin? I laughed. Even if I shared with her, which I wouldn't, Phoebs was incapable of understanding the depth of my love for Eli, and how special that evening had been.

Phoebe would never know it was the anniversary of Eli's first time. No, never; I'd never tell Phoebe. She would make some snide remark about Mary Poppins and imply that Eli was frigid. Eli, frigid? What a laugh.

I didn't know I was laughing out loud until I noticed Phoebe starring, her small brown eyes crinkled in confusion. But really, the idea that anyone could think Eli was frigid; preposterous.

Tonight I should have been with Eli celebrating, re-creating that evening. Well, not literally. I would have taken Eli out to dinner this time so she wouldn't get sick on the champagne. And of course, she was no longer a virgin.

Phoebe leaned her head against my shoulder, her hand coming to rest on my chest. She quietly kissed my cheek again. I lifted her hand and removed it.

"Not tonight," I murmured.

"Too wasted?" Phoebe asked, or was it a factual statement.

"Yeah," I answered, my voice hazy.

Let Phoebe think whatever she wanted. I would never spend tonight with her or any other woman. Tonight was sacred. If I couldn't be with Eli, I'd rather be alone, wasted and depressed, an empty hole where my heart once beat joyously.

I took another deep drag of the joint. Yeah, Phoebe wouldn't understand. A girl like Eli was beyond her comprehension. Phoebe could never understand that there still existed an eighteen year-old girl, no, a woman, who waited until she found a man she had fallen in love with.

Sorrow and grief overwhelmed the emotional balance of that man who loved her so much.

And so, the weekend finally ended. Emotionally bankrupt, I was surviving, but barely. Crunch time was here. Research papers and my film project were coming due.

The advantage of the long hours logged with Rachel in the editing suite was the enforced sobriety. I didn't have time to get wasted, nor did I want to. Mental acuity was a must. I wouldn't jeopardize our grades.

The disadvantage of the long hours; enforced sobriety and celibacy. After an evening of post-production, I had neither the time nor inclination. Worse, I couldn't stop thinking about Eli. If I were with Eli, she'd be there for me in the morning when I did have the energy. I'd wake up and she'd be smiling that beautiful smile that never failed to start my day off right. My heart ached from loneliness.

These days I felt as though I was living with Rachel. We had ten days to complete our project. The Film Department building had become our temporary home. I didn't leave except to attend classes and sleep. Even eating was done here. Today I had to take a break, a legitimate break. I was going to crack if I didn't.

A good nap followed by dinner with the guys, was what I needed. My body and soul craved it. Sitting at an actual table, eating food that wasn't pizza or a sandwich, hot food that actually needed silverware. Nirvana! The dining hall's plain china plates had never been so appealing.

I caught up to Rachel after she left dining with Eli, and we wordlessly walked back to editorial. My conscience was somewhat soothed knowing Eli was being looked after. I doubted I could have finished my film if I had to obsess over her well-being.

Why did all my thoughts eventually lead back to Elizabeth?

Before Rachel and I reached the film building she broke the silence,

"I need to stop at the ticket office," she said.

The Student Center was on our way so it made sense to stop there first.

"What are you getting tickets for?" I asked.

"Chloe and I are going to Elizabeth's dance performance on Tuesday. It's like her final."

"You need tickets?"

I raised an eyebrown, surprised. Tickets to attend somebody's final? You didn't need them for student film screenings. Weird.

"They're free, but it's a small venue, and the performance is well-attended. So you need a ticket."

"Can I get a ticket? I'll go with you?"

Rachel stopped in her tracks.

"Are you serious?" she asked disbelieving me.

"Of course I'm serious. I've never seen Elizabeth dance. Remember, she was injured last year?"

Rachel chuckled, acknowledging my fault in the broken ankle caper.

"You like dance? It's ballet and modern," she explained.

I laughed. "I've never been to a ballet."

"So why not start now by watching your ex dance in one?" she said sarcastically.

"I want to give Elizabeth my support because…"

"Don't start that again, Danny. You know my answer."

"Okay. Well this way if my mother asks, I can tell her how Eli did."

"Your mother!" Rachel laughed and couldn't stop. "Your mother? Danny, do you know how ridiculous that sounds?"

I laughed too, then shrugged.

"Be honest, Danny. You want an excuse to stare at Elizabeth while she's wearing a leotard so you can fantasize how she'd look without it."

"You're so crude, Rachel. Eli's your best friend."

"Crude, but true Danny."

"Wrong," I said flippantly. "I can have that fantasy anytime I want. I have an excellent memory."

"You're impossible."

"That's me," I answered with an impish grin.

We had arrived at the ticket both.

"Are you getting me a ticket? I'll sit alone if I have to, but I'd rather not."

"Fine. If I must. But I won't tell Elizabeth you're coming."

"Thanks, Mom."

I would enjoy watching Elizabeth in a leotard. But I would never admit it to Rachel.

CHAPTER TWENTY-NINE - ELIZABETH

Stop staring at me! What was with Danny's constant staring from across the classroom? It was difficult enough concentrating. Tonight's upcoming dance final had turned me into a bundle of nervous energy.

Since Albany, life had gotten easier. Not better, easier. Similar to Elizabeth Kubler-Ross' stages of grieving, I found myself going through the break-up version. I was no longer angry, in denial, or waiting for Danny to come to his senses and beg me back. I existed day-to-day, confined to a state of perpetual numbness. Devoid of emotion. I dragged through life.

Sadly, I doubted anyone noticed. Either I was a better actress than I gave myself credit for, or my friends had tired of trying to cheer me up. I had been this pathetic for so long they accepted it as normal, not worth a second thought.

Danny glanced my way, yet again. This was not delusional ex-girlfriend thinking either. Danny definitely looked my way. From his seat, he practically had to do a one-eighty. His glances could only be deliberate.

I tried not to look, but Danny sat between me and Professor Denison. I looked to his side; I looked beyond him; anything to avoid eye contact. It was torturous. The expression on Danny's face did not waver. His eyes danced. An impish smile flitted across his lips. I tried reading him, analyzing him. What did it mean?

If a month hadn't passed since we'd last spoken, I'd have thought that Danny was doing a poor job of concealing a secret from me. The eyes, and the grin that accompanied them screamed, "I know something you don't know." How juvenile.

What could he know? Nothing about me, that's for sure. My life was beyond boring. I had no secrets. Well, there was one, but not even my parents or Rachel knew yet. My curiosity peeked by a website Grandma Margie nagged me to scroll through, I applied for a summer program in Israel. My acceptance had arrived yesterday.

Spending the summer in Israel was appealing. I had never been there, and it was 7,600 miles from Danny. The opportunity to visit the biblical and historical sites intrigued me, and they were continents away from Danny. Grandma would be proud when I told her if she didn't first give me the, "I told you so," treatment.

I would be on my own, your average American college student abroad, spending the summer someplace where the names Jacobs and Newman meant nothing; no famous or influential family friends to help me.

Israel was as far east of the 405 as I could get. It was equally as far from Danny. I craved the separation. I needed a summer where we couldn't possibly cross paths. I would be free to be me. I could find out who "me" was. And did I mention, Israel was 7,600 miles away from Danny.

Thankfully class ended. I scooped up my books and dashed out, avoiding Danny.

I always got wound up on performance day, and Danny's earlier attentions exacerbated that. But as soon as I arrived at the theatre, I would be fine. I always was.

Call time was two hours before the eight o'clock curtain. A warm-up barre was mandatory, followed by hair, make-up and wardrobe.

Backstage before the curtain went up, Kelsey and I checked our hair and make-up – again.

"I can hear the audience," she whispered, excitement in her voice.

Her parents had driven in from Boston to catch the performance. I was disappointed that Dad's parents didn't do the same, but we didn't have that kind of relationship. At times like this I regretted being so far from home.

I couldn't dwell on who was not in the audience. The choreographer expected beautiful dancers, not melancholy ones. Mom's voice took over my consciousness.

"Performers leave their private lives in the dressing room, Elizabeth."

I would heed her advice. At least Rachel, Chloe, and a group from the yearbook would be in the audience supporting me.

CHAPTER THIRTY - DANIEL

Paging Leitia Baldrige! What is the proper etiquette for attending your ex-girlfriend's dance performance? I pondered this for most of the afternoon. My sentimental side won out, and I ended up at the local florist. Ms. Baldrige's ghost smiled down.

Now what? The appropriate bouquet for you ex was certainly not the usual order. Eli's favorite, roses, was out, and the bouquet couldn't be too large. That would send the wrong message. But what message did I want to send? I settled on a small bouquet of autumn colored flowers I couldn't identify. It seemed emotionally neutral.

I met Rachel and Chloe in the lobby of the dance venue.

"You brought flowers!" Rachel exclaimed when she saw the bouquet. "You didn't?"

I gave it right back noting her empty hands. Rachel would not make me feel any more uncomfortable than I already did.

"Danny, I think it's very sweet. Elizabeth will love them."

Chloe's overbearing reassurance that I'd done the right thing was cloying.

"Thanks, Chlo," I responded. I playfully stuck my tongue out at Rachel, behaving oh so maturely this evening.

The venue didn't hold more than one hundred fifty seats. There was no place to hide. If Elizabeth glanced at the audience, she would certainly find me. I didn't want her to find me. She might make a mistake or worse, get hurt. Eli was prone to that.

I settled into my tenth row center seat, eyes darting everywhere, certain everyone was starring at me, the man who didn't belong. Rachel might have been right; an emotional decision made in haste. It was too late now. The row had filled. I felt awkward and fidgety. My long legs did not fit comfortably.

The house lights went down. Rachel reached for my hand and quickly squeezed it. Huh? I stared at her. This kind gesture underscored how pathetic I felt. We were the closest of friends, but Rachel was not the touchy-feely type. We didn't even exchange air kisses. Rachel squeezing my hand was a big deal, her acknowledging my emotionally charged evening.

"I'll be fine," I whispered as the spotlights rose and the music began.

According to the program, the first act featured a new ballet performed to a classical piece written by a senior music major. So not only was I about to watch a ballet, an activity I had spent twenty years avoiding, but I wouldn't even know the music. Why couldn't ballet be performed to rock music?

There was only one reason for my attendance, and there she was!

Elizabeth was breathtaking as she leaped across the stage. Her costume, a unitard of green and brown tie-dye, gave her the appearance of a lighter-than-air woodland nymph. It clung to every luscious curve I ever held in my arms. Sadly Elizabeth was less curvy than usual. That I didn't like.

Near where the sheer gossamer fabric of the same pattern was attached to look like soft wings, Elizabeth's collarbone stuck out prominently. Obvious to anyone who knew her as well as I did, and I assumed that number was zero, she'd lost weight that she couldn't afford to lose. Again the urge to protect Elizabeth welled up inside me.

I had no idea what the steps were called, but Elizabeth was working hard and doing an amazing job. I was particularly impressed when she went up on pointe, pleased that her ankle was strong again. Elizabeth glided through the performance, seemingly effortlessly. How did she do it?

Rachel was right. I hated that about her. She was almost always right about what I was thinking before I even thought it. Sitting here, starring at Elizabeth, her auburn hair in a long, glossy ponytail that whipped around every time she did, pure torture. The unitard left little to my imagination. I was relieved knowing I was the only bored man in the audience that knew what lay beneath.

It had been three months, and my longings for Elizabeth were getting the better of me. With nothing else to do but focus on her, the pain of our separation stabbed me relentlessly.

What was my problem? I had been afraid of honesty and commitment, but in retrospect, I had not even looked at another girl in all this time. Except for that night at Vassar, I had been celibate, a state that surprised even me.

It was foolishness on my part. I should have confided and told Elizabeth the truth. Either we would have lived happily ever after, or we'd have split, but it would have been a real split, one based on animosity. This split, where we both knew we wanted the other, was tortuous.

Epiphany hit me, and a grin stretched across my face. I had the power to end this heartache. I would give in. After the show I would speak with Elizabeth. I would tell her everything, beg her forgiveness, and give her the promises she wanted.

As my thoughts completed, the lights went up for Intermission.

"It's ending tonight," I said to myself, but Rachel heard me and perked up.

"I've made a decision. After the show, I'm talking to Eli. She wins."

It felt good just saying it.

I tried hard, concentrating on the second half of the performance, but I was too focused on afterwards. Elizabeth's second dance was a blur, like watching a still photograph come to life. I fixated on Elizabeth's face and her athletic grace, but I couldn't absorb anything. The performance was seen by my eyes, not my heart. My heart was all about anticipation. How sweet tonight would be.

I stood beside Rachel, fidgeting, as we waited for Eli after the performance. Chloe had left at intermission to meet up with her study group. Rachel swatted my arm.

"What?" I asked.

"I've never seen you like this. You're a nervous wreck."

I smiled sheepishly at my uncharacteristic behavior.

Then Rachel hugged me and said, "You'll be fine. She wants you too."

I needed that; confident reassurance. As soon as Rachel finished the words, I released her hold on my shoulders and grinned from ear-to-ear.

Soon, Elizabeth appeared dressed in lavender velour sweats tucked into Uggs, a white long-sleeved tee, and her unzipped ski jacket. She carried her large black dance bag on her narrow shoulder. The weight of it seemed an unbearable burden.

Elizabeth's ponytail hung limp with sweat while tendrils curled and stuck to her neck. She was exhausted. No matter, Elizabeth was still the most beautiful girl I had ever laid eyes on.

My heart beat rapidly as I stood frozen for a moment starring at her. I couldn't wait to cross the room and fold her into my arms. Nothing could stop me.

Out of nowhere, Jackson Shaw appeared carrying a large bouquet; much larger than the one I was holding. Other yearbook staff accompanied him. Worse, he got to Elizabeth before I did, leaving me standing with Rachel, half way across the room, alone and unseen.

What I saw next made me ill. Jackson, all preppy perfection, kissed Elizabeth's cheek, and he handed her his bouquet. I gasped, and had to keep myself from yelling, "Get away, she's mine." Elizabeth kissed him back, and her eyes were alive again. They chatted, animated. Elizabeth appeared refreshed, alive with energy.

My mind was reeling, my stomach churning. I recognized what I was witnessing. Angry, I turned on Rachel.

"Why didn't you tell me she was dating Jackson?" I seethed between gritted teeth.

"What!" Rachel was stunned by my reaction though I couldn't imagine why. How had she kept this from me? I was furious with her betrayal.

I was furious with Jackson, too. How dare he pursue my girl? I was furious at myself too for having missed my opportunity. Most of all I was furious with Elizabeth. How could she be over me? I was the love of her life! I wasn't over her.

I shoved the flowers at Rachel's surprised arms.

"I am so out of here," I hissed and stormed out.

Several hours later, I woke with the fierce headache of a class A hangover. Jackhammers in my skull would have been kinder. The Mojave held more moisture than my mouth, and the stale sour taste was relentless. I tried focusing. Where was I? My eyesight was blurry, but I could see it was still dark outside.

This bed and my surroundings were unfamiliar. Slowly, any faster and I might throw-up, I turned my head toward the body lying next to me. Wearing nothing but the sheet loosely covering us, Phoebe.

Now my head spun even worse. How had I'd gotten here? From our lack of clothing it was obvious what had gone on. Disgust filled me. Knowing Phoebe would do it again just for the asking, no attachments needed, saddened me. I had to get out of here.

I carefully rose from the bed. I didn't want to wake her. Phoebe might not let me leave. I threw on my clothes and crept out. Elizabeth would never have let me make love to her if I showed up in this condition. With Phoebe, it wasn't making love. She had probably been equally wasted. With Phoebe, it was just something you did when you drank, an amusement, a physical release.

CHAPTER THIRTY-ONE - ELIZABETH

After getting past my initial reaction to Ellen's presence, I surprised myself by enjoying my vacation.

"Elizabeth, we're just three women out for a good time," Ellen had said.

Seems Ellen felt equally uncomfortable. Soon we shared a laugh and moved on, glad to dispense with the awkwardness.

Mostly I enjoyed the sun and the surf, absorbing their healing powers as I baked. I spent hours at the beach, sometimes alone, sometimes playing with vacationing children who adopted me as their big sister. Such fun! I enjoyed having a purpose.

My days filled with activity. One morning of outrigger canoeing stretched to half the afternoon. For the first time, I defied my mother and took surfing lessons. Mom, so determined to end my depression, even encouraged me.

I played tennis against the resort pro at least a half dozen times, and the challenge suited my mood. Other days, Ellen, Mom and I went to the spa for massages and other treatments. At night we dined in the finest restaurants. I even persuaded Mom to go to a luau. Total tourist! But I loved letting my hair down and joining the crowds.

Two weeks in Hawaii flew by. Before I knew it, Mom and I returned to Santa Monica where I had one more week before returning to Donnelly.

Between my deep russet tan and the weight I gained, I looked the healthiest I had in months. I felt psychologically stronger too. Did I dare harbor optimism that my depression could have turned the corner to recovery?

At eight o'clock the following morning I joined Mom for breakfast on the patio. For January, it was unusually sunny and warm. Already seated at the table, Mom appeared agitated. Underneath her tan, she had paled. She held the phone palm up, starring at the receiver, disturbed.

Dad! Teddy! Had something happened to them? A skiing accident?

"Mom, what's wrong?" I asked, unable to conceal my fear.

Mom laid the phone down and looked at me with concern. "Ellen called."

"Is she okay?"

"Not exactly," Mom answered, and she motioned me into my chair. Obedient, I sat and looked at her expectantly.

"Is it Steve?"

Mom took a deep breath before responding.

"Elizabeth …"

"Oh, no!" I groaned. "Danny…?"

Mom nodded affirmatively.

"Elizabeth, we've spent the last two weeks shielding you, but I can't any longer." Then she paused, thoughtful. "I hate doing this. You've made such good progress," she fretted.

Mom's grimace was disheartening. Whatever it was must be very important for her to risk hurting me. Mom took my hands, and pulled me into her arms. Then she hugged me.

"Elizabeth, you're so vulnerable, but Ellen is frantic and you're the only one who can shed any light."

I drew back, and stared at Mom. She was practically in tears. I panicked.

"Did something happen to Danny?" I blurted out, petrified. I couldn't live if something bad happened to Danny.

"He's not in a hospital or anything like that, but Ellen's scared."

"What's happened to Danny?" I insisted.

"Are you aware that he's in New Orleans?"

"At Duncan's." I shivered at the name.

"Each time Ellen calls him," Mom paused. "Danny doesn't sound right. Ellen thinks it's drugs."

"Probably. He's with Duncan."

The dull ache in my heart that I thought had vanished reasserted itself.

Mom raised her hand, stopping me. "Danny called Ellen at two this morning."

"That's four in New Orleans," I fretted.

Mom nodded gravely. "Danny sounded so out of it, Ellen talked nonsense to him for over an hour until he finally showed signs of snapping out of it. Ellen feared hanging up. She thought if she did, Danny might pass out and never wake."

Sobs I didn't know I still felt for Danny let loose. Mom held me in her arms and rubbed my back as I continued crying.

"It's okay," Mom said in a soothing voice. "Danny called back at six."

"He did?" I trembled in a little girl voice.

Mom nodded. "I hate putting you through this. Who is this Duncan? Should Ellen be concerned or is she just being Ellen and overreacting?"

I looked at Mom to answer firmly. "Ellen should get on her plane and bring Danny home. Now!"

"It's that bad?"

"Worse than you know."

"Tell me, Elizabeth," Mom prodded, her voice gentle. Tears spilled down my cheeks. "I wouldn't put you through this if it wasn't important."

"I know, Mom." I tried hard to regain my composure, and I chewed my lip. "Mom, I want to help," I stammered. "If something bad happens to

Danny, and I hadn't tried… I couldn't live with myself. I love him so much."

"Shhh, honey. You're doing the right thing."

"Duncan is another reason we're not together. Danny had a choice, and he chose Duncan." I dissolved into a new round of tears.

"I'm sure it's not like that. Danny wouldn't choose Duncan, or anyone else over you. Danny loves you."

"I think he does, but I just don't know anymore."

"I do. Danny still loves you. Now tell me about Duncan."

"Duncan and I hate each other. If Danny were a cartoon character, I'd be the angel with a halo perched on one shoulder, while Duncan as the devil would sit on Danny's other shoulder. We'd be locked in mortal combat over Danny's soul."

"Surely you're being overly dramatic."

"No. That's really how we are. From the moment we first met, Duncan sensed my importance to Danny, and he didn't like that."

"Why?"

"I don't know. Afraid of losing his banker, perhaps. Danny has always kept us apart. He tried to protect me."

"From what?"

"A night with Duncan's friends means heavy drinking and drugs with the sleaziest girls at Donnelly."

"Lovely," Mom said with sarcasm. "I can't imagine why Danny wants to be with them."

"It makes him feel popular. His years at Bromley were cruel."

"Ellen never said," Mom answered sadly.

I nodded in response. "Danny kept that to himself. Steve and Ellen had enough problems of their own back then. He didn't want to add to them," I said.

Mom nodded. Ellen confided everything to her.

"Twice Danny took me to Duncan's parties," I continued. "When he injured his face, Danny was in so much pain. It frightened him, and he needed my support." Tears spilled at the memory. "The other time, Danny's band was rehearsing. Duncan's a great musician."

"So Lucifer has one redeeming quality."

I laughed at Mom's sarcasm, but I was uncomfortable as I remembered the events of that evening. I would have to suck it up. Mom would still love me.

"Elizabeth?"

"It was so boring. Danny was busy playing his bass, and nobody would talk to me. From the moment we arrived, the girls gawked like I was an alien or something. They didn't even know Danny had a girlfriend, and I didn't understand how they didn't know. I thought everybody knew. We were inseparable."

"So what happened, Elizabeth?"

I blushed. "This girl sitting next to me on a couch was rolling joints, lots of them…," I began awkwardly.

"And you got stoned?" Mom laughed.

"You think that's funny?" I exclaimed.

"Yes. Elizabeth, my straight-laced daughter stoned. I find that very funny. Danny must have been a happy man that night."

"No. He was not."

"Elizabeth, there is not a man alive who is not happy when his girlfriend gets stoned. I'm sure Danny enjoyed taking advantage of your state."

"Mom!"

I turned the deepest shade of red imaginable. It was difficult enough talking about Danny. I couldn't discuss my sex life with my mother. That was too personal, when I clearly remembered how uninhibited I had become, and how Danny had to restrain me from behaving inappropriately.

"Anyway," I stamered, "Danny's a hypocrite. His girlfriend is not supposed to get wasted."

"What do you think set him off this time?"

"I've no idea. It's not as if I've run off with a new boyfriend. If that ever happens, he'll really go off the deep-end. Danny won't tolerate me being with another man," I stammered.

I shuddered. Tears flowed again. Damn you, Daniel! Why did you have to do this to me? Just when I was finally, maybe getting over you.

Instead I tearfully confessed, "If Danny rang the doorbell right now, I would be out the door in a heartbeat. I love Danny so much."

"I know you do, Elizabeth."

"Call Ellen. Now. She's got to go this instant."

Mom's conversation with Ellen was short and to the point, finishing up with, "Do not tell Danny Elizabeth's involved."

By eleven, Ellen had departed for New Orleans.

Mom insisted on retail therapy, and I willingly complied. The morning had been difficult. We both feared a reversal of my recent progress.

Noon on this beautiful sun-drenched day found us seated at a patio table at The Ivy, enjoying their signature chopped salad. After a relaxing mother-daughter luncheon, it was off to the boutiques that lined Robertson Boulevard. In spite of everything, I enjoyed the carefree outing. We didn't even mind the occasional stares from passersby who recognized Miranda Jordan.

While completing our purchases at a trendy shop, the text message we had been waiting all day for came through. Mom showed me her phone as the clerk folded the clothing I was buying into a shopping bag. The text read "D on plane. Take off 5 min. Call u l8r." I was so relieved I hugged Mom.

CHAPTER THIRTY-TWO - ELIZABETH

Good feelings accompanied me to Donnelly the following week. At my insistence, Ellen agreed that Danny would never learn of my involvement in saving him unless I divulged it myself. Elated, the new semester began on a high note.

Danny was faring poorly. Ellen had called after returning from New Orleans and seeing Danny to bed. Distraught, she had cried to Mom. Ellen had found Danny strung out, nearly unresponsive. And with no explanation, Steve refused to leave Aspen to return home to his family. Mom and I were furious. What was wrong with him? Danny was his only child, and he almost lost him.

Danny then spent the week convincing Ellen not to withdraw him from Donnelly and put him in rehab. She believed him when he swore that the responsibilities of going to classes and studying would keep him from too much partying.

I love Ellen, but when it comes to her son she can be so gullible. I would never have let Danny return to Donnelly without rehab, or at least committing to therapy in New York. If I were still his girlfriend, I would have instituted a "no touch" policy until he cleaned himself up. I frowned. If I were still his girlfriend, this never would have happened.

I didn't care that classes were starting early the next morning. After a month with Mom, I needed to blow off steam. I knocked on Rachel's door.

"Let's go to The Cellar."

"Seriously?" Rachel exclaimed, stunned by my sudden desire to be social. "I'll text Chloe."

The Cellar was crowded when we arrived with everyone excited to be back after the lengthy break.

"You seem like you again," Chloe observed.

"I hope so. I'm not ready to declare victory, but I'm cautiously optimistic," I said, and I sipped my beer.

"Why cautiously?"

"Because Elizabeth hasn't seen Danny in a month, and she isn't sure how she'll react when she does," Rachel answered.

"Exactly. So I can't declare victory yet. The real test will be when the American Presidency class meets for the first time."

"Why do you do that?" Chloe asked.

"She's a masochist, isn't she?" Rachel said.

"I understood last semester. You were the hottest couple on campus when you registered for that class, but now. Why torture yourself?"

"Chloe, I like Professor Denison, and I enjoy his classes. Danny could drop the class just as easily. Why should I have to be the one?"

"Because you're the one who's been walking around in a deep depression all year," Rachel answered. "And it's Danny's major."

"Thanks, guys. Thanks for reminding me of something I hope is now in the past."

"We'll see," Rachel said skeptically. "Something could soon be back in your future."

Chloe leaned in close across the small round table toward me, and whispered, "Guess who just walked in?"

She nodded toward my right. My stomach clenched. Danny!

I slowly turned my head. A gasp escaped my lips as I spied Danny at a table that included Duncan, Ron, and Kirk plus Phoebe's posse. His arm around Phoebe's shoulder held her close so he could speak into her ear and be heard above the noisy bar scene.

As though linked by radar, Danny's eyes found mine. I jerked my head away. He shouldn't see my hurt.

"When did that happen?" I hissed.

"I don't know," Chloe answered.

"The last time Danny and I spoke," Rachel explained, "He told me he wanted to make things right with you."

"Well, obviously not."

As I reached for my jacket, Chloe said, "I'm so sorry, Elizabeth."

All I could do was nod. The familiar numbness returned, and I pushed back from the table, rising up.

"I've got to get out of here before I throw-up."

I bolted for the exit not knowing that Danny's sad eyes were following me.

For the first time, the realization that our relationship was unsalvageable, that Danny had moved on, sunk in. I woke up to the fact that I had never before believed it had been the end. Now it was painfully clear, and I mourned the finality for the first time.

CHAPTER THIRTY-THREE - DANIEL

Shit! Elizabeth! It was the perfect storm if you liked being in the center of an F5 tornado. Eli rarely went out, yet here she was. Phoebe rarely left the Village, yet here she was. And at the vortex of it all, me.

The expression on Eli's face when our eyes met killed me. Eli was devastated. To her it looked as though I was on a date with Phoebe. I sighed. I had brought Phoebe, but to me a date should be special and include romantic feelings, two notions that didn't apply to Phoebe.

"I've got to get out of here," I said to Phoebe and I threw a twenty on the table.

Why had I even brought Phoebe? On my way to meet her I had run into Jackson Shaw and a girl he introduced as his fiancee. She was visiting from Wellesley where classes did not begin until next week.

I now knew my reaction to Jackson at the dance performance had been just that; a pig-headed, jealous, over-reaction. He never dated Elizabeth. Upon learning this, if I'd had any brains at all, I should have said, "to hell with Phoebe,"and dashed off to make up with Elizabeth.

But no, Phoebe was expecting me, and not showing was rude. Why the hell did I care? Phoebe wouldn't have. She'd have stood me up if something better had come along. Meanwhile, I would have enjoyed my long overdue reunion with my sweetheart, the girl who saved my life last week.

Eli thought I didn't know, but who else had my mother's ear, and the information that would get Mom on a plane? That had been proof enough that Elizabeth still loved me.

Instead, I returned to Berkeley Hall alone, not knowing what to say or do. If Rachel weren't still at The Cellar, I would have sought her advice. Rachel was tired of being put in the middle, but if she gave me the right advice, there wouldn't be a middle to get into anymore.

What the hell was I going to do?

Urgent knocking on my door startled me; Rachel? In my state, I couldn't tolerate anyone else. I needed her steadfast reliability to right me. A worse person in this world than me did not exist. Of that I was completely convinced. What kind of man repeatedly hurts the woman he loves?

I opened the door. Rachel wrinkled her nose, disgusted at the sight of the partially smoked joint in my hand.

"Give me that," she snapped, and she swiped the joint from my hand.

"Rach!" I protested.

She tapped the joint out in the ceramic ashtray and then, ignoring me crushed it with single-minded determination. Message received, Rach.

I slunk over to the edge of my bed and sat down. Rachel had this way of making me feel like a naughty little boy. Of course that could be because the only time she ever came to my room was when I behaved like a naughty little boy.

My eyes found the ground, unable to make eye contact with Rachel. I strongly suspected where she'd been, so I asked, "How's Eli?"

"You bastard!" Rachel seethed. "Too bad you didn't consider Elizabeth two hours ago. How do you think she is?"

I hoped that was rhetorical. The answer was obvious, and I was ashamed.

"What the hell game are you playing, Danny?"

I had no answer. Instead I parried back.

"Why did Eli have to save my life last week? Everyone would be better off if I were dead. They would mourn, and Eli could finally move on," I thought to myself, although I must actually have said the words, because Rachel reacted strongly.

"Damn it, Danny! Don't pull that shit! The death card won't work with me."

"Eli deserves so much better than me."

"What do you mean Elizabeth saved your life?"

I explained my exploits in New Orleans and the aftermath.

"Dad was in Aspen with Mike, oblivious. I love my mother, but she is not a take-charge person. That's why she's such good friends with Randi. Randi's a powerhouse.

Elizabeth is a kinder, gentler version, but when the need arises, she knows what to do. I can almost hear Elizabeth ordering, 'Ellen, get on a plane.' Otherwise, Mom would have waited for Dad, and it might have been too late. Swear you won't tell Eli that I've figured it out?"

Rachel groaned. "You have my word. Now give me your word that you won't do anything stupid. With all your talk of death..."

I laughed. "I won't do anything stupid."

"Good. I'd miss you. Who else would tolerate being my film class partner?"

"Probably nobody." We both laughed, a rare occurrence for me. Then I turned serious again. "Rach, promise me you won't tell Eli I think she deserves better than me."

"Daniel!" Rachel exploded.

"Rach, Eli deserves so much better than me, but I don't want her to find better. Then she won't want me, and I want her so badly."

"Can I strangle you? I can't take it anymore. I have her secrets. I have your secrets. I'm afraid to go beyond 'hello' for fear I'll spill a secret. One day I'm going to lock you both in a room until you tell each other every damned secret! You'll kiss and make-up, and I won't be having a nervous breakdown anymore!"

"Rach, chill. You're losing it."

"Damn right I am, Danny!"

The next day I was no better off as I went through the motions of attending class.

If only I were a pill popper. I'd reached this conclusion sometime during my Intermediate Micro-Economics class.

Being the first class of the semester, I didn't miss much while zoning-out most of it. Instead I contemplated the pros and cons of getting drunk versus getting wasted before my one o'clock American Presidency class.

Eighteen students, two of whom were Elizabeth and I, were enrolled in AP. Taught seminar-style, the tables were arranged in a way to facilitate conversation. There would be no place for us to hide from each other.

I needed something to take the edge off. A few beers would do the trick and give me the desired light buzz. But it would not be cool to come to class smelling like beer. Owen would kill me. Cross that idea off the list.

Smoking half a joint would also provide the desired buzz, but again I would smell, and I actually did care about my reputation, favorable until now. I was considering a run for student government president, and I was on probation with Mom. I couldn't jeopardize either by coming to class smelling of pot.

A shower and changed clothes would eliminate the odor, but the activity would sober me up. I considered smoking the entire joint. I would get completely blitzed and then shower away the scent. That wasted, I would still feel the buzz afterwards. Then again, I was equally likely to fall asleep long before I remembered that I was supposed to shower and change my clothes, or that I even had a class to attend. Cross this idea off the list too.

Which led me to contemplating pills. On the upside, pills are odorless. Showers and clothing changes were removed from the equation. On the downside, I wasn't a pill-popper, and I wasn't about to become one. Once in prep school I had taken half a Quaalude. It made me so loopy I had been petrified. Never again.

Pills were real drugs. They were easily addictive, and the smallest mistake in dosage could be fatal. Despite telling Rachel everyone would be better off without me, I didn't want to die. I might be messed up at the moment, but I was preternaturally optimistic enough to think I could turn it around.

And so, I entered the seminar room sober, an early arrival. I grimaced, my worst fears confirmed. With the rectangular configuration, Elizabeth would be visible at all times, no matter where either of us sat. I chose the third seat up from the front on the window side of the room, knowing full-well I'd piss-off whoever sat in the second seat. They would spend the semester trying to avoid bumping elbows with me; lefty's revenge. I was not in an accommodating mood.

Elizabeth made her grand entrance. I gasped; my breath taken away. Wow! I couldn't help staring. Her deep Hawaiian tan had not faded and Eli played it up.

Tight jeans tucked into Uggs were once again tight, accentuating her shapely ass, the way I liked it to be. Elizabeth tossed her glossy hair as she removed her ski jacket and set it on the back of her chair. The v-necked apricot cashmere sweater Eli wore clung to delectable curves that had returned after a month of good food.

The heart necklace I had given her lay just so, drawing my eyes to her alluring cleavage. I noted her diamond bracelet delicately resting on her left wrist too.

My jaw dropped. My heart skipped at least a few beats while starring at the beauty that had belonged to me. Now I understood. Elizabeth planned to show up looking like a fashion model twice a week. Certainly she knew the effect it had on me. Even she wasn't naïve enough to think otherwise.

It took all my self-control not to pick her up and carry her to the nearest empty room.

CHAPTER THIRTY-FOUR - ELIZABETH

Daunted by the prospect of the small enrollment in the American Presidency class, I considered what Mom would do. She was the expert. Mom could handle any situation with aplomb no matter how difficult.

If Mom were I, she'd give it the full star treatment, choosing clothing that would burn Danny's eyes. Add a little make-up and the right jewelry, hold her head high, and exude confidence she didn't really have.

"Play the part, Elizabeth," Mom would coach me.

I would no longer be Elizabeth Jacobs attending my AP seminar. I would be an actress playing the part of Elizabeth Jacobs, college student. This slim distinction, this one degree of separation, allowed me to confidently enter the classroom.

Danny was already seated on the far side of the room making eye contact unavoidable when I entered. Keep smiling, Elizabeth, I coached myself. It was easier than I imagined. Danny starred, his mouth momentarily agape. I smiled, butterflies tickling my stomach, pleased that I had won round one. Danny looked positively ready to pounce across the room and devour me. In my head, I giggled.

With his two-day stubble, tousled hair, and well-defined muscles under his open-neck button-down shirt, Danny was hot! I would have embraced his pounce and eagerly been devoured, but for the professor standing directly behind me.

I took a seat toward the back of the near side of the rectangle and willed myself not to glance at Danny.

Ninety minutes later, the class ended. I had survived. As soon as Professor Denison dismissed the students, I jumped up and exited. I did not want to cross paths with Danny. It had been a draining experience, and I did not see how I would repeat my performance twice a week for thirteen more weeks! I was not meant to be in a touring company.

Fighting the urge to return to my room, I headed to The Café for a cup of tea. If I had any chance for recovery, I needed to put myself out there, embrace opportunities to engage in social interactions. It was out of my comfort zone, but I had to try. My mental health required it.

None of my friends, or even remote acquaintances, were in The Café when I arrived. Unfortunately, as I sipped my tea, there was nothing to do but let my mind wander. Hot as Danny looked today, he belonged to someone else now. Phoebe would be enjoying his strong arms, and the feel of his perfectly sculpted chest. He would be sharing Phoebe's bed, not mine.

Phoebe! Why her? With her stringy hair, black rose tattoo, and constant inebriation; she was not Danny's type. Was she his transitional relationship, someone he hooked up with in the interim before he entered another serious relationship?

My new best friend, the dull ache returned. I tried so hard to fight it, but I didn't have the strength, and so I succumbed. I should return to my room, but the malaise left me powerless to move. Leaving the table would require logical, ordered steps, and my synapses were not firing. Against my better judgment I sat paralyzed, unable to complete the simplest task even though it would save me.

Then Chloe, all upbeat smiles, arrived accompanied by a student I'd never seen before.

"Hi Elizabeth," she cheerfully greeted me. "Can we join you?"

Without waiting for an answer, they both sat down, steaming cups of coffee in their hands. I was stuck. I had no option but to force a smile and attempt being social. Why did this annoy me? Wasn't that why I had come to The Café in the first place?

"Elizabeth, this is Scott," Chloe said as an introduction.

Scott had kind, brown eyes set in a face neither angular nor round. His lips upturned in what must be a perpetual smile, but when Chloe introduced him, dimples punctuated his cheeks, resulting in a most charming affect.

Topping it off was thick, curly hair, dark brown and close-cropped. I smiled. His mother must have forced him to get it cut before returning from break. I smiled again, this time from deep inside, as I responded, "I'm Elizabeth Jacobs."

I didn't know Scott, but curiously smiling came easily in his presence.

"Elizabeth was my roommate last year," Chloe explained. "Scottie went to Scarsdale with me. We're sort of like you and Danny, except without the sex."

"Chloe!" I frowned. Danny was not Scott's business.

"Who's Danny?" Scott asked. How could he not after Chloe's set-up?

"Elizabeth's ex. I'll introduce you sometime. Maybe you can come with me on Saturday night. It's his birth... day party," Chloe answered, stumbling over her final words. "I'm so sorry, Elizabeth. I didn't think."

I glanced down at my cup, speechless.

"It was a nasty divorce," she told Scott.

I took a deep breath and steeled myself. "So how come I've never met you before?" I asked Scott, trying to change the subject to something neutral.

My eyes met his dimpled smile again. I couldn't help smiling back.

"I just checked-in. I took a gap year that lasted a year and a half," Scott laughed, an easy, self-deprecating laugh that put me at ease. Nobody ever put me at ease on first meeting.

"I went abroad for a community service program," he continued. "Asia, Africa, Latin America; at every stop I worked on a different project. I really got to know the people."

Chloe and I spent the remainder of the afternoon in awe as Scott explained in great detail the projects he had participated in, and the people he had met. He was proud of his accomplishments, and rightly so.

"You can't understand true poverty until you go to a third-world nation. Think about the poorest place you've ever been," he challenged us.

"When I go to the city, Metro-North goes through some pretty rachet parts of the Bronx," said Chloe.

"I served meals at a homeless shelter when I was in high school," I volunteered, recalling the field trips my temple youth group had taken on Sunday afternoons. "It was in a gritty neighborhood with boarded-up dilapidated houses."

"But there were houses," Scott pointed out.

"But the siding was peeling and some windows were covered in waxed paper and cardboard where the glass panes were missing," I explained.

"But they had running water and electricity?"

"I guess so. I couldn't tell from the bus."

"Where I travelled, homes didn't have utilities. And the dwellings were made of cardboard, not the windows. We built schools. The kids had to walk miles, some without shoes. And when they arrived, there weren't enough desks. Imagine sitting on the floor all day in order to learn."

I didn't know what to say. It was difficult to imagine. I was ashamed that all I knew of the desperate level of poverty Scott described was from news exposés. To have served these people, what an incredible young man Scott was.

CHAPTER THIRTY-FIVE - DANIEL

Twenty-one! Finally! Today I become a legal adult. Let the party begin, but first…

I started the day prudently sleeping-in. The one interruption, the phone.

"Teddy? Hey, what's going on, bro?"

"What's going on? Dude, did you think your baby brother would forget your birthday? Happy twenty-one, big guy."

My baby brother. Eli and I had isolated Teddy from our troubles. He and I managed to remain close. Teddy's birthday greeting warmed me.

"Thanks, bro. You have no idea what your calling means to me."

Teddy really had no idea. Just the sound of his voice lifted my spirits. Perhaps this wouldn't be such an awful day after all.

"Whatever happened between you and Elizabeth, you're still my brother."

Whenever we spoke, Teddy danced around the issue, hoping I'd latch onto it and spill the details.

"Thanks, Teddy. How's it going?" I asked, changing the subject.

"Fantastic! Your advice has paid off in spades!"

Teddy returned to being an exuberant fifteen-year old, albeit an incredibly spoiled and immature one.

For the first time in a long time, I smiled. "Which advice was that?" I asked, though I was pretty certain I knew.

"The advice where you told me sex was all about pleasing the girl. It works. They're all over me." Teddy bragged.

"That's great, Teddy."

"There are two upperclassmen I'm banging pretty regularly. I'm not ready for the girlfriend thing."

I laughed. Teddy, so much like me, should have been my real brother.

"I'm happy for you, Teddy."

Baby brother was growing up.

"Danny, what happened with you and Elizabeth? It's gross… I mean, she's my sister… Did you forget it should be all about pleasing the girl?"

I sighed. Teddy had such a simplistic view of relationships. But in a nutshell, he was right. I hadn't been thinking of how to please Elizabeth when I cheated on her.

"I violated my own rule, Teddy. I made Eli miserable."

"I thought you loved her."

"I did, and I do. I always will."

"You weren't ready to be married?"

"Probably not, but I handled it badly. Eli found out I cheated, and she can't live with a man she can't trust, even though she loves me."

"That's gotta hurt, for both of you."

"It does. Especially today."

"You're a stud, Danny. I'm sure a lot of girls would love to make it a happy birthday for you," he chuckled.

"That's not the same, Teddy. I can't expect you to understand. You're only fifteen."

"And you are too young to be married."

"Fair point, well made," I answered, and took a deep breath. "Teddy, my time with Eli was the best. When you fall in love, everything, and I mean everything, is so much better."

"I hate you sounding so sad on your birthday. Go find Elizabeth. Maybe as a birthday present she'll forgive you."

"I wish it were that simple."

After that, I couldn't fall back to sleep. I tossed and turned, haunted by memories of my last birthday and what was so blatantly missing from this one; Elizabeth.

Later, Mom and Dad, yes even Dad, called with birthday wishes. Since Vancouver, we had not spoken. Today it was unavoidable. In unspoken agreement, out of respect to Mom, we were civil. Mom still had no clue that anything was amiss. She giggled, excited by the big day though she mourned my official passage out of childhood.

Then came Mom's admonition. "Danny, don't go crazy tonight," she warned. "Call me in the morning so I'll know you're alright."

It was as close as she would come to reminding me of her recent trip to New Orleans. Message received, loud and clear, Mom.

Later, Fedex delivered the legal papers I'd been waiting my entire life for. Another reminder of my new status as an adult; once signed, notarized and returned to my attorney, I would have authority to make withdrawals of principal from my trust fund without parental approval. I was now a wealthy man in my own right, a fact that would not leave my room. Happy Birthday, Daniel!

The biggest surprise of the day came in late afternoon. Alone in my room, quietly playing the guitar to kill time until dinner, the phone rang. Michael!

"Happy Birthday, Danny!" he exclaimed as though nothing were the matter.

Mike tried as much as possible to stay out of my relationship woes, but rightly so, he sided with his daughter. Still, I am his godson, and it was a milestone birthday.

Suspicious, I finally asked, "Where's Randi?"

"At the club with your mother," he answered sheepishly.

Just as I thought. Mike had waited until Randi wasn't around before calling. If Randi were my wife, I'd have done the same.

Dinner at a local steak house was boisterous. With Shane, Cam, Rachel and Chloe, I relaxed. And the round table we were seated at made it less obvious that someone was missing. Still, if they were all with me, this left Eli alone. I frowned.

When the young waitress came to take our drink order, Chloe took control. Seated beside me, and ordering first, guaranteed I would go last. We laughed as my friends ordered soft drinks, knowing full-well my obligation to order something harder.

All eyes were on me as the waitress paused at my side. I felt bad for her. The pert brunette couldn't be more than a few years my senior, and the staring flustered her.

"I'll have a vodka martini," I ordered, a broad grin stretching across my face.

"Card him!" Shane called out.

The others followed his lead, chanting, "Card him! Card him!"

Shit! Could my friends be any more embarrassing?

Diners at adjacent tables stared, not pleased with the disturbance. My face turned scarlet, something it never did.

As quickly as possible, I reached into my rear pants pocket, took out my wallet, and showed the waitress my driver's license. Good-natured, she smiled through the noise.

"You've been through this before, haven't you?" I asked.

"Yes. Every year," she said, and she handed me back my wallet. "Happy Birthday, Mr. Newman," she added, and she gave me her rehearsed flirty grin.

Later came the party to end all hall parties. Cam, Shane and I threw open the doors to our rooms scattered down the seven-room corridor. One other single, and three suites of three freshmen each, completed the hallway.

The Resident Advisor had long ago given up on protecting his advisees from our corrupting ways. With freshmen like Ian on the hall, it was the RA that needed protecting.

Our hall had earned the reputation as **the** party place in Berkeley Hall, and within a short time everyone on the hall joined the party. Lots of students, including some of the prettiest girls in the dorm, arrived as well; over one hundred people in all crushed in the narrow space.

By ten-thirty several things were apparent: the guests were having a great time; this was probably the most successful party of the year; and I was miserable. I wanted to be alone, and there was no place to go. It was my party.

If Berkeley Hall were a straightened letter 'C,' my hall would be the top rung on our floor. The short corridor, and its twin on the bottom, each dead-ended at large picture windows. Urban legend claimed that in the mid-1970's a student had been so inebriated he had crashed through the window, fell three stories, and survived with only a broken leg. Waist-high polished wood railings now installed before each window would stop the momentum of any similarly high-flying student.

After grabbing a fresh bottle of beer, I pushed through the crowd to lean in solitude against the railing and stare out at the evening darkness. It didn't work. My mind wandered to Eli and my last birthday.

Tonight I found myself turning my head toward the closed fire doors at the other end of the hall in anticipation of who might next step through them. Frustrated, I downed the beer and placed the empty bottle on the floor beyond the railing.

I pressed my hands against the top of the smooth wood and stretched my back, my neck, and my arms. As I straightened, a gentle hand rubbed my back, but it was not the hand I wanted to feel. I turned toward the hand, and Chloe kissed my cheek.

"She's not coming, is she?" Chloe said softly. Sadness tinged her voice.

"Thanks, Chlo. You understand," I answered quietly.

"I've been watching you. Every time the door opens, you turn."

"I'm that obvious?"

"To me, you are."

I was grateful for Chloe's presence. I needed a friend to lean on, and girls were more sensitive to my troubles than guys were. Cam and Shane encouraged me to get laid as often as possible, as though a fling with some slut would ever be a substitute for Elizabeth. How little they knew. I sighed. The guys meant well.

"Hey," she began. Chloe's hand rested on my shoulder. She tried her best to be cheerful. "I've spotted at least half a dozen attractive girls here who would probably be thrilled to make your birthday a happy one."

"I don't think so, Chlo." I didn't want a hook-up.

"Your heart is not in a good place."

"You're right."

I pulled a joint from my pocket and lit it, inhaling deeply. Chloe wouldn't want any. After too many hook-ups last year, she didn't smoke anymore.

"It's interesting, Rachel can read my mind, and you can read my heart. If I combined you into one person, I'd have the perfect girlfriend."

"No. You'd have Elizabeth. She's your perfect girlfriend."

"Yeah," I said somberly. I took another hit, desperate to forget.

Chloe hugged me. She understood my pain.

"I feel so bad. You love her so much."

"That I do," I said.

I picked up the beer bottle and tapped the joint against it until it went out.

"Then what are you doing here? Go downstairs. I'm sure Elizabeth is home."

"I don't think so."

"This may be your only chance at having a happy birthday," Chloe warned.

"Hey, Newman!" A buoyant Ian clapped me on the back, startling me. "Happy Birthday, man."

I jerked around toward him. Ian stood with a guy I didn't recognize; another freshman I presumed.

"Thanks, Ian." I responded with a forced grin, the expected response from the birthday boy, and I extended my hand to shake his.

"Say, you're with Chloe tonight," Ian observed.

"She's cheering me up," I answered.

Flatered, Chloe smiled as she often did.

"Good. That's real good." Ian grinned a snarky grin I didn't trust. "Then you won't mind me calling on Elizabeth."

"What!" Ian wanted my lady. No way!

"A hot babe like Elizabeth shouldn't be spending the evening alone."

Never! My hands fisted, poised to strike. Elizabeth would never let the likes of Ian anywhere near her.

Chloe raced to the rescue before I throttled him. "She's studying at the library," Chloe stammered. She knew where Eli's heart lay.

Straightening my posture, I had several inches over Ian, and I now used it to my advantage. Hands on hips emphasized my broader shoulders and well-developed muscles. A formidable glare met Ian's smirk.

"Elizabeth is not available," I said sternly.

Ian shrugged. "Hey, she's a free agent. Let her decide. I'm just giving you a heads-up, Newman."

Wisely, Ian and his friend turned and left me with Chloe. It took all my control not to raise my fists and deck him. I was seething.

"Putz!" I spat out loud enough that only Chloe heard.

"Asshole," she agreed.

"There's no way Eli would ever let that guy near her."

"Danny, go to Elizabeth. She's in her room," Chloe insisted. "I'll clean-up and lock your door."

I smiled. Chloe understood. I embraced her, and kissed her cheek.

"Thanks, Chloe. I'll catch you tomorrow,"

Minutes later, I tentatively knocked on Elizabeth's door. What was I doing? All I could do was go with the flow.

"It's open," Eli called, her voice soft.

I entered, hesitant. Then I squared my shoulders, more confident. I had nothing to lose. What was the worst that could happen? Sadly, I knew the answer all too well. Eli could throw me out. Then I'd be as miserable as I already was. It couldn't get worse.

Reclining on her bed reading, Eli's jaw dropped, emerald eyes opened wide as saucers. A panoply of emotions crossed her lovely face; surprise, confusion, and finally, fear. I closed the door behind me and out of habit turned the lock.

"Hey, Eli," I said as casually as possible.

"What are you doing here?" Her quivering voice bordered on panic. How could Elizabeth be fearful? I loved her.

"I needed to see you," I answered.

Eli followed my staring eyes. Her long, coltish legs, covered to mid-thigh by an Oxford shirt with cuffed-up sleeves beckoned.

"Why?" she asked in a near whisper. Eli's lower lip trembled.

Flustered and uncomfortable, Eli placed her book on the adjacent desk, nearly dropping it. Then she grabbed the nearest pillow, clutched it to her chest as if for protection, and cowered in the corner.

"Why are you here?" Elizabeth stammered.

Long, thick lashes hid her emerald eyes from my view. I smiled shyly and shrugged.

"It's my birthday," I answered.

Horror crossed her face. Eli gave me a hard stare.

"I am not your present, Daniel," she said sharply. "Get out!"

Get out? No! I had no contingency for expulsion. I panicked.

"No, Eli! That's not what I meant," I said, apologetic.

Though it had occurred to me. What better birthday present than a night with my enchanting love? But I didn't want to frighten her. It had been months. It had even been a couple of months since our last conversation.

How would I have reacted if Eli suddenly turned up in my room this late at night? Scrap that thought. I knew exactly how I would react. That's why Eli was frightened.

"Shouldn't you be upstairs at your party?" she asked.

I shock my head in response. Then I walked over to the bed and sat down. Eli let me take her hand. Its soft familiarity filled me with warmth.

"I was miserable," I said, and I looked straight at her.

A tear slowly rolled down Eli's cheek.

"Everyone was there, except the one person who matters." I smiled at her gentle green eyes.

"Me?" Eli whispered.

"Yeah," I answered softly. "Do you want to get dressed and go upstairs with me?"

I pictured how happy everyone would be if I returned to the party with Elizabeth.

"No, I don't think so," Eli answered quietly.

Of course; Eli's eyes were red and her face was tear-stained.

"You've been crying," I said with gentle surprise.

Embarrassed, Eli averted her gaze.

"I was remembering last year," she quivered. Tears flowed down her cheeks. My heart ached.

"Me too." I smiled at the memory. "That was the best birthday ever. Starting at midnight and ending at midnight." I carefully played with her fingers. "Someone adored me that day. I couldn't wait to see what she would do this year."

Eli wiped her eyes with a sleeve. "I spent the summer planning."

She looked down again, pain etched across her face. It tore my gut apart.

"That's why I had to see you tonight, baby."

I released Eli's hand and stood for a moment to remove the joint and matches from my pants' pocket. Eli needed this. After all this time, she was still so emotional.

As I sat down again, Eli watched me light the joint and inhale.

"Here," I said as I passed it to her.

Eli considered the joint, then said, "I don't think so. You know how I get."

A faint blush tinged her cheeks. I certainly did know how she got, and I smiled.

"You're tense, baby." I practically ordered her to inhale.

"Of course I'm tense," Eli snapped. "You show up at my door. What do you expect?"

"E, c'mon baby," I said in a soothing voice.

Despite her objection, Eli inhaled deeply and then passed the joint back. I hated that I unnerved her. I inhaled, but not too deeply. I didn't want to get wasted.

After a few more hits, Eli relaxed. She let go of her pillow, unaware that the movement made her shirt ride up to skim the top of her thighs.

Focused on Eli's attire I realized, "That's my shirt, isn't it?"

"Yes," she giggled, well on her way to being wasted. I smiled at Eli's hazy eyes.

"I like to sleep in this," she cooed, sounding like a little girl. "It feels like you're with me 'cause it smells like you."

Eli had possessed the shirt for over five months. It couldn't possibly smell like me.

"Doesn't it smell like you or your detergent?"

Eli took another hit of the joint. "I don't wash it. It won't smell like you if I do."

Wasted, Eli was pleased to share this tidbit. What had become of my immaculate lady? Being sober, the thought of her sleeping in a shirt that hadn't been laundered since early September struck me as disgusting. I leaned into her and risked taking a whiff.

Not wanting to offend her I said, "Eli, that shirt doesn't smell like me."

"It doesn't?" She screwed up her face, a combination of confusion and disappointment.

"No, it's much better than that. Babe, it smells like you."

"Oh," she said sadly."I want it to smell like you."

"Here's an idea," I said cheerfully, "let's swap. I love your scent."

Eli's childlike face lit up at my idea.

"Okay!" she said enthusiastically.

I stood up, removed the shirt, and dropped it on the back of the desk chair. Eli noticed the blue-gray t-shirt I was wearing underneath.

"Can I have that one too?" she giggled.

"Sure," I readily agreed.

"I bought those for you in Malibu," she happily recalled.

"Yes, you did," I answered as though I were addressing a child. "Thank you."

I pulled the shirt over my head and let it fall to the floor. Eli let out a gasp of delight as she stared at my bare chest. In her wasted state, she failed to comprehend the obvious; that when I removed the shirt, I would be bare-chested.

I lay down on the bed behind Eli, and propped myself up on my elbow, facing her. "Better?"

"Much better," Eli answered in a flirty voice.

"You can shop for me anytime you want."

Eli grinned, happy with that prospect. Sunshine. The warmth of her smile filled me with joy. This is what had been missing from my life. Now I wanted more.

I gently brushed a few stray hairs off Eli's face and inhaled. Her light floral perfume had been replaced with the pungent aroma of pot. I frowned. This was wrong.

"Be right back," I said.

I scampered off the bed, and in two strides I reached the bureau in this small room. Sitting on top, as always, was a crystal bottle of Eli's signature fragrance, light floral with delicate vanilla undertones. I grabbed the bottle and hurried back to her side.

Eli giggled; her captivating eyes never left me. Then I lifted her chin, and aimed the bottle toward her neck, squeezing the atomizer twice.

"There," I declared, and I inhaled deeply. "That's more like it. You smell like my Eli again."

I placed the bottle on the desk and crawled back onto the bed.

Eli was content; my happy kitten. I inhaled deeply several times, wanting to imprint her scent in my memory. If she never let me be this close to her again, let me remember her scent forever.

I reached up and unbuttoned the first button of Eli's shirt. She didn't object. Her gold Peretti heart was visible, lying in her bra-less cleavage. As I lovingly fingered the heart she smiled at both my gesture and my touch.

"You're still wearing this," I said softly, amazed. I wasn't sure what I had expected Eli to do with the piece, hide it away in a drawer or something, though I would have been disappointed if she had.

"Someone who used to love me gave this to me," she answered wistfully, and a tear escaped her eye.

I opened the next shirt button. There were only two left.

"Someone still does love you." Overwhelming emotion filled me. "I've never stopped loving you, Eli."

Relief flooded me. These were the words I had wanted to tell Eli for so long.

Tears streamed down her cheeks. I didn't know if they were from sadness, or from happiness. I carefully brushed Eli's cheeks with my fingertip.

"Babe, don't cry."

"I love you too, Daniel."

"I know," I assured her.

The brightest smile I hadn't seen on Eli's face since the summer lit her face like the stars on a clear Malibu evening. Eli eagerly let me open the remaining button, and I pushed her shirt open.

"I haven't had any love in a long time," Eli whispered.

I moved my hand to hold her face. Slowly, I kissed Eli's beautiful, full lips that I missed so much. I didn't want to force her into anything she would regret in the morning, so I asked very gently. "You want my love?"

Eli looked so small as she nodded. "There's nobody else's love that I want."

She held out her slender arms to me. My heart filled, elated to the point of bursting. Recently I'd had sex with a couple of girls, but it had been four long months since I had made love to anyone. No other girl ever had that effect on me. This was love, pure and intoxicating. Elizabeth owned my heart.

While one hand held her close and we kissed, Eli opened my belt buckle. My other hand found her hips and lifted the band of her lacy bikini. Eli flexed her hips making their removal easier.

I felt so full. This was where I belonged.

"I love you, baby," I whispered, fearful that tears of joy would form in my eyes.

Happy birthday, indeed.

CHAPTER THIRTY-SIX - ELIZABETH

Still as I tried to be, I sensed Danny's awareness that I had woken. The familiar arm wrapped around my waist tightened into an affectionate hug. Danny's unique aroma, a blend of his faded citrus cologne that reminded me of the beach, and his musky perspiration, filled my nostrils with joy.

Melted against Danny's strong sculpted chest, for the first time in months I felt so right. But it was so wrong. Warm kisses played upon my neck and shoulder, sending shivers of excitement through me. Involuntarily I pressed against him. I always did. It was reflexive, or was it a learned response like that of Pavlov's dog; if Danny touched me a certain way, I responded in a certain way.

I was disappointed by my inability to control myself. Danny interpreted my response as a sign of encouragement. Understandable given that we'd made love twice before falling into deep sleep, easily the best sleep I'd enjoyed since early September.

Now I faced the dilemma of my life as Danny's hand slipped between my thighs and his fingers gently parted me. I purred. I wanted him so badly.

No! Snap out of it. Elizabeth! There is no dilemma.

"Please remove your hand," I requested in a sharp voice.

"Eli?" Danny expressed surprise, and then disappointment.

Of course he did. I had been an enthusiastic participant last night, even after I sobered up. He assumed that in the morning I still would be. How I longed to be, but I couldn't afford to be.

Danny turned me around to face him. Those dammed seductive sapphire eyes locked on me. My heart melted. I couldn't let my resolve do the same.

Danny smoothed an unruly wave off of my face. I tingled at his touch.

"I love you Eli," he whispered.

Tears filled my eyes.

"I love you too," I whispered back.

Danny's lips met mine, and he kissed me, our mouths molding together, a perfect fit. How do you tell the man you love that you can't be? How do you tell him when he's holding you in his arms while you're lying in bed naked from a night of passion?

I placed my hand against Danny's cheek and released my lips from his.

"Danny, I can't."

"Eli, I love you. You love me. C'mon Sweetheart, what we shared last night was beautiful. I want you, baby."

"I know you do," I said sadly. "It was great." I smiled. "But I don't want only one night. I'm not a one-night-stand."

Danny let out a loud whoop of laughter. "Babe, you? We've been together so long you get a free pass for life. You can sleep with me whenever you want."

"Danny, that's not what I mean. If I periodically sleep with you, how am I ever going to move on and find someone who will give me what I want?"

"Maybe I don't want you moving on, Eli. I don't want one night either, baby. I want to make love to you every night, and every morning. I want to make love to you every in between. It can be just like…"

"… like we used to be?"

"Exactly! Like we used to be." Danny sounded hopeful.

"I can't be like we used to be," I protested.

"We're so good together, baby."

"We are. But I want better, Danny."

"I'm miserable without you."

"So am I. But we can't be."

"Eli, I love you," he pleaded.

"I deserve better, Danny. Until you're ready to change… I can't live with your lies and deceptions."

I trembled as tears began flowing. Danny enveloped me in his arms and wiped them away with the corner of the top sheet.

"You betrayed me with Vanessa," I sobbed. "What a fool I was. We were living together. You called me your wife. But Vanessa knew differently. She must have had a good laugh."

"Nobody laughed at you."

"That afternoon when she came by our room," I stammered. "Vanessa didn't know I was in town. That's why she was so shocked to see me. Especially in my robe, and you in a towel. Vanessa wasn't looking for Steve. She was looking for you. I spoiled her plans!"

"Eli, don't go that way. It's in the past. It's over." Danny hugged me tighter.

"My life has shattered. Your lies…," I quivered.

"Eli, I'm so sorry. I hope you believe how much I love you."

"Yes, I believe you. And despite all the hurt, I still love you. I must be mental because I do love you."

"Eli, can't we wipe the slate clean, and start over? I love you."

"Not if it's going to be the same. I deserve better. I can't risk getting hurt again. I'm so depressed."

"So am I. It's awful without you, Eli. I want you, baby."

"I can't, Danny. I can't be your girlfriend if I can't trust you. Without guarantees…" I shrugged out of his hold. "Maybe Zac will invite you to visit him at Harvard. I would hate myself for the questions I would ask when you returned. My self-esteem is at stake. I may be miserable and depressed, but at least I have my self-esteem."

"Speaking of Zac, I'm visiting him next weekend."

"Oh no! You know the first words out of his mouth are going to be, 'Are you and Elizabeth still together?'" I fretted.

"Baby, it's none of Zac's business."

"And what if you meet a cute little coed?"

"I would never publicly humiliate you like that."

"Yeah. You only humiliate me privately."

"Eli, I promise," Danny pleaded, "Zac will never know we're having problems."

"Problems?" I laughed. "Is that what you call this? I thought we'd broken up."

"We love each other. We're not broken up, Eli. We're separated. We're taking a hiatus until I get my shit together. You're my girl, baby."

"Danny, do you know how deranged that sounds?"

"I guess I do," he laughed. "Maybe I should be in your Abnormal Psych class."

"I could have done my oral presentation last week about you, Exhibit A. You know that's the worst part about being separated."

"I couldn't be your psych class exhibit?" Danny smirked.

"No. I miss not having my best friend."

Again I began crying, shaking. Danny wrapped his arms around me and held me tightly.

"Eli…"

"Danny, that was the best day. My presentation was awesome. The professor was impressed, and she's very tough. Nobody ever impresses her. After class other students came up to me, congratulating me."

"That's great!"

"Yeah, it was. I was stoked. I ran back here on autopilot, excited to share my triumph with you. Then I walked through the front door. Reality came crashing down. I ran for my room," I cried. "I didn't have my best friend to share it with. That was the worst."

Danny hugged me close and kissed my cheek.

"I hate this," he said. "I don't want you crying."

"I miss our friendship, Danny. We could share everything. You cared. You would listen. Nobody else does."

"I still care, Eli. My door is always open for you."

I shook my head sadly. "I can't. We both know what would have happened. I was excited. You would have been too. Then you would have hugged me, and kissed me, and… This is so fucked," I complained. Danny grinned. "Until you open up and let me help you, until you commit to me, we have to stay apart. I can't risk it."

Danny cradled my face with his soft hands and gently kissed my lips. My pulse instantly quickened. I turned my head away.

"Danny, please go. I'm afraid if you stay we'll end up making love again. Then I'll hate myself for letting it happen."

Danny laughed and kissed my shoulder.

"Okay, I'll go. You've never thrown me out before, Eli."

"There's always a first time for everything."

Danny rose from the bed and pulled on his jeans. I clutched the sheet under my chin to hide my nakedness. Danny turned to face me while he fastened his button and his belt. He smiled warmly through tired blue eyes.

His beauty took my breath away. I couldn't help but stare at his perfectly sculpted chest and chiseled abs. He reached for his shirt, remembered our swap, and took the old one, putting it on, but leaving it open.

Tears wracked me again. In an instant, Danny returned to my side. He hugged me and kissed my shoulder.

"I want so badly to stay," he whispered.

"I want that too," I stammered. My heart ripped in two.

I felt a tear fall on my shoulder, and I stared at Danny. It was his face that was wet, not mine.

"You're crying," I said softly, and I tenderly wiped his tears away.

Danny was embarrassed.

"Don't tell anyone."

"Of course not. Who would believe me?" I teased.

"Remember what I said at the premiere? About us?"

"When you declared us married?"

"Exactly. Well we still are. This is just a bump. One day we'll look back at this year and, and, agree that it made us stronger. We have to believe that."

"I don't know that I can."

"I'm hurting Eli. I am so messed up. I'm spiraling downward, and I'm so scared."

"Oh, Danny." My heart went out to him. This was worse than horrible. "Are you working on you?"

"No. I've been wallowing in self-pity over hurting the only girl I've ever loved."

"That girl wants you to stop wallowing and start working," I smiled at Danny. "You need help. I'll go with you."

"I'm not ready. I have to hit bottom."

"I'm frightened, Danny. What does bottom mean?"

"Baby, I'm not going to die. I love you too much."

"You should go. This is too much for me to process."

"Would it be easier if I didn't love you?"

"I need to shower," I said ignoring Danny's question. "Feeling you on my skin is depressing. I want so badly for you to take off those jeans and get back into my bed."

"You'd hate yourself for compromising your values. I don't want that, Eli."

"Thank you for saving me from myself," I smiled weakly. "Can you please bring me my robe?" I asked.

Danny rose and brought my fluffy pink robe from the hook on the back of the door. He turned his back to me while I rose and put it on. Then I smiled and reached for his hand.

Danny pulled me into his arms. "You feel so good, Eli."

"You should go."

"What are you going to do today?"

"Bury my head in my pillow and cry," I said matter-of-factly. "How about you?"

"Go upstairs and get wasted."

"We're a great pair."

"That we are. I love you, Elizabeth. Believe that I do."

"I believe you, Daniel," I whispered.

I went up on tip-toe and pulled his face down to mine for one last passionate kiss. Danny's arms wrapped around my back and waist, pressing my body against his. My robe opened, and he grinned. I pulled it closed.

"I better go, or I'm gonna scoop you up and take you back to bed."

Then he kissed my nose, and left.

I wrapped my arms around my middle clutching tightly, trying to hold myself together. This beautiful, brilliant man loved me. This dear, sensitive man was damaged, broken really, and not able to seek the help he so badly needed. My poor Danny.

Later, I would either be on the road to permanent recovery, or I would crash. My heart-of-hearts told me that this had finally been good-bye.

CHAPTER THIRTY-SEVEN - ELIZABETH

What I enjoy most about studying in the basement stacks is the solitude it affords. Save for the occasional student engaged in research, the only noises are electrical, or the quiet padding of feet. Both easily blotted out.

Deep in concentration, footsteps startled me. They were not the quiet slow ones of a student looking for books, or the quicker, but similarly quiet steps, of a student walking toward a vacant cubicle they wanted to claim.

These footsteps were urgent, rushed as though on a mission. I could almost hear the heavy breathing of their attached body as the feet stopped not more than two or three carrels from mine.

"Chris, you'll never believe who just spoke to me!" an excited high-pitched voice exclaimed.

Oh, great! Gossip. This interuption better not last long. I had work.

"Who, Lindsay? The captain of the football team? God?"

I snickered, barely containing the laughter that fought to break loose. Donnelly didn't have a football team. I must meet this Chris. We were on the same wavelength. She seemed as annoyed by the disturbance as I was.

"Just about," Lindsay continued in a squeal. "Adonis if you ask me."

"Adonis?" Chris asked doubtfully.

"Might as well be. He's only the hottest guy in our class."

"That Adonis," Chris answered knowingly, interest peaking in her voice. "Get out of here! Why would Danny Newman speak to you? He's never even acknowledged your existence."

"I went for coffee, and he stopped me. Danny needed my notes from this morning," Lindsay explained. Then she whispered, "He said he missed class because of a hangover."

Hangover! Missed class! My stomach did unpleasant flip-flops hearing those words. Danny, what are you doing? Danny didn't miss classes. He always came to our class sober. Why was he so drunk on a Tuesday night that he couldn't get to class on Wednesday morning?

"Hungover?" Chris laughed. "That sounds about right."

I frowned, hurting at Danny's damaged reputation.

"Maybe. But what a bod!" Lindsay exclaimed. "While I sent Danny my notes, he removed his sweatshirt. His t-shirt rode up. Oh my god! Talk about six-pack abs! And his jeans hung so low…" Lindsay about swooned.

It pained me hearing Danny being discussed as though he were a piece of meat. I thought of how I enjoyed running my fingertips over his six pack. My six pack. And the top of the vee peeking from his waistband that led down to… Stop it, Elizabeth!

"So why are you down here?" Chris' voice jarred me back to reality.

"Once Danny received my notes, he left to study."

I smirked. Of course he went to study, you twit! How did they think Danny managed straight A's? Osmosis?

"Lindsay, get back up there and flirt," Chris ordered. "He's single."

My ears perked up again.

"I thought Danny lived with his girlfriend."

"Where have you been? That's so last year," Chris explained. "He split from Elizabeth after the summer. I can't blame him. She's so snobby, strutting around in designer clothes every day. She thinks she's so great because her mother's a movie star," Chris added. "Elizabeth is an ice princess. That's probably why they split. A man as hot as Danny Newman requires a girl with steam."

"Exactly," Lindsay responded with enthusiasm.

"So get back upstairs," Chris ordered. "Danny needs a new girlfriend."

I crossed my arms over my book, collapsed my head, and silently wept. What hurt more? That they discussed Danny as though he were a commodity? That Danny was getting drunk on Tuesdays now? Or the realization that girls were openly pursuing him? All three crushed me.

They called me a snob and an ice princess! Just because I wear nice clothes, clothes that Danny loves seeing me in, some of which he selected. How dare they! Clearly they were uninformed or they would know that Danny considered me the hottest girl he'd ever met. He had told me as much often enough, including after making love to me only three days ago.

"Elizabeth?" a male voice whispered.

I lifted my head to meet Shane's kind face.

"Elizabeth, what's wrong?"

Shane registered concern. His eyes bounced from my wet cheeks to the tear stains on the open page of my book.

"Shane. I'm okay," I answered meekly.

"No you're not. Speak to me, Elizabeth. What's wrong?"

Shane pulled the desk chair from the next cubicle over and sat down. Now we were eye-to-eye, and he reached for my hands. With tear filled eyes, I told him what I overheard.

"I'm scared, Shane. Why is Danny so drunk on a Tuesday that he can't get out of bed on Wednesday?"

"I don't know. We're buddies, but Danny doesn't let me into his head. Cam and I try to keep an eye on him, but we can't be with him every moment of the day. We have lives too."

I flushed, embarrassed. "Of course you do. I didn't mean to imply."

Shane nodded. "You and Danny have been impossible since your split.

It's very difficult for us."

"Why does everyone assume that we broke up?" I asked.

"Because you used to be inseparable, and now you're apart. When was the last time you and Danny were together, or even spoke to each other?"

"It's been a while," I lied. I refused to tell Shane that Danny and I had spent Saturday night together even if this knowledge would boost my argument. It was not Shane's business.

"But that doesn't mean we split up. Not forever."

"It doesn't? Then what does it mean, Elizabeth?'

"We're on a hiatus," I explained, using Danny's phrase. "Danny has some issues to work out, and he wants to do it without me."

"And when he does, you'll live happily ever after?" Shane asked caustically.

"Something like that," I said triumphantly.

"Do you know how delusional you sound?"

"Danny loves me. He told me so."

"When was that, Elizabeth?" Shane gently asked.

"A while ago," I hated admitting.

"Elizabeth, I'm you're friend. You have to know, Danny's changed."

"He would tell me if he didn't love me anymore. Danny doesn't lie to me." I was aware that I sounded like a petulant child.

Shane gathered me in his arms like the brother I desperately needed.

"Oh, Elizabeth," he murmured. I began crying again.

"He does love me, Shane. Danny and I, we're life partners. This is just a hiccup," I told him aping Danny's phrasing again.

"Elizabeth, you're crying, and you're miserable. Danny's wasted most nights, and he sometimes spends them with other girls. Get a divorce. This marriage is killing you, honey."

I hated crying all over Shane. It was humiliating, but I couldn't stop. His words hurt me all over again. How dare Shane tell me to get a divorce! And what girls was he talking about? I'd seen Danny with Phoebe. She was a slut, and Phoebe was singular, not plural, like Shane had put it.

Lifting my face from Shane's shoulder, I wiped my eyes with my hand.

"You okay now?"

Biting my lip I nodded, 'yes,' and searched for a tissue in my totebag. After finding a wrinkled one, I dabbed at my eyes and cheeks.

"Shane," I had to ask, "Am I an ice princess? That girl said Danny and I split because I was an ice princess and he wanted someone hotter."

Shane burst into uninhibited laughter. In the acoustics of the stacks, his loudness carried, echoing off the metal shelves. A nearby student popped her head out of her cubicle and glared. Chris?

"Sorry," Shane laughed in apology to her. "Elizabeth, you an ice princess? They obviously don't know you. As you're former roommate, I can attest that Mrs. Danny Newman is the farthest thing from an ice princess that there is. When you and Danny are together there's always fire in the room."

"Liz?"

I turned at the sound of a soft male voice as I exited the restroom. Scott's warm brown eyes and dimpled smile made me smile, no easy task. I had just splashed water on my face to clear my tear-stained cheeks after my conversation with Shane.

There was an innate kindness about Chloe's high school friend that after only one meeting I already found appealing. I didn't even mind that Scott had called me, "Liz," a name I had rarely been called.

I detested being called, "Liz." That hard "z" sound had always grated on my ear and was why I had gone by the softer "Leelee" when I was a child. But when Scott called me Liz, it didn't sound so bad. It sounded nice, actually.

"Scott? What brings you to the dungeon?" I asked in an attempt at humor.

Scott held up the book he was carrying. "Finding material for my History of World Religions class."

I noted the impressive girth of the black cloth volume. "A little light reading, I see," and I arched an eyebrow.

Scott smiled at my humor, and and flipped to the last page. "Sort of. It's only 732 pages."

"That's light?" I laughed.

Scott shrugged. Then he carefully assessed my appearance. "Are you all right?" he asked.

"I'm fine. My lens tore," I shrugged, "And I waited too long before removing it."

Scott didn't know that as soon as I was old enough I'd had Lasiks surgery. After four tortuous years of contact lenses, I never got comfortable with them.

I smiled at Scott and shrugged again. "I was in the middle of a chapter. Big mistake. I should have removed the lens then. The chapter could have waited."

Scott smiled as he realized, "Since you're at a stopping point, want to join me for a cup of coffee?"

"I don't drink coffee, but I could use a break."

CHAPTER THIRTY-EIGHT - DANIEL

"Yo, Danny."

Shane's unexpected appearance at my carrel caused me to look up from my laptop. I was reading notes from the class I had missed this morning. The manicotti I ate at dinner last night had left me up half the night retching, so I slept in to be alert for my afternoon film class.

I hoped the girl who had sent me her notes hadn't taken it seriously when I'd told her I'd missed the class because I'd been hungover. It was fun watching the geeky girl's reaction. She had tried so hard not to look shocked, it was laughable.

I had quickly thanked her for her notes and cut the conversation short before the girl had the chance to flirt and make a real fool of herself. Eli would kill me if she knew I'd played with her that way.

"What's up Shane?"

"Haven't seen you today. You all right?"

"I'm doing better. I couldn't bring myself to eat dining hall food today after last night's food poisoning."

"Food poisoning?" This was news to Shane.

"Yeah. Should have followed you and Cam and eaten the chicken last night. The manicotti nearly killed me. I spent half the night hugging the toilet."

Shane recoiled. His face soured.

"Don't sweat it. I'm fine now," I assured him.

"Danny, find me when you're ready to leave. We haven't hung out lately."

"The Cellar would be good," I suggested.

"Not tonight. I need a clear head for my computer class in the morning," Shane answered. "How about some good coffee at The Café?"

I glanced into my cup of lukewarm vending machine crap and grimaced.

"Fifteen minutes, Shane," I told him.

I took a bite of buttery pound cake followed by a large swallow of coffee. Nirvana. The Café sold Starbucks.

Shane took a gulp of coffee too, and he sat down next to me at the small bistro table. He put his cup down and picked it up again. Then he put it down. He crossed his legs then just as quickly uncrossed them. Shane's fidgets made me nervous. What gives?

"Shane, what number cup is this for you," I finally asked.

I tried keeping it light, but he was taken aback anyway.

"It's my first," Shane answered defensively while straightening his posture.

"It is? Dude, you're wired."

"Sorry." Shane paused, then hesitated. "Danny, I've tried staying out of this. I figured it's not my business, and you'd come to me if you wanted it to be. I'm only asking you now because I ran into Elizabeth earlier. She's scaring me."

"What's wrong with Eli?" I asked, sitting up straighter.

I was alarmed thinking something might be the matter with her. Then I grinned. Elizabeth had been more than fine Sunday morning. I wiped the smile off my face and replaced it with a more appropriate grimace.

"Nothing. Everything. That girl's a mess, and she said some outlandish things. I'm trying to determine if she's losing it and maybe needs help."

"What do you mean she's a mess, and she's losing it? Eli's not a mess. She's, she's Eli. She's beautiful."

"I meant emotionally, not physically. Hell, Elizabeth's gorgeous. Except when she's crying."

"Eli's crying?" I was dumbfounded. Everything had seemed settled when I left her Sunday morning. "Why was she crying?" I didn't want Eli to cry.

"Maybe because she's not with the man she loves. You are so obtuse, Newman!"

Shane's words cut to the core, stabbing me through the heart.

"I meant what set her off?"

"This time? Elizabeth overheard some girl tell her friend who has a thing for you that you're single and she should pursue you."

"It's so unfair that Eli has to be poisoned by this gossip. She knows better."

Shane let out a deep exhale, perplexed.

"Danny, if you don't want to tell me, don't, but what's the story with you and Elizabeth? You were the perfect couple. It was both beautiful and disgusting to be around. I was certain yours would be the first wedding in our group. Hell, you were living together in your own house."

"Shane! Enough!"

If he wanted to discuss Eli, I needed something more potent than coffee. My heart ached from being reminded of how great it was.

"Elizabeth's depressed, Danny," Shane began. "And you, you're almost always drunk or wasted. It's amazing seeing you sober tonight, my friend. So why'd you break up? You're both miserable without the other. Why can't you guys make things right?"

"Shane, thank you for your concern, but I'm sober most of the time."

"No, you're not. And it scares me. As much as Elizabeth's depression does."

"I'm going through some bad shit. I don't want to take Eli down."

"You already have."

"Don't say that! I love Eli. She knows it. Eli's the best thing in my life."

"Except that she isn't. You're as delusional as she is."

"Shane! Eli is my lady."

"Then why aren't you with her? You love her. She loves you. I'm missing something here, Danny." Shane was exasperated.

"I can't go into it. We didn't break up. We're on a hiatus. Eli knows I have to work on me, and I need some space."

"Space? Is that what sleeping with Phoebe is? Space?" Shane's voice was rising. "I don't think Elizabeth would see it that way."

"Shane, you were right. It's not your business," I said sharply.

I forcefully pushed back from the table, grabbed my coffee, and stomped away. I threw back the last drop, smashed the paper cup, and threw it in the trash. Shane didn't know squat!

CHAPTER THIRTY-NINE - ELIZABETH

January soon became February, and time did not heal me. The only bright spot was Scott. Without intention, we spent more and more time together. I found his dimpled smile and affable personality appealing.

I experienced no pressure when I was with Scott, and a true friendship blossomed. Scott couldn't fill the void left by Danny, but he did provide the male companionship I hadn't known I was craving.

Most important, Scott was my friend, not Danny's. Hell, I didn't even know if they'd ever met. As far as he let on, Scott knew I'd had a boyfriend named Danny, and now I didn't. Case closed. Subject never to be discussed. It lifted my heart having a friend who focused on me in the present, not my past.

Then one cold Monday evening, Scott walked me back to Berkeley Hall after we left the library. Halfway down the path, Scott smiled shyly and reached for my mitten-covered hand. Without hesitation, I let him take it. My heart fluttered nervously.

It wasn't Scott that made me nervous. During the time I'd known him I'd found Scott to be not only an intelligent young man, but he was kind, sensitive, and he genuinely cared about the world. From his travels, Scott had acquired maturity beyond his years. Scott was thoroughly decent. And he was certainly attractive.

So why be nervous? Holding hands was innocuous enough. The symbolism of what it represented frightened me. Was I ready to risk dating again? I didn't know. If I got involved with Scott, it would mean I had finally, completely, gotten over Danny. But had I? I didn't know, at least not with certainty.

I didn't even know if I wanted to be over Danny. What had kept me going all year was the belief that one day Danny and I would be back together. Would dating Scott mean I no longer held that belief? Perhaps it meant that I was now strong enough to no longer need to cling to that belief; I could now confidently go forward.

Maybe what I needed to do was just go with the flow for once. Stop overthinking everything. He was just holding my hand.

Nearing Berkeley Hall, Scott squeezed my hand. Again he smiled and I smiled back. Scott's hand felt nice. It was soft, but the strength of his grip was decidedly masculine. The warmth radiating from his fingers comforted me on this chilly evening.

Entering the dorm, Scott dropped my hand and opened the heavy front door.

"Let me walk you to your room," Scott suggested in a deferential tone.

Momentary fear gripped me. Would Scott expect to be invited in? And then what?

Scott sensed my hesitation and smiled warmly, nearly laughing and said, "Don't worry, Liz. I only want to talk."

"Thank you," I responded.

I relaxed, appreciating Scott's sensitivity.

Scott followed me into my room and closed the door. Awkward, I didn't know what to do next. My closet-sized room felt tight like a trap. Where do you sit when the only furniture is a desk chair or a bed? I nervously looked around for an answer.

I never had this dilemma when Danny entered my room. We both went for the bed. What's wrong with me? Scott was in my room, and my brain wanders to thoughts of Danny. Help! I'm pathetic.

"Let's sit," Scott suggested. "I won't bite," he teased as though reading my mind.

Scott waited for me to sit down on the edge of the bed. Then he joined me.

"Liz," he began. Then Scott took my hands. "I like you," he said.

Uncomfortable, I looked at Scott. He smiled. I didn't know how to respond. Men didn't say things like that to me.

"I like you, too," I answered with uncertainty.

"I mean, I really like you, Liz. I'd like for us to go out some time."

"I'd like that," I surprised myself by answering.

Scott exhaled, visibly relaxing. "I didn't know if you would."

I looked at Scott, uncertain of what he meant.

"Liz, you haven't discussed it, but Chloe told me about you and Danny Newman. I know you were in a serious relationship with him and I don't want to get hurt. I need you to confirm that you're over Danny."

I sat quiet, not knowing how to answer. I didn't have an answer. Yes, I did. There was only one answer; the truth.

"Scott, I like you, and I don't want to hurt you. The truth is, I don't know. I'd like to think I'm over Danny, but I won't be sure unless I do go out with you. Does that make any sense?"

Scott smiled warmly. I flushed with relief.

"You make lots of sense. I appreciate your honesty, Liz," he answered. "Let's give it a try. We'll go to a movie next Friday. How's that?"

"I'd like that," I responded.

"We'll take it slow. I won't push you, Liz."

But first I had to get through tomorrow, Valentine's Day. Despite being cheered by Scott's invitation, I cried after he left, cursing Danny for putting me in this position.

Valentine's Day! Why did it have to be Valentine's Day tomorrow? That had to be the worst possible day of the year if you were trying to get over your ex.

Thankfully it fell on Tuesday this year. Even Danny couldn't have planned too big a celebration for a holiday falling on Tuesday.

Scrap that thought. Last year, Valentine's Day fell on Monday and Danny had planned an over-the-top romantic celebration. We spent the long weekend skiing in Vermont where we stayed in a luxurious suite with wood-burning fireplaces and a two-person spa tub.

I buried my head in my pillow at the memory. This year Danny would certainly have taken me someplace even more spectacular, perhaps a private club in St. Barts. My crying became gut-wrenching sobs. I was shaking.

"Damn you, Daniel!"

I pounded the mattress with my fists before falling into a fitful sleep.

In the morning I woke and forced myself out of bed. The loneliness of Valentine's Day might have me down, but I couldn't stay in my room and mope. I had classes to attend.

Drop/Add period had passed. Stubborn beyond reason, I remained enrolled in the American Presidency class. It was getting more and more difficult to play my part. Doing the hair/make-up/wardrobe routine was easy, but I could no longer strike a confident pose and smile. That was too hard, especially today.

Was Danny affected by the date? A furtive glance across the room provided the answer. Danny was a no-show. Danny never cut Professor Denison's classes. Did that mean he couldn't bear facing me?

Danny the sentimental romantic had to hurt as much as I did. I imagined him hungover, trying to forget last year. Danny was probably waiting for the acceptable hour to get wasted in an effort not to think about what might have been. When class ended, I planned on returning to my room to mourn the day with tears.

"Elizabeth!" Rachel called out.

She and Chloe were approaching Berkeley Hall from the left side path at the same time I was approaching from the right. I waved to them and waited at the entrance.

Truthfully I didn't want them to catch up to me. I wanted to retreat to my room.

Together we entered the dorm.

"Do you have any Advil or Tylenol?" Chloe asked, a pained expression on her face. "Cramps," she moaned.

"I'm all out," Rachel answered.

"I have both," I offered.

Oh, great! I really didn't want Chloe or anyone else coming to my room. I wanted to be alone!

"Elizabeth! Delivery!" Wendy, phone plastered to her ear, nodded toward the side table covered with at least half a dozen vases of flowers. I quirked an eyebrow, confused.

"Second from the left. The pink ones," Wendy explained.

"Thank you," I answered, and I picked up the heavy vase filled with one dozen, long-stemmed pink roses.

"Who are those from?" Chloe asked, excited.

Rachel glared at Chloe. They both knew I didn't have a boyfriend.

"They're probably from Dad. He sends me flowers every year."

Rachel and Chloe followed me down the hall to my room. I paused by the door, uncertain over my next move. My hands were full with the vase, and my keycard was in the outside pocket of my small purse.

"I'll take those," Chloe offered, and I handed her the vase.

Chloe grinned at Rachel. Why was she giddy when she had cramps? Strange.

I removed my key card, opened the door, and was immediately grateful that Chloe had taken the vase. What greeted me would have made me drop the flowers.

"Oh my god!" I exclaimed. My jaw dropped open.

Rachel and Chloe laughed at my reaction. Strung across the room, horizontal, vertical, and on both diagonals were strings of cut-out cardboard hearts in red and pink.

Affixed to the window shade pull was a large pink, 3D paper heart. Tacked to my bulletin board a plastic banner proclaimed, "Happy Valentine's Day."

On my desk sat another vase, this one filled with mixed pink and white flowers. A plate held six large heart-shaped cookies iced in red. Beside them was a thick stack of cards.

Then I noticed two more vases atop the bureau. Absolutely unbelievable!

"Where did all this come from?" I exclaimed.

Chloe and Rachel were giddy from my joy.

"Happy Valentine's Day," Rachel said.

"We knew today would be difficult," Chloe explained, "So we thought let's tackle it head-on and turn it into a happy occasion."

"You guys did all this?" I was amazed by their love, and I enthusiastically embraced them. Group hug! "You're the best! How did you do this?"

Danny was the only person with a copy of my keycard. They wouldn't have enlisted his assistance.

"We lied," Chloe laughed. "And cajoled. Until Bonnie Preston-Smith let us in."

"So who sent all these flowers?" Rachel asked.

"Oh," I answered. I opened the card from the roses I'd brought from the lobby and read it. "Just as I thought. Dad," I smiled.

I opened the card from the next vase "Teddy! That's so sweet."

I never thought Teddy would send me flowers. The third vase was from Mom, and the last was from Chloe and Rachel.

"Thank you. You didn't have to. You did all this," I said indicating the room.

"It was fun," Rachel said.

"Well, thank you. This has turned out to be a great day."

The following week Professor Denison addressed the class. Applications for the student government elections had been announced. The professor explained the process for getting on the ballot for the six positions: President, Vice President, Treasurer, Secretary, and two Senators representing each class. Interested students needed to file an application, and obtain fifty signatures, twenty for Senators.

"Each year students from this class apply," the professor said. "To encourage you, I will allow all potential candidates to pass their petitions for signature during class. Understand that this does not commit you to voting for each other. It just promotes comraderie, and I expect your compliance."

Candidates could thus obtain seventeen signatures without effort.

I contemplated running. The yearbook kept me busy, but student government was different. It was more social with the officers required to attend school events. Student government would provide the kick in the butt I needed to get going again.

So I considered running for Secretary. I would be part of the team, but not leading it. Plus, unlike President and Vice President, positions often held by seniors, it was not unusual for a junior to be Secretary. My chances for winning were better than for the top of the ticket.

"What do you think?" I asked Scott while we took a break from our studies at the library that evening.

"You'd be great, Liz. You should go for it."

When I called my parents, they echoed Scott's upbeat opnion.

By the following class I finalized my decision to run, and Professor Denison was pleased to help me obtain my signatures.

Friday evening as we walked to the movie theater, Scott again voiced enthusiasm.

"I'm proud that you filed," he declared. "You're going to be a great candidate and an even better Secretary!"

Scott's energy was infectious, and by the time we entered the theater I believed victory was possible.

After purchasing the tickets, Scott and I stood on the refreshment line.

"Popcorn?" Scott aasked.

"Of course," I giggled. "What else?"

Scott laughed. "A large bucket it is."

"With butter?"

"Of course," Scott smiled. "Just not too much."

When the counter worker handed Scott the bucket, he passed it to me.

"Liz, you put the butter on while I get our drinks."

A happy grin broke out on my face. I went up on toe and kissed Scott's cheek.

"Thanks," I said cheerfully.

It was going to be an excellent evening. Unbeknownst to him, Scott had passed the popcorn test with flying colors.

The following week, Danny filed his application to run for President. If we both won, we'd be serving together, but we wouldn't take office until the following school year. Certainly by August we could tolerate each other again. Besides, it probably would never become an issue. I was confident Danny would win. My chances were less certain.

If Lindsay and Chris were any indication, Donnelly students found me snobbish and cold. In contrast, Danny was popular with everyone. Apparently for an attractive man, everything was acceptable.

Knowing that Danny loved me did not prevent a return of my depression. Nor did dating Scott. Each time I saw Danny in class, it tore me up. He would always be beautiful to me, but now he looked haggard, and the twinkle in his sapphire eyes was missing. Less biased eyes than mine would say he looked like hell.

Attending Professor Denison's class became progressively more difficult. I had to make an extra effort not to glance toward Danny. At the same time, I spent the class furtively engaged in trying to catch him looking my way. If by the end of the class Danny had not, I left feeling hurt, convinced he didn't love me anymore.

I wanted to be pursued. I wanted to feel his love again. It was important, and I no longer understood why. I had Scott. Whenever I spent time with Scott I thoroughly enjoyed myself. Scott left me happy and carefree. So why did Danny still affect me?

Through the grapevine I knew Danny was still seeing Phoebe. Nobody had told me, but my friends actively sheltered me. Rachel and Chloe had me swear to never bring up the subject in return for their promise to tell me immediately if Danny's status had changed. So far, there had been no breaking news bulletins.

What disturbed me more was the other gossip I heard, and not from Rachel or Chloe. Danny was back to hardcore partying, drinking too much too often, and getting wasted just as frequently. Why was he doing this? What was he trying to escape from?

So, much as I wanted to get over Danny and concentrate on Scott, Danny's behavior worried me, and it presented a challenging dilemma. Self-preservation, mine, not his, told me to ignore the gossip; he was of no concern to me.

Twenty years of caring could not be turned off, and that made it impossible to ignore. I knew I would intervene if it got really bad, but what defined 'really bad,' and what would I do? I was clueless.

Except for when I was with Scott, the black cloud weighed heavily on me. Some days I barely functioned. I even missed classes because I couldn't motivate myself to get up and get dressed.

Spring break was mercifully just a week away. February had opened with optimism, and then had faltered. March at least held the promise of getting away for two weeks, and returning to warmer temperatures after the break.

Danny was off to Palm Beach with Cam and Shane. I was going home with a stop in Dallas to visit Mom. Two weeks, no Danny. Yes!

CHAPTER FORTY - ELIZABETH

Officially Spring Break began as soon as my last class concluded on Thursday, but I wasn't leaving until Saturday. First stop – Dallas. Mom was on location, even working Saturdays, so it was pointless for me to arrive before late that afternoon.

I was only visiting for a few days, then on to Santa Monica. Much as we wanted to spend more time together, with Mom's schedule, it was impossible.

After I landed a car took me directly to the downtown set. Mom's workday would soon end, and she didn't want me waiting alone in the hotel. I didn't want that either. Hotel rooms got boring, fast.

It was good to be still. My stomach had felt out of sorts for most of the day. As I stepped out of the car, no longer in motion, it hadn't yet settled. "I'd better not be getting a virus," I fretted.

In recent weeks the flu had been making the rounds at Donnelly. The last thing I wanted was to be laid up during Spring Break.

As I spotted Mom stepping out of a trailer, I forced a smile. No need for her to worry. If I got sick, she would know then.

"Elizabeth!" Mom called out, excited to see me.

Mom was in costume, including stiletto-heeled pumps that seriously impeded her progress. I chuckled as she cautiously teetered while trying to hurry toward me. Accommodating her shoes, I met Mom more than half-way. The star twisting her ankle would be irresponsible.

I felt incredibly petit. In stilettos, Mom towered over me. She grabbed me by my shoulders for an arms-length hug, and an exchange of air kisses. I didn't take it personally. She was in full makeup for her next scene. A woman with a hairbrush had tailed her and was now fluffing her mane.

"My daughter, Elizabeth," Mom explained.

The woman had frowned when Mom and I embraced. I assumed she was fearful that we'd mess up her work product, and the star would be late to the next take. The star would never be blamed though it would have been no one's fault but Mom's.

At the introduction, the hairstylist's grim expression became all smiles.

"Ms. Jordan's daughter!" she gushed. "Of course! You're as lovely as your mother. If you'd like me to do your hair later…"

"Thank you," I answered. The fawning left me self-conscious.

"We're a little behind schedule," Mom explained. "One more scene and we wrap."

I nodded my understanding. Then Mom stopped in her tracks and took a good look at me. She frowned. Her brow knotted.

"You don't look well, honey. Are you alright?"

"I'm just tired from travel," I assured her.

The star must be free of worry while she is working.

"We'll talk later. Come," she beckoned.

I followed Mom to the set and watched Miranda Jordan go to work. I was in awe. Mom's talent was incredible to observe. Her nuanced performance imbued with natural realism, came effortlessly.

After a leisurely dinner in the hotel restaurant, Mom and I adjourned to her suite. The star's accommodations were fit for royalty. The sumptuous suite contained two bedrooms and three bathrooms. Apart from me, Dad had been her only guest. Once. For a three-day weekend.

"It feels so good to finally relax," I told Mom as I kicked off my shoes.

Then Mom, despite her long workday, sprang into action, opening my garment bag, hanging my clothes in the closet and putting my toiletries in the bathroom. In my state of exhaustion, I readily let Mom be a mom, taking care of me.

A large yawn escaped me.

"Elizabeth, change into your pajamas," she ordered.

I had no choice but to obey. She was Mom.

When I returned from the bathroom gripping my clothes, Mom pried them from my arms and I burst into tears.

"Elizabeth?"

Mom sat me down at the edge of the bed and held me close in her loving arms, rocking me gently while rubbing my back. Oh, Mom. I didn't blame her for being puzzled, but I couldn't confess to what had set me off. It was too embarrassing.

While changing my clothes, I realized I was wearing my own pajamas and not Danny's shirt. Afraid of Mom's reaction, I was careful to bring my own pajamas for this trip, and I left his shirt at Donnelly. Mom would have been angry, and would have accused me of not trying to get over him.

I couldn't stop crying. Even for me I was being overly emotional.

"Is this about Danny?" she asked, concerned.

I nodded 'yes.' What else would it be?

Mom smoothed my hair as she spoke. "Elizabeth, I'm worried about you, honey. I know you're hurting, but I thought by now you'd have moved on."

"I'm trying," I cried. "I'm sort of dating someone, but I'm not sure."

"You're dating someone?" Mom exclaimed.

I had never discussed Scott with her before. There seemed no point unless a relationship materialized.

"Scott's very nice. He's good-looking too. But I can't shake Danny from my heart. When I'm with Scott I'm happy, but when I'm not…" My voice tailed off. "Every day I try, but I can't. It's impossible. Danny's everywhere."

"Are you sleeping with Scott?"

I shook my head.

"Maybe you should be."

"Mom! I'm not ready."

"Oh, Elizabeth! Get over it. You're not a virgin anymore. It's not that big a deal if you like the boy."

"It is to me," I grumbled.

Mom sighed, exasperated. "I should never have let you lose your virginity to a boy you actually want to spend the rest of your life with. You've built it into something much too important."

"Sorry if I wanted love," I responded, my voice heavy with sarcasm.

"This Scott must really like you if he's willing to wait. Don't make him wait too long, Elizabeth."

"He knows about Danny. Scott's willing to go slowly."

"I never should have let you return after Christmas. Elizabeth, you'll never get over Danny as long as you're at Donnelly. You have the same friends. You live in the same dorm. It's too small. Why you take the same classes as Danny, I'll never understand. Surely you could study something else. The course catalogue is extensive."

"Danny will not intimidate me from studying what I want," I wailed.

Mom sighed loudly. "I'm glad you're going away for the summer, but Dad and I don't understand why Israel when we're not even religious." Mom sighed again. "At least it's away from Danny."

"Mom!"

"Elizabeth, Dad and I don't want you returning to Donnelly next year. Come home. Transfer to UCLA or USC."

"I don't want to be home. That's why I'm at Donnelly. To be away. Besides, I'm sure the deadlines are passed."

"Not for you. With your grades, one phone call and you're in."

"Not SC."

"Okay. Not SC. Then pick a UC. If you don't want to be near home, what about Berkeley? That's one of the best universities in the country. Or how about UCSD? La Jolla's a great town. We'll buy you a condo on the beach."

Mom was trying her best to entice me, but all it did was make me quiver, saddened by the reality caused by the demise of my love life. I felt like a failure.

"Or, I know where! Santa Barbara! You'd love it at UCSB. It's excellent academically, and it's, well it's Santa Barbara. What's not to like? And we would secure you invites to all the best parties in Montecito. You would meet the right type of boys who would be dying to fall in love with you."

"Mom! I don't want boys falling in love with me."

"Yes, you do, Elizabeth. You just don't know it yet."

"I've missed the deadlines," I pointed out, hoping that would end it. Alas, not with pig-headed Mom once she had a cause to pursue.

"Elizabeth, do you have any idea how much money Dad and I have raised for the governor over the years? Let's just say he owes us big time. Tell me which campus you want to attend, I'll phone the governor, and you're in."

And that will be that, all settled. Mom!

"I don't have to answer today, do I?"

"Of course not," Mom softened her voice. "It's a big decision. Just consider it, honey."

Thankfully Mom did not bring up the subject again.

Rachel was arriving in Los Angeles on Friday. If I transferred, how would I see her or any of my Donnelly friends? Where they too big a price for getting over Danny? Was I even ready to get over Danny? I didn't know. Perhaps Scott was the answer.

Friday morning found me gripping a baggage trolley at the luggage carousel at the American Airlines terminal at LAX. Hopefully Rachel had slept on the plane. She had taken the eight o'clock flight to maximize her vacation. If you considered time zone differences, Rachel had probably been up since one in the morning. Now I was concerned that she might crash, though I was so tired from my travels, that I might crash first.

There she was! Her dark, frizzy hair falling half-way down her back made Rachel stand out in any crowd. "Rach!" I called.

Wearing my darkest sunglasses, anxious not to be recognized, I pushed my way through the crowded baggage area to greet her.

"Elizabeth," she exclaimed. "I can't believe I'm here."

Rachel's eyes darted about, taking in the environment. We hugged each other warmly, and squeezed through the crowd to reach the front of the luggage carousel.

"How was your flight?" I asked.

Rachel shrugged. "I don't know. I slept though most of it."

Good. I was relieved. Rachel could keep up with the busy day I had planned.

Rachel's luggage came quickly enough and we steered the trolley across the sun-baked road to the parking structure. She starred at the swaying palm trees and soaked in the perfect seventy-two degree temperature.

"First stop, my parents' house," I announced, at once proud but also nervous. Would Rachel recognize it from last summer's Archetectual Digest spread? I hoped not.

Rachel was anxious to see my parents' home, which made me completely self-conscious. We would unload her luggage, and I would switch to a more appropriate car. I hated Mom's car. It screamed, "You're driving your parents' car." But not knowing how much luggage Rachel would bring, the large black Mercedes S600 with its impressive power that could easily outrun the paparazzi and had a huge trunk made sense.

"This is your house!" Rachel exclaimed in awe as we drove through the gates of Casa de Jacobs as my family lovingly referred to it.

I hadn't considered Rachel's reaction to the fortress-like environment, the car park that could easily accommodate eight cars, or the generally over-sized proportions of the house, but there she was, gawking. Until last summer I had always lived here, and my friends had grown up here too. To me it was simply home.

Flora carried Rachel's luggage up to my room. Meanwhile, I gave Rachel a tour. With her eyes wide as saucers as I showed her around the first floor, Rachel didn't understand how awkward this was for me. I smiled pleasantly to keep her from knowing, Then we entered the kitchen.

"My god! The size of this kitchen!" she exclaimed. Yes, it's large.

I cringed, forced to explain, "It's a kosher kitchen. There's two of everything."

I omitted the part about the space required by the caterers we hired at least a few times every year for my parents' elaborate gatherings.

"Miranda Jordan keeps kosher?" she gaped.

"So do I, when I'm home," I answered, though a bit of an exaggeration. I enjoyed the shrimp Danny grilled on the patio too much. If we kept shellfish in the outdoor refrigerator only, the kitchen would still be kosher, wouldn't it? Hmmm, I'd have to ask Grandma Margie. She was the expert on all things Jewish.

Mom keeping kosher often surprised people. Why did nobody react when it was revealed that a glamorous star was a strict Christian, but an observant Jew was shockingly unheard of? I frowned. At home, Mom was not Miranda Jordan. She was Mrs. Michael Jacobs, a Jewish Santa Monica wife and mother of two.

"Grandma was raised orthodox," I explained. Then I reached for two pieces of fruit from a bowl. "Have a peach," I said, and I handed one to Rachel.

After completeing the brief tour I announced, "Let's go."

There was plenty of time to get to our lunch reservation, but I needed a car. I was desperate to ditch Mom's, and I had been disappointed to find no other cars parked at the house. Where was my BMW328?

"What's wrong with this car?" Rachel asked.

I could understand her confusion. It was top-of-the-line, but it wasn't me. It wasn't how I wanted to show Rachel L.A. I grabbed a set of keys from my desk drawer and smiled mischievously. I knew exactly which car I wanted, and where to get it.

The Newman house was only a short drive. When I turned left at the Allenford Avenue traffic light, Rachel asked, "Where are we going?"

"To get my car," I answered. "It's at the Newman's."

"We're going to…"

"Steve and Ellen's," I cut Rachel off before she uttered Danny's name.

"Why is your car there?"

I understood Rachel's confusion. Most families didn't share cars the way the Jacobs and Newmans did.

"This is Danny's house!" Rachel exclaimed when we arrived at the Newman's home on upper North Kentner a short time later.

"No, this is his parents' house. Danny's house is in Malibu."

"Right. With you. Except that you haven't spoken to each other in months. And you're dating Scott."

Rachel shook her head in frustration. I rolled my eyes, ignoring her comment.

Rachel was awestruck when I pressed the security code for the ornate ironwork gates to open. The opulent 35,000 square foot Tuscan villa dwarfed my parents' home in both size and opulence. Though still quite spacious, my parents low-key Mediteranean exuded warmth and hominess. My parents weren't ostentatious like Steve. He insisted on doing everything larger than life, and Ellen eagerly embraced her husband's desires.

Ellen must have seen us on the security monitors, because she threw open the massive front doors as we climbed out of the Mercedes.

"Elizabeth!" she cried out.

"Ellen!" I shrieked as I ran to her welcoming arms, and we warmly embraced. "This is Rachel Bergman," I said to Ellen.

"Nice to meet you, Mrs. Newman."

"Call me Ellen, dear. With Daniel always talking about you, it's as though we've already met." Then Ellen grinned. "There's only one girl Daniel talks about more than you, and we all know who that is."

"I doubt he's said anything about me in a long time, Ellen," I said sadly.

"Then you'd be surprised."

"I would be," I answered.

"Elizabeth, when are you and Daniel getting back together? This split is killing me."

"I'm sorry for the inconvenience, Ellen. I doubt we're ever getting back together. Danny doesn't have any interest in a relationship with me. If he did, well he knows where to find me."

"You know where to find him too, dear."

"I can't. Danny knows my bottom line," I answered sadly.

"What do you think, Rachel?"

"The truth?"

"Yes, of course. Daniel says you can always count on Rachel to give you her real opinion, so don't ask unless you want it." I smirked at his accuracy.

Rachel paused, and looked directly at Ellen, and then me. "I think I was a very happy camper last week in Westport where no one has ever heard of Elizabeth Jacobs or Danny Newman. For the first time in months nobody asked me about them."

"Oh dear," Ellen answered, clearly taken aback.

"Ellen, Rachel is sick of being put in the middle."

"I understand. It must be difficult, Rachel."

"It is," Rachel answered politely.

"Elizabeth, what does bring you girls here?" Ellen asked, changing the subject.

"I need a car."

Ellen smiled. "Of course," she said, and she led us toward the front three-car garage. There was a second garage in the back.

Ellen pushed a button on the security control panel. The garage doors opened revealing a glossy, silver, seven series BMW sedan, a white convertible BMW328, and a convertible Porsche Carrera, shiny black and showroom clean.

"Your car's right here," Ellen nodded toward the BMW328.

"I want my other car," I smiled, a mischievous glint in my eyes.

"Elizabeth!"

Ellen looked at me in disbelief. She understood.

"I have the keys," I said slyly.

I removed the keys to the Porsche from my purse, and dangled them.

"Elizabeth, if you take that car, what will I tell Danny?"

"Nothing. Tell him absolutely nothing," I said arrogantly. "He's not going to ask. Besides, I'm allowed to drive it. Who do you think gave me the key?"

With the top down, the Carerra roared eastbound along Sunset Boulevard toward Beverly Hills and our luncheon at the Polo Lounge.

"I can't believe Danny owns a car like this, and drives it only during vacations!"

"Sweet, huh? Lucky us, he's not home." I laughed, enjoying the ride as I whipped around the curves, and Rachel gripped the dashboard.

"And his car at school is also ridiculously expensive, and he can't use it half the year because of snow. Absolutely incredible. Danny has got to be the most spoiled person in American. And to you this is normal?"

"It's normal if you're Danny."

"And you're enjoying every moment of this joy ride," Rachel said in frustration.

"I certainly am. To paraphrase Shakespeare, 'Hell hath no fury like a rich girl scorned by an even richer boy,'" I laughed. "Sometimes I love my life."

I smiled at Rachel's frown as I whipped around another curve, pleased that the traffic was unusually light.

Arriving at the Beverly Hills Hotel, the attentive valets opened the doors to the Carerra for us.

"Welcome back, Miss Jacobs. Are you dining with us, or checking in?"

"We're dining. Thank you," I smiled sweetly to the attractive young valet.

Out of earshot Rachel asked, "He knows you?"

"No. It's his job. He's paid to recognize me. Besides, he'll want me to put in a good word with my father when he pitches his screenplay."

"He's writing one? How do you know?"

"Every valet in Los Angeles is a writer, unless they're an actor."

We walked through the opulent lobby to reach the entrance of the iconic Polo Lounge.

"Good afternoon, Miss Jacobs," the attractive blonde maitre'd greeted me.

"Good afternoon," I pleasantly replied, my head held aloft.

I sensed Rachel looking around, taking it all in, scanning the faces of the other diners for familiarity. That was exactly why I had selected the Polo Lounge. Welcome to Hollywood, Rachel!

"Your table is ready," the maitre'd informed me, and she led us out to the garden to a prime table with an umbrella to keep us shaded from the sun.

"Thank you," I smiled, and while shaking the maitre'd's hand, I slipped her $20.

"Do you come here often?" Rachel asked.

"Not too often. I was probably here last summer."

"Let me guess. She gets paid to recognize you."

I shrugged and smiled mischievously.

After lunch, I gave Rachel the obligatory tour of Beverly Hills. Wonder filled her eyes as we strolled Rodeo Drive and passed the world-famous boutiques.

Gucci's window stopped me in my tracks. There was the sweater I'd fallen in love with in the pages of the latest issue of Vogue. In person, I loved it more.

"Come. We're going in," I declared. "I must get that sweater."

Rachel rolled her eyes as I dragged her through the doors. "Someday, Rachel will get over her rebellious grunge stage and enjoy shopping as she should," I thought.

"Would you like to try the trousers we're showing it with?" the salesman asked.

The skin-tight leather jeans pared with the sweater were stunning, but oddly I hesitated.

"I don't know that I have any place to wear them. I'm a student." I studied the outfit a bit longer. "Danny would die if I wore these," I mused.

"Yes, but you're not with him anymore," Rachel snapped back, and I frowned.

"I'll just try the sweater," I said with confidence that masked my sadness.

The sweater fit perfectly. The pants would have been divine.

"I'll put it on this," I told the salesman as I took out an American Express Black Card, and handed it to him.

Eagle-eyed Rachel noted the name on the card. "That's Danny's. How can you charge a sweater to him?" she scolded.

"He'd want me to. Danny likes me to wear the latest styles."

"But you're not talking to him."

I shrugged. If Danny were with me instead of Rachel, he'd be buying me the sweater. Hell! He'd have insisted on the leather pants too. And shoes and a purse, and... And I would have said, "yes" because if I were with Danny, I'd have someplace to wear them.

The salesman returned with the sweater, now wrapped, the card, and the receipt for me to sign. I smiled at Rachel, shrugged, and quickly signed for the purchase.

"Incredible! You charged a Gucci sweater to Danny without even asking," Rachel exclaimed once we were outside again.

"Danny loves to spoil me," I answered. "He wants me to always look my best."

While Rachel unpacked her suitcase, I snuck down the hall to my parents' room. If she knew I was calling Gucci, she would kill me. But I had to have those pants.

"It's Elizabeth Jacobs," I said when the salesman was reached.

"Charge it to the same card," I told him. "Excellent. I'll have my driver pick it up tomorrow."

Step one accomplished. Now for step two. I placed another phone call.

"Hi Daddy! Can Armando do a pick up at Gucci for me tomorrow?"

Later, I found myself yawning, barely able to stay awake while Rachel and I enjoyed a movie in the twelve-seat screening room after dinner.

"You have your own theater," Rachel had exclaimed when we entered. I shrugged. Why was she surprised?

"Want some popcorn?" I offered.

CHAPTER FORTY-ONE - ELIZABETH

Was it really ten o'clock already? But there sat Rachel, wide-awake in bed the next morning, and reading a book.

"Sorry," I sheepishly apologized.

"You were out for eleven hours. Are you all right?"

"I'm fine. I didn't sleep well in Dallas," I answered.

I really was fine. Once I thought about it, I realized my body had finally recovered from months of poor sleep.

We hurriedly pulled ourselves together, getting ready for the day.

"I can't wait to show you our house," I squealed as we headed north on Pacific Coast Highway in my white BMW 328 with the top down.

It was a perfect day in Malibu with plenty of sunshine and the temperature hovering near seventy.

"Are you sure about this?" Rachel sounded concerned.

"Of course. It's my home," I answered smugly.

Rachel gave me a sidewards glance that told me she believed otherwise.

"Okay. Maybe," I backtracked. "We'll know when I get there."

Truthfully, I couldn't predict how I would react until I opened the door. If Rachel wasn't visiting, I wouldn't be here. Or perhaps Rachel was an excuse. I wanted so badly to see my home. My home; Danny's home.

"We need to buy food," I said as I turned into the Malibu Colony Plaza. "Let's hope Graci emptied the frig," I laughed.

The thought of any food remaining sickened me. The house had been vacant since August.

Rachel's eyes darted around as we walked through the parking lot.

"Even strip malls are nicer here," she remarked.

"I guess," I laughed.

What fun it was watching Rachel! Her eyes surveyed the scene, while her body tried its best at nonchalance.

"Before we go to Ralph's, I need to stop at the bank for cash."

When we entered the branch, instead of using the ATM, I approached a teller. I wanted to confirm the balance. Before I used the joint account, I needed to know if Danny had written any large checks.

"The balance on this account is $97,587.23," the teller informed me.

What? "Are you sure?" I exclaimed.

According to my check register, I should have only about twenty-two thousand in the account. When had seventy-five thousand dollars been added?

"Something wrong?" Rachel asked.

"No, the opposite. $75,000 has been added to my account."

"I wish someone would add $75,000 to my account," Rachel gripped.

"Would you please tell me when the last deposit was made?" I asked the teller.

After a few quick keystrokes she replied, "It was transferred internally from another account."

Then she turned the computer for me to see the entry on the screen. There it was! I noted the amount and date of the transfer in my registry.

"Thank you," I said cheerfully. Then I cashed a check for five hundred dollars.

"Why do you care?" Rachel asked when we left the bank. "I don't understand why you'd want to use this account," she persisted.

"When we opened it, Danny said it was for the house or anything I wanted if I was north of Topanga. Anything."

"You haven't spoken in months. How can you keep spending Danny's money?"

I didn't have a good answer. Rachel would berate the joy this tenuous connection to Danny gave me.

Instead, "He wants me to," I answered.

"Right. Telepathy. Danny told you?" Rachel asked sarcastically.

"Pretty much so."

"I don't get it. You and Danny haven't spoken in months. Did he send you a text message?"

I shook my head. "Rach, do you remember Danny's birthday?"

"Yeah. We took him to dinner, and afterwards there was that colossal hall party," Rachel recited. Then she paused for a beat. "Danny was miserable because you weren't there."

"Danny wasn't miserable when I saw him."

"When you saw him?" Rachel's eyes opened wide. "You weren't at the party."

"Danny missed me. He came to my room."

"He what!?" Rachel was dumbfounded.

"The next morning Danny wanted to stay but I wouldn't let him."

"Whoa! Hold on a minute. You spent the night together! In January? Then why aren't you together?" Rachel raised her voice.

"Danny's not ready to give me what I need, so I told him to leave."

"Because he still won't commit. Yeah, yeah, we know this already. But you slept with him!" Rachel's voice grew even louder.

"Rachel!" I exclaimed. Her insolence annoyed me. "I never told you this because, well I know how you are. You're like, like this. Anyway, before he left, Danny told me he still loved me."

"Of course he did," she said cynically. "He'd just spent the night with you."

"Rachel! That's not why."

"I'm sure in his own warped Danny way he does love you."

"Danny was sincere. He doesn't consider us split. He insists this is only a hiatus."

"And that's why you haven't slept with Scott. Oh lordy, help me!"

"Rachel!"

"Elizabeth, that was two months ago. And you're still not talking to each other."

"Don't remind me," I said sadly.

"I'm sorry, Elizabeth," Rachel relented. "I'm being insensitive. So why do you think Danny wants you to use that account?"

"The deposit. It was made the next day," I said proudly.

"Wow! So that must make you the highest paid hooker in America. Seventy-five thousand dollars for one night. I doubt Julia Roberts even made out that well in Pretty Woman."

"Rachel!"

I was appalled by her analogy. She knew damned well how much I loved Danny.

"It's not like that! This is Danny's way of saying he doesn't want me moving out, and he still wants to take care of me. He knew I was coming home for Spring Break."

"I give up!" Rachel said in frustration. "Let's buy some food already."

"Fine. But tomorrow we're going shopping. Malibu has great boutiques."

"And let me guess, Danny wants to buy you new clothes."

"And you too. You're our guest."

"Amazing!" Rachel exclaimed when I gave her a tour of the first floor.

"I want to redo the kitchen."

"Why? It's lovely."

"Danny says after graduation I can do whatever I want, even gut it. I want to expand it and build a kosher kitchen like Mom has, except not as large."

Why didn't Rachel get it? The way you made a house your home was to renovate. Everyone knew that.

Rachel stopped by the couch and studied the mural.

"Is that?"

"Yeah, that's us," I completed her thought.

"It's nice."

"Thanks. I had it commissioned last summer. The artist almost didn't finish in time, but he made it. I had it installed just before Danny returned. I wanted so badly to surprise him."

My eyes filled with tears that I successfully blinked away. The memory of Danny's lack of interest saddened me. That should have been the first clue that something was amiss. Instead I had ignored it, attributing his indifference to exhaustion.

"Let me show you around upstairs," I offered.

I had to get my focus off the mural. It's reminder of a future spent with Danny, one filled with love and promise, depressed me.

First I showed Rachel the two smaller bedrooms and told her which had been mine when I was a child. Then I lead her down to the other end of the hall and threw open the double-doors.

"And this is our room," I proudly announced.

Rachel followed me into the spacious master suite. I watched as her eyes darted around the room, and then slowly returned to examine the furnishings more closely.

"This is beautiful. Everything's so white," she exclaimed in awe.

Then Rachel focused on the view. Her eyes lit up, and she walked rapidly toward the wall of glass. I was pleased to find the white-painted wooden vertical blinds pulled to one side, fully revealing the magnificent Pacific. Thank you, Graci.

Rachel slid open the door and strode out onto the balcony. She stared at the horizon while leaning against the rail, and I watched as she breathed in the salty air.

"Amazing," I heard her murmur.

Rachel came back in, grinning.

"I can't imagine waking up to that view every morning. And you even have a fireplace," she exclaimed. "No wonder you and Danny love it here."

It wasn't the view that I loved. Rather, the allure of the man snuggled next to me made this bedroom amazing. My heart sank. I blinked hard to keep back the tears that threatened.

Maybe showing Rachel Malibu was a mistake. All it did was depress me. My mind drifted to endless nights with Danny. I even felt the warmth of his arms around me.

My eyes lighted on the small, crystal Tiffany box sitting on the table untouched for all these months. I crossed the room and opened it. Inside I found my gold hoop earrings carved in a filigree of roses. I delicately removed one earring from the box, and lovingly fingered it, lost in memory.

"What's that?" Rachel asked.

"Earrings. Grandma Frankie gave them to me for my sixteenth birthday."

As I answered, I lifted my gaze, and that's when I saw it. The lone white rose made of silk, in full bloom as always, stood straight in the otherwise empty vase. I began to shake. My stomach knotted up, and my eyes filled with tears. This was too much. Gut-wrenching sobs overtook me. I collapsed into the small white chair beside the table.

"Elizabeth?" Rachel was instantly at my side.

I lifted the rose and cradled it to my chest.

"What is that?"

"The night we moved in," I sniffled, "Danny had bouquets of roses everywhere, including a dozen of the freshest white roses. The buds were so tight. And in the middle was this one."

"It's silk, isn't it?"

"Yes. Danny said it symbolized our love. It would never die."

Sobbing wracked me again. Rachel hugged me as a sister would.

"He really said that?" she asked in a gentle voice.

"Yes," I whimpered, "and the next morning after breakfast we went to the bank, and he opened that account."

"You never told me."

"I never had the chance. Everything unraveled so quickly once we returned to Donnelly."

"What the hell happened to him in Vancouver?" Rachel mused.

"I don't know. That's what kills me. Danny won't tell me. All he says is that he's going through a bad time, but he won't discuss it. You know all that."

"It was a rhetorical question, Elizabeth."

I returned the rose to the vase and pictured a day when it would once more be surrounded by real ones. "What's the point?" I thought, and I sighed.

"Rach, let's change and get to the beach."

Once Rachel left the room, I opened the door to the nearly empty closet to find a bathing suit. I stopped in my tracks. It was unhealthy. I knew I shouldn't, but I couldn't help myself. It was unbearable, the side of the closet where Danny's clothing hung, preserved in time.

There weren't more than a dozen items, but there they were; t-shirts, light-weight cotton button-down shirts, and several brightly colored Tommy Bahamas. I smiled, picturing Danny wearing them; Malibu dress shirts.

I lovingly fingered my favorite, a cotton chambray that made Danny's sapphire eyes pop when he wore it. I hugged it as though my love was wearing it now. The shirt was soft, wonderfully masculine.

Tears spilled down my cheeks as my nose detected the faint scent of Danny's cologne, faded after so many months. How I missed him! I continued hugging the shirt.

"I love you," I whispered to it.

"Are you sure about this?" Rachel asked when I told her my old room would be hers for the night. "I can sleep on the couch. I don't want to make a mess for you."

"Don't be ridiculous," I laughed. "That's why we have guest rooms. Besides, it will give Graci something to do this week."

"You have a housekeeper even though no one's living here? Unbelievable."

"It's good for security," I explained, "And nothing ever gets dusty."

Now as I tossed and turned, I was glad all over again that I had insisted on Rachel taking the guest room. This room and this bed, they were filled with too many memories.

Every time I turned, I expected Danny's strong arms to capture me with their love. Soft fingertips should be gently sweeping my hair to the side. I expected to find Danny's toes playfully teasing mine beneath the warm blanket. I expected his handsome face and killer blue eyes to be resting upon his pillow. I expected his lips to devour mine.

I turned to face the other direction. My insides felt hollow. Grief consumed me. I openly wept. I missed Danny so much.

"I want my life back!"

I punched the pillow and more tears came. Emptiness consumed me in a way that I had not experienced in months. Without Danny beside me, I couldn't sleep in this bed. Without Danny, this wasn't my home.

Careful not to wake Rachel, I silently padded down the stairs, carrying a pillow in my arms. I flicked on the television, immediately lowered the volume, and settled on the Food Network. A rerun of "Chopped" should do the job.

Setting the volume low enough that I could fall asleep, but still loud enough that I didn't strain to hear it until I did fall asleep, I made myself comfortable on the couch. I placed my pillow just so, and set the television timer for the maximum two hours.

Pulling the chenille blanket around me felt cozy, but I was quickly consumed with the woven in memories of Danny and I down on the beach making love on that blanket. Tears spilled again as I gripped the chenille tight, hoping to glimpse a scent of long-ago.

It was time to let go and move on. I didn't want to, but I had to. When a blanket makes you cry, when you can't sleep in your own bed, it's time … Was this why Rachel hadn't protested my suggestion to stay the night? A brilliant strategy forcing me to face the reality I had been denying.

Chef Amanda Freitag speculating over the appropriate use of a marinade was the last thing I remembered before finally succumbing to sleep.

"What are we doing?" Rachel demanded.

She had a valid point. We had already been through the Country Mart without buying anything, and now I dragged her to the Lumberyard. Rachel groaned. She hated shopping.

"I have to get something, Rach. It's spring."

I frowned. Nothing seemed right today.

"Elizabeth, you can't force it. If you really don't find anything you love."

"I'll write a check," I told the sales girl at the next boutique.

Finally I had found some clothes to buy. So what if it wasn't really clothes. Lorna Jane sold the cutest shorts and yoga wear in cheerful Australian colors. The tees and tanks with their encouraging slogans were just what my psyche needed; inspiration splashed against a backdrop of pink, orange, and lime. I even bought two for Rachel. Actually Danny purchaesd them.

"We're north of Topanga Canyon," I reminded a scowling Rachel. "Danny wants to buy these," I insisted again. "Otherwise he wouldn't have deposited more money into our account."

Rachel wasn't aware of the life-changing decision I had made at two o'clock this morning. This was the last time I would use this account. I had no plans to be north of Topanga Canyon again.

Leaving the house had shattered me. While Rachel waited in the car, for the last time I brought my fingertips to my lips, moistened them with a kiss, and delicately touched the happy Danny depicted on the wall.

"Good-bye," I said to the mural with finality.

I trembled with emotion. Living in this house had brought me such joy. Now that was over. My heart ached from the unbearable loss. No matter what Danny had said to me in January, I now understood that our love story was over. Time to face reality and move on, Elizabeth. Time to concentrate on Scott and give him the chance he deserved. Scott was a good man.

Distracted by the finality of the transaction, I handed the salesgirl my check, which she studied carefully. Then she looked at me and smiled shyly.

"I'm a music major at Pepperdine," the young woman explained. "I love your father-in-law's compositions. Is he scoring anything new," she asked.

"Huh?" I responded. What was she talking about?

The girl blushed, embarrassed. "I'm sorry," she said. "I shouldn't have assumed. You're not one of the music Newmans, I guess."

I enjoyed the recognition the Newman name received, but I felt bad for her. This had happened before. The musical Newmans also lived in the Westside coastal communities.

"No, not music. We're the Steven Newmans," I explained to make her feel better.

Sadness threatened me again. When I was stronger I would mail the checkbook back to Danny. Never again would anyone mistake me for being a Newman.

"Oh," the girl's face lit up, even more impressed. "I can't wait to see his latest film when it opens. It's getting great buzz. Vanessa Rogers! Don't you love her? Steven Newman casts the best actors every time," she gushed.

"What was that about?" Rachel asked as we walked to the car.

"Mistaken identity."

CHAPTER FORTY-TWO - ELIZABETH

Glammed for clubbing, me in a scandalously short skin-tight emerald dress, and Rachel, more staid in a less form-fitting basic black, we left the house pumped for a night on the strip.

A long foreboding line in front of the club, filled with young, attractive, well-dressed people waiting to be granted admission dampened Rachel's spirits.

"We should go elsewhere," Rachel said. "It could be midnight before we get in."

"You're with me, Rach. We don't stand on line," I said with a touch of arrogance as I pulled up to the valet. Opening my door his mouth momentarily dropped. The valet stared at my face, then my legs, considerably lengthened by the short dress and Louboutain stilettos. I smiled sweetly, as though I dressed like this every day.

"We'll take good care of your car Miss Jacobs," said the eager young man.

"Thank you," I answered sweetly.

With an impressed Rachel in tow, I confidently approached the well-dressed, muscular bouncer at the door.

"Good evening, Miss Jacobs," he greeted me, and the red velvet rope was lifted, granting us admission to the club.

Once inside, a slender young woman with perfect blonde hair hanging halfway down her back, the longest legs I'd ever seen extending from an even minier than mine mini-skirt, and expertly applied make-up, escorted us to the roped off VIP section. Rachel's attempt at nonchalance was an epic failure. I couldn't help giggling, and thankfully she laughed too.

"You're in my town, Rach," I chuckled as I stopped to check the crowd.

The VIP section was filled with members of the young Hollywood elite; those who were famous in their own right, and those like me, the children and siblings of the famous. Everyone wore the latest designer styles, and there were more attractive young women than at a beauty pageant. The staff, equally attractive were likely aspiring actors hoping to connect with the exclusive clientele.

"Over there," I said to Rachel, and I led her through the crowd to the table where Grant Barnes, the English-speaking world's hottest young actor was seated.

"Hey Grant," I said, and I leaned down to kiss the handsome superstar's cheek, rough with three-day stubble.

"It's Lizzie J!"

Grant greeted me with his trademark British accent that made most women melt. Not this woman. I was immune to his boyish charms. When you've seen a disheveled man standing in your yard wearing nothing but boxers, and having a nicotine fit at seven in the morning; it turned me off for life.

Grant rose, and we exchanged warm hugs and kisses.

"This is Rachel. She's visiting from Connecticut."

"This is Luke," Grant said, indicating the attractive young man seated beside him. "He's my entourage for the evening. Luke's visiting from Los Feliz," he smirked

We laughed at Grant's teasing, as did Luke.

"Lizzie J, where's your man?" Grant asked as we sat down.

"Florida," I answered while trying to sound casual about it. "Where's Courtney?"

Grant recently shared that he was secretly dating his former co-star. Like Mom, Courtney Sullivan was a rarity. She had survived the pitfalls of childhood fame, and at twenty, Courtney appeared to be making a successful transition to an adult career.

"Court's in New York, and your man's in Florida. Why didn't he take you with him? You're ravishing in a bikini. I've seen you."

"Thanks, Grant," I answered with a smile.

Rachel stared. Most women would die to get a compliment from Grant Barnes. I took it in stride.

"We're having marital problems," I explained.

"Nice euphemism," Rachel said, but I ignored her.

"No divorce, I hope. I liked Mr. Steven Newman's kid."

I rolled my eyes at Grant's description. Clearly he'd forgotten Danny's name since the one time they'd met last year.

"Danny. His name is Danny, Grant."

Grant raised his martini glass.

"Well, here's to you and Danny patching things up. I want to see a smile on your face the next time we meet."

Rachel's joy as we danced with Grant and Luke pleased me. It was her vacation, and I wanted it to be a memorable one. Even I had fun for once. I could understand how girls easily fell for Grant's casual British charm and manners. I wished I could run into Grant every night.

Time passed quickly. We had been at the club for at least a few hours when Grant said, "I've got to get back to the Chateau, Lizzie J. I'm due at ADR tomorrow morning."

With Courtney in New York, Grant had decamped to the Chateau Marmont, one of Hollywood's favorite hotels. With his girlfriend's house often staked-out by the paparazzi, their relationship would be a secret no longer if he stayed there.

"We'll walk out with you."

With Grant leaving, the night would go downhill from here.

Grant glanced around the room, studying the crowd, and strategizing the best way out.

"How am I going to escape?" he mused.

"I have an idea."

I whispered a plan in Grant's ear, and he smiled mischievously.

"I like it," Grant exclaimed. "If you weren't already married, I could want you."

I laughed at the words most women would die to here. Maybe it was time to leave the Newman world and join the human race. Then I'd feel free to pursue Grant like everyone else did. I even had an advantage; pre-existing friendship.

Rising from our table, Grant took my hand while Luke accompanied Rachel. Women stared at Grant as we pushed our way through the crowd. They glared at me, jealous. It was exactly what he wanted.

When we reached the door, Grant wrapped his arm around my shoulder, and held me close, just as we'd planned.

"Let's give the paparazzi something to talk about," I said.

Grant and I exchanged mischievous grins. Club security pulled open the door, and we walked out, appearing to be a happy couple extending the evening.

When we reached the photographer filled street I leaned into Grant for a passionate kiss. This had been better as a plan. Kissing Grant without grimacing was difficult. Our plan called for me to act crazy in lust. But the hottest man on earth tasted like a chimney! Gross! I hadn't considered Grant's noxious cigarette habit.

"Rach, go with Luke. We'll meet you at the Chateau," I explained as Grant and I got into my car with camera flashes going off all around us.

After reuniting with Rachel and Luke at the Chateau Marmont, Grant and I shared one more kiss, just in case any photographers had followed us.

"Lizzie J," Grant said in a dreamy voice, "You've grown up. You can kiss me like that anytime. To hell with Mr. Steven Newman's kid and Courtney."

I smiled at Grant, flattered by his compliment.

"Grant," I said as we dropped hands, "You don't stand a chance with me unless you stop smoking."

"Yeah," Grant grinned. "I'll work on it."

As he opened the car door for me, Grant and I exchanged knowing smiles, pleased for different reasons that our plan had worked. But how would this ultimately play out?

Rachel and I spent the next few days playing tourist. While initially a reluctant participant, somewhere on the freeway to Anaheim Rachel began singing, "Yo-ho, yo-ho, a pirate's lfe for me," in her laughable off-key voice. I forced myself to get with the program.

"You can't be grumpy at Disneyland unless you're a dwarf," Dad had said as we left the house ridiculously early to beat the traffic.

Rachel had never been to the original, "happiest place on earth," and I delighted in being her guide, until…

"Splash Mountain! C'mon," Rachel exclaimed, and I blanched.

I hate that ride! I despise all rollercoasters.

"I'll wait for you at the exit," I said.

"You won't go on it?"

I couldn't tell if Rachel was angry or in shock.

"I hate that sinking feeling you get on the steep drops," I answered sheepishly, "And my legs feel like spaghetti when I get off."

"Chicken," Rachel sneered, "You're going." A Rachel order was not to be disobeyed, and she dragged me to the ride.

I learned that by screaming on the plunges, I didn't get that sinking feeling, and I actually enjoyed myself. We went on Splash Mountain two more times.

The glee carried over to the next day spent visiting Dad. Rachel appreciated my private tour of the Sony lot, and we enjoyed lunch at the celebrity chef designed commissary.

At the end of the week spent playing tourist, hiking in the canyons, and louning at the beacah, came the highlight of Rachel's trip. We visited Steve on the set of his latest film. Rachel was a wreck.

"Do you think I look alright? How's my hair?" she fretted, uncharacteristic for Rachel, before we left the house.

"You look great, Rach," I laughed. "Why don't you borrow this necklace?"

They'd never met before, and Rachel idolized Steve. I knew everyone people generally idolized, thus I had never idolized anyone. It was difficult for me to relate to her emotions, but I tried.

"Hey Steve!" I greeted him with a warm daughterly embrace and cheek kiss at the entrance to the lunch tent.

"Elizabeth!" Steve spun me around and hugged me tight. "You must be Rachel," he said after releasing me. "Danny's spoken so fondly of you."

Rachel smiled and seemed to relax. Then we entered the tent.

"How are you doing this film?" I asked Steve as we approached a picnic table. "Isn't the Vancouver project still in post?"

Steve grinned, "You're right. It's unusual to start something new when we're not even out of previews. Ellen isn't happy," he smirked, thinking of his grueling schedule. "I really wanted to do this project, and it had to be shot now, or I'd have lost my star."

"Why the interest? This is too low a budget for a Steven Newman film."

Steve smiled warmly. His blue eyes twinkled so much like his son's that it saddened me.

"Elizabeth, you're right. This isn't my usual, but it has compelling characters I wanted to explore, and a stellar cast of up-and-coming actors."

Perhaps it was Rachel's presence, but I felt sassy today. As Steven Newman's goddaughter I could get away with anything while everyone else cowered in his presence. Who would stop me?

Just before taking my seat on the bench across from Steve, I plucked a crouton off his salad, mischievously smiled, and popped it into my mouth.

"Elizabeth!" Steve scolded, but he was smiling so we both knew he was playing.

Now seated beside Rachel, I reached across to snatch another crouton, but Steve playfully swatted my hand.

"Thief! Go get your own," he chuckled.

"They're crispy."

"You can have croutons with your fish," said Rachel, "Get some."

I glanced at my grilled salmon accompanied by rice pilaf and green beans. There was more than enough starch on my plate.

"I'll pass."

"Lazy, Elizabeth?" Steve smirked. His raised eyebrow teased. "Or are you still tired from your wild night out with Grant Barnes?"

"Huh?" Wild night? Me? Right! "Rachel and I were home by midnight," I clarified. "How did you know?"

Steve frowned. He opened his iPad and scrolled. Then he turned the tablet toward me, revealing a popular Hollywood gossip blog. Steve stretched the entry to full-screen size in case I tried denying the obvious. It was exactly as Grant and I planned.

"Fantastic! Grant will love it!" The photo was of us kissing.

"Grant Burns!" the headline screamed.

"Elizabeth?" Steve questioned.

"Oh, Steve. Grant and I are old friends. We were playing."

"Playing at what? Making Danny jealous?"

"No. I was doing Grant a favor." I leaned forward toward Steve to whisper. "Grant's secretly dating someone. With the paparazzi following him everywhere, I was helping him keep his relationship quiet."

"Grant's no longer with Courtney Sullivan?" Steve asked in his full voice.

I was disappointed. "You know about Grant and Courtney?"

Steve smirked. "Doesn't everyone?"

"Well, they think they're doing a good job of keeping it secret," I laughed.

"I'm glad you didn't know," Steve grinned. "It means you're studying."

I hated when Steve grinned. His face lit up, and his blue eyes twinkled, identical to his son's. Only the hair was different.

I recalled what Steve had said earlier. "Do you really think Danny will be jealous?" Please say 'yes.'

"Doubtful, Elizabeth." My face fell a little.

"How can you say that?" I asked with dismay.

Rachel laughed. How dare she! I scowled.

"Danny would hate thinking I was with another man. He loves me!" My voice rose in anguish.

"Elizabeth," Steve said in a calm voice, "Of course Danny would hate the idea of you with another man, but it's Grant Barnes."

"Well, yeah. Grant's only the second most desirable man in the English-speaking world," I responded. Rachel couldn't stop laughing. "Why are you laughing?" I scolded.

"Because, what Mr. Newman…,"

"Please, call me Steven," he interrupted.

"Thank you. What Steven is saying is Danny won't be jealous because he can tell the photo was staged."

"It was real," I protested.

"I was there," Rachel laughed.

"Rachel is right, honey. Danny knows there's nothing between you and Grant. Danny knows you're old friends. Hell, you introduced them."

I furrowed my brow and frowned. What had been the point? Grant's secret wasn't one, and both Rachel and Steve were convinced Danny wouldn't be jealous.

"If you wanted Danny's attention, you probably succeeded. Read the rest," Steve ordered. "Danny won't be happy."

Confused, I obeyed. Scrolling down the page, there was a second photo. Tears filled my eyes. It was of Danny and I at Steve's premiere last year. Danny must have just kissed me because we were holding hands, our eyes and smiles filled with so much love.

How I longed to relive that evening when our future held such promise. I wiped a tear away. The photo featured a thick squiggle line drawn down the center symbolizing a split, and there was a thick red question mark.

I skimmed the article. My stomach lurched.

"Steve, they're implying that I'm cheating on Danny!"

"Do you know how embarrassing this is for him?"

"Danny knows I would never cheat on him."

"The rest of the world doesn't, Elizabeth," Steve said sternly.

"Oh, no!" I can't hurt Danny that way. When he sees this, he'll be humiliated. "What have I done?"

I buried my head in my hands. What was I to do? I know…

"Rachel," I perked up, "You'll have to tell Danny the truth. He'll listen to you."

"I will do nothing of the sort. I refuse to get in the middle."

I frowned. I thought Rachel was my friend. Then another idea formed.

"I'll call my publicist. She'll make them issue a retraction."

Steve laughed. I glared. There I was a frantic mess, and Steve was laughing at me?

Steve reached across the table and took my hands. The size of his hands and the love emanating from them mimicked his son's.

"Honey." Steve massaged my knuckles and continued. "Call your publicist. It's time you issued a statement announcing your split from Danny. Then you're not cheating. You're a single woman out with an attractive man. Do it for Danny."

I frowned. A knife painfully stabbed at my heart.

"I can't," I protested. "That's not fair to Danny. How awful to read on the internet that you're split up, even if it contains the usual bullshit about being amicable, remaining best friends, and still loving each other." I sniffled at those last words.

"But honey," Steve pleaded, "Danny knows you're split."

"It's not official. We never agreed," I pouted in protest.

"Oh, no! Not this hiatus crap again," Rachel said in frustration.

Steve looked at her expectantly. Rachel shrugged and nodded toward me for my explanation that was not forthcoming. I scowled.

"I have to talk to Danny first. I can't blindside him. I owe him that much."

Steve smiled. "That's my girl! I know this is difficult, but it's for the best. I'm sure there's no harm if you wait until you see Danny next week. One or two more weeks won't make a difference."

I wiped a tear from my cheek. I was shaking.

"I'm scared," I confessed.

"It's difficult for you to acknowledge it's over," Steve said with empathy.

"That's not it. I'm afraid to speak to Danny."

"I'm sure he'll be supportive."

"He won't bite," Rachel laughed.

"Of course he won't." I was embarrassed with Steve part of the conversation, but I had no choice. "Every time Danny and I have been alone this year, we end up in bed."

A loud guffaw burst from Steve. I turned beet red. Everyone seated at nearby tables turned, momentarily stunned by their director's outburst.

I glared at Steve and he shut up. "If that happens this time, how can we issue a statement saying we're split?"

"Because there's a difference between being in a relationship and having an occasional tryst," Steve answered. "Of course that happens. You and

Danny shared a lot of love. Issuing a statement doesn't slam the door, Elizabeth. You and Danny can work things out if you want to at a later date."

"I know," I said glumly. I didn't like the new reality Steve was proposing, but he was probably right.

"Elizabeth, issuing a statement not only protects Danny from looking like a fool, it also protects your reputation. We don't want the world to think you're the type of girl who cheats on her boyfriend."

"Oh, Steve! Why did I have to be so stupid and kiss Grant?"

Steve smiled. "Because you're young, and you weren't thinking. Now you've learned. Danny's ego may be bruised, but he knows your heart. He knows you wouldn't intentionally hurt him."

"I love Danny. I would never hurt him."

"What about Scott?" Rachel asked. "He won't like seeing you making out with Grant, and they've never met."

"Shit! Scott! He doesn't understand our world. The photo with Grant will devastate him," I fretted.

"Who's Scott?" Steve asked, puzzled.

"A guy at Donnelly that Elizabeth started dating," Rachel volunteered.

"Whoa!" Steve exclaimed. "Let's back up a step. Elizabeth, you're going on and on about Danny, but you're dating someone else?"

"It's not how it sounds," I said sheepishly.

"Then how does it sound, Elizabeth?" Steve asked sternly.

It was bizarre discussing Scott with Danny's father, but Steve's motives were pure and Dad-like.

"Scott's a nice guy. I like him, but it's not serious."

Steve raised an eyebrow. I sighed, resigned.

"I'm not sleeping with Scott."

Steve grinned, pleased.

I smiled. "Danny and I haven't officially broken up. How would it look?"

Steve rose from the bench. "Elizabeth, come here," he ordered, but he was grinning.

I walked around to Steve's side of the table. We embraced, and I reached up to kiss his cheek.

"I love you, Steve," I said.

Then I sat down beside him on the bench. Steve wrapped his arms around my shoulders and playfully hugged me. He kissed my forehead.

"I love this girl so much," Steve said to Rachel. "She's the daughter Ellen and I never had but wish we did."

I smiled back.

"I thought we were going to get you too," Steve said sadly.

"Oh, no. I'm so sick of this," Rachel said.

"What are you sick of, Rachel? My son?"

"Yes! No. I love your son, I'm just sick of hearing about him." Rachel swallowed hard. She gazed at her now clenched hands before looking up at Steve.

"This is really difficult for me," she said slowly. "I've never met you before, and you're Steven Newman. Yikes!"

"Rachel," Steve held his hands out, palms up. "I'm Danny's dad. Nothing more. If there's something I should know … " He smiled at her warmly.

I love Steve. His concern for not only Danny and I, but Rachel too, impressed me, and filled me with pride.

"Sorry, Elizabeth. You're first," Rachel began.

"I thought this was about Danny," I protested.

"Like it or not, you come as a pair and your parents haven't given me this access."

"Rachel, I appreciate this," Steve said.

Steve tilted his head down, giving me his serious 'I'm a Dad,' expression which made me squirm. I should not be the topic of conversation. Steve tightened his hug. As Rachel began, I frowned.

I was not happy listening to her run-down of how messed up I was.

"What are we going to do about you, Elizabeth?" Steve asked with concern.

I was so embarrassed. "Mom wants me to transfer," I shyly answered.

"No!" Rachel exclaimed, hearing this for the first time.

"That might not be a bad idea. Do you want to?" Steve asked.

"I don't know. I'll think about it this summer."

"Can you make it until then?"

"It's only two more months. I'm tough." I smiled.

"Yes, you are honey."

"I'm getting some fruit," I announced, eager to escape from the table, and I made a hasty escape to the salad bar.

When I returned, and I purposely took my time, I found Steve leaning across the table as Rachel completed her dissertation on his son.

"I'm frightened," Rachel was concluding as I sat down. "Danny's drinking and drug use are getting out of control." She turned to me. "You don't see it, Elizabeth. Danny hides it well, and he always shows up sober for class. But in his down time… Danny needs help, Steven. I'm frightened. I don't want anything bad to happen to him."

CHAPTER FORTY-THREE - ELIZABETH

Scott was meeting me at The Café this morning and I couldn't wait!

Sunday had been an exhausting day spent travelling. I had collapsed in my bed upon arrival back at Donnelly. Yesterday, not quite recovered, I opted for a quiet evening in my room, though I did speak briefly to Scott by phone. Too tired and mumbling incoherently, Scott laughed at my jet-lagged attempt at conversation, and suggested meeting this morning.

I woke clear-headed and full of energy. After two weeks apart I longed to see Scott. Absence made me appreciate how important he had become in my life.

With students passing through between classes, the Café was busy at this time of day. Arriving before Scott, I grabbed a bottle of water and claimed a small table. I gulped some water, and there he was! Scott leaned over, kissed my cheek, and took the seat beside me. He placed his books on the table and took a swallow from his own water bottle. Scott smiled warmly.

"Hey, dear," he said. I blushed at the endearment.

"Hey, yourself," I responded cheerfully, and I kissed Scott's smooth cheek.

From the corner of my eye, I spotted Danny exiting the service area with a large steaming cup of coffee. He was tan from Florida, but his eyes behind his glasses were worn. He looked like hell. That Danny was wearing eyeglasses was a testament to the hard partying he must have engaged in last night. The sorry sight of him deflated the joy of being with Scott.

"Elizabeth, what's the meaning of this?" Scott asked drawing back my attention.

Elizabeth? Scott always called me Liz. So much for dispensing with niceties.

Scott unfolded two sheets of paper and handed them to me. His smile had vanished, replaced by a grim countenance. The first sheet was the gossip blog photo of Grant kissing me. The second sheet was the article planted by my publicist explaining that, "knowing Grant had been followed by the paparazzi, the two old friends decided to play with them."

Scott had used his green highlighter pen to mark the paragraph that I assumed bothered him the most. "A source close to Ms. Jacobs tells us, 'Elizabeth is embarrassed by how this prank went down. She has always been faithful to Danny Newman, and would never do anything to humiliate him. Elizabeth loves Danny and respects him.'"

"I thought you were over Danny," Scott said in slow measured tones. "I thought we had something special going on."

Inhaling deeply, I re-folded the pages and set them down on the table. Noting Danny leaving The Café without spotting me put me at ease. I smiled and reached for Scott's hand. Then I kissed his cheek.

"I am, and we do," I answered.

Then I explained my escapade with Grant, and my need to plant the second article to keep Danny's honor and mine, intact.

"I couldn't let people think I was cheating on him. How humiliating. I can't be known as the kind of girl who cheats on her man."

"I understand the part about you and Grant. Neither of you considered the unintended consequences."

"Exactly!" Relief. Scott got it! "Two old friends having fun. It was short-sighted of me."

"But why this charade with Danny? Everyone knows you split months ago, and you've been with me for weeks now."

"Privately, at Donnelly, yes. Publicly, no."

"Privately? Publicly? You've lost me Elizabeth."

"Danny and I never officially broke up."

"Officially? Am I from another planet?" Scott's voice rose. "What the hell does that mean? Do you put an ad in the fucking New York Times?" Scott was frustrated, and I didn't blame him.

"You're not far off," I explained. The celebrity world I lived in was like another planet. "When Danny and I attended Steve's premiere last year, photos of us together ended up in the press. Our relationship became public. A public relationship has to be ended, well, publicly."

"I'm not following you, Liz. Does that mean you and Danny have to have a big fight while out on a date?"

"God, no! Nothing messy. Our publicist simply has to issue a statement saying we split several months ago, it was amicable, we remain the closest of friends who love and respect each other, and please, respect our privacy. The usual Hollywood bullshit to save face and prevent anyone from asking uncomfortable questions."

"You and Danny have a publicist? Unbelievable!" Scott exclaimed.

"No, of course we don't. Our parents retain publicists. Actually, they use the same firm."

"How cozy," Scott said, his voice laced with bitterness.

"Scottie, c'mon," I said softly. I touched Scott's face and kissed the corner of his mouth. "This is just how it's done in our world."

"Your world," Scott contemplated. "I don't know if I'll ever understand your world. Do I even belong in your world?"

"Of course you do. It's really not that complicated. It's a game."

"Then why didn't you make the split public instead of that bullshit about being faithful to Danny?"

"Don't be angry, Scottie. You have to understand. I couldn't do that to Danny without discussing it with him. He was in Florida, and I was in LA. It would have been devastating for him to learn via the internet that we had broken up."

"I don't give a crap about Newman's feelings. He knows you broke up. Elizabeth, it's been months."

"Please understand. I couldn't do it unilaterally. Remember, Danny and I have a twenty year history."

"Who could ever forget that?" Scott said sarcastically.

"Scottie," I pleaded. "The statement has to be crafted with care."

"So when does this happen? I wouldn't want anyone to think your cheating on Danny by being with me."

"Nobody thinks that. Our relationship exists at Donnelly."

"This is so confusing." Scott exhaled loudly, frustrated.

"I'm sorry. I know it is." I kissed his cheek again.

The upset in Scott's expression tore at my heart. Would this be the end of us? I would have nobody to blame but myself if it was.

"I promise I'll talk to Danny by the end of the week. After that, it will probably take another week or two and I'll be publicly single again."

"And that means what for us?"

"On a practical basis, nothing. Though we could go down to New York, party in clubs, and be stalked by the paparazzi."

"Oh, joy! Do we want that?" Scott frowned, unhappy with this idea.

"Probably not. I hate publicity, but that's what the statement means."

I reached for Scott, determined to cheer him up.

"Welcome to my world," I concluded, and I kissed Scott on his full, warm lips.

CHAPTER FORTY-FOUR - DANIEL

"Phoebs, take this," I said, and I handed her the joint I was smoking.

Safely tucked away in the back pocket of my jeans, my phone vibrated. Seated on the worn sofa at Duncan's place in The Village, I dug it out without rising.

"Shit!" I exclaimed as I read the caller ID. "It's my mother." Phoebe giggled, amused by my reaction. I grimaced.

"Hi, Mom," I answered. With music blaring, I covered my ear to understand her.

"It sounds like I caught you at a party," Mom screamed in an attempt to be heard. "Is it a bad time?"

That was certainly an understatement. "I'm good, Mom," I lied. "Let me walk outside where it's quieter."

As I stood, I pressed the mute button to keep Mom from focusing on the noise.

Phoebe followed me out the front door, and tucked herself under my arm. Without considering the weather, we had left our jackets inside. It was freezing!

Out of necessity, Phoebe and I huddled together. Whatever Mom had to say better not be confidential. But first, I took a long pull on the joint, precautionary fortification.

"Hey, Mom. What's going on?" I asked.

"At least I can hear you now," she answered.

"What's up?" I replied, ignoring her comment.

"Daniel, what are you doing at a loud party on a weekday?"

Oh, lord! The last thing I needed was a well-meaning parental lecture.

"Mom, chill. I have no classes tomorrow."

I took another long pull on the joint. Then I appraised the remaining length held in my fingers. If Phoebe didn't share, I estimated it should last through the call.

"Daniel!" Mom scolded, and I tried not to laugh. "What the hell are you doing?"

"Mom, I'm getting wasted. And then I plan on getting laid."

"Daniel!" Mom was either angry or shocked. Probably angry. Mom knew me well enough not to be shocked. "You'd better be joking."

I took another hit. Relaxation flowed through my veins to every muscle.

"No, Mom," I said, my voice getting hazy. "I'm serious. I'm seriously wasted, and if I don't get too wasted I'm certain about the getting laid part too."

Phoebe giggled, knowing she would be a very happy girl later.

"I hope you're using protection," Mom warned. "Unless it's Elizabeth, I'm not ready to be a grandmother, Daniel."

Thanks, Mom. With Phoebe standing so close, and hearing every word, the getting laid part was now questionable.

"Don't worry, mother." Oy!

Even wasted, I always used a condom except with Eli. I tightened my hold on Phoebe and held her closer. I must not think about Elizabeth.

"Don't be sassy, Daniel."

"Mom, why are you calling? It's freezing out here."

I listened without responding. When Mom finished, I slammed off my phone.

"Shit!"

Late in the morning of the last Friday in March, I entered the lobby of Berkeley Hall from the stairwell. Carrying my black leather backpack heavy with books, and a Prada overnight duffel, trepidation filled me. Since leaving Vancouver, Dad and I had not spoken, so why was he here?

"Keep an open mind, Daniel," Mom implored me.

Mom had deliberately been left in the dark, but she knew my relationship with Dad was… how had she put it? Strained. Dad and I both understood the latest episode with Vanessa would have sent Mom running, straight to the nearest divorce lawyer.

Thus, Dad shared none of the facts with Mom to preserve their marriage. And I, the dutiful son, also kept the truth from Mom, to protect her. More than anything, I hated the prospect of hurting her. That might be the only thing Dad and I had in common anymore – undying love for Mom.

Immediately after hanging up on Mom last night, I made my decision. I would get blitzed and spend the night with Phoebe. To hell with Dad! I might be forced to spend the weekend with him, but I didn't have to go quietly.

Dad stood waiting for me at the front desk when I'd stumbled through the Berkeley Hall lobby half an hour earlier. Knowing I smelled from a combination of pot and sex, I smirked when I spotted him.

"Dad! Great to see you!" I had sneered.

If looks could kill, I'd be dead already. One look at his unkempt son, and one whiff of my odors, revulsion spread across Dad's face. Yes! Score!

"Daniel," he said sternly, "Get upstairs and shower. Don't come down until you're respectable."

A couple of students passing through the lobby overheard our exchange and stared at my disheveled appearance. I slunk away, mortified.

So here I was, cleaned up, and ready to humor Mom.

"Give Dad a chance," She had pleaded. "He's even more stubborn than you are. Apologies do not come easily for Steven."

"We'll see," I thought. Mom could not begin to understand the enormity of what he was apologizing for.

Crap! I spotted Dad across the lobby chatting with Elizabeth, acting as though it were an everyday occurrence. Seeing Elizabeth shouldn't have surprised me. I would have done the same had it been Mike. But now I couldn't avoid speaking to her. Unexpectedly I cringed with guilt over my antics with Phoebe.

I hadn't been avoiding Eli, but I knew she had been trying her damndest to avoid me. Eli had to feel awkward having me see her with Scott. She was right. If I didn't see it, the pleasures he was giving her didn't exist for me.

Observing the woman you love enjoying the company of another man was unbearably painful, more painful than anything I'd ever experienced. It hurt even worse knowing it was my fault, and that I felt powerless to change. Lately I'd been numbing the pain more frequently.

Still, I couldn't stay rooted in place by the fire door, much as that would have been the easy thing to do. So I affixed a confident, nonchalant expression to my face, hoping that neither of them would notice how forced it was, and I swaggered over.

"Dad!" I said, hoping my voice contained enough genuine sounding pleasure to mask the stress of standing this close to both him and Eli.

Dad and I embraced, and the warmth, and more surprisingly, the love emanating from his hug put me at ease. This wasn't what I expected. I wanted to taste bitterness. I wanted to challenge him to regain my love. But I hadn't realized until this moment how badly I needed his love. It shouldn't be this easy for him.

Now Dad's arrival pleased me. My battered psyche needed a break from everyone and everything Donnelly, especially the beautiful angel chatting with Dad.

"Glad you're ready," Dad said brusquely.

I regarded Elizabeth tentatively, knowing I had to say something, anything, even if it sounded lame.

"Hi Eli," I tried smiling, but doubted if I'd succeeded. "How's your new beau, Grant?"

"Hello, Daniel," she answered icily, ignoring my crack. I'd earned the cold shoulder, but I tried not to show its impact on me.

"Nice of you to let the world think you're cheating on me. Do you know how humiliated I've been?"

"Then you didn't read the follow-up," she answered curtly.

I had in fact read the follow-up. Eli had obviously tried protecting me, but I couldn't admit that to her. Hell! I hadn't even been humiliated. I knew nothing was going on with Eli and Grant. I simply wanted to get to her.

Eli turned back to Dad. "Steve, I've got to go".

Eli tried hard not to show her emotions, but I knew Elizabeth too well. I detected the slight quiver of her lower lip.

"Wait. Elizabeth." Dad grabbed Eli for a good-bye embrace. "When we return on Sunday I'm taking you both out to an early dinner before my plane leaves."

Eli responded sadly. "I ... I... don't count on me, Steve." And she avoided eye-contact with him as she spoke.

With difficulty I kept my eyes on her. Eli looked so deflated, and it was my fault. It pained me. Seeing me with Phoebe had killed her spirit. My heart ached.

"You have no choice," Dad answered. "I would never hear the end of it from Mike and Randi if they found out I came to Donnelly and didn't feed you. Five-thirty, Sunday. Be dressed." Eli was wearing only a leotard and sweats.

Elizabeth sighed in resignation, recognizing her defeat. Shit! She couldn't even stomach the thought of a quick meal with me.

"I'll be there. For you Steve," she responded pointedly.

Eli took a deep breath as though summoning strength. "Danny, I need to talk to you anyway," she added. What? My spirits rose, slightly.

Then Eli left for the elevator while Dad and I went out the back door to the parking lot.

The drive down to New York was quiet by Newman standards. Dad and I periodically engaged in guarded small talk. Our usual easy banter was absent.

What did Eli want to talk to me about? I thought she hated me. Maybe not. Hmm. Curious. I closed my eyes trying to sleep, or at least trying to let Dad think I was sleeping, so I wouldn't have to talk. I feared he would bring up Elizabeth, and I didn't know what I would say.

A conversation about Elizabeth would force me to confront my deepest emotions. I had successfully avoided, there was that word again, this conversation, even with myself. The truth was buried, but not too far below the surface, and I had been running from it for months.

Why must I have these thoughts now when trapped in a car with Dad? Usually when I tortured myself with thoughts of Elizabeth, I would get wasted, and seek out Phoebe. Then she and I would get blitzed, and the pain would subside until another day.

Phoebe was the opposite of Elizabeth, which was why I hooked up with her. She demanded nothing of me. If I saw her fine; if I didn't, oh well. It didn't matter to me and I doubted it mattered to her either.

Phoebe was not monogamous, and we had absolutely no commitment to each other. She served a purpose. Phoebe provided the ultimate disposable relationship. The moment I had my head in a different place, I would easily shed Phoebe. I simply had no idea when that would be

When the limo stopped in front of the Four Seasons Hotel I sensed this would not be a pleasurable father-son weekend. Dad's choice of hotels telegraphed loud and clear that his agenda did not include enjoying my company.

The Four Seasons is one of the best hotels in New York City, but it's not our usual place. The Regency is. Dad had a reason for booking a hotel where the doting staff would not be asking about my mother, or worse, my girlfriend. By choosing a hotel where we could come and go as anonymously as is possible for a world-renowned director, confirmed that I was in trouble.

After checking in to our two-bedroom suite, Dad and I went down to the bar for a casual late lunch. Not having eaten since last night's pizza, I was starving.

The waiter approached. "May I take your drink order sir?" He asked Dad.

"I'll have a Corona with a lime and my son will have…"

"I'll have one too." I added.

Dad turned to the waiter. "No, he won't. My son will have a Panna water or a Coke with his lime."

"Both," I mumbled.

"Thank you sir," the waiter answered before taking his leave.

I was dumbfounded. "Dad, what gives? I'm twenty-one. I drink beer all the time," I protested.

"Daniel, that's the problem," he responded curtly.

What! It was just a beer. I badly needed one, probably more than one, to make it through lunch. Actually, I needed something much more potent than a Corona, but if Dad wasn't even buying me a beer… I sat back in my chair sulking bitterly, and nibbled on a breadstick.

What ensued was the quietest meal I ever shared with my father. He appeared to be waiting for the right time, whatever that meant, and whenever that might be, to pounce. I feared giving him the opening, so I said nothing. Instead, I played with my food and absorbed the tension permeating the table.

My Chicken Cesaer salad, which ordinarily I would have found delicious, stuck in my throat. I was that stressed. It was like being on death row waiting for the execution. Only the judge never told you which method they would employ to kill you. So you sat in your cell, imagining the worst done to you in at least three different ways.

At last the waiter came to clear Dad's near-empty plate. He noticed my barely-touched salad.

"Are you still working on that sir?"

"Not anymore," I scowled, stabbing my fork through some romaine so it stood up straight in the bowl. The waiter took my bowl and departed. Dad looked me straight in the eyes, his expression unreadable.

"You're not hungry today?" he asked.

"No. I'm hungry. It's difficult to eat when you're waiting for the other shoe to drop."

"I wouldn't put it that way. But you're right. We need to talk."

"Right here?" I hoped that would lead to a delay.

Dad nodded. "There are no distractions here."

I sighed loudly, surrendering this round. Daniel Newman does not like to lose.

Dad leaned in closely to speak in barely louder than a whisper. "Daniel."

Dad never called me Daniel unless I was in hot water. I sensed it boiling.

"Your mother and I love you very much. But we're both extremely concerned."

"There's nothing to worry about. I'm an A student," I assured him.

"This isn't about your grades."

I knew that, but I sure as hell wouldn't admit it.

"I haven't told Mom because I didn't want to upset her, but I know what's going on with your constant partying; the drinking, the drugs, and the women."

"How would you know what I am or am not doing? You're three thousand miles away," I answered indignantly.

This conversation, though not unexpected, made me anxious. I needed a shot of something. My nerves were frayed.

"People talk." Dad leaned in closer. "Remember who you are. That makes you someone people enjoy talking about, and you've been giving them plenty of fodder," He said through gritted teeth, exasperated. Good. Hypocrite!

"Does this have anything to do with Eli?" I asked trying to turn down the heat. "Did Eli say something to Randi, and she repeated it to Mom?"

"I wouldn't know what Elizabeth says to her mother, but she knows about discretion. You can trust her."

I nodded, agreeing. This was how I knew the Grant Barnes photos had been staged. Eli had grown up with a heightened regard for privacy. She never uttered a word outside of our bedroom that she would not have felt comfortable finding quoted on Google the next morning.

Our bedroom. I sighed. Memories of our good times together percolated up from the abyss where they lay buried. The shovel scraped away the top layer of dirt, uncovering my hidden emotions. My heart pounded. I desperately needed something stronger than Panna water. I feared I would fall apart, right here, right now, if I didn't get a drink.

Again, Dad inched closer, now in my face.

"Danny, I love you. You're my son, and I think the world of you. But you strut around, arrogant, brimming with a tremendous amount of confidence. You lead a charmed life where everyone fawns over you. You're a brilliant student, you're attractive, especially to the girls, and you come from a prominent family.

If I were someone who wasn't part of your inner circle, I would get my pleasure seeing you taken down a few notches. So don't be so naïve. When I say people are talking, believe me, they're talking. And I'm not happy with the text."

Dad sat back quiet, nothing left to say for now. I could breathe again and digest what he'd said. Interesting how Dad chose to ignore the reason why I was so fucked up. I forgot; he didn't have a mirror with him.

Thoughts of Elizabeth flooded my brain. I flashed back to the highlights of our relationship – there had been so many. I focused on how she always made me smile; always. Eli was so beautiful, both inside and out. I remembered the joy of holding her in my arms, the sweetness of her kisses, and our passionates night together. We had shared two halves of the same heart. Then I blew it.

I hadn't been able to admit why I betrayed Eli's trust. The shovel reached paydirt. My insides quaked. I felt nauseas. I couldn't take it anymore. The truth won out.

I needed my sunshine back, and I couldn't get it until I confronted Dad. He had to know the pain and hatred I felt, and the terrible guilt I harbored. Dad had betrayed both Mom and I, and I didn't know how to broach it. But I had to. A relationship cannot be built on lies and deceptions.

I lay my head down in my arms on the table. Dad gently rubbed my back.

After a minute or two, I half lifted my head. Tears stung my eyes. I spoke, keeping my voice soft, fearing a complete breakdown.

"Dad, I'm sorry. I didn't mean to disappoint you," I stammered.

"You haven't disappointed me, Danny," he answered, his voice calm and measured. "Part of me expected this when you left for college."

I forced myself to refocus. Dad was talking about drugs and drinking. He wasn't referring to the Vanessa mess. "You did?" I asked.

Dad nodded. "But not to the degree I'm hearing about. Please, correct me if I'm wrong. I want to be wrong. My understanding is that you're barely functioning some days. That scares me."

"I'm barely functioning now," I wanted to reply, but didn't. I let Dad continue.

"I battled my own demons when I was younger. I don't want you going through that. Mom and I don't want to lose you. We love you very much, Daniel."

I understood the demons Dad referred to better than he imagined, and I shuddered. The twin demons – Vanessa and drugs; a Newman family saga.

I ceased functioning. A knot formed in my chest. My throat constricted. Tears streamed down my face. I didn't even care that I was sitting in the middle of the bar at the Four Seasons Hotel. I was a wreck.

I looked at Dad through glassy eyes. I knew what I wanted to say, but I couldn't. Speaking came with difficulty. I concentrated on transmitting the words in my head out through my lips, These were the words Dad wanted to hear, not the ones I was feeling.

"Dad, I'm sorry." I trembled. "I love you and Mom so much. And Elizabeth, too. Please help me."

Dad drew me to his chest to offer comfort. Holding me tight he said softly, "The worst is over, Danny. The worst is over."

Upstairs in my bedroom, I overheard Dad in the living room on the phone with Mom. I fought through my sleepiness to listen.

"El," Dad said, "Danny's in bad shape. I'm worried."

He paused for Mom's response, inaudible for me.

"We're talking at least, so that's good." Another pause.

"Yeah. I saw her this morning."

Eli! My ears perked up.

"Elizabeth's a mess, too. Completely depressed."

Eli's a mess? I felt as though I'd been punched in the gut. It was my fault, and I couldn't stand it. Never would I want Eli to hurt and be depressed, but of course I bore witness everyday.

I fought to refocus on Dad's voice. I had to keep her out of my mind.

"He's depressed too," Dad said into the phone before another pause.

"Yeah, El. They should sit around and be depressed together." Dad said with sarcasm in response to what, I didn't know. "Only I get the feeling," he continued, "If they were forced together, then neither of them would be depressed any longer. You should have seen them when Danny met me in the dorm lobby. Elizabeth almost burst into tears, and Danny tried so hard to sound normal it was pitiful."

So I hadn't fooled anybody. Great!

"I should give them both a swift kick in the butt and lock them in a room until they work it out. They're both miserable. It's so much fun, El."

Another pause, then, "I'm tired, El. It's been a long day and an emotional afternoon. Danny's sleeping. He needs his rest. Opening up has been challenging. I'll speak to you when I can. I love you, El."

Tears came to my tired eyes. Hearing Dad say, "I love you" to Mom ripped my heart in two. I used to say, "I love you" to Eli all the time. I missed her so much. Was Eli saying those words to Scott now? I forced myself to block the thought.

Could I ever make things right again? I had to confess everything to Dad and to Eli. Everything. Even if she wouldn't take me back, Eli had to know.

Lying alone in the large hotel bed, I imagined Elizabeth beside me. If only I could touch her. She would be real. Absolute misery swept over me. Exhaustion claimed me, and soon I fell into a fitful sleep.

CHAPTER FORTY-FIVE - DANIEL

After sleeping in the next day, Dad wanted to take a walk, and I wanted to eat, so we struck a compromise. We would go to the Carnegie Deli, a New York institution, where sandwiches big enough to feed an entire family are named for celebrities. As the deli is on the west side and our hotel is on the east side, by definition we would be taking his much-desired walk.

Dad insisted. "Walking is the best transportation there is in New York, Daniel," he said as though I'd never visited the city before.

I began to think Dad had read in some parenting handbook that if you wanted to connect with your troubled son, take a walk with him, and if they're genuinely fucked up like me, make it a chilly day at that.

I splashed cold water on my face and put on my eyeglasses before reaching for my jacket. When I woke, I had found a small, hard plastic blob stuck on my cheek, a contact lens. A box of spares lay on the bathroom sink. My eyes were sore from yesterday's tears, and Eli always liked the way I looked in my glasses, so why not?

Again I let Dad take the lead in conversation as we strolled to the deli. It was easy not to speak. The streets of New York on a late Saturday morning in early spring provided enough distractions to hold our attention.

Near the hotel well-dressed folks scurried about, some shopping, others entering fine restaurants. Tourist families in jeans and sweatshirts stopped to keep their children in tow as they took in the sights. Homeless beggars sat slumped in doorways hoping for handouts.

A trio of attractive women, probably only a few years older than me, caught my attention. Fashionably dressed, they enjoyed a good laugh as they headed south toward Saks Fifth Avenue.

Dad furtively glanced at me and smiled, undoubtedly pleased to see I wasn't a complete basket case if I still appreciated pretty girls.

"Daniel?" he asked.

"What?" I pretended not to have interpreted his cocked eyebrow and sly grin.

"What's on your mind?"

"The truth?" Dad nodeded. I doubted he would like my answer. "As attractive as those girls are," I grinned, "They pale in comparison to Elizabeth."

Dad sipped a bowl of matzah ball soup while I devoured my mountainous turkey on white sandwich. I insisted he share and cut off a quarter for him. Dad didn't want much because he had eaten breakfast in the suite while I slept.

I was tempted to offer another quarter to the two giggly teenaged girls staring at us from across the diningroom.

Perhaps Dad hadn't considered it, but this close to the theater district, customers at the deli easily recognized entertainment personalities. The girls and several other patrons' stares said they noticed Dad. Did they know I was his son? We bore some resemblance although I had Mom's coloring. It wasn't like being Eli though. A full burqua was required to prevent people from guessing her identity.

"Let's have some fun." I said to Dad. A wicked grin crossed my face.

"Daniel, what are you planning?" he asked. Amusement tinged Dad's voice pleased to see my playful humor had returned.

"You'll see."

I waved a waiter over and asked for a bread plate. When he brought it, I set the remaining untouched quarter of my sandwich on the plate and poked a frilly toothpick in the middle. As an added touch, I garnished the little sandwich with two pickle spears.

"You see those two girls," I motioned to the young, giggly pair still staring at us, "Please deliver this to them." I slipped the waiter ten dollars.

"Daniel!" Dad exclaimed, appalled, but when I started laughing he joined in.

The girls blushed as they received my gift. After that, they still giggled, but at least they stopped watching our every move.

"Brilliant move," Dad admitted once the results became apparent. Now the girls had a story to post on Facebook.

Unwittingly, this provided the opening Dad had been waiting for. When we were once again protected by the anonymity provided by the streets, he spoke freely. I was not in the mood.

"I'm glad to see you're better today," Dad started.

"You know me. I find it difficult to remain morose for long," I answered sarcastically, hoping Dad would return to less personal chatter. Not to be.

"Daniel, stop it," he scolded. "You're suffering from serious problems, and sarcasm won't solve them."

"Fine." I shoved my hands deep in my jacket pockets and slouched.

"What are you doing?" Dad asked of my uncharacteristic posture.

"I thought you'd be happy. I've been the perfect son all day doing what you want. I've even been charming for your fans."

"I don't need you charming my fans. Nor do I want you to be perfect. What I want is for you to consider what you want in life."

"You mean what I want provided I start with being clean, sober and celibate."

Dad grimaced. He fumed. Exactly my intention.

"I am certainly not advocating complete abstinence in any of those areas. It's about control, Daniel. Getting your life under control and deciding what you want. Do you have any idea what you want?"

I didn't have to consider it for long. There were no doubts as to what I wanted. I wanted my life back, but how? I stopped still in the middle of Fifty-Eighth Street. Dad skidded to a stop, barely avoiding colliding with me.

"I want Elizabeth," I said while looking directly at Dad. My world fell into place when she was in it.

"Elizabeth." Dad mulled this over. "Do you even know if she wants you?"

"Dad! Why wouldn't she?" But I had my doubts. Scott.

"Because she's a fine, lovely girl and you're a mess. Because she's dating someone else?"

It was one thing for me to think of him, but why did Dad have to throw Scott in my face?

"Eli loves me."

"Oh, really?" Dad raised a doubt-filled eyebrow.

"She said so. The last time we talked."

"And when was that, Daniel?"

"It's been a while," I hated admitting.

"Then maybe she's changed her mind."

"Thanks so much, Dad," I said with sarcasm. "I overheard you telling Mom that Eli is miserable without me."

"I did. She is. But she'll get over you if you leave her alone."

"I thought you were on my side," I groused.

Why else had Dad invited Elizabeth to dinner on Sunday? To torment me? To torment her? That would be cruel, not at all like Dad.

"I am on your side," Dad continued. "I'm on her side too. Elizabeth's happiness is as important to me as yours is. Elizabeth isn't some girl you met in your dorm. If she were, I wouldn't care what happened between you. I would counsel you to get over it and move on. But it is Elizabeth, and whether it's you or someone else whom she eventually marries, I'll be at her wedding toasting the bride."

"It will be me," I seethed. It will. That's why reconciling with Eli posed such a challenge. The knowledge that she, hell everyone, would know that once we reconciled we were as good as married. That permanency panicked me.

"If that's what you want, I hope so. But first you need to be honest with yourself, Daniel. What went wrong between you and Elizabeth? One minute you're living like newlyweds in Malibu. A few weeks later, you're not even talking. Are you ready to be honest and repair the damage?"

Dad backed off for me to consider this. Opening up was difficult, but I recognized the time to come clean approaching. Dad wanted to help, and I needed the help, badly. I just wasn't sure if he possessed the necessary objectivity.

Emotionally exhausted, I was relieved to enter the hotel. I used the time now available to gin up my courage. Dad wouldn't expect me to continue such an intimate conversation in the lobby or the elevator. I needed the release. I yawned deeply. It could wait until tomorrow when my stamina returned.

Once inside the suite, I backtracked. My tomorrows had run out. I couldn't wait any longer. The silence was killing me.

I could never make an honest attempt at winning Eli back if I didn't confront Dad. I needed to tell her the truth, and I couldn't unless it first played out with Dad.

"You really want to know what went wrong between me and Eli?" I asked.

Dad looked up from hanging his jacket in the front closet. His eyebrow rose. Yeah, for once I had Dad's full attention.

I took a deep breath, steeling myself. Here goes nothing. Everything.

"It was my fault," I began. That didn't sound right.

I drew in another deep breath. This was painful. How do you tell your father his long-ago foibles are now yours? Try again?

"The last thing I wanted was to be twenty years old and in a serious relationship."

"So I've heard, Danny." Dad cut me off. "You weren't looking for love. Then you reunite with your BFF. Only now your BFF is a gorgeous young woman. You discover whole new areas of compatibilities. Then one morning you realize holy crap! I'm in love! Fast-forward, and you want out. But you don't want to lose her because she's Elizabeth, the woman who you'd love to cast as the mother of your children. If only you can keep her on hold until you're ready. Did I omit anything?"

"Wrong," I snapped. How that man can piss me off! "Dad. I didn't want to fall in love with Eli, but I'm not unhappy that I did. She's the best thing that's ever happened to me. And no, I don't want to keep her on hold, because…"

"Then pick up your story where I went wrong, Daniel," he said caustically.

"I love Eli, Dad. Then this summer…"

"You sabotaged it with Vanessa. You couldn't keep your pants zipped for half the week."

I shuddered at her name. How much did Dad think I knew? Little, or so he hoped.

"This affair wasn't about Eli. Otherwise I would have confessed and begged forgiveness months ago. This is bigger Dad. And it's tawdry." I paused and noted his lack of reaction.

"Tawdry? An interesting choice of words, Danny."

Dad was being cagey. Like a champion poker player, he refused to reveal the cards dealt to him until he was forced to do so.

"Yes, but appropriate. Dad, I feel dirty and disgusted. I've been hurt and manipulated. The foundations of my very being have been ripped out. The one person who might have helped me, Eli would have seen me through this. I'm too ashamed to discuss it with her. Dad, this involves you more than it does Eli. Don't deny it." I gave him a steely stare.

"What does that mean, Daniel?"

The color in Dad's face rose in anticipation. Time to face the music, Steven Newman.

"Vanessa." I spat out the name with venom. "Vanessa told me everything." I stared at Dad, a murderous glare.

"Vanessa set her sights on me," I continued in measured cadence. "She's a cunning bitch. When she found out Mike was Eli's father... What better way to settle a grudge with your former lover than destroying his son and his best friend's daughter."

I waited for Dad's explosive reaction. Instead, his shoulders slumped accompanied by a vacant stare.

I forced myself to take a deep breath. I needed to tell Dad everything. All the hatred and contempt I'd kept inside since August begged to come out. My gut twisted and my head threatened to explode.

The 'great' Steven Newman was about to be taken down. "If only the world knew the real Steven Newman," I thought derisively.

Over the years Dad's team of publicists carefully cultivated the image of a creative genius that was also a devoted family man. There had been countless photos of "Award winning director Steven Newman and his beautiful wife of X years, Ellen." Articles touted how long the "college sweethearts" had been married. A rare Hollywood success story they proclaimed. If only the truth had ever been revealed.

The narrative included photos of me, posing as the 'adorable little boy.' Most were with Dad, some with Mom too, as I grew up enjoying typical family activities. The photos were taken at Dodger games, the beach, Disneyland, skiing, and other wholesome locales. What a cliché!

Over the years, regular readers of People Magazine and similar publications might have wondered when Steven Newman had time to direct all those movies. He was always frolicking with his wife and son.

Then Eli was added to the storyline. The 'adorable little boy,' now a man, had a breathtaking girlfriend who owned an equally impressive Hollywood pedigree. My life had become a publicist's dream.

I proudly appeared with Elizabeth in print. Who wouldn't? She always looked amazing. I was thrilled to have the world see me with her. It hadn't occurred to me until now that Dad's image had been enhanced, not mine.

I was tired of being the living prop in this fictional tale.

I fixed my glare back on Dad. Did I detect a quiver? Was Steven Newman's veneer about to crack? I steeled myself to disclose everything.

When I finished, I looked Dad directly in the eyes. It was painful. The mighty Steven Newman had tears in his eyes. Good! Let him suffer. I had. Mom had. Eli had. And we still were.

"Vanessa told me everything. I know why Mom kicked you out. She should have kept you out. You bastard! What you did to us!" I was shaking.

Hurt, shock, and worse. Pain swept across Dad's face. He slouched in despair. Humiliated, Dad realized the truth he had worked tirelessly for years to shield me from was out.

I kept my glare on Dad as I spit out the rest. Venom laced my shaking voice.

"After the wrap party Vanessa and I returned to her suite for the final time. She revealed everything.

'Did you ever wonder why I chose you?' Vanessa purred as she handed me a glass of wine and took a sip from her own.

'You found me attractive and thought I would be fun,' I answered with unparalleled arrogance.

'Grow up, Danny. You're just a boy,' she said coldly. 'And you're not that much fun. You're a rather ordinary lover.'

Ouch! That cut to the quick. I was stunned. She'd always seemed more than satisfied when I left her bed.

What reason besides great sex could there be for having a casual, fling with a younger man? So what was Vanessa talking about?

'You're Steven's son,' she said in a strong voice, a complete counterpoint from her usual kittenish purr.

I did not understand what she meant beyond the obvious, but the little hairs at the base of my scalp prickled. Petrified, for the first time I felt very young, and as inexperienced and naïve as Eli.

'Don't get me wrong, Danny.' Vanessa went back to her usual seductive purr. 'I'm a professional, and I desperately wanted this part. This will be the biggest film of the year, not to mention of my career, and I will catapult to the top.'

'Then why defy Dad?'

'It's a fact. Steven didn't want me on this film. My agent went directly to the studio. Steven couldn't reveal why he didn't want to work with me, so he relented.'

'Why didn't Dad want you? You were perfect for this part.'

Vanessa smiled, like a mask not touching her eyes.

'Six years ago I worked with Steven, my first and last time, until now. He cast me in a small part, but it was Steven Newman. At the time, I'd have been happy to be a walk-on just to say I'd worked with him.'

Vanessa ran her long, pointy-nailed finger down my jawline. Her eyes met mine. Fierce. I gulped. She scared the hell out of me.

'I had an affair with your father. Very passionate, although the drugs probably played a part. I brought an amazing stash from L.A. that I eagerly shared.' She laughed, a low throaty laugh. 'We were so wasted I don't know how filming was ever completed.'

She looked for my reaction. I tried not to. All I felt was pure revulsion.

'No offense Danny, but I prefer the maturity of Newman senior.'

I stared at her, immobile. My stomach dropped. Nausea overwhelmed me. My hands fisted. I wanted to strangle Vanessa.

'It was you!' was all my tongue-tied tongue could muster.

'I was young and stupid. Never again. I actually thought Steven cared for me, and that it would last. Wrong, wrong, and more wrong. After we wrapped, he went home to the wife and kid. I've never been hurt by any man again, not even my philandering ex.'

Dumbstruck, I stared, wide-eyed. Vanessa's true self, revealed at last. Rather than the spoiled diva she presented, Vanessa was an evil, vindictive bitch.

Vanessa delighted in having had an affair with a married man. And now she gloated about it to his son, the victim in a warped revenge scheme. What a stupid kid I had been, lured into the spider's web.

'I understand your mother kicked Steven out and didn't take him back until he completed rehab. I was a very naughty girl. Influenced him terribly. My bad,' she trilled.

Vanessa, the ultimate manipulator, had taken advantage of me. Abused by her power, my strings had skillfully been pulled. I had felt so sophisticated thinking this beautiful, older woman found me interesting and had wanted me.

In the few minutes it took to return to my room that evening, my anger, no my shame, become indescribable. I knew you cheated on Mom, but to have the 'other woman' stand there and tell me about it was unbearable."

"How could you have done this to me and Mom?" I screamed at Dad.

Only the knowledge that celebrity outbursts at hotels eventually make their way to CNN kept my temper under control. I wanted to smash the mirror, or throw a chair through the window. I was enraged, but I didn't want to end up in jail or on the news. I considered Mom. Poor Mom.

Why hadn't Dad resisted Vanessa? What was going on in our home that had made him vulnerable to her? And all those drugs? Was Mom partially to blame? Of course not. Mom was the one bright light in the Newman household. She was Mom.

Had it been my fault? I volunteered to enroll at Bromley Hall because my parents were having problems. They could spend more time together if I went to boarding school. Could I have been their problem? At the time,

Dad constantly shot films on location. I had been a handful. Did I misbehave because Dad was away, or was Dad absent to avoid being around me?

Now I desperately needed to know what had been going on at home back then.

"Danny, please!" Dad pleaded.

For the first time ever, Dad seemed small, despite his strong voice.

"Vanessa is a sick, vengeful woman. That was years ago. Mom and I were having problems before I left for Utah. Vanessa appeared at a bad time in my life, and she made things worse. But it's in the past."

"Not for me, Dad. This is my present. And my future." I paused. **My** future. "My future won't even talk to me because of what you set in motion. I don't have a future."

"Danny, you're only twenty-one. You have a long and very bright future."

"My future is gone," I sobbed bitterly. "Elizabeth will never want me back."

"Your mother took me back, and what I did was much worse."

"Was I your problem?" I had to know. "Be honest," I demanded.

"Of course you weren't the problem. You never were. You don't think you had anything to do with…? Danny, no! You've always been the light of my life. No man could ask for a better son than you." Dad wiped a tear from his eye. "Get that thought out of your head. You've always been what's best in my life."

Somewhat relieved, I breathed again. This was hard enough to process. I couldn't live with myself if I had been the cause of my parents' problems.

"Danny," Dad continued. "At the time, my ego had inflated too much for my own good. I strutted around, invincible. A gold statuette sat on the mantle; my passport to immortality. I could do whatever I liked without consequence. So I started taking drugs and cheated on your mother."

"I don't want to hear this!"

"Well you're going to Daniel. You're an adult now. Act it," he replied curtly. "Vanessa may have been the last, but she wasn't the first. By the time we met, I hadn't been a good husband for years. Your mother suffered silently. She would smile for the cameras, but at home she cried her eyes out."

"I heard her," I said sternly. "Nobody would tell me anything."

"You were too young. Mom and I love you more than anything, Danny. We tried to protect you. It seems we didn't succeed."

"You're right, you didn't." I bit my trembling lower lip. I didn't want to cry like a child. I blinked hard.

"I was out of control. Mom threw me out. She was protecting you, and her own sanity, but she never stopped loving me."

"She should have. It would have spared us all."

"Danny, don't say that. I know you're bitter, but please give me a chance," Dad pleaded. "After Mom kicked me out, it took months before I crashed. I hit bottom the night I was busted. It should have been a routine speeding ticket, except for the thick smell the officer couldn't escape when I rolled down my window. She found a stash of joints and pills in the glove compartment, and cocaine in my pocket. The wasted girl in the passenger seat wasn't Mom."

My stomach churned with revulsion. The girl wasn't Mom. How could he?

"I've never heard this," I said soberly.

"It's nothing Mom and I wanted to discuss with you. It's in the past, and we prefer keeping it there. It was the darkest time of my life, and I had hoped to spare you the pain of finding out. This is embarrassing, Daniel. I wanted to be my son's hero.

Michael rescued me that night. Thank god my best friend is an attorney. But Michael had one condition. He would only bail me out if I agreed to go directly to rehab.

Michael was brutal. "What about Danny? Think about Danny. What kind of father do you want to be?" he kept saying. I considered how Michael was the perfect father. He was always there for Elizabeth and Teddy.

I pictured the amazing boy I had at home, and those blue eyes that always looked at me with adoration. I was ashamed of myself. I was not the father I wanted to be. You deserved so much better than a drug-addicted bum.

That's when I realized how bad off I was. Like a baby, I broke down crying in Michael's arms. When had my personal life gone so wrong? I wanted to give you Elizabeth's life, full of love and stability. She's always safe, protected by Michael and Randi. She's safe now, protected by you.

Michael convinced the judge to dismiss the charges. He drove me straight to Betty Ford where I stayed for three months. Despite everything, Ellen still loved me. She believed I was sincere about changing, and took me back. I've been clean for five years.

After Betty Ford, Mom and I went to counseling. We matured and our marriage recovered. We've been through hell, and we've come out stronger because of it. Mom has forgiven me. You should too."

"I can't. This is all new to me. Mom lived through it. She had time to figure it out. I haven't. Don't you see? I considered you the perfect father. Then I find out you cheated on Mom. Now this. Our family has been one fraud after another."

Salty tears stung my eyes. I brushed them away.

"Danny. We can work it out," Dad pleaded.

I shook my head. "I've got to get out of here," I said, and I bolted from the suite, slamming the door behind me.

CHAPTER FORTY-SIX - ELIZABETH

After Steve had called earlier to postpone tomorrow's dinner, I went for a swim. Steve sounded agitated as he explained that they were staying in the city for a few more days. He said he would call later in the week to reschedule our meal.

If I was willing to let Danny get under my skin I would have been curious over Steve's call and wondered why the delay. To be honest, that was why I went swimming. Steve's unusual agitation got to me, and a relaxing swim would put Danny where I needed him to be, out of my mind.

Now, my phone was ringing as I reached for my room key. All I wanted was to get ready for dinner, but my phone... I whipped it out of the small zippered pocket of my totebag. Steve? Again? Twice in three hours. Hmm.

I quickly entered my room and answered.

"Steve?"

"Elizabeth. Good, you're there." Steve's curt greeting stuck me as unwarranted. What was his problem? "Have you heard from Danny?"

"Danny? Not in months," I answered brusquely.

"What about today?"

"Of course not. Why would Danny call me? We don't talk, remember?"

Why didn't Steve understand this? Then again, why didn't he know where his son was? They were sharing a hotel suite.

"I'm grasping at straws, Elizabeth. I don't know where Danny is. We were having an emotional conversation, and he ran out. Three hours ago."

"Maybe he's shopping. You're in New York. Danny loves shopping."

"Elizabeth, don't be flippant," Steve scolded. "Danny was very upset, and he said some disturbing things before storming out of the suite."

"What did he say?" My voice rose an octave from its usual alto.

"He doesn't think he has a future."

Those words hit like a ton of bricks. Even in my darkest depression I thought I had a future. If I could make it through the next two years, I would graduate, get away from Danny, and finally find happiness. Or I could marry Scott. Not that he had proposed.

"Oh my god, Steve! You don't think?"

"I don't know what to think, Elizabeth."

"Have you tried calling him?"

"Of course I've tried calling him," Steve snapped as though I were the biggest idiot. "Look Elizabeth, Ellen and I are frantic. You're our only hope. Can you please call Danny? Or at least text him? If he sees it's you, maybe he'll answer."

"Steve, I don't know," I fretted.

"Elizabeth, Danny hurt you, and you're vulnerable. I wouldn't ask if it wasn't an emergency. Danny could be anywhere. I've got to find him. I'm afraid he might do something stupid."

"Oh, Steve! When you put it that way." 'Something stupid.' Steve's scenario tore at my insides.

"Thank you, honey," Steve sounded relieved.

"How am I supposed to get over Danny when you and Ellen keep drawing me back into his life?" I moaned.

"Maybe you're not supposed to, Elizabeth," Steve said quietly.

"That's a happy thought," I answered sarcastically.

"Honey, be honest. Do you still love Danny?"

I pondered this for a moment. Steve was asking a powerful question. I shouldn't answer hastily. I had avoided thinking about Danny that way. It was painful, and counterproductive.

"I do love Danny," I finally admitted, "but that's not the same as being in love."

"Understood."

"Alright, I'll try to reach him, Steve. If I don't try and something bad happens, I couldn't live with myself."

CHAPTER FORTY-SEVEN - DANIEL

An incoming text message? After three chilly hours of wandering around Manhattan, I finally stopped at a Starbucks for a latte and a slice of lemon pound cake. I considered going to a bar. Several old-fashioned neighborhood Irish taverns, the type where you could tell all your troubles to the kindly barkeep, and inexpensively, by New York standards, get drunk, still lined Ninth Avenue. Dad would go there if he was I, but I vowed not to do anything Dad would do.

Curiosity got the better of me. I glanced at my phone. Eli! And on our shared thread. Why would Eli text me? I couldn't remember the last time she had done so. Her message was simple and direct. "Call me," it said.

Before Dad's revelations, I would have filled with joy over Eli wanting me to call her. Now I was cynical. Had Dad gotten to her? Was she his pawn? Dad had texted me several times, and I refused to answer. I wouldn't put it past him to coerce Eli into calling me. He knew I couldn't resist her. "That's really low, Dad," I thought.

I refused to respond; a first. I never ignored Eli's texts.

Having finished my pound cake and latte, I wandered over to the west side. Recalling those bars made me curious. The hell with what Dad would do. Eli's text had rattled me. I needed a drink.

I sat at the antique mahogany bar with its highly polished surface and shiny brass rail, finishing my second shot of Jack Daniels when I received another text from Eli.

"I'm worried. Call me." This was too much to process. I downed the Jack and ordered a third.

Within minutes I received an additional text. Eli sounded frantic.

"D, R U alright? Call me. I love u. E."

Eli loved me? I found it hard to believe, but there it was, in text. Eli would never admit to loving me on orders from Dad. It had to be sincere. How could she love me? I was scum. But I didn't want Eli worrying unnecessarily. I loved her. I needed to protect her. So I texted back;

"I'm OK. Can't call now. Love U 2. D."

The Jacks kicked in with their desired effect, numbing me from the world.

It occurred to me that it was late afternoon, and I was in New York City. I should have been back at Donnelly by now. Well, I guess I was now officially AWOL. The shock! The scandal! What would my professors say when I failed to show? What would the gossips say? I felt myself laugh out loud. Who cared if anyone stared?

I better tell Eli. She would be frantic when I didn't show for our class tomorrow. We had lost everything, but we still had "our" class.

I picked up my phone to text her again when she beat me to it.

"D, Where R U? – E."

I'd let her stew before answering. I didn't know what to tell her. The truth hurt too much. The truth was all I had.

CHAPTER FORTY-EIGHT- ELIZABETH

Breathe Elizabeth, breathe. My pulse quickened. Danny's agitating texts disturbed me. If I kept him talking, maybe I could help, or at least find out where he was.

Why had he run out on Steve? What had they argued about? Was this related to whatever had happened in Vancouver?

Rachel came to fetch me for dinner. Twenty minutes had passed without word from Danny. I affixed my best Hollywood calm. Stressed and frazzled, I didn't want her to notice my agitation and ask questions, the answers of which would anger her.

"What happened to dinner with the Newmans?" Rachel asked as we left for the dining hall.

"Postponed. They're staying in the City a little longer." I wanted to sound nonchalant. Why worry Rachel?

"Danny's missing class?" Rachel exclaimed. Danny never missed class. "What's going on?"

I was about to answer that I didn't know when Danny finally responded. I stopped and glanced at my phone.

"At a bar. Drunk."

"With whom?" I immediately texted back.

"Alone."

No! I shuddered. Danny was getting drunk alone. My poor boy!

"Talk 2 me, Sweetie," I begged while blinking back tears.

"What's going on?" Rachel asked, indicating my phone. The chimes of the incoming texts, and my rapid response could not be ignored.

"It's Danny."

"Danny?" she said skeptically. "You're talking again?"

"No, just texting." I answered. "I'm scared, Rach." I could no longer keep it bottled inside. "Steve called earlier. Danny ran out on him. Something happened. Danny's alone in a bar and drunk."

"Let Mr. Newman handle it. Why should you care?"

I rolled my eyes. What a stupid question.

"It's Danny." My answer said it all.

I might be numb from the pain he'd inflicted on me, but Danny... well he was Danny. I 'd always love Danny, even if I was no longer in love with him. What didn't Rachel get?

We entered the dining hall and my phone chimed again.

"I need u Eli."

Tears stung in my eyes. Danny needed me, and I wasn't there.

"I'm here," I furiously typed back.

Oblivious to my surroundings, somehow a complete meal materialized on my plate. What food I'd selected, I didn't know.

With my hands full, I couldn't answer my phone when it next chimed. I hated making Danny wait when he was in such a state.

As soon as I placed my plate, drink and cutlery on the table I read the latest message from Danny. I blocked out Rachel, Shane, Cam and Chloe's presence at the table. For the moment, my friends didn't exist. Only Danny mattered.

"Bad shit is happening," he typed.

"What?" I answered.

"Steve. I hate him."

"He's ur dad."

"No."

"Y?"

"2 much 2 xplain."

"Danny…"

"Can't say."

"Tell me."

"Not like this."

"Can I help?"

"U alrdy R."

I trembled, and tears silently flowed down my cheek.

"What's she doing?" Cam asked Rachel.

"Talking to Danny," she answered.

"But she's crying," Cam observed. Rachel shrugged.

I hugged the phone to my chest and cried to it. It chimed again.

"E, don't cry."

I wiped my eyes with a napkin and smiled at the phone. Mindreader.

"How did u no?"

"Who nos u best. Evn f I'm drunk."

"Not fair."

"Fair."

"Where r u?"

"Ninth Ave. The 40's. McSomethings."

I furiously opened a new thread and texted this information to Steve.

By now I had completely blocked out my surroundings. I had to keep Danny texting until Steve got to him.

"What r u drnkng?"

"Jack."

"Ur fav. How much?"

"Idk lol."

"More than enuf?"

"Yeah. Eli?"

"Yes."

"Gve me ur fingers."

"Here."

What was he doing? A lump formed in my throat. My emotions got the better of me. Tears stung my eyes again. Why must Danny get gushy when he was drunk? It always got to me, and apparently it still did.

"I luv holding ur hand. Soft & sweet. Lik u."

"Thanks," was all I could type.

"I mis u Eli."

"Ur drunk."

"I am. I mis u Eli."

"Don't…"

"crying again?"

"Yes."

"Dad is here."

"Go w/him. He loves u."

"Yes. I'll go. I h8 hm."

"No u don't."

"Bt I love u Eli. Always."

"D – Kisses –E."

I collapsed, crying into my arms on the table. Shane, the person nearest to me, tried comforting me, but his clumsiness made it awkward for both of us.

"Does this mean you're never getting back together?" Shane asked.

"This has nothing to do with me. Danny's drunk. He's had a breakdown," I snapped. "I hope Steve can help. I can't stand seeing him like this," I whimpered.

"All that from texting?" Cam said scratching his head.

Back in the privacy of my room, I buried my head in the pillows and sobbed. I lay on my back, held my phone at arms length, and addressed it.

"Damn you, Daniel!" I exclaimed. "Get out of my head," I cried.

Get out of my heart, too.

Later that night Steve called. I was restless worrying over Danny, not sleeping anyway. When would it end already? I needed to get on with my life.

I resented Steve calling me, and dragging me back in. Was this how it would always be? Would Steve make me his go-to girl whenever there was an issue with Danny? That sucked!

Did some cosmic connection exist between Danny and I that could never be severed? Steve had to know how this episode affected me. This crisis probably set my recovery back at least several weeks. Didn't he care about my mental health?

"Thanks, honey," Steve said in a voice so soft it was nearly a whisper.

Danny must be nearby I surmised.

"You didn't give me any choice, Steven," I answered bitterly.

Steven Newman was accustomed to everybody doing his biding and being thrilled at the opportunity. I was not one of those people. He had forgotten my equal status. My frankness reminded him.

"Elizabeth," Steve said, trying to assuage me, "I owe you big time. You saved Danny. He was in real bad shape when I found him."

"This is my second save of the year, and it's only March. I'm tired of it, Steven. I am not Daniel's guardian angel. I need to get on with my own life."

"Of course you do, honey," Steve answered. "But isn't it possible that Danny is your life?"

"Where were you last night? I missed you, Liz."

Scott greeted me with a chaste kiss on my cheek as we sat at a table in The Café. The kiss felt awkward; my cheek revolted in a state of betrayal I hoped I could mask.

"I stayed in," I answered, simple and to the point.

"Danny," Chloe injected. Chloe was already seated with Scott when I had joined them. "He had Elizabeth crying over text messages at dinner."

"Chloe!" I scolded. How dare she bring up Danny in front of Scott.

"I'm tired of this, Elizabeth. I don't want Newman messing with you. When will he get it through his head that you're not his girl anymore?"

"I'm okay, Scottie. Danny was in distress and he reached out. He trusts me. Nothing more." A pang of guilt vibrated through me as I recalled our text stream. It wasn't 'nothing' more.

"I don't like it," Scott complained.

I didn't blame him. If his ex-girlfriend kept surfacing, it would piss the hell out of me.

"You cried at dinner," Chloe pointed out.

"Danny's in trouble. It disturbed me," I answered in a clipped tone.

"I want him out of your life. Your not his girlfriend anymore," Scott said firmly.

Later, to prove to Scott who counted in my life, I accepted his invitation to accompany him to Thursday evening's Astronomy Department lecture. I had no interest in astronomy. I didn't know Ursa Major from Minor. I had never identified either Dipper or any other constellation. Stargazing was impossible in the urban sky over Santa Monica. The motivated drove out to the desert to find a dark enough expanse. I was not one of them.

CHAPTER FORTY-NINE - DANIEL

A psychiatrist recommended by Dad's internist met us at the suite upon our return from the bar. Dad must have paid the shrink a fortune because the good doctor didn't leave until Thursday after dinner. He even slept in an adjoining room.

Much of Monday and Tuesday was a foggy haze with watchful eyes upon me. I didn't leave my room, but when I got dressed I noticed my belt and tie, even my bathrobe sash, were missing. Had my shoes not been slip-ons, would the laces have been removed too? C'mon, Dad, I'm not suicidal.

The doctor presided over my care, anticipating the sweating, shaking, and nausea from detox that didn't come. Meanwhile, Dad ordered healthy foods specially delivered from a local organic gourmet market for me. Why didn't they believe me when I said I wasn't an addict? I was simply a messed up kid who self-medicated to blunt the pain.

By Tuesday afternoon, my rebellion bored me. Dad had even removed the television and my laptop from my bedroom, leaving me no choice but to venture into the living room. Crap! I should have remained in isolation.

"Daniel, please have a seat," The good doctor pounced on me and launched his therapy program.

By Wednesday I began to feel human again.

There was a downside to feeling human. My heart ached when I thought of all the pain I caused Mom and Eli. Mom was easier to deal with. She had been worried sick on Sunday, and when I called her Wednesday morning, she seemed relieved to find her son back with the living. Damage repaired.

Eli. Several times I re-read our text thread. Her words were so caring. Eli said she loved me. She'd given me her hand, and signed off with kisses. Yet what did that mean? Did Eli harbor feelings for me, or was she frightened and feeling pity? I couldn't exactly call and ask.

As a treat for being a good patient, or perhaps to spell Dad for a couple of hours so he could get some work done, my afternoon therapy session moved outside. The doctor accompanied me on a long walk on this warm, sunny spring day. I enjoyed getting out and about, the cobwebs finally cleared from my skull.

The psychiatrist had a pleasing personality, and genuinely cared about me. I don't open up to people, but I found it easy to open up to him.

By the time we returned, I didn't hate Dad anymore. I recognized that Dad too was human. I needed to take him off the pedestal I had placed him on and own up to Dad not being infallible.

I learned about and came to accept Dad's drug and alcohol dependencies. His affairs with women, most notably Vanessa, were more difficult to reconcile. My forgiveness would take time. I understood that Dad's life had spiraled out of control, and women and drugs were his way of coping. It was the women that hurt. That was personal. Dad had betrayed Mom and I. My wounds ran deep.

Twice during the week my opinion of my mother changed. At first I was angry. I'd never been angry with Mom before. I always considered her an innocent victim like myself. Now I blamed her for not being stronger and standing up to Dad to stop his freefall.

Days later I came to realize her immense strength. Mom had understood that the only way to help Dad was to let him crash and burn. How heartbreaking it must have been for her watching the man she loved plummet, while knowing the best thing for him was to wait and do nothing, letting it play out. And all the while Mom had protected me from the ugliness. My respect for this incredible woman soared.

It was not lost on me that I put Eli through a nearly identical experience. My heart ached. What had I done? How could I put someone I loved through this? If only Eli would let me back in her life. I would do whatever it took to make it right.

I no longer blamed Dad for my shortcomings. I needed to take responsibility for my actions. Dad didn't make me sleep with Vanessa. How could I have sabotaged the most important relationship in my life?

I shared with the doctor everything about Eli. The only solution was honesty. Either Eli would forgive me, or she wouldn't. Painful as that might be, we could finally close this chapter and move on. I shuddered, petrified. I didn't want to close this chapter. I wanted to turn the page and start the next one.

Figuring out why I'd screwed it up, and identifying my motivations, the doctor told me would take time, more time than we had together. Before he left Thursday evening, the doctor scheduled an appointment for me with a therapist in Beverly Hills via Skype.

CHAPTER FIFTY - ELIZABETH

Donnelly College is known for its impressive observatory. The modern state-of-the art facility sits majestically atop a hill on the eastern edge of the campus. Until moments ago when Scott helped me from the car and led me inside, I had never seen it before.

"I'll show you around," Scott said enthusiastically. "We have two telescopes."

His child-like glee was infectious, and I smiled. The dimpled grin I received in response filled me with a warm tingle.

Scott took my hand and guided me to the closer telescope.

"This scope with its twenty-inch reflector is used it for public observation, but not tonight."

I nodded my understanding, and smiled shyly. Okay, so I had no idea what he was talking about, but damn, Scott was smart!

Then Scott led me to an even larger telescope.

"We use this one for class and research. It's a forty-inch reflector," he bragged.

I hated my ignorance3; Scott's passion told me I should be in awe, but his words meant nothing to me.

"It's quite impressive," I responded, hoping my voice reflected the right level of enthusiasm.

Scott chuckled and grinned at me. "You have no idea what I'm talking about," he said good-naturedly. I blushed. How astute.

The guest lecturer, a researcher from the Keck Observatory in Hawaii, delivered a fascinating presentation that even an amateur like me could understand.

Afterwards, Scott led me over to the larger telescope. Under Scott's expert tutelage, for the first time I clearly discerned the constellations high in the clear night sky.

"This is fantastic!" I exclaimed, and I meant it. "It really is shaped like a ladle."

Scott laughed. "You've discovered a new constellation, dear, the Large Ladle," he teased.

"For scooping moon cheese, of course," I giggled.

Our easy repartee carried us through the evening. I always relaxed around Scott. He was kind, smart, and witty. And when Scott took my hand as we strolled through the obsesrvatory's exhibits, it felt natural and full of warmth.

Eventually we made our way to The Aerie, Donnelly's alcohol-free under-21 hang-out. Until I met Scott, I never went there. Armed with authentic-looking fake IDs, Danny and I, along with our close friends, had frequented The Cellar. Of course, now Danny actually was twenty-one.

Why did going to The Aerie make me think of Danny? Ugh!

Scott's friends, a diverse welcoming group, made it easy for me to push Danny from my mind. As a result, I enjoyed myself in a way I hadn't in months. When we left, Scott walked me back to Berkeley Hall.

"Can I come in?" he asked when we arrived at my door. It was early, just after eleven. Scott's warm dimpled smile caused my heart to skip a beat.

I grinned as I opened the door, and Scott followed me inside. While I dropped my purse on the desk, Scott removed his parka and draped it across the back of the chair.

"I had a really good time tonight," I told Scott as I hung my jacket on the hook behind the door.

Scott reached for me and pulled me into his embrace.

"Let's make it even better, dear," he suggested.

My pulse quickened. Scott's response didn't surprise me, but did I want that? I wasn't certain, but I was excited that he did. I giggled, a nervous giggle.

Not giving me time to answer, Scott brought his lips to mine, and I eagerly responded, parting mine to let his tongue explore. It had been so long.

My heart beat rapidly in anticipation. This was not like my first time with Danny last year. No longer a timid virgin, I knew what to expect.

Scott led me to the bed. The power of his kiss awakened a hunger that lay dormant for so long. Together we fell onto the bed, our lips locked together. We smiled at each other when we stopped to breathe.

"You are so beautiful tonight, dear," Scott whispered.

The compliment made me self-conscious.

"Thank you," I giggled, nervous again.

"I love your giggle. It's cute."

I blushed. "I'm a little nervous," I admitted.

"Don't be. We'll take it slow."

Scott didn't wait for an answer. He reached for my face and brought our lips together again. His thumb held my chin firmly. Then he pulled my blouse out of my jeans. I gasped at his touch while my stomach flip-flopped. Scott clumsily opened the small pearl buttons. He was clearly not as experienced as Danny, or else he was as nervous as I was.

Danny! I tried pushing him from my thoughts by reaching for Scott's shirt that I began unbuttoning. My fingers trembled.

Scott smiled. He took my hands and kissed them. "It's okay," he assured me.

I never had any problems with Danny's buttons. Danny!

Scott pushed my blouse off my shoulders. In nothing but my skin-toned bra, I felt so exposed. I never experienced this sensation when Danny undressed me. I eagerly welcomed it. No, I relished it; my feminine powers unleashed.

My clumsy fingers finished with the buttons, and I removed Scott's shirt. In the time that I'd known him, it had been winter. I'd never seen Scott shirtless before, and now I carefully studied his physique.

Scott's shoulders were average, not broad. He was slender, his chest and arms not well developed. Clearly Scott did not frequent the weight room. I resisted frowning from disappointment.

How else did Scott differ from Danny? I shouldn't compare, but I couldn't help it. Danny was all I knew. My pulse escalated, elevating me to borderline petrified.

Scott folded me into his arms. His skin against mine was warm. I hoped its heat would stop my trembling. Scott reached his hand to hold my face, and he smiled.

"Hey," he said softly. "It will be good."

Then Scott leaned in and joined his lips to mine. Searing heat did not course through me. It always did when Danny kissed me.

Scott unbuttoned my jeans and pulled the zipper down. Shit! Did I want what came next? My breathing became shallow as my body found itself rebelling from his expectations.

I didn't want a man to be different from Danny. What if I didn't enjoy different? I wanted a man to be just like Danny. I wanted my man to be Danny!

A smile that Scott could not see behind masked my internal chaos. He had no hint of my turmoil. Was the window on the truth I tried so hard to bury opening?

Scott brought my hand to his crotch for me to feel his hardness, for me to lower his zipper. For me to anticipate...

In that innocuous motion I found clarity. I did not want to open Scott's jeans. I did not want to unleash his masculinity. I did not want to touch him, not there. I did not want him inside me. Not tonight. Not ever. I only wanted to open Danny's jeans. I only wanted Danny!

I loved Danny. The words I'd texted him were the truth. I couldn't fight it any longer. My heart knew me better than my head did.

I abruptly dropped my hand, shaking with fear, knowing what I had to do.

"I can't," I cried. "Scottie, I can't do this."

Tears rolled down my cheeks. I sat straight up, coming face-to-face with a very bewildered Scott. I hated disappointing him. Scott, so decent, deserved better.

"Elizabeth?" Scott asked as I reached for my shirt.

"I'm sorry. I thought I could, but I can't," I stammered, while crossing my arms protectively across my chest.

Scott grabbed his shirt, and buttoned two buttons, enough to hold it closed.

"I thought we had something special here, Elizabeth," he said, hurt now that reality had registered.

"I thought so too," my tear-filled voice quivered.

"Newman!" Scott spat out the name of a man he'd never met with venom. Actual poison would have been more palatable.

"I thought I was over him," I stammered.

"And it took you until now to realize you aren't?" Bitterness laced Scott's accusation. I couldn't blame him. My timing sucked.

"I'm sorry. I don't want to hurt you. I like you, Scott. Very much."

I knew the moment the words tumbled out of my mouth how lame they sounded. Nothing would make this awkward moment any less so.

"Clearly not enough," Scott snapped. He was right.

Scott grabbed his jacket from the chair. "I like you a lot, Elizabeth, but I'll never be Newman. Nobody ever will be. You're going to be a very unhappy girl if you don't hurry up and get over him."

"I'm sorry," I said, and the tears continued streaming down my face. Scott stormed out of my room, the door closing loudly behind him.

I buried my head in a pillow and sobbed.

How could I hurt a man as nice as Scott? I felt terrible, but now that I realized I still loved Danny, better to get it over sooner than later. It would have been so much worse if I had slept with Scott.

Guilt nagged my conscious. No! Don't! I had always been honest with Scott. From the first, I told him I wasn't certain I was over Danny. But we spent so much time together, he was not wrong in assuming that I had.

No! I had not led Scott on! It was the normal thing to do, completely appropriate. Dating a man is the only way to discover if you are right for each other. It's the only way to advance a relationship. Unfortunately, Scott learned tonight that I was incapable of doing so.

Now what? The vivid realization that I still loved Danny, despite the passage of months, despite dating Scott, hit me powerfully.

Danny was a lying, cheating bastard. How could I possibly love him?

Memories of our happy times together came flooding back. The mundane; the touch of Danny's fingers brushing against mine as we wheeled a cart through the supermarket, his smile as he teased me for keeping score at Dodger games, our daily lives. And special times; that glorious evening at the premiere of Steve's movie, and the day we moved into our own home.

I fingered the diamond bracelet Danny gave me for my birthday. I had never removed it. Danny's love was potent as I fingered the platinum and diamonds. I missed him so much.

Danny was a lying, cheating bastard. I hurt, badly. Danny said he loved me. Danny couldn't commit to not having occasional dalliances with other women. But he could never keep his hands off of me.

Memories of our romantic times together became powerfully vivid; our first night together, the hot tub in Aspen, making love on our beach, and my birthday spent making love on a sailboat in Vancouver.

Danny was a lying, cheating bastard. But he was my lying, cheating bastard. I owned up to the truth, now plain as could be. I was miserable without Danny. I wanted him so badly!

I was tough. I could turn a blind eye and live with his deceptions. I had done it in the past. The alternative was far worse. I now knew that for sure. I had been living a nightmare, and I couldn't stand it. No more! I couldn't go on like this. I wanted Danny!

As long as he would spend every night with me, I could ignore the sordid possibilities of the few times we would be apart. Soon, eventually, probably in the next few years, Danny would mature and my concerns would be erased. I wanted Danny so badly I could feel him.

Now what? Danny's text confirmed that he loved me. Of course, he had been plastered at the time. No, he loved me. Danny in a crisis turned to me. He trusted me. He could depend on his Eli, because as much as my heart knew he loved me, Danny's knew I loved him.

Sunday! Steve presented the perfect opportunity. I'd already told Danny we needed to speak. Of course at the time it was meant as a vehicle to get his agreement on issuing our formal break-up notice. I certainly didn't want that anymore.

Dinner with Danny and Steve was the perfect opening. Seated at the same table, we would have to speak to each other. The ice would be broken. I had my pride even if I did deperately want him back. I would make him pursue me. It had to be Danny's idea even if I predetermined the outcome.

But what if Danny didn't want one thing to lead to another?

CHAPTER FIFTY-ONE - DANIEL

I woke Friday morning with an epiphany. I loved Dad, and he loved me. I considered how much Dad had sacrificed to be here and get me the help I needed. He had more than proven himself.

Dad should have spent the week in an editorial suite working on his director's cut. Now his film was behind schedule and over budget. But Dad was paying for the crew and mitigating other expenses incurred due to his absence.

Adding everything up, this week had cost Dad a small fortune. Unconditional love.

"Dad, thank you," I told him over breakfast in our suite.

"I'm glad to have my son back," Dad answered, and he wiped away a tear.

That night we took the subway to Citifield to catch the Mets. Dad's long-time secretary Maureen had made the arrangements. Regrettably, Mo recently told Dad she'd be retiring at the end of the year and moving to Oregon. We loved Mo like a member of our extended family.

It wasn't the Dodgers, but what a match-up! Mets pitching versus Cardinal hitting. Anytime the Cards played the Mets it was an important game. Only the buzz of the crowd made the chilly, dank evening bearable. I eagerly gulped hot coffee, not missing my usual stadium staple, beer, for a moment.

At Citifield Dad and I relaxed for the first time all week. Hell, for the first time all year! Dad and I felt comfortable around each other, unheard of since June.

Dad and I shared this bonding opportunity, relieved that the strife was behind us and we could return to our previous closeness while moving forward

The chilly night air invigorated while we walked back to the hotel from Grand Central Station. We strolled silently up Fifth Avenue to the Apple store where I needed to purchase a new iPhone charger.

I slowed to take in the windows of Saks Fifth Avenue. Designer-clad mannikins posed as though enjoying a picnic in the country caught my attention. One, adorned with a long, wavy brown wig, and dressed in denim capris and a sleeveless lavender shirt tied to reveal her midriff, stood out from the rest. Eli!

"God, I miss her." I said sadly.

"Elizabeth?" Dad asked. I hadn't realized I had spoken out loud.

"Yeah. I was thinking how beautiful she'd look in that outfit."

"She would." Dad paused. "Elizabeth was good for you, Daniel. Her love made you stronger and kept you on track."

I nodded my agreement. "Eli's the best." My heart ached.

"You want Elizabeth back, don't you?"

"I've never stopped loving Eli," I answered. "You know, we never officially broke up. The last time we spoke, we called it a hiatus. Neither of us wanted the finality of an actual split. We both wanted to keep the door open."

"You have a difficult decision, Daniel," Dad's understanding buoyed me. "Elizabeth's a serious girl. She won't want you back if it's business as usual. You have to promise that you'll stay clean, and that you will never so much as look at another girl."

"I know," I answered soberly.

"Can you make that commitment and be the man Elizabeth deserves? You don't need to answer right now."

"I can answer now. Dad, I want to be that man. I'm ready to make that commitment. Maybe I needed to see how miserable I'd be without her to realize that forsaking all others is easy compared with forsaking Elizabeth. How could I have been so stupid, Dad?"

"You're a kid, Danny. Don't be so hard on yourself."

"We were so happy. Eli's the most amazing girl. She's the only girl who ever puts me in my place and I need that sometimes."

"You enjoy being put in your place?" Dad laughed.

"Only by Elizabeth. She does it out of love, and she's always right," I confided. "I need Eli back."

"Of course you do, and she needs you. You'll see. You'll both be happy again. Give it some time." Dad reassured me. I lacked his confidence.

"What if she doesn't believe I've changed?" My voice cracked in panic as we entered the lobby of the Four Seasons.

"We'll take care of that tomorrow," Dad promised. I raised an eyebrow, confused. "Danny, I did much worse to your mother and she took me back. Elizabeth will see you're sincere. Have you ever lied to her?"

"Never," I smirked. "Even when it would have helped me."

"Then Elizabeth will have no reason to doubt you."

Dad let me sleep in so I didn't rise until after ten. When I did, despite the gray sky, I felt the best I had in months. My head was clear instead of hungover. And I was cautiously optimistic. I had a future again.

Breakfast arrived while I showered. Under the hot pulsating jet I pondered what Dad said last night about convincing Elizabeth of my sincerity. Dad remained silent, cagey even, as though he harbored a state secret.

As soon as we ate and dressed, we left the hotel for wherever it was we were going to accomplish this. Strolling down Fifty-Seventh Street in the light, chilly rain I turned up the collar of my cashmere sportcoat to keep warm. I considered the designer stores we passed where I would love shopping for Elizabeth. I would have to bring her down for a weekend and spoil her.

Daniel, stop daydreaming! What if it really was over? Don't think that way! Daniel, don't spoil your mood.

We turned at Fifth Avenue, packed with shoppers and tourists, despite the unseasonable weather. The latter, with their cameras slung around their necks and color-coordinated family outfits, clogged the sidewalk as they stopped without consideration to pose for pictures in front of Trump Tower.

Dad turned to me "There is one thing guaranteed to help you win Elizabeth back. It always works with women. It's even helped me with your mother," Dad explained, a touch of arrogance in his voice.

"What?" I asked, curious.

"Jewelry. She can't deny your sincerity if you give her an important piece of jewelry," Dad answered.

Of course! And Dad \purposely timed his words, for there we were at the massive doors to Tiffany's. That I hadn't thought of this myself was testament to the dangerous place my mind was in.

Elizabeth cherished the diamond bracelet I'd given her for her birthday, just as she loved the Perretti heart I'd given her our first night together. After the pain I'd inflicted on her this year, something more significant was required. And there it was, in the window: Tiffany keys.

What could be more perfect! No matter how corny it sounded, I would give Elizabeth the key to my heart, something only she would ever have.

The saleswoman, an attractive woman near thirty years old with a flippy blonde ponytail showed us the various designs and sizes the keys came in. If she recognized us, she was doing a superb job of hiding it.

I decided to purchase a large key, one with diamonds, but which? The Enchant Primrose – perfect! The mostly platinum key with its top shaped like a flower was as dazzling as Elizabeth. Covered in round and Marquise diamonds, with a center cluster set in rose gold, the two-inch long key was as eye-catching as Eli.

I turned to Dad who shook his head.

"No. Not that one."

"But it's as dazzling as Elizabeth," I protested.

"Elizabeth won't feel comfortable with it. You know she hates being stared at."

Then he said to the saleswoman "She's the most beautiful young woman you've ever seen, but she's modest." She nodded her understanding

"Daniel, Elizabeth could be seated in a 200-person lecture hall and students on the other side of the room would take notice. That's not what you want."

"Okay. I get it. Something with less bling."

"Do you have a photo of your girlfriend?" the saleswoman asked. "It would help me assist you better."

"Sure," I answered automatically, and I pulled a small photo out of my wallet.

I was almost as surprised as Dad that I had a photo of Eli with me after all these months. The saleswoman looked at the photo and smiled.

"She's beautiful," she said after studying the photo. "Your girlfriend looks like she could be Miranda Jordan's daughter."

"She is Miranda Jordan's daughter," I answered bluntly.

"Oh." The saleswoman was flustered by my admission but quickly recovered. "Then your father is right. She doesn't need bling."

"What about this one?" I asked while fingering a plainer gold key. "It's like Elizabeth, understated but elegant."

"That one's perfect," Dad said.

"The Crown Key. A good choice," the saleswoman agreed.

She held it up tp her neck. I was pleased that it fell low enough that Eli could wear it with her Peretti heart. Then I frowned. I didn't want the Crown Key.

"I'm sorry, Dad. I want the bling. Everyone should pay Eli attention. I'll take the Enchant Primrose." I removed my American Express Card from my wallet and handed it to the saleswoman.

Now I anxiously waited for tomorrow. I wanted to return to Donnelly and have our dinner with Eli so I could get our lives back on track. I wouldn't give her the key until it was the right time. I would carry it in my backpack because you never knew when the right time would present itself, and I didn't want to miss it.

CHAPTER FIFTY-TWO - ELIZABETH

Sunday afternoon found me refreshed from a nap; ready for dinner with Steve and Danny. In just over an hour… My stress level at Defcom One, terror alert level red, must be controlled. Get a grip, Elizabeth.

Rachel, one of the most fashion-challenged people I ever met, tried calming me by helping to choose my outfit. Was there really a proper outfit to wear when dining with your ex?

"I can't believe I said yes to this," I fretted. "Just when I've convinced myself I can put Danny behind and finally move on with life. What's wrong with me?"

I didn't dare share my decision with Rachel. After the hell we'd put her through, she would be enraged by my planned capitulation. I felt mild guilt deceiving Rachel.

"You said Steven gave you no choice," said Rachel.

"True. And after Danny's texts, I need to confirm he's okay."

I paused and sat down on my bed. I stared earnestly at Rachel, my best friend and confidante. "I'm frightened, Rach. I've finally progressed. I can't backslide."

"You have to be strong. You are strong."

"I don't know," I hesitated. "Dining with Danny. Even with Steve there, you know what Danny does to me. I don't want to get torn up again."

"Then don't," Rachel firmly advised. "You're a formidable woman. You have the power. Don't let Danny take it from you."

She was right, except for the formidable part. Mom was formidable, not me.

Time was running out. I desperately needed to get dressed. I went rummaging through my closet. Again.

"I want to look nice, but not too nice. It shouldn't seem like I care, but I want Danny to hurt looking at me. This is so frustrating!"

"You'll figure it out. Just make sure you're comfortable so you don't fidget."

I pulled out a navy cashmere sweater. "How about this?"

"Too wintry."

Then I pulled out a pink tank.

"We're in upstate New York, not Santa Monica!"

"Right." I slunk down on the bed and held my head. "I don't know what to do!"

"You're turning into a basket case." Rachel frowned.

Then she strode over to my closet and pulled out a black woolen miniskirt and the sweater from Gucci.

"Wear this. It's perfect. Let Danny see what he bought you," Rachel smirked.

It was such an obvious choice. Why had it eluded me?

Rachel continued searching through my closet. Finally she pulled out black high-heeled boots. "Wear these," she ordered.

Soon Rachel left. I swapped the skirt for the leather Gucci trousers, and I got to work getting dressed, applying makeup, and finishing with a spritz of perfume, a fragrance Danny had selected for me.

A half hour later I was ready, brushing my hair once again, when a knock came on the door.

"I'll be right out." I called sweetly.

My stomach clenched. Show time! Then I stretched my jaw muscles so a smile would come more easily, and I grabbed my small black quilted Chanel purse by its gold chain.

Although it made prefect sense, I was surprised to find Steve with Danny when I threw open the door. Despite the hell he'd been through, dressed preppy perfect in chinos, a pin striped button down, and his navy cashmere sportcoat, Danny was as handsome as ever. He'd even trimmed his unruly hair.

I flashed Danny a thousand megawatt smile in counterpoint to his twinkling sapphire eyes. His mouth dropped open, and then quickly recovered. Danny's eyes opened wide, taking in all my curves set off to perfection in the body-hugging pants and sweater. Suffer!

"You look great. I mean it's great to see you Elizabeth," he stammered.

"Nice sweater," said Steve.

"Thank you," I answered, smiling. They had no idea the real reason for my thanks. "I got it when I was home," I added.

Hmm, I'd known Danny all his life, but somehow he seemed different this evening; quieter, perhaps more subdued. Danny had lost some of his usual swagger, a trait I had always associated with him. Sitting beside each other at the small restaurant table I was glad that he had. I didn't want to be the only uncomfortable one.

The waiter came for our drink order, and giving no one else a chance, Steve ordered a bottle of Panna water for the table. Reminding him that women order first, or should, I quickly voiced my selection.

"I'd like a Margarita, please," I told the waiter.

Steve glared at me as though I had committed a heinous crime. Danny scowled though I didn't understand why.

"Must you Elizabeth," Steve implored.

"Yes. I really want a Margarita," I insisted.

"Thank you," the waiter said, and he scurried away before the men could change my mind.

Danny turned away, but Steve gave me a severe look.

"What?" I asked. What was their problem?

"We're not having any alcohol tonight," Steve said sternly.

"I must not have received that email. I'll fire my secretary," I responded sarcastically.

"Elizabeth…"

"Steven, you know how uncomfortable this is. I'm only here because you forced me. So if I need a Margarita, if that's the only way I can tolerate being at the same table as your son, so be it."

I was being rude, but hey. I didn't want Danny to suspect. I was the woman who had been scorned. Danny needed to pursue me.

But Danny was having no part of my plan. Instead, he threw down his napkin, muttered, "Excuse me," and left the table in a snit. He stormed toward the restroom. Maybe I'd gone a little too far

Angered, Steve leaned over, closing the gap between us, and he grabbed my wrist.

"What are you doing, Elizabeth?" he barked.

"I'm sorry, Steve. You know how I feel."

Steve released my wrist and smiled, a fatherly smile.

"Elizabeth," he said gently. "I know Danny hurt you. But what if he wants to make amends?"

"Right."

"Elizabeth, what if Danny wants to change? What if he already is changing? Would you take him back?"

I stared at Steve. Did Danny want to reconcile? I couldn't appear too eager.

"Steve, what are you saying?"

"I don't speak for my son, but he's been miserable without you. I think Danny's ready to make it up to you."

My head was swimming. Wasn't this what I wanted? I couldn't believe it. I shuddered.

"Do you mean what I think you mean?" I was trembling.

"Danny knows it will take time, but he's prepared to be patient. So if any part of you would consider forgiving him, please stop the nastiness. Danny's vulnerable right now, and he'll interpret it as a rejection."

"Okay. I'll be nice," I whispered, still not believing this conversation.

Soon Danny returned to the table, and dinner continued smoothly. Thanks to Steve it was the most relaxed time I'd had in months. Steve had that knack at putting everyone at ease. He had spent his career assuaging egotistic, temperamental actors. A couple of messed-up college students who hadn't spoken to each other in months had to be a breeze.

Steve excused himself from the table while Danny and I finished our entrees. An awkward silence fell. We hadn't been alone together while sober since September. I sensed Danny looking at me, but I didn't want to raise my eyes from my plate to confirm it.

"There's a drop of sauce on your cheek," Danny said quietly.

I blushed, embarrassed. I wanted to look perfect tonight and a smudge of bolognese on my cheek was not perfection. I wiped my cheek with my napkin while averting my eyes.

"Here, let me," Danny offered.

Danny lifted his napkin by the corner, giving me no choice. He delicately dabbed at my cheek, but when he placed his right hand on my face to steady it, I felt his strong softness. Our eyes locked, green on blue, and I gasped, my usual reaction. My heart skipped several beats.

Danny gave me his warmest smile that never failed to melt me, and it did so now. It had been so long. I'd forgotten its power over me. Instinctively I placed my hand over his, and I pressed it against my cheek.

Danny leaned in closer.

Built-up longing threatened to overwhelm me. My heart thumping wildly, I felt his breath on my face, and then his lips against mine, as Danny tentatively kissed me.

That was too much. I didn't want to melt at the dinner table. He couldn't think I was caving. I jumped up and ran out to the street.

"Shit," I heard Danny mutter as I left.

Clutching myself, trying to literally hold myself together, I gulped deep breaths of the chilly night air. Control, Elizabeth; do not lose control. Breathe. Hyperventilating would not do me any good.

That Danny had followed me outside, I didn't realize until he wrapped me in his arms. I broke down sobbing on his broad shoulder, a place where I always found comfort. Stroking my hair Danny gently intoned, "Eli, don't cry. Don't cry baby."

I shuddered. Danny calling me 'baby' was too much to take. The agony of the last seven months welled up inside me. A new round of sobs rose from my chest. Danny continued to hold and comfort me.

"Baby, don't cry. Please? I hate when you cry."

I couldn't help it. The heartbreak finally found its release.

Danny's strong arms around me felt so good. I had missed them so much. Finally, I stopped crying and looked up at his kind smile. Danny took my hand and squeezed it.

"Feeling better?" he asked. Amazingly, I did. The curative power of a good cry.

"Yes," I smiled back. "Steve will wonder where we are," I added.

"Dad will figure it out. I'm sorry I kissed you, Eli. I wasn't thinking."

CHAPTER FIFTY-THREE - ELIZABETH

My stomach twitched, dinner threatening to ruin the evening and my new sweater. I swallowed hard, defensively. Keep it together, Elizabeth. The silence in the car was deafening, and though the ride was short, less than twenty minutes in duration. That was twenty minutes too long with my nerves stretched to their maximum.

I clenched my fists together, the skin nearly breaking from the pressure of my nails. When we returned to Berkeley Hall, I hated saying good-night to Steve, my last bastion of defense. I wouldn't see him until mid-May at the earliest. How I loved this man!

Steve and I embraced. "I'll tell Michael how well you're doing."

"Yes, please," I smiled, and I kissed his cheek. "Give my best to Ellen."

Then I turned to walk to my room. Danny soon caught up, just as I anticipated. Or dreaded?

"We need to talk," Danny said. "I'll come by after I see Dad off."

Upon entering my room I cued my Bose Wave. Keeping the music soft, I changed into flannel PJ pants and a t-shirt. Music would calm my nerves. Maybe. Then I went to the bathroom to brush my teeth. Garlic breath would not do. Anticipation made my heart flutter and my breathing shallow. Stay calm, Elizabeth!

Soon a knock came on the door. Danny! My stomach lurched. That long forgotten, but familiar shiver, the one that threatened to drive all reason from my mind whenever we were alone, woke from its long slumber.

"Hey, Eli," Danny greeted me. His voice soft, uncertain even.

"Hey," I responded with a shy smile. "You changed your clothes."

No longer New England preppy, Danny morphed into the California beach boy that I loved. He had shed the sport coat and loafers, and had changed into flannel pants, a t-shirt and flip-flops. With the form-fitting tee tucked into his pants, Danny's narrow hips and muscular chest were emphasized. I couldn't help staring.

When our eyes met, we both laughed. We looked like fraternal twins.

I needed this laugh to cut the tension. I had forgotten the flip-flops my heart made whenever I looked into Danny's sapphire eyes. With his hair still neatly groomed, Danny was more handsome than any A-list actor.

"It's comfortable," Danny said as he carefully closed the door, hung my do not disturb sign on the outside knob, and engaged the deadbolt. Nobody would interrupt us.

"That was a really nice dinner," I said. "I love seeing Steve."

"Dad has always been a big fan of yours."

We both spoke tentatively, avoiding why we were together in my room at this moment.

An awkward silence enveloped us. Another indication of our current status. Danny and I never experienced awkward silences. We'd always been comfortable with quiet. But that was then, and so much had changed in recent months.

Danny's usual confidence was missing. Though standing still, he appeared to be moving. Danny would look at me and then avert his eyes. It was as though he needed to summon the nerve to speak and then backed off. I gave him the time he required.

"Elizabeth, we need to talk."

"So you said," I answered coolly.

Danny smiled awkwardly. "You have every reason not to trust me, but I'm clean." Danny pulled his pockets inside out.

I relaxed only slightly, relieved that Danny couldn't get me wasted and take advantage like he had in the past, though maybe I wanted him to.

"What makes you think I want to talk?" I asked.

"You let me in." Danny stated the obvious.

"Oh," was all I could respond.

"You might not need to talk, but I do." Danny paused. "Eli," he continued in a soft voice, and Danny took my hand, kneading my knuckles.

Danny fingered my diamond bracelet, concentrating on the stones, as though he expected them to give him strength. "Thanks," he smiled nervously. Danny had never been awkward around me before. "You make me feel safe."

I didn't know what to say. What was better than the knowledge that you provided your man with comfort?

"Thank you," I mumbled, uncomfortable with this accolade.

"Eli, Sweetheart." Danny looked at me, uncertain. "I stand before you humbled and contrite."

"Humbled?" I laughed, breaking the tension. "Danny, you're never humble."

"Thanks, Elizabeth," he scowled. "I didn't know you found me so arrogant."

"I'm sorry. I didn't mean that. It was a funny choice of words. That's all."

I didn't want to keep Danny from whatever he wanted to discuss. He found this difficult enough.

"I guess it was. I am humbled though."

Danny continued holding my hands, his soft strength radiating through his touch. Then Danny looked directly into my eyes, and I smiled, shy once more.

"Eli, you saved me. Your texts saved me. The words were so kind. No matter what happens, I'm glad you still care."

"Danny. Don't. I did what any friend would have done." I emphasized the word friend though I had ended the thread with 'kisses,' and had included "I love you."

"I've re-read the thread several times," he pointed out.

"Oh." There was no hiding from the truth and Danny smiled at my awkward blush.

"Dad found me. I was so out of it. Sneaky, Eli. You got me to reveal my location, and then you texted Dad." Danny raised an eyebrow and smirked.

I shrugged, embarrassed. Had it really taken him this long to figure it out?

"Are you angry?"

"No. I might have been if I hadn't been so drunk. You did the right thing." Then Danny laughed. "You always do."

"Occupational hazard?" I shrugged.

Danny massaged my fingertips out of nervousness.

"Babe, I hurt you. Badly. I'm finally ready to tell you everything. I want to come clean, Eli. I have to be honest. Complete honesty is the only way you'll trust me again."

"You're right."

"Babe, I don't know if anything I do or say will make a difference." Danny paused. "Hell, I've seen you with Scott," he said with an air of resigned rejection. "You look good together. I bet he's not fucked up, like I am. Must be nice to have a normal boyfriend for once."

"I wouldn't know," I whispered.

"But Chloe told me…" Danny responded with a mixture of confusion and what sounded like… hope.

"You sort of ruined it for me."

"How? I've never even spoken to the guy."

"Scott's real nice. He's attractive, he's kind. I liked him a lot. But after a while…" This was too awkward to admit to Danny.

"What? He wasn't good enough in bed?" Danny laughed.

Typical Danny. Did all men need affirmation that they had been your best lover ever? Of course Danny actually had been. Then again, he'd been my only lover.

I turned away, unable to look at him. This was so uncomfortable.

"It didn't get that far," I stammered.

"It didn't?" Danny asked. He was surprised, but I detected glee in his voice. "You never slept with Scott."

"I wanted to, but… I really liked Scott. When the time came and I… Scott never got past opening a few buttons on my blouse. It felt wrong. I didn't love him."

A warm smile spread across Danny's face.

"You're the one who's always cheating, and I got wracked by guilt, like I was doing you wrong. And we aren't even together."

"Baby, that's fantastic," Danny exclaimed with relief.

I glared.

"I mean, I'm sorry I ruined things for you." The words stumbled out.

"No, you're not. Be honest, Daniel."

Danny smiled sheepishly knowing I was right. "Is that why you've never removed your heart or your bracelet?"

"I would think about it, but then... I couldn't part with them," I quickly added.

Danny smiled, and I glanced away. It was Danny I couldn't part with. Now he knew.

"Scott's much more tolerant than me," Danny explained. "I wouldn't date a girl who refused to put away gifts from her ex."

"I never said they were from you."

I looked down, focusing on my bracelet, unable to face Danny and his uncanny ability to read though my façade.

"I ... I don't ..." I stammered. "Maybe I wasn't ready to move on." I lifted my face, and peeked through my lashes into Danny's intense sapphire eyes. "When we split, Scott said he deserved a girlfriend who wasn't in love with another man. He was right."

"You're in love with..." Danny grinned.

I began crying at the memory of my recent humiliation. Danny gathered me in his arms and stroked my back.

"E, that's fantastic," he began in a gentle voice, "If it helps, I'm glad you didn't sleep with Scott. If you hadn't been a virgin, I wouldn't care. But I like knowing I'm the only man you've been with. It killed me thinking you and Scott...I want you sleeping only with me."

"That's great, Daniel. But we're not sleeping together anymore."

Then Danny lifted my chin and looked at me with pleading eyes.

"I want you back, baby. Please give me a chance."

"I'm afraid to," I sniffled.

Then I broke down, shaking with emotion. Hadn't I been waiting months for this moment? Hadn't I decided when Scott left me that I would make this happen? That Danny handed me the decision to make overwhelmed me. Tears flowed.

Danny held me close, his strong arms comforting me as always.

"Baby, don't cry," he whispered against my temple. "I want to make things right."

"I believe you," I trembled through my tears. I really did. "Tissue?"

Danny smiled and reached across to the box on my desk. "Here. Let me." He tenderly dabbed my eyes and cheeks.

As Danny's hand lingered on my face, I held my hand over his and enjoyed its masculine feel. When he smiled again, I abruptly dropped it.

"Elizabeth, I've been going through hell since Vancouver. I'm sorry I put you through it."

"Danny what happened? What went wrong with us?"

"Nothing went wrong with us," he said contritely. "It was me. I take full responsibility."

"We were living together. I assumed…"

"It was the beginning of forever," Danny answered sadly.

More tears spilled, and I wiped them away.

"That was my intention, E." Danny paused again. "Damn! I hate myself."

"Danny. Don't."

Now Danny shed a few tears. I had seen him cry only once before. Danny had always been my rock. I had to be his.

"Baby, I'm so sorry. I never wanted to hurt you," he choked out through his tears.

I held Danny close and gently caressed his strong back. I let him cry. He needed to release the pain.

Danny's weight proved too much. We fell back against the pillows, Danny still in my arms. His crying ceased, and he moved to my side, though we still held each other.

I wiped Danny's tear-stained cheeks with my fingertips like he had done for me. Danny smiled a shy smile, his face against mine.

"Thanks, Eli. I'm so embarrassed."

"Don't be, Danny. It's me you're with."

Danny continued holding my hand. We lay next to each other, comfortable, like we had so many times before.

"I hurt someone I love, and I couldn't live with myself. Every time I saw you, or even thought about you, I did something stupid just to dull the pain. It didn't work. And then I'd do something stupider which made it even worse."

"Oh, Danny," I put my hand on his cheek, and hugged him.

"Dad made me realize if I kept it up I'd soon be dead."

Tears quietly ran down my cheeks. Danny held me close. In his arms, I was home.

"This week with a live-in psychiatrist brought me clarity. I confronted Dad and came to terms with my real issues. I'm straightening up, Eli. I want to make things right."

I nodded, poised to listen.

"Now the hardest part." Danny began to mindlessly twirl strands of my hair. "This is so difficult. I need to be honest, but it's going to open old wounds and hurt you all over again. I'm sorry, Eli, but I have no choice."

I squeezed Danny's hands. "I'm tougher than you think," I smiled. "After all, I live with Daniel Newman."

Danny smiled. "You do, don't you?" Then he took a deep breath.

Danny began at the beginning, taking us back to Malibu. The memory of those idyllic days in May broke my heart.

"I was determined that no one would ever come between us. We were rock solid when I left for Vancouver."

I shook my head. "We must not have been or what happened wouldn't have."

"No. We were solid," Danny protested. Regret over what he had spoiled filled his voice. "I had every intention of remaining true. Then, enter Vanessa. I take full responsibility, but she played to my insecurities. I tried so hard to say no. I didn't try hard enough," Danny said sadly.

My stomach churned. His confession tore me apart, but it needed airing.

"I was part of a larger plan, Eli," Danny began.

Slowly, the details of the tawdry affair unfolded. By what I assumed was the end, I was crying and Danny's eyes were moist. I hurt so much.

Danny held me tight, soothing me, hoping it would provide him with the comfort he so desperately needed.

"It gets worse, Eli," Danny cautioned. I didn't see how it possibly could.

With my emotions a twisted morass, it killed me to hear Danny's explanation of his betrayal. At the same time, my heart went out to him. Danny was in agony. Now, I understood why he had spent most of the school year wasted. How had Danny lived with this bottled up inside?

"After we wrapped, on her final evening in Vancouver, Vanessa dropped the final bomb. Her motives became clear."

Danny wiped fresh tears off my face, and I gave him my rapt attention.

"E, I was with Vanessa. She and I were, uh, together."

"I don't want to hear this," I wailed.

"I know, baby. I'm near the end."

Danny and Vanessa; I couldn't allow myself to picture them. The thought made me ill. I concentrated with all my might. My brain had to block out this vision.

I shivered, cold from fear. What could possibly be worse than what Danny had already shared?

"This is so difficult," Danny said slowly. "Elizabeth, I… God, this is so hard. I hate hurting you more." Danny paused, summoning the inner strength he needed. "What Vanessa said next tore the fabric of my existence into little pieces."

Danny was not one for dramatics, so this had to be big. I took his hands and kissed his cheek.

"I'm here for you, honey," I assured him. "I won't judge."

Danny nodded. "Once when I tried ending things with Vanessa, she warned me that only one man had ever broken up with her, and he was paying the price for the rest of his life." Danny stopped and looked me straight in the eyes. There was fear in his sapphires.

"Eli, that man is Dad. Seven years ago Dad had an affair with Vanessa."

"What!" I jumped up to sitting, jerking out of Danny's hold. "Oh my god!" I exclaimed. Shocked, overcome by revulsion, now I understood. "Utah?" I stammered.

Danny nodded. His usually brilliant sapphire eyes filled with sorrow.

"She was responsible for my parents nearly splitting up. Vanessa was conniving, but she was young, and somewhat naïve. She assumed Dad loved her back and would leave Mom. Of course, Dad had no intention of doing that. He didn't love Vanessa. To him, she was one of many. Dad loves Mom and always has. This is so fucked up.;"

I had to agree. "Danny, this is intense," I said in a soft, shocked voice. Unbelievable was more like it.

Danny pulled me back down to the mattress, holding me tight.

"Vanessa was an unknown getting her first break with a high-profile director. Mom and Dad were going through a rough patch. Dad drank too much and did drugs. Mom lost her tolerance and stayed home with me.

Vanessa was ambitious. Initiating an affair with Steven Newman seemed like a good career move. If all went well, she would become Mrs. Celebrity Director, and her career would soar."

"Danny, I'm so sorry. How devastating for you."

"Eli, why are you sorry? I cheated on you with Vanessa. Like father, like son right?"

"Don't say that. You are not Steve. He was married. He had a son. Steve willingly got involved with her. You, she played. And I am too allowed to feel sorry. That bitch hurt someone I love. Several someones if you add in Steve and Ellen."

Danny smiled. "Don't forget yourself. That bitch hurt someone I love, too."

He'd said it. I grinned. Danny loved me!

"I don't get it. Why go after Steven Newman and Michael Jacobs?"

"Vanessa thinks after this film opens she'll be in such demand it won't matter."

"Just for revenge? If it wasn't our Dads' film I'd pray for it to bomb."

"Oh, Eli." Danny smiled. "Hmm. We don't need the money, and it won't hurt our Dads' reputations. Let it bomb."

"Danny, you don't mean that."

"I do, Eli. Screw Vanessa. Dad has his next three projects lined up. I'm sure Mike does too." Danny took a deep breath. "Let me finish. There's more."

"More?" Wasn't this enough?

"Elizabeth," Danny, gripped by fear anticipated my reaction. "I have… a sister."

"What!" Absolutely incredible!

I clutched Danny tightly while he held me as though he was going to collapse. "How?" I cried in shock.

"Vanessa."

That much I had figured out. My head swam with questions, grief, and repulsion, all in equal parts. How do you sleep with your daughter's half-brother?

"She wouldn't get an abortion," Danny answered the unasked question.

"I've never heard that Vanessa had a child."

"She was an unknown. Dad paid her to leave town until after the birth to keep it secret. He's still paying to care for the child."

Unfuckingbelievable!

"My sister's name is Stephanie Nicole."

"Clever," I said sarcastically. "Only Vanessa would get pregnant by a married man and name the baby after him."

"She attends a residential school. Near Camarillo. Vanessa' drug habit damaged the fetus. Stephanie is six years old, and has special needs."

"I'm so sorry." How tragic. Despite her parentage, I knew Danny would have been thrilled to have a sister. As a child he longed for the closeness I shared with Teddy.

"That's why Steve taught you to never trust girls about birth control."

"Probably."

"Does Ellen know?" I dreaded the answer.

"About me, no. About Stephanie, yes," Danny answered, his voice filled with remorse. "That was the last straw. Mom threw Dad out. She even refused to let him see me."

"Danny, I don't know what to say."

"Eli, I couldn't face Dad. I hated him. I hated me. I blamed Dad for everything. I hated him all over again for hurting Mom and disrupting our family. I hated him for turning Vanessa into a vindictive bitch.

I felt betrayed, devastated to learn I'd been a pawn in a sick game all summer. And I couldn't tell anyone. The hatred built up inside me over the months.

I didn't come home at Christmas because the thought of seeing Dad made me ill. My guilt toward Mom was unimaginable. That's when I lost it."

"We thought we'd lost you. Permanently." Tears formed in my eyes again as I relived the frightful day. "When Ellen got your call from New Orleans, and you were so out of it. She was frantic. I was worse because I understood. Duncan. I forced her to get on the plane."

Danny squeezed my hand. I recognized the hurt in his eyes from learning of the pain he had caused his mother and I.

"I had a feeling my personal angel was looking out for me." Danny smiled, briefly. "But as soon as I returned to Donnelly, I resumed partying. It helped for a while, and then I would do it again. The pain was incredible."

"Did the partying solve anything?"

"No. I would see you, or hear from Mom, and guilt consumed me all over again. I couldn't face you or Dad sober."

"But now?"

"Dad got me to open up. He's very strong. Dad made it safe for me to share how much I despised him, and how I hated what he did to Mom and I. And he wouldn't let me near anything stronger than Diet Coke. Dad restocked the mini-fridge with non-alcoholic beverages only."

"You don't really hate Steve, do you?"

Danny shrugged. "I'm not sure. No, probably not hate. Dad proved his love in New York. I was a mess, but he took care of me."

Tears spilled down my cheeks.

"Eli, baby don't cry," Danny said tenderly. He brushed his thumb along my cheek and jaw. His eyes twinkled at me. "I got through it." Danny smiled proudly. "Dad and I came clean about everything. I realized that six years later I still hurt because they had kept me in the dark. I asked him why he did this to me and Mom."

I looked at Danny expectantly, waiting.

"Dad said he'd gotten too full of himself. He believed his press clippings. After he won the Oscar that spring, he felt invincible. When Mom kicked him out, and then with the arrest, he crashed back to earth.

Dad loves his family more than anything. You included. He never wanted to hurt us. Instead, he nearly lost us all. Babe, I understand. You love Dad, and this is shocking."

"It is. You poor thing," I reached for Danny, and I kissed his cheek.

"Thanks, E. Only your parents know. When Dad hit rock bottom, Mike bailed him out of jail, and somehow managed to keep it quiet. Mike drove Dad straight from the courthouse to Betty Ford. Only after he completed his program did Mom agree to even consider if their marriage could be saved."

A lock of hair had fallen across Danny's forehead. I tenderly brushed it back and let my fingertips linger on his cheek.

Danny cradled my hand, then kissed my palm and smiled, his deep sapphire eyes dancing. The familiarity of his lips filled me with warmth. God, how I'd missed this. More than anything, I hated that our separation had kept us from the endless hours of conversation we had always enjoyed.

"Why didn't you tell me any of this when you got home? I could have helped."

"You had expectations. I had encouraged them, and you were disappointed."

"I didn't understand what had changed. Only two weeks had passed since I'd seen you. I thought you were suffering from exhaustion."

Danny nervously massaged my knuckles.

"By the way, I love the mural, especially the depictions of us as kids." Then he smiled and squeezed my hand. "I felt like a lying, cheating bastard, scum of the lowest kind. After I told you to make the house our home, you did just that and I... I wasn't in the right mind to receive it."

"I didn't think you noticed."

"Of course I did. I didn't feel worthy." Danny frowned. "I was ashamed. I didn't deserve you. Eli, you're a proper girl. I couldn't exactly come home to my fiancée and say 'honey, I've been cheating on you with a psycho all summer, please help me.'"

"I'm your fiancée?" This was news.

"Well, we live together, so yeah."

We do? Danny still considered us to be living together? This really was a hiatus? Whoa! Did that mean I cheated when I dated Scott? I instantly dismissed that thought from my brain.

"So now you were ready to tell me?"

"Babe, I've been going through hell. I've needed you so badly."

"You were a mess when you texted me from New York."

"I was. But before I could begin to heal, I had to confront Dad. I stormed out of Vancouver and never spoke to Dad again. When I texted you, I was reaching out for help. There I was, sitting alone in a bar. How pathetic. Your love saved me, baby."

I nodded. "I couldn't let you go down in flames."

"Dad had a psychiatrist waiting. Despite the anger, he still loves me."

"Of course he does. I do too," I confessed. "You're very loveable."

Danny relaxed. He smiled, and his eyes twinkled again.

"The doctor was great. We had continuous sessions, only taking breaks for meals and working out. Dad knows I'm angry and disappointed, but now I understand what was going on in his life back then."

Danny looked at me expectantly. His story ended, I tried processing everything I had learned. Were I not a principal in this sordid tale, I would have felt sorry for him.

Instead my insides were quaking. Nausea threatened. I had listened to Danny explain how he'd gotten involved with Vanessa, and how he had kept it secret. I couldn't hold back any longer. Torrents spilled down my face. I didn't know what to think. I was so confused.

Danny had needed to tell me the truth. Our relationship had to be based on trust. But this truth was unbearable. This was the ugliest truth I'd ever learned.

The composure I'd fought so valiantly to keep was gone. I shook. I cried.

Danny wrapped his arms around me and held me tight.

"I thought I was past it. I hurt, Danny," I cried, feeling the anguish in my gut.

"I know you do, baby. I know," Danny said gently. "You had to learn the truth. Please don't hate me, Eli. I'm so sorry. You've got to believe me," he pleaded. "I love you. E, I will do anything to make us right again."

Danny brushed a damp hair off of my wet face. His eyes searched my face, hoping for a positive reaction. "If we love each other enough anything is possible."

"I don't know how. We can't go back in time and pretend Vanessa never happened."

"We can go forward," Danny pleaded. "Dad and I are. We have a long way to go, but at least we're headed in the right direction."

"That's good, Danny," I said sincerely. Still, I sniffled.

Danny took my hands. His eyes studied my soul. "Elizabeth," he began tentatively. "I'd like us to head in the right direction, too."

"What does that mean?" I asked, although I had a premonition what the answer was going to be.

The gentle, loving warmth in Danny's sapphire eyes as he looked at me; the touch of his fingers against my jawbone, told me all I needed to know.

"I've never stopped being in love with you, Elizabeth. I want you back. I promise I will never hurt you again. If you give me another chance, it will be the last one you ever have to give me. Baby, I want us to be us again. Only better."

Danny took my face in his hands, brought his lips to mine, and kissed me. Unlike at the restaurant, this time I responded, welcoming his breath and his probing tongue, wrapping my arms around his neck, and holding tightly.

Bolts of electricity connected us. The power of our shared need pushed me down on the bed. We were laying joined, lips glued together, as though we were making up for all those lost months in one kiss.

When we stopped to breathe we found ourselves in each other's arms smiling, our foreheads touching. Kissing Danny felt so right.

"I shouldn't have done that," he said softly.

"No," I answered in a drunken haze, "You shouldn't have."

Then I reached for Danny, and initiated the next kiss. Danny tightened his hold on me once more; one strong hand around my shoulders, the other caressing my back. God, I'd missed this so much.

"What's wrong with me?" I asked, abruptly ending our kiss.

"You love me?" Danny answered, an impish grin highlighting his boyish charm.

"But why? You're a two-timing cheating cad. And you just shared all the sordid details with me."

"I'm your two-timing cheating cad." Danny shrugged. I frowned. "Babe, that was last summer."

I quickly rose to my knees. My hair fell like a curtain across my face. I looked directly at Danny.

"You're asking a lot."

"I know I am baby, but I'm not like that anymore. Eli, I've changed. Please let me prove myself. I love you." Danny's expression was so sincere.

"You don't know what love is, Danny."

"Yes I do." Danny tucked my hair behind my ear and lifted my chin. His touch so gentle, yet so masculine, melted my heart. "Love means every night I go to sleep with you in my arms, and every morning I wake up with you in my arms, and in between I don't touch, look, or even think about another woman for the rest of my life."

"You mean that? Seriously?"

"Seriously," Danny laughed. "Babe, after I crash landed, I realized what I spent all last year denying. I love you. I really love you. You're it for me, Elizabeth."

"You're not just saying that because you're horny?" I smiled.

Danny raised an eyebrow. "No. I'm being sincere. E, have I ever lied to you?"

"No. You've always been brutally honest, even when the truth hurt your cause."

"Exactly." Then Danny smiled mischievously. "And I am horny."

"Aha!" I laughed.

"What do you expect?" Danny chuckled. "I'm lying in bed with the love of my life, whom I haven't touched in months."

"You're asking me not only to forgive but to forget. I don't know if I can."

"Which is more difficult?"

"Forgiveness comes from the heart, Forgetting comes from the head. It's much more difficult to forget." I paused for a beat. "Danny, I believe you. You've been open tonight like never before. I trust you, so I think I can forgive."

Danny smiled. His eyes brightened as he digested the meaning of what I had said. "Babe," Danny said as he took my hand. "I've been miserable. I can't live without you."

I stared into Danny's twinkling sapphire eyes. "I feel the same," I murmured while smiling down at him.

"What will make you forget?"

"I don't know if I ever can," I paused to think. "Time. Time will dull the bad memories. Creating new good memories will replace the bad ones."

Danny looked at me thoughtfully, processing my needs.

"Let me take you out to dinner tomorrow, Elizabeth. It's been so long since we've gone out together. I'll make it special."

I smiled warmly at Danny's proposal, but I had a better idea. "I'd rather have a study date tomorrow. I have so much work to do."

The wattage of Danny's sapphire eyes dulled a notch. Again I smiled warmly. It was not a rejection.

"I don't want to wait until tomorrow. Can't we create a new memory tonight?"

Danny's eyes opened wide as he digested my message. "You mean you want to…?" he asked hopefully. I nodded, my grin stretched wider. "Oh, babe. Do you have any idea how much I love you?"

"Actually, I do," I said. I really did. "Let's make love, Daniel. It's been so long. I'm dying to."

Danny laughed. I frowned. "Why are you laughing?" I asked.

"I love your directness, Eli. Whatever happened to that shy little virgin?"

"She grew up, married you, and toughened up to survive."

"Oh, really?" Danny smirked and raised an eyebrow.

"Mrs. Daniel Newman cannot be a timid mouse."

"You're right, and you're not. If you were, we wouldn't be here. I'd have kept cheating on you without giving it a thought. You played me right, Mrs. Newman."

I collapsed against Danny and planted a quick smacker on his check. "Now I have to be honest." Intermittent guilt had bothered me since Rachel scolded me in Gucci.

"What did you do, babe? Cheat on your taxes?" Danny couldn't imagine there was anything I needed to come clean over.

"The outfit I was wearing tonight," I began tentatively.

"Yeah, it's great. Absolutely stunning on you, baby," Danny grinned. "I can't wait to see it on you again. Every curve. Why? Did you shoplift?"

"Of course not!" I snapped. "No, you bought it for me."

"I did?"

"Spring break. Gucci. I used your credit card."

"So? You always wear nice clothes. Did you really think I would mind?"

"No, but Rachel gave me a hard time."

"Don't sweat it, babe. I would have bought it had I been there."

"That's what I told Rach. She doesn't understand us." I tilted my head toward his. "Let's make love, Daniel."

"You're sure you don't want to wait until Friday?" Danny laughed, referring to our aborted reconcilliation last September.

"I can't wait another minute. Daniel, you showed true courage tonight. You opened up and let me into your darkest secrets. Then you gave me what I wanted most in the world; you gave me your pledge. You gave me you, all of you. I want to give you what you want most – me."

I pulled off my shirt, tossing it aside. Danny stared at my breasts, barely concealed in a lacy demi-bra.

"God, you're gorgeous Eli," he exclaimed. I blushed, delighted with his reaction. "Copper?" Danny noted the color of my bra with pleasure.

"To match the sweater," I insisted. "While I was in Beverly Hills, I bought some new colors at that shop we like."

"For Scott? I hope I didn't buy them." Danny frowned. "Couldn't he have seen your old stuff? He wouldn't know the difference."

I laughed. "Daniel Martin Newman, you're jealous!" I taunted.

"No, I'm not," Danny insisted, but discomfort crossed his face.

"Scott never saw my underwear, old or new. I told you that. I couldn't." I sighed. Happy. Finally. "You were always on my mind."

Danny's frown vanished, replaced by a twinkling grin. "You bought these for me?"

I nodded. "Rachel wanted to kill me. She thought I was having a breakdown. Maybe she was right. Using your Amex card at Gucci made me believe that maybe it really was only a hiatus."

Danny chuckled. "And of course being Mrs. Danny Newman, I bet you purchased the entire collection because you knew that would please Mr. Newman."

"Maybe not the entire collection. I didn't like the shade of green they were showing. And no, you didn't buy them. I did. What if you saw the Amex statement?"

Danny smirked. "I would have wondered why a girl I wasn't even talking to was charging an entire wardrobe of sexy underwear to me. Eli, you're a nut," Danny laughed. "Is there a matching thong?" he asked eagerly.

"You'll have to find out for yourself," I answered, shamelessly flirting.

I grinned as Danny scooched over, and slowly and dramatically, eased my flannel pants over my hips, down my thighs and then completely off, revealing the matching copper-colored thong. With a flourish, he threw the pants on the floor, and I smirked.

At Danny's touch, I shivered. The chemistry between us was incredible. Lightning bolts shot through me. My heart raced out of control. I barely breathed.

"E, you are the most amazing girl I've ever met," Danny declared.

Then he pressed his lips to my stomach, below the hipbone where the narrow band of the thong rested, securing the miniature triangle of copper satin in place.

I gasped, white heat coursing through me. "Like it?" I asked provocatively, my back arching, challenging Danny for more.

"Oh, yeah," he answered, and he raised his head.

Danny grinned, recognizing my aroused state. "You wore this for me?"

"Daniel!" I was embarrassed because of course I had.

"Lizzie!" he teased. "You planned all along how you wanted tonight to end."

"Daniel!" I squealed again; heat flushing my face.

"Awww, baby, you wanted to look nice for me," Danny laughed.

"Of course I did," I said, resigned. I could never conceal my feelings from him.

Danny smiled and he held my glance, sapphire eyes twinkling devilishly. His fingertips gently lifted the copper fabric, and he kissed me below where it had rested, sending renewed shivers of excitement through me.

"Danny!" I gasped. Another inch. It had been so long.

"You're sure?" Danny asked as though any girl as aroused as I was could possibly say no.

"I've never been more sure of anything," I answered. I reached behind my back, and removed my bra, flinging it toward his head.

Danny grinned as he ducked and squeezed my breasts. "God, how I've missed these," he said, and Danny kissed each one, his tongue lingering, tantalizing me.

"They've missed you too," I gasped, and we both laughed.

Then Danny lifted the band of my thong at each hip and slowly eased it off. After tossing it aside, Danny nuzzled his head between my thighs, kissing them, his tongue lapping, teasing me. I grasped his hair, as I writhed from the intense pleasure, my back arching, encouraging him.

Danny raised his head, and our lust filled smiles met. He inched his body upward. Our lips met, crushing together, seven months of longing to make up for. I reached for the waistband of Danny's pants, and I hurriedly pulled them down, freeing him. Dispensing with his clothing, we enjoyed the pleasure of our bare skin twining together.

Our kisses grew more powerful. And when I felt I could not take the intensity any longer, Danny plunged into me more forcefully than ever before. His rhythm increased, and my back arched, meeting his every thrust.

My throaty moans were answered as Danny thrust even more powerfully. My nails dug into his strong back, holding on for dear life. Brought to new heights of ecstasy, we soon exploded together. In our shared passions, a new memory was made. Our long nightmare was over.

CHAPTER FIFTY-FOUR - ELIZABETH

Rapid knocking on the door woke me. Fuzzy-headed from staying up half the night t alking to Danny, and then making love again, the noise didn't register.

I glanced at Danny, wrapped around me like a warm blanket. His eyes fluttered open. So it hadn't been a dream! His skin against mine, the smile on his sleepy lips, they brought back the memory of last night's passion and the promise of more. If we kept this up, yeah, forgetting the past seven months would be easier than I imagined.

"You're really here!" I whispered. Danny laughed.

Knock, knock, knock.

"Elizabeth, you coming to breakfast?" Rachel called from the other side of the door.

Now wide-awake, Danny snickered, on the verge of a full crack-up, and he squeezed me tightly to prevent it.

"Shit!" I whispered. "She can't know you're here."

I clamped my hand over Danny's mouth and felt his muffled laughter vibrating against my palm.

"Shit! I've overslept, Rach," I called out, my voice genuinely in panic.

Time was running out on keeping Danny quiet.

"Then I'll catch you later. I'm dying to hear about dinner."

Danny chose this moment to run a finger up my spine causing me to squirm.

"Okay," I responded while cringing to stifle a giggle.

"Stop that!" I muttered while releasing my hand from over Danny's mouth.

Danny's laughter burst free. "You're afraid of Rachel!" he choked out.

"No, I'm not," I snapped. Caught! "It's just, she'll think I caved."

Danny nuzzled my neck and kissed my shoulder. "Do you think you caved?"

"Well, I really didn't want to sleep with you, at least not yet."

"If I recall, it was your idea." Danny twirled a lock of my hair.

"Grrr… Daniel!"

"Oh, c'mon Eli. I love you, baby, but be honest. Don't deny it."

"I wanted you to make the first move," I complained.

Danny laughed. "I did make the first move, knucklehead. I came to your door."

Then Danny pressed his lips to mine, igniting my passion, and his kiss ended the discussion.

When our lips parted, Danny gently moved an errant wave off my face. Holding my head, our noses touched, and we smiled. Taking in his sparkling sapphire eyes, my heart fluttered.

"Elizabeth, for twenty years you've been my most enjoyable playmate."

Danny ran his fingertip over my hip and down my thigh. I shivered.

"And you played me perfectly. I don't know how you did it, but you are a lot tougher than you look."

I ran my fingertip along Danny's lower lip and smiled.

"Mrs. Danny Newman has to be tough if she wants to remain being Mrs. Danny Newman."

"Is life with me really that bad?"

"On certain days it is," I quipped.

Danny smirked. "What about today?"

"Today?" Uncontrollable giggles overwhelmed me. I fell back against the pillows. "Oh my god, Danny! Today it's great!"

I stretched my arms and enthusiastically clasped them around his neck. I briefly kissed Danny's lips. He grinned.

"Today I love being Mrs. Danny Newman!"

I rolled on top of Danny, playfully straddling him. Then I gave him a smacker of a kiss on his cheek. "This is who I am. This is where I want to be," I joyously declared.

Danny wrapped his arms around me, pulling me beside him on the mattress. "Everyday will be as good as today," he promised.

Then Danny crushed his lips to mine. My heart skipped a beat as his power pulsed through me. Danny rubbed against me, his hardness probing.

"Danny, no!" I objected in a fit of giggles. "I can't. I'm so sore. I'll never be able to walk again."

He looked at me with soulful blue eyes. "E? I won't see you all morning. Don't you want me to start the day happy?"

"Danny!" I laughed. "That sounds so pathetic. You've already stated the day happy. You woke up in my bed."

"E?" Danny pleaded, and he slipped his hand between my thighs. "I love you."

"Danny, we made love three times in the last eight hours," I laughed.

His fingers entered me causing every muscle to clench. "Can't we have a playdate later?" I barely eked out as my arousal intensified.

Danny grinned, so boyish. "I like later too," he said as he rolled on top of me.

I wrapped my arms around Danny's back in surrender. "Now is good," I said breathlessly, and he entered me.

"Make-up sex is the best!" I gasped.

"And why is that?" Danny asked as he began his rhythmic thrusting.

"The promise of more to come," I giggled.

Danny groaned at my double entendre. Then he crushed his lips to mine, probably to shut me up.

Soon we shared our climax, and I snuggled up to Danny, sore but content. We exchanged delicate kisses borne of our rediscovered intimacy and love.

"E, time to get up," Danny whispered within what seemed too short a time.

"Do we have to? I want more make-up sex."

Danny kissed my nose. "I've got to be the world's luckiest man. My girlfriend is gorgeous, and she doesn't want to leave my bed. Unfortunately, you have class, and I'm meeting with the Dean. I can't be late."

"The Dean! Are you in trouble?"

"No, it's perfunctory. Dad called last week and told him where I was. I'm sure all he wants is to confirm that I'm alive and living. But I can't be late. It's the Dean."

Leaving me with another smacker of a kiss, Danny disengaged and climbed out of the bed. As he pulled on his flannel pants, our eyes didn't leave each other. Then Danny leaned down for one last kiss.

"Remember when Dad and I were leaving for New York, you said you wanted to talk to me? E, what was it you wanted to discuss?"

"It's moot now." I laughed.

"E?"

My cheeks were hot with embarrassment.

"I wanted to discuss issuing a formal statement announcing our split."

Danny grinned and ruffled my hair. "So you could be free to smooch with Grant," he laughed.

I frowned. "So nobody would think I was cheating on you."

Returning from the shower, I steeled myself for what I knew I must do. I hadn't even told Danny; he might have tried talking me out of it. I reached for my phone and dialed the person I dreaded but felt obligated to call.

Awkward as it was, it was best to be direct. Prolonging the inevitable would not make it more pleasant. But I knew it was the right thing to do.

"Hey, Scottie," I said.

CHAPTER FIFTY-FIVE - ELIZABETH

"Hey, you!" an exuberant Danny greeted me outside the dining hall.

I had just taken back-to-back dance classes, and my appearance was not on par with the Adonis who greeted me. My ponytail hung damp with sweat, limp against my neck and back. Danny's shaggy mane was perfect, falling just so, flopping across his brow as though he'd planned it that way.

In contrast to Danny's snug designer jeans that emphasized his narrow hips, and the Nordic sweater that accentuated his broad shoulders, I was a mess. Capri-length yoga pants were worn over cut-off tights, and a zip-up hoodie was open over my tank leotard.

Danny didn't care. His strong arms grabbed me around the waist. Then he lifted me off the ground, and twirled me in a circle, leaving me in a fit of giggles, clutching his muscular biceps for safety. Finally he put me down, a gentle touchdown.

"How was your morning, beautiful?"

"Beautiful? I'm all sweaty. I've got to take a shower."

"Baby, you're always beautiful," Danny responded. "Hey, I see you can walk," he teased before quickly kissing my cheek.

Danny's kiss set my heart to fluttering. "Barely," I confessed. A broad smile lit my face. "I missed you. I haven't seen you in three hours," I teased back.

"Poor you," Danny laughed. "How was class?"

"I don't know," I admitted. "My legs are so sore. I'm lucky I didn't fall. All I could think about was last night."

"And this morning?" Danny grinned, and he took my hands.

"That too," I giggled, "Danny, I can't wait for tonight. Must we wait?" I sighed.

Danny laughed and squeezed my hands. "You said you were sore."

"I am, but I miss you." My adoring emeralds met his sapphires. Judging by their twinkle, he was feeling as much a love sick fool as I was today.

"Same, but I can't skip class. I missed too much last week."

"I hate when I don't get what I want," I pouted.

"Spoiled," Danny laughed. I frowned. "Let's eat fast. I'll help you shower."

Every muscle south of my waist clenched. My heart beat rapidly. I grinned. How I wish I didn't need food so badly. After ballet and jazz, I was starving, and my body needed the fuel.

"I don't want anyone to know about us yet," I said, as Danny opened the heavy glass door for me.

"Then why are you holding my hand?" I abruptly dropped his hand, and Danny took it back. "Honey, you're a ditz." Danny laughed again, and we entered the building.

"I called Scott," I blurted.

Cued up by the salad bar, Danny stared at me, stunned.

"It was the right thing to do. Scott's a good guy. I didn't want to hurt him if he found out about us through the grapevine. Or worse; what if he saw us together?"

"How did Scott react?"

"Resigned. He didn't have a fit if that's what you're implying. Scott's a gentleman."

"If he's such a gentleman, why was Scott trying to get in my girl's panties?"

I rolled my eyes. "Daniel! C'mon. You and I were split."

Was he always going to throw Scott in my face? Danny had no right to be jealous.

"Okay, fine. I still don't like that you almost gave him what was mine."

"But I didn't. Leave it at that, Daniel."

I frowned. If he didn't stop this, I would shower alone.

Danny glanced at me and recognized my ire. "I'm sorry. Of course guys wanted you. All that matters is that you didn't want them. I'll get over it. So, what did Scott say?"

"He thanked me for my sensitivity, and for letting him have closure."

"I'm glad you called him. Chloe says Scott's a stand-up guy. You did the honorable thing, Eli."

"Thanks. What about Phoebe?"

"Phoebs?" Danny said awkwardly. "I didn't have time," he stammered.

I knew he was lying. Danny probably hadn't given her a second thought. "Daniel?"

Danny smiled sheepishly. "Phoebs isn't like Scott."

"You were sleeping with her." I pointed out the obvious, much as I hated reminding myself of it.

"Only sometimes. She won't care. E, Phoebs is a slut. She'll find someone new."

I frowned; disappointed that Danny seemed intimidated by Phoebe.

"I'll call her later," Danny relented after noting my disapproval. "You're right. I should tie up the loose ends."

I kissed Danny's cheek. "Thank you."

Reaching for a plate as we inched our way up the service line, I asked Danny in a soft voice, "Do you think anyone has figured out that we're back together?"

For some reason, and much as I had spent the entire jazz class trying to figure it out, I didn't want people to know.

"Probably not yet."

"Oh, good." I was relieved.

Danny shot me a devilish grin. "Of course, ardent royal watchers might suspect I'm banging my wife again."

"Danny!" I rolled my eyes. "That's crass." Danny laughed.

"We'll they've probably noticed we're standing together, and we are chatting amiably." I frowned. "Babe, your face gives it away. You're wearing a smile that won't quit, and you're looking at me with adoring eyes that scream, 'I love this man. We had amazing sex last night. I want more!'"

"I'm that obvious?" I fretted.

"So am I. One look at me, and it's obvious I spent a wild night with a certain red-head, and would do anything to do it again."

I frowned once more.

"Eli?" Danny recaptured my attention, and I smiled up at him. Then, without warning, Danny reached for my face, brought his lips to mine, and kissed me. My response was immediate and heartfelt. I wrapped my hands around Danny's neck, careful not to hit his skull with my plate. I luxuriated in his embrace.

"Now everyone in the dining hall knows," Danny murmured.

"Yeah. They do, don't they?" I responded in a love-induced haze.

Danny noticed the shrinking line and released me. "Hey, we're next."

Danny was right. Only two more students were in front of us for the salad bar. I quickly glanced around the cavernous room.

"Danny," I said, "A few new students have entered. They don't know." I smiled shyly, went up on toe, and kissed him.

"You've changed your mind?"

"It's too difficult to hide."

Danny's smile teased me. He tenderly smoothed stray hairs off my face. "I love you, babe. You're a nut."

As Danny kissed me again, I heard the frustrated server call out, "Next." I couldn't help giggling as our lips parted.

"Just like old times," Danny said as he slid into the seat beside me. I let his right hand take my left once he settled in.

"Only better," I smirked.

Danny lifted my hand, locked eyes with me, and kissed my knuckles. I filled with joy. How I'd missed this. There was no better way to enjoy a salad than by holding hands with Danny.

Soon, we spotted Cam, Rachel and Shane, led by a buoyant Chloe. We abruptly dropped hands.

"You're back together!" Chloe squealed.

Danny and I exchanged surprised glances and then stared at Chloe. How did she figure it out? Had she seen us?

"Uh, yeah. Thanks," Danny answered awkwardly. "How'd you know?"

"Your faces. You're both happy," she pointed out. That of course led to a renewal of our smiles. "Plus," Chloe grinned, "From the line I saw you holding hands."

I blushed. So busted!

"Which means you weren't sleeping when I knocked," Rachel accused me. "You had company."

"Guilty?" I answered rather guiltily.

"Oh, thank god," Shane exclaimed. "Danny's an unbearable son of a bitch when he isn't getting laid."

I blushed deep crimson while Danny smirked. Before I could object to Shane, Danny leaned over and planted a chaste kiss on my lips. I beamed with joy.

"This is awesome!" Chloe gushed. "I love a happy ending."

"Chloe, get real," Rachel snapped. "Happy ending? Until it isn't."

"Rach!" Danny said sharply. "You wanted us back together."

"Yes, but twenty-four hours ago, you weren't even talking to each other."

"Dad got us started. We couldn't exactly sit through dinner and remain silent," Danny explained defensively.

"Wow! Steven Newman must be the most fucking brilliant man in America. Not only does he win Academy Awards, in his spare time he's a marriage counselor," Rachel said sarcastically. "Two hours with Dr. Newman, and you go from hostility to honeymooners. Unfucking believable!"

"Rachel! It wasn't like that," I protested. "Danny and I were up half the night talking."

Danny brushed a lock of hair off my face. "Babe, what Rachel objects to is the other half of the night."

"I thought she'd be happy for us," I trembled.

Danny furrowed his brow. "Don't be sad. Rachel can't spoil our day."

Unexpectedly, a tear escaped down my cheek.

Danny gathered me in his embrace, holding me against his chest.

"Shhhh," he gently murmured. "No tears, baby." Then Danny turned to Rachel. "You will not ruin my girlfriend's day," he said sternly.

"Rachel," Chloe interjected, her calmness serving as an emotional counterpoint. "Remember, Danny and Elizabeth never stopped loving each other. I'm sure it wasn't difficult for them to find common ground."

"I'm trying to protect her. I don't want to see Elizabeth hurt again."

I released myself from Danny's embrace. "I can take care of myself!" I declared forcefully.

CHAPTER FIFTY-SIX - DANIEL

"Let's go, Rach," I ordered. I kissed Eli's cheek. "I'll be right back."

I led Rachel to an alcove off the lobby where we could enjoy some privacy.

"Look, Rach," I began sternly, my hands on my hips. "You've said it yourself, Eli and I have been driving you nuts all year. Now we make-up, and you're still unhappy. What's your problem, Rach? It's making my lady sad, and she's suffered too much sadness this year."

"Really? Then maybe you shouldn't be sleeping with her. You're setting Elizabeth up for even greater heartbreak."

"What the hell are you talking about?" I asked, concentrating on keeping my volume down. I was furious, but aware of passersby staring. "I love Elizabeth. So what heartbreak do you foresee?"

"Danny, don't pull that innocence crap. Remember, there are things I know that Elizabeth doesn't."

So that's where this was going. Would I ever escape my past? Rachel's regard for Eli made me smile.

"Oh, Rach," I said, and I embraced her. Stunned, Rachel couldn't respond. "We're so lucky to have a friend like you who really care," and I released a bewildered Rachel.

"Then you know what I'm referring to," she snarled, recovering her composure.

I smiled. "You have nothing to be concerned about. I've changed, Rachel."

"In one week? I want to believe it, but how can I?"

"Rach, I hit rock bottom in New York. I went through hell, but in my darkest moment, Eli's love was there for me. I vowed if I made it through the night, I would do whatever it would take to win her back."

"But you were a drunken mess," Rachel pointed out.

"No matter. Once my head cleared, I felt it even more profoundly. Dad was skeptical at first too."

"I can understand why."

"Dad had a therapist staying in our suite."

"You're kidding, right?"

I smiled, embarrassed. "Hey, he's Steven Newman. Whatever Dad wants, Dad gets. In this case, he wanted his son's brain repaired quickly and quietly."

"Amazing." Rachel was more than a little stunned.

"It worked. See anything on the internet?"

Rachel brightened. "I did see one photo of you and your Dad. It was real nice. You were strolling on Fifth Avenue. The caption made it out to be a father-son shopping trip. I printed it out for you."

"Thanks. My point made."

"Did Steven plant it?" Rachel smirked.

"Possibly," I laughed. "We did go shopping one afternoon. I took a break from the round-the-clock head shrinking. Hell! Shopping with Dad was probably part of the therapy. We had a lot to work on."

"I'm sorry. I hope you can patch things up."

"It's coming. Through everything my desire to right things with Eli never wavered, despite the shrink's objection. He claims a girlfriend will distract from my recovery. The hell with that! I told him, and Dad agreed, 'Eli is not negotiable.'"

Rachel laughed at my blatant disobedience.

"Don't you think the doctor might know better?" Rachel protested. "Isn't it wrong to burden Elizabeth with your recovery?"

"The doctor does not know better, and I am not burdening Elizabeth. It's not like I was a strung-out junkie. I had some personal issues I couldn't deal with, and I went a bit crazy. I told Eli what was going on, and… Yeah, she knows."

Rachel looked expectantly at me.

I chuckled as I answered, "Sorry, Rach. It's between me and my wife."

"Your wife? I didn't mean to presume…" she answered awkwardly.

"Rach, I always knew what Elizabeth wanted. She deserves no less. Now I'm able to commit to her. Hell, I finally can admit it to myself. No more games. No more cheating. Eli's it."

Rachel starred wide-eyed. "You mean it, don't you?" She asked hopefully.

"I let Eli declare victory last night," I smiled. "And I couldn't be happier. Best decision I ever made."

Elizabeth rested her tote bag against my desk while I packed my laptop and reading materials into my backpack. I brushed by her to reach across the desk for my favorite pen and Elizabeth's hands encircled my waist.

"What?" I laughed as I turned in her hold to face her.

Eli's complexion glowed; her damp hair a potent reminder of the best shower I'd had in months. Those emerald eyes twinkling in my direction were more than alluring. I recognized that look. Eli had enjoyed the shower as much as I had.

"Class starts in fifteen minutes," I said.

Riing up on toe in a way that only a dancer can do, Elizabeth tightened her grip. "Must we?" she asked in a breathy whisper. Then Eli kissed me.

I unwrapped her hands. "Message received, babe," I told her with a chuckle. "But we can't. I missed too many classes when I was in New York."

Elizabeth frowned. "You can't miss just one more?"

I hated disappointing her. After our long separation, I wanted to spend the afternoon with Eli just as much as she wanted to spend it with me.

I pulled Elizabeth back into my arms, reinvigorating her smile. "How's this? We attend class like good little students, and afterwards you and I will celebrate with an epic late-afternoon date."

Miraculously, Elizabeth and I arrived at the classroom before Owen did.

I pulled Eli back into the hall to enjoy a few moments of alone time before the class began. She leaned against the wall, and I faced her, captivated by her smile and those dancing emerald eyes.

Elizabeth was irresistible. I lifted her chin and ran my index finger down her jawline. She grinned, and I felt her shudder. I wanted Eli so badly. Damn, class!

I leaned in and pressed my lips to hers. This kiss would have to carry me through until the class ended. The taste of her lips was sweeter than any candy; Eli felt it too.

She wrapped her delicate hands around my neck, and my body pressed her into the wall. The soft moan emitted from her parted lips was intoxicating, urging me on. I plunged my tongue into her mouth, exploring every bit. Our tongues met, and danced their own slow, seductive, dance.

"Ahem, Mr. Newman."

Shit! Owen!

Our mouths flew apart, though Eli's hands remained around my neck, holding me close.

"Class, folks," Owen added, and he smirked at what he had interrupted.

Eli turned the reddest red I'd ever seen, and I knew my coloring wasn't more than a shade or two paler.

"Coming, professor," I mumbled.

As the seminar ended, I quickly loaded my backpack and met Elizabeth at her seat. As always, she meticulously packed her tote bag.

Eli rose, and she took my hands. Her sassy grin melted me.

"Ready for our date?" I asked, with the broadest smile lighting my face.

"You betcha," Elizabeth answered playfully.

Her smile said it all. I leaned in to kiss Elizabeth, eager to take her back to my room.

"Danny, I need to speak with you," Professor Dennison called as our lips met.

I abruptly pulled back, awkwardly ending our PDA.

"I'll wait outside." Elizabeth's smile told me she didn't mind the delay.

"Thanks, babe. I won't be long," and I tapped her nose.

I joined Professor Dennison at the front of the empty classroom.

"Owen, what's up?" I asked.

"Congratulations."

I smiled sheepishly, embarrassed. "Uh, yeah. Thanks."

"When did this happen?"

"Last night. Dad was visiting, and he forced Elizabeth to join us for dinner."

"And nobody says no to Steven Newman?"

"Not exactly," I laughed. "But Dad made it impossible for Eli to say no. Then after he left, she and I started talking. And talking. And talking."

"That was fast."

"I was lucky," I admitted. "Elizabeth was still in love with me, and we only had two issues to work out."

Owen raised an eyebrow, inquisitive. He wanted to know more, but wouldn't ask. He was a professor, after all.

"I promised Elizabeth that I was done with the drinking and the drugs, and what really did us in. I'm embarrassed to admit it. Ugh! I hate myself for what I did, Owen. Eli should have dumped me sooner. There were times when I went home with someone else."

"I could see where that would be a deal-breaker," he said drily. "Elizabeth's convinced that won't happen again?"

"Yeah. Eli trusts me now. Owen, I was so stupid. I thought I was being cool. Instead, I hurt the one I should have been protecting. Now I know, what's cool is being with Elizabeth, and only Elizabeth. She's the most amazing girl I will ever meet, and I've promised her I will never go near another."

"Congratulations, Danny. You're now a man. When's the wedding?"

"Owen!" I exclaimed. "I don't know. We're not engaged. But we'll invite you."

"I'd like that. Maybe now I can have you both over to the house. I'd like Annabelle to meet the real you this time."

"Sorry about the Christmas party."

All I remembered of the party at the Dennison's house was getting drunk and acting like an ass. In retrospect, I wish the ground had swallowed me up that evening. I doubted I could ever face Mrs. Dennison again.

"There's a lot of evenings I'm sorry about," I said apologetically.

"I'm sure there are," Owen agreed. "Listen Danny. I don't want to keep you from Elizabeth, but I heard from Dean Colton. He said you met with him this morning."

"I can't believe he put me on probation," I complained.

"You don't realize how close he came to suspending you."

"Are you kidding me? Owen, I'm an A student!" I was enraged.

"That's what I told him when he met with me on Thursday. He relented when I pointed out that this late in the year Miss Bergman couldn't start her film over, and she would unnecessarily be penalized and lose credit."

And Rachel's father isn't Steven Newman. Her career would go down in flames before it ever began.

"Thanks, Owen," I said contritely. "You don't know how much I appreciate it."

"I think I do. Just promise me you won't do anything stupid and blow it."

"I promise. God, if I get suspended, I'd be so embarrassed. My parents would be humiliated, well Mom would be. I don't want to imagine the headlines."

"I feel for you. That's an added pressure most of us will never know. Danny, I'm your advisor, and your friend. I'm here to give you whatever support you need."

I nodded. "Thanks, Owen. I still have to tell Elizabeth. I didn't want this to spoil our reconciliation."

"Do you really think it's wise to have a girlfriend right now?"

"Elizabeth is not negotiable, Owen," I said firmly.

CHAPTER FIFTY-SEVEN - ELIZABETH

"Babe, I've missed these afternoons so badly."

Entwined between the sheets of Danny's bed, we smiled at each other, basking in the afterglow of our lovemaking. He ran his fingertip up my spine and I shivered.

"Never again," I trilled. "I'm free any afternoon you want."

Danny grinned. "That is so tempting."

Joyously I threw my hands around his neck. I still couldn't believe how radically our lives had changed. No two people could be happier.

I must have dozed because I didn't remember time passing, but I opened my eyes in the most wonderful place. Warm, loving arms held me, not wanting to let me go. Expressive sapphire eyes twinkled in my direction. Danny's lips kissed me.

"Hey, sleepyhead. Ready to get up?" he asked in a soft voice.

I yawned, and then stretched my arms like a kitten, a very contented kitten.

"No, not really. I'm too cozy."

"Me too. All afternoon in bed with you isn't long enough."

"Then let's stay," I giggled.

"Okay." Then Danny sat up and gave me a quick kiss. "I'll be right back, babe."

Danny climbed over me, leaving our bed, and found a towel that he wrapped around his narrow waist. I watched his every move, awestruck. I love watching Danny. I could stare at his magnificent body all day. And night. Every night.

Danny abruptly turned back toward me. Caught! He grinned. "Love ya," he called before going out the door. I chuckled to myself. Bathroom.

I lay back on the pillows and stretched again, so cozy. A smile lit my face. I knew how I really felt; at home. Reunited with Danny, I was home.

The phone interrupted my reverie. I rolled over and picked up Danny's iPhone. The display identified Steve as the caller.

"Newman residence," I answered in a perky voice.

"Newman residence?" Steve laughed.

"Well, it's Danny's phone, and this is his residence."

"Have you moved back in?"

"Not yet, Steve. We're only been back together for about sixteen hours."

Steve chuckled. "I'm happy for you, Elizabeth."

I wasn't sure how to respond. Steve was single-handedly responsible for the misery I'd experienced this year. Steve was also responsible for the pleasure I was experiencing in his son's bed.

My knowledge of Steve's affairs was too fresh to grant forgiveness. I was furious. His behavior had damaged Danny. I owed Danny my loyalty.

But Danny had forgiven Steve. I sighed. It wouldn't help anyone if I held a grudge. Danny was fragile, in the early stages of recovery. Our relationship seemed solid, but I was acutely aware that it was equally fragile.

Danny would appreciate the support from me that letting bygones be bygones would bring him.

"Thank you, Steve," I responded sweetly. "You worked miracles last night. We owe you."

At that moment, Danny bounced back into the room. It had been a long time since I'd seen him this happy.

"Who's on the phone, babe?" Danny asked as he returned to my side.

Now within my reach, I playfully pulled off his towel, and Danny grinned. "It's Steve," I answered.

Danny sat down on the bed and took the phone. I perched against his shoulder, the sheet slipping down, and leaned in close to listen.

"Hey, Dad. Catching up with my lady?"

"I certainly am. You work fast, son." I couldn't help giggling. "Whatever you said to Elizabeth last night sure was effective."

Danny lay down, propped against the pillows and pulled me down into his arms. "Yes, Dad. Everything is good again." He pressed his lips to my forehead. "Can we speak later? Eli and I don't like interruptions."

"Okay. I get it. I'll tell Mom you're fine. Enjoy your afternoon," he chuckled.

"We are, Dad."

Danny set the phone down on the desk.

"Shower?" he asked. Again?

Belt pulled tightly closed, the shoulder seams of Danny's bathrobe lay halfway down my arms. The hem reached my ankles. My body was lost in endless yards of navy terry cloth.

Danny smirked. He could laugh. The bathsheet he wore tucked around his waist fit perfectly, and showed off his swoon-worthy pecs.

I was relieved when we walked into the bathroom and found it empty. I relaxed. Privacy.

Entering the shower stall, I locked the door while Danny pulled aside the curtain and turned on the water. Our eyes met. Danny grinned, I giggled, and then we kissed. The electricity between us was palpable.

Danny whipped off his towel. My eyes opened wide. Then I hung my robe on a hook. It was Danny's turn to stare. Dancing sapphire eyes took in every inch of me. My heart filled. I loved pleasing Danny! And I loved knowing only I made him feel this way.

The warm water splashing my face and spilling down my body was envigorating yet somehow calming. Danny held me close and pressed his lips to mine as the water continued to cascade over us.

I reached for the soap, musky with the scent of a distant forest. The bar was slippery and I giggled when I almost dropped it. Safer was pressing it against Danny's chest, rubbing it against his scant chest hairs. He enjoyed my hands lathering the soap and sliding it across his sculpted chest, and I loved the feel of his taut muscles and well-defined abs beneath my fingertips.

"This is so much fun!" I squealed. "Second time today."

Danny laughed. "I haven't been this clean in months."

Then I joyously threw my hands around his neck and kissed him hard. I didn't even mind the fragrant bubbles tickling my nose.

Meanwhile, Danny slipped the soap bar from my hand into his. Lovingly, he caressed my back with it. Clinging to him, I shuddered from his gentle touch.

My head in the clouds, I was intoxicated. The soap glided across my rear and I gasped.

"Danny," I murmured.

"You like that?" he whispered.

My head, resting against his chest, nodded.

"I know what else you like," he whispered. His breath against my ear tingled.

I gasped again as Danny gently parted my thighs. Then two fingers entered me. My heartbeat accelerated. All my muscles clenched. I clung to him for dear life. The pleasure was unbearable.

"Oh, Danny," I murmured.

In the background a toilet flushed, making me alert again

"Danny!" I cautioned, but I kept my voice low, "He'll hear us."

"The water muffles us." And then he kissed me hard to shut me up.

"Who's with Newman?" I heard one male voice asking another.

"Guess he's over the ice princess," Ian answered, and his friend laughed.

"It's Ian! Shit!" I whispered. He never thought I was an ice princess when he was trying to get in my panties. Hypocrite!

But I couldn't protest for long. Danny's lips were glued to mine, and his kiss had removed all common sense and reason from my brain.

Then Danny turned me around, my back against his front, holding me with his hands firmly pressing my breasts, his lips nuzzling my neck, and he plunged into me.

"Ready for dinner?" Danny asked as he entered my room.

"Just about," I responded.

I took his hands and greeted him with a warm kiss. "Can we talk a minute?" I asked cautiously.

"Is something the matter?" Danny fretted.

After the afternoon we'd shared, he couldn't imagine anything could be the matter. And it wasn't. No, quite the opposite.

I smiled warmly, putting Danny at ease. Then I squeezed his hands.

"Not at all," I answered. "This afternoon was incredible."

"I'm glad you're happy," Danny grinned.

"You made me more than happy. I can't wait for tonight," I trilled.

"Baby, I'm wiped," Danny laughed. "All I'll be doing tonight is sleeping."

"Thank god," I said, relieved. "I can hardly walk, but I still can't wait for tonight. As long as I'm cuddled up in your arms, it will be a great evening."

"You're okay with only sleeping?"

"As long as we're together," I assured him. "Being depressed was so exhausting. When I woke this morning, and I was happy, I had all this energy."

Danny drew me close and looked at me with his magnetic eyes. He took my face in his hands and kissed me.

"Eli, I love you. I really love you."

"Same. Though after this afternoon, I thought it was rather obvious," I giggled. "Danny, today I felt like us again; completely, totally us again. Danny, I'm ready to put this year behind us and go back to how we were. You can say no if you think it's too fast. We'll take things slower if you'd like. Danny, I want to be with you every night. I'm ready for us to live together again."

"E, this is the best news ever." Excitement filled his voice.

Danny grabbed me by my waist, lifted me off the ground, and swung me around. Glee shone on his face. I squealed, delighted.

"E, I have something for you." Danny grinned like a joyful little boy.

He hefted his backpack on to the desk. I was puzzled. What had him so excited?

"I bought this in New York," Danny said as he opened his bag and searched through it. "I was waiting for the right time. I didn't want to pressure you by giving this to you before you were sure of us."

Finally Danny pulled a Tiffany box out of his backpack and handed it to me. "I hope you like this."

My heart filled with love. I didn't care what was in the box. A gift was unexpected.

I pulled at the white satin ribbon and opened the blue box. "Danny! It's stunning!" I exclaimed as I pulled out a diamond-encrusted platinum key hanging on a platinum link chain.

Immediately I thought of all those girls I'd seen flirting with Danny from across the political science classroom or at the Café. Oh, Lindsay and Chris from the library! I smirked at the lovely shade of green their faces would turn.

"Everyone will see this and know we're solid again," I said excitedly. "Help me with the clasp?"

Danny delighted in my reaction. He took the necklace from my hands, and I experienced familiar electricity through his touch. Ah! I lifted my hair out of the way, and Danny fastened the clasp. I ran to the mirror and fingered my gift while admiring it.

"This really is beautiful," I gushed. "It's perfect!"

But something wasn't right. I threw my shirt off over my head and tossed it to an astonished Danny. His eyes opened wide now that I was only in my bra. I threw open my closet and thrust a hanger into his hands.

"Hang this up, honey?" I requested.

Too surprised to say no, Danny obeyed as I rifled through my closet. There! A royal blue silk t-shirt was what I was looking for. I slipped it over my head, tucked it into my jeans, and re-buckled my belt.

After pulling my hair out of the neck, I adjusted the key against the fabric. Contrasted against solid royal, it would immediately be noticed.

All the while, Danny watched with amusement.

"I love it," I told him once again as I proudly fingered my gift.

Rachel walked with us to the library. The three amigos; it truly felt like old times.

As we entered the building, Danny headed to the front desk.

"I have to pick up a key," he explained.

A key? What key? I didn't have a clue, but I proudly fingered my key.

"Gift?" Rachel asked. She had not dined with us.

"Isn't it beautiful," I effused. "Danny gave me this before dinner."

"Nobody else would have," she answered drily. "It's very sparkly. I didn't think you liked bling. It sort of shouts, 'I'm sleeping with Danny Newman again.'"

"I know. Isn't that great?"

"You're right, Rach. It does. I love spoiling my lady."

Danny had returned to my side having not missed a beat of our conversation.

Rachel rolled her eyes.

"And I love being spoiled by you," I purred, and I kissed his cheek. "What's that for?" I asked regarding the small key on a six-inch long silver colored chain that Danny was holding.

"The Dean gave me a study room for the rest of the term."

"For real?" Wow! Typically those rooms were for seniors writing their thesis.

"I don't understand," a puzzled Rachel added.

Danny's eyes darted around the foyer, searching, but for what? Several students were passing through.

"I'll tell you downstairs," Danny said in a hushed voice, and we followed him.

Along the back wall of the library's lower level was a cluster of small rooms with glass-windowed steel doors. Danny stopped at a door with a black plate announcing Room 27, and he inserted the key. Rachel and I followed him in.

In contrast to the upstairs study rooms that we had used in the past, this room was small. Its rectangular table stood against a sidewall for easy access to electrical outlets with a desk catty-cornered. A low bookcase against the back wall provided storage for research materials, and there were two desk chairs.

"E, hold the door, babe," Danny requested. I shrugged.

Danny swiped a chair from a nearby study carrel.

"Okay," he said as he closed the door. "Now we can talk."

Danny was being so mysterious. I felt oddly shy and stood quietly.

"So how did you land this room?" Rachel asked, "Newman charm? Or a sizeable donation to the library?"

Danny rolled his eyes, pacing uncomfortably before continuing. "No Rach, neither charm nor money."

Danny took a seat, and I sat down in the chair beside him. Rachel remained standing despite the extra chair Danny had dragged in. Then he reached for my hand. Danny leaned toward me and his sapphire eyes locked on me. Was that fear?

"Babe, don't get upset. I was planning all along on telling you tonight. I wanted nothing to get in the way of us before."

"What is it, Daniel?" I fretted.

"Don't be angry, E."

Nothing good ever starts with the words "don't be angry." My hackles rose. I withdrew my hand.

"Daniel," I said, narrowing my eyes. "If you had told me this last night, would I have said no to us?"

"I hope not. You might have said let's wait."

"I thought I could trust you," I said angrily. "What are you keeping from me?"

"Maybe I should go," Rachel said.

Danny shook his head. "Stay, Rach." Then he took back my hand.

"You can trust me, E. I only found out this morning."

I eyed Danny suspiciously.

"I'm sorry, E. I wanted so badly for us to enjoy the afternoon. I didn't want anything to spoil it. Forgive me?"

Then Danny reached for my face and pressed his lips to mine. As always, his kiss won me back.

"Rach, I can trust you. This stays in this room, okay?"

She and I exchanged confused glances.

"I won't say a word."

"Thanks. This is so embarrassing. Only my parents know." Danny tightened his grip on my hand. "The Dean gave me this room because he put me on probation."

"But you're an A student!" I protested.

"That doesn't make sense," Rachel agreed.

"He wanted to suspend me."

"No!" I was horrified.

"He told me I should take time off to work on my 'health issues,' was how he put it. But Rach, you saved me."

"How did I save you? I've never met the Dean."

"Owen appealed to Dean Colton by explaining that you would lose credit if he suspended me. He had to back down. Probation was the compromise."

"That sucks! Danny, this is awful," Rachel exclaimed.

"Maybe now isn't a good time for us," I said fearfully.

"Definitely no. That's why I didn't tell you this afternoon, Eli. We are not breaking up again." Danny was adamant.

"Danny, I would hate myself if you were suspended because of spending too much time with me."

Danny shook his head. "Rach, my lady worries too much." Then he squeezed my shoulder. "Eli. Baby, there isn't a class I'm not already getting an A in. All I need to do is not skip any classes for the remainder of the term. The Dean wants my professors to report my attendance. Sort of like academic bed-check."

"The Dean better not check your bed," Rachel laughed.

"That would be embarrassing," I agreed.

"And that's why you can't leave me over this, Elizabeth. Who's the morning person in our house?"

"I couldn't get up today," I said with a naughty smile.

"Okay," Danny laughed. "Not today, but usually?"

"Me? I almost always wake up before you do."

"And you're much more pleasant than an alarm clock."

"Gag me," Rachel exclaimed.

Danny and I laughed. "Well, she is. Eli, you can't leave me baby. I need you to get me up every morning."

"Daniel! How romantic. Not."

Danny wrapped his arms around me and kissed my forehead.

"Oh c'mon, Eli. You know we can't live without each other."

Exasperated, I sighed. "Why does he always win?"

Rachel rolled her eyes. "Time for me to leave this love fest."

"Rach, remember," Danny warned. "This stays here."

After Danny closed the door behind Rachel, he removed and hung his denim jacket on the hook above the door's window.

"I don't want anyone to see I'm in here. Too many questions, Eli."

Danny paced the room, full of angry energy. Finally he lifted the chair he had brought in for Rachel and slammed it down hard. Startled, my heart leaped.

"Daniel!" I exclaimed.

There was outrage in his sapphire eyes and it frightened me.

"Damn it, Lizzie! This is so unfair. How could he do this to me?" Danny shouted.

I rose and wrapped my arms around Danny to calm him. He tried shaking me off. I resisted, holding on to him with all my strength.

"Danny, calm down," I said softly. "People will hear you."

"The room's soundproofed," Danny snarled, but he cracked a smile.

I caressed his broad shoulders knotted with tension.

"Honey, we'll get through this," I said calmly.

Danny shrugged with all his strength, effectively disengaging me. "Danny," I said angrily, "I'm on your side."

He paced one more lap, brooding all the way.

"Damn it!" he exclaimed. Danny violently swept his books off the table. They crashed to the floor in an angry clatter. I cowered against the wall, eyes wide in fear.

"And I was supposed to be grateful. He didn't even care about who I was." Danny stopped in front of me, rage in his eyes. "Hell Liz, that's probably why he did this; revenge, power play. He thinks I'm some spoiled rich kid, and he's in the position of power. And I had to stand there and take it! I'm supposed to be grateful!"

Danny pounded his fist on the table. "Here's what really sucks. Dad thought he was doing the right thing. He called the Dean and told him why I was in New York. If Dad hadn't called, he wouldn't have known. I'm being punished for having integrity!"

Danny picked up the chair and slammed it down again.

"Danny! You're frightening me."

Ignoring my plea, his rant continued. "You know what I learned today? Damn, fucking Dean. You can be a goddamn junkie like Duncan, but as long as you stay below the radar, they don't care what you do! But god forbid you admit to a problem… Damn it, Lizzie!"

Danny furiously slammed the chair down again. I pressed as hard as I could against the wall, sinking down to my knees, hoping to disappear, and be swallowed up by the plaster.

This was a Danny I'd never seen before. And he was running out of furniture to attack. Would I be next? I was shaking, petrified. I broke down.

"Danny, please. Stop! You're scaring me," I cried.

I buried my face in my hands and wept. I shook.

In an instant, Danny was at my side. He gathered me in his arms and held me tight. My crying had broken the spell that had consumed him.

"Oh, babe. I am so sorry," Danny said contritely. "I didn't mean to frighten you. I love you, baby. I love you."

"I've never seen you like this before," I said in a raised voice. "I don't like this, Danny."

"Eli, please. I'm frustrated, babe. It's been a perfect day, except for the Dean."

Danny reached for my face, wanting to kiss me. I swatted his hand away.

"You're reacting irrationally, Daniel. The Dean gave you a slap on the wrist."

"He put me on probation, Elizabeth," Danny said indignantly.

"So your ego is bruised. Get over it, Daniel. All you have to do is continue to get good grades and attend all your classes. You rarely cut anyway, so what really is your problem?"

"It should be my choice, not his," Danny groused.

I threw up my hands in disgust. "I give up," I muttered.

Ending the conversation before I came to the point of storming out, I reached for my tote bag, removed my laptop and book, and placed them on the table.

"Let's get to work," I said as I took my seat and opened the computer. "We have a lot of material to cover."

Unsettled was the best word to describe my state. I didn't know what to make of Danny's earlier tirade. He had explained it all in a tidy way that made sense intellectually, but my gut emotions had been ravaged.

Danny's outburst was a complete contradiction to the lifelong image I had of him. My Danny was a kind, gentle soul. Even when he was a boy, hell, always, I felt physically safe with Danny. Not tonight. Though once we began studying, and surface level normalcy had been restored, I still felt uneasy.

Returning from the library, I donned an oxford shirt, crawled into bed, and turned my back on Danny. Having put his tantrum behind him, he didn't understand its continued affect on me.

Danny affectionately wrapped an arm around my very frigid shoulder and kissed my cheek. I did not respond.

"Oh c'mon, Eli. Don't do this," he pleaded.

"You said after this afternoon you were too tired," I said icily.

"That was before. I don't like you being angry."

I turned onto my back. If we were engaging in protracted conversation, I wanted to face him.

Danny propped on his elbow used those damned sapphire eyes to bewitch me. I wouldn't let them.

"So sex is the answer?" I asked.

Danny smiled. "Maybe. I can try." He ran his fingertip along my jawline, causing me to squirm. Then he brought his lips down to kiss mine. I turned my head.

"Stop that," I said forcefully.

"Eli, you should never go to sleep angry."

"Tonight I may have to," I answered bitterly.

Danny slipped his hand under my shirt and mindlessly caressed my breasts.

"What are you doing?" I asked. My hands gripped the sheet, trying so hard not to respond.

"I like to touch you. Your skin is so soft."

"You're impossible," I gasped, fighting the exciting clench of my muscles.

"Elizabeth, we're back together for only one day and already we're fighting."

I pushed Danny's hand out from under my shirt.

"Maybe Rachel was right. We shouldn't have moved so fast."

"Don't say that! I can't lose you, baby." Danny panicked.

"You haven't. Yet. I'm here, aren't I?" I said coldly.

"Tell me what you need."

"Time, Daniel. Give me some time. You frightened me, and I'm not over it. I saw a side of you I didn't know existed. It tore at a basic tenet of our relationship; my security. Until tonight I never had reason to doubt my safety when I was with you."

Danny inhaled sharply. "Elizabeth, you didn't think…? I would never hurt you. I love you."

"Danny, you were out of control."

"I was. But that was furniture. I would never lay a hand on you, or any other girl, no matter how angry I might get. I thought you knew that."

"I do know that. That's part of why I've always loved you. Danny, please. You have to make me understand what was going on tonight."

Danny nodded. "E, ever since this morning I've kept my anger bottled up."

"Why didn't you say anything?"

"I didn't want to dampen your spirits. I thought our date would cure me," he smiled. "E, you have to understand. When I left the Dean, I was devastated. But I didn't want anyone to know, so I had to press on and show my happy face. Do you know what I really wanted to do? I've been fighting it all day."

Of course! Why hadn't I realized it? I had been so consumed by our romance I hadn't stopped to consider the emotional upheaval Danny had been through that had nothing to do with me.

"Danny, I'm so sorry. I wasn't thinking. After last night, I wanted to believe our lives were perfect again."

"And I wanted that for you. When I left New York, you were my top priority. E, I've spent the last twenty-four hours sheltering you from me. Maybe I shouldn't have. You need the truth about me so you can decide what you want."

"I know what I want."

Danny shook his head no. "You want the old me. That's not who I am anymore."

"Good. Because the old you was a hard-partying, lying, cheating bastard."

Danny smiled. "I deserve that. E, I'm not carefree now. I can't be. My life is in disarray. I'm a work in progress. Does that make sense?"

"Yes. And I'm here to support you, Danny."

"First, see if you want to. This is new to me, Eli. It's going to be a long process, and right now I could easily fail."

My poor, vulnerable Danny. Admitting to weakness was so painful. I nodded my understanding.

"God, how I hate saying that. You've always relied on me to be the strong one. Now I'm weak."

"You're a very strong man, Danny. Only a strong man could admit this."

"Baby, understand, I wasn't addicted so I'm not having physical cravings, but I have psychological cravings. When I left the Dean, I wanted to get wasted, really badly."

"Danny, don't say that."

"Why not? It's the truth. That's how I handle my problems. Any disappointments, I'd get wasted. That's who I've become, Eli. I'm not proud."

"I understand how difficult this is, but I'm proud of you, Danny. You've come to terms with your problems, and you're getting the help you need."

"You're right. I am. The doctor in New York set me up with a psychiatrist in Beverly Hills. Harlan is treating me via Skype until I get home. After my meeting with the Dean, I had a session. I'm seeing him five days a week to start. Harlan will help me find a healthier way to cope. "

"Thank you for trusting me."

"Eli, I'm in a bad place. I don't want to drag you down."

"Are you breaking up with me? I'm lying in your bed."

Danny smiled. "That would be stinky. I don't want to break up with you. I want you to break up with me."

"If I leave you tonight, that's it, Danny. Forever. It won't be a hiatus. I won't be coming back."

"I can't live without you. Elizabeth."

"So what are you saying, Danny?"

"Eli, I'm trying to protect you."

I smiled. "Danny, do you remember what you said at Steve's premiere last year?"

"Are you referring to when I declared us married, and I kissed my bride?"

"I took my vows seriously even if the ceremony was conducted by the groom and wasn't at all legally binding."

"It probably was in some states. After all, we moved into our own house and opened a joint bank account."

"My point was in the vows, where I promised to take you in sickness and health."

"I'm healthy."

"Don't be flippant. Right now you're suffering. If you believe in our vows, what kind of wife would I be if I cut and run? I won't do that. Get it through your thick skull, Daniel. I'm yours for life."

"I don't want to lose you, Eli. I wanted to give you options."

I fingered my key. "Options? You don't give a girl a diamond necklace if you want her to have options. You gave me this as a symbol of your commitment, and I accepted it as a symbol of mine."

Danny smiled uncomfortably, caught in his own bullshit.

"I don't want you to feel trapped," he said, recovering.

"Daniel, I know all your flaws yet I want to be with you. I don't feel trapped. Nothing is more important than giving you my support. We'll get through this together. That's how we always do it."

CHAPTER FIFTY-EIGHT - DANIEL

"Babe, there's whipped cream on your chin," I said to Elizabeth.

Afternoon found us once more at our favorite table at The Café, the only place at Donnelly that served Starbucks. I was enjoying my venti brew black. Eli was nursing her usual hot chocolate with too much whipped cream.

How she consumed that many calories on a more or less regular basis and not gain an ounce was a wonder. The charmed life of a dancer. Then I smirked at the memory of our last twenty-four hours. I'd put Eli through several intense workouts. Burning calories the Newman way!

Lifting a small paper napkin, I poised to dab Elizabeth's chin. As I leaned toward her, I took her face in my hand and brought my lips to hers.

I lied. There was no whipped cream on her chin. It was an excuse to kiss her; not that I needed one.

"Ahem. Danny," a hesitant female voice caught my attention.

Shit! Mandy! And she was standing nearly on top of us by the side of the table. Mandy and I had a study date for her to explain the material from the Economics classes that I missed last week.

Embarrassed, I broke off the kiss, though I continued holding Elizabeth's face.

"Hi, Mandy. Great timing," I said sarcastically.

Mandy smirked, and Elizabeth blushed.

"If you don't want to study, I'll understand," she said coyly.

"No, no. We have a date. I need to go over this material now or I won't get through the readings tonight." I glanced at Eli. "Do you mind? I've got to catch up."

"Don't worry. I can amuse myself," Eli answered with a grin.

Eli reached for her totebag and removed her laptop. Meanwhile, Mandy took the seat on my other side, and removed her laptop from her backpack.

"I'm gonna go out on a limb and assume you're Elizabeth."

Eli nodded as she turned on her computer.

"Sorry," I answered awkwardly. "Eli, this is Mandy, my Econ buddy."

"Danny's not usually this rude," Eli explained. "He's been distracted lately." And Eli flashed me a wicked grin and winked.

She winked! I loved playful Eli. Hell. I loved every version of Eli. If only Mandy weren't here. I wanted so badly to hold Eli in my arms and kiss her.

"Glad to meet you, Elizabeth. This guy has been crying over you all year. I'm so glad I won't have to wipe up his tears anymore."

"You make me sound so pathetic," I complained.

"Danny, you have been pathetic," Mandy answered.

"Thanks…"

There! That brainy girl from Physics entered the food service area. I desperately needed the notes from last week. What was her name? It was on the tip of my tongue. I pictured hearing the professor say it. Her name was…? Uhm… Bridget! It was Bridget!

I jumped up from my seat surprising my two ladies.

"I need the notes from Physics," I explained."I'll be right back."

Then I kissed Eli's forehead, and bounded up to the bewildered Bridget who was now carrying a packaged coffee cake and a bottle of Coke, besides a heavy load of books and a laptop.

"Hey, it's Bridget? Right?" I asked, just in case I had her name wrong.

"Uh, yeah," she answered, awkward as a middle school student.

Bridget, a freshman, was in my sophomore-level physics class thanks to having scored perfect fives on two levels of AP Physics exams. And she looked it; all pale skin, mousy hair, and non-descript clothing. Even nuns had more sex appeal.

She was the perfect student to borrow notes from. Bridget was probably the only student in the class other than myself who was getting an A.

"I missed physics last week," I began.

I shoved my hands into the front pockets of my jeans and affixed a shy smile to my face. Bridget seemed easily intimidated.

"You were gone," she stammered.

"Yeah. I was out sick for a couple of days. Do you think I could borrow your notes? The professor wouldn't help me."

"Sure," she nodded, "I'll email them to you."

"That's great, Bridget."

"There's also an outline. I can send that too."

"Perfect. My email is DanielMNewman@Donnelly.edu. I really appreciate it. You're a lifesaver, Bridget."

Then I kissed her forehead, leaving a very flustered Bridget in my wake.

"What was that about?" a puzzled Eli asked.

"Oh, no!" I groaned.

Until that moment, I hadn't realized that I had kissed Bridget. It was simply exuberance at a problem being solved so easily.

An hour later, Mandy packed her laptop and economics textbook, leaving Elizabeth and I alone, at last.

"Now where were we?" I asked, as I wrapped my arm around Eli, and held her close, ready for the kiss Mandy had interrupted.

"You were pretending to wipe non-existent whipped cream off my face."

Elizabeth giggled, having read through my transparent rouse.

"You can't fault a man for trying," I laughed.

"I don't. But you could have been direct. I'd have said yes."

"Eli, you're a nut," I laughed.

Then I lifted her chin and brought our lips together for the kiss I hoped would last us until after dinner.

"Dan?" An unwelcome voice suddenly standing beside me interrupted our fun.

Shit! Phoebe! And Duncan was with her. Phoebe always called me "Dan," and I hated it.

I froze in place holding Elizabeth's face. I had been spending so much time either with Elizabeth or thinking about her that I hadn't spent even one second considering Phoebe. She was so unimportant that in the two weeks since last seeing her, she hadn't even crossed my mind.

Phoebe was a loose thread I should have tied up earlier this week, but I had been too busy re-igniting my relationship with Elizabeth.

If Phoebe were a normal girl I would have excused myself and taken her to a quiet corner to talk. We had been seeing each other for only two months, and sporadically at that, far from attaining girlfriend-boyfriend status. Phoebe knew, hell everyone knew, that Elizabeth and I had been deeply in love before our hiatus. It should come as no surprise to her that Elizabeth and I might work it out.

Another girl would have interpreted the significance of me kissing Elizabeth at The Cafe, and would have called me later to scream, shout, or cry. Instead, Phoebe was a spiteful loose cannon, and Duncan at her side added fuel to the fire.

Why Duncan hated Elizabeth I never understood, but it would give him pleasure to see her miserable. I had the feeling my dream afternoon was about to become a nightmare. It had to be handled with utmost care.

"Hey Phoebs, Duncan," I said as casually as possible.

"Lois Lane," Duncan sneered.

Eli ignored this insult. I understood immediately that she planned on remaining silent, deferring to me to deal with them. Duncan, and Phoebe were my problems.

"Where have you been Dan? I've missed you," Phoebe purred provocatively, completely ignoring that she had found me kissing my girlfriend.

Elizabeth simply stared. She fingered her key necklace, and then glanced at me for non-verbal guidance. I didn't give any, hoping Phoebe and Duncan would disappear and be swallowed up by a black hole.

No such luck. Phoebe put her hands up to my face in an attempt to kiss my unresponsive lips. I immediately shoved her hands back.

"Phoebs, we've got to talk," I said firmly.

"Certainly, Dan," she purred.

Duncan starred at Elizabeth, waiting, watching her reaction. I couldn't look at her. I felt the energy leave her body, and was certain Elizabeth's beautiful smile had been replaced by disappointment and hurt.

Why wouldn't it be? Just minutes had passed since we'd been kissing, knowing we would soon adjourn to our bedroom for the remainder of the afternoon. Now another woman was trying to kiss me. If I were Elizabeth, this would be too much for me to handle.

I rose from the table. I wanted to take Phoebe aside where we could talk privately without Duncan lurking and interfering.

"Danny, I've got to go," Eli stammered. I turned toward Elizabeth's beautiful face, now crestfallen.

She looked like she had been punched in the gut, and metaphorically, she had been. I felt her fighting to keep her composure. My brave girl. She would not let Phoebe or Duncan see her cry.

"I have to pick something up. From yearbook. Upstairs."

She was trying so hard as she grabbed her jacket and books. I wanted her to understand that this encounter was of no concern. I would take care of everything.

"I'll meet you there in a few," I said while trying to smile and sound reassuring.

"Later, Lois," Duncan sneered, and Eli again ignored him.

I squeezed Elizabeth's hand and kissed her cheek as she hurried off.

"Poor Mary Poppins," Phoebe emphasized loudly enough that Elizabeth could hear. "Did she really think she could get you back?"

"Elizabeth and I are back together," I barked. "You better not have ruined it."

Furor, absolute furor. My blood was boiling. I doubted I could control the rage I was feeling. I took one gulp of the steaming coffee and slammed the cup down on the table. I had to catch up to Elizabeth. And I had to keep myself from throttling both Phoebe with her sneer, and Duncan with his slimy smile of victory.

"I hope you're happy," I growled at them as I ran out.

CHAPTER FIFTY-NINE - ELIZABETH

After the run-in with Phoebe, I didn't feel social. I feared leaving Berkeley Hall, with its thick brick walls insulating me from the evildoers, I mean Danny's former lovers. How many more crazies were waiting to ambush me?

Was I overreacting? Possibly. I knew Danny had a past. Hell! Except for possibly only me, didn't everyone? Phoebe was part of his past, the very recent past. But past was the operative word. Danny claimed she meant nothing to him. I shouldn't let her get to me. I believed him.

Danny had offered me every reassurance when he caught up to me at the yearbook office within minutes of me fleeing the Café. The rapidity with which he joined me spoke volumes. Phoebe was a dead issue. Nonetheless, it was an uncomfortable episode, and I wasn't ready for a repeat encounter. Not this soon.

Phoebe's nastiness… what was her problem? She knew she was never more than the most casual of relationships for Danny. Phoebe, with Duncan egging her on, relished her role as a spoiler. She couldn't get to me. I wouldn't let it. Bring it on!

I hoped Danny would follow my example by staying in tonight. His sobriety was a challenge. I would not, could not, be his babysitter, but I would give Danny all the support he needed.

So early on I changed into cozy cotton yoga pants and a tank top in case the history book I was tackling put me to sleep. I needed to get through about forty pages. Sitting at my desk seemed the best strategy for staying alert.

Surprisingly, the assignment turned out to be an interesting chapter on the inventions of the late nineteenth century. I hadn't realized how many important things we take for granted, including refrigerators, telephones, and cameras, had originated during that period. And proudly, they were all American inventions.

I eagerly read ahead and was well into pre-World War I inventions when a light knock came on my door.

"It's open," I called out. How had it become ten-thirty?

Danny, looking like Adonis in sweat pants, a t-shirt and eyeglasses, closed and locked the door. His scent, and the taste of his kiss, told me that he had been a good boy. His appearance told me he intended on spending the night.

"Five more minutes," I said indicating my book.

There were just a few pages left in the chapter. I didn't want to lose momentum. In one fluid motion, Danny picked up my iPad and bounded onto my bed, propping himself up on my pillows, making himself at home. Arrogance came naturally to Danny. It was what gave him his infectious charisma and made Danny, well, Danny. Arrogance was also what gave him the confidence to be absolutely wrongly certain that Phoebe would not care that he had made up with me. And it spilled over. When I was with Danny, I too believed that all was not only possible it was probable.

I completed my work and turned my attention to Danny. Giving him my high wattage smile, he tossed away the iPad.

"Don't I get a proper greeting?" he asked. Rising from my desk chair, I eased into Danny's welcoming arms, joining him on the bed.

"I wasn't expecting you," I murmured against Danny's freshly shaved cheek. I ran my fingertips down his smooth jaw to his lips, and kissed him.

"You weren't?" Danny held my hair back off my face, and looked into my eyes. He seemed perplexed.

"I was studying," I explained. "I wasn't thinking about us."

Danny cradled my face in between his wam palms.

"You will be now," he said, his breath seducing my senses. Then Danny kissed me hard. A girl could get used to this.

"How's my sweetheart?" he asked.

I smiled at his inquiry, yet I had to be honest. Logic told me I had no reason to doubt Danny, but I had been mulling this over for hours.

"Phoebe," was my strained answer. I averted my eyes. Danny shouldn't see the tears that were forming.

"So that's why you're not in our room?"

I nodded. "I needed some space."

From behind, Danny wrapped his arms around me, and pulled my back against his chest.

"Baby, don't," Danny pleaded softly. "This afternoon was unfortunate, but you're Mrs. Danny Newman, and Phoebe…" he paused to find the right words. "Phoebe never was, and never will be. Don't let her sully what we have. She's nothing to us."

I turned my face toward Danny. "I know," I agreed. I really did know. My reaction had been purely emotional, not rational. "Bare with me? It might take some time."

"Done," he said with finality.

If Danny wanted something done, he decreed it as such, and then it was.

Danny kissed the top of my head. I smiled. "How was your evening?" I asked.

"After Shane caught me up on computer science, we were all set to go out when Dad called to Skype."

"Good. You're supposed to be staying out of trouble, remember?"

"That's why Dad called; checking up on me."

"Did you pass muster?" I asked.

"I think so," Danny laughed. "I told him I was going to see you."

"Is that why you're here? So Steve can check with me and you're not lying?"

"Absolutely not. I always planned to end up here." Danny squeezed me, and kissed the sensitive sport below my ear. I shuddered. "You are where I want to be."

"We'll make sure you stay out of trouble," I said to encourage him. "Here's my plan for tomorrow. We go to the library and prep for Owen. I don't want him thinking I'm not keeping up any longer because we're back together."

"And after the library?"

"Your room, of course," I smiled up at Danny and pressed against him, my hands on this thighs providing leverage.

"Our room."

"Yes, our room."

Danny examined my face while I spoke.

"I could study your freckles," he teased.

"What freckles? I have flawless skin," I protested.

Danny gently touched my nose. "There's one," and he brushed my jawline with his fingertips before settling on my lips. "And here's another." I gasped at his touch.

"Get me into trouble," I begged.

"Oh, baby."

Then Danny kissed me so furiously my head spun. I could barely breathe. My response was immediate. I swiveled around and moved to straddle his lap. My back arched, pressing my front against him. Danny stopped his kiss, and striped off my clothes, discarding them where they fell. This was exactly where I wanted to be.

Shortly before the alarm clock was set to ring, I woke to find Danny still holding me. God, this felt good. I reached out to shut the alarm. This subtle motion made him stir. Danny breathed in the scent of my shampoo, and pulled me closer, kissing my head and purring in my ear. I nearly convulsed. I could get used to a wake-up like this, and fast.

Danny brushed a few hairs off my face. "You're so beautiful, even this early in the morning," he whispered, and I blushed.

"I love you, Daniel." Before I had time to think about it, we were making love all over again.

Afterwards, we lay entwined in each other's arms, "E," Danny began, "neither of us has classes on Friday. Let's go home for the weekend."

CHAPTER SIXTY - DANNY

The moment the flight attendant secured the door of the Gulfstream for take-off, the tension I didn't know I was suffering immediately lifted like a noose being removed from around my neck.

To say that Elizabeth felt the same was an understatement. I laughed at the goofiest, most joyous grin worn like a little girl on Christmas morning.

"Danny, I can't wait to be home already!" squealed the girl who had thoroughly objected to making this trip. "This is the best idea ever!"

After fretting over my homework load, and what if the Dean found out, I was relieved that Elizabeth had changed her mind. This was the best idea ever. Three days devoted to us. No Dean, no dorm, nobody. In Malibu I was not on probation. In Malibu there was no Phoebe, or Scott. In Malibu prying eyes did not gawk at us. In Malibu, we just were.

Spending the weekend at home would be therapeutic. We would return to Donnelly Sunday evening refreshed, and able to relegate the last seven months to the dustbin of our personal history.

I squeezed Elizabeth's dainty hand and settled back awaiting take-off.

Six hours later, Elizabeth danced into the house ahead of me. Without hesitation she crossed the living room, threw open the glass slider, and skipped out onto the patio.

I caught up to her as she was deeply inhaling the crisp salty air. Elizabeth beamed in delight as my arms wrapped around her from behind. We were both transfixed, starring at the white-capped waves breaking against the darkening night sky.

"It's so good to be home," Elizabeth said, her voice as calm as the still evening.

"It certainly is," I agreed, and I kissed the back of her shoulder.

Then Elizabeth pivoted, clasped her hands around my neck, and smiled.

"I love you, Daniel. You make all my dreams come true," and she kissed me. Elizabeth jumped into my arms and wrapped her legs around my hips. "You're the best," she whispered.

"No," I answered, "But I'm working at it."

Not caring about my self-opinion, Eli smothered me with kisses. Laughing at her playfulness, I carried Elizabeth to the nearest chaise. Her giddiness was infectious, and oh, so arousing. I immediately striped off her clothes and made love to her.

The fresh breeze wafting through the slightly open bedroom slider invigorated us. Having forgotten to close the blinds, the early morning sun woke us. We didn't care.

Eli pounced on me, playful as a happy kitten, and I pounced back. There was something so magical about being home. It infected us both. Every sensation was heightened; the serenity of the environment, the beauty of the girl beside me, her auburn waves scattered across the pillow, and most important, my deepening love for Elizabeth.

Sharing our passions did not diminish our energy. Instead of snuggling in my arms afterwards, warm and content, Elizabeth jumped out of bed.

"I've got to step outside," she declared. "The air smells so good!"

Eli grabbed a fluffy white towel from the bathroom and wrapped it like a terry-cloth dress.

I caught up to her on the balcony after wrapping my own towel around my waist. The breeze off the ocean was blowing her hair back off of her face. Elizabeth's eyes were as clear as the water as she gazed at the white caps. It was a picture-perfect morning with barely a cloud to mar the blue sky.

Sensing my presence, Eli turned in my direction and our lips joined. When she raised her arms to reach around my neck, her towel slipped down to her hips. Elizabeth shrugged an impish grin, not caring.

"We're twins now," Eli laughed, gripping my shoulder for balance.

We stood side-by-side, starring at the horizon where the waves were breaking with high tide ferocity. Mostly I watched Elizabeth, the contented picture of serenity.

Eli held the rail with her delicate hands. Messy auburn waves cascaded down her back. Her chin pointed upward and out. Expressive emerald eyes studied the horizon. Eli breathed deeply, absorbing the fresh ocean air.

I marveled at her confidence. Elizabeth, standing topless, facing the beach, did not waver for even a moment. She was completely secure.

Studying her every movement, her every expression, I knew without doubt that the most beautiful woman I would ever lay eyes on, was standing beside me. And she was mine, for life, if I didn't blow it.

Irresistible was the only way to describe her. I wrapped my hands around Elizabeth's waist, then ran my fingers up the sides of her torso until my palms rested on her breasts and my fingers explored them. She was lovely, firm and soft at the same time.

Elizabeth gasped as I gently squeezed her. "Oh, Danny," she murmured while leaning back and into me. I kissed her delicate shoulder and her neck, both pale from the long New York winter, while my fingers teased her breasts.

"E, where's your camera?" I asked. Eli never travelled without her Nikon SLR.

"On the living room table," she murmured without removing her eyes from the ocean.

"I'll be right back. Don't move," I instructed.

"No!" she didn't want me leaving. Eli was so aroused, but this couldn't wait. Within moments I returned with the camera and pointed it at her profile.

"Danny! I'm topless," Elizabeth objected, but she giggled.

"Personal consumption, babe. Nobody will see these but me," I promised. Then I kissed her cheek. "You look more beautiful today than ever. I've got to capture it."

Elizabeth smiled sassy, and turned to face me. "Full frontal?" she asked.

"Actually, no," I laughed, though I was delighted with her offer.

I had been enchanted by Eli's profile, the tumbling auburn waves cascading down her back, bare until the towel covered her at her hips, the hint of breast, fleeting or not depending on arm placement. It was artsy, not salacious.

"Stand as you were and ignore me," I instructed.

Like an experienced model, Eli followed my directions perfectly. I shot frame after frame, subtle movements and posture changes, marking the differences.

"My turn," Eli declared as I lowered the camera. "I want pictures of my handsome photographer," she said, and Eli kissed me. "Too bad we don't have a tripod. A photo with both of us would be nice."

I turned toward the ocean and mimicked her poses. After some shots, "Turn towards me," Eli ordered. "I want to see your face."

Complying with her directive, I smiled at her giddiness. Eli was having so much fun with this.

Placing the camera on the small teak table when she finished, I was rewarded with deep kisses from my photographer. While she went up on toe, one hand holding my neck for balance, Eli's other hand loosened her towel, and it dropped to the ground.

"E!" I gasped, and she shrugged, comfortable with her nakedness.

"It's early. The beach is empty," she assured me. Then Eli grinned. "I thought you might like more photos. Personal consumption."

I laughed. "My personal will definitely enjoy consuming these."

I marveled at her ease, and her complete trust in me. Eli posed as before and I positioned the camera to capture her complete vertical image. Elizabeth was perfection. Every curve captured was a beauty to behold.

Soon I returned the camera to the table and came up behind her. I wrapped my hands around her hips, enjoying the feel of her softness, and I gave a little squeeze. My pulse beat rapidly. Eli turned her head and reached for my lips. My heart melted from her potent sensuality as we kissed.

Keeping one hand on her hip, I again ran my other up her torso and caressed her breasts.

"Mmmm," Eli murmured, intoxicated.

Then she reached for my towel, loosened the knot, and let it fall before returning her hands to around my neck.

I continued caressing Elizabeth, knowing it was filling her with insane pleasure. Eli arched her back, pressing against my front, her arms around my neck. Her soft groan threatened to push me over the edge. I slid my hand from her hip and gently parted her silky thighs. In moments I would need to pull her back inside to the bedroom.

"Oh, yes," she sighed, as I stroked her with feathery fingertips.

"Right here?" I whispered, my breath tickling her ear.

Eli nodded. "Now," she moaned.

The electricity pulsating between us was unbearable. Elizabeth's hands moved to hold the rail for balance as I kissed her neck and then her shoulder while my fingers entered her.

"Danny, please," Eli begged in a breathless whisper.

My breathing quickened. We were both in as heightened a state of arousal as we could ever be. Clasping Eli's waist, I entered her, and soon we exploded together.

Wobbly, Elizabeth pivoted in my arms, clinging to me, while we kissed, enjoying the after-effects of our love. I held her firmly, enjoying every inch of her, soft and lightly fragrant from the perfume she had applied yesterday morning.

"Daniel," Eli sighed in ecstasy.

"Maybe we should go inside," I whispered, and I kissed her again.

I scooped Elizabeth up in my arms, uncertain of whether she could walk without stumbling. Then I grabbed the camera, and we entered the bedroom.

"More pictures?" Elizabeth asked, a saucy smile playing upon her lips as I deposited her on the bed.

For the next fifteen minutes Elizabeth posed on the bed, provocatively using the sheets and pillows as props for our very private photo shoot. I was in awe at the trust she placed in me, a trust I would never violate.

"How about the Grove?" Eli answered when I asked where she'd like to spend the afternoon.

The Grove, Los Angeles' trendy outdoor shopping mall, attached to the historic Farmer's Market, was a favorite of ours. It was the favorite of most everyone in our crowd, too. Therein lay the problem. We were practically guaranteed to run into someone we knew. By nightfall, our secret weekend would no longer be one.

Dad would kill me if he found out I was here.

"How about Third Street?" I countered.

I pulled Elizabeth into my arms and tipped her chin up. Sapphire eyes locked on emeralds.

"We're less likely to run into anyone." Then I chastely kissed her lips. "I want you all to myself."

Eli grinned. "Okay," she answered, and Eli wrapped her hands around my neck, and kissed me hard.

The morning was nearly over by the time we showered and dressed, me in jeans, a tee and an open chambray shirt; Eli in a short flippy shirt and lavender cropped polo.

"We can go shopping, and then have an early dinner and see a movie. Or an early movie and then dinner," she added.

A relaxing dinner and a movie; that was about the right speed for me. Enjoyable as it had been, I could not manage a replay of the last twelve hours, and I doubted Eli could either.

By mid-afternoon, Eli and I found ourselves at the Third Street Promenade in Santa Monica. Locals, tourists, men, women, children, and beasts of all kinds, could be found in equal parts strolling on this magnificent spring day. With the strong ocean breeze blowing, I was glad Eli had taken a cardigan.

Every sort of humanity, from the sublime to the outrageous, could be encountered on the three-block long pedestrian thoroughfare spanning from Broadway to Wilshire Boulevard. If God had seen fit to create it, eventually it would show up on Third Street.

Tourist families were out in droves, gathering the "you won't believe what we saw when we were in L.A." stories and photos to share on Facebook and Instagram. They crowded the streets, watching the street performers and shoppers with equal fascination.

Locals ignored the performers as they pushed through the crowds on their way to Urban Outfitters, Anthropologie, Barnes & Noble, or several mutiplexes. Fashionable Westside mothers avoiding the prevalent beggars, pushed designer-clad babies in Maclaren strollers while sipping on lattes. Children eating frozen yogurt were herded into the Gap. This was home.

Elizabeth wasn't ready to take the plunge.

"Let's go to Bloomingdale's first," she announced after I handed the BMW X5 to the valet at Santa Monica Place, the elegant outdoor mall that anchored the southern end of Third Street.

I had half-expected this. The upscale shops of the mall were more to Eli's liking than the mid-range stores lining the Promenade. Hell, they were more to mine, too.

In the end, we didn't buy much. After over-ruling Elizabeth at least half a dozen time, she purchased a few tops, a couple of skirts, and a pair of ice-blue capris. They were the perfect compliment to a sweater I insisted upon.

Usually I hate when Eli wears anything oversized unless it's mine. Then it's cute, in that high school cheerleader wearing her quarterback boyfriend's letter jacket kind of way. This sweater was an exception to my rule. Soft, pale pink cashmere, with a large red heart on the front, and in navy knitted script, "Malibu."

I had discovered the display of knitware, and when I handed her the sweater, Elizabeth had giggled, memories of this morning still fresh.

"It's perfect," she declared. And on Elizabeth, it was.

We opted for an early dinner before going to a movie and left two large shopping bags with the valet. After checking the theater's schedule, we went for sushi at Sugarfish, a block away on Second Street. It would take no time to stroll over to the theater on Third Street afterwards.

Elizabeth and I emerged from the theater laughing at the implausible plot of a film I wish I hadn't wasted two hours of my life attending, I pulled Eli into my arms. I starred into her emerald eyes, preparing to kiss her. But she couldn't stop giggling.

"How did they expect anyone to believe that?" she guffawed. "That was the lamest storyline. Who green-lighted that movie?"

"At least nobody named Jacobs or Newman," I grinned.

"Our dads know better. And the actors, don't they read scripts before signing on to a project?"

"Apparently not," I choked. "Maybe they needed the money. Jace just went through a messy divorce."

Eli nodded agreement, but her eyes and thoughtful expression told me she was still contemplating the film.

"The stars had no chemistry, and we're supposed to believe they're in love."

"Like us?"

"No. We have chemistry. We should have taken those parts," she chuckled.

"You want to be an actor? 'Cause I certainly don't."

"No, of course not. I'm going to work for Dad for a few years, and them become one of those spandex-clad, Maclaren stroller moms."

She laughed so I knew she was teasing. Hmm, Eli in spandex. How hot would that be? My jeans tightened. Shit! Third Street was not the place.

"Jace should stick to his TV show," Eli continued on about the movie, totally oblivious to the discomfort her visual had caused me.

Eli shivered from the passing breeze, and I tightened my hold around her.

"Eli," I teased. "You are one tough customer."

"Not with you," she said with a smile.

If it was possible, Third Street was more crowded now than earlier, but I didn't care. I swept Elizabeth's hair back from her face and brought my lips to hers. I held her tightly, one arm around her shoulder, the other around her hip. The result was immediate electricity.

"You're right, we have chemistry," I whispered, and Elizabeth giggled.

I leaned down and kissed her again. Then I heard, "Daniel?"

I stopped in my tracks, my lips jerked back from Elizabeth's, while she pivoted to face, "Dad?" What was he doing here?

Dad was walking down the middle of Third Street with an Asian man in his early thirties that I didn't recognize. As Dad realized it was Elizabeth in my arms, he smiled momentarily, before giving me a severe glare.

"Daniel, William Chang," Dad said in introduction.

I stuck out my hand to shake Mr. Chang's. William Chang was a hot screenwriter Dad had been courting for a project, and my lifesaver. Dad would not chastise me in front of him.

"Will, my son Daniel, and his girlfriend, Elizabeth Jordan Jacobs."

Dad was **the** Steven Newman. Why did he feel the need to impress William Chang, or anyone for that matter, by emphasizing Eli's name?

Mr. Chang nodded. Point made, Dad.

"Dad, what are you doing here?" Steven Newman rarely went out this publicly.

"Will and I met for dinner. Then we stopped at Barnes &… What do you mean what am I doing here? What are you doing here, Daniel? You're supposed to be in upstate New York studying."

"We were shopping and decided to have dinner and go to a movie."

"This is what happens when spoiled kids grow up," Dad cautioned Mr. Chang, but he was smiling. "Ellen and I gave them our house in Malibu. Now we're building a new one."

"You are?" This was news.

"Mom and I missed the beach, so we bought two acres a couple of miles further north."

"We'll give you the house back if you want it," Elizabeth offered.

"That's okay," Dad smiled. "Ellen and I finally realized it wasn't Malibu that we didn't like, it was the house. It's tired, and it needs work."

"We've noticed. After graduation, we've got to renovate it. Dad, Eli and I can't live there full-time without a major re-do."

"When I saw them in New York last weekend," Dad explained to Mr. Chang, "They had barely spoken since September. Now they're back to living together."

Elizabeth released my hand and stepped over to Dad.

"Steve, thank you. You worked a miracle," she whispered. Elizabeth and Dad embraced, and she kissed his cheek.

Dad fingered Eli's key necklace. "When did Danny give you this?"

"You knew?"

Dad smiled. I smirked. Of course he knew. Eli flushed.

"Monday. Before dinner," I answered.

"That was fast. Elizabeth, what happened to the girl who was only having dinner with us so she could get over Danny and date someone else?"

"Say what?" Unbelievable.

"I thought by spending time with you I would find that I didn't have feelings anymore," Eli answered uncomfortably."Obviously I was wrong. When you dabbed that sauce off my cheek, I knew then that I was never getting over you."

Dad embraced Elizabeth again. "I'm glad you were wrong. Ellen and I need you in our family as much as Danny does."

"Can we go home now?" I asked as I stifled a yawn.

"Not until you tell me what you're doing in Los Angeles."

"Shopping. The stores near Donnelly suck," Eli answered without missing a beat.

Dad rolled his eyes. I couldn't help laughing.

"Eli and I needed quality time together, so we came home for the weekend." I smiled, and I hugged Eli to my side.

"I'm sure you could get quality time somewhere closer to Donnelly. Daniel, you'd better not be missing any classes," he warned.

"No, Dad. We left after our last classes on Thursday. Neither of us had any today. We fly back Sunday. Mo arranged it."

"Mo. My secretary knew, but I didn't. What about Mom?"

"I had to tell her. We needed Graci to stock the kitchen. Just make sure Mike and Randi don't find out. They won't be happy."

"I'm not happy either, Daniel. The Dean had better not find out. I'm certain he won't approve of a student on probation going home for the weekend when home is three thousand miles away," Dad said. His rising voice made his disapproval crystal clear.

"Understood, Dad. We'll be back in the dorm by nine. We took the G-5."

"Is that wise?"

"Dad! It's not like its winter and we have to worry about snow."

CHAPTER SIXTY-ONE - DANIEL

Thunderstorms! We didn't have to worry about snow on Sunday, but I had forgotten the more likely April weather culprit that could wreak havoc on flight plans.

"Thanks, Mo," I said when I put down the phone after receiving her call.

Our flight to Donnelly was delayed due to a line of severe storms forecast to move into that section of New York at the time our plane was scheduled to land.

"Now what?" Eli asked expectantly.

"We enjoy two more hours at the beach," I said cheerfully.

Eli was fretting, and I didn't want her to worry unnecessarily.

"I hate this. Our day is in a holding pattern."

"Its only two hours, babe."

I tried reassuring us both. Part of me feared we were in for a long day.

An hour later the phone rang again.

"Mr. Newman." This time it was the pilot calling. "The storms have become stationary. They're moving more slowly than expected."

I sighed in exasperation. "So when do we take off?" If the delay was going to last several hours, we could spend the afternoon at the beach.

"Enjoy your day, Mr. Newman. We have a situation here. We're butting up against curfew. The airport in New York closes at 2300. We won't make it."

"What are you saying?! We've got to get back to Donnelly! I can't miss my class on Monday!" My voice rose. Elizabeth watched with fear in her eyes.

"New York reopens at zero seven hundred."

"So we can't take off until midnight? I hate it, but if that's the best we can do."

Eli and I would be exhausted. If we boarded the plane at eleven, we could fall asleep in the stateroom, and if we slept through the flight, that might work.

"We can't do that either. Mr. Newman, Santa Monica also has a curfew."

"Shit!" My dream weekend with Eli was turning into a nightmare.

"We have two choices. We can layover at either McCarran or O'Hare and then head to New York. Either way we're wheels-up at 2200."

I pondered the choices. "McCarran," I told the pilot.

Las Vegas was not subject to the unpredictable weather of Chicago. The last thing I needed was to land at O'Hare and be stuck on the ground because of weather.

"Yes, sir. Anything else I can do for you Mr. Newman?"

"Uh, yeah. Can you please have Deliah stock the galley for breakfast? Omelettes, croissants, extra Starbucks?"

"Sure thing. We'll see you this evening, Mr. Newman."

"Damn!" I exclaimed, and I slammed down the phone. "This is unfucking believable!"

Good news is never delivered personally by the pilot. When I realized he was walking up the aisle of the Gulfstream seeking me out, I tensed. Freak-out time!

"Mr. Newman," the captain began, disappointed and fearful of my reaction, "We can't get clearance for McCarran."

"Shit!" I exclaimed.

"I'm sorry, Sir," he apologized. "We'll be laying over at O'Hare, estimated arrival, three-thirty local time. We'll be wheels-up at 2245."

"Eli, I'm screwed," I moaned.

Elizabeth rubbed my shoulder. "Not yet. It's only an hour and a half from Chicago to New York, plus an hour for the time zone difference," she said calmly.

"What time do we leave Chicago?" I asked half dreading the answer.

"We'll be wheels up at six-thirty, sir."

"We land at nine! That's cutting it close. My class is at ten," I seethed.

"It's the best I can do, sir," the pilot answered respectfully.

"I know. You're doing what you can. Thank you," and the pilot left for the cockpit.

"Danny, the airport's just fifteen minutes from Donnelly," Eli reminded me.

"Okay," I said tersely, while I contemplated my lack of options. "Anymore delays, and I will be officially screwed."

"The Dean will understand. It's not your fault that bad weather delayed our flight."

"Oh, Eli," I moaned, and I dropped my head into my arms resting on my knees. Usually I found Elizabeth's naivete refreshing. At times like this, I wanted to clobber her. I sat back up, pissed that I had to state the obvious.

"The Dean will not be sympathetic. How do you think it will sound when I plead for leniency because I flew home with my girlfriend for the weekend, and due to the weather my private jet couldn't take-off? Think, Elizabeth!" I was exasperated.

"Well, it's not your fault. You didn't know there were going to be severe thunderstorms when you filed our flight plan."

"Eli!" I said sharply. Was she really this obtuse? "The Dean will think

I'm a spoiled rich boy who thinks he can flagrantly break the rules and get away with it. He'll enjoy throwing the book at me. I know I would."

"You can blame me. I should have objected more firmly when you told me you wanted to go home."

"Eli? You didn't object."

"I'm trying to help here, Daniel."

"You thought it was the best idea you'd ever heard."

"It was. We both wanted to come home, and we had a great time. So Danny, stop fretting about the Dean. Our love is so much more important."

"Oh, Eli!" Why did she have to see things so simplistically at times?

How long had I been asleep? I yawned and stretched my arms overhead, dislodging my blanket. Where had that come from? My eyes darted around the cabin. Elizabeth was nestled in her chair sound asleep, soft snores coming with each exhale, a contented smile on her face.

I wanted to kiss my beautiful lady, but I didn't chance waking her. She needed rest for today's classes.

What time was it anyway? I had reset my Rolex to east coast time before leaving Malibu. Now I glanced at my watch. Eight-thirty! I bolted straight up. I had instructed the flight attendant to wake us an hour before landing so we could eat breakfast. It wasn't like the usually efficient Deliah to be late. There could be only one reason… and I was about to explode.

I unfastened my seatbelt and strode to the galley. Deliah looked up in surprise.

"Hungry, Mr. Newman? Breakfast will be out in ten minutes," she said, pleasant and all matter-of-fact.

I was flustered. My stress level was rising to off-the-charts levels.

"When do we land?" I asked with agitation.

"We're scheduled to touch down at nine-forty," she replied.

"Nine-forty!" I bellowed, and Deliah recoiled. "I have Econ at ten! Shit!"

I raced back to Elizabeth and shook her. "Eli, wake up!" I urged, and I shook her some more. Elizabeth's emerald eyes popped open and struggled to focus on me.

"Danny?" she said sleepily.

"Eli, I'm screwed!" I was in full panic. "We don't touch down until nine-forty!"

"Breathe! Danny, breathe." Now alert, she ordered me as I plopped back down.

Trying to calm was impossible. My head was on the chopping block. I inhaled deeply. Elizabeth was trying her best. She understood I needed to restore my equilibrium. I inhaled again.

"Donnelly's only fifteen minutes from the airport," she said.

"What if we're further delayed? What if there's traffic?" I slumped in the seat, and held my head in my hands. "Eli, any more delays and I'm totally screwed."

Eli rubbed my muscular shoulders, knotted from tension. It was role reversal time. She had to be the strong one. I was petrified, and reacting irrationally. Eli cradled me against her breast, and stroked my unkept hair.

Success at Donnelly was of utmost importance to me. Eli understood. No matter what happened in our race against the clock, she would do whatever it took to keep me from being suspended.

Eli lifted my head from her breast, and kissed my unresponsive lips. "Let's eat breakfast," she suggested, trying to sound cheerful."You'll feel better."

"I don't know," I glumly responded. "I don't have an appetite."

Eli smoothed a lock of hair from my brow and smiled. "I know," she quietly replied, "But this is the only chance you'll have to eat until lunch."

I wasn't convinced. "Please? Just an omelette," Eli insisted. "Protein will do you good."

Eli leaned forward.and kissed my cheek. "I. Love. You," she said slowly, emphasizing each word, while patting my head.

"Thanks, E. You understand." I smiled weakly. "I'll have that omelette now."

Grabbing a to-go cup of coffee, I sprinted down the Gulfstream's steps, my backpack thumping against my hip. Reaching the tarmac, I was bewildered to find that running supplied me with no advantage. Light as we had travelled with just one garment bag each, our luggage was not yet transferred from the plane to our waiting ride.

"C'mon, c'mon," I silently urged, tapping my foot. Where was the porter? Elizabeth looked as anxious as I felt. A quick glance at my Rolex told me it was 9:50. Add in the drive time to Donnelly, and I was doomed.

"I'm late for class. Please hurry," I instructed the driver as we settled into the black Town Car.

Elizabeth took my hand and squeezed it. I was too anxious to have any part of my body held, so I untangled my fingers from Eli's, and took a large gulp of coffee.

Based on my calculations, I deduced that I'd had no more than three hours of sleep. Strong coffee would have to power me through Economics. Additional cups would hopefully keep me awake through Political Science. There wasn't enough time between the former ending and the latter beginning for me to schedule a nap.

Eli's loud yawn got my attention. An exhausted pale face with puffy green eyes met my unexpected smile. The evening had been hard on Elizabeth, an inglorious end to a perfect weekend. I smiled at her, a warm smile, while I placed my coffee cup in the cupholder. Then I took her soft hands and caressed them, their softness filling my heart.

"E, as soon as we reach Donnelly, I'm off running." Elizabeth nodded.

"We'll drop you off first. It'll be okay. Maybe not you, but people are late to class everyday."

"Thank you. E, I probably won't have time to tell you, but this weekend was the best." I kissed her knuckles, and smiled at my content but sleepy kitten.

"It was, wasn't it," Eli agreed, her eyes showing more life. "Danny, thank you for taking us home."

"We needed this. I feel as though we're back to where we used to be."

"We are,"she smiled shyly, peeking up at me through long lashes.

"E," I smiled, "I wish we could have stayed longer. It was epic."

I reached for Elizabeth's face, cupped it in my hands, and kissed her with all my heart. We broke apart when we cleared the Donnelly gate, and I gave the driver directions to the social science building.

"I'll manage the luggage," Elizabeth offered. Lateness didn't matter to her. She wasn't on probation.

"Thanks, babe. See you at lunch."

One more quick kiss, and I was out the door, running to Economics

Professor Nash raised her eyebrow at me, acknowledging my late entrance to the Intermediate Micro-Economics class. I had steeled myself for this. There was no subtle way to enter a twenty-student class when you're ten minutes late.

Settling in as quietly as possible, I forced myself to remain alert and follow the strategy I had crafted: participation, participation, participation. If I participated in today's discussion and asked intelligent, well-thought out questions, then Dr. Nash would forgive my lateness.

"Daniel," Dr. Nash, a kind, scholarly woman in her thirties, summoned me when class concluded. I tentatively approached her at the front of the room.

"Yes, professor," I confidently responded, trying to mask my insecurity.

"I don't understand the Dean. Academic probation? It makes no sense with your grades. I'm supposed to report if you're absent or late, but I won't. Your participation today was superior to the students who arrived on time, but please don't be late again. I don't want to be put in this position."

"Thank you Dr. Nash. I won't disappoint you."

A shower and lunch would hopefully provide the boost I needed to get through Political Science. Afterwards, Eli and I could sleep until dinner.

I unlocked the door to my room. A grin stretched across my face. Awww! I had no choice but to smile. Cuddled up under the comforter, Elizabeth was sleeping, softly snoring. It was obvious she hadn't even tried getting to her class. Can't say I blamed her. I wish I could have done the same.

CHAPTER SIXTY-TWO - DANIEL

A steaming cup of coffee on this unseasonably chilly April morning should warm me. I hoped. I grabbed the first empty table I could find at the Café, teeming with students and faculty at this hour, and I settled in to enjoy my Starbuck's. Ah!

Elizabeth would soon be joining me. She had a long trek from her class on the other side of campus. I inhaled deeply. The enticing aroma of the coffee warmed me, and I hadn't taken a sip.

I opened my denim jacket and removed it. Twisting around, I draped the jacket on the back of my chair. As I returned to my coffee, towering over me, a steely glare from her small brown eyes eviscerating me, was Phoebe. Shit! What the hell did she want?

How to ruin a perfect cup of coffee! If looks could kill, her narrowed eyes and sneer would have ended me. Phoebe flipped open an iPad and shoved it under my nose, nearly toppling my coffee. I looked at her, puzzled and annoyed. Phoebe had better be gone before Eli arrived.

"Dan, what's the meaning of this?" Phoebe demanded.

There on a popular celebrity gossip blog was a photo of Elizabeth and me on the balcony outside our bedroom in Malibu. We were in a clinch and kissing. Though only Eli's profile, and her bare back, down to the dimple above her shapely rear were visible, Eli's nudity was apparent to anyone viewing the photograph.

What the fuck? I sat up ramrod straight.

"Where the hell did this come from?!" I exclaimed. I was enraged. Elizabeth and I had had our privacy violated; big time.

"How would I know," Phoebe snapped back. "It's not my blog. Or photo."

The beach had been empty, or so we had thought. Only the longest of long lenses could have snapped this without our knowing.

Phoebe snatched the iPad from my clutches.

"Phoebs, wait. I want to read the caption."

I snatched it back. "Grant who?" the headline screamed. I couldn't help laughing as I read. I was angry at the intimate nature of the photo, but I loved its effect.

"Either Grant Barnes and Elizabeth Jacobs really were playing with the paps as they claimed when they were caught smooching last month, or Daniel Newman is the most forgiving man since RPatz. You decide. The long-term Donnelly College lovebirds were spotted over the weekend enjoying the scenery from the balcony of their Malibu love nest. They can't do this in the dorm. Lolz. Sorry, Grant. The lady looks like she's taken."

"Perfect!" Absolutely perfect. "Thanks, Phoebs," I grinned like an utter fool.

"What the hell is this, Dan?" Phoebe demanded.

"Eli and I were having sex on the balcony off of our bedroom," I answered dryly. So what? We're both consenting adults.

"How could you do this? It's humiliating!"

"Phoebs, do what?" Had I heard her correctly? I hadn't done anything to Phoebe.

"We had something special going, Dan."

"Whoa! Hold on. What we had did not qualify as special. You knew Elizabeth was my lady. I never led you on."

"You weren't with her anymore."

I drew in a deep breath. Why was Phoebe giving me such a hard time? I glanced around. Duncan wasn't here.

"Look, Phoebe, what we had was nice, but it wasn't serious. It was short-lived. We saw each other so infrequently, it barely qualifies."

"We were together," Phoebe insisted.

"I was going through a hard time, and you helped me through it. But it's over. You know that."

Phoebe glared. "You do not always get your way. I'd keep an eye on your 'lady' if I were you."

I stared at Phoebe, not believing what I'd just heard. "Are you threatening Elizabeth?"

"Think what you want," Phoebe snarled, and she strode away.

What the hell? I didn't know whether to feel sorry for Phoebe or be fearful of her. I buried my head in my arms. Out of frustration I banged my fist on the table. Repeatedly. Eli would freak when she saw that photo.

"Danny?" a kind female voice said my name. I put down my fist and lifted my head, embarrassed.

"Hey, Chloe." A frown marred her lovely face.

"What are you doing?" she asked, concerned.

"Phoebe," I said with a strong exhale. The name alone spoke volumes and would keep Chloe from an inquiry.

"Phoebe? Isn't she out of your life?"

"I thought so, but she doesn't want to face…"

Shit! What a great morning this was turning out to be. For the first time I recognized the guy accompanying Chloe. Scott!

I took a large gulp of coffee and immediately spit it back into the cup. Ew! It was ice cold.

"Reality. Phoebe won't face reality. Me and Eli," I stammered.

I had never been in a conversation with Scott. Hell, we had never even been introduced. And Eli was due to join me at any moment. The perfect storm was brewing.

It was up to me to make the fist move. I had no bones to pick with Scott. I'd won. Time to be a mensch.

"Join me?" I asked Chloe and Scott. "Elizabeth's meeting me."

Chloe glanced at Scott, uncertain. I smiled warmly at them both. Scott nodded.

As Chloe slid onto the chair to my right, I rose and extended my hand to Scott. Time to be charming.

"Daniel Newman," I said. "Nice to meet you, Scott." I smiled warmly. It was important that he knew I was being sincere.

Despite his obvious discomfort, Scott took my hand, and we shook.

"Good to meet you too," he responded pleasantly, and we both sat.

Across the small table I made eye contact with Scott, using this opportunity to size him up. How could I not? Elizabeth, my Elizabeth, had fallen for this guy. I was desperate to figure out why.

"Scott, I want to thank you, and I mean it."

"Thank me for what?" He knotted his brows.

"Look, this is awkward for both of us, but Chloe tells me you're a stand-up guy. I'm glad you were there for Elizabeth."

Scott glared at me as his response. Then confusion washed over his face.

I smiled, uncomfortable. It was difficult to put my feelings into words, and fluency was evading me.

"Let me re-phrase this because I sounded like an arrogant prick, and I'm not."

Scott's eyes laughed their silent agreement. Hmm. He had warm brown eyes. Had that been the attraction? But I thought Eli only liked men with blue eyes. I pouted. She'd always told ME that.

"I treated Elizabeth terribly this year," I began. "I won't go into it because it's between Eli and me, but yeah, I hurt her badly. I pushed Eli into an awful depression. It frightened me, but I was unable to take the steps to end it, until recently, of course.

When she was with you, I saw glimpses of the old Eli trying to emerge. You made her happy when I couldn't. So, thank you. You got her through a bad time."

Scott's jaw dropped open. "You'll understand if I don't say 'your welcome.'"

"Of course," I laughed. "Eli probably made the wrong choice, because you're much more decent that I am."

"Don't be so hard on yourself. But you're right. You are an arrogant prick." Scott smiled, so I knew he was joking. The tension left the table. "Danny, I'm not saying we can all be friends now."

"And sing Kumbaya?"

"And sing Kumbaya," Scott laughed. "Maybe you, but not me. You've never heard my singing voice."

"I have," Chloe giggled. "You don't want Scott singing anything, Danny."

Scott extended his hand to shake mine. "There's no reason we can't get along. For Elizabeth."

My earlier assessment was correct. Scott was a mensch. That's why Eli had fallen for him. She deserved no less.

"Scott, let your presence remind me not to blow it, or I'll lose Eli to you for good."

"Don't I have a say?" Elizabeth giggled her arrival.

"Eli!" I nervously laughed.

Elizabeth leaned down to kiss my cheek. I nearly got whacked by the tote bag hanging from her shoulder.

"Whoops!" she giggled, and laughing, I kissed her on her lips where her hair had fallen across her face. I wiped auburn strands off my face.

"Here," Elizabeth chirped as she handed me a steaming cup of coffee.

"Thanks, babe. I needed this. Mine's cold."

Elizabeth placed her water bottle on the table, set her tote bag on the floor, and looked for a chair. Finding none, I pulled her onto my lap and held her securely around her hips. Sorry, Scott. The victor gets the girl on his lap.

"Oh my god!" Elizabeth finally realized whom we were sharing a table with.

She jumped up, and I pulled her back down to my lap. Then she turned to me, uncomfortable and unsure of what to do.

"Scott?" Elizabeth asked tentatively.

"It's okay, Elizabeth," Scott smiled. "Given that we're all friends with Chloe, I'm going to have to get used to seeing you with Danny. Don't sweat it, dear."

"Thank you," Eli answered. She exhaled, relieved.

I took a large swallow of coffee and returned my cup to the table. Then I swept Elizabeth's hair to the shoulder away from my face to avoid getting another mouthful. I planted a soft kiss on her neck and was rewarded with her subtle shiver. I looked at Scott who was battling against reacting.

"Hey, E, do you have your iPad in there?" I asked.

"Uh, yeah."

I leaned over to Eli's tote and removed her tablet. She eyed me curious, as did Chloe and Scott. A few keyboard clicks and finger swipes later, and I had what I wanted up on the screen.

"Look at this," I somberly instructed, and I handed Eli the tablet. Better she finds out from me.

Much to my surprise, a smile lit her face.

"This is a great photo," Elizabeth said, excited.

"You like this?" I was flummoxed.

"Yeah. It captures the moment," she answered dreamily, her eyes reliving that morning.

"Eli, focus. It's a gossip blog," I said sternly.

Elizabeth's innocent emerald eyes met my disturbed blue ones. She sat bolt upright. Reality had struck.

"Oh god! How did they get that?" Elizabeth exclaimed. "Danny, there was nobody on the beach but a couple of joggers."

"What is it, dear?" Scott asked.

"We went home last weekend," I explained.

"Paparazzi," Elizabeth added. "It was a glorious morning, and I ran out onto the bedroom balcony. The ocean was so beautiful." Then Elizabeth frowned. "That was a private moment. How did they get this?" she cried.

"High-powered zoom," I answered.

"From where? I feel so violated. It looks like I'm not wearing anything."

"Uh, Eli," I grinned, "You weren't."

"Let me see that, dear," Scott smirked.

"No!" Elizabeth exclaimed, and she hugged the iPad to her chest, hiding the tablet. I frowned at the obvious while Scott grinned and took out his phone.

"It's on the internet, dear. I can Google it."

Elizabeth and I both scowled; Eli because she was now faced with Scott seeing the photo, and me because if Scott called Eli 'dear' one more time I was going to lose it.

Begrudgingly, Eli handed the tablet to Scott. Chloe looked over his shoulder.

"That is a great photo!" Chloe declared. "Very romantic."

"Hot damn!" Scott laughed. "You're a lucky SOB, Danny. I would have enjoyed being the man in that photo. You look great, dear."

"Thank you?" Eli responded, uncertain how to react.

I inhaled deeply to keep from throttling Scott.

"How is it we dated for two months and the most I ever saw was your bra? If I had known a trip to Malibu was the answer, I'd have taken you there myself, dear."

Elizabeth turned toward me, and leaned her head against my chest, trying to hide. Her emerald eyes welled with tears she fought to keep at bay.

Time to put Scott in his place. "Never could have happened. I own the house, and I don't lend it out."

I hugged Eli tightly and kissed her hair. A sexy smile returned. "Elizabeth doesn't need Malibu. She only needs me."

My lady was frowning again, but Ian was approaching so I couldn't ask why.

"Hey, Newman!" he greeted me with a clap on the shoulder. "Back from the beach? So that's why I haven't seen you around."

"It was a quick trip. Got back yesterday morning."

"Great photo, Elizabeth," Ian said with a smirk. "You ever get bored with Newman, you can take me to Malibu."

"Daniel!" Elizabeth seethed. I smiled at Ian and hugged Elizabeth.

"That's never going to happen, Ian. I'm hers for life."

"Whatev. Keep me posted, Elizabeth. I'm available if you want a real man next time." Ian laughed at his own perceived humor.

"I have a real man," Eli answered indignantly.

"And I have a class. Remember, if you change your mind, Elizabeth, I'm your man."

"She won't," I answered curtly.

Ian shrugged and left for another table. Scott chuckled.

"Shut-up, Scott," Eli scowled, and he stopped. "Danny, what are we going to do?" she asked.

"Enjoy the attention. By tomorrow everyone will be on to the next story."

"What if there are more photos?" Eli fretted.

"The story's out. There's nothing more."

I smiled at Elizabeth. "Hey, just think, at least this lays the Grant Barnes story to rest. Nobody who sees this picture could possibly believe there's anything going on with you and Grant."

Elizabeth rolled her eyes. That did not comfort her. "But what if there are more?"

Elizabeth's voice was rising frantically.

"Baby, we're not important enough. There's no scandal. We were both with the person we're supposed to be with."

"What else is there?" Chloe asked.

"Uh, nothing," Eli answered rapidly.

"There's only one thing you could be dreading, dear." Scott smiled and his eyes twinkled mischievously.

Chloe gasped. "Video! You were having sex on that balcony."

"Next time, take me dear," Scott added with a chuckle.

Eli's face turned purple. Unable to face her friends, she burrowed against me.

"That's it!" I snapped, accidentally jarring Elizabeth. It was bad enough that Scott had thoroughly embarrassed Eli, some sort of sick revenge I was certain. This was the last straw. "If you don't stop calling my fiancée 'dear' already! I will throttle you. And that is not a threat."

"Fiancee?" Scott asked. "I didn't know."

Eli lifted her head. Her face back to its normal color, she proudly smiled at me.

"We live together," I barked, "and I don't take kindly to other men calling my lady by endearments."

"Sorry," Scott relented. "It's a habit I'll have to break."

"Danny, good digital cameras have video capability. We have to do something."

"Shit!" I exclaimed. Why had that gone over my head? "We'll figure it out, Eli."

She was desperate. I had to calm her. In this case, I was clueless as to how.

"Hey," I said gently, "At least you were with the right guy."

Then I grinned at Eli and squeezed her shoulders. I felt Eli relax, but only by the smallest increment.

She turned and kissed my cheek. "Yeah. I certainly am."

Eli understood, but I felt compelled to voice it, not for her consumption but for our audience.

"E, we're a team. We'll get through this together. At worst, we'll suffer a few days of embarrassment, but we'll be embarrassed together."

Elizabeth smiled, a weak smile. I was certain she was considering her parents and dreading it. Mike and Randi didn't even know we had gone to Malibu.

To hell with Scott. I was going to do what I wanted to do, namely give my lady the comfort she so desperately craved.

I reached for Elizabeth's troubled face, leaned in, and kissed her luscious lips. Eli's smile returned. She leaned her head against my shoulder and hugged me.

"What are you going to do?" Chloe asked.

Eli bolted upright, wired, in fighting mode. So much for the lasting effects of a comforting kiss.

"Danny, we need to call our lawyer to fix it for us," Eli declared in a manic tone. Her demeanor had returned to a state just short of panic, and she wasn't thinking clearly.

"Uhm, Eli," I began while I stroked her upper arm, "We don't have a lawyer. We only have a publicist."

Scott snickered again, pleased that his ex's former and current couldn't fulfill her every desire.

"That won't do," Eli declared. "Surely Steve has somebody on retainer..."

"Yeah, if we have tax issues or need a contract negotiated."

"Wait!" Eli was energized. "The last time Steve had a discrete matter he... "

"Called Mike."

"Exactly! I'll call Daddy. He'll know what to do."

I couldn't help the laughter I was trying to stifle from exploding in loud whoops, and Scott joined me.

"Why are you laughing?" Elizabeth was so confused. It was the first time all morning that Scott and I had reached agreement.

"Sorry, baby." I apologized.

There was no one I trusted more than Michael, but I couldn't imagine Elizabeth explaining our predicament to her doting father.

Eli grabbed her tote bag and rifled through it.

"Where's my phone?" she muttered. Finally she pulled it from her bag. "I'm calling Daddy right now!" she announced, and then she jumped off my lap.

"Whoa, Eli!" I reached for her arm and held her back. "Really? Mike?"

"Daddy will know what to do."

"How are you going to explain to Mike that there might be a sex tape staring his favorite daughter floating around?"

Eli stopped in her tracks. "Ew. This is so awkward." She frowned. "Danny, I don't know what to do. It's embarrassing, but we didn't do anything wrong. We were at home. Our privacy has been violated. We're the victims here."

"I'll go along with whatever you feel comfortable doing, baby."

"I certainly don't feel comfortable, but it's time to be an adult, right? I'll just have to suck it up and confess to Dad." Elizabeth paused, thoughtfully. "Maybe I'll call Kathy instead."

CHAPTER SIXTY-THREE - ELIZABETH

"How's my girl?" Danny greeted me outside the dining hall entrance with joy and affection, wrapping his arm around my shoulders.

"People keep starring at me," I complained.

Danny's warm embrace and buoyant greeting had nonetheless put a smile on my face.

"Lizzie," Danny laughed, and he tightened his hug, "People have always starred at you, babe."

Then he lifted me up, my toes skimming the ground. I giggled in delight. My hands flew around Danny's neck as I crushed my lips to his. To hell with the public. I loved this man, and I didn't care who knew. With internet blogs reporting on us, the whole world knew anyway.

"You're not coming?" Danny asked.

We were in his room after dinner. Danny was fitting his laptop into his backpack.

"I'm still recovering from yesterday. I'll be here reading."

"You're sure?" Danny zipped his backpack closed.

"Yeah," I nodded. "You go ahead."

Danny raised his eyebrow and grinned. "E, you don't want to face the public."

I turned away, embarrassed by the truth. Despite my earlier bravado, the stares we'd received at dinner unnerved me. If I could avoid public places as much as possible for a couple of days, it would all blow over.

Morning found me in a better mood. Perhaps it was the passage of time, perhaps it was from feeling rested, at last recovered from our travel. Or perhaps it was from the security that comes with waking in the arms of the right man.

The 'right man' was gently snoring. I doubted he'd come home late, but Danny wasn't back when I had fallen asleep at around ten. My head resting on his shoulder, I smiled as I glanced at his boyish face. Asleep, there was only one word to describe Danny; adorable!

Lifting my head just an inch or two allowed me to see the clock on the desk. It was early, seven o'clock. Our classes started at ten. I was bored. Of course! Email. Cautiously, I leaned my arm across Danny's chest. It was a long stretch to reach my phone that lay by the clock, but I could reach it.

A strong hand clamped my wrist, startling me.

"E, what are you doing?" Danny's wry smile greeted me.

"I didn't want to wake you. I thought I'd check my emails."

A mischievous twinkle in his deep sapphire eyes stopped me. "No," Danny said firmly, "Not now." Then he grabbed me, crushed his lips to mine, and climbed on top of me.

"Okay, so that was much better than checking emails," I admitted as we snuggled together after making love.

"Ya think?" Danny said with a grin.

"I think," I agreed, and I kissed him.

"This is how I want to wake up everyday, Lizzie."

"Me too," I chirped. Since when did Danny call me 'Lizzie?' He sounded like Grant Barnes. "Can I check my emails now?" I asked.

Danny laughed and ran his finger up my snaked pine causing me to shudder from the sparks. "Why are you so anxious about your emails this morning? Are you expecting a howler from Grant?"

"Not exactly." I rolled my eyes, and I reached for my phone.

"E?"

"Grrr! Danny!" I laughed, and I covered my face with my hands, mortified.

"E?" he asked again.

"Ugh! This is so embarrassing," I began. "After yesterday when I seemed to be the last person to know."

"Except for poor, <u>dear</u> Scott," Danny said, his voice dripping with sarcasm.

"Except for Scott," I frowned.

Either Danny was jealous of what I'd had with Scott, or he was gloating over what Scott never had, and never would have with me. I couldn't decide, and I wished Danny would stop.

"I should be the first person to know about me." I glanced at Danny uncertain as to how this would sound. "I signed up for a Google News Alert."

"Seriously?" Danny laughed out loud.

"I knew you'd make fun of me," I pouted.

"No, no, Eli. It's brilliant. So let's see what's news about you. And me too, I guess."

Danny handed me the phone. I touched the email icon, and saw that we were once again in the news. I tapped on the link where yesterday's story had been supplemented with reader comments.

"This one's negative, but I agree. It says, 'They may be hot, but who cares? Just because their parents are Hollywood royalty doesn't make them news-worthy.'"

"Yeah, I agree too. What else, E?"

"This one's simple. It says, 'Smokin.' Another one says, 'They're so in love. It's beautiful.'"

Danny laughed. "At least that one's true."

"Yes it is," I replied, and then I kissed Danny. "There's just two more. 'If my man looked like Daniel, I'd do it on the balcony too.'"

"Thank you, thank you. I have a fan club," he smirked.

"Oh, cut it out!" I playfully swatted Danny's arm. "You'll like the last one. 'Poor Grant Barnes. Elizabeth is so much hotter than Courtney.'"

"You certainly are. Poor Grant. He'll never know what he missed out on. Any new articles posted?"

"I'm scrolling."

Danny anxiously studied me as I did so.

"Wait! Here's one."

There was a photo of Danny and I at the Santa Monica Place mall. Danny was carrying two large brown bags from Bloomingdale's while I held a small one. We were eating cones of gelato while laughing and enjoying ourselves.

The caption read, "Adorabz! Elizabeth and Daniel's Shopping Funzies."

I grinned at Danny and passed him the phone. "Nice photo," I said, pleased.

Danny reached for his eyeglasses. "That is a good photo. Did you read the article?"

"Not yet. Read it to me?"

"'Our favorite young Hollywood couple, caught taking a gelato break. Elizabeth and her boyfriend Daniel are adorable shopping in Santa Monica. Wonder if there's anything for me in those brown bags. A source says… '"

"No, not 'a source!' That always sounds so bogus."

"You didn't file this story, did you?" Danny teased.

"Very funny! Of course not."

"Let me continue," and he feigned clearing his throat. "'A source says, *they're so in love. They couldn't keep their eyes off each other. Danny was holding Elizabeth's hand, and they were laughing. Sometimes they were kissing.'* We can't wait for the Donnelly College lovebirds to come home for summer. Might there be an engagement?'"

"An engagement?" I exclaimed.

"Remember, those blogs don't know we split. Any couple that's together as long as we are, they start speculating."

"It was a nice write-up though."

Danny smiled and stroked my arm. "You're getting more comfortable with publicity," he commented.

"Maybe. So long as this is the end."

"It should be. We were only home for three days."

Danny returned the phone to the desk. "Now, where were we?" he asked.

I rolled on top of Danny and straddled him. "Let's kill some time."

Chilly temperatures made it an ideal day to wear my new baby blue capris and oversized cashmere Malibu sweater. With a tee underneath and Toms on my feet, I felt cozy and ready to face the world.

By late-morning the sun was shining strong, and the temperature had risen. When I stepped out of the History building, I removed my sweater and tied it around my waist. The Malibu heart now covered my butt.

I hoped nobody would stare at me as I walked to the dining hall. Danny was waiting there, and I looked forward to the security he provided me. I'd had enough of the attention.

Behind my Ray-Bans, I could avoid making eye contact with whomever I passed. Earlier, Danny had walked me to my history class before he continued on to physics. Now I was alone for the cross-campus trek. The history building was located in an isolated corner of Donnelly, on a quiet subsidiary path. I welcomed its seclusion.

Just after merging onto the main path for the final leg of my walk, I heard a taunting voice behind me call, "Princess Elizabeth."

I stood stock still, then turned and came face-to-face with Ian and his snarky grin. He was with two guys I didn't recognize. Mocking grins were on their faces. Had they been laughing at me? Or was Ian trying to impress them because he knew me?

"Ian," I coolly responded. Why had I bothered stopping?

"Nice, sweater. Malibu."

"Thank you," I answered tersely.

Where was this going? Ian couldn't care less about my wardrobe.

"A momento?" Ian chuckled.

He was so crass. I didn't even blush. To let Ian see my discomfort was for him to declare victory. I opted for a different tactic.

"Pretty much," I answered cheerfully. "Danny wanted me to have a reminder of our amazing weekend at home. Not that I needed one."

Ian closed the gap between us. His encroachment in my personal space sent queasy prickles up my spine. Then Ian brushed a lock of hair off my shoulder and let his hand linger. I flinched.

"The hottest babe at Donnelly shouldn't be constrained by one man," he said.

I swatted his hand off my shoulder, and gave Ian a steely glare.

"I'm not constrained," I countered firmly. "Danny is my choice."

"She'll come around," he assured his friends.

"I wouldn't wait if I were you. I've got to go. Danny's expecting me."

"We'll escort you. Got to keep you safe," Ian laughed.

Safe? Ian was the only one I needed protecting from.

I turned and quick-stepped away, continuing down the path again. But Ian and his friends rapidly caught up.

"We don't have any balconies at Berkeley Hall, but you can leave the window shades up."

"In your dreams," I answered curtly.

Danny was waiting when I arrived at the dining hall minutes later. I warmly announced my arrival by collapsing into his arms and kissing him.

"I missed you," I murmured.

Danny hugged me back, then noticed Ian's proximity.

"Hey, Danny." Ian greeted him so friendly, as though he hadn't just been hitting on me.

"Hey, Ian. What's up?"

"Ran into Elizabeth. Kept your lady safe until I could deliver her to you. Body guarding, sort of say," Ian replied, and he flashed me a snarky grin. I frowned.

"Uh, thanks, Ian," Danny responded uncertainly. "We were about to have lunch. I'll catch you later."

"That prick!" Danny muttered as we entered the building. "Nobody guards your body except for me."

With Danny by my side for most of the afternoon, I confidently navigated my way through lunch, political science, and dinner. By the time we arrived at the library, yesterday's gossip was gone from my consciousness.

I gave it no thought when Danny and I prepared to part ways at his study room.

"Whenever you want to take a break, come get me, babe."

"Okay," I answered. "I won't be far."

Then Danny kissed me, and I left to find a nearby cubicle.

After organizing my work I realized I needed additional research materials before writing my paper. Psychology books were shelved in the basement stacks, but they were two rooms over from where I sat.

Brrrr! The room housing Psychology books was freezing! Who turned the heat off? I was glad I was wearing my sweater.

"Excuse me," I said politely to two girls blocking the entrance to the stack I needed to browse.

Scouring the shelves with no success, I realized my mistake. I needed to be one stack over. When I reached the end of the row, I turned and entered the next stack. Half way down, I found the applicable section of books. I quickly discovered two sources that were spot-on. But I wanted an additional one.

While browsing the shelves, I heard the giggles of the girls from the other side of the stack. Ugh! Couldn't they be quiet? This was a library! I wanted to concentrate.

"That was her," one of the girls whispered.

Great! They must be directly on the other side of the stack I was standing in front of. And now I was being subjected to their gossip about some poor girl.

"She thinks all she has to do is appear, bat her eyes, and everyone will move out of her way," said the other.

"Like the parting of the Red Sea," the first girl added. Then they giggled.

"Oh, shut up!" I wanted to scream, but wouldn't dare do.

"Did you notice her sweater?" asked the first girl.

"Yeah," laughed the other. "I heart Malibu! As though everyone doesn't already know where she spent the weekend," she sneered.

"And how," the other snickered.

Shit! Jealous bitches! So I was the girl they were gossiping about. I wanted to flee, but I also wanted to hear what else they might say.

"It's really gross," the second girl said. "She's like, I'm Miranda Jordan's daughter, and my boyfriend flies me to his Malibu beach house for the weekend," she mocked.

"Disgusting," her friend agreed.

"She's so full of herself. Now that Danny took her back, she snootier than ever."

"Why does he want her? Danny's so hot and she's, well she's not."

"You saw that photo," the first girl explained. "They were outside on a balcony doing it. That's why Danny took her back. She's a slut."

A slut! How could she? I slouched against the bookcase and held myself tightly. My eyes welled up with tears. I had to get out of this stack, but how? They would see me. I gasped. Oh my god! They knew I was here, trapped, forced to listen to their venom.

Despite the chilly air, perspiration beaded up on my forehead. I was panicking.

"And what about today? What student has photographers following them?"

"Yeah, Bloomindale's and ice cream. How sweet," the first girl said sarcastically. "I bet her publicist..."

"She has a publicist?" the second girl asked in surprise.

"Everyone in Hollywood has a publicist. After yesterday, I'll bet her mother ordered her publicist to have a photographer follow them until they were doing something wholesome, and voila, ice cream at the mall."

The girls burst into raucous laughter.

Perfect! I would take advantage and make my escape. Thank god my flat Tom's made no noise.

Undetected, I scampered to the far end of the stack, zipped past the stack the laughter was coming from, and fast-walked my way out of the room and through the next one. I didn't slow until I reached Danny's study room where I urgently knocked on the door.

Almost immediately, Danny opened the door. I collapsed into his strong, comforting arms. As soon as I heard the door click locked, I broke down sobbing.

Danny tightened his hold and stroked my back. "Baby, what is it?"

"People hate me," I sobbed.

"That can't be. You're wonderful."

Danny guided me toward the desk. He pushed his books to the side and sat me down on the now empty spot. Then Danny pulled up his chair, sat between my dangling legs, and took my hands.

"What happened, babe?"

"You a slut?" Danny laughed when I finished telling him everything I'd heard. "Everyone knows I'm the whore here."

"Danny! Don't say that. You are not."

"I used to be."

I frowned. "Lizzie, if I were a girl, that's what they'd have called me, a whore. I'm not proud of it, but men don't get labeled."

"As you said, that's the past."

Danny nodded and leaned up to kiss me.

"And everybody knows you took me back, not the other way around. Have you seen the latest?"

"What now?" I groaned in frustration.

Danny reached for his phone and accessed the latest entry.

This photo, taken on Third Street, was of Steve embracing me and kissing my cheek while a pleased Danny stood beside me.

The headline announced, "Elizabeth and Daniel's Family Affair."

"Catchy," I remarked.

"It's nice. Read it," Danny directed me.

"*Elizabeth Jacobs apparently holds the key to the heart of not one, but both Newman men. While boyfriend Daniel proudly looks on, director Steven Newman plants an affectionate smacker on her cheek. Seems this love match has Daddy's approval. Can wedding bells be far away?*" An insert was a close-up of my left hand; my ring finger was circled with the caption, "*waiting for my ring,*" across it.

"Not another wedding rumor?" I groaned.

"At least I'm the groom."

"Yeah," I smiled, "But it's got to be on our timetable."

"Agreed," Danny said, and he kissed me.

"I can't believe how we were followed around all weekend. That nasty girl had a point. It's as though we called our publicist and gave her our itinerary."

"Uh, Eli," Danny hesitated. "Don't be angry. Please? I called Kathy."

"What! You did what!?" I was outraged. "You know how I hate publicity!"

"Eli, easy baby."

I glared at Danny. Then I realized… "Oh my god! You knew there was a photogorapher on the beach. You let me… I thought I could count on you to protect me!"

"Elizabeth, I always protect you," Danny pleaded. "I love you. I swear, I didn't know. I would have wrapped you in my towel."

"How could you?" I sobbed. "I trusted you, Danny!"

"E, listen to me."

Danny jumped to his feet, and grabbed my shoulders. I had no choice but to make eye contact.

"I told Kathy we were coming home," he said sternly. "I wanted photos placed from when we went out. I told her where we would be on Friday afternoon. Not morning."

"I thought I could trust you," I sobbed.

Danny's face dropped, crestfallen. He abruptly released my shoulders.

"Elizabeth, please go," Danny said sadly.

I stared, stunned. What? Go where? Why?

"If you don't believe me… Hell, Eli, if you don't trust me, then what have we got? I can't live with a woman who doesn't trust me."

"Danny, what are you saying?" I didn't understand.

"Elizabeth, I don't want this. Please go."

I gasped, horrified, as I realized what Danny was saying.

"Are you breaking up with me?"

"Yes. I am."

"No! Danny, you can't do that! You love me. And I love you," I blurted out, panicking.

"You can't love me if you don't trust me, Elizabeth."

I hugged myself to Danny, but he didn't hug back. No! No! No!

"I trust you," I cried through my tears. "I trust you with my life, Danny. I trust you with everything." I was desperate. "Please believe me," I begged. "I overreacted. All this attention has me stressed."

Danny wrapped his arms around me with calming effect. "You know I can't live without you, babe."

"Then we're not breaking up?"

"You're certain you trust me?"

"Of course I'm certain. I love you."

Danny handed me a tissue. I wiped my eyes and cheeks and then blew my nose.

Danny took my shoulders again. Molten cobalt eyes bored into me.

"I called Kathy as soon as I saw that photo," Danny explained. "That wasn't her photographer."

"Then whose was it?"

"Apparently we have a new neighbor, Bart Reilly. He stars in a new series."

"Never heard of him."

"That's because we never have time to watch television at nine o'clock on Tuesday night."

"We'll have to make a point to watch so we recognize him when we see him."

"Yeah, fine. Whatever."

"We need to know our neighbors," I insisted. "It's the friendly thing to do."

Isolated on the family estate, I had never had relationships with neighbors while growing up. I wanted this.

"Eli, focus. Kathy said the photographer was stalking Bart. Seems our neighbor has a new gal pal. The photographer was hunting for an exclusive. But when he spied a stunning redhead on our balcony, he refocused his camera, realized who it was, and..."

"The rest is history," I said gleefully. "We were a mistake."

"That's one way to put it, E. We were a mistake."

I leaned forward and grabbed Danny's face to kiss him. "We're never a mistake."

Danny rose from his chair to keep me from falling off the desk. His arms wrapped around me as he lowered my back to the desk. I wrapped my left leg around his hips for Danny to fit between my legs

"Why did you want a photographer following us?" I asked.

Our faces, separated by inches, couldn't hide the truth. Danny blushed.

"You're embarrassed," I giggled. "Were you still hung up on Grant Barnes?" I felt gleeful knowing I was right.

Danny crushed his lips to mine, silencing me by reigniting our kiss. Then, holding me tight, Danny reached beneath my t-shirt, and unclasped my bra. I gasped at his touch.

"Danny, what are you doing?" I whispered.

"Eradicating Grant Barnes from your consciousness," he sneered.

"Grant who?" I giggled. Only one man counted in my life, and Danny knew damned well who that was.

Then Danny joined his lips with mine once again. At the same time, he flipped off my shoes. Then Danny unbuttoned my capris and pulled down the zipper. His hand entered my panties, and he thrust two fingers into me. Again I gasped. But I couldn't object. Danny's lips were glued to mine.

My arms, wrapped around Danny's back, pulled us closer. Instinctively my hips lifted, and he removed my capris and panties. I stared at Danny, my eyes opened wide in disbelief.

Our lips still joined, our tongues exploring each other's mouths, Danny continued pressing against me, hard and strained against his jeans.

What were we doing? It was the library!

Danny grinned. "The door's locked," he answered my unanswered question.

"But it's the library!" I protested, to no avail. I could not prevent the inevitable, and my hips rising against him, anticipating, rejected all logic thoughts.

"I never want to hear Barnes' name again," Danny said as he unbuckled his belt, opened his jeans, and pulled them down so they fell to his ankles. This was insane; sex in the library. But I was so aroused.

Powerless. I gasped as I stared at Danny's masculinity. His hand was under my shirt again, fondling my breasts. I moaned; all sense vanished. I would do anything Danny wanted if it would lead to an orgasm.

"No Grant. Not ever," I stammered breathlessly as he squeezed my breast. "I swear it," I gasped, and Danny plunged into me.

"Wipe that snarky grin off your face," I scolded Danny though I was equally giddy. We were nearing the entrance to the library break room.

"Can't help it, babe," Danny laughed, "What about yours?"

"Stop," I scowled, and I held up my hand as I abruptly stopped walking. "We are not entering that room until we sober up," I said firmly.

Danny raised his eyebrow and again I burst into giggles. "Sober up? I don't get drunk anymore, Liz," he teased.

I swatted Danny's head. He was grinning ear to ear. "You know what I mean," I hissed, trying to look somber, but failing miserably. "We're so obvious, we might as well hold up a sign."

Danny let out a whoop of laughter. A student at a book trolley glared.

"Lizzie!" he laughed and Danny pulled me into his arms for a kiss. "I love you, baby," Danny whispered.

"I love you too, but I don't want everyone to know that we were, you know, in the library," I whispered uncomfortably.

Danny twirled a lock of my hair. "Is the girl from the balcony growing back her modesty?" he teased.

"I never lost my modesty. We thought that was a private moment."

Fighting hard to keep straight faces, Danny took a careful sip of steaming coffee while I nervously sipped from my water bottle. I was certain everyone was staring at us though when I looked around nobody was. The other students in the room were engrossed in their own lives, their own conversations.

I leaned my back against the tall ad-covered metal beverage vending machine, while Danny, his hand placed above my shoulder, stood over me, leaving me hidden. This afforded me the most privacy I could expect in this most public of places.

From the corner of my eye... Shit! The two girls from the stacks had entered and were buying coffee.

"E?"

"Sorry. I spaced."

Danny laughed. "I've ruined you for the evening, haven't I?"

I grinned back. I'd let Danny think that. Not that it wasn't true, but it was the arrival of those girls that had me rattled, and I wanted to keep it from Danny.

Then I spotted Rachel.

"Rach is here," I said.

"Good. I need to see her."

Except before we could approach her, Rachel found those girls from the stacks, and was now chatting with them.

I slumped in dismay.

"E?"

"Rachel is talking to those awful girls from the stacks."

I nodded in their direction. Danny's eyes followed mine.

"I can't believe she's friends with them. Those girls hate me," I whispered through gritted teeth, though in case they noticed me, I plastered a smile on my face.

"I need to discuss business with Rach. We're going over."

I gave Danny a pained look. "But they hate me," I complained.

"They won't once they meet you," Danny replied confidently.

I wasn't convinced. "But, Danny..." I protested.

He leaned in and pressed his lips to mine. "E, all you have to do is turn on the Newman charm."

His breath on my face sent bolts of electricity through me.

"But I'm not a Newman," I whispered.

Danny reached his hand to my face. His palm held me still as he kissed me again. My heart beat rapidly as always. Danny grinned. His sapphires twinkled. He was well aware of his effect on me. I smiled back, newly confident.

"Yes, I'm a Newman," I whispered.

Danny took my hand, so soft, yet strong, and led me toward Rachel.

"Sorry to interrupt," Danny addressed the girls while flashing his most sincere smile, the smile guaranteed to make any woman melt, save for Rachel. "When you have a moment, we have business to discuss, Rach."

Rachel laughed. "My, you're polite this evening."

I couldn't help but giggle as Danny flushed and then grinned.

"Uh, yeah. I didn't want your friends forming the wrong opinion," he stammered.

"Right. You're running for office," Rachel acknowledged. "Should I do the introductions?"

"No, that's okay," Danny answered sheepishly.

He turned to the girls standing beside Rachel. They flushed. Predictible.

"Daniel Newman," he smiled. Then he raised our joined hands, "My spouse, the notorious, Elizabeth Jacobs."

I laughed, understanding that Danny had purposely used the term to give me an opening. The girls smiled politely, confused.

"Kelly," the first girl volunteered.

"And I'm Jill," the second one added.

"Nice to meet you, Kelly and Jill," Danny answered for us both.

"I am not notorious," I laughed.

"Yes, you are, babe," Danny grinned.

"Ugh! I am never going to live down that photo. It's so embarrassing."

"Which part?" Rachel asked.

"Huh?" We stared at her as one.

"The fact that you were caught on your balcony naked, or the publicizing that you have your own beach house in Malibu?"

I blushed. "I'm not embarrassed by my house. I love my house. I'm embarrassed at how our privacy was violated by a hidden mega-zoom lens."

Kelly and Jill nodded their understanding, though not being in my shoes, they couldn't really understand.

"What I didn't like, because that's a gorgeous photo, babe…"

"Typical man," I interrupted, and we shared a laugh at Danny's expense.

"I'm serious. I don't like the world knowing where we live. It's a security risk."

"Stalkers?" Jill asked with concern.

"Possibly," Danny replied.

"There are so many crazies out there," Kelly added. "It's a good thing you're safe at Donnelly. Can you do anything about it?"

Danny had been right. Engaging Kelly and Jill in conversation was the best way to overcome their negativity toward me. By the time we returned to our studies, Kelly and Jill had become friendly acquaintances whom I actually found myself liking.

CHAPTER SIXTY-FOUR - ELIZABETH

Election night. After being offered the Associate Editor position for next year's yearbook, I had dropped out of the race for Secretary. I only had Danny to worry about though I couldn't imagine him not winning the race for student government president. But you never know.

Our friends gathered early in The Cellar to wait for the results. Danny was holding up much better than I was. By ten o'clock Danny was still nursing his only beer of the night. Meanwhile, I was halfway through my second Margarita.

Hanging out with our gang did nothing to calm me. Periodically, Cam disappeared upstairs to the student government office for updates. His body in constant motion was distracting and causing me angst. I wished he would just disappear until he actually had news report.

I tried ignoring Cam by listening to the music, usually an effective way of mentally removing myself from most situations. I desperately needed a good dance song. There! I jumped up from my chair and grabbed Danny's hand.

"Let's dance," I demanded.

Danny and I joined several other couples on the dance floor. The romantic, slower rhythms were only to be shared with a lover.

Danny placed one hand around my waist and held my hand up to his shoulder. I held my other hand on his back and leaned my head against him. Bliss. Three and a half minutes of uninterrupted bliss. I sighed and our eyes met.

"Your eyes are sparkling like the finest emeralds," Danny whispered with obvious pleasure. His breath against my ear made me tingle.

"Yeah," I answered with a dreamy smile, intoxicated in his arms.

A shiver went through me as our eyes met again, and we exchanged knowing smiles. Danny removed his hand from mine, which I kept on his shoulder. He lifted my chin, and still smiling, tenderly kissed my lips.

White heat coursed through my entire being. All logical thinking left me as we wrapped our arms around each other and continued with our passionate display. Who cared if The Cellar was packed? Nobody else mattered to me; only Danny did.

A short time later, Cam came bounding down the stairs, excitement in every step. He ran to our table and threw his arms around Danny.

"You won, man! You won!" Cam screamed, clapping him on the back.

Whoops of joy erupted. I threw my arms around Danny. He picked me up by my waist and twirled me around while we both grinned in our shared excitement.

"You did it!" I squealed.

Danny folded me into his arms and held me tight. His massive smile said it all. "I did it, babe."

"I'm so proud," I pressed my lips against Danny's in a victory kiss.

Our entire group had jumped up. They were screaming, hugging, and high-fiving. Without their support Danny would not have won.

Then Danny took my hand and gently squeezed it. "Come with me," he said, and Danny lead me back to the dance floor.

A victory dance! Danny's arms around my waist held me close against his strong chest. My hands instinctively clasped around his neck, pulling him closer. Danny's strength flowed through me as our eyes locked on each other. Molten cobalt mirroring my emeralds melted me. My legs, turned to jelly, and quivered.

"You don't regret not running?" Danny asked in a soft voice.

I shook my head and smiled. "Danny, I'm fine. I really am. This is for the better."

"E, be honest. We could have been partners."

"But we are. We're life partners. That's much more important."

"Yes it is," Danny grinned. "But baby, you must be disappointed."

"I'm not. I have yearbook." I smiled sweetly and kissed his cheek. "This makes your life easier."

"How is that?"

"Think about it. There are five people on the Executive Council. What if there was a two-two split. and I had to vote?"

"You'd vote with me of course."

I narrowed my eyes and frowned.

"Not necessarily. And that's my point. If I voted with you, everyone would say, 'Elizabeth only voted that way because she's Danny's girlfriend.'"

"No. they wouldn't," Danny objected.

I raised an eyebrow.

"Yes they would," Danny relented with a sigh.

I went up on toe and kissed Danny's lips.

"I have the best of both worlds. I can influence what goes on because you'll want my opinion. And I don't have the responsibility. I don't have to attend meetings. I'll have more time for you."

Danny smiled warmly. "No meetings," he chuckled. "You may be the lucky one."

Then he inclined his head toward mine and kissed my nose. The tickling sensation made me giggle.

"I don't need an official title. I'm your first lady."

"My first lady," Danny pondered.

I held up my Tiffany key and looked directly into Danny's soul through those riveting sapphire eyes. Then I smiled, feeling an inner glow I hadn't felt in I didn't know how long.

Danny grinned from ear to ear. I hadn't seen him this happy since May. Then he grabbed my waist and twirled me in a circle. When my feet touched the ground again, we were both laughing.

"Being president is for a year. Being with you, baby you're for life."

Danny gathered me in his arms, pressed me against his body, and passionately kissed me. My heart raced. His sapphire eyes bored into my soul as our eyes met in a steamy stare. I didn't hesitate as my hands pulled his lips to mine for another kiss.

"Oh, babe. I love you so much. You have no idea how happy I am," Danny whispered against my ear. His breath sent more shivers through me.

Sunlight peaking through the window shade woke me. I grinned at the man asleep next to me. With Danny, life was exciting and comforting all at once.

Danny moved his head closer to mine and kissed my hair. "You smell nice," he murmured, and I kissed his stubbled cheek as my response.

Neither of us wanted to leave our cozy nest and face the world. It was the world part that was objectionable. I think we would easily have gotten out of bed if a private villa waited outside our door. But a noisy dorm, that was indeed a rude awakening on such a perfect day.

Then my phone rang. Another rude awakening. As I reached for it I noted the caller I.D. Oh, no!

"Hi, Mom," I answered sleepily, followed by a yawn.

"How was the election, Elizabeth?"

"Danny won, of course." I yawned again. "Sorry, I'm sleepy."

"Isn't it after eleven?"

"It is?" I didn't know it was that late.

Danny tried suppressing a laugh, and coughed. I glared.

"Hi, Randi," Danny cheerfully chimed in. I rolled my eyes.

"Is that Danny?" Her voice was chilly.

Danny laughed. "It better be me or Elizabeth isn't my girlfriend anymore."

Mom sighed, resigned to the fact she didn't approve of.

"Daniel, it's going to take time for me to accept this. I'm not necessarily happy. You hurt my daughter. Badly."

"I know, Randi, and I paid the price. Let me assure you, I'm clean and I can truthfully say I will never do anything to ever hurt Elizabeth again. She's too important."

"I want to believe you. I'm not sure that I can. Daniel, you need to earn back my trust. I'm not as forgiving as my daughter."

"Understood."

Mom took a deep breath. "You need each other," she admitted. "Neither of you was right without the other."

"Mom, thanks for understanding."

"And Danny, congratulations on your election."

"Thanks, Randi."

"I'll speak to you later. Elizabeth. Give Danny a kiss from me."

"Sure thing. Bye Mom." I clicked off and put down the phone.

"Where's that kiss from Randi?" Danny asked, and he grinned.

"This is so embarrassing." I quickly pecked his cheek.

"You can do better," he teased.

I rolled my eyes. Then Danny swept my hair out of the way before bringing his lips toward mine.

"We're never getting up today, are we?" I asked.

"No," Danny answered, and we started kissing all over again.

When Steve called thirty minutes later we decided we had better get up. It was embarrassing being repeatedly found in bed by our parents three time zones away.

Danny's eyes followed me as I went to get my robe from the hook on the back of the door. I was having a difficult time. My head was in the clouds, and my legs wobbled like jello. I could barely stand, and I felt self-conscious with Danny watching my every step as I stumbled across the room. I put on my robe, protected in its soft chenille.

Danny chuckled as he pulled on his jeans. Then he embraced me and held me upright.

"A hot shower will do you good," Danny said tenderly as he planted a soft kiss on my swollen lips. "I'll come by in an hour."

His smoldering sapphires looked directly at me. A shiver ran up my spine once more. Danny's touch and his gaze overwhelmed my senses.

"I love you, baby," he whispered, his breath on my face seducing me.

Then Danny opened the door and left. It had been a heady last twenty-four hours. At Danny's side, anything was possible. I was alive again.

Early spring warmth made it the perfect afternoon to enjoy some ice cream!

Danny and I shared giddy laughter as we left The Café with his iced tea, and my treat. I rapidly licked my vanilla soft serve cone aware of the sun beating down.

Unexpectedly, Danny squeezed my shoulder and kissed cold vanilla lips.

"Yum!" he exclaimed, sapphire eyes twinkling mischievously.

"You're making me drip," I scolded with laughter.

Then he joined me in licking the ice cream at the base of the cone. When our tongues met, our eyes locked, and we cracked-up. I loved playful Danny.

I took a bite off the top of the swirl and Danny wrapped his arm around my shoulder.

"It's amazing how you can eat so much junk food and never gain an ounce," he said as he took a swig of iced tea.

"I get a lot of exercise," I deadpanned.

Iced tea squirted out of Danny's nose as he broke into laughter that became a choking cough. Doubled over, Danny tried catching his breath, and I patted his back.

"Are you okay?" I asked, concerned.

His coughing subsided. "I'm good," he croaked.

Recovered, Danny straightened and hugged my shoulders. "You certainly do get a lot of exercise," he chuckled.

I glanced at him over the top of the half-eaten ice cream and flashed a devilish smile. "Want to put me through another work-out? You're the best personal trainer."

Danny smirked. "I'd love to babe, but I'm meeting Riley Watson in half an hour. The current prez is orienting the future prez."

"And so it begins. The lonely life of a political wife," I teased.

"Never."

Danny guided me to a nearby bench surprisingly vacant on this pleasant day. It was relaxing to sit in the sunshine and breath in the fresh spring air. My legs curled under my short skirt. Danny held my left hand and played with my fingers while I finished eating. It reminded me of early last year when we had first rekindled our friendship. Similar afternoons spent sitting on benches, talking, resulted in us eventually falling in love. That memory made being together like this even more enjoyable.

Danny leaned in to kiss my neck, just below my earlobe, and I shivered.

"You're so beautiful today. You're glowing, Eli," Danny breathed in my perfume. "You smell nice, too."

I'm pretty sure I glowed even more upon hearing Danny's words. I might have blushed too.

Danny turned serious. "You're happy?" he asked.

I took my last bite of ice cream cone, savouring its crunch. "Of course," I smiled, fingering my key. "Aren't you?" If not, he was hiding it well.

Danny's brow knitted. "Life with you, most definitely. With me, maybe not so much."

"What's wrong?" I asked.

Danny took both of my hands and looked directly at me.

"I'm afraid I'm going to disappoint you," Danny said sadly. "I might not live up to your expectations. E, I can't hurt you again."

"I don't think that's possible," I chirped, forcing optimism. "I love you, and you love me. There's nothing we can't conquer together."

"It's not that simple," Danny replied, and he averted his gaze.

I touched my hand gently against his cheek and whispered, "Hey, what is it?"

Danny paused for a beat. "Remember when we discussed my issues, and I said I needed to work on me?"

"I thought all was good. You haven't taken anything, have you?"

"No. It's just… I've been so caught up in us. I wanted to shelter you. I didn't want my struggles to get in the way of us getting back together."

"You've been struggling?" I was surprised; Danny had not even hinted.

"A little. Sometimes. When I'm down at The Cellar or when I'm hanging out with the guys."

"I've wondered. For someone working on sobriety you have been spending a lot of time in a bar. I feel bad for not speaking up. But… well because, I didn't want to be that overbearing wife."

"I appreciate it, babe. I wanted one less thing for you to worry about."

"That wasn't complete honesty." I reminded Danny of our pledge.

Danny nodded. "It's been hard. I want you to think I'm invincible."

"I don't need a superhero." Then I realized, "I haven't been the most supportive. No more Margaritas. I don't need them."

"Thanks, baby." Danny patted my hand and paused before continuing. "Cam and Shane have been very supportive. They won't party in front of me. Other than an occasional beer, they go elsewhere."

"That's good. They're good friends," I answered sincerely.

"They are, but it makes it harder. I feel left out. I don't like being the only one not at the party," Danny said sadly.

"You're used to being the center of the universe. Your universe needs changing."

I kissed Danny's cheek. I felt bad for him. Danny hadn't yet come to terms with the obvious; he needed new friends, sober friends.

"Dad is right. When I'm home this summer, and I see Harlan in person, things will improve."

"I respect you so much for saying that." I smiled at Danny.

"Don't. I have to earn your respect."

Danny squeezed my hand. The little hairs on the back of my neck prickled. Danny was hiding the truth.

"What are you not telling me? Danny, you sound as though you anticipate something bad happening."

"I hope I'm wrong." He sounded worried. Why?

"You must remain strong. Remember, you have me on your team."

Danny smiled. "I know I have you. My beautiful head cheerleader and coach, my first lady who I love so much. But I have other friends I enjoy too. I haven't hung out with them lately. I want to. Summer's coming and I won't see them."

Oh, shit! "Duncan! That's what this is about." I snarled. Unbelievable!

"The guys are jamming tomorrow night. I miss my friends, babe."

"Can't you ever say 'no' to him? After all the hurt he inflicted on us."

"Duncan's done some awful things, but I don't want to say no. You know how much I enjoy playing my bass and he's the best keyboardist around. Ron and Kirk will be there too. I blew it for the band this year. I want to make it up to them. I owe the guys that much."

I could deal with him hanging out with Duncan, but…

"Shit! Phoebe will be there too!" I was enraged. My perfect day now lay in ruins.

"Don't worry about Phoebe," Danny pleaded. "She's easily ignored."

"No she isn't. Phoebe will be all over you, all touchy-feeley, to make a point."

"And what point is that?"

I shrugged, uncertain of what it was. "That she can," I said.

"There's a definite lack of trust here, Elizabeth." Danny sounded hurt.

"I trust you, Daniel," I insisted. I really did trust him. It was the others…

"It doesn't sound that way, Liz," Danny answered angrily.

I turned away, embarrassed, and pulled my knees up to hide my face. If we were going to fight, it shouldn't be over Phoebe. We were better than this. Tears flowed, and I was shaking. Danny clasped his arms around my cocooned body.

"I feel so stupid," I wailed. He laughed.

"I forgive you," Danny said tenderly "After what I've put you through this year, I don't know if I would completely trust me either."

I turned back to Danny and wrapped my arms around him. I needed the hug probably more than he did.

"I do trust you. I love you, Danny. Otherwise, what am I doing here? It's Duncan and his friends that I don't trust. Most of all its that vindictive bitch, Phoebe!"

Danny chuckled. "You don't mince words, do you, babe?"

"Not where Duncan and Phoebe are concerned," I growled.

"I'm not sure I trust them either, but I want to play. I miss the scene."

"You miss the scene?" I asked incredulously. "If you're sober, it won't be the same."

"You could be right. I have to find out for myself."

I appreciated Danny's honesty, still I was fearful. I pictured my memories of "the scene," and I couldn't imagine what it was about a roomful of wasted people that one could miss. And Phoebe would be there! Ugh!

"I'm coming with you."

"No, Eli. I don't need a baby sitter. Besides, you and Duncan always get into fights. And if Phoebe shows up, it's better if I handle her alone."

That was true. She was a powderkeg that might blow. I couldn't guarantee that I wouldn't provide the ignition. "Let sleeping dogs lie," Grandma Margie always said. Staying away was safer for everyone.

"But you'll be here, always," Danny said indicating his heart. I couldn't help smiling. Then he softly kissed my lips.

"Shane and Cam are going. It's boys' night."

That made me feels only marginally better. I trusted Shane and Cam.

"Just remember who I'll be coming home to," Danny smiled. His sapphires twinkled.

I took his hands and held his gaze. "I know you will do the right thing, Danny. You're strong. Know that I trust you."

"I will never violate that trust. Nothing is more important to me than you, Elizabeth." Danny pulled me into his arms and pressed his lips to mine for a powerful kiss that made us both forget that we were sitting on a bench near the student center.

CHAPTER SIXTY-FIVE – ELIZABETH

The next morning, in response to my texting, Rachel stopped by. She found me unpacking purchases that had arrived yesterday from Neiman Marcus.

"Did you buy a new wardrobe," Rachel asked in a surly tone.

"Just a few things," I answered tersely.

I held up two dresses, one by Diane von Furstenberg and the other by Missoni, that I was about to hang in the closet.

"What do you think?"

"Aren't those formal for school?"

"No. I like wearing dresses in the warm weather, and these are pretty casual," I answered matter-of-factly.

"You like dresses? I've never noticed."

I ignored her. "Dresses and skirts are more comfortable than jeans."

Rachel opened another box and pulled out a pair of Kate Spade flats and a matching purse.

"Killer," she said sarcastically.

"They are adorable, aren't they?" I responded.

Exasperated, Rachel silently nodded. It was not like my friend to withhold her opinion.

"What are you doing?" Rachel sounded like the inquisition.

"I'm putting clothing away?" I answered innocently. "You don't expect me to let them lie around and wrinkle."

"No, we wouldn't want you to have to iron," she muttered. "You're going home in only a few more weeks. I'm sure you have enough clothes to last until then."

"Maybe that's why I wanted new things. To me, it's more than only a few more weeks at Donnelly. It's only a few more weeks with Danny before we separate for the summer. Again," I said angrily.

"Isn't everything peachy-keen? I've seen the pictures," she teased.

"It is, but I'm not naive. Our relationship is fragile. I won't feel secure until I return from Israel."

"You don't have to go. Danny would prefer if you stay home."

"Danny understands. Much as we hate being apart, in the long run, it's better. I must prove that I can live independent of him and our families and succeed." I picked up a shipping carton and slammed it against the wardrobe door. "I hate this. I really do," I sobbed. "I'm going to miss Danny so much. But I have to go. If I don't, I will wake up one morning and regret it."

"So until then you'll prance around like a Barbie doll?"

"Wanting to look nice, does not make me a Barbie doll," I replied indignantly. "You should try it sometime."

"You really don't see it, do you?" Rachel asked, ignoring my insult.

Rachel was right; I didn't.

"You and Danny are all over each other. Everyone turns and stares. And the gossip blogs? Do you really think anybody cares who the Donnelly student government president is sleeping with?"

Rachel was doing a good job of spoiling my day. I'd never pegged her as the jealous type. Nothing else explained her outburst.

"That wasn't my intention," I explained defensively. "You know how uncomfortable I get when people look at me."

"Good point," Rachel said, now softer. "You are a privacy freak. Funny that you'd end up with the one guy at Donnelly that everyone is always staring at."

"Rach, I didn't invite you over to criticize my boyfriend. Is there a point to your tirade?" She was getting on my nerves.

"You're changing," she blurted out. "Like weekends in Malibu, and this sudden interest in designer clothes."

"Danny and I went home for the weekend. So what? You've done it. Everyone does it. And I've always liked nice clothes."

"But your home is Malibu, not Westport or Framingham."

"I can't help where I live."

I rolled my eyes. After the long separation, I suppose it was easier for my friends, even Rachel, to believe I was changing. In fact, it was Danny who felt the need to change. I was the same me I had always been. I was finally confident enough to let it show.

"Rach, you were in my house. Did it ever enter your mind that maybe that is who I am? I'm tired of the charade I've been living. You more than anyone should understand. I've always shared my fears with you."

"You were afraid of people taking advantage of you."

"I was young, immature and naïve. But I was smart enough to know that I was all of those things. I understood that I had grown up in a bubble. Life in that bubble didn't give me the tools to make the quick decisions I needed to make about the people I was meeting. So I hid behind a façade. It bought me time to grow up, and time to develop friendships I could trust. Then I didn't feel vulnerable or like somebody's prey."

"You feel like prey?"

"Sometimes. Like when I go to Film Department events. I don't even know those people, but the way they swarm around me."

"I wouldn't trust them either if I were you."

"You know, I'd love to take an acting class, but forget it." I frowned.

"I'm sorry it has to be that way."

"Now I'm free to be me," I smiled. "I don't need to hide behind a façade."

"Because of Danny?"

"Yes, because of Danny. You two are good friends, but I know Danny better than anyone. I'm twenty years old, and except for when he was in prep school, Danny and I have been like this." I held up my first two fingers twisted together to illustrate. "For twenty years."

"Like an old married couple," Rachel laughed.

"Except we have passion," I giggled. Then I sighed, remembering last night's bliss. "Danny is an incredible person. People assume he's arrogant, but he's the most grounded person I know. Danny is confident, and he's handsome, brilliant, and excellent at everything. So of course he's accused of arrogance."

Rachel smiled. "Spoken like a woman in love."

"Well, I am." I smiled back.

"Doesn't it bother you having him show you off like you're arm candy?"

"Danny doesn't consider me arm candy," I grimaced. "We're equals. Now back to why I asked you to come by," I said as I filled the Kate Spade bag. "Let's do girls' night out tonight. You, me and Chloe. The new Liam Hemsworth film is playing across the street."

"It's Saturday night. You're not seeing Danny?" Rachel was surprised.

"Saturday night isn't the same when you see a man every night."

"Won't Danny mind?"

"Nope. Danny is already doing boys' night out."

"Aha! The truth comes out."

"Rachel, I need a distraction."

"Liam Hemsworth will do that," she teased.

"He's not my type, but he is great to look at."

Rachel glanced at me curiously. "You know him, don't you?"

I nodded, and looked down, nervously twisting the fabric of my shirt.

"I'm, I'm concerned about tonight."

"What's going on?"

"I trust Danny. I really do. It's just," I stammered. "He said it's only jamming. I'm not stupid, Rachel. I know how these things go." Tears rolled down my cheeks.

"You're crying," Rachel observed as she sat down beside me. "Elizabeth, where is Danny going?"

"Duncan's," I cried.

"And you're afraid Danny will come home wasted after he's been making such good progress."

I nodded. "Rach, I'm having this really bad premonition."

"Did you ask him not to go?"

"Of course I did. Danny was reassuring. I trust him. But it's Duncan..."

DANA AYNN LEVIN

"I love your boyfriend, but he's a jerk. What is it about Duncan that he can't ever say no to him?"

I shrugged. "Danny says he misses the music, but I think in a strange way he's intimidated. Duncan's like this dark side Danny knows he could never join. There's something enticing about it."

"Then Mr. Perfect isn't. Why does Danny find Duncan worth risking his relationships with you and his father? He needs help."

"I wish I could understand it." Tears trickled down my cheeks. "It's like Danny's flirting with diaster, challenging himself to get through the night sober. He doesn't need to do this. And there's nothing I can do. I've tried."

"Do not blame yourself. Danny has to want this himself."

"I know."

"Now let's work on you. You can control you. Liam Hemsworth sounds good to me. I'll get Chloe on board."

By the time Danny arrived to meet me for dinner, I had cleansed my face, put on a little makeup, donned my new blouse and acid-washed capris, and had straightened my room. There were no signs of my earlier distress.

"Hey, princess," Danny's cheerful voice greeted me through the ajar door. I closed it behind him, threw my arms around his neck, and gave him a welcoming kiss.

"I missed you," I said.

Dressed in low-cut jeans that emphasized his narrow hips and toned butt, a t-shirt that showed off his sculpted pecs and delts, and his faded denim jacket, Danny took my breath away. I couldn't let go.

"I missed you too, babe." Danny's arms wrapped around me, and his lips joined with mine for a passionate kiss.

"Did you guess that I've been avoiding you today?" Danny asked.

I raised an eyebrow, surprised. "Weren't you studying?" I replied.

"Not so much. My thoughts kept returning to you."

"Really?" I squealed, and my muscles clenched, so aroused.

"I thought you were angry about tonight and wouldn't want to see me," Danny explained. I frowned.

"I'm not happy, but I always want to see you," I answered.

Danny smiled warmly. We both understood that our love ran much deeper than whatever happened tonight.

"I don't understand what you're doing," I admitted. "If you're trying to test yourself…"

"Understood. Opinion noted," Danny replied, cutting me off, but I didn't change his mind. "You're as protective of me as I am of you."

I was pleased that he really did understand. Other guys might interpret my reaction as being that of a possessive girlfriend, trying to keep her man from his friends. Danny understood that wasn't me.

"Don't worry, baby. I have a game plan," Danny began. "Two beers. That's my limit. And I promise to return here, no later than one o'clock."

Then Danny tenderly tucked a lock of hair behind my ear. His eyes were full of sincerity. I knew I could trust every word he said.

"If my kiss tastes like anything besides beer, or if I'm behaving like I've drunk more than two," Danny continued. "Then you can kick my sorry butt out that door and I will have to live with the consequences of having blown the best thing that's ever happened in my life."

I laughed. "You have thought this out, haven't you?"

"Yes. See, no secrets, Eli."

"I still don't like it."

"I know," he answered, and he kissed my hair for us both to feel better.

Leaving the dining hall with Rachel and Chloe, Danny draped his jacket around my shoulders.

"I don't want you getting a chill," he explained.

I appreciated his concern, and the cozy softness of the aged fabric. He had owned this favorite jacket since prep school at Bromley Hall. I inhaled sharply. The scent of Danny, and his cologne, filled my senses. If he didn't take the jacket back when we reached my room, I would wear it tonight. In this jacket, Danny would be with me.

Danny accompanied me to my room while I waited for Rachel and Chloe. He wasn't going to Duncan's until later.

Once inside, Danny leaned his strong hands on my shoulders and looked me in the eyes. "Elizabeth. I love you. I won't do anything to jeopardize us. If it gets too difficult, I'll leave." Danny stated with conviction. I had no choice but to believe him.

"I trust you. It's what you can't control that worries me."

"There's only one thing I can't control," he smirked, "but as Rachel and Chloe are about to knock on the door…"

We both laughed as sure enough a knock came on the door.

"She'll be right out," Danny called.

Smiling, he lifted my chin up for our lips to meet. Then there was another knock. I didn't want to let Danny go. Dread returned. Why did I feel that this might be our last kiss? Ever.

"Okay, okay. She's coming," Danny called.

I reached for my wristlet and shoved my keycard into the pocket of Danny's jacket as we opened the door for Chloe and Rachel.

"You be good," Rachel warned Danny.

"Yes, ma'am," he saluted her, and then Danny turned to me. "You have a good time," he said. "I'll be home later, baby."

"Behave yourself," I admonished.

Masking my dread, I squeezed Danny's hand, and smiled. Then I went up on toe to whisper in his ear. "You're hotter than Liam," I giggled..

Going to the movie proved therapeutic. For two hours I relaxed and took my mind off of Danny. Liam Hemsworth could take your mind off of anything.

The only reminder was when my phone vibrated with a text message from Danny. It said, "I love you," and attached was a download of a red rose.

Earlier in the day, it would have made me anxious all over again, but lost in the story on the screen, it filled me with its intended warmth. I pulled Danny's jacket closer to feel his presence.

Afterwards, Rachel, Chloe and I went to the frozen yogurt shop down the street from the theatre.

"This is so good," I said as my tongue glided over the creamsicle flavored yogurt swirl. After the saltiness of a small bag of movie theater popcorn, it hit the spot.

"Let's get a table," Chloe suggested. "I can't eat and walk."

Rachel and I glanced at the large cup Chloe was holding. Chloe's yogurt was drenched in chocolate syrup, and it was smothered with berries that threatened to roll off the pointy vanilla swirl.

Like me, Rachel had ordered a simple cone; vanilla covered in chocolate sprinkles.

"If we're staying, I'm getting an iced tea," Rachel responded.

Chloe and I turned our heads toward the growing line. The yogurt shop was always crowded after a movie let out.

"That's at least a fifteen minute wait," I pointed out.

Chloe spied the last empty table and marched over to claim it.

"You're not in a rush, are you?" she asked.

"Not, really." I frowned. Danny wouldn't be home for hours.

Sitting at the table was a good ploy for prolonging my night out. Rachel and Chloe understood that once I returned to my room I would become a jangle of nerves until Danny came home.

Once our yogurts were eaten, I was anxious to get home. It was early, ten o'clock, but there was nothing I wanted to do beside get comfortable and wait for Danny.

"Go have some fun." I ordered Rachel and Chloe, after we returned to Berkeley Hall. It was Saturday. No need for them to cut short the night.

After all the time I'd been spending with Danny lately, I had enjoyed a night out with the girls. I needed to do this more often. I relished being with my friends.

CHAPTER SIXTY-SIX – ELIZABETH

Eleven o'clock found me sitting in my bed attempting to read. When I had returned from the movie, I changed to silk pajama bottoms and a cotton tank top. When Danny came home. I would at least look as though I had been trying to sleep.

Unable to concentrate, I re-read the same page for probably the fifth time, the words devoid of meaning.

Loud, rapid knocking on the door startled me.

"Elizabeth?" Cam! He sounded frantic.

"Cam?" I called out, my voice squeaked, terrified.

What did Cam want? Where was Danny? With him, right?

Cam burst in, worry etched across his brow. I'd never seen my laid-back friend frantic before. My heart leaped into my throat.

"It's Danny!" he exclaimed, "c'mon."

"What!" The book dropped out of my hands and fell to the bed. My stomach lurched. "What's wrong?" I jumped out of the bed.

"It's bad, Elizabeth," Cam said with urgency. "You've got to take Danny to the hospital."

"Hospital!"

All color drained from my face. I threw on Danny's jacket, shoved my feet into my Ugg slippers, and grabbed my wristlet and car keys, both lying on the desk where I'd thrown them earlier.

"Where's Danny? Cam, where is he?" Panic clenched my throat. My voice was barely audible.

"With Shane. At your car."

We ran at warp speed, down the hall to the back door that led to the Berkeley Hall parking lot. Danny, looking white as a ghost and unsure of his footing, was leaning against my Range Rover while Shane supported him. Something was terribly wrong.

I gathered Danny in my arms, and he slumped, his weight causing my knees to buckle. I smoothed hair off his face, kissed his cheek for reassurance, and smiled.

"I'm here," I whispered. There was no doubting my love. Then springing into action, "Get Danny in the back," I ordered Cam and Shane.

My adrenaline surged as I jumped into the driver's seat.

"Shane, Cam, keep him awake," I barked.

Whatever it was, I had learned from watching too many television dramas that they needed to keep Danny conscious.

"E," Danny mumbled, his voice weak and thready. "I'm sorry."

"I know," I responded while furiously blinking back tears. "You'll be alright."

"Keep it together, Elizabeth," I silently willed myself, "You must be strong."

Now was not the time for crying or hysterics. They would cloud my vision, and my thinking. Danny needed my mental acuity.

Thank god my Rover had a GPS. I had never driven to the local hospital, and I had no idea where it was located. Time was Danny's enemy. I couldn't afford to get lost.

I tore out of the lot, and off the Donnelly campus at top speed. I raced through the streets the GPS instructed me to take while tearing through stop signs and red lights.

"How's Danny?" Several times I called to Cam and Shane.

Danny was hanging in, barely conscious.

I was petrified, but I had to hold it together and get to the hospital. I called the emergency room to have a gurney meet us. Then I remembered the rules of hospital bureaucracies. I needed Danny's insurance card, and possession of his valuables.

"Cam," I barked like an army officer, "Get Danny's wallet and watch, and any other valuables he has on him. Give them to me at the hospital."

"There it is!" Shane shrieked.

I made a final left turn straight into the driveway entrance of the Emergency Room. An orderly stood waiting outside.

"Help!" I yelled to him, and the next few minutes were a blur.

Everyone moved at lightning speed. Orderlies lifted Danny out of the car, onto a gurney, and ran into the emergency room, while I jogged by his side. Inside, two nurses took over.

"What drugs did he take?" one of the nurses growled at me.

"I don't know. I wasn't there," I trembled, clutching myself around my stomach. "Danny doesn't… He wouldn't..." I stammered. The nurse's glare intimidated me.

Then she called out a code to another nurse.

At the electronic doors to the exam area, the first nurse stopped me cold. "You can't come in here," she said firmly.

"What do you mean? But I'm. He's uh…" I stumbled while trying not to weep. "Danny!" I cried.

"Only medical staff," she said brusquely.

I was shaking, but she meant business so I didn't protest. Fear gripped me. Turning back to his nearly still body, I forced a smile. Danny couldn't see how petrified I was. Danny needed me strong. "Newmans and Jacobs are strong," I thought. I couldn't let Danny or our parents down tonight.

For what I prayed wouldn't be the last time, I squeezed Danny's unusually clammy hand. Then I leaned down to kiss his parched, colorless lips. "I love you," I whispered, and the staff hustled Danny out of sight.

The heavy doors slammed shut in my face. I stood transfixed, staring at them. Grief, fear, panic, and love – all these emotions simultaneously overcame me. My heart hurt so badly. I trembled. Huge sobs wracked my body. I shook uncontrollably.

If Cam and Shane hadn't been standing beside me, I would have collapsed. Instead, Cam pulled me to his chest and comforted me, like the brother I needed. Oh, Teddy! I need you.

All I could do was cry and then cry some more.

"Elizabeth, shh, shh. He'll be all right," Cam murmured while gently rubbing my back. "The doctors will take care of him. Danny is strong."

"What if they can't?" I cried, and I got hysterical all over again.

The thought of living without Danny was unbearable. And Ellen and Steve; the burden crushed me.

"Don't even think that," Cam whispered. "We have to be positive. For Danny."

I nodded. "For Danny," I whispered.

My shaking subsided and finally stopped. Cam led me over to a gray leatherette sofa. He kept his arm around my shoulder. Perhaps it brought him comfort too. All for one, and one for all.

Shane settled in on my other side. He had purchased three bottles of water, and now he handed one each to Cam and myself.

"Here, drink this," he mumbled.

I looked at Shane's face, and then Cam's, for the first time since Cam had summoned me. Fear; it was etched across their knitted brows and evident in their ever-moving fingers. Danny's best friends were as frightened as I was. Even Cam's mocha colored complexion had paled.

It struck me how young and inexperienced we were. Huddled together, each of us tried to keep the others from falling apart. We needed a parent.

How I longed for my mother. With her forceful, take no prisoners demeanor, Mom would already know Danny's condition. Mom wouldn't let a couple of nurses keep her from the exam room. It would have taken the National Guard to keep her out.

Thoughts of Mom made me cry again. Her name alone opened doors.

"C'mon Elizabeth. Crying won't help Danny," Shane said.

"I want my mother," I blurted. "I'm so scared."

"We all are," Cam replied, and he grasped my hand.

"Should I call her for you?" Shane offered.

I shook my head no. What would I tell her? Sadly, I knew her response would be that Danny needed rehab, not me.

It dawned on me that neither Shane nor Cam had told me what happened. They were both sober, a sign that it hadn't been a particularly raucous party. I wiped my eyes with my fingertips and sat straight up. I looked at them through red, swollen eyes.

"Danny promised he wouldn't have more than a couple of beers. What happened?"

"I didn't see anything," Shane responded sadly. "I was hanging with Jazz."

"I stuck pretty close to Danny," Cam said. "Remember, you threatened me?" I had indeed done so. I smiled for the first time.

"And you're both sober. So what happened? I've seen Danny drunk. I've seen him wasted. Danny never does real drugs. How did this happen?" I demanded.

"I don't know," Cam began. "Danny was great, just playing his bass and nursing a beer. There was a lot of tequila and pot in the house. I even said something to him, but Danny went on about how you were too important and he wouldn't jeopardize it."

"He did?" Cam nodded, and I grinned, proud of my man. "You're going to make me cry again." I felt Danny's love in Cam's words. "How did things go so wrong?" I asked.

"Danny took a break from playing, and he picked up his beer. He'd left it on a table in the corner. He was nursing it, using the bottle mostly as a prop. Danny was resolute. He was coming home sober. After a few sips, he put the bottle down and returned to playing. I was watching him, not the beer. Within minutes he abruptly laid down the bass and found me. Danny said he felt weird. He panicked. That's when we left to get you."

"Someone spiked his beer! Those bastards!"

"It looks that way," Cam answered with downcast eyes.

I shook my head and took a deep breath. "I've had a bad feeling all night. Why would Duncan do this!?."

"It wasn't Duncan," Shane said. "He was too busy playing."

"Who else was there?" I demanded. "Who hates Danny that much?"

"We can't prove anything, Elizabeth," Cam answered.

Could it get any worse? My love was lying in this hospital, in a condition I could only imagine, and somewhere, somebody wanted him dead. I shuddered at the thought, and I pulled my knees up to my chest for protection.

New tears welled up in my eyes. My head slouched forward. I buried myself against my knees. Everyone loved Danny. Who would want to harm him?

"Be strong, be strong," I willed myself. Think positive thoughts. Danny's young, Danny's strong, Danny's in top condition. If anyone could get through this, it was Danny. Oh, Danny!

I suddenly had a thought of surprising clarity. "Damage control, guys. We've got to do damage control."

Shane and Cam stared at me, possibly because it was the most lucid thing I had said in the hour that we had been sitting in the waiting room, and probably because it seemed so cold-hearted and calculating. Me, sounding like a publicist was the last thing they expected.

The stabilizing effect of having a mission to concentrate on was appealing. My brain needed this to focus on, and I needed to do all I could for Danny.

"Elizabeth, what are you talking about?" Shane asked.

"Somebody is out to get Danny." Cam and Shane nodded their agreement. "We don't know their identity, but they know what they've done. They probably didn't mean for it," I paused looking for words that wouldn't frighten me, "to go this far. I can't imagine anyone wanting to kill Danny. He's so popular. Who would have a grudge?"

"A lot of people are jealous of Danny," said Shane.

"They call Danny Donnelly's golden boy," Cam added. "He has everything, and hatever he wants he gets. Now Danny's added student government president, and he's back with his killer girlfriend." Cam smirked at me.

I blushed. "Do people really think that about me?"

"Yes," they answered simultaneously. I blushed again.

"I'm flattered. I think."

Cam ruffled my hair. "Let's make you a little less perfect." I laughed for a moment and then returned to our task.

"Here's our plan. Do not say a word to anyone, not even Rachel and Chloe. What happened tonight stays between the four of us and whoever did this," I said. "They can't brag, because they deserve prison, but given that all the suspects are stoners, the perp will probably slip-up."

"You can count on us," Cam said.

"We have to protect Danny. If this gets out the Dean will suspend him, or worse. With Danny's history no one will believe your story. They'll chalk it up as another accidental overdose. We know that's not Danny."

I blinked hard. A lump caught in my throat. "That's not my Danny." My head fell back to my knees, and I wept.

"Calm down, Elizabeth," Shane said gently, and he rubbed my back.

"I'm sorry. I'm trying to hold it together," I stammered.

"Of course you are."

Then another frightening thought occurred to me. "The media! Do not even think of Twitter, Facebook, Instagram, email or texting. This cannot make the internet. It would ruin us."

"Elizabeth, reality check," Shane reminded me, "We're in a small town in upstate New York."

"Just heed my warning, and be wary. Thanks to those gossip blogs, Danny and I are targets. Do not utter our names, even here. You never know who is listening."

"You sound paranoid," Cam said, as he glanced around the empty waiting room.

"I know what I'm talking about," I scowled. "I've lived this long enough. We can't be too careful."

Nearing one o'clock, we still had no news. I had to think positively, I had to, but my mind assumed the worst. I sat on the edge of the sofa, my head in my hands starring down at the white with gray speckled floor tile. One, two, hmm. How many speckles per square foot were there? Meanwhile, Shane absent-mindedly rubbed my neck and Cam paced in circles while reading his phone.

Had it been only last week when Danny and I had been home? I replayed the weekend in my mind. What an amazing three days. After the hell we'd been through, our short stay in Malibu had been the final step in repairing our relationship. Our love solidified, the future belonged to Danny and I. The future. I blinked back tears. There might not be a future. Despair filled me. I wept again.

During his rounds, Cam stopped a nurse we had seen go in and out of the exam area several times. He addressed her in his most polite, deferential voice.

"Excuse me ma'am."

The nurse turned her attention toward him, and Cam continued. "It's been a long time. We haven't heard anything about our friend."

"What is your relationship to the patient?" she asked brusquely.

"We're his roommates," Cam answered.

"All of you?" Her eyes bored into me.

Cam chuckled. "Well, really only she is. Shane and I roomed with Danny last year."

"I see," she responded crisply, unmoved.

"Ma'am, my friend's on the verge of a complete breakdown," he said indicating me. "Her fiancé is lying in there, and nobody will tell her if he's even alive."

"Fiance?" the nurse answered doubtfully.

"You see the diamond necklace she's wearing? Fiancee."

"I'm not sure what I can do. She's not his family."

"Maybe not on paper, but Elizabeth is most definitely Danny's family."

I sensed the nurse softening as Cam continued on a new track.

"Ma'am, how would you feel if your husband was in there, and nobody would tell you anything?"

344

"That's different. We're married."

"Ma'am?" Cam pleaded. "They're as good as married."

"All right. I'll find out what I can," she relented

"Thank you ma'am. You're an angel."

Cam returned to the sofa and took my hands. "That nurse is going to help us," he said confidently.

It seemed like forever, but it was probably only fifteen minutes later when the nurse approached. She sat down beside me and reached for my hands. I looked into her kind eyes and trembled. It was the moment of truth I'd been wanting and dreading at the same time. She smiled, surely a good sign. Pleeeease.

"Honey, he's stabile."

"What does that mean?"

"Your fiancé will recover. They need to run a few more tests and clean him up. Then you can see him."

A wave of relief poured over me. I released the breath I didn't know I was holding. My heartbeat calmed. Danny was alive! He would recover!

"When? I have to see Danny," I said through the tears of happiness flowing down my cheeks.

"In about an hour."

"Thank you," I squealed. I wiped my face with my sleeve, and hugged her. The nurse rose and left for her station. Shane, Cam and I group hugged.

"He's going to live," I exclaimed, relieved, wiping my face again.

Now that Danny would be alright, I realized the time, almost two o'clock, and turned to Shane and Cam. "You should go. It's late," I said.

"We don't want to leave you," Shane replied.

"I'm fine. It's better if you go."

"What if someone asks where you and Danny are?" Shane asked.

"They won't," Cam answered. "It's Sunday. Everyone will assume they're uh, sleeping in." He raised an eyebrow, and I blushed.

Time passed, and the nurse approached me again. "I told Danny you're here. He can't talk, but he smiled."

"Thank you. I feel much better."

"Where can we get a cab?" Shane asked the nurse.

"They can call you one at the security desk."

"That's going to be expensive," I told Shane. "Let Danny pay for it."

I removed Danny's wallet from the denim jacket's pocket and gasped.

"That's me!"

Inside the wallet, was a photo Danny had taken of me while we were sailing in Vancouver.

Warmth filled me. I quietly wept, touched by Danny's love. Cam placed his arm around my shoulder.

"Danny loved that photo. He had me make some prints," Cam said. "Don't you ever come up to his room?"

"Of course I do, but we've mostly been downstairs this week."

"The 5x7 is on his desk."

"That's so sweet," I beamed. That really was sweet!

Now that I was smiling, the nurse examined both me, and the photo, carefully. "You're an exquisite girl."

"Thank you," I answered, suddenly aware that I was only wearing pajama bottoms and a tank top underneath my jacket.

She glanced at the photo again. "I think you may be even prettier than she is, but has anyone ever told you how much you look like Miranda Jordan?"

Was the nurse baiting me? Had she read somewhere that I was enrolled at Donnelly?

I smiled politely, and responded, "I've heard that before, but my eyes are green not brown, and her hair is brown not auburn. You really think I'm prettier?"

"Oh, yes," she replied.

I was glowing as the nurse returned to her station. Other than Danny, nobody had ever said that to me before. Mom was known worldwide for her beauty, and here, unsolicited, a nurse tells me I'm prettier than her. It was heady.

Shane and Cam worked hard at keeping straight faces, smirking at my vanity. Meanwhile I pulled out a wad of bills from Danny's wallet. I counted out five twenties and gave them to Cam.

"Danny won't mind you spending his money?" he asked.

"Of course not," I answered crossly, offended by his question. "We have joint accounts."

I returned the wallet to my pocket. Then I turned to Shane and Cam who appeared taken aback by my revelation.

"These are some things I want you to put in Danny's backpack. Do it before you crash and leave it in front of my door." I handed Cam a piece of paper and Danny's room key. "And remember to put the key in the bag."

"Yes, ma'am," Cam replied, saluted, grinning.

Once Shane and Cam departed, I felt more alone than ever. I hadn't realized how comforting they had been. Even when they had sat silently beside me, their presence had soothed me.

Despite knowing Danny would recover, the raw emotions of the evening took over. I was happy. I was angry. Most of all, I was relieved. Overtired and overwrought, uncontrollable tears overtook me again. Only this time, Shane and Cam weren't there to comfort me.

A kind arm unexpectedly wrapped around my shoulder.

"Come sit by me, honey. No need to be alone," the nurse said. "Can you fill in some forms? I need your fiance's insurance card, if you have it."

I numbly assented, and then realized, "I need to call Danny's father."

"Of course."

This was the most difficult phone call I'd ever placed. Steve was probably on a mixing stage so I texted him, "9-1-1 Call me." He would drop everything and call immediately from a private room.

My phone rang a moment later. "What the hell is going on, Elizabeth?" Steve barked.

I hadn't been thinking. One look at the clock, and Steve would know something was horribly wrong. Only bad news comes in phone calls placed at two in the morning.

"It's Danny," I stammered.

I was petrified, anticipating his over-the-top reaction, and I was right.

"What the hell did my son do now?" he snarled.

After I filled Steve in, he exploded, expletive after expletive hurled at me. He was angry with Danny. He was angry with me. Why didn't he understand? Danny was innocent here.

Steve was furious. He barked at me as though tonight had been my fault.

"How could you let Danny do this, Elizabeth?" Steve screamed. "You're irresponsible! Running off to a movie so Danny could party! Fuck this, Elizabeth! I thought you loved him. You've let Danny down and me!"

I shook, crying and distraught. Not Steve, not my parents, nobody had ever screamed at me like this before. I snapped.

"I'm not his babysitter! Danny's a grown man, Steven!" I screamed back.

"You're supposed to be taking care of Danny."

"I do take care of Danny. But I can't hold him prisoner."

"You're nothing but a child, Elizabeth. You don't know what love is. You think love is nothing more than sharing a bed. That's sex, Elizabeth, not love!"

"Steven! How dare you! I know what love is. Love means trusting your partner and I trust mine!"

"Fuck! My son is in a hospital because of your negligence!"

I couldn't take Steve's tirade anymore. I was exhausted. My nerves were shot. How could it be my fault? Everyone else said I had saved the day. I lost it. In my entire life I had never blown up at Steve, but now I did. It felt so awful, so wrong, yet so necessary.

"You do not speak to me this way! I am not some little P.A. in awe of the great Steven Newman! I am Elizabeth Jacobs, and there's a good reason why your son loves me so much."

"Yeah, you'll have sex with him almost anywhere?"

"What!" I gasped loudly. "How dare you!" That was rich coming from a man who had spent years chronically cheating on his wife. "Do you want my father to hear how his best friend insulted his daughter?" I scolded.

"I'm sorry. I take it back."

"That you could even think that! Danny loves me because I always have his back, and I won't take any crap from him. And I won't take any crap from you either, Steven."

"Calm down, Elizabeth," he begged.

"I will not calm down, Steven!" I yelled into the phone. "I have been doing everything right! I got Danny to the hospital even when I didn't know where it was. I sat here for three hours not knowing if Danny was alive or not, and I spared you by not calling until I knew. I'm sorry if you don't think I did a very good job at keeping Danny out of trouble, but I'm just his girlfriend, not his nanny! It's nearly three in the morning, and I'm alone at a hospital. I can't handle this anymore!"

And I slammed the phone off. I was shaking. Feeling cold and alone, I burst into sobs. My nightmare seemed to be cloning more nightmares.

Moments later, the phone rang. Steve was back to being Steve.

"I'm sorry, honey. You've been great tonight Elizabeth. I don't blame you for this. It's not your fault Danny went to a party," Steve relented. "When I get my hands on my son, I'm going to kill him! Danny's very lucky to have you."

"Thanks," I answered, still numb from his earlier tirade.

"You're a lot stronger than anyone gives you credit for, Elizabeth. Hang in there." I sniffled to mask my fresh tears. "I love you, honey. Please don't cry anymore."

"Okay," I answered in a trembling voice.

"Is there anyone you can sit with?"

"There's a nurse. She's nice," I responded in a whimper.

"Go. I don't want you alone."

"Okay. I love you, Steve."

"Whenever you want, call me. I'm never asleep for you," Steve added. "Now can you get me the nurse? I want to speak with her."

Dutifully I obeyed Steve and sought out the nurse. It was the first time all evening that someone had told me what to do. It was liberating to have the burden of responsibility lifted.

I went to the nurse's station and handed her my phone. I couldn't hear Steve's questions, so I was forced to figure it out by listening to her responses.

The nurse took down Steve's cell phone number and said the doctor would call him in about half an hour. Then she noted on Danny's chart that Miss Jacobs was family, meaning I could see Danny whenever I wanted, and the doctors would have to answer my questions. I liked having Steve in charge. Things got done.

The nurse was named Beverly, and she was a dedicated, caring professional. Beverly hated the pain I was in, and her chattering helped.

At the same time, she made me uneasy. I had hoped that Danny and I could get through this ordeal with anonymity. I dreaded what the media, and especially those outlets that had no obligation to even attempt to find facts, would do to Danny.

And then there was my involvement. This evening had the potential for becoming our publicist's worst nightmare. Twenty years of good reputations gone. I excused myself to call Kathy.

Kathy expected clients to call her at all hours of the day and night, so I didn't hesitate for a moment, even knowing it was midnight in Los Angeles.

"More sexy photos, Elizabeth?" She asked upon hearing my voice.

"Worse than that, Kathy. I need crisis management. We have a situation here," I somberly told her.

Beverly was a big movie fan as her Miranda Jordan comment had shown and she had just spoken to Steve. When she entered Danny's insurance information, it became impossible to keep his identity secret. Being under twenty-six, Danny was covered by Steve's policy. The name Steven Newman was printed on the insurance card that bore the imprint of the Director's Guild of America.

Beverly eyed me as she typed.

"You're Miranda Jordan's daughter, the girl on the balcony," she observed, though she wasn't judgmental.

I blushed. Even at a hospital in upstate New York, I couldn't escape that photo.

"He's very handsome. Even tonight," said Beverly.

"Thank you, but Danny's so much more than that."

"It's obvious that you love him very much."

"I do. Danny's an incredible man."

"Like his father."

"Yes, like his father." No, not at all like his father, if you knew his father like I did. But it was simpler to agree. "Please don't let anyone know who we are," I begged. "If it gets out that I brought Danny to an emergency room for a drug overdose, it'll be a disaster."

"Don't worry," Beverly assured me, "This is upstate New York, not Hollywood. There's nobody to find out."

"People tweet and blog," I pointed out.

"Hospital staff is required to uphold patient confidentiality," she promised.

Then my phone rang bringing further comfort.

"It's my Mom," I told Beverly.

The nurse seemed unsure of how to process that her favorite actress was on the phone. Her eyes opened wide in disbelief, then recovered. Beverly motioned me to a small room where I would have privacy.

"Hi, Mom," I said, and the warmth of her presence calmed me.

"Hi, Sweetie. I just heard from Steve. How are you holding up?"

Finally! Someone who understood the hell I'd been through.

"Better, now that you're on the phone," I said.

"I'm so sorry you're alone. I wish I was there with you."

"Me too," I whispered.

After talking for about ten minutes, Beverly knocked on the door and pointed toward the exam rooms. I could finally see Danny! It was nearly 3:00. It seemed like forever.

"Mom, they're gonna let me see Danny," I said with relief.

"You go, Elizabeth. Call me tomorrow. Or sooner, if you need me."

"I will, Mom."

"Give Danny a kiss from us. We love you; him too."

My emotions threatened to overtake me again. I was elated to finally see Danny, but I was scared. I didn't know what to expect. I'd never been to an emergency room before. I talked myself down. It would not do any good for Danny to see the wreck I had become.

Beverly escorted me through the electric doors and down the corridor. She paused by the door leading to Danny's room.

"You can have five minutes. They're moving him upstairs to a private room." Beverly patted my hand and opened the door for me to enter.

Danny needed me to be strong all over again. I summoned all the acting ability I hoped I'd inherited from my mother to present a good face. With red, swollen eyes, I had to look awful.

The man lying in the hospital bed did not look like Danny. My tall, athletic boyfriend appeared small. Instead of strong and muscular, he seemed slight and weak.

Danny's usually tanned face was pale, drained of color. He appeared vulnerable, too. The twinkle was missing from his usually expressive sapphire eyes. Danny was attached to an IV hook-up and several monitors. Oxygen flowed through plastic tubing at his nose.

A second nurse scribbled on his chart and then left the room. Tentatively I walked over to the left side of Danny's bed while giving him a reassuring smile. Beverly had cautioned me that Danny was unable to speak tonight. She would not divulge the details, but told me that the stomach pumping process left his throat raw.

Instead, I contented myself on watching Danny's facial expressions. After fearing the worst all evening, Danny's appearance did not matter. Only his health did.

Relieved, I stared at his chest, rising and falling in a regular rhythm. The heartbeat monitor indicated his strong pulse. I took Danny's hand, and before I squeezed his, he pulsed mine. My heart melted. Everything was going to be all right.

"I love you," I whispered, and Danny responded with another squeeze to my hand. Gently, I kissed his parched lips, and I laid my head on his shoulder. I didn't want Danny to see my fresh tears, this time from happiness.

Waves of relief washed over me as Danny, fingers fumbling, awkwardly stroked my hair. With all the hook-ups, it was difficult, but it was important for him to show affection in the only way he could.

All too soon Beverly returned to admit Danny to a private room. I could have stayed in his room for what remained of the night, but I needed the deep sleep only a real bed and the solitude of my room would provide.

Danny squeezed my hand once more. His eyes smiled, the twinkle trying to return. "I love you," I told him. "I'll be back after I get some sleep." I gave Danny another kiss and forced myself to leave.

Danny's backpack was waiting in front of my door when I arrived at Berkeley Hall shortly before four o'clock. I noiselessly opened the door, noted that the "do not disturb" sign was in place, and closed it behind me.

As though my body knew it had done all that was required from it, the adrenaline drained from my system, and exhaustion overtook me. As soon as I peeled off Danny's jacket, I collapsed onto my bed and fell into a deep sleep.

CHAPTER SIXTY-SEVEN - ELIZABETH

The hallway was silent as it should be on a Sunday morning when I woke. I tip-toed down to the bathroom undetected. Nobody, not even Rachel, would ever know about last night.

Shortly before noon I arrived at the hospital, having first made a few stops. Hungry from skipping breakfast, I stopped at McDonald's for a quick Egg McMuffin. Next stop, the local Wal-Mart, where I picked up a box of Charms lollipops. Danny's favorite flavor was cherry. I also grabbed a bag of lemon Ricola drops; perfect for his raw throat. Lastly, at the adjacent strip mall, I purchased a bouquet of spring flowers.

The guard manning the desk in the hospital lobby directed me to Danny's room. Stepping off the elevator on the third floor I easily found it. I paused at the door to regain my composure before entering. My heart beat rapidly. Given Danny's condition last night, I didn't know what to expect.

Steeling myself for the worst, I hoped for the best. I took a few deep cleansing breaths and satisfied myself that all was well. Danny would see that I believed Cam and Shane about the party. He needed complete confidence in our love.

Tears pricked my eyes. Don't cry, don't cry! Damn it, Elizabeth! Don't cry! I'd almost lost Danny for good. That thought was unbearable. I tried to smile. My smile had to be natural. Otherwise Danny would read right through it.

Tentatively I knocked on the door, then entered. Danny, dressed in a regulation hospital gown, was sitting in bed, propped against two thin pillows. An IV remained hooked up to his right hand. The tray table held an empty jello cup, and a partially eaten second one. Hunger, always a good sign.

Danny turned his head toward me. His color had returned, and his shy smile melted my heart. A weight lifted. With newfound lightness in my step, I strode over to the side of the bed and placed the flowers on his nightstand. Awkward, sunglasses still on, I leaned over the bed's metal safety rail to embrace Danny. I strained to reach his lips. We wanted to kiss, but the height of the bar and position of the tray table prevented us from doing so. I frowned.

The backpack slipped off my shoulder and onto the mattress. I lay my purse on the floor beside the nightstand. As I examined the metal bar, I jiggled it, and tried lowering it. Stuck. I frowned. Danny smiled mischievously, laughing at my failed effort. I shrugged and smiled back.

"How the hell does this work?" I was frustrated. I wanted my kiss! Danny smirked and pointed at something just past my right hand.

"Button," he said, his voice low and graveled, like sandpaper.

"Your throat!" I exclaimed as I found the button and finally lowered the bar. Danny sounded awful.

"Wicked pain, E," Danny slowly whispered, croaking, "Like it's on fire."

Then Danny slid over to make room for me. I removed my denim jacket and threw it across the room where it landed on an orange leatherette club chair. Wearing his jacket brought me great pleasure. In it, I was surrounded by the faint scent of Danny's cologne, and the cozy softness of the fabric that felt like Danny's embrace. Today that brought more comfort than usual.

All enthusiastic, I jumped onto the bed. Then I smoothed down my short skirt. My eyes filled with mischief as I playfully dipped my finger in the jello and licked it. Danny grinned at my impish smile.

"Yum, red," I teased while smiling at Danny. I dipped my finger into the jello again and pressed it into his mouth. Grinning, Danny sucked the jello off my finger. Then he pushed the tray table away and pulled me into his strong arms for a soft kiss.

"I have something for you," I said, and I reached for the backpack from which I removed the box of lollipops and bag of Ricolas.

"Cherry?" he whispered. I nodded. "My favorite."

"Shh. I know," I said, laughing at my little boy. I took out a lollipop, unwrapped it and handed it to Danny.

"You're the best, E." Danny smiled, and before he could put the candy in his mouth, I quickly kissed his lips.

I let Danny suck on the lollypop as I snuggled against him, his arm wrapped around my shoulders. His throat needed both the candy and to be quiet. I didn't mind. After last night, I was content to lie in Danny's arms and let our eyes do the talking.

"I was so scared," I finally whispered after Danny put the clean lollypop stick down on the food tray. "I thought I'd lost you."

Danny stroked my hair, and looked at me tenderly "E, I'm so sorry," he whispered, his voice only slightly less hoarse than before.

"Shane and Cam told me everything. It wasn't your fault," I reassured him.

"You believe me?"

"Of course I do. When I took you back it was because I trusted you. About everything. Always. I love you, Danny."

Danny leaned over to kiss me, but first his fingers reached out to lift my sunglasses.

"Don't," I said, and I raised my hand to prevent him from doing so.

"You've been crying," Danny stated more than asked. I nodded. "I assumed as much." Danny removed my Ray-Bans. "Babe, you cry too easily." Danny smiled, and he kissed my forehead.

"It was awful," I whispered. "They wouldn't tell me anything. I didn't know if you were dead or alive. I waited more than three hours. They said I wasn't family."

Danny frowned. "You're family. I don't understand," he said.

"My last name isn't Newman," I explained. "Girlfriends don't count in hospitals."

Danny lifted my chin so our gaze could meet. "We'll have to change that," he smiled, pleased with his suggestion.

Was Danny implying…? I certainly couldn't hold him to something voiced out of frustration with hospital bureaucracy. I kept it light, made difficult because Danny's breath on my face was intoxicating.

"Eventually," I answered breathlessly with a glimmer in my still puffy eyes.

"E, I love you," Danny whispered, and he pressed his parched lips against my moist ones.

Electricity radiated through us as we held each other and kissed. My hand reached into Danny's thick hair and brought our faces even closer together. I was so grateful. Danny was alive!

Our kiss deepened. His free hand held me tightly, reaching under my short skirt, feeling my tush, exposed in a lace thong. I moaned into his mouth. Danny's fingers slipped under the waistband and stroked me. I writhed from the presure. Mmm. This was a hospital. Under Danny's spell, I was beyond caring.

A knock on the door stopped us mid-kiss. Danny abruptly removed his hand and patted my skirt down in place. We stared at each other, Danny amused by my frustration, and I red-faced, embarrassed by the intrusion.

A nurse dressed in blue scrubs entered. "Time to check your vitals, Mr. Newman," she cheerfully said.

The next day after my dance classes, I quickly showered and braided my hair. I applied eye make-up and blush, dressed in a short skirt and feminine top, and checked that I looked pretty for Danny. After his ordeal, everything should be perfect for him.

When I arrived at the hospital, Danny was dressed in the jeans he'd been wearing on Saturday, and the fresh shirt I had brought him yesterday. His back to the door, Danny sat on the bed stuffing his belongings into the backpack.

I tiptoed in and threw my arms around Danny's shoulders from behind, surprising him. I kissed his neck and cheerfully greeted him, "Hey, Sweetheart," I chirped.

Danny smiled at me. "Hey, beautiful," he said, his voice sounding raw, but improving. Then Danny hugged my arms closer around him.

"Ready to go home?" I asked, and I kissed his cheek.

Danny placed his book in the backpack and zippered it closed. "I am now."

CHAPTER SIXTY-EIGHT - ELIZABETH

Emotionally drained, Danny and I entered Berkeley Hall, silent. Danny's grip, strong on my hand, stood in contrast to the slouch of his shoulders. He had no energy.

Danny didn't even try to hide his yawn as he opened the door to his room.

"I've got to take a nap." He yawned again as he threw his backpack on the floor and kicked off his shoes.

"I'll see you later." I rose up on my toes and kissed Danny's cheek.

"E, stay. Please?"

"You didn't sleep well at the hospital?"

"People keep coming into your room. Even in the middle of the night they want to take your blood pressure."

"Don't hospitals always give out sleeping pills?"

Danny burst into laughter. Unable to contain himself he wiped tears from his eyes. I frowned. What was so funny? And that made him laugh even harder.

"E... Ow, my throat," Danny winced. He was choking on his laughter. "E, they don't give sleeping pills to patients admitted for a drug overdose."

I blushed crimson. Then I laughed with him. "I'm sorry. I wasn't thinking. I mean it isn't like you really take drugs."

"Oh, baby," Danny laughed, and he hugged me closer. "I love your innocence, Elizabeth. Don't ever lose that. It's endearing." Danny kissed my forehead. "Stay with me, baby. I don't like to be alone. It's hard for me to sleep."

I gave Danny a curious stare. "How did you sleep all those nights I wasn't with you?" I wasn't afraid of the answer because apart from me, Danny had rarely spent an entire night with a girl.

"Do you mean recently, or all my life?"

"Both, I guess." It seemed strange that Danny had sleep problems, and I had never heard of it before.

"You've had sleep problems all your life?"

"Not all, but close." Danny sat down on the bed. He took my hand and massaged my knuckles. "Except when I'm with you. You make me feel safe." And he smiled.

I kissed Danny's cheek. "I'm glad that I do."

I already knew that getting drunk made Danny fearful. I didn't know he felt uneasy even when sober.

"That's part of why I drank so frequently."

"To fall asleep?" Danny nodded. "That's awful," I said, and I held him tight.

"Promise you won't laugh at me?"

I raised an eyebrow. "I promise," I answered. Whatever it was must be very odd.

"When I was born, someone gave me a stuffed animal, a soft, squishy cow. Every night I slept with him."

"I remember that cow from when we were kids."

"As long as I held that cow I was able to sleep at night."

"You were little, Danny. I slept with a blankie, but I gave it up by the time I was six or seven."

"I didn't until I went to Bromley."

I starred at Danny in disbelief. He had been nearly fifteen and had already lost his virginity.

"Our parents may be best friends, but our home lives haven't been similar. You grew up in the perfect family. I didn't. My parents had problems for years. As an only child, it was stressful. Dad was one fucked-up dude. The arguing was constant, usually at night. My parents assumed I was sleeping. But who could sleep with all that going on?"

I reached for Danny's cheek and softly touched it. My heart ached for him. "Danny, I'm so sorry."

"Eventually my parents worked things out, but I couldn't. Well, maybe now I have."

I hugged Danny tightly for support and he smiled back. "How did you sleep once you went to Bromley? I know you weren't wasted every night."

"You mean when I didn't have a sexy redhead to cuddle up to?"

"Yeah," I grinned. "All those years without me."

"I'd wear myself out to the point of exhaustion."

I frowned. "That's why you were never without a girl?"

"No, E." Danny laughed. "I went to the gym every night. Then I'd stay up reading until my eyes wouldn't stay open. Pretty fucked, aren't I?"

"I wouldn't put it that way." Actually, I would, but I loved Danny too much to tell him how truly odd this was. "You needed a coping mechanism, and you found one. Think how well-read you are because of this!"

"Yeah, that's why I'm straight As." Danny replied sarcastically.

I rolled my eyes and grimaced.

"I knew you'd think I was weird. E, you can leave me if you want."

Oh, Danny. I smirked. Why are you so insecure?

"I can't leave you. Nobody else would ever want me."

"Of course they would. You're beautiful, smart, and sexy. You're perfect."

"No, I'm suspect. If you're this weird, I must be even weirder to live with you."

"Okay. You're weirder," Danny laughed.

"Promise me you'll discuss this with Harlan."

"I'll put it on the list."

Sweet, gentle kisses on my neck and shoulders, accompanied by hands pressing me closer woke me from my nap.

"Mmm," I murmured. Danny's light, feathery touch aroused all my senses.

"I missed you," Danny whispered.

"Moo," I answered, not able to contain myself.

"Not funny, Elizabeth," Danny said crossly.

Then he quickly turned me around and tickled me.

"I will never, ever confide in you again, Elizabeth," he said while continuing his torture.

"I'm sorry. I'm sorry," I laughed, squirming. "I was only teasing you, Daniel."

"Good. 'Cause I had a different tease in mind." Danny pressed up against me, his lips centimeters from mine.

"Aren't you too tired?"

"We haven't had sex since Saturday morning."

"It's only Monday afternoon," I reminded him.

"That's almost three whole days, E."

"My poor baby," I purred, and kissed his lips.

"Does this mean yes?"

"It's open to interpretation," I answered saucily.

CHAPTER SIXTY-NINE - DANIEL

Returning to Berkeley Hall from dinner, I covered my mouth as a large yawn escaped. Dinner had been one long stress fest with Shane and Cam's frequent glances, Eli on edge, ready to pounce like a mama lion, and me battling to behave as though everything was normal, when life was anything but. I couldn't reach my room fast enough.

Another yawn. Elizabeth turned to me, her face full of worry.

"Are you alright?" Her soft voice jumped half an octave, unable to hide her concern.

"Yeah," I smiled and rubbed her back. "I'm beat. A wild woman attacked me this afternoon."

Eli giggled. "Let's stay in tonight and study. I'll tuck you in early."

I nodded my agreement and kissed Eli's head.

How did I get this lucky? My lady cherished me and gave me total devotion. She always had my back.

This weekend was the most significant manifestation of her love yet. Not only had Elizabeth saved my life for the second time this year, but she had saved my reputation too. My overprotected, seemingly fragile Hollywood princess had proven to be a dynamo in action. I was in awe.

Elizabeth owned my heart, and my entire being. And she knew it. I was perfectly content with that. Elizabeth was the person I trusted the most in this world, and I would never violate that trust.

"Key?" I asked Elizabeth as we arrived at her door. She removed it from her jacket pocket. It was actually my jacket, but Eli seemed to be living in it lately. She placed the card in my hand.

"You're such a gentleman," she giggled. And I placed the card in the slot.

The door locked behind us after we entered the room. Elizabeth took my hands and tilted her head upwards. Her beautiful emerald eyes met my blue ones, but they did not twinkle. They scrunched, confused, and her lips were downturned.

"Daniel, are you okay? You said you were hungry, but you didn't eat much."

"My throat's still scratchy," I answered in a whisper. It hurt less this way.

"You didn't say anything."

"I didn't want to draw attention, so I tried to sound normal." I spoke slowly to save my throat.

"Tomorrow you'll have strep," she suggested.

Eli moved her hand up to my cheek and gently caressed it. I reached for it and kissed her palm. Every man should be this loved by a woman.

"I'm sorry you're not better yet." Eli's soft voice touched my heart.

"I'll be okay," I assured her, but my voice cracked halfway through. It was like going through puberty again.

Elizabeth clasped her arms around my neck and went up on her toes to kiss me. I needed this.

Light as a feather, I scooped her up without our lips separating. Eli wrapped her slender legs around my waist. Her heart beat rapidly as I held her close. When we broke apart to breath we smiled at each other, eyes twinkling, and she said, "I thought you were tired."

"I am," I whispered. "That doesn't mean we can't do some hard-core kissing."

Eli giggled and pressed her lips to mine. She tasted so fine.

I carried Eli over to the bed and delicately placed her on her back. Eli's arms reached out, beckoning me to join her. I eagerly complied.

Elizabeth's lithe body moved closer to me than I thought possible. Excitement pulsated between us. Involuntarily she flexed her hips against me, telegraphing how badly she wanted more than I could give.

Despite my exhaustion, I opened the button and zipper on her jeans. Eli gasped and giggled in delight. Boy, she was in a giddy mood today.

"I thought you were too tired," she whispered in a flirty voice.

"I am."

Puzzled by my contradictory behavior, Eli lifter her hips anyway. I quickly dispatched with her jeans.

My eyes sprung open. "Eli!" I exclaimed. She had nothing on underneath! My girl never stopped surprising me.

Elizabeth gave me a saucy giggle knowing she had thoroughly delighted me. Then she reached for my jeans' zipper. Appreciating how badly she wanted me, I summoned every last ounce of energy to satisfy her.

My thoroughly contented lady lay purring in my arms. Elizabeth glowed. I kissed her hair. A teasing smile flitted across my lips.

"Don't ask me to do that again until at least tomorrow," I croaked. I was spent. I needed a nap.

When I woke, I didn't know how long I had been sleeping. It couldn't have been too long, Eli appeared not to have moved, and her eyes were wide open, a satisfied smile on her face. I winced in pain. My throat felt as though it was under attack from tiny beings wielding miniature knives. I pointed to it.

"It hurts?"she asked. I nodded. I couldn't talk. Eli twisted around and reached for a bottle of water on the nearby desk. "Here, Danny. Drink."

I took a couple of large stinging gulps. I was still in pain, but without the dryness I could at least speak, limited as my ability was. This was the punishment for getting through dinner speaking normally.

"Can I get you anything?" Eli asked, reading the pain in my face. I hated giving her something new to be concerned with. She had been through enough.

"Lollypop." I croaked. Eli hugged my head to her bare chest.

"Daniel, you sound awful. Are they upstairs?" I nodded.

Eli kissed me and rose. What an ass! I starred at her amazing body as she confidently strode over to the hook on the door and reached for plaid flannel pants and a tee shirt. Only when Eli turned and saw me starring did she blush.

"Anything else?" she asked, as she dressed.

"Sweats, tee shirt," I answered using my throat sparingly.

Eli rifled through the pockets of my jeans and found my key. She gathered my clothing in her arms.

"I'll be right back." Eli smiled and blew me a kiss. My heart melted.

CHAPTER SEVENTY - ELIZABETH

Less than ten minutes later, my arms loaded down with fresh clothing and the box of lollypops, I fumbled with my room key. If I dropped anything, let it be the clothes, not the lollypops.

Opening the door to my room, I couldn't believe what I saw! I burst into laughter, big guffaws emanating from deep inside of me, and making me shake. I couldn't remember the last time I had laughed so hard. It felt so good. I needed this.

I tried to control myself, but looking across at Danny, I burst into laughter all over again. What a sight! Hands on hips, Danny struck a pose while wearing my fluffy pink bathrobe!

The sleeves barely reached his elbows, and compared to its mid-calf length on me, the robe fell to mid-thigh on him. Barely belted, the sides unable to meet, Danny's impressive pecs peeked through.

We both laughed so hard though Danny tried and failed miserably to keep a straight face. I stumbled over to him, my ribs sore from convulsing. Somehow I remembered to safely set my bundle down on the desk.

"You're adorable," I sputtered, choking on the words.

Danny feigned girlish modesty by trying to hold the robe closed and adapting a coy posture, batting his eyelashes.

"Thank you," he began in a falsetto that wasn't really happening because of his raw throat. "I'm so glad you like my new dress."

Danny winced in pain, and I forced myself to stop laughing.

"That must kill," I said. I didn't want him inflicting permanent damage on his vocal chords.

"Big time," he rasped.

I touched Danny's cheek affectionately. Then I kissed his lips, and whispered, "Have a lollypop. I won't sleep with a man whose voice is higher than mine," and I winked, all flirty.

Danny grinned, and opened his arms to hug me, but I stopped him cold.

"Take off my robe before it rips," I ordered.

Danny peeled off the robe. I gasped. He was wearing nothing!

"Let's go to The Café. I'm hungry," Danny murmured in my ear. So much for a romantic moment. Boys and their stomachs.

"You might want to wear something," I teased.

I strode over to the desk where I'd dropped Danny's sweats and tee. I snatched them up, along with a lollypop that I unwrapped.

"Here," I said, handing him the clothes and the candy.

Danny stuck the lollypop in his mouth and sucked. Then he twirled his tongue across the cherry candy, his eyes twinkling, never leaving my gaze. My heart beat rapidly. He knew his effect on me.

Danny casually handed me back the lollypop. While he put on his shirt and sweats, I sucked, tasting his unique Danny flavor on the cherry sweetness.

"Hey! That's mine?" Danny exclaimed when he finished dressing.

"I'm keeping it moist," I answered.

"No, I'm keeping you moist," and he winked.

I blushed crimson, and we grinned at each other. I handed Danny back the lollypop.

Then I shoved my arms into the denim jacket while Danny threw his sweatshirt over his head. I attempted to brush my bedhead hair, but surrendered to the tangles and made a quick ponytail. We walked out, Danny's arm around my shoulders. But first I grabbed a grape lollypop. Now we truly matched.

We silently walked to The Café. Danny's embrace radiated quiet strength. He held me close, more protective than usual. He had been that way all day. Beginning when I had picked him up at the hospital, Danny had been in physical contact with me. It was as though he feared something bad would happen if we didn't touch.

Part way to the Student Center, Danny removed his hand from my shoulder. He took my hands and stopped to tenderly kiss me. My heart fluttered. Danny stared into my eyes, his deep in thought, troubled thought. Patiently, I waited. I squeezed his hand, telling him everything was good.

"I was so frightened," Danny began.

He kept his raspy voice low. I didn't want him to talk. It was painful, but it was more painful for him not to share what had happened on Saturday night.

I nodded for Danny to continue.

"I had played a few songs. My throat was dry from singing. I reached for the beer I'd been drinking earlier. The bottle was still cold and I took a couple of long pulls. Almost immediately I felt really weird." Danny paused for a moment to suck the lollypop.

"E, something was terribly wrong. I freaked. I had ingested some evil shit, but I didn't know what. I was terrified. Shane and Cam wanted to take me to the hospital, but I demanded they take me to you."

Tears filled my eyes. "You stupid bastard," I scolded. "You wasted critical time. You could have died."

Danny smiled. "It was stupid. Eli, I was so scared. I needed you."

Oh, Daniel! My poor, frightened boy. I went up on toe and gave him a warm hug. Reliving Saturday was too painful.

"Somehow, it wasn't... My gut instincts knew. I felt it here," Danny indicated his heart. "If you were with me, nothing bad would happen. You wouldn't let it. You'd protect me. I needed you, E."

Tears flowed down my cheeks. Danny wiped them with his thumb. "No tears," he ordered. "Now we get to live happily ever after."

Then he gathered me in his arms. I had never experienced such powerful emotions before.

"I love you so much, Elizabeth," Danny whispered.

"And I feel the same," I responded in a soft voice.

At the Café, nearly empty at this time of night, we selected steaming plates of macaroni and cheese. Rich and creamy, with a lightly browned crust, not only was it the delicious comfort food we both craved, but it would be easy on Danny's bruised throat.

Usually I ordered the half-sized portion, but tonight I selected the regular size. Danny could eat whatever I left over. He was that hungry!

Placing our plates on a table, we realized we'd forgotten beverages.

"I'll get the drinks. You get the forks," Danny said. "Diet Coke?"

"Yes, please," I answered.

Danny returned to our table and placed the paper cups and straws on the table. Then he helped me remove my jacket, placing it on the back of the chair. I glanced down at my pajama bottoms and tank, and grimmaced.

Danny glanced around at the nearby tables, all vacant and shrugged. "Nobody's looking," he said as he removed his sweatshirt. Then Danny enveloped me in his arms. "They can't see you now," he laughed, his heart-stopping sapphire eyes twinkled mischievously, and he kissed my lips. "I forgot dessert," he teased. "You'll provide my sweetness." Danny smiled, and he held my face for another kiss, setting my heart aflutter.

"That's so trite," I scolded while smiling into merry blue eyes. "You're impossible."

"I am at that. I've earned it, Princess."

"Earned what, Mr. Newman?"

A deep voice startled us. The voice belonged to Dean Robert Colton, an elegant man in his forties. I was mortified by my appearance. Let the ground swallow me up.

Without missing a beat, a grinning Danny answered in his usual voice.

"Earned the right to give Miss Jacobs a hard time," Danny teased. I cringed, imagining his pain.

I had never met the Dean before, and wearing pajamas was not the impression I wanted to make. The Dean grimaced. He had noticed.

"Pajama party, Daniel?" he asked with a raised eyebrow.

"Sorry, Dean Colton," Danny answered sheepishly, "It's casual night."

"This could be a little too casual."

"Yeah, maybe."

And maybe I could sink through the floor and disappear. Instead I tried to project confidence, and I straightened my posture.

"Do you know my better half?" Danny asked the Dean.

"The girl on the balcony," he answered with amusement.

Even the Dean had seen the photo. Heat filled my cheeks, turning them crimson. Damn the hard tile floor! No escape. I was mortified.

"Yeah, that's her," Danny admitted with cheerful pride.

"We haven't met," Dean Colton answered. Then he smiled warmly. "Which is a good thing. It means you're a young lady who stays out of trouble."

"My future fiancée most certainly does," Danny agreed.

I stopped still and starred at him. Future fiancée! That was news to me.

I turned toward the Dean and stuck out my hand to shake his.

"Elizabeth Jacobs." My name stumbled off my lips.

"Elizabeth," he pondered as we shook hands.

"I'll try to continue staying out of your office," I answered.

Dean Colton smiled, and Danny grinned.

"Elizabeth will be accompanying me to events next year. She's my first lady."

"Then I'll be seeing much more of you."

"And I promise to be better dressed," I smiled.

"I'm sure you will be," Dean Colton said. "Danny, Owen tells me you're fulfilling your attendance requirements."

"Elizabeth knows. We don't have secrets."

"Then you have her support, but please, no more weekend trips to Malibu." Danny nodded his compliance. "I enjoyed meeting you, Elizabeth. Have a good evening."

"We will," Danny answered.

"Goodnight," I added, and the Dean left with his coffee.

Finally, we could sit down to eat our macaroni and cheese. I picked up a steaming forkful and starred at Danny who wolfed his down.

"What?" he asked while devouring another forkful.

"You told the Dean I was your future fiancée."

Danny put down his fork and lifted my left hand.

"Sometime in the future I will be purchasing a sizeable diamond to place on that finger." He kissed the top of my finger where the ring would sit.

"You are?" We had never discussed this. "What if I don't want that? You haven't even asked me."

Danny smiled. "Relax. I was going to ask you before giving you the ring, and it's not anytime soon. I'm not ready, and neither are you."

"Then why tell the Dean?"

"Because you are. Because when I do ask, it will be when I'm confident you'll say yes."

"You're very sure of yourself."

"Yes I am," Danny smiled, and he kissed my hand again. Then he gulped down the remainder of his macaroni.

"But why tell the Dean?" I didn't understand.

"The Dean recognized you as the girl on the balcony. I wanted him to know you weren't a casual fling, or an ordinary girlfriend. Lots of guys have girlfriends. But how many will be together by the start of the next school year?"

"Not many," I guessed.

"Are you done with that?' he asked, indicating my barely touched macaroni.

"You can have it," I answered, and Danny slid my plate over to himself.

"And who will you be waking up with on September 24?" he asked, and then dug into the creamy pasta.

"What day of the week is that?"

"I don't know. Doesn't matter."

"You, of course. You just promised me a diamond."

"Exactly. In two words the Dean understood that we are in a mature relationship." Danny paused, then frowned. "Also, if anything were to ever happen…"

"Like at the hospital?"

"Yeah, only if it's on campus. The Dean won't keep either of us out of the loop."

After finishing our macaroni, and Danny consumed almost half of mine, we rose to leave. Danny sucked on the straw in his Diet Coke. I laughed at the futility as he made an exaggerated slurping sound of mostly air rising up.

"Empty," he grinned, as he jiggled the cup. "I'm getting a refill. Want one?"

"No, thanks. We have water at home."

Danny kissed my forehead and left to refill his cup. I readied myself, putting on my jacket. Then I went to throw our trash in the nearby receptacle.

"Lois Lane!"

A voice startled me as I turned from the trash bin. I found myself face-to-face with Duncan, the last person I wanted to run into, especially tonight. Duncan and trash – how apropos!

"Pajamas? Poor princess," Duncan's Louisiana drawl dripped with sarcasm. "The Cafe wouldn't deliver? Or did you give the servants the night off?" he smirked.

My face heated with anger. This was my first encounter with Duncan since the afternoon when he had encouraged Phoebe to paw at Danny in front of me.

I had to contain myself from smacking the slimy sneer off his face. Instead, warm, familiar arms wrapped themselves around my shoulders, and brought me back down.

"We're dining out tonight. What of it?" Danny answered for me, while hugging my back against his chest. My hero to the rescue!

"Newman. Why am I not surprised? You two are joined at the hip lately."

"Mostly we've been joined elsewhere lately," Danny smiled, and he hugged my shoulders again. I blushed crimson. Daniel!

"That's a visual I don't need," Duncan smirked. "Where'd you disappear to the other night? The party had just gotten started."

"I had a date," Danny answered.

"Tell Lois to loosen the reigns."

"Saturday, Duncan. Date night." Danny hugged me and kissed my hair. Triumph.

"So bring her next time," Duncan blurted, frustrated. "If your prissy wife will even come. I need my bass player."

"I am not prissy," I said, defending myself.

"Newman, you were a lot more fun when you were with Phoebe." Duncan said deliberately, glancing at me for my reaction.

A stab of pain went through my heart. Phoebe! But Danny felt my pulse increase, and he hugged me tighter, protectively. I succeeded at keeping my expression neutral.

"No, I was a lot more stupid then," Danny answered in measured tones.

"Whatever." Duncan brushed off Danny's response. "You should have seen her after you left. Phoebe went nuts, completely crazed. Ever since you went back to Lois, Phoebs has been totally whacked-out. She was really into you, you know."

The mere sound of Phoebe's name caused the little hairs on the back of my neck to stand at attention. I tried so hard not to show it. Duncan shouldn't see he was getting to me. I pressed myself close against Danny. Duncan couldn't hurt me if I was in Danny's protective embrace.

Danny glanced at Duncan, then at me and back to Duncan. I'd never seen him so tentative before. Danny wanted to speak, but with me standing in his arms, and with the subject being Phoebe, he hesitated.

"Duncan, excuse us for a moment."

Danny took my hand and guided me far enough away from Duncan so as not to be overheard.

"I'm apologizing in advance," Danny said softly, so his voice wouldn't carry. "I don't want to have this conversation, especially not in front of you, but I'm fishing."

I frowned. "I understand," I whispered.

As uncomfortable as Danny discussing Phoebe would be, if it would answer our questions about Saturday, it would be worth it.

"You're okay with this, baby? If you're not, we'll walk away."

"I'm okay. They can't hurt us anymore." In reality, I was anything but okay.

"Trust me," Danny said, almost as a question.

"Always," I answered. I smiled weakly. I would always trust Danny.

Danny and I returned to Duncan. Presenting a united front, we stood squarely facing him, Danny holding me tucked under his arm.

"Phoebe can't be into me. We were hardly even together. She's delusional," Danny said to Duncan.

"Well she was. She may not show it, but Phoebe fell hard. Now she's like a powder keg, ready to explode."

"I don't understand," Danny began carefully.

"You dumped her, man. Even for a girl like Phoebs, it had to hurt."

"Phoebe was never mine to dump. Duncan, you know as well as she did, hell, everyone knows, there's only one girl for me, and you're looking at her. Elizabeth and I may have been going through difficult times, but we never called it quits."

I placed my hand on Danny's back and gently stroked it. This was so difficult for him.

Danny turned toward me; sorrow filled his eyes. Whatever he had to say next was going to be the most painful part for me to endure.

"Phoebe was available. I didn't seek her out. I needed comfort during a bleak period, and she provided it. I gave her no reason for expectations."

"I know you didn't," I whispered.

"My relationship," Danny choked on the word, "With Phoebe, if you can call it that, may have lasted for a couple of months, but it was sporadic at best. If we were at the same party, I'd be with her. I never took Phoebe on anything that resembled a date."

A sudden sharp pange of guilt stung my stomach. A date. I'd enjoyed several with Scott. No. Stop. Scott had always understood my status.

Duncan's expression softened. "Phoebe's a nut-case," he said.

For the first time since I'd met him, Duncan reacted like a friend.

"I feel for you, man. If what she said Saturday is true, Phoebe's turning her wrath on you, a full-blown vendetta."

"I should have handled this better," Danny replied. "I didn't know I meant anything to Phoebe. All that time I thought she was doing me because she enjoyed hurting Elizabeth."

I cringed. That was a visual so repulsive I didn't know how I would expunge it from my mind.

"We thought when we patched things up, that would be that. Phoebe would be out of our lives," I added.

"What planet are you guys from?" Duncan blurted. "Or is it something they put in the bottled water in Beverly Hills?"

"We're not from Beverly Hills!" Danny and I answered in unison.

"Whatever. Close enough. Newman, you're as naïve as Lois. Look, it's like divorce, and I know about divorce. My mother's on husband three."

"We're not married, Duncan," Danny protested.

"Newman, I'm saying this as your friend. Phoebe's interpretation of life has gone over your head. And except for some legal mumbo-jumbo, you and Lois are married. Shit. You're both wearing pajamas, so hear me out."

Danny and I stared at Duncan, dumbfounded. Duncan was never this direct. Perhaps it was because for once he wasn't wasted.

Duncan continued, "It's like you were separated from you wife, so you had an affair. Sure it meant nothing to you. You knew you loved your wife. But Phoebe didn't know or want to.

So then she hears you're back with your wife. But Phoebs has her pride. How do you think she felt when she saw the pictures where you're doing it on a balcony? Or your weekend in L.A? And the gossip all over Donnelly is what a cute couple, you and Lois; that's what everyone's saying.

Maybe you don't hear it because it's about you, but even I've heard the latest about Danny Newman and his movie star girlfriend. And I actively avoid gossip. So I'm sure Phoebs heard it, and it's got to hurt."

Danny stepped back as though the air had been sucked out of him.

"Newman, why are you so surprised?"

"I never meant to hurt her," he replied apologetically.

"Danny, I'm your friend. I believe you. But Phoebs is a nutcase. That's why no one ever spends more than a night or two with her. You're the first guy to risk spending real time with Phoebe. Either you're the bravest SOB on earth, or the most messed up one."

I shuddered, thoroughly revolted. I dug my nails into my palms to blunt the pain.

"Like I said," Danny answered sheepishly, "I was wasted all the time."

Duncan nodded. He'd been there and seen it all. "Anyway, if what Phoebs said Saturday is true, she's out to get you, and in a bad way."

"What did she say?" I demanded.

"Chill, Lois," Duncan cautioned. "Phoebs was wild, beyond stoned. She showed me a fistful of pills. I don't know what they were, but she was off the reservation. Phoebs ranted that she'd thrown some in your beer, and I'd hear about it on the news."

"What!" I exclaimed. "She didn't!" I couldn't control my shaking voice.

Danny calmed me, rubbing my shoulder.

"Phoebs was chanting, 'I've killed him. I've killed Dan.' It was all very believable." Duncan paused for a breath. "I'm glad I ran into you tonight, even if you are with Lois, and you look like you were just fucking. I don't know what Phoebe meant. You look fine to me. You're certainly not dead."

"I'll verify that. Danny is definitely alive," I smiled.

"That's more information than I need, Lois."

"She better not say those things. Danny has his reputation."

"Claws in kitten," Danny laughed and folded my fingers.

"What if she tells people you took those drugs!"

"She can't hurt us," he replied.

I realized my potential gaffe. I turned and stared at him, searching for forgiveness. Would Duncan catch my meaning?

"Phoebe can say whatever she wants," Danny continued. "Who's going to believe her? I'm the new student government president, and she's a girl with severe drug and mental health issues."

"We should get a restraining order," I said, my voice rising.

"Newman, rein in your wife. She's scaring me."

"Elizabeth, take a chill pill."

"Chill pill! Isn't that our problem? Phoebe wanted you to permanently chill."

Danny sighed and pulled me to his chest for a comforting hug.

"Elizabeth, stop freaking."

I buried my head against the soft fleece of his sweatshirt and trembled. Danny felt my body vibrate. He gently stroked my hair.

"Why are you crying?" he whispered.

I lifted my head. "I'm scared," I whimpered. "She wants you dead."

Danny gave me a reassuring smile. "She won't hurt us." Then he kissed my forehead and hugged me against his chest again.

"Duncan, isn't it nice to be loved this much?" Danny laughed.

"Actually, it's scaring me. I am so not ready for that."

"I thought I wasn't either. Until one day I woke up and realized I was already living it. It's an amazing feeling."

"And then you dumped Phoebe," Duncan countered.

"I found my way back to where I belonged, and I could not be happier. Even if Elizabeth does have this annoying habit of soaking my shirts with tears."

Danny kissed the top of my head as I continued holding on to him.

"I really don't want to be in the middle of this," Duncan said. "I'm going to The Cellar. I didn't mean to interrupt your pajama party." And he winked.

"Wait. We need a plan. What do we do about Phoebe? I still think we should get a restraining order."

"You've been watching half of too many TV shows, baby," Danny responded.

"What does that mean?"

"It means if you'd watched entire episodes you'd know it's a public court proceeding. I can't think of any member of the Jacobs-Newman clan that wants to open this up to such scrutiny."

"Oh," I answered. Then, what?

Danny turned to Duncan.

"You and Elizabeth may not like each other, but this is for me. I need to know that you are loyal to me, not Phoebe."

"Of course. This is serious shit," Duncan answered immediately.

Danny smiled. "Here's my plan. We do and say nothing."

Huh? How was that a plan?

"Duncan, do not tell anyone you ran into us tonight. Meanwhile, I'll lay low. With my workload that's not difficult. There's less than a month until we go home. Maybe she'll cool off. If nothing else, if Phoebe's kept wondering, she won't be hatching Plan B."

"That should buy you this week," Duncan said.

"I hope so. Meanwhile, if you hear anything, text me, 24/7."

"I'm on it."

"Thanks, Duncan."

"I know you're not doing this for me, but thank you," I told him. "Nothing is more important to me than keeping Danny safe."

Once outside and alone, I confessed, "I'm scared, Danny. What do you think Phoebe will try next?"

"Baby, she's just a drugged-up kid. Phoebe isn't a professional assassin. I'm not that important. She'll give up, and study for her finals."

"I hope you're right. I can make it through a month." Then I frowned. "Danny, what did you mean by laying low?"

"Curtailing our public life. Stay out of The Cellar and away from parties. And please don't cry, pout or kill me, but the formal is out."

"Again." I said, disappointed.

"I said no pouting."

"We never get to go," I complained.

"Eli," Danny scolded, and I sighed.

"Keeping you safe is what's important," I relented. "If anything happened to you, I would die."

Danny stopped to kiss me.

"I will make it up to you. I am already hatching a plan. Remember the last time I made it up to you," he grinned, remembering the missed formal that led to our first night together.

"We can't do that again," I giggled, grinning from ear-to-ear. I could only give him my virginity once.

I threw my arms around Danny's neck and pressed my eager lips against his.

"Let's relive that night right now," Danny whispered.

"I love you, Daniel." I smiled and kissed him again. Intoxicated.

Laying low was relatively easy. We had too much studying and too many papers to write. Other than classes and the dining hall, the only place we went was the library.

When he wasn't with me, Danny was locked away in his editing bay with Rachel. Their film was due next week; not a moment too soon as far as Rachel was concerned.

"What is with your boyfriend?" she had complained earlier in the week. "He keeps the door locked while we're working. Even when I go to the bathroom, I have to knock on the door to get back in!"

"Spies," I had responded with a shrug. "You know Danny. He's probably afraid that someone wants to copy your film."

"And he's afraid if I'm in the bathroom they'll barge in and pepper spray him to steal it?" Rachel shook her head, perplexed.

Okay, so spys wasn't as plausible as I'd thought. I had shrugged her off by saying, "Danny is insufferably self-important. Don't you know," I laughed, "The world is waiting for Steven Newman's son's school project, so he must protect it against an upstate-New York film piracy gang."

As I hoped, Rachel had laughed at this over-the-top scenario. Later, I cautioned Danny that his security obsession had been noticed.

Several times that week I had rehearsals for my year-end dance performance, now less than three weeks away. It was like being under modified house arrest. Either Danny accompanied me, or he arranged for Shane or Cam to mysteriously? accidentally? appear to escort me. I employed my best acting skills to mask my annoyance with having bodyguards, and to make it seem like a fun, coincidental run-in.

The frightening part was, I knew Danny wasn't overreacting.

CHAPTER SEVENTY-ONE - ELIZABETH

Relief. The followingThursday afternoon Danny and I left Donnelly as soon as our American Presidency class ended. Danny hadn't disclosed our destination. Like a mischevious little boy, his face lit up whenever the subject of our weekend came up.

"Uh, no. Elizabeth, I'm not telling you. Trust me. We will have a great time," he bragged. "Much better than the formal."

Danny's infectious grin melted my heart and temporarily erased the tension. The stress had reached epic proportions. We relaxed only when entwined in bed. Even then, unexpected noises in the hall caused my heart to jump.

"Let me see your gown," Rachel had said when she stopped by my room Wednesday afternoon.

Rachel had only recently woken having pulled an all-nighter with Danny to complete their film before the nine in the morning deadline. Our paths had crossed briefly in the lobby at eight as I left for breakfast and they stumbled in, exhausted from having met their deadline.

Rachel nodded to me then as she headed for her room. I had quickly hugged Danny, and with a quick kiss I sent him off to bed.

"Gown?" Huh?

"For the formal," she insisted.

Of course. The formal. She expected Danny and I to attend. Didn't everyone?

"Danny and I aren't going." I forgot I hadn't told Rachel.

"You're not? But Danny's student government president!"

"He's taking me away for the weekend."

"You'll never go, will you?"

"There's always next year." Unless that psycho Phoebe is still after us.

"And he'll have another excuse. This is pathetic. You've been together for two years already. And Danny even owns a tuxedo. It's a no-brainer."

"Except for Danny," I laughed.

"Where are you going? Malibu?"

"No. Danny won't tell me. He's enjoying the intrigue way too much. He's even packing for me. Danny doesn't want me to guess where we're going, so he's insisted on selecting all my clothes."

"Danny's a fucking control freak."

I laughed. "I think it's romantic."

"You would."

"Your chariot awaits, m'lady," Danny announced as soon as AP ended.

I flashed him my brightest smile as he collected my books. Those were the most reassuring, comforting words I'd heard since Danny left the hospital. I sighed. Going away was far better than going to the formal.

"Top down?" I asked as I adjusted my sunglasses and settled into the passenger seat of Danny's BMW convertible.

The sky was clear with the sun beating down, but early May was too chilly for the top to be down when we reached highway speeds. Still, I wanted the sense of freedom it brought me. Danny climbed in the car and started the engine. At the roar of the turbo, and the receding hardtop, the tension melted away. I placed my hand over Danny's, ready to shift the car into reverse, and squeezed. He grinned with anticipation.

"Ready?" he asked. Danny's lips brushed against mine and then together we shifted the car into reverse.

The cool breeze blowing through my hair was therapeutic. My shoulders dropped, and a smile emanating from deep inside shone on my face. I felt light as a butterfly aloft in the air current. I cranked up the volume on the stereo and sang along with the upbeat tune. I couldn't see them through his dark glasses, but I knew Danny's sapphire eyes twinkled with amusement.

"Eli, you need help, babe?" Danny laughed. Then he joined in and sang along, his superior tenor keeping me in tune. Our weekend was already willed with joy, and we hadn't even gotten beyond the main gate of Donnelly yet.

"We're not stopping for anything," Danny cautioned when the song ended. "We have a dinner reservation at eight."

Control freak, I smirked.

"Which restaurant?" I asked innocently.

"Uh no, Elizabeth. I'm not divulging classified information." Danny laughed.

After the first hour, I gave up trying to guess our destination. We headed south, but that didn't narrow the possibilities except to eliminate Canada from contention.

There were too many east-west interchanges to consider. Boston, Buffalo, Pittsburgh? It couldn't be Pittsburgh. We'd never get there by eight. But there were too many attractive destinations in-between. The Berkshires, the mid-Hudson Valley, Litchfield?

I sighed and succumbed to drowsiness. If nothing else, we'd both sleep well this weekend, no matter our destination.

I must have dozed, for when I opened my eyes, there was no doubting our destination – New York City! The familiar, run-down grime of The Bronx greeted me like an old friend.

"New York!" I squealed, thoroughly pleased with Danny's surprise.

"Good morning, Princess," Danny laughed as I wiped my eyes. "Sleep well?"

"I'm sorry. I couldn't help it. I've been sleeping so poorly lately."

"Me too. But not this weekend." Danny grinned. "You smiled in your sleep. Must have been a good dream."

"I don't remember, but my dreams are always good when you're with me. So, what are we doing in New York?"

"It's a secret. But, I promise, it will be different than last time."

"Well, yeah. Of course. It's not Thanksgiving and our parents aren't here. It has to be different."

Danny laughed. "Be patient."

I hate being patient. I am not good at being patient. And he knew that.

Cabs zig-zagging, and horns blaring; downtown traffic was slow as to be expected during the evening rush that we found ourselves mired in. At six-thirty Danny pulled the BMW up to the front of the Crosby Street Hotel in SoHo.

Okay, difference number one from last time. I had never stayed downtown before, but the Crosby Street Hotel had an excellent reputation, and it was popular with young Hollywood A-listers.

Getting off the elevator on the uppermost floor, we were shown to our room, a romantic junior suite. Spacious, with floor-to-ceiling windows letting in natural light, and a cozy sitting area, this would be our weekend home.

Luxuriously appointed, I loved the purple accents that gave the suite's otherwise neutral pallet a pop of unexpected color. Grinning like a kid, I fell backward on to the king-sized bed.

"This is great," I exclaimed when my back hit the comfortable mattress.

Danny pulled my up by my hand, back to my feet and into his arms. His strength held me around my waist, and my hands encircled his neck. We laughed as we held each other and playfully kissed; not a care in the world.

A knock on the door abruptly interrupted our fun. The bellman delivered the luggage we'd forgotten.

I unpacked my garment bag, trying to guess our itinerary based on its contents. Inside were two mini-skirts, denim capris, and four feminine shirts. Sweats and a couple of t-shirts were also included. Danny had packed my light blue Converse sneakers plus my pink ballet flats. No heels. Hmm. Casual?

Then I laughed at the contents of the large zippered front pouch; color-coordinated thongs and bras. Danny had indeed remembered everything I would need, but for what? As I put my clothing away, I caught his mischievous grin.

In two strides Danny was at my side. He gathered me into his arms and kissed me tenderly. My arms held Danny tightly around his neck as I stood on my toes to gaze at his perfect face. Danny's lips were upturned in a playful smile that lit up his entire being. A devilish twinkle shone in his sapphire eyes.

My heart was racing. Danny's arms around my back tightened as he held me securely. My heart beat rapidly. I tilted my chin upward, and our lips met again. Sweet kisses went on forever as we were freed of the shackles of the past ten months. There had been lies, infidelity, misunderstandings, loss of trust, and now, Phoebe.

We might have begun our reconciliation weeks ago, but in the kisses we now shared, I realized it was an evolution. It had taken the quiet privacy of this afternoon, but the process was now complete. Any hidden doubts I may have harbored had vanished along with the remaining tension. Our hearts were truly bound together again.

I didn't realize until we'd driven away from Donnelly that I hadn't been completely honest with myself, or with Danny either. I had been so eager for us to reconcile that I had subjugated my feelings.

The relief I'd experienced from being back together had not left time for reflection. Nor had the life or death saga we found ourselves embroiled in. There had been too much drama in our lives; an us against the world dynamic.

The little niggly sensation buried in my heart for convenience became full-fledged in the car. The realization that it had been a long time since I completely trusted Danny; possibly I had never completely trusted him before, rushed to the forefront of my mind.

Observing Danny from out of the corner of my eye while he drove, the major events of the past two years came flooding back, my own personal replay system. Before falling asleep, I examined the evolution of our relationship, from our first date to our first night together, up through this year. When I reached the dinner we shared with Steve in March, I exhaled, a deep cleansing breath. With it the doubts, insecurities, and lack of trust melded with the wind.

I smiled, warmth spreading inside me, filing every crevice. Without Danny noticing, I sat back in the leather seat examining his face, not for its obvious beauty, but for character. The heat enveloping my soul was trust and true love, for I genuinely approved of what Danny's face held for me.

Here was the man I loved, but now in a mature, adult way. Danny's face radiated kindness, love and intelligence. He adored me as I did him. And Danny loved to show it by spoiling me as he was now doing. He would always protect me, watch over me, and see to my happiness.

At last I was secure in my satisfaction, secure in the permanency of my position in the life of this amazing man. Most important, I was secure that we were finally equals. I was no longer the mousy adolescent with a crush on the popular boy, grateful to be spoken to.

Danny scooped me up and carried me to the bed. He propped himself against the headboard, and placed me on his lap. I rested my head against his soft cotton shirt and inhaled, taking in his unique Danny scent. While he played with my hair, I traced patterns with my fingertips. I felt whole again, healed. There was no place else I would ever want to be. In Danny's arms, I was home.

Danny lifted my hand from his chest and kissed my palm.

"Something's different," he said, reading my mind in his telepathic way.

"I've recovered," I answered happily.

Danny smiled back, understanding. "I hoped you would. I knew it would take time, but it's taken less time than I thought."

"You knew?" I was surprised at how perceptive he was.

"Of course I did. We're soul mates, Elizabeth. I always know what you're feeling."

"You do, don't you," I sighed. "Daniel, I love you so much it hurts."

"I feel the same, baby."

"We'll never be apart again."

"Never, E. It's you and me forever."

"Forever. I like that," I whispered. We kissed, passionate, yet tender. This was the manifestation of love, not lust.

When we broke apart Danny whispered, "I want to shower before we leave for dinner. Let me take out what you should wear."

"Okay," I answered obediently.

We scrambled off the bed, and went to the closet where Danny took out a black mini-skirt and a silk chiffon blouse with a large pink floral pattern and a plunging, ruffle-bordered neckline.

"I want to look perfect for you tonight."

Danny kissed my nose. "You're always perfect. It's me who's fucked up."

He kissed my lips once more before entering the bathroom.

I changed as quickly as I could and brushed my hair until it was smooth and glossy. A little blush, lipgloss, and a spritz of cologne, and I was good to go. I wanted to be ready before Danny left the bathroom. Perfection should greet him.

Moments later, Danny emerged from the bathroom wearing only a towel around his waist. Whoa! My eyes opened wide, pupils dilating My pulse galloped. Did he have any idea of the effect on me?

Danny gasped as he took in my appearance.

"Wow! E, you're stunning!"

I blushed, smiling shyly. I had a difficult time with compliments. Danny strutted over, his upper body still glistening from rivulets dripping down from his hair.

"They have bathrobes here," I giggled, and he laughed too.

"I'll get dressed. Then I'll kiss you properly."

Danny removed the towel and dried his arms, chest and hair.

"Do you mind?" I asked the incredibly built man standing naked in front of me, towel now slung over his shoulder. My arousal was obvious.

Danny moved closer, pressed against me, and kissed my lips. I emitted a low moan. I wanted him so badly.

"Am I giving you ideas, Elizabeth?"

"No," I mewed.

Then Danny gathered my face in his hands and kissed me hard. Instinctively my hands wrapped around his waist, finding their way to his smooth, bare backside. Who cared about dinner?

"You're such a liar," he laughed.

"Maybe," I trembled. Danny rolled his eyes. "Yes," I reconsidered, " but we have a reservation, don't we?"

"Shame," he said arrogantly. "It's so much fun to tease you, Liz."

As Danny walked toward the bed where his clothing was laid out, I pulled the towel off his shoulder, and snapped it at his firm butt.

"Ouch!" he exclaimed.

"It's so much fun to tease you," I giggled.

"I deserved that," he answered rubbing where the towel had struck.

Then he slowly dressed, leaving the buttons on his shirt for last. Yummy. My own Danny floorshow. I was panting.

"Hmm, preppy?" I observed.

Danny tucked his striped oxford buttondown shirt into khaki pants. He shoved his bare feet into oxblood loafers.

"I am a Bromley Hall grad, Elizabeth," Danny answered while fastening his brown leather Gucci belt with its golden "G" buckle.

"Sure you can stand being seen with a mere day-school girl?"

Danny slipped on his navy sport coat and adjusted his shirt collar.

"There is nothing mere about you Elizabeth."

An exclusive, celebrity-chef owned Italian in Greenwich Village was our destination. One of the most coveted restaurants in the city, it was nearly impossible to get a table at this small establishment without reserving one weeks in advance.

I hadn't met Steve's new assistant Lila, but if Danny's choice for dinner was any indication, he must have driven her crazy with his arrangements for our weekend.

Lila was ambitious, and only two years out of UCLA. I imagined her

DANA AYNN LEVIN

displeasure with Danny's requests. Catering to Mr. Newman Junior had to be the least favorite part of the job, but keeping Steven's son happy came with the prestige of being Steven Newman's assistant.

CHAPTER SEVENTY-TWO - DANIEL

Part of the restaurant's charm was its location in an antique building with a narrow staircase and uneven floorboards. The focal point when you entered in through the bar was a sizeble fireplace with stone surround that provided unnecessary warmth on this mild evening.

After a short wait, the maitre'd led us to a cozy table for two on the small, open second floor.

"Excuse me a minute," I said to Elizabeth as she settled into her chair. I smiled at her beautiful face and leaned in to kiss her. She glowed.

I quickened my pace toward the stairs to catch up to the maitre'd. I stopped him at the bottom of the stairs. Anticipating Elizabeth's reaction to my next surprise filled me with joy.

"Sir?" he asked politely.

I answered in a low voice, not that Elizabeth could hear me from upstairs.

"I want to surprise my girlfriend with a bottle of champagne."

He smiled knowingly. "We carry several. I'll send the sommelier over."

"Please, no. I don't want her to know. Just bring me the best one."

The maitre'd looked directly at me, his smile broadening. "Is tonight a special occasion?"

"Maybe?" I answered, unsure of what he was getting at. An evening out with Eli was always a special occasion.

"Don't be nervous. I've worked here a long time. I'm sure she'll say yes, sir. They always do."

"Say, yes?"

"To your proposal, sir."

My jaw dropped open. "Proposal?" Yikes! Of course, champagne. What else would he assume?

"Then why are you ordering our finest champagne?"

"Because I can," would have been an arrogant reply. Instead, I considered his question. My reason for ordering the champagne was to evoke memories of our first night together. But why? Unless I wanted to create another even more important memory.

It all made perfect sense. Only earlier Elizabeth and I had declared our intentions to spend forever together. Why not make it official? I turned to the maitre'd and smiled shyly. I couldn't believe I was doing this.

"I don't have a ring," I said.

"Tell her you want her to select it, but here, take this." He removed a cigar from his jacket pocket and handed me the ring-shaped paper label.

"Now I am nervous," I chuckled. I couldn't remember anything except taking Eli out on our first date ever petrifying me like this.

"I'll have the sommelier get your champagne. Good luck, sir."

I started back to the table, a wobbly-legged wreck. Certainly in recent weeks I had grown to recognize that one day I would propose to Elizabeth, but that day should have been at least another year away. Hell, Eli was only nineteen. We were young, immature, and shared a rocky recent history. Three solid strikes against us.

"Hey. I'm back," I said as I reached Elizabeth.

I bent over to kiss her, and took my seat. Her smile melted my heart. I took her hands, marveling at their softness. A giggle escaped her lips.

"What?" I asked.

"You have no idea how you look, do you?" There was a musical lilt in her voice.

"Is something wrong with how I look?" I asked, now even more self-conscious.

"No," Eli softly laughed. "It's just, you have the goofiest grin on your face, like a little boy up to no good. If I were your fifth grade teacher, I'd be afraid to turn my back."

There was nothing to say. Instead, I turned her palms upward and kissed them.

"Now it's my turn to be excused for a minute," she said, and Eli rose. "Danny, please order me a drink when the waiter comes."

I nodded, speechless.

CHAPTER SEVENTY-THREE - ELIZABETH

I felt lighter than air as I walked back to the table, grinning at the excitement of being alone with Danny in the most vibrant city in the world. Then I stopped short. All eyes were on me, watching my every movement. Why? I eyed the nearby diners suspiciously. Had they recognized me as the girl from the balcony?

Danny jumped up and pulled my chair out. He was grinning like a mischievous ten year old. I raised a suspicious eyebrow at him, and he shrugged. Hmm.

After we were both seated again, he reached across the table for my hands and caressed my knuckles. I leaned forward and whispered through gritted teeth, "People are starring at us?"

"That's because you're the most beautiful woman in the restaurant," Danny answered, sapphires in full twinkle mode.

My cheeks flushed, and I furtively glanced around. We really were being watched.

"They recognize us from the balcony," I whispered. "People don't look at you for this long because you're attractive. Nobody even stares at Mom for this long. They take a quick peak and turn away. They don't want to be caught."

I glanced out of the corner of my eye again and noticed the silver standing ice bucket containing a bottle. For the first time I recognized two crystal flutes on the table filled with an unmistakable bubbly beverage.

"Champagne? I thought you couldn't."

After the overdose, Danny had sworn off all alcohol, even beer.

"I'm sure a glass or two with dinner won't hurt me," Danny whispered while still anxiously kneading my hands. Why was he so tense?

Danny gazed intently into my eyes and held them. My heart skipped a beat, several actually, and lodged in my throat. Danny gripped my hands even more tightly.

"Elizabeth, you know me better than anyone ever will," Danny began. "You're my biggest booster, and my fiercest critic. You're loyal, but you're just as likely to kick my butt. E, you keep me grounded. I trust you with my life. And you know I mean that. How many men have had their girlfriends literally save their lives?"

I smiled shyly, trying hard to remain composed. My pulse galloped.

"And I'd do it again, but hopefully I won't have to." My shaky voice came out an octave too high.

Danny smiled back. "Yeah, hopefully."

He took another deep breath and continued.

"Elizabeth, their will never be anyone who compares to you. I'm a blessed man. I have my best friend with me on this journey called life, and she's the sexiest, most beautiful woman I've ever laid eyes on. I hate getting out of bed in the morning. The things you do, the way you make me feel, I've never had this much fun with anyone. You look at me like you're doing now, and I die. This is love. You drive me crazy, baby."

"Danny," I blushed, speechless. Where was all this emotion coming from?

"Elizabeth, you are my world. You're it, baby. The forever we talked about this afternoon, I want it to start now. Let's make it official. I would be the happiest man in the world if you would say yes to becoming my wife."

Wife! My eyes popped open wide as saucers. Stunned! This was so unexpected.

"You're serious?" I gasped. "This is not a hypothetical?"

Danny gave me a wicked smile that set my already fluttering heart beating even more rapidly. He was serious!

"Elizabeth Jacobs-Newman is a beautiful name, babe."

"Our parents will kill us. They'll be like you've only just gotten back together and Elizabeth's off to Israel for the summer, why not wait?" I replied in rapid-fire speed.

"They don't know our hearts."

"But they'd have a point. I'm leaving. Soon," I said plaintively.

"Then I won't have to worry about you taking up with any Israeli guys. Many girls find those dark-haired IDF types very attractive. So I'm told."

"Oh, Danny," I laughed. Not this girl.

"E, stop being logical. I would be the happiest man if you said yes."

"I wasn't expecting this."

Danny laughed. "Elizabeth, you've been waiting at least fifteen years for me to propose."

"This is so sudden."

"Maybe you weren't expecting this tonight, but c'mon. Elizabeth, I spied you playing wedding with your Barbies when you were little."

"Oh, no! You didn't?" I turned bright red. As a little girl I called my Ken doll, 'Danny,' and my Barbie, 'Lizzie.' "Ugh! This is so embarrassing!"

"Elizabeth, you were four years old. It was adorable and you still are. Baby, you want to say yes."

"Can't my answer be yes to you asking me a year from now?"

"No. The question is on the table right now, tonight," he said firmly. "I want to spend the rest of my life with you. Nobody else. Only you, Elizabeth."

"You really are making this difficult."

"Difficult? Elizabeth, I'm the one putting my heart on the line here."

I stopped, ashamed of my insensitivity.

"Of course you are. I'm so sorry, Daniel. You caught me off guard. This wasn't even on my radar."

"Nor mine. The maitre'd assumed when I ordered the champagne. I don't even have a real ring."

"That will make a good story to tell the kids. Dad proposed because the maitre'd thought it was a good idea," I laughed.

"Those children will want legally wed parents, E."

"If I say yes, we can't tell anybody until I'm ready."

"Whatever you want, baby."

"Danny, I love you so much. I've already spent my entire life with you. I can't imagine not spending the entire rest of my life with you. I will be the proudest woman on earth to become Mrs. Daniel Martin Newman."

"Is that a yes, Elizabeth?"

A smile stretched across my face and I nodded enthusiastically.

With his grin matching mine, Danny dug into his coat pocket, removed a paper ring, and slipped it onto my finger. "This will have to do for now," he said.

I was too overwhelmed to say anything. Then Danny leaned further across the table. He gathered my face in his warm hands and tenderly kissed me. Nearby diners applauded. We blushed at the attention the most important moment of our lives had attracted.

Danny lifted his flute, and I did the same.

"To my future bride," he said brimming in delight.

"To my future husband," I stammered.

The words, an unexpected addition to my lexicon, came out with difficulty. I would have to get used to it. We tapped our glasses together and slowly sipped the delicious champagne.

After we returned the flutes to the table, it sunk in.

"I can't believe it!" I squealed.

Danny took my left hand and kissed the cigar wrapper ring.

"I can't either, but I sure am glad." Danny was all smiles.

I paused for a moment. I didn't want to share our news with anyone, yet something was missing. For an engagement, it didn't seem official.

Shyly I asked, "Can we go shopping tomorrow?"

Danny smirked. He understood. "You want a real ring, don't you?" he teased.

"Yes," I admitted sheepishly. "Do you mind? I want to feel official."

"Of course you do," Danny laughed. "I expected as much."

"You did?"

"You're a girl, Elizabeth. All girls want diamonds." Danny grinned. "I thought you wanted to keep this secret."

"I do. I don't want a big diamond until we're ready to go public. But I still want a ring, something that won't draw attention. Only we'll know what it means."

"Tomorrow, Mrs. N."

A shiver of excitement ran up my spine. Mrs. N!

What a waste of a good meal. My head was floating in the clouds and my appetite had vanished. Despite being at one of the best restaurants in New York, I could barely eat dinner though Danny insisted that I try.

Across the table, we stared at each other, dreamy-eyed. Our fingers touched, and our legs brushed against each other. Several restaurant guests stopped to congratulate us. Graciously we thanked them for their well-wishes. It was as though we had thrown ourselves an engagement party.

"Let's walk back," Danny suggested after dessert. It was a beautiful night, clear skies, a slight chill, and streets busy with folks taking advantage of springtime in the city.

"Look at where we are," I said, pointing out the famous arch of Washington Square Park, directly north of where we walked on Waverly Place.

"NYU. The scene of the crime," Danny teased referring to where Steve, Ellen and Dad had met so many years ago.

"We've got to take a selfie and send it to our parents," I insisted as I pulled Danny across the empty road.

Ellen called in tears within moments of receiving our text.

"Oh, Mom. Cut it out," Danny teased, and then he turned serious. "Don't tell anyone where we are," he warned her.

"Danny, are you in trouble?"

"Of course not. I'm with Eli." And he wrapped his arm around my shoulders.

"Then why the intrigue? Whom would I be discussing your whereabouts with anyway other than the three other recipients of this picture?"

"There's no intrigue, Mom. We wanted our privacy so we're not telling anyone where we are. Aren't I allowed to spend a weekend in the city with my girlfriend?"

"Not when finals are around the corner and you were just in Malibu."

"Mom! C'mon! Alright, so the Dean won't like it, but we didn't skip any classes and we're studying."

"Right. Sure. I'm still suspicious. Daniel, you're hiding something and I will find out what. When you get home… You've never been able to lie to me in person."

"I love you too, Mom. Bye!"

Danny starred at the phone in frustration.

"Why did I talk to my mother? I should have given the phone to you."

I rubbed the back of Danny's neck.

"So what? By the time we get home, Phoebe won't matter to us."

"You know something I don't?"

"No. But she'll be 3,000 miles away."

"Mom will find out and then she'll spend the next two years worrying. She will find out, Elizabeth. Mom's right. I am incapable of keeping secrets from her."

"Are you going to let this ruin the best day of my life?" I teased.

Danny stopped short and smiled at me. My heart jumped, all fluttery.

"Come here, Mrs. Newman," Danny said and he embraced me.

CHAPTER SEVENTY-FOUR - ELIZABETH

On what should have been a morning of languorous celebration, Danny had placed a wake-up call. Apparently, whatever he had planned for this evening required us to get an early start.

"We could stay in bed longer if you would just let me go to Tiffany's," Danny complained.

On this I wouldn't budge. A Tiffany diamond would scream what I wanted kept secret. Our wedding wouldn't be for at least two more years. Why rush the engagement announcement until we were certain ALL our parents would approve? At this point, probably only Ellen did.

A glorious day beckoned. Another cloudless sky filled with early May warmth. I laughed that Danny would not tell me his plans beyond ring shopping. Based on the clothing he had chosen, it was clear the itinerary called for casual. But casual for what?

Cheerfully, I donned denim capris with an emerald colored plaid cotton tunic. I left the top three buttons open and belted the shirt with a wide brown leather belt. On my feet I wore sky-blue Converse. Danny also wore jeans and sneakers, his white buttondown shirt casually open over a black t-shirt.

Why did it matter? I assumed it would become apparent.

Another girl would have found him maddening. Rachel would not have tolerated a man choosing her wardrobe. I found it charmingly amusing. I enjoyed Danny's love of surprises, and I took immense pleasure in his unique way of turning this special day into an extraordinary one.

Our plan, strolling the streets of Manhattan in search of the perfect ring didn't go exactly as intended. By two o'clock, I still had not found the one I wanted. I sensed Danny's mounting frustration.

We were on a small side street, about to enter a promising store advertising antique and estate jewelry, when Danny pulled me aside.

"We have been in so many stores, I don't even know where we are anymore. I could hail a cab to drive us to the hotel and find out it's only two blocks away. That's how lost I feel. Elizabeth, here's the deal." Danny took my hands and looked directly into my eyes. "If you don't find anything in this store, we are taking a cab up to Tiffany's."

"Daniel," I pleaded, "That's not fair."

"It is fair. I'm getting tired, and it's getting late. Tiffany's has lots of rings that aren't solitaires."

I looked at Danny's handsome face, his sapphire eyes ablaze. I didn't want his day marred by anger. I sighed, resigned. He was the one making the purchase after all.

"Okay, Daniel. It's a deal."

We entered the small, nondescript store. One side of the narrow showroom was lined with glass-fronted jewelry cases. Behind then stood an older, balding man dressed in creased trousers and a rumpled shirt.

"Good afternoon," he greeted us with a faint German accent.

"She'd like to look at rings," Danny answered in a bored voice. "Nothing showy, but it should be nice," he added.

"Perhaps in this case," the man replied, and he directed me to the right.

Danny wandered off to the left, uninterested. He pulled out his phone and scrolled through emails. Danny disagreed with my desire for an interim ring that wouldn't catch anyone's attention, and he hadn't been shy with expressing his opinion. He wanted to go straight for the rock.

Finally, a ring caught my eye. Set on a white gold band were three light purple amethysts separated by two diamonds of the same discrete size.

"I'd like to see that one," I told the man as I pointed.

"A beautiful ring, miss," he answered as he removed it from the case and placed it on a black velvet mat. I picked it up and noticed the sparkle of the stones. Placing it on my ring finger it fit, perfectly, as though the ring had been waiting for me.

"Daniel! I've found my ring," I squealed, and I lifted my hand.

Danny walked over to examine my finger.

"It's nice, Elizabeth," he said without emotion.

"You're not thrilled." His reaction disappointed me.

"It's nice for what you want. No one will suspect it's an engagement ring."

"It's one of a kind," the owner said. "The same family owned it for three generations."

"It must have been painful for them to part with it," I said.

"No," he answered. "The owner passed away last year. The estate is selling it."

"Shame. There were no heirs?"

Danny lifted my hand and examined the ring.

"Beautiful stones," the storeowner commented, but Danny didn't seem convinced. "GIA certified. Finest grade and clarity."

Sensing my happiness, Danny relented.

"This is the ring you should wear," Danny declared, beaming with pride as we both stared at my hand.

The broadest grin stretched across my face. Our eyes locked, green to blue, and back again. The ring was perfect. I loved it. It even felt perfect.

"Its unique quality comes at a price, sir," the storeowner said.

Having noticed our youth, he was being polite, intimating that it could be beyond our budget. Dressed down, Danny certainly didn't appear to be a man worth millions.

Danny looked directly at the man and firmly answered. "My fiancée deserves nothing less than the best."

My heart skipped a beat. Fiancée. I would have to get used to it.

"The main stones are half a karat each," the man said. "But they're flawless."

"So is my fiancée," Danny answered. Then he quickly kissed my lips causing me to blush. "Excuse us a moment," he told the merchant.

I reluctantly removed the ring and placed it carefully on the velvet mat. Danny led me to a corner to talk privately.

"Elizabeth, if you want this ring it's yours." I frowned. Danny smiled, he understood. "You want an obvious engagement ring, don't you?" Danny asked.

I nodded sadly. "I wish it were a year from now."

"We don't have to wait."

"Yes, we do," I answered glumly.

Danny took my face in his hands and spoke frankly. "I respect your desire to keep our engagement private for as long as you feel necessary. We'll say this ring signifies our commitment to each other, or something like that. But when we get home, I'm talking you to Sarah Reid for a fitting. While you're in Israel, he and I will design your real ring."

"Sarah Reid! Oh my god! You're the best. Danny, I love you so much!" I squealed and threw my arms around Danny's neck.

Danny laughed and he kissed me. "I love you too, Sweetheart."

"We've made a decision," Danny began as we returned to the counter holding hands, excited smiles on our faces.. "We love that ring. It's perfect."

The merchant was pleased, but uncertain.

"This ring is priced at eight thousand dollars. It's been a slow season so I can let you have it for five thousand."

Danny paused for a moment, while I kept my eyes on the man, knowing he doubted Danny's ability to afford the purchase. It was probably why he lowered the price. He doesn't believe he has a real sale.

"Do you take American Express?" Danny asked, and he took out his wallet.

"Yes," the bewildered man stammered.

Danny removed a black credit card I had not seen him use before.

"Won't Steve see the statement?"

"No. This is my account, Elizabeth. The statement goes directly to my banker. Dad never sees it."

Danny took my hands and looked into my eyes. His expression was all mature adult and serious. "If I couldn't afford the ring, how could I expect to support the girl?"

The merchant polished the stones, and Danny slipped the ring on my finger. I held up my hand and admired it, grinning like a love-sick fool. The ring was a magnificent addition on my ring finger.

Outside the jewelry store, Danny and I grabbed a cab to the hotel. With his arm around my shoulder, and a grin that wouldn't quit, Danny pulled me to the elevator. As soon as the doors closed, he pressed me against the wall, his hips grinding into me, and his lips attacked mine. My arms flew around Danny's neck, pulling him closer. We were all hands and lips.

In the short time it took for the elevator to reach our floor, my shirt became unbuttoned to my waist and my hair was a tousled mess.

The door to our suite barely closed before we ripped off each other's clothes in a frenzy of passion. Shirts, sneakers, jeans, and belts, carelessly tossed wherever they fell. Danny scooped me up and carried me to the bed. We were on fire.

Our lips locked together, our tongues dancing, enjoying each other's taste. Danny was like the sweetest wine. His breath on me was intoxicating. Danny's hands on me heightened every sensation, sending wave after wave pulsing through me. And under my touch, his muscles were taught, his skin smooth and warm.

My head was spinning. Danny grabbed my thong and pulled it down. I thought I would burst. With urgency, we pressed closer and closer until entwined, he entered me, and we became one. Our passioned frenzy escalated to levels we had never experienced before. I gasped, digging my nails into Danny's shoulder to stifle the scream that threatened to escape. Finally we shared our explosive climax. Then we collapsed, exhausted in each other's arms.

Danny and I held each other, silent. Words would have been wrong. Light feathery caresses, and gentle kisses, said it all.

"I hate to break the spell," Danny murmured after we'd made love again. He Held my face and delicately kissed my lips to blunt my expected disappointment. "Time to get ready for the evening."

Danny had not shared his plans. "Can't we do something else?"

I planted a slow, sensuous kiss on his lips and rubbed up against him to make my point.

"Elizabeth,"

"Yeah," I answered dreamily, and I kissed him again.

Danny took my hands. "This will have to wait until later. We have tickets," he firmly stated.

Tickets! Broadway? We had plenty of time until the curtain. Dinner?

Danny eased up to sitting, his magnificent body on full display.

"You're not being very spontaneous this weekend, are you?" I pouted.

Danny looked at me in hurt surprise. "How can you say that Elizabeth Newman? I made the biggest decision of my life," he declared as he held up my left hand, "Because a restaurant worker said I should. I think that's pretty damned spontaneous."

I flushed, embarrassed. No longer wearing even the sheet, I felt completely exposed with nowhere to hide.

"I'm sorry. I didn't mean that. Of course you're spontaneous. That's one of the things I love about you."

"But you're a spoiled little girl who didn't get her way?" he teased.

"No," I countered with a megawatt smile, "I'm a deliriously happy woman who was having too much fun fooling around with her fiancé, and didn't want to stop."

Not too much later, after Danny had more than satisfied me again, we showered, and then dressed in the same clothes as earlier. Per Danny's instructions I swept my hair into a ponytail. After donning our jackets, ready to leave the suite, I found out why.

"We have to wear these," Danny said, and he produced two Dodgers' baseball caps, placing one on himself, and the other on me. While lifting my ponytail through the back hole he added, "We're going to Citifield. Dodgers play the Mets tonight."

Now I knew why Danny wouldn't change our plans. When he had tickets to the Dodgers, nothing kept him from the stadium. The Jacobs and Newmans had always had season tickets. Danny and I had grown up at Dodger Stadium. Fortunately, I enjoyed baseball as much as he did.

The rocking motion of the subway pushed us against each other as we held tightly to the center pole. The train was crowded with a combination of shoppers headed home, and fans headed to the game. We were more than a little conspicuous riding the Number Seven train to Citifield. Unfriendly glares directed our way were expected when dressed in enemy caps while riding the Mets express.

Danny gave me a reassuring smile. My hand clutched his so tightly it had to hurt. Still Danny smiled. He was right. The train passengers seemed non-threatening. I loosened my grip only slightly, confident that my athletic fiance could protect me.

As we exited the station, I looked around every which way, bewildered. Before us was Citifield, but we were in the middle of an urban neighborhood. Parking seemed haphazard at best, with few formal lots. Now I understood why Danny had insisted on taking the train.

"This is so odd," I said, as we found ourselves at the entrance to the

Jackie Robinson Rotunda. Why had the Mets named part of their stadium after a Dodger legend? I made a mental note to ask Danny once we found our seats. He knew everything about baseball. Surely, he would know this.

"We're standing in the old Shea parking lot," Danny said thoughtfully, as though that should mean something to me. And what did that have to do with Jackie Robinson?

I glanced around. I couldn't imagine it as a parking lot, but it looked like finding a cab on this busy street would be doable when the game ended. This environment was so foreign. I was used to Dodger Stadium. Palm trees, and acres and acres of blacktop surrounded its near perfect roundness. I followed Danny through security at the entrance to the steep escalator.

Despite the upscale food stalls, Danny and I agreed the only dinner to eat at a ballgame was hotdogs with fries, and a cold beer. We slathered the dogs with mustard and drenched the fries in ketchup. I enjoyed licking a drop of mustard that had smeared on my fingertip.

When Danny added chopped onion to his dog, I frowned.

"You will pay for that later," I teased.

Danny laughed. "Deal with it, Elizabeth," and he gave me my last sweet tasting kiss of the night.

Front row, on the home plate side of the visitor's dugout. I expected no less. Danny, no we, owed Lila big time for securing us the best seats.

Baseball games in New York were a substantially different experience than ones at Dodger Stadium. The crowd was more passionate. Most every seat was filled before the first pitch was even thrown. At home, fans routinely arrived during the second or even third inning.

Other than some glares, nobody bothered us while we cheered for the Dodgers. And though the Dodgers were up by five runs, barely anyone left before the ninth inning, convinced that the Mets would come back.

Danny and I enjoyed ourselves immensely; easy when your team wins 7-4. After the last pitch, a called strike three, Danny kissed me, excited over the Dodger victory. Ugh! Onion-beer breath!

"You are not kissing me again until you brush your teeth," I admonished.

Danny laughed and hugged me. "Deal with it, Liz." Then he leaned in to kiss me again, and I pressed my hands against him to keep Danny at bay.

"I'm serious, Daniel," I tried protesting, "You have oniony beer breath." Danny batted my arms down, and kissed me anyway.

CHAPTER SEVENTY-FIVE - DANIEL

Buzzzzz. Buzzzzz. My arm stretched to the nightstand and fumbled to reach the phone. Groggy with sleep, I answered my phone. "Newman."

"Danny, it's Shane."

"Huh?"

"It's Shane," he persisted.

"Shane?" What the hell?

I looked around. The room was dark. Elizabeth lay curled up beside me sleeping, the prettiest smile on her full lips.

"What time is it?" I whispered, trying not to wake Eli.

"I don't know. Three, maybe?"

"Why are you calling me at three in the morning?" I whisper scolded.

"Why are you whispering?" he asked.

What kind of asinine question was that?

"Because it's three in the morning a-hole. I don't want to wake Elizabeth."

"You're sleeping?"

"Of course I'm sleeping. Why aren't you?"

"It's Saturday," Shane answered, as though that explained it all.

"Remind me to find you a girlfriend. Then you'd be sleeping instead of making phone calls. Why are you calling me anyway?"

"It's Phoebe."

"Phoebe!"

I sat bolt upright, my attention all on Shane. Elizabeth didn't stir, sleeping through my abrupt movement. "Phoebe hasn't found us, has she?" I fretted.

"I don't even know where you are," Shane answered. "Tonight was the formal."

"Completely forgot. We've been having too good a time. Went to the Dodger game tonight. They slaughtered the Mets. It was sweet. Nice stadium though."

"You're in New York?"

"Shit"! Me and my big mouth. "Don't tell anyone."

"It's okay. You're safe. Phoebe came to the formal with Duncan."

"Duncan? No shit! I'm having a hard time picturing a girl who never even brushes her hair, going to the formal."

"I know. Phoebe in a gown – kind of blows you away. She's not bad _ooking when she cleans up. I can sort of see how you hooked up with _ner."

"Shane!" Phoebe was a mistake I did not want to be reminded of. I glanced over at Elizabeth, peacefully sleeping. "Focus, Shane. I want to get _ack to sleep."

"So, Phoebe was looking for you. When it became apparent that you were a no-show, she went ballistic. Total breakdown. Phoebe had all these _ills, and Duncan said she swallowed a bunch. The Dean was called, and an ambulance took her away."

"She'll be back by Monday," I said drily.

"Doubtful. Chloe was standing by some faculty chaperones. She overheard them saying something about the Dean calling her parents to come collect her and her stuff."

"Serious?"

"Danny, this isn't like getting wasted in a dorm room. This was _ossession of a large quantity of controlled substances. In public. At the formal."

"You sound like a lawyer."

"When you grow up with one in the house... Anyway, Phoebs will be _ucky if expulsion is the only thing she gets."

"And this was all because of me?"

I found it hard to believe that I had caused the girl to crack. If I had, that confirmed Phoebe's mental instability. Part of me felt guilty, but another larger part, felt pure relief.

"Don't go there, Danny. Don't let her ruin what you have."

Elizabeth turned toward me, still sleeping. "You're right. I just can't believe it. I hope she gets the help she needs. Phoebe's really not a bad person."

"She tried to kill you, Danny."

"Just let Phoebe be out of our lives. I'm too happy to hold a grudge."

"When you have a girl as hot as Elizabeth, you can enjoy married life. I'm not ready yet. I never thought you would be either."

"I'll have to find you the right girl. Now can I get back to mine?"

"Sure. I'll see you when you get back."

"Shane. Thanks for calling. Even if it is the middle of the night."

After returning the phone to the nightstand, I smiled at Elizabeth. The call hadn't disturbed her sleep. I would tell her the news in the morning.

A wave of relief swept over me. The muscles I hadn't known were tense relaxed. Phoebe was gone! We were free to be us again.

I leaned over Elizabeth's bare shoulder and kissed her check. My beautiful sleeping angel, her loose curls cascading down her back, smiled and wiggled closer, pressing against me. Instant arousal. I skimmed her cheek with my fingertips. She moved her face, letting my lips press onto hers.

"Mmm," she murmured like a happy kitten. Sleepy eyes half opened, Elizabeth purred, "Is it morning?" she mumbled.

"Shh," I whispered.

I found mostly asleep Elizabeth incredibly appealing.

"It's the middle of the night," I whispered.

"Oh," Elizabeth answered, and she snuggled even closer.

Content with our future, I brought my lips down to hers again, and kissed her, but with more passion. Elizabeth brought her hands up around my neck, and responded with her own innocent, sleepy passion. As gently as I could, I didn't want to fully wake her, I parted her thighs and carefully made love to Elizabeth.

My contented angel fell back to sleep, protected in my loving arms. I was certain that come morning, Elizabeth would think it had been a lovely dream.

CHAPTER SEVENTY-SIX - ELIZABETH

I woke with a grin, feeling wonderfully well-rested and incredibly alive. My joy mirrored the sun streaming in through the sheer curtains. I found myself snuggled in Danny's embrace, always a great way to start the day.

Sleepy sapphire eyes soon fluttered open, and I grinned. Danny pressed his lips to mine, and our bodies entwined. After our shared explosion of love, nestled in each other's embrace, Danny shared his phone call with Shane. What incredible news! How had I slept through their lengthy conversation?

Unexpectedly, I experienced conflict. Juxtaposed with my relief that we were free from danger, I felt sorry for Phoebe, and that disturbed me. That nobody had recognized Phoebe's fragile mental state bothered me. So did another thought. How had Danny ever been involved with her? I fingered my ring, a powerful symbol of what was most important, and pushed those thoughts out of my mind before they ruined our day.

Thursday was my dance performance. What a difference a semester made! With bittersweet memories I recalled December's performance. Jealousy, because Kelsey's parents drove in from Boston and mine were no shows, mixed with overwhelming sadness because as far as I knew at the time, Danny had not been there either.

Much as I wanted to let loose Wednesday evening after the last of my classes, Danny insisted we leave The Cellar by eleven. He wanted me well rested for Thursday.

"E, let's get going," Danny ordered. He grabbed my hands as we stood with our friends.

"Not yet," I protested, "I want to dance." Bossy Danny was infuriating.

Then Rachel arrived. I hadn't seen her all week. Did she even know that we'd been to New York?

"Hey, lovebirds," she teased.

I blushed, and Danny answered for us both. "Hey, Mom. What's up?"

"Ready for Friday?" she asked.

Friday. Rachel and Danny's film screened on Friday. It would be one of five student films premiering that evening.

"Sure. There's nothing left for us to do but show up," Danny answered. "It's not like Elizabeth who goes live tomorrow, if she'll ever let me take her home."

"I'm waiting for a slow dance, " I explained.

"E, we can slow dance at home."

There was frustration in Danny's voice. He squeezed me around my clavicle, and tilted my head to the side so he could kiss my throat. A stray hair fell across my face, and I brushed it back with my right hand.

"What's that?" Rachel asked, regarding my ring.

Danny grinned. "A small purchase I made in New York."

"This isn't? You didn't get…" she stammered.

"Calm down, Rach. I just want everyone Elizabeth meets this summer to know she's taken."

"You got me nervous."

I couldn't help giggling. Danny and I had lied straight-faced to Rachel and succeeded. He squeezed me. It was my secret, and my giggling jeopardized it.

"Rach, you know me better than that. When the time comes, I'm buying Elizabeth a rock."

"I expect no less from you," Rachel answered.

I frowned. Why was Rachel pleased that we weren't engaged?

A favorite slow song began playing.

"I love this song," I said, and I guided Danny to the dance floor. I circled my arms around his neck, and we held each other close. His arms tightened around my waist, and we swayed to the beat. Danny smiled, his eyes full of love, and we kissed, melting into each other.

My heart beat rapidly. I couldn't make it through the song. "Let's go," I whispered. "I can't resist you anymore."

Thursday morning I couldn't sit still. I wasn't nervous about tonight's performance, but. I couldn't concentrate. I drove Danny nuts. He sat on the bed, leaning against the wall, attempting to read an article for his economics final.

"E, one of us is leaving this room, and it isn't me."

"But it's my room," I complained.

Danny put down the article, strode over to me, and clasped his hands on my shoulders. He looked deep into my eyes.

"You're a bundle of nervous energy, Elizabeth. Either go to the gym or swim."

"Daniel!" I protested.

"And don't come back until lunch," he added. Danny dismissed me with a kiss to my forehead.

CHAPTER SEVENTY-SEVEN - DANIEL

Settling into my seat beside Rachel, I relaxed. This time I belonged here. Across the auditorium, I spotted Elizabeth's yearbook friends, here to support her. Jackson Pruitt and I exchanged smiles. How stupid to have been jealous of him. I chuckled. Nothing would bother me tonight.

I scanned the audience. Parents who lived within driving distance filled the seats. At events like this, I regretted being so far from home. Eli didn't say it, but I'm sure she agreed.

Wistfully I considered my screening tomorrow evening. I missed my parents terribly. They would be so proud if only they could be here. But not to be. Dad was busy in post-production, and he couldn't drop everything. Again I was doubly glad I had Elizabeth.

Moments before the lights went down, a middle-aged woman noisily hurried to her seat behind me.

"There you are," the man beside her said.

"Bob, you'll never guess who I just saw in the restroom," she said excitedly. "Miranda Jordan!"

Rachel's jaw dropped, and she gaped at me. I whipped my head around.

"Randi? You saw Randi?" I exclaimed.

The couple looked at me like I was crazed.

"I said Miranda Jordan," she answered pointedly.

"Yeah, I heard you. Was she with anyone?" Elizabeth would be thrilled. I hoped my mom was here too. Randi rarely flew solo.

"I don't know. It was the restroom." She said, annoyed.

"You couldn't tell if Randi was with anyone?" I insisted.

"Randi?" She looked down her nose at me, not understanding.

By this time Rachel had turned her head toward the conversation.

"Randi's here," I told her excitedly.

"Is your mom with her?"

"I'm trying to find out."

"My, don't you sound overly familiar," the woman, said derisively.

My temper flared. I might lose it. Why wouldn't this woman just answer my questions?

"Miranda is my godmother," I told her.

"Of course she is." Her sarcasm said she did not believe me. Why would anyone make this up?

"Miranda Jordan is his godmother," Rachel interjected. "He's always called her Randi. Her daughter is in the show."

Then the lights went down before I got an answer about Mom. The darkness made it impossible to look for either Randi or Mom.

Like an angel floating on air, Elizabeth danced across the stage. Mesmerized, I stared, in awe of her grace and elegance. How did she do it?

"Elizabeth's so beautiful," I whispered to Rachel. She squeezed my hand and grinned.

"You're adorable," she whispered back.

Adorable? I was a lot of things, but adorable? Uh, no.

Rachel continued in hushed tones. "Your face is full of pride. It's obvious how much you love her."

"That's because I do."

"When's the wedding?"

"You know?" How? Eli wanted our engagement kept quiet. Why did she tell Rachel?

"I do now," Rachel answered with a smug, triumphant expression on her face.

I smacked my hand against my forehead, not believing I'd fallen into her trap so easily.

"After graduation," I answered. "Don't say a word. Especially not to Elizabeth, or our parents."

"Doesn't she know?"

I rolled my eyes. "Of course Eli knows. But she can't know you guessed. Nobody is supposed to know, especially the Jacobs. I'm still in Randi's doghouse."

"Tonight she'll see how happy Elizabeth is."

I shook my head. "It's going to take a lot more than this to earn Randi's trust."

"When am I allowed to know?"

"When Eli shows you her ring."

"I saw it."

"Not that ring. The real one. I'm designing it over the summer."

"Shh," came a harsh voice from behind us. Ugh. That woman. Rachel giggled. Rachel never giggled.

I lifted my finger to my lips signaling this conversation was over. I wanted to concentrate on Elizabeth.

Intermission couldn't come soon enough. I jumped out of my seat, determined, and forged my way toward the lobby. I was so anxious I could have knocked over anyone in my way. The grouchy woman behind me topped the list.

Finally. After passing through a crowd packed as tightly as a mosh pit, I reached the lobby. There! Not only was Randi here, so were Mom, Dad and Michael. And they were surrounded by fans!

This was so incredibly unfair. Tonight was my fiancée's performance. These were our parents! It was demeaning to push through the crowd to reach my own parents. At this rate, intermission might be over before I even had a chance to utter "hello".

Dad was so busy being fawned over he didn't notice me as I pressed forward. My aggressiveness pissed off his adoring fans. Too bad. He was my dad, not theirs.

"Danny!" Mom called out.

"Mom!" We came together in a warm embrace.

Mom kissed me and held me tight. When had I last seen my mother? It had been so long. I was embarrassed remembering it had been Winter Break when she saved me in New Orleans.

Mom's arms felt warm and welcoming. I loved her so much. Despite having given her so much grief over the years, I knew how much she loved me. I was proud that phase of my life was over. Mom smiled appraisingly, enjoying her son.

"Danny, you look great. And happy. Elizabeth must take good care of you."

"Yes, Mom," I laughed. "And I love being me again."

"Steven," Mom tried getting Dad's attention. "Don't you recognize your own son?" she giggled.

"Of course I do," Dad sneered while completing his autograph on a girl's program.

Then Dad turned away from the crowd. Showtime was over.

"Danny!" he said enthusiastically, and he gathered me in his arms for a bear hug.

Then Dad pulled backand critically examined my appearance.

"You look like a new person, son."

"I feel like one too, Dad."

"I can tell."

Dad leaned his head toward mine to speak in a low voice intended only for me to hear.

"Danny, I'm proud of you."

I considered Phoebe, and the fate that could have befallen me if Dad hadn't loved me enough to drag me from my hell.

"Thanks for kicking my butt and getting me the help I needed, Dad."

"That's the job of being a dad. Enjoy New York?" he asked, changing tacks.

"Amazing," I smiled. "Did Lila receive our thank-you gift?"

"Yes," he nodded. "She thinks you and Elizabeth are the most spoiled kids she's ever seen," Dad laughed. "I'm glad your bills don't go through her."

"Maybe when I meet her she'll find I'm not so bad."

"Before you work on winning Lila over, there's somebody more important you have to make up with, dear," Mom reminded me. "Randi is not happy about yet another weekend getaway. Actually, she's not happy with you at all."

"I had to get Elizabeth away from that psychopath." After the fact, I had shared the Phoebe drama with Mom.

"Of course you did, but Randi blames you for their being a psychopath in her daughter's life to begin with," Mom answered.

"Dad," I began to protest. "Alright, I'll give her that. The psychopath was my fault. But it was unintentional. Phoebe's gone now. Can't Randi let it go?"

"Danny, Randi blames you for all the unhappiness Elizabeth went through this year. She's not as forgiving as her daughter."

"Mom, doesn't she see how happy Elizabeth is now?"

"Danny," Mom tried softening the blow, but there really was no way to do so. "This drama reinforced Randi's position. She doesn't trust you. She's afraid Elizabeth will get hurt again."

"But I love Eli," I protested. "I would never hurt her."

"Randi hopes that while Elizabeth is in Israel she'll get over you."

"That's not gonna happen."

"Of course it won't. Elizabeth loves you very much. That will never change."

Mom and Dad looked at me with a seriousness that had been missing until now. Was I on trial? Then I noticed a student milling about, just behind Dad, waiting to get his attention.

"This is a private, family conversation," I snapped.

The guy turned red, embarrassed, and backed away. Good! I was sick of it. Mom glared at me. Didn't she understand?

"I'm sorry, Mom. I'm not in the mood for the circus tonight."

"It's Elizabeth's night," Dad said agreeing with me.

"And Randi has to understand how much we love each other."

"Unless you do something stupid again, Danny," Dad added.

Mom nodded her agreement. Crap! Skeletons from the past that I did not want brought up again ever, rearing their ugly heads. Did no one, save for Elizabeth, have any faith in me?

"Mom, Dad," I began contritely "I would never do anything like that again. I've changed. I would never jeopardize my relationship with Elizabeth."

"I know that Danny. You're lucky to have each other. Dad and I love Elizabeth as much as we love you."

"Thanks, Mom, Dad." I quickly hugged Mom. Then I gave Dad a longer hug.

"Randi will have to understand," said Dad, "but it may take time."

"Randi better get over it and fast. Elizabeth and I plan to rent a house next year."

Where had that come from? I caught myself. Elizabeth and I had not discussed moving off-campus. But now that I thought about it…. Tonight I would tell her. It made perfect sense. In Los Angeles we had our own home. Why not here where we spent most of the year? It was an excellent idea Eli was certain to love.

"Randi will not like that."

"To hell with Randi, Mom. There's nothing she can do about it."

"She could cut Elizabeth off and force her to transfer."

"That won't work. I can support Elizabeth, and Randi knows it."

"I doubt Shakespeare ever envisioned Romeo with a trust fund," Dad interjected with a smile that lightened the mood.

"Daniel," Mom started. Uh-oh.

"Mother," I said back.

"Daniel, don't sass me," she smiled. "Miranda has loved you all your life. She wants to forgive you. Give her a reason to. Be a model citizen this summer, okay?"

"Can I be a citizen model instead?" I was purposely being surly.

"Daniel! This is for your own good," she said. "Stay sober and drug-free, work hard at TAG, and don't go near any women. Randi will notice, especially that last one."

"That's the easy one. It's the first one that might be difficult, especially without Elizabeth."

"Danny," Dad said supportively, "That's why you have me, your mother, and a therapist."

"Thanks, Dad," I said, and I hugged him. Dad whispered so Mom wouldn't hear.

"You really think two months of celibacy is going to be easy?"

Given Dad's history of cheating, it didn't surprise me that he would find sexual abstinence more difficult than sobriety.

I answered pointedly. "There's only one woman I want to be with."

"No drugs, no drinking, and no sex. Are you sure you're my son? What will you do for fun this summer?"

"Maybe I'm Mom's son. I have my priorities straight."

"Danny, I'm teasing. Mom and I are prepared to do whatever it takes to support you."

"Thanks, Dad."

"I'll catch you later." Rachel excused herself when the final curtain came down. She understood that Elizabeth and I would want alone time with our parents.

As they remained in their seats waiting for the audience to thin out, I hurried to the front. I'd catch Elizabeth as she came from backstage. She had performed brilliantly. I wanted her to know how proud I was.

Soon Elizabeth burst through the door wearing shorts over her leotard, and tights rolled up to below her knees. The broadest smile lit her face like the most powerful of stars.

"E, you were great!" I declared enthusiastically.

Completely energized, she threw her arms around my neck. I drew her lithe, sweaty body to mine for a hug and kissed her full pink lips.

"You think so?" she asked..

"Oh, yes," I nodded.

"Me too. I agree."

We shared a laugh and kissed again.

"Where are they?" I had sent Eli a note before intermission ended. She knew our parents were here.

I took Elizabeth's hand to stop her forward motion.

"You should know. Randi is livid over our trip to New York."

"That's silly. Mom will see how happy I am," Elizabeth laughed.

"She doesn't trust me. Randi thinks I'm going to hurt you again."

"Well, she would be wrong. I trust you, so Mom has to."

"Elizabeth, you're being naïve."

"No, I'm not." Eli reached up and pressed her lips against mine for a warm kiss.

Not caring what Randi, who was certainly watching us thought, I deepened the kiss, and kissed my fiancée the way a man should kiss his fiancée.

CHAPTER SEVENTY- EIGHT - ELIZABETH

"Mom! Dad!" When Danny finally released me I ran to their warm, welcoming arms.

While we hugged and kissed, I truly believed everything was right in my world.

Danny had to be wrong. Mom's smile seemed genuine. Danny was probably over-sensitive because of the news we were keeping from our parents.

Then I noticed, Steve and Ellen! I was so excited to see them.

"What are you all doing here?" I asked both sets of parents.

"Can't I see my daughter dance?" Mom asked.

"And I wanted to see my son's film," Ellen added.

"And we figured, if they were both coming... What the hell," Dad said.

"Elizabeth, you look great. Like a different girl since last time I saw you."

"Thank you, Steve." Going up on toe, I kissed his cheek, and whispered, "You saved my life."

Pulling me into a bear hug, Steve whispered back, "Glad I could help. I'm enjoying your happiness."

"Mom isn't," I pointed out.

"I don't want her spoiling my favorite girl's night."

I hugged him back. "I love you, Steve."

If my mother didn't approve of my love life, at least Steve and Ellen did. Mom would have to get on board.

After joining our parents for a light bite at a local diner, Danny and I walked back to Berkeley Hall. Immediately after entering our room, I pulled off my shorts, relieved to remove the uncomfortable sweat-soaked garment.

"I feel so gross," I said as I stripped off my leotard.

Down to nothing but my flesh-colored footless tights, Danny's eyes, wide as saucers starred at my bare torso.

"Whoa! Elizabeth!"

Hands on hips, I answered, "Uh, no. Not until I shower. I'm sweaty and disgusting."

"I'm not listening, Eli," Danny said, and he grabbed my hands, pulling me close.

I gasped. Danny's hands on my bare back, whoa! Electricity spread throughout my entire being. Helpless, I stared at him. Sapphire eyes twinkled mischievously. I was defenseless and Danny knew it.

Danny's hands pushed my tights down past my hips. He had me. I'd worn nothing underneath my leotard and tights. My hands flew around Danny's neck, and I forcefully kissed him. He ran his hands up and down my outer thighs. I shuddered. Yeah, I was all his.

"You're so soft, and sweet and beautiful," Danny whispered.

"I'm sweaty and I smell," I protested as I stepped out of the tights and kicked them away.

Danny inhaled deeply. "Mm. Sweat, faded perfume, and Lizzie J. – my favorite scent."

I giggled. Seriously, Daniel? My sweat could not possibly be his, or anyone else's favorite scent.

Then Danny moved his hands up to my scalp. He yanked out my ponytail and unsuccessfully tried fluffing my damp hair.

"I love how uninhibited you are. Eli, do you have any idea how incredibly sexy you are stripping off your clothes like that?"

"I had to remove them. They're gross. Hand me my robe, please?"

"That's why it's so sexy," Danny said, ignoring my request. "You weren't thinking about it. Now it's my turn to get sweaty."

"Danny!" I giggled, as he pulled his polo shirt over his head, and tossed it aside.

Danny grinned. "We'll shower later."

Why fight it? "I can't resist you either." I said, and Danny carried me to the bed.

"Ready for that shower?" Danny murmured. We were snuggled under the crisp sheets, Danny holding me close in his loving arms while I traced patterns on his chest with my fingertips.

"No." Then I yawned. "I don't want to get up. I'm too sleepy."

Danny laughed softly.

"What's so funny?"

"You are. First you're like 'don't come near me. I'm sweaty and gross.' Now you're like 'I'm too sleepy to shower. I can't get up.' You're so contradictory. It's cute."

"Well now it doesn't matter. You're sweaty, too. We're the same."

I couldn't resist kissing Danny. His eyes were twinkling like the brightest stars, and his beautiful smile melted me. Danny's lips curved upward. He was so content.

I took Danny's face in my hands and kissed him. Nothing was better than sharing my love with Danny.

"You have no idea how happy you make me, E," Danny said.

He held me as close as he could, relaxed in our post-love making bliss. I was sleepy, but this was when Danny often opened-up, sharing his most intimate feelings. I encouraged hin to continue.

"As happy as you make me?"

Danny smiled thoughtfully. "Probably."

"Do you think we'll always be this happy?" I asked.

"There may be a few bumps along the way, but nothing we can't get through together," he replied. "As long as you promise to never stop talking to me."

"I promise. What a disaster that was!"

Danny brought his lips to mine for another sweet kiss. His hand caressed my cheek.

"Eli, how am I going to live without you this summer?"

"Danny, we've been through that. We have email, Twitter, Facebook, What'sApp, Skype, and parents who don't care how high the phone bill gets. We'll hardly know we're apart."

"It doesn't take your place, babe. I can take a laptop out for the evening, but it certainly won't be making love to me."

I tilted my head down against Danny's chest, hiding my face. A tear escaped my eye. I had tried so hard to put a positive spin on our upcoming separation, but no matter how much technology would assist us, there was no getting around the physical separation we would endure.

Except for his hospital stay, we had not spent an evening apart since we had reconciled. Each day began and ended identically, with me entwined in Danny's arms. Two long months apart would be painful for us.

"I'll miss you too, Danny. You can't imagine how much."

"Yes, I can."

"Okay, you can, because it will be just as bad for you, but there's got to be an upside."

"E, you don't have to be all merry sunshine. You can be sad."

"I am sad. But it will be good. Especially for you."

"How will being nine time zones away be good for me?"

I had to think fast. I didn't want Danny to see through the veneer and realize I was making this up as I went along.

"I won't be in your way."

"You're never in my way, baby."

"I would be this summer. There's a lot going on in your life. It will be easier if I'm not there."

"I'm not following you, babe."

"Men are so dense."

"Thanks, Eli."

"Don't take it the wrong way. I love you, but you're not looking beyond the surface."

"And you are?"

"Yes. As always," I said, and I took a deep breath, buying time to formulate my response. "Danny, your internship at TAG is going to be more intense than you think. They'll expect you to put in long hours. You would not be happy constantly cancelling me. Danny, you would feel guilty that I hadn't made plans with my friends instead."

"E, I would still come home to you every night."

"Forget about us for a moment."

"I can't. Dammit, Eli! I don't want you to go!"

I turned away for a moment, blinking back tears. Stay strong, Elizabeth.

"What about you, Danny?" I asked, eyes on him again. "You promised not only to see a therapist this summer, but to spend time with Steve resolving your issues with him."

"I will. It's important Eli."

"It is. And it will be better with me away. Same with sobriety. Let's be honest, Daniel. It's much easier for you to stay sober when you're with me. You know I'll keep you in line."

"Ouch! You crack a tough whip, Elizabeth," he laughed.

"Daniel!" I rolled my eyes. "You have to know you can do it on your own, not because I'll kick your butt."

"You're right, Eli," Danny sighed, resigned. "You're right."

I tenderly kissed his lips. "You'll be so proud of yourself knowing you did it without me."

Danny stroked my thigh; light, feathery strokes.

"You know what else would make me proud?"

"Yes. When the summer is over, and you've proven to yourself that you are the man I should spend my life with, I will proudly go public with our engagement."

"You mean that, Eli?" Danny was elated.

"Yes," I answered. A megawatt smile crept across my face. "When you've done everything you're planning to do this summer, even my mother will be impressed and know I'm right about you."

"E, I promise to make amends with Randi."

"I have faith that you will."

"E!" Danny smiled brightly. He pulled my head to his chest for a hug and kissed my head. "That's my girl," Danny laughed, and he kissed me again.

"Now can we shower?" I asked.

"Later for that."

Danny took my face in his hands and kissed me hard. He pressed me against the pillows, and made love to me again.

CHAPTER SEVENTY- NINE - ELIZABETH

"E, where have you been?" Danny exclaimed as I entered our room. It was just past three in the afternoon, not particularly late. What was his problem?

"When did you get back?" I countered. Wasn't I allowed to go out? He had spent the day playing golf with our dads.

"About an hour ago." Danny, sat on the bed propped against the wall by pillows. He held an open paperback. "I sucked big time." His sapphire eyes twinkled devilishly. "For some reason, I couldn't concentrate on my game," he laughed.

"I was at the pool doing laps," I answered shyly. Though with my wet hair, it was obvious.

Danny raised his eyebrows. "Didn't you get enough exercise last night?"

I rolled my eyes and blushed. Then Danny reached for my wrists and pulled me down to sitting on the bed.

"I'm glad you're back. I need to stop at the screening room. Come."

"Give me ten minutes to dry my hair." If I didn't blow it now, I would be stuck with unruly waves for the evening.

Danny smoothed a damp lock off my face. "Don't." Then he touched my face gently and kissed me. "I like your waves. They're natural. You look more like Elizabeth and much less like Miranda."

I melted, all giggly inside. Danny was the most amazing, brilliant man. I had been thrilled with my parents attending my performance last night, but either Danny was a mind-reader, or I was that transparent, either way, he knew that my parents rattled me. His reference to Mom signaled that. Danny never called her Miranda.

I laughed when I discovered Danny's reason for getting to the screening room – seat saving. He had printed out six pieces of paper with "Newman" in large type, and four similarly printed with "Bergman" for Rachel.

After trying out a few seats, Danny found the row he wanted to sit in.

"Aren't you getting a bit carried away?" I asked. "This isn't a premiere."

"It is for me, Elizabeth." Danny answered petulantly. He sounded like a hurt little boy.

"I'm sorry. I know it's an important evening for you."

Danny taped the first two "Newman" tags on the seats closest to the aisle.

"I'll sit on the aisle. The inside one's for you," he explained.

"Where are you putting our parents?" Tension crept into my voice.

"Next to us?" Danny asked tentatively.

"Then move me."

Danny frowned. He put his hands on his hips, and sighed, frustrated.

"Eli? Where do you want me to put them?"

"Mars." That would still not be far enough away.

"Elizabeth?"

"I hate having my parents here. I've worked so hard to be known as me and not as their appendage."

"Everyone at Donnelly knows you as you."

"Tonight I'm stepping backwards."

"Elizabeth, other parents will be here too."

"But who else will have their girlfriend's parents here?"

"You've got me on that. I don't know. Who cares? I don't even know who has a girlfriend, or boyfriend."

"They're not the Smiths."

Danny took me by my shoulders and looked at me sternly.

"Elizabeth," he said firmly "Get a grip."

"I don't want this attention." I pouted. "If it were only Steve and Ellen that would be fine."

"I can't uninvite Mike and Randi just because you're freaking."

"I am not freaking!" I hissed, loudly. "I hate the attention."

"What do you think will happen when I give you that ring?"

"We'll live happily ever after?"

"Yeah," Danny laughed. "If you make it through the publicity."

"Publicity?"

"Come here, baby," Danny said softly, and he gathered me into his protective embrace. Then he lifted my chin and held my glance.

"If it were any old Mr. and Mrs. Jacobs' daughter getting engaged, you're right, few would care. But when the bride's parents are Michael Jacobs and Miranda Jordan, and the groom's father is Steven Newman, you're being naïve if you don't think Kathy and Nancy will have a field day issuing press releases and photos."

"I hate this. I love you, but I hate this."

"And I'm not choosing a career that lets me fade into obscurity. E, this is the life you were born into, and it's the one you're signing on to with me. I don't know what you're thinking, but this is our world, babe."

"I know," I said glumly.

"Hey. Elizabeth, I want to spend the rest of my life with you, despite who your parents are, and all the baggage that comes with it."

"Daniel."

"Maybe it's good that you're going away this summer. You need time to consider what it really means to become Mrs. Danny Newman, and I mean everything. The entire package. Because if you're not absolutely certain, we can postpone that ring until you are."

"Of course, I'm certain I want to be Mrs. Danny Newman."

"I need you to think it all out. Promise you'll do that? I'll gladly wait if you need more time, or we can just live together and never get married."

I rolled my eyes. "I don't need more time. The moment we announce our engagement, no matter when that is, the media will descend on us."

"You're okay with that?"

"Not really. But Kathy can release some photos and quotes, along with a request to honor our privacy. Interest will die quickly. We're not public figures. We're only their offspring." I paused, and then I grinned. "See. I'm better with this than I used to be."

"We'll be in it together. Like on the balcony."

I blushed. "That's the only thing that makes it bearable."

"Sure you don't want to go back to Scott?"

"Daniel!" I growled. I took his hands and smiled into mischievous sapphire eyes that said he was teasing. "You're stuck with me for life."

"I certainly hope so, Elizabeth."

We met our parents for an early dinner at the restaurant where Danny and I had dined with Steve. That significance was not lost on us.

Danny and I were in a particularly happy mood as we waited for our table. I smirked at our wardrobe choices, appropriate, in contrast to what we wore to last spring's screening. Then we'd dressed for a premiere, me in a cocktail dress, and Danny in a suit. I shivered at the memory of his hands all over me.

This year, I wore an orange silk t-shirt, a yellow mini-skirt and orange ballet flats. My heart and my key necklaces stood out against the brightly colored shirt. Danny beamed with pride, pleased with the way my thick waves tumbled over my shoulders.

Wearing a grey sport coat over a pale yellow shirt and jeans, Danny was so handsome this evening. His face glowed with confidence. I couldn't stop staring.

Our parents were dressed casually, in jeans and no jackets. They were attending the screening as parents, nothing more. They understood. Tonight belonged to Danny.

"Margarita, Elizabeth?" Steve asked as the waiter took our drink order. When he smiled, his blue eyes twinkled like his son's.

"Steve!" I laughed, reminded of the last time we dined at this restaurant. Needed the fortification that evening. Not tonight. I glanced at Danny. "No thanks. I'm good."

Dinner was delicious. I ordered filet of sole served with a delicate lemon sauce. Danny had ravioli filled with butternut squash and topped with brown butter. Yum! My eyes filled with longing.

"You want one?" he asked, taking my hint.

My mouth watered as Danny cut one of the pasta pillows in half with his fork. Then, holding his hand beneath it to catch drips, he placed it in my mouth.

"Mmm!" I said, enchanted with the rich, nut-like flavor. It was like autumn on a plate. Danny held up his fork again.

"Here. Have the other half." I opened my mouth for Danny to feed me. "Can I taste your fish?"

"Sure," and I lifted a forkful toward Danny's lips as soon as I swallowed the ravioli.

Mom slammed down her fork. We froze, startled, Danny in mid-bite.

"Elizabeth, I'm sure Daniel is perfectly capable of feeding himself."

I turned crimson; my face heated. "Sorry," I responded meekly.

Mom's harshness brought tears to my eyes. I fought to contain myself, blinking hard. Danny squeezing my hand calmed me as did Ellen's immediate retort.

"Miranda! Can't you see how happy the kids are?"

"I'm sorry, Ellen. Unlike the rest of you, I am not so quick to forget the pain your son inflicted on my daughter," Mom answered sharply.

I stared at my mother, then Ellen, and finally Danny, who was trying to keep his composure. Mom wasn't thrilled by us being back together, but her level of hostility startled me.

"Randi, please," Dad cautioned in his usual calm voice. "This isn't the time or the place." He took Mom's hand to steady her.

"Then when is the time and place, Michael? This seems as good as any. We're all here."

"Miranda!" Dad muttered sharply.

Mom sighed and drew in a deep breath. Her perfect brow furrowed.

"Michael, I have held my tongue for weeks. I kept quiet while pictures of our daughter having sex with Daniel were plastered across the internet. I remained silent when they went to New York. I can't do this anymore."

"Mom! I thought you loved Danny."

"I do love Daniel. I've always loved Daniel. As a person, not as your lover. I'm trying to protect you, Elizabeth."

"I don't need protecting." I glared at Mom, and I grasped Danny's hand.

"Elizabeth, I'm not going to argue. That's how I feel. Deal with it."

"Randi, I love Elizabeth. I will never hurt her. I swear it."

"You say that now, Daniel. I think you mean it. Bottom line – I don't trust you."

"Mother!" I was shaking, and I looked to Danny. "I trust you," I whispered.

"I know you do, baby," Danny whispered back, his forehead touching mine.

"I'm sorry you feel that way, Miranda," Ellen said in an unusually assertive tone. "I remember all too clearly the last time I saw the kids. Danny was drugged-out in New Orleans, and Elizabeth was a walking zombie. Her only sign of life came from driving Danny's car."

"You drove my Porsche!" Danny exclaimed, clearly not amused by my spring break antics.

I moaned. "You were in Florida. I wanted to show Rachel a good time."

"I didn't say you could drive it. You didn't even ask."

"We weren't talking to each other."

"So you drove over and took my Porsche?" He was stunned.

"I'm allowed to," I said defensively. "You gave me the key. Do you want it back? I'll gladly swap it for the Range Rover's."

"E, no! How would I get around in the winter? I need the Rover."

"Get rid of the BMW and buy one for yourself."

"I can't do that. I love my..."

Danny stopped abruptly, having noticed my mother's look of triumph. Shit! Our little spat, which was at least partially in jest, had been interpreted as proof of our immaturity, and as further evidence that all was not right in paradise.

"You win," Danny relented. "The Porsche is yours whenever you want."

"Danny," Dad said, "if Elizabeth damages your car I'll get it repaired. I think I'm good for it."

"It's okay, Mike. Elizabeth's my responsibility."

"There was no damage. It's back in the garage as perfect as when it left," Ellen added, smiling at us.

Then Ellen took Steve's hand and looked at him, her eyes full of love.

"Steven, I don't know what you did, but to see our son this happy and clear-headed is the greatest gift you've given me."

Steve leaned over and kissed Ellen. She wiped a tear from her eye. Danny squeezed my hand as he noticed my mother's awkward flinch. Dad smiled.

"Mom, don't cry," said Danny.

"I'm sorry," she laughed nervously. "To see you so healthy and Elizabeth back to being herself, and both of you so in love. I couldn't ask for more."

Danny blushed, and said, "Mom, you're being way too mushy."

"Now I know where you get it from," I teased. I reached my right hand up to Danny's cheek and quickly kissed his lips.

"Elizabeth, what's that?" Mom asked, and she pointed to my ring.

"A gift from Danny." I tried sounding nonchalant although I felt anything but. I prayed it didn't show.

"It's a ring," Mom said pointedly.

"I wanted to buy Eli a gift when we were in New York, and she has more than enough necklaces for her one neck," Danny answered flippantly.

"But I have ten fingers," I smirked and held up both hands.

"It's a ring, Daniel," Mom said, icily this time.

"Mom, if it were what you're thinking, it would have been a substantial diamond. Danny wouldn't let me wear anything less."

Mom exhaled loudly. "You're right, Elizabeth. Danny would want your ring to be visible from across the room."

Danny grinned. "I won't be disappointed if the guys Eli meets in Israel assume it's an engagement ring," he explained, and I giggled.

"Good thinking, son," Steve agreed.

"It sure is. Nobody will bother me."

"It might be good if they did bother you, Elizabeth."

"Mom! You may not like it, but I'm taken, and I couldn't be happier. Get over it!"

"Steven?" Mom asked as an accusation. "Danny had your permission?"

"Daniel?" Steve asked sternly and looked at Danny.

Mom smirked as though she had won a round.

"I have my own money." Danny pointedly reminded them. I smirked, so proud of my man. "Sorry Randi. You can't blame Dad."

We left our parents early before dessert. I had to escape from my mother, and Danny was anxious to get to the screening room.

It was a quiet ride to campus with both of us deep in thought. Pulling into our parking spot at the film center, Danny started laughing. Loud peels of laughter filled his small car.

"What?" I asked, bewildered.

"I love how you answered Randi." He grabbed my face and kissed me hard.

"She was pissing me off," I answered.

"I could tell. We could all tell. It was great, Eli. I like this new confidence."

CHAPTER EIGHTY - ELIZABETH

The cavernous lobby of the modern film center was empty. Our footsteps echoed on the marble tile. At least an hour remained before the screenings would begin. Danny laid his hands on my shoulders, a distracted look on his face. Now that we had arrived, I the enormity of the event had hit him.

Tonight was exponentially more important to him than originally; the stakes for Danny critically high. Much as he was thrilled for Steve to be here, his presence was a game changer. None of the other parents attending had a Best Director Oscar sitting in their den.

I clasped my hands around Danny's neck, and I delicately kissed his lips.

"For luck," I whispered.

"You can do better than that," Danny teased.

I reached for Danny again. My hands pulled his face to mine, and I pressed my lips against his warm welcoming ones. Danny held me close, one arm around my back, his other hand holding my face, while we continued kissing.

"Hey, guys," Rachel interrupted. "I knew you'd be early."

Our lips broke apart, but Danny continued holding me against his chest, stroking my hair.

"Your timing sucks." Danny scowled. "Can't a guy kiss his girl without being interrupted?"

"Sorry. As you were." Rachel laughed, without embarrassment or remorse. Danny rolled his eyes. "Enjoy dinner with the folks?" she asked.

Danny and I exchanged grim glances.

"That good, huh?"

"Mom's trying to break us up," I explained.

"Eli told Randi off. Boy was that sweet. I'm so proud of her." Danny grinned; his eyes twinkled.

"I always miss all the fun," Rachel smirked.

The lights dimmed signaling the program to begin. Danny re-assigned the aisle seat to me for him to sit beside Rachel. Chloe, Shane and Cam sat on her other side. Our parents sat a row behind.

Five, fifteen minute long films would be shown. Before each one, its filmmakers would say a few words as introduction. In my mind, they were saving the best for last.

As the evening progressed, Danny's stress increased. The gentle hand holding mine increased in pressure to a death grip. I flexed my fingers to let Danny know it hurt.

"Sorry," he whispered, and lifted my hand to kiss my sore knuckles.

It was time. Danny rose to go forward, and he quickly kissed me. I gave his hand a gentle squeeze, and smiled at him and Rachel as she followed.

My heart thumped wildly. I was a nervous wreck. While Danny was seated beside me, I had been the calm one. Watching Danny stride to the front of the auditorium brought home the enormity of the event.

Rachel spoke first, briefly. She hated public speaking. As she always explained, preferring to stay in the back ground was why she was a writer.

"Working on this film has been a great experience. My thanks to our cast, our crew, and Mr. Rose, our faculty advisor. Most of all, thank you to my co-producer and fabulously talented director. He drove me nuts with his attention to detail, and perfectionism at all costs. But it paid off, even if at least a few times I wanted to kill you, Danny. Sorry. You know I love you."

The audience chuckled. I laughed out loud. That's my man!

Danny grinned and kissed Rachel on the cheek. He hugged her affectionately.

"Thank you, Rachel. We never could have completed this film if she had been successful at any of her homicidal attempts," Danny laughed. "Lucky for me, Rachel is a much more talented writer than murderer."

Danny stopped laughing and became serious.

"I've been blessed. Rachel is an extraordinary screenwriter, an awesome production partner, and a great friend who isn't shy with telling me off when I need it. And I've needed it, 'cause I've put her through hell this year."

I blushed. Danny was not the only one who had put Rachel through hell. I had no outlet to publically apologize, though. Instead I nodded across the auditorium and mouthed, 'me too.' Rachel smiled back. Message received.

Danny continued with his speech. "We had the most amazing cast and crew. They made our jobs so much easier. Thanks, guys."

Many of the student cast and crew members were present for the screening. They stopped Danny with their applause while he acknowledged them with his own applause.

"Mr. Rose, thank you for your patience and sage advice. We couldn't have asked for a better advisor. I also want to thank my parents for their love and support. I can't believe you're here."

I turned to see Ellen, always emotional, wipe a tear from her eyes. Steve, beaming with pride, squeezed her hand.

"Thank you to our special technical advisor, Steven Newman, who was available at all hours of the day or night. And yes, Dad, I always did manage to get at least a few hours of sleep."

I smirked, remembering the last week of post-production when Danny staggered into bed only a couple of hours before I woke.

"Lastly, there's one more person without whom I couldn't have made this film."

Danny looked directly at me, his piercing blue eyes sparkling brightly, his smile turning me to molten lava.

"Elizabeth, you inspire me to do my best every day. I love you."

All eyes in the auditorium turned to me as one. Ellen leaned forward and patted my shoulder, then kissed my cheek. Tears filled my eyes. I blinked hard. Smeared mascara would not do. Then I turned my head. Even my mother dabbed her eyes.

I barely heard Danny conclude, telling the audience, "Please enjoy our film," before I stood to let him and Rachel back into our row. Danny grasped my hands and kissed me hard before we sat back down.

"Do I really inspire you?" I whispered.

"Every day, E."

"That's the nicest thing anyone's ever said to me."

The lights went down. "Showtime," he whispered.

Danny left his arm around my shoulders as I settled against him. My hand clutched his thigh as the screening began. Nails digging through denim, Danny winced. He removed his arm from my shoulder and took up my hand. I gripped his tightly. I wanted more than I'd ever wanted anything before, to absolutely love his film.

It did not disappoint. They really had saved the best for last. Rachel's superb script exhibited the maturity and natural sounding dialogue of a seasoned pro. Danny's direction was masterful. He had extracted wonderfully nuanced performances from his actors, and had ventured away from Donnelly to find more varied locations. My car was featured in a scene filmed at a snow-covered beach. Steven Newman's son would not settle for less.

As the final credits rolled, I placed my hand on Danny's cheek, and my eyes met his twinkling ones. "You're amazing. It was great!" I squealed.

"You really liked it?" Danny asked, his voice laced with doubt.

"Why would I make this up?" I effused. "I love it."

Thrilled, Danny pulled me into his arms and kissed me.

In the lobby, everyone congratulated Rachel and Danny. It was their night, and I was content to stand beside them, beaming with pride. I enjoyed watching our parents, so accustomed to the spotlight take a few steps back. They respected that it was Danny's night. He was the star.

Once the well-wishers had moved on, our parents rejoined us.

"Danny, can I get a copy?" Steve asked.

"Sure, Dad. What for?"

"For a public screening."

"It's a student film, Dad."

"Danny, you don't realize how good your film is. I want it qualified for Academy consideration."

"Dad! Are you serious?" Danny's exclaimed.

Academy consideration! An Oscar! I was speechless.

"I wouldn't put my name on the line if I couldn't completely support it."

"Rach, did you hear that?" Danny exclaimed. He was soaring. Steve's offer was the career starter any aspiring director would jump at.

Along with our parents, Danny, Rachel, and I joined our friends at a large table in The Cellar. How awkward to be with my parents, but soon my discomfort stopped and our celebration was in full flow.

Despite Danny holding me on his lap, I was ignored while he held court. The film students looked over my head, catching his eye, talking to him. To them, I didn't exist. Not so, Danny His arms around my waist warmed me, and his breath against my nec as he spoke made my heart flutter.

"May I borrow my daughter?" Dad asked Danny, interrupting my boredom.

I turned to Danny and nodded my desire to go with Dad. "She's all yours, Mike," he conceded, and he released his hold on me.

"May I have this dance, Elizabeth?" Dad asked, and he took my hand as I hopped off Danny's lap.

"I was wondering when you were going to ask," I answered, and I winked.

Dad led me to the dance floor. I hadn't danced with him in a long time; a shame, as Dad was a good dancer. The first couple of songs that played were fast, upbeat pop. Michael Jacobs easily kept up with the kids.

Then came a slow song. Dad was pleased to hold me in his arms.

"I haven't done this in a long time."

"Oh, Dad." So sentimental. "You can dance with me anytime you want."

"Danny will let me?" he teased.

"For you, anything," I laughed.

Dad gave me a warm, fatherly hug, his arms strong, yet tender. It was soothing. I felt more loved at this moment than ever before.

"Danny makes you happy," he stated. It was not a question.

"Very," I agreed. "We love each other."

"I'm glad," he admitted. "I always wanted you to end up with him."

"You did?" I was surprised, especially as Dad often remained silent while allowing Mom to rant. "Does Mom know this?"

Dad laughed, uncomfortable. He ignored my question. "Danny's had his problems, but he's a great kid. He's grown up this year, and I know who got him there."

"Me?"

"Yes," Dad smiled. "And he knows it. Danny loves you very much. It's obvious. Not since I met Miranda have I seen a young man be that much in love."

I grinned at Dad, and I felt the color rising in my cheeks.

"He treats me like a princess," I whispered.

Dad smirked. "Yeah. Steve shares everything with me."

"Right. The Amex statements." We both laughed.

"Danny's very generous with Steve's money."

"Dad!" I exclaimed. "Danny has his own money."

"Of course. He's twenty-one now." Dad paused. "You trust Danny?"

"Completely," I answered, without hesitation.

"So do I, but Mom doesn't. I'll work on her this summer."

"Thanks, Dad."

"Anything to keep that smile on your face."

"I love you, Daddy."

Dad had always been my ultimate protector.

"May I cut in?" A rich tenor voice as lovely as the beautiful man it came from asked.

"No," I answered, dreamily. My head rested content against Dad's shoulder.

"No?" Danny was taken aback. I smiled brightestly to blunt his disappointment.

"Danny, don't pout. I'll save a dance for you," I said sweetly.

"Promise?"

"Of course." I lifted my head from Dad's shoulder and kissed Danny's cheek.

Danny brought his mouth to my ear. "I can't wait," he whispered, a big grin on his face.

I shuddered from his nearness and blushed. Danny laughed. "Later for you, mister. My dance partner is waiting."

Danny kissed the top of my head and left us.

I returned to Dad, my head once more against his shoulder.

"Daddy?"

"Yes, Leelee."

"Leelee! You haven't called me that since…"

"…about the last time you called me Daddy." We both laughed.

"I don't know. Sometimes I like feeling like a little girl. I suddenly think I'm growing up too quickly, and I want to stop time."

"Danny?"

"I love Danny."

"But? I hear a but coming, Elizabeth."

"There's no but," I said with certainty. I sighed. Maybe Dad was right.

Maybe there was a but. I lacked the words to describe my exact emotions.

"Stop me when I make a mistake," Dad began. "You love Danny, but you weren't prepared for the intensity. He gave you a ring, honey."

"It's not that kind of ring."

"Still, it's a ring. Now you're thinking, maybe things are going faster than you feel comfortable with. You're only nineteen."

"Dad! There will never be anyone else for me."

"I agree." I gave Dad a pleased smile. "Still, I think you want a slower pace. More time to be boyfriend and girlfriend before graduating to fiancée."

"I don't know. I like that 'f' word," I grinned.

"Of course you do, Cinderella."

"Dad!"

"Your relationship with Danny is operating in some sort of hyper-drive. Slow it down, honey. You love each other and that's terrific. But this wasn't your plan. You imagined yourself graduating, getting a job, and moving into your own house. Independence and personal success are important to you."

"You're right, Daddy. What am I to do?"

"You and Danny will be apart this summer. There will be plenty of time for you to think. But keep this in mind; no matter your decision, twenty years from now will you regret not having gone the other way?"

"You don't want me to be a frustrated forty year old thinking 'what if?'"

"Exactly. Danny wants to rent a place with you in the fall. Don't do it unless you're absolutely certain you won't regret not having had a bachelorette pad first."

I nodded, understanding his point. At the very least, Dad gave me fodder to focus my thoughts on. "Dad, Steve promoting Danny's film changes things. Every girl in L.A. will be after him."

"Not when they see the beautiful woman Danny already lives with."

"If he still wants me when I come home."

"Elizabeth! Danny is crazy in love with you."

"He is," I agreed.

"This summer will be good for him, too. He needs to know, you both need to know, that he can stay sober without having you as a crutch."

"We've discussed that. So even you think I'm a crutch?"

Dad nodded. "Elizabeth, Danny knows when he's with you he's safe. He's secure. That's good. That's how it should be. This summer will be a test. Is he secure enough when he's not with you?"

"I hope so."

"I do too. I don't want you saddled with a substance abuser. It's been hell for Ellen. Danny, too."

"I won't be," I said confidently. "Danny's spending the summer in therapy. He's very motivated."

"I want you to be right, Elizabeth. I love Danny."

Later, I danced with Danny. He held me close. His strength pulsating through me so powerfully my heart raced.

Danny tightened his grip around my waist. My breath was taken away as he dipped me low, and bent down to plant a languorous kiss on my lips. I gasped. My head spun. Would Danny always have this effect on me? I hoped so.

Danny held me impossibly close. His hands sandwiched my face, and again his eyes twinkled fiercely. I looked at him with dreamy, drunken eyes.

"When can we go?" I asked in an urgent whisper.

"Soon," Danny kissed me again. His passion left me wobbly kneed. I couldn't stay on my feet any longer.

"I'm so wasted," I whispered.

"You look it too, babe," Danny smiled.

"Yeah," I answered, and I smiled. More shivers coursed through me. I had to fight the urge to jump into Danny's arms and rip off all my clothes.

"I want you so badly," I answered dreamily in a love-clouded haze. I was so aroused.

"I know, baby. I want you too."

I pulled Danny to me, and this time I kissed him, my tongue begging entrance to explore his mouth. Massive bolts of electricity shot through me. I was on fire, and Danny grinned, his eyes filled with overpowering lust.

"E, time to ditch the parents."

Ditching our parents was easier said than done. At the table, Danny perched me on his lap again. He held me firmly around my hips, his hands resting on my thighs. I was practically panting.

Much to my chagrin, Danny then became engrossed in conversation with Dad and Steve. I desperately wanted to leave, and they had him discussing business. What had been a minor student film two hours earlier, had been co-opted by the two masters. They were brainstorming turning it into an Oscar contender. And Danny was eating it up. This was exactly the positive attention from Steve that he had always craved.

I tried paying attention to the men's conversation, but I wasn't succeeding. Any strategizing regarding Danny's career was in effect about my future so of course I was interested, but my brain would not focus. I wanted Danny, and I wanted him now!

Whenever Danny leaned forward to speak, his hands pressed against me. Purposely. He kept his lips close to my neck. Danny's breath against my ear made me shiver. My arousal was impossible to ignore. Mom sent a scowl in my direction. She recognized it too. If we didn't leave soon, I would explode.

I turned my head and quickly kissed Danny's warm lips. Can we go? Please?

Danny nodded and whispered in my ear, "Soon, Eli." Then he kissed my neck, and that made my head spin all over again. Danny settled his chin into my shoulder, and hugged me tighter, bringing an excited grin to my face.

"We can talk in the morning," Steve said.

Before they left for home, we were meeting our parents for brunch.

"You kids look like you want to leave," he added.

I turned scarlet because it was true.

"Steven!" Dad scolded sharply.

"Michael, the way they're carrying on, it's obvious."

I buried my face against Danny's chest.

"Dad, you're embarrassing Elizabeth," Danny admonished.

"Why? You're living together. You gave Elizabeth a ring." Steve leaned forward. "Now go. Take her home. We'll see you in the morning."

CHAPTER EIGHTY-ONE - ELIZABETH

Two weeks later, Danny and I settled into the Gulfstream for our trip home, so similar, yet so different from the same flight just weeks ago. Now our relationship was solid and we were secure in its stability. I grinned in joyous anticipation. Home! Yes!

As we prepared for take off, Danny held my left hand and twirled my ring. As soon as the door to the limo closed, speeding us away from Donnelly, he had insisted on moving my ring to my left hand.

It may have taken seemingly forever before Danny could commit, but now that he had taken the ultimate plunge, he wanted to tell everyone.

After moving my ring, Danny took my hands in his. Fierce sapphire eyes met timid emeralds. "Elizabeth, from this moment forward we are on."

Then he delicately lifted my chin. Those deep sapphires twinkled at me, so full of love. My resistance melted away. Danny's lips found mine, and with tender sweetness, his slow kiss left my heart racing and my head spinning.

During the last two weeks I had engaged in much soul searching. Many times I replayed my conversation with Dad. I had spent my youth envisioning a future where I would assert my independence by working and living on my own. I had spent even more years fantasizing about a future with Danny. The two were contradictory. Trying to reconcile them resulted in turmoil.

Which choice would leave me with regrets when I was forty? Dad begged me to consider the long-term.

That kiss in the limo sealed my fate. Danny's love was undeniable. All at once I knew with certainty what I wanted. To hell with living on my own! To experience Danny's love every day was what I wanted. Not living with him is what I would regret when I was forty.

I would not be trapped in a gilded cage. I could assert my independence with Danny, not apart from him. We were both trying to free ourselves from powerful parents. We would do it together.

I enthusiastically kissed Danny back, all doubts removed. "I'm yours," I whispered, brimming with excitement. "We're on."

Smiling broadly, Danny held my face against his. He kissed me again, even more enthusiastically.

"You are my life, Elizabeth."

"And you are mine, Daniel."

After one more kiss, Danny stretched his long legs out on the adjacent bench seat and I leaned back against him. His arm around my shoulders held me protectively close. Content in the life I had chosen.

We touched down at Santa Monica Airport shortly before nine at night after a long, exhausting day. Our luggage was loaded into the waiting limo while Danny and I settled in for the drive to my parents' house. My brain was so fuzzy from sleep-deprivation. All I wanted was to crawl into bed.

Morning would come, and Flora would have breakfast prepared exactly the way I liked it. And my shower, with its rainhead and multiple wall-mounted jets, was waiting to caress me with pulsating power. Or maybe I'd take a bath. Yes, that's what I'd do! They didn't have Bain Ultra tubs in the dorm. Nirvana – a good bed, good food, and a hot whirlpool bath!

I was jarred from my reverie when the driver entered the westbound Santa Monica Freeway instead of jogging over to Twenty-Sixth Street to reach San Vicente. That didn't make any sense. Maybe I'd missed something. I was so tired.

"This isn't the way," I complained.

"Yes, it is," Danny smiled.

Now I understood, and it brought a smile to my lips. It was so like Danny.

"You want to prolong the drive," I remarked, and then yawned.

"E, wake-up," he laughed, "we're going to **our** house."

"Our house? We're going to Malibu?" I gushed, instantly awake.

"Where else would we be going? We live there, Elizabeth."

I yawned. "I didn't think. A dorm isn't really living together."

"That's why we'll get our own place next year."

"We will?"

"Boy, you really are tired," Danny laughed.

I shrugged with as much amused enthusiasm as my weary self could muster. "I can't wait to get home."

"You mean it, Eli?"

"You know how much I love living with you at the beach. Remember last time?"

Danny grinned at the fresh memory. "I certainly do, balcony girl."

I giggled, and flushed. "But what about my mother?"

"I sent Mike an email yesterday."

"Email, huh?" I raised an eyebrow.

"I wimped," Danny laughed. "I didn't want to risk the wrath of Randi by calling. What if she'd answered the phone instead of Mike?"

"Add this to your summer to-do list."

"Another fence to mend with Randi."

"Yep. Too bad Malibu Lumber isn't a lumberyard anymore. You need supplies."

"As long as I have you, who cares?" Danny answered, and he leaned in to kiss me once again, slipping his hand between my thighs.

CHAPTER EIGHTY-TWO - DANIEL

"Harlan wants to meet you tomorrow," I told Eli a couple of days later while I set the table for dinner.

I knew Elizabeth wouldn't be thrilled, but her reaction was unexpected. A fork fell from her fingers and loudly crashed against the pickled hardwood floor. Her eyes filled with apprehension.

"Baby?" I asked as I stopped in mid-stride.

"Harlan wants to see me? Why?"

I placed two large dinner plates on the table. Then I crossed the room to Eli at the kitchen counter. Picking up large maple-wood tongs, she tossed a chef salad in a sizable matching bowl. I gathered her into my arms and she dropped the tongs into the bowl.

"He's met my folks. Now it's your turn. Harlan wants to meet my entire family. Especially my most important family member."

Eli frowned. I kissed the top of her head, an attempt to comfort her. I didn't understand her apprehension. I wasn't suggesting she become his patient too, though that probably wasn't a bad idea.

Eli cautiously lifted her head from my shoulder. She seemed so small. "I'm scared," she tentatively admitted. "What if Harlan doesn't like me?"

"That's preposterous." I summoned all my control not to laugh. The result was a snarky grin I tried hard to remove from my face. The effort hurt my ribs.

"Of course he'll like you. Everybody likes you. You're the best part of my life."

"That doesn't mean Harlan will like me," Elizabeth protested.

"Who cares?" I declared. "All that matters is that I love you."

CHAPTER EIGHTY-THREE - ELIZABETH

The next morning an appointment in Beverly Hills with jeweler Sarah Reid tempered my emotions. The moment we entered the tan stucco-covered building housing her shop on Robertson Boulevard, all thoughts of impending doom vanished.

Harlan doesn't have to like me, I thought smugly. Danny's love was undeniable. We were ring shopping.

Danny had already informed Ms. Reid that no design decisions were being made today. This was just an opportunity for the designer to meet her clients.

"Elizabeth's going to Israel for the summer. We'll have plenty of time to complete the design while she's away," Danny explained.

He made clear his intent on participating in the process, insuring that I would love the end result.

Then Ms. Reid carefully sized my finger. She visually examined my hand, and the overall size and shape of my fingers. Danny and I were shown settings, some simple, others quite the opposite. I modeled all different shapes and sizes of diamonds. I hoped they picked up on my hints as to which I preferred. But would Ms. Reid find my fingers too petite to accommodate the rock I'd always dreamed of?

In the end, Danny and Ms. Reid successfully kept poker faces; exactly as Danny intended. I hadn't a clue what my ring would look like.

After lunch nearby at The Ivy, we arrived at the office of Dr. Harlan Rivers. As one of the few people I knew who had never been to a psychiatrist, in Hollywood kids get assigned to one practically at birth, I was especially anxious. I didn't know what to expect or what my role at this meeting was.

Danny had dressed casually enough in jeans and a red Burberry-plaid cotton shirt. He did not tuck the shirt in and had cuffed the sleeves above his elbow. I followed his lead wearing a short, casual skirt topped by a conservative white cotton blouse with small pearl buttons and eyelet trim at the short-sleeves and waist.

Despite its comfortable leather furnishings, I was too antsy to take a seat in the waiting room. Instead, I stood facing Danny who held my hands. His warm smile was reassuring.

Soon, a pleasant man in his thirties, and dressed like a college professor, in jeans and an oxford shirt, entered the room. Dr. Rivers approached with a warm, genuine smile on his face. Danny slid his hands out from mine and moved to my side. He placed one hand behind my back and let it rest protectively on my waist. A smile lit his face.

"Good afternoon, Danny," the doctor said cheerfully.

"Harlan, I'd like you to meet my lady, Elizabeth."

Danny's exuberant introduction made me feel shy. I cringed, clenching my hands into fists at my side.

More than an office, we followed Dr. Rivers into a spacious living space containing several conversational seating areas. A cozy fabric-covered couch with throw pillows in contrasting muted shades predominated the room. Catty-cornered, two over-stuffed armchairs completed the central seating area. A glass-topped coffee table held a silver tray with a carafe of water and three crystal glasses.

To the left stood the doctor's elegant cherry-wood desk with a matching credenza against the wall behind it. Facing the desk were two gray leather chairs. Another area of the office held a round glass-topped table, large enough for a family session with five of the same leather chairs encircling it and room for several more. Lastly, another leather chair sat beside a fully reclining club chair. No matter your preference, there was a seating area to make you comfortable.

Danny guided me to the couch. As we sat down, he placed a pillow behind my back. I was too small to sit against the backrest without being swallowed-up by the deep seat.

Dr. Rivers took the chair nearest Danny. I clutched Danny's hand, and he rubbed my fingers. He was smiling, pleased to have his doctor meet me.

"Elizabeth, this is a safe environment. Feel free to say whatever's on your mind or to ask me any questions." Dr. Rivers spoke in a soft, well-articulated voice that soothed my nerves. Temporarily. I nodded my understanding.

I looked into Danny's magnetic blue eyes, took a deep breath, and figured I ought to say something. That was why we were here.

"Dr. Rivers," I stammered, "Danny knows…" I took another deep breath, afraid to get to the heart of the matter. "I'm afraid you won't like me."

"Elizabeth, I am not here to judge you."

I let out my breath, relieved.

"You're not my patient. Danny is. I don't have to like you. Danny says he loves you, and you're important in his life. That's good enough for me. I wanted to meet you because my patient wanted me to. I'll determine whether anything about you would adversely impact Danny's recovery."

I sat stunned by the doctor's frankness. Never before had anyone told me it didn't matter whether or not they liked me. Danny's eyes opened wide, angry.

"Harlan. Eli is my fiancée. She's a great influence on me."

"All I care about is Danny getting better," I added.

"I'm sure you do," Dr. Rivers said in a flat tone that left me unsure as to whether or not he believed me. "Elizabeth," he continued, now leaning toward me, "How will you react the first time you want to get wasted at a party, and Danny can't join you?"

My eyes narrowed in disdain. "Relieved," I answered immediately. "I hate when Danny gets wasted. It's like I'm his nurse. I have to keep Danny safe, hold his hand while he barfs, and put him to bed. But you asked about me. I don't get wasted."

"Yeah," Danny agreed. "Harlan, Eli doesn't party. I got her drunk on champagne our first night together. Eli got so sick, she was afraid it would end up being our last night too. Then the one time she did get wasted. Eli turned into a wild woman. If I hadn't stopped her…" Danny grinned at the memory.

My cheeks flamed. "Danny, you're embarrassing me." I seethed. Why did he have to bring up that night? Was that part of the therapeutic process? You revealed it all, even at the expense of your loved ones?

Danny kissed my knuckles. "I'm sorry, baby. Harlan needs to understand in no uncertain terms that you are not a party girl." He turned toward the doctor. "I would never be engaged to her if she were. Eli wants me sober and has for a long time."

"You've told me as much," Harlan replied. "I wanted to see Elizabeth's reaction."

I frowned. "Did I pass the test?" I asked sarcastically.

"Of course you did," Danny answered

We looked at the doctor expectantly, waiting for his approval. Instead he smiled, but at the same time, he looked grim.

"As I said, this isn't about whether I like you. Elizabeth, it's about how you'll influence my patient."

Harlan adjusted his body, directly addressing me again. "Elizabeth, Danny already knows my opinion. For the sake of his recovery, I would prefer that he had no fiancée living with him. Danny needs stability. The rockiness of your relationship makes it anything but."

I stared at Danny, horrified. Tears welled in my eyes. Were we here so the doctor could do Danny's dirty work? I turned back to the doctor, outraged.

"You want us to break up?" I exclaimed. "Danny, do you want that too?"

"No, baby. Of course not," Danny answered immediately.

"Calm down, Elizabeth. Danny already told me you're not negotiable."

I looked at Danny, relieved by his warm smile. He placed his hand gently against my face.

"Baby, I've already told Harlan. We are rock solid."

I pressed his hand and nodded.

"We are. Then why does Dr. Rivers think that we're not?"

"Danny's told me your history as a couple. Elizabeth, he's not always been a good boyfriend."

I turned directly toward the doctor again, thoughts of our visit to Sarah Reid at the forefront.

"Danny is an amazing fiance," I spat out. "He is my best friend and the love of my life. Danny treats me with respect and kindness. He's always there for me. I trust him with my life. Danny loves me, and I love him."

"Bravo! Your parents must be so proud. Danny sounds like the perfect mate," Dr. Rivers said sarcastically. "Except for three major flaws that you're ignoring: too many drugs, too much drinking, and I'll let you ponder the last one. It's usually a deal breaker for most woman."

I knew exactly what Dr. Rivers was alluding to. I leaned forward, hiding my head in my knees, thoroughly embarrassed. Our dirty laundry was just that; ours. How dare he!

Dr. Rivers made our past problems sound much worse than they were. But maybe they really had been that bad. I didn't know. It was different when you were the one living through it.

Danny's gentle fingers rubbing my back gave me assurance that it was safe to utter the last unspoken flaw. I lifted my head and sheepishly stared at Dr. Rivers as he waited for me to complete his sentence.

Very quickly I rattled off, "Danny sometimes slept with other women."

Humiliated, I couldn't look at Danny. The old pain had bubbled up from where it had lain dormant since we'd reconciled. I felt nauseated.

"How did that make you feel?" Dr. Rivers asked.

"How do you think?" I snapped. "Terrible, of course."

"But you stayed with Danny?"

"The first time, I was in shock. Danny warned me on our first date that he wasn't ready for the level of commitment I desired. I naïvely chose to ignore his warning. When I learned he'd cheated, Danny felt awful. Then he gave me his room key. Nobody cheats on a girl who has their room key."

"I thought so too," Danny said sadly.

I smiled at him. "Hey, it's in the past," I whispered.

"Danny did it again, and yet you stayed with him."

"So many weeks had passed. In the interim Danny had changed, or so I thought. He said he considered us married. My heart told me it would never happen again."

"But your heart was wrong."

No! No! No! I did not want to go there. I quivered. Tears spilled down my face. The whole Danny-Steve-Vanessa triangle was beyond painful. It was raw; gut-wrenching.

"Harlan, this is too difficult for Eli," Danny said firmly. "Don't make her re-live this. It's in the past."

Danny gathered me into his strong arms to soothe me. I twisted free, violently dislodging him. I did not want Danny touching me.

"That was the worst time of my life." I reached for a tissue from the box on the table. "Danny cheated, but he broke up with me."

"It was a hiatus," Danny interrupted.

"You broke up with me, Daniel," I scowled. "His indiscretions were too painful for him to face me."

I started crying again, loudly sobbing, doubled over in grief I thought I was long past. It was as though a knife was twisting in my heart.

"Baby, it's okay," Danny said in a soothing voice while he rubbed my back.

"Maybe it's not," I wailed. "I've forgiven you, Danny, but I haven't forgotten. As long as we don't discuss it, I can pretend, but the minute it comes up… The hurt is raw, and it's powerful. I don't want it to be, but it is."

"E, we've been through this," Danny pleaded. "We've been open and shared it all. I thought you wanted to be past this and go forward."

"I do. But it still hurts. Especially hearing someone else say it."

Danny gently wiped my tears with his thumb.

"Elizabeth, why did you reconcile with Danny?"

"It was a long process. Danny wanted me back within a week of our initial breakup. A movie night with our friends turned into a date. I was happy for a couple of days. But Danny wouldn't make me the promises I wanted."

"And those were?" Dr. Rivers asked, though I was certain he knew the answer.

"The promise to settle down and stop cheating."

I dabbed my eyes with the tissue already moist from my tears.

"I couldn't do it. I wasn't ready." Danny sounded so sad. "I was so messed up after Vancouver. I wanted Eli more than anything. But she deserved better."

I buried my face in my hands and quietly wept. Danny put his arms around me.

"Baby, don't cry. You have better now, much better. I've given you the most powerful promise I can," he said while fingering my ring.

I nodded. "You have," I whispered.

I lifted my head, and Danny's sapphire eyes twinkled.

"We didn't talk again until late January, my birthday," he told Dr. Rivers.

"Danny came to my room on his birthday. I was shocked to see him. I let him get me wasted, and he spent the night. In the morning, he told me he had never stopped loving me. After all that time, Danny wanted us back together. He said we could be like we used to be. But I couldn't. I wanted more."

"Danny, how did you feel?"

"Disappointed, but I respected Eli's decision. She was right."

"But two months later you're living together?"

I took Danny's hand, and I smiled.

"We never stopped loving each other, Dr. Rivers."

"No, we never did," Danny agreed, and he kissed the top of my fingers. I felt the warmth of his love flow through my arm to my heart.

"Steve came to Donnelly to take Danny to New York for the weekend. Before they left, he invited me to dinner for when they returned. It wasn't optional. You don't say no to Steve Newman." Then I blushed. "Well, maybe I wanted to see Danny, too."

Danny grinned as he kissed my knuckles again.

"After dinner, Danny came to my room, sober. He said he had all intention of us both staying that way. Then I learned the purpose of Steve's visit, an intervention. I also learned the truth about last summer."

"We stayed up most of the night talking," Danny added.

"By the time we fell asleep," I told Dr. Rivers, "We had decided on a trial reconciliation."

Danny squeezed my knee, and we exchanged smiles.

"I could finally make the promises Eli deserved. Then we came home for the weekend, and that cemented things."

I grinned. "We were whole again," I added.

"And then I took you to New York."

Danny took my hands, and we smiled into each other's eyes.

"And you proposed!"

"And we couldn't be happier."

Danny pulled me into his arms. Our lips met for a brief kiss.

"Harlan, I can't live without this lady. She's my inspiration. I trust her with my life. Eli only wants what's good for me."

"I have high expectations for this man."

"And I plan on living up to them. I don't want to ever disappoint you again."

"I believe you, Daniel." I kissed his cheek.

"If only you weren't going away for the summer," Danny sad sadly.

"How do you feel about that, Danny?" Harlan asked.

"I'm not happy. I don't want Eli to go."

"It will be good," I assured him. "I need to know I can succeed on my own. And you need to work on yourself and your summer job. You'll have no distractions."

"No!" Danny shouted. He jumped up. First, he looked at me, fire in his eyes, then he turned to Dr. Rivers. "Harlan, it will not be good for me."

Usually I enjoy waking on Saturday because Saturday morning invariably follows an amazing Friday night. But today was different. I lay in bed watching Danny sleep. He looked so peaceful as his chest constricted and expanded with every breath. It would be my last opportunity until August. I would be heartbroken if I squandered it.

Even with his eyes closed, I felt the magnetic power of Danny's sapphire eyes. He was more handsome than ever with his shaggy mane framing his face. Danny knew how sexy I found this longer length, and he had put off cutting his hair until later today. Monday Danny's internship would begin.

Monday. The thought hit me with powerful sadness. Monday followed Sunday, and I was leaving tomorrow. My eyes welled up. I wouldn't be here on Monday. Danny's first day at TAG, and he would wake up alone. There would be no morning kisses or love making. I would not be smoothing Danny's shirt collar, or serving him breakfast, before sending him off in his Porsche. I smiled. No intern would be driving a nicer car.

My smile rapidly collapsed into a frown, as I considered all that I would miss. Danny would come home ready to share the highlights of his day, and I wouldn't be here. He couldn't even call me when he got home. It would be three in the morning in Israel!

I didn't have to feel them to know tears were falling down my face. How selfish. If I was depending on Danny to be my rock, and keep my spirits buoyed until take-off, who would be his rock? It had to be me. Danny needed me to be the strong one, more than I needed him to be it for me. Afterall, I was the one leaving, and as I had learned last summer, it was much more difficult to be the one left behind.

For now I would focus on the sculpted chest rhythmically going up and down. The blanket barely covered any part of Danny's body, an indication of a night of restless sleep. I would imprint this vision in my brain. It would have to stay with me for the next ten weeks.

Ten weeks! Tears welled-up again. I needed to prevent their spilling. There was only one solution. I slid over and pressed my bare front against his. Involuntarily Danny wrapped his arms around my waist as my arms went around his neck. I brought my lips to his sleepy ones. Danny's immediate response filled me with sweetness. Sleepy sapphires opened and twinkled. He instantly became hard against my thigh. I grinned. Danny knew exactly what I wanted.

In the warm cocoon provided by Danny's embrace, silence enveloped us. Deep in thought, I could only imagine what he was thinking as he held me dearly. Probably the mirror image of my thoughts.

I turned my head ever so slightly and noted sadness hiding behind his lovely smile. Danny was trying to keep this Saturday normal, but it was anything but. Guilt that I was hurting him forced me to turn so my back nestled against his front, his arms still around me. My head tucked against the pillow, tears spilled. My face became a wet mess.

Danny's embrace tightened. More tears. I tried so hard to control myself, but couldn't. I shook.

"Baby, don't cry," his gentle, love-filled voice pleaded.

"I'm not crying," I lied, my voice quivering.

"Yes, you are. Your whole body is trembling, babe."

I sniffled loudly. Then, my secret out, I buried my head against Danny's chest and sobbed.

"E, don't cry, baby. Don't cry," he whispered while stroking my back.

"I'm going to miss you so much. It's not like you can visit me on weekends."

"No, I can't do that. And I'm just as unhappy as you are. Eli, this is our last day together for a long time. I don't want it ruined by tears. Let's make a good memory."

After spending the morning on the beach, I packed most of the clothes I had brought from Donnelly. We were stopping at my parents' house before taking Danny for his haircut. Flora would unpack and press everything. When we returned I would decide what to take to Israel.

At the beach, I had delicately brought up the topic of Danny's summer residency.

"I want you living in Brentwood," I said firmly. "I don't want you here alone."

"Are you afraid I'll pick up some girl at the beach and bring her home?" he teased.

I looked directly in his sapphire eyes and confidently replied.

"Not at all. We've been down that road, and you know as well as I that it's a disaster. And this time I would never forgive you."

"I'd never forgive me too, so you have nothing to worry about."

"I have other things to worry about. I don't want you living alone. Danny, your recovery means you're vulnerable. It's still very early in your recovery. You need a support system. Your parents and Harlan will give you that."

"I hate when you say that. You make it sound like I'm an alcoholic or something."

I raised an eyebrow. "Aren't you?"

"That hurt, Eli. Low blow," Danny protested. "Stop worrying. I've been thinking the same. I don't want to be here without you. Once all our stuff is moved in and we make it our own, and we meet the neighbors, then I could stay alone. We would know Malibu people. It would feel like home. Hell, it would be home."

Neighbors? I had never experienced neighbors. Danny probably hadn't either. We had both grown up in gated fortresses, intimidating estates that screamed, "Stay away! You're not welcome!" because of course, uninvited guests were not at all welcome. Everyone was a potential security risk; even Girl Scouts selling cookies.

We were dining with our parents tonight. After stopping at the Newman's for my now handsomely coiffed love to change from surfer dude to Beverly Hills stud, we would have just over an hour for me to pack and change.

I loved Danny's new haircut. Short at the sides, and sexy rock star long on top, it was incredible that this beautiful man was now even more so. I ran my fingertips through its softness and kissed him before we got out of the car at my parents.

"Hello, dear." Mom greeted me with a peck on the cheek after we entered the house.

"Hi, Randi." Danny leaned down and kissed her unreceptive cheek. At least he was trying to be friendly.

"Daniel," Mom responded icily. "It's about time you brought my daughter home. I was afraid I wasn't going to see her again."

"Mother!" I exclaimed. "You knew where I was, and you knew I was coming by to pack."

"Coming by, Elizabeth? Don't you mean coming home?"

"Sure, whatever," I answered awkwardly.

"Eli, let's go upstairs and get it done," Danny said, and he led me up the staircase.

Danny's idea of helping was to drape his sport coat across the chair back, stretch out on the bed, and give his approval or disapproval to my selections.

"Remember, they dress more casually in Israel. You won't need more than a couple of nice things," he instructed

A pattern developed. I might have been reading into it, but the plainer more ordinary items were "perfect" according to Danny, whereas the feminine fabrics and prints that he liked to see me wear were deemed, "too dressy."

Frustration mounted. When Danny again said "no," as I folded my favorite silk peasant blouse, I snapped.

"Nobody asked for your opinion, Daniel. I know how to pack," I barked.

Danny put his fingers up to his lips and cautioned, "Shh. Come here."

I walked over and sat down facing him. Danny pointed to the door my mother had insisted we keep open. Mom was treating us like high school kids.

Danny took my hands. "We're both under a lot of stress. Let's not give Randi reason to gloat," he said in a near whisper.

I leaned forward and stretched out. Lying down in his arms, sadness returned. I blinked hard to keep tears back, but some managed to escape. Danny's arms wrapped around me. He tried soothing me.

"E, no tears. I want every head in the restaurant to turn when you walk in tonight. It's my last chance to show the world that my fiancée is the most beautiful girl in Los Angeles. Red eyes won't do."

I smiled at Danny, not wanting to disappoint him.

"Okay. One beautiful, smiling fiancée for the evening. I'll cry later when we get home."

"That's my girl," he smiled, and then gently pressed his lips against mine.

Danny's kiss deepened, while he tightened his embrace. He ran his fingertips up and down my thigh, his hand finally settling on my rear. Each time we would stop to breathe, Danny would kiss me again. My heart fluttered. My head felt light. No sadness now. The pleasure of the moment was too intense.

A knock on the door abruptly interrupted us. Danny and I forcibly unlocked our lips. I felt the heat rise in my cheeks as I saw who was at the door.

"How's the packing going?" Mom asked calmly as though she had found me filling a suitcase. Her nonchalance made me even more uncomfortable about being caught in bed kissing Danny, our bodies curled around each other.

"Mom!" I answered, surprised.

"Hey, Randi," Danny calmly greeted her while keeping me in his embrace.

"How's the packing?" she coldly asked again, completely ignoring Danny.

"Not very well," I answered. "Danny's not a good helper."

"I can see that," she said raising her eyebrow at us.

"Every time I take out something nice, Danny tells me I won't need it."

Mom laughed her low throaty laugh and smirked.

"Danny Newman! You're insecure!"

Now I laughed too. Danny blushed. Spot-on, Mom!

"Miranda!" He hissed, unhappy at being exposed. I giggled, and kissed his cheek.

"I still love you. Even if you are only human," I said.

"Danny, Elizabeth would look good in a burlap sack. There's nothing you can do except trust her."

"A burlap sack? That's an idea."

"A bad one. Too itchy," I retorted.

Mom smiled and sat down on the bed. Danny pulled me over a few inches to make room for her.

"Danny's afraid every man between Tel Aviv and Jerusalem is going to make a play for you."

"That's ridiculous!"

"They want to in Los Angeles," Danny answered drily.

"Not that I've noticed," I declared. "If anyone does, it's because they mistake me for Mom."

"Nobody thinks you're Randi," Danny laughed as he wrapped an arm around my collar, pressed my back against his chest, and rubbed his knuckles against my right temple. "What a knucklehead! Randi, where did you go wrong with her? How does Elizabeth not know that she turns heads wherever she goes?"

"I don't know, Daniel. Guess I did too good a job teaching her to be modest, and have humility," Mom laughed. "Or else it was too many years at an all-girls school."

"That must be it. Blame Archer," Danny laughed.

"Seriously, you're exaggerating Daniel." I was admanent. "Even if you're right, I'm not looking back. Why would I? I'm not interested in anyone but you."

"It's different. Here everybody know's we're together. In Israel…" His voice tailed off wistfully.

"Danny, you have nothing to worry about. Elizabeth loves you, and she's faithful. It's not as though she's going to have a secret fling with an actor."

"Mom!" I exclaimed sharply, angry that Vanessa had been raised for the second time in recent days.

"You know about that?" Danny asked uncomfortably.

"Of course I do," Mom smirked. "I know about everything that affects my daughter, Daniel. Whether you want me to or not."

"And you don't trust me because it's another summer, and Elizabeth and I are apart once again."

"Mom, you're not being fair. I trust Danny. You have to also," I said with urgency.

Danny took my hands and spoke in a soothing voice. "It's okay, Eli. Randi's trying to protect you."

"You're right, Daniel."

"But things have changed," I protested. "You've changed, Danny."

"I know it, and you know it. Randi loves you, and she doesn't want you to get hurt again. It's going to take time, but I'm prepared for that."

"You understand my concern given your history and where you're working."

"Yes, Randi. But my plan is to be the hardest working boy in Hollywood. I have a reputation to build. And when Eli comes home, I want her to be proud."

"I believe you Danny, but we'll see," Mom answered. Then she noticed the clock on the nightstand and stood up.

"Elizabeth, get dressed. We're leaving in ten minutes."

"Mom, after dinner will you help me pack?"

"I'd be happy to," she answered as Danny and I stood. "Danny, come downstairs so Elizabeth isn't distracted. We're short on time."

He reached for his sports coat from the chair and left with Mom. As I returned to the closet. I heard Mom say, "I'm rooting for you, Daniel."

CHAPTER EIGHTY-FOUR - ELIZABETH

Danny smoothed the chenille blanket out on our favorite patch of sand; close enough to watch the waves break, far enough back not to get wet when the tide came in. He took my hands and pulled me into his strong arms for a quick kiss that promised more later.

We lowered ourselves onto the blanket. Danny wrapped his arms protectively around my shoulders, drawing my back into his chest. Silence. Tomorrow's separation loomed over us like a thick layer of fog.

In my heart, leaving was the right thing. But the knowledge that I would not be home for ten weeks, sharing my favorite place with the man I loved, saddened me beyond belief. I tried so hard to hide it.

I turned my head toward Danny and smiled weakly. Then I brought myself up to my knees. Cradling Danny's face in my hands, I kissed him long and hard. He smiled, but his joy quickly faded. Danny was incapable of masking his emotions. I slid down to sitting, nestled silently in his arms, Danny's warmth filling me.

Soon I sensed his eyes upon me, and I turned to meet Danny's sad gaze. I gently squeezed his thigh, the only place comfortably within reach. He took my hand and brought it to his lips for a kiss. I gave Danny the best smile I could summon, and squeezed his hand, encouraging him to speak, before time ticked away for us.

Danny gripped my hand, his eyes never leaving mine.

"You don't have to go," he began tentatively. "Nobody would think any less of you for changing your mind, especially now that we're together again."

"I don't want to leave you, but I want to go. Can you understand that?"

"Not really. When you applied for this program you wanted to be as far away from me as possible. I got that. It's not the case anymore." Danny leaned over and gently kissed my lips.

"You were never why I wanted to go. Sure, when I got my acceptance travelling half-way around the world seemed like a great way to finally get over you. But I applied to this program to do something for me, and this still is about me."

"You'd have to go way further than half way around the world, and for much longer than ten weeks, to get over me," he teased.

I giggled. "Probably so." I kissed Danny again.

"We could spend the entire summer here." Danny raised an eyebrow. "You would be my trophy wife!"

"Trophy wife!" I laughed. "You're a little young, Daniel."

Danny smirked. "E, just think, you can work on your tan, and get your nails done. You'll go shopping."

I glared at Danny.

"The gym?"

"Every day?"

"Alternate with yoga and pilates."

"Daniel! I'm not a trophy wife!"

"E, we'd have every night alone. My parents would be thrilled."

"You mean your mother."

"No, Dad, too. I think they love you more than they love me. You never cause them any grief, and they know I'd be safe living with my own personal lifesaver." Danny's eyes pleaded with me.

"You've forgotten my parents. Dad will go along with whatever Mom decides, and you are most definitely still in her doghouse."

"You're nearly twenty. You can do whatever you want."

"They'd cut me off."

"So?"

"I have a $65,000 tuition bill coming due."

"I'll pay it."

"Danny," I said firmly "Your parents will not get in the middle to piss-off mine."

"You're right. I'll be the one pissing them off. Elizabeth, **I** can pay your tuition. I can pay your everything." Danny looked intently into my eyes, "My money. Not Dad's. I'm twenty-one. Trust fund assets transferred to me on my birthday. I have more than enough for us to live on. Hell, I can even buy us this house if you'd like."

Was he nuts? "That's incredibly generous, Danny. But I can't defy my parents."

"And your mother would hate me more."

"Probably. You have a lot to prove with my mother as it is, so don't make it worse. I want us all seated around the same table at Thanksgiving."

"Agreed. I'll work on it this summer. I don't like being persona non gratis with Randi. I have a long way to go toward earning her trust back, but I will."

"You will," I agreed, and I smoothed a lock of hair off Danny's forehead. "Although Mom still hopes I'll come home and be over you."

"You better not. I hear women find those dark-haired Sabre types very sexy," Danny teased, and he traced my lips with his fingertip.

"I like my men blue-eyed and with sandy-colored hair."

"You do?" I laughed at the obvious. "You do," Danny agreed, and he kissed me.

"You're the wallpaper, on all my devices. Every time I log on there you'll be, even if it's the middle of the night here." I said.

Danny kissed me again. "You've been my wallpaper all year. Phone too."

"I have?" He never failed to surprise me. To think, even when we weren't talking, Danny had put me front and center in his life. He was such a complicated man.

Danny playfully kissed my nose. "It really pissed-off Phoebe," Danny smirked.

"Sucked for her. No wonder she tried to kill you." I laughed. "I can't imagine sleeping with a guy, and his ex is plastered all over his devices. You are such a cad."

"I'm your cad," Danny grinned. "You only find that funny because you were the ex."

"Not anymore, I'm not."

"Yeah, not anymore, or ever." Danny pushed me down on the blanket, our lips joined. His love transmitted so powerfully, it almost hurt. Our hands were all over each other. My head spun. I could barely breathe. Danny's heart beat rapidly against my chest. Mine kept pace.

"I recently updated your photo," he whispered.

"To which one?"

"The balcony."

"The one where I'm looking at you, and I'm thinking how badly I want to make love to you?"

"Yeah, that one," Danny grinned "And you're giving me that same look now."

At ten o'clock at night the beach was deserted, with the sky dark except for the moon, and its reflection off the Pacific. I flashed Danny my wickedest smile and pushed the hook on the waistband of his shorts open.

Later, Danny smoothed my skirt, and we lay quietly in each other's arms trading soft kisses and gentle touches.

"Elizabeth, this is killing me. You tell me all the time how much you love me, and you certainly show it. I can't understand why you're leaving tomorrow."

"It's not about us. I've told you, it's about me. I have issues."

"So do I. But I'm not leaving the country to solve them. You could stay right here and spend the summer in analysis."

"I don't need analysis. I understand what my issues are, including having a pig-headed boyfriend who won't shut up long enough for me to get a word in."

Stunned by my outburst, Danny fell silent.

"Thank you," I smiled sweetly. "When I returned to Donnelly last August everyone was discussing their summer jobs. No matter what they did, they had real employers. But what had I done?"

"When you weren't visiting your adoring boyfriend in Vancouver?"

"Yes. When I wasn't being made an international fool."

"You weren't an international fool. I was. You were a junior executive for one of the largest production companies in Hollywood, a job most kids would die for."

"It sounds so much more impressive when you say it."

"Elizabeth, it was impressive. Mike told Dad what an asset you were. Everyone at J4 respected you. They saw how hard you worked."

"Who told you this?"

"Jacobs-Newman golf classic. Eighteen holes of Dad talk."

"Oh."

"You felt inadequate because your boss was named Jacobs."

I shook my head. "Not until I returned to Donnelly. Working for Dad was great. I would gladly do it again." I paused. "Dad understands, and so should you. I need to get out of the cocoon. Didn't you experience the same working for Steve?"

"Maybe I felt self-conscious, especially the first week, but never inadequate. I worked twice as hard, and put in longer hours than any other P.A. Everyone realized how serious I was, and they forgot who I was."

Danny smiled at me and brushed his lips against mine.

"Of course, then Miranda Jordan's drop-dead gorgeous daughter would fly in on her Gulfstream, and expect to be taken to the best restaurants and hottest clubs. I was the only P.A. whose photo made the Vancouver Sun. That rather blew my cover."

"Sorry," I shrugged. I smiled at the memory of the concert we had attended. The photo featured us backstage chatting with the headliner.

Danny lifted my chin and gazed into my eyes. "There were some perks I was not going to give up." Danny kissed me again.

"When Grandma suggested I go to Israel for the summer, I laughed. Typical Grandma, trying to inject religion in my life," I explained. "Then I learned of this program. It seemed perfect; a place where nobody would know my name. I would simply be Elizabeth Jacobs, an ordinary American college student spending the summer abroad, getting in touch with her heritage. Even if we're miserable, I need to know I can succeed on my own."

Danny smirked. Then he tenderly put his hand on my cheek and turned my face toward his.

"Elizabeth, I understand. I did the same, sort of."

"You did?" I sat up, intrigued to learn something new about Danny.

"Dad didn't know I'd applied to TAG until after they accepted me. I purposely chose TAG because he's not their client. I used my Donnelly address on my resume so they wouldn't suspect. I even interviewed at TAG's New York office because everyone recognizes me in Beverly Hills."

Danny never failed to surprise me. I was so impressed. It was comforting to learn we had yet another thing in common. "You're sure nobody knows it's you?"

"I can't be certain, but I've done everything possible." Then Danny gave me a devilish grin. "I even ditched my glamorous girlfriend," he laughed. Then he tickled me.

"Daniel!" I laughed, squirming from his teasing. "They'll figure out who you are on Monday."

"Probably, but they'll respect me for trying to distance myself from Dad."

"I'm proud of you, Danny. It's difficult to get those internships. You took a chance, and they saw your merits. Your hard work at Donnelly paid off."

"Thanks, babe. I'm proud of you too. But couldn't you have picked a program closer to home?"

"It's better this way. I'm almost twenty years old, and I've spent my entire life sheltered. I've never had to develop decision-making skills. If I screw up, my name or influence saves me."

"You never screw up. You make great decisions. Every day. I've seen you."

"It seems more like luck than ability. I don't trust myself. I don't trust people. I'm sure you've noticed, I have the smallest inner circle of anyone."

"I've noticed."

"It's not that I wouldn't like more friends, but I don't trust my ability to distinguish between those who are genuine and those who may want something. I wish I had your confidence."

"Being wary isn't a bad thing."

"I'm beyond wary. I border on paranoia. It started in nursery school. Mothers were trying to insinuate their children into my lives. If they learned what dance class I enrolled in, or sport I was doing, they would join too."

"It could have been coincidental."

"Daniel!"

"Okay, if you say so."

"It was suspicious. Their fathers worked in the industry."

"That's scary. Soccer moms stalking a four year old," Danny laughed.

"It wasn't funny. We were very careful with divulging my interests after that."

"At Donnelly you're not this secretive."

"That's why I chose Donnelly. There's more diversity. As long as I stay away from film students..."

Danny chuckled. "Which is why both your best friend and your fiancée are film students. That makes perfect sense for someone trying to stay away from film students."

"Rachel, I trust. She is the most ethical person I've ever met. And you, well you're you. I don't count you as a film student. You're you."

"And you're you," Danny quickly kissed me. "I never knew you were so insecure, baby."

"I'm not when I'm with you," I answered. "You, I trust completely. I always have."

"I thought that was one of our issues this year. You didn't trust me."

"I didn't trust you as a boyfriend. I always trusted you as a person. Even when we weren't speaking, I knew if something blew up in my face, I could call you, and you'd be by my side before I'd even put the phone down."

"I sure would have been. Rescuing my fair damsel, with pleasure."

"And that's exactly why I have to go. I need to stand on my own two feet." Danny leaned over to kiss my hands that he had been holding.

"I don't like it, but I understand. If this trip will give you the confidence you're lacking, then I fully support your decision."

"Thank you," I squealed, and I threw my arms around Danny's neck to kiss him.

"I miss you already."

"Same. But the separation will be good for you too. I'm a distraction."

"I love when you distract me." Danny said, and I smirked.

"I love you so much Daniel, but you are one messed up dude."

"So why do you want me, Elizabeth?" Danny laughed.

"You're an excellent lover," I deadpanned.

"Elizabeth!" I smiled and shrugged. It was fun shocking Danny.

Sleep did not come easily. When today is beautiful and tomorrow is dreaded, what incentive is there to find sleep? Every time I moved, so did Danny. I tossed, he turned, we kissed. We even made love. A bittersweet pattern developed.

By five o'clock, and perhaps with one hour of sleep under our belts, we gave up and lay in each other's arms, afraid to let go. When the alarm we no longer needed sounded, Danny rolled over, groaned, and turned it off. Tomorrow was here.

I didn't see that Danny had reached into the nightstand drawer, until he turned back holding a blue-ribboned white box that screamed, "jewelry."

"A little something to remember me by." Danny forced a smile as he handed me the box.

"Like I could ever forget you?" I tried smiling back. It wasn't happening.

Real smiles were impossible to come by this morning. I untied the ribbon and opened the box. Inside a black case was a wristwatch. It wasn't just any watch. Its oversized face and strap were pink. The bezel was heart-shaped.

The heart was divided in two. The symbolism was not lost on me. Each half of the heart was surrounded by pale pink Swarovski crystals and contained its own timepiece, one side set to Los Angeles, and the other set to Tel Aviv. Whenever I looked at it, I would instantly know what time it was at home.

"It's beautiful," I said, while I lifted the watch out of the box. "Thank you," and I kissed Danny's lips.

"You'll know if I'm awake, but you can call even if I'm not," Danny explained. "You'll know where I'll be."

This time I really did smile, a genuine smile that even touched my eyes. After all the times I hadn't trusted Danny, I enjoyed knowing he would be sleeping in Brentwood every night, at his parents house, alone.

"Come here," he commanded. Danny's sapphire eyes twinkled full force as he smiled back. I returned the watch to the nightstand, leaned into his strong welcoming arms, and sighed.

"I love you, Daniel," I said, as I reached my arms around his neck, and pressed my lips to his. There was no mistaking how badly I wanted this moment to last.

"E, I'm gonna miss you so badly," Danny said breathlessly in between kisses. He held me as close as possible, stroking me, cherishing my softness, and we made love for the last time until August.

Beyond exhausted, we might easily have fallen asleep, but there wasn't time. A shower with Danny tenderly washing me did not bring me back to life.

"E, your eyes!" Danny exclaimed as he toweled dried me. I glanced in the mirror and blinked. Dark circles from lack of sleep surrounded dull green. Ugh!

I turned back to Danny. "Yours are just as bad." His eyes not only had dark circles, they were blood-shot. "We look like emo raccoons!"

Danny chuckled. Then he turned me into his arms and gazed into my eyes. "Hey, I don't care. You're the most beautiful emo raccoon I've ever seen. Don't forget that."

"I'm glad you have that picture of me on the balcony so this isn't what you remember me by."

Danny kissed me again. I'd lost count of how many times he'd done so this morning.

Finally we could avoid it no longer. We had to leave. Heaviness filled my heart as I took one final glance out the patio doors to the ocean beyond. My ocean.

We paused in front of the mural. Starring at the little boy and the little girl playing in the sand, filled my eyes with tears, and I trembled. Danny cradled me in his arms and let me have a good cry.

"Baby, you'll be back soon. I promise," he tried calming me.

This was our private paradise. What was wrong with me? How could I leave?

Danny helped me into the Porsche. Behind my Ray-Bans fresh tears escaped. Before turning on the engine, he leaned over and lifted my chin.

"Babe, we don't have to do this. We can go back inside, cancel your trip, and go to bed."

"You just want to sleep," I teased.

"I'll get mine later. I have nothing else to do today."

"Me too. I have fifteen hours of nothing to do."

Top down, Danny backed out of the garage, and onto Pacific Coast Highway. I inhaled deeply, wanting to imprint on my memory the tangy, salt-laced air that was Malibu. My Malibu. My home. I would miss this place so much. Our time at the beach was always so special. It was all about us. Nobody intruded. Not even our parents.

Danny sensed my wistfulness. He took my hand and smiled.

"Hey, ten weeks is nothing," he said, and kissed my knuckles. "We'll have four weeks when you return. I won't let anyone touch your pillow 'til then."

I involuntarily returned his smile. The beach, our home. It was our home.

Until our left turn up the California Incline, en route to my parents' house for breakfast before leaving for the airport, I kept my eyes peeled on my ocean, almost fearful that I would never see it again.

CHAPTER EIGHTY-FIVE - ELIZABETH

Dad drove us to the airport. Thankfully, Mom remained quiet. I didn't want to talk to her, or be subjected to an anti-Danny barrage. All I wanted was to sit in the back seat of the Mercedes snuggled against Danny, his arm protectively around my shoulders, my hands gripping his free one.

"Elizabeth, put your seatbelt on," Dad admonished.

"I'll take my chances," I answered in a sour voice that matched my mood.

"I'll keep her safe, Mike," Danny said.

Didn't Dad see how miserable I felt? Perhaps making inane conversation was his way of coping. He didn't want me to leave. After being away all year, I had hardly been home. Dad had hoped I'd be working with him again, like last summer. He failed at hiding his disappointment.

Danny read my mind, and my heart. He brought his hand up to my face and kissed me. I kissed him back, deepening the kiss. I didn't care if Dad glanced in the rear-view mirror, or if Mom turned around and snarled. Nothing would keep us apart until we got to airport security.

All too soon we arrived at El Al in the Tom Bradley Terminal. An escort greeted me. I had dressed modestly in a mid-calf length, tiered cotton yellow skirt with a sleeveless white eyelet blouse topped by a lightweight white cardigan. The escort voicelessly approved of my conservative attire.

Now my parents were saying goodbye. Mom embraced me and kissed my cheek.

"Elizabeth, I don't want you worrying about anything at home," she whispered with an eye pointed toward Danny. "This trip is about you. I want you to take advantage of all that's offered and have fun. You've earned it. I love you, sweetheart."

"I love you too, Mom. I'll miss you."

Then Dad folded me into his strong, protective arms. A tear escaped as I clutched him. Tomorrow I should have been reporting to work. With Dad. I couldn't let go of him.

"You're going to have the best time. Don't feel guilty that you're deserting me." I smiled. He'd read my mind. "I know you'll miss Danny, but it will be worse for him, so chin up."

"Thanks, Daddy." My voice shook, betraying my misery.

"Honey, you don't have to do this. Say the word, and I'll get your luggage back. Elizabeth, nobody would think any less of you for changing your mind."

I smiled weakly. "I want to go, but thank you for giving me an out."

I would miss Mom and Dad terribly, but with the schedules they followed, I had been saying goodbye to them for most of my life. In fact, Dad was off to London tomorrow. We kissed, we hugged, and I promised to text when I landed.

The moment I dreaded was here. Danny stood stoically, waiting his turn. I couldn't look directly at him. The dam of tears would burst.

Danny enveloped me in his arms. He held me so close. His heart beat rapidly, but in my grief the familiar shiver was missing. Danny's strong arms always brought me comfort. I clung to him now for support, my head against his chest, afraid to let go. He buried his head against my hair, gently kissing me.

Danny was the brave one. Murmuring, "No tears, Eli, no tears," he lifted my chin. Then he removed my sunglasses, and tucked them into my neckline, touching my skin, his fingers searching for the jewelry I wasn't wearing. Earlier, I had given him my necklaces, mindful that the two Tiffany pieces screamed "American."

"I look awful," I whispered.

"Not to me you don't. Never. I wanted to see your eyes before you go."

"You too," I answered, and I removed Danny's sunglasses. I forced a smile at the sapphires that usually set my head spinning. Today my head wouldn't spin. Danny's eyes were so tired from lack of sleep. They were unfocused too, now that I had removed the sunglasses I had forgotten were prescription.

"I'm blurry, aren't I?" I asked.

"Yeah," Danny smiled, and I placed the sunglasses back on him.

"Better?"

"Much," he answered with a smile. Danny took my hands and fingered my ring. "You be a good girl, Eli."

"Aren't I always?"

"Yes, but I won't be there to keep you out of trouble."

"I'll be fine. You're the only one who ever gets me into trouble. Daniel, you're the one who needs to stay out of trouble. I won't be here to save you."

"No problem, E. I'm going to make you proud. I start work tomorrow and I'll be seeing Harlan three times a week. I plan on spending a lot of time at the gym, too."

"What about Steve?"

Danny had to get the acrimony resolved. "I'll deal with him."

"I know that will be difficult, but I'm with you. Always."

Always? I was leaving. So not always. A few tears trickled out despite my efforts to control them.

"No tears, Eli," Danny said again, and he lifted my chin and kissed me. My hands went around his neck as I deepened the kiss. I wouldn't let go. I didn't want the kiss to end.

"You don't have to go," Danny whispered in my ear, giving me one last chance to back out. His breath made me tingle making this so difficult. I had to remain strong.

"I want to go. I just can't bear leaving you. I hate goodbyes."

"I do too. Promise you'll text me the minute you land."

"I promise."

"And we'll Skype or email everyday."

"I promise."

"I'll miss you so much, babe."

Danny pulled me close again. The warmth, the pressure, the strength of his arms; I concentrated on imprinting them in my memory, ready to recall on demand.

"One more kiss?" I asked timidly.

"For you, anything." Danny smiled warmly before obliging. The sensation of his lips, and his tongue dancing with mine, I would imprint these as well. We couldn't let go of each other.

"I love you so much, Danny Newman."

"I love you too, Elizabeth Jacobs." Danny pressed my ring against the flesh of my finger. "Always," he added and Danny kissed me one last time.

I gathered my inner strength and accompanied the escort through the terminal. Don't look back! It would be too painful. If Danny and my parents caught my eye, the crying would start. Even worse would be the emptiness in my soul if they had already exited.

Surrendering myself to the escort's authority, I followed along through security to the First Class lounge, going through the motions, engaging in the expected pleasantries. We discussed my trip. She recommended places I might enjoy; restaurants, shopping, and culture.

Time to board. At the gate, I thanked the escort for her assistance. Then the upbeat flight attendant showed me to an oversized leather seat, my private home for the next fourteen and a half hours.

I hoped there were some good movies to choose from though I had loaded several favorites onto my laptop. They were my failsafe for combating homesickness. I even included Mom's movies so if I missed her…

Danny and I had made videos for each other, G-rated, because you never knew who might be around when we needed a dose of each other. We were cognizant that with the nine-hour time difference, Skype sessions might be rare. The videos weren't the same as live, but at least it was Danny's voice and face.

"Would you like a glass of champagne?" the flight attendant interrupted my reverie.

Ten minutes until take-off. I had returned to my seat from changing into soft yoga pants, a tee, and socks.

"Yes, thank you," I responded.

I glanced at my new watch. Hm. Eleven at night in Tel Aviv. Sleeping early in the flight would be a good start toward putting my body clock on local time.

I was tired from last night's restlessness, but at the same time, I was wired. Champagne should make me drowsy enough to sleep. The flight attendant would make up my bed once we reached cruising altitude. Then I could stretch out.

As the plane taxied, I stared out the window. Trembling, I fought my emotions, trying not to lose my composure. There was no one on board to comfort me. Wasn't that why I was here? I needed to learn to be an adult. Crying on a plane over missing one's fiance was not what adults did.

I hoped Danny was in Brentwood sleeping. He was exhausted from last night. I grinned, remembering my contribution to his state. I didn't want anything to happen to him. Tears stung my eyes once again. I missed Danny so much already.

College was half over. In two years, when I graduated and went out into the real world, I would face challenges of much greater magnitude than being apart from Danny for the summer. If nothing else, I would learn to stand on my own. Failure was not an option.

Take-off. With the flight path initially westbound over the Pacific, my window faced north. Focusing on the coast, my eyes picked up the Hyperion water treatment plant in El Segundo. Then I spotted the Santa Monica Pier, and beyond the cliffs of the Palisades was Malibu, my Malibu, our Malibu. I couldn't pick it out, the plane had climbed too high, but I imagined a glimpse of our home.

I bit my lip. "No tears, Eli," Danny's voice intoned in my head. I wouldn't cry. I would text him this later. Danny would be proud.

Pangs of loneliness stabbed my heart. I missed Danny and our life in Malibu so badly. I kissed my fingertips and silently blew the kiss toward the window and down to our home where I imagined Danny catching it.

"I love you, Daniel. I'll be back soon."

The plane banked to turn eastward, abruptly ending my last view of home for the next ten weeks.

To Be Continued

ABOUT THE AUTHOR

Born and raised in New York City, I was always a California girl at heart, obsessed with sports cars in a town with no parking. I couldn't wait to leave. So I did.

After graduating from Vassar College where I studied Psychology and Economics, I headed to Los Angeles. Then, after a brief stint in Washington, D.C., to earn my MBA, I headed back to the beach, and became a film production accountant, working on films you've probably never heard of.

I wrote my first novel at the age of six, and didn't write another until Hollywood Princess. I'm a news junkie and a baseball addict who loves a good love story. There are too many tragedies in the world. Why not provide an escape?

Now living in Connecticut, I'm married to a New York-based film producer. We have three children; two are not yet old enough to read this book, though one keeps trying to peek.

www.danayannlevin.com
www.facebook.com/DanaAynnLevin
twitter.com/OfficialDLevin

www.ingramcontent.com/pod-product-compliance
Lightning Source LLC
Chambersburg PA
CBHW070613260626
47161CB00007B/2416